D0032038

"Charlie and Constance are something special: middle-aged, decidedly unglamorous, and sharing the kind of subtly conveyed emotional intimacy that is the antithesis of hard-boiled."

—*Booklist*

"Author Wilhelm is considered a grande dame of science fiction, but, as she proves with this latest Meiklejohn mystery, she is also a shining star when writing murder in the present."

—Charleston *News and Courier*

"Kate Wilhelm always knows how to make the world symbolize the inner self, how to suggest psychological conditions from narrative events. [She] brings delight both through fine feeling and fine writing."

—*Los Angeles Times*

"Wilhelm is a master. . . . Her plots are taut, compelling, and insightful."

—*Library Journal*

"One of the masters of psychological fiction in America."

—*San Francisco Chronicle*

"An outstandingly fluent, sensitive writer, Kate Wilhelm is able to really get inside her characters' heads; she makes those small observations of behavior and emotion that go further toward defining human psychology than all the poetry and virtuosity in the world."

—*Minneapolis Star-Tribune*

THE CASEBOOK OF

Constance and Charlie

VOLUME I

ALSO BY KATE WILHELM

No Defense (forthcoming)
Defense for the Devil (1999)
The Good Children (1998)
Malice Prepense (1996)
A Flush of Shadows (1995)
The Best Defense (1994)
Justice for Some (1993)
Seven Kinds of Death (1992)
Naming the Flowers (1992)
And the Angels Sing (1992)
Death Qualified (1991)
State of Grace (1991)
Sweet, Sweet Poison (1990)
Cambio Bay (1990)
Children of the Wind (1989)
Smart House (1989)
The Dark Door (1988)
Crazy Time (1988)
The Hamlet Trap (1987)
The Hills Are Dancing (with Richard Wilhelm) (1986)
Huysman's Pets (1986)
Welcome Chaos (1983)
Oh, Susannah! (1982)
A Sense of Shadow (1981)
Listen, Listen (1981)

Better than One (with Damon Knight) (1980)
Juniper Time (1979)
Somerset Dreams and Other Fictions (1978)
Fault Lines (1977)
Where Late the Sweet Birds Sang (1976)
The Clewiston Test (1976)
The Infinity Box (1975)
City of Cain (1974)
Margaret and I (1971)
Abyss (1971)
Year of the Cloud (with Theodore L. Thomas) (1970)
Let the Fire Fall (1969)
The Downstairs Room and Other Speculative Fiction (1968)
The Killer Thing (1967)
The Nevermore Affair (1966)
The Clone (with Theodore L. Thomas) (1965)
The Mile-Long Spaceship (1963)
More Bitter than Death (1963)

THE CASEBOOK OF

Constance and Charlie

VOLUME I

Kate Wilhelm

ST. MARTIN'S MINOTAUR
NEW YORK

THE CASEBOOK OF CONSTANCE AND CHARLIE: VOLUME 1. Copyright © 1987, 1989, 1992, 1999 by Kate Wilhelm. All rights reserved. Printed in the United States of America. No part of this book may be used or reproduced in any manner whatsoever without written permission except in the case of brief quotations embodied in critical articles or reviews. For information, address St. Martin's Press, 175 Fifth Avenue, New York, N.Y. 10010.

The Hamlet Trap by Kate Wilhelm. Copyright © 1987 by Kate Wilhelm.
Smart House by Kate Wilhelm. Copyright © 1989 by Kate Wilhelm.
Seven Kinds of Death by Kate Wilhelm. Copyright © 1992 by Kate Wilhelm.

Design by Nancy Resnick

ISBN 0-312-24501-7

First St. Martin's Minotaur Edition: December 1999

10 9 8 7 6 5 4 3 2 1

FIC
WILHELM
v. 1

Contents

THE CASEBOOK OF
Constance and Charlie

VOLUME I

The Hamlet Trap

1

Roman Cavanaugh closed his eyes and turned his head away when he saw Ginnie sailing down Pioneer Street on her ten-speed. The next time he looked, she had crossed Main safely and was slowing down for Lithia Way. He took the breath he had not dared attempt and walked around the theater to the stage door. He was smiling slightly, but his fear had been real and heart-stopping. Ginnie was his only living relative and he sometimes thought that if anyone loved another person more than he loved Ginnie, he would die of it.

He seldom saw the theater anymore, unless he was showing it off. It was perfect—from the brass hinges and copper spittoons to the cherubs on the ceiling, from the acres of scarlet velvet drapes everywhere to the twenty-foot-diameter cut- and stained-glass chandelier in the lobby. Perfect. He had resisted the temptation to rename it after himself and stuck to the original: Harley's Theater.

"Morning, Ro," William called out from the stage, where he was examining one of the traps. William Tessler, in his sixties, Ro's age, had been the technician so long that people said when the builders started excavating they had uncovered him and he'd refused to go away. Ro waved to him and headed toward his office. William had looked at him with candor when Ro said his niece was going to work with Harriet, the set designer. Is she good? William had asked. Ro had assured him that Ginnie was very good and he had nodded. So why're you telling me this? his nod had implied. Ro had asked him how he felt about working under a twenty-four-year-old girl.

"If she's good, what else is there to bother with?"

William was not a designer, but he could put together anything Ginnie said she wanted, from the Eiffel Tower to a swarmy dungeon to a surreal black-and-white dreamscape. It was as if they had been built to work together. Now, with Harriet retired,

Ginnie was the only set designer they had, and this team simply got better every year. This was Ginnie's fifth season.

In his office Ro heard Ginnie enter and yell to William and Spotty, the watchman, who would be leaving along about now. You always knew when Ginnie had arrived. Ro's smile was broader as he started coffee before approaching his messy desk.

Ginnie stuck her head in, as he knew she would, and greeted him. "Hear from Wonder Boy yet?"

"He called from Bend last night. He'll get in this afternoon. Underestimated how long the drive would take. No one from back East believes the distances out here."

"Got a cup of coffee?"

"Come on in," he said in mock resignation. "And, Ginnie, stop calling him Wonder Boy. You'll forget and say it in front of him. And please don't swear like a sailor, at least until he gets to know you."

"Sure," she said, taking the coffee cup from him. "Thanks. In fact, I quit cussing. Haven't you noticed?"

"When?"

"Couple of weeks ago. You know, I started it when I realized I'd never grow t——" She looked at the ceiling and said primly, "One day it occurred to me that I probably would never become a voluptuous woman and no one would believe I was grown up, so I decided to use language to make the point."

"And you gave it up?"

"Right. I decided what the h——. I decided I didn't give a f——. I decided I didn't care."

Laughing, he poured himself more coffee. Ginnie was rangy, with dark curly hair that she kept too short. She wore sweatshirts, blue jeans, and crazy T-shirts and sneakers. Today her shirt had a smoking dragon on it. Ginnie had lived with him after her mother died, then she had gone away to school and at twenty-four had returned, two years into her master's program. She didn't give a shit about the degree, she had said cheerfully then. She had hung on for the experience of designing sets and now she was ready to go to work for Harriet. She had shown him her portfolio and half a dozen models, and he had hired her.

He had been anxious and watchful in the beginning. When she hung around the theater before, as a kid, she had been colt-

ish, childlike, obviously sexually immature, in no real danger.
She was still too young, but with a difference: She was now
independent. The first smooth-talking, handsome actor who
came down the pike and saw a good thing in her because of
who she was, who her uncle was, would twist her like wet spaghetti, he had thought, and he had been wrong. She treated
them all with affection, like pets. Now he felt sympathetic amusement for the fresh young actors just out of school who came
along and got a crush on her, and many of them did, whether
or not she had developed a womanly figure.

"Has Wonder Boy picked out the winner yet?" she asked
when she finished her coffee and was leaving his office.

"Ginnie, please. No, he hasn't."

"Well, sh———oot," she said, and winked at him. "How can I
start thinking about the set when I don't know what for?"

"There'll be time, plenty of time. Now get. I've got work to
do."

Ginnie wandered backstage greeting various people who were
arriving: Anna Kaminsky, grumbling about the way the actors
mistreated their costumes, as if she had nothing better to do
than take up this seam, let out that one . . . And clean them.
Always, clean them. She was leaving Monday for a vacation in
Phoenix. Eric Hendrickson arrived, his brow more furrowed than
usual. "Henry Dahl is sick," he said in a tone of disbelief, incredulity. How dare Henry Dahl get sick now! he was actually saying. Two more shows to go! He'd pump him full of penicillin
personally. . . . Gary Boynton had to see William right now—he
had found such a deal on redwood one-by-eights! Jessica Myers
slouched her way toward props, her eyes distant and dreamy.
Jessica had a new friend, her third this year. They were planning
a long trip, starting Sunday night. . . .

Bobby Philpott and Brenda Gearhart arrived together and
flushed when Ginnie raised an eyebrow at them. Bobby was
lights; Brenda, sound.

"When I go take that workshop on laser lighting," Bobby said
diffidently, "we thought Brenda might look in on some new
sound techniques."

"Her technique looks pretty sound to me as it is," Ginnie said.
Brenda blushed even more.

Could there be such a thing as a simultaneous manic depression? she wondered. Everyone always got manic at the end of the run, and it was always coupled with a depression amid the talk of vacations and trips and new affairs and whatever.

One show tonight, she mused, two on Saturday, and a matinee on Sunday that would finish the season with the last performance of *Harvey*. Finis. End of season. Already the theater felt different, as if a presentiment of loneliness had invaded it. Ginnie had been gone much of the summer and would not be leaving again until after the new season was well launched. She knew her Uncle Ro was grooming her to take over for him one day; he had asked her to sit in on the selection process for the next season, be in on the precasting decisions, budgets, everything. She was not certain she was ready for those responsibilities yet.

She glimpsed Kirby Schultz conferring with Eric. Kirby was the director who was leaving to make his fortune in television. She wished him well and thought it was just silly of Uncle Ro to be furious with him. Even if Uncle Ro was right and Kirby ended up hating it, he had to try, she had decided months ago, and tended to side with Kirby every time the subject came up.

"They're sloppy," Kirby was saying to Eric when she got within earshot. "I timed it on Wednesday and they're running nine minutes longer than they were a month ago. Timing's everything in a play like *Dracula*, everything. Take them through the second act, that's where it bogs down."

Eric nodded silently. Poor Eric, she thought, passing them, waving. He had been so certain he would get Kirby's job.

"Not creative enough," Uncle Ro had said when she questioned him about it. "A director's got to be as creative as the writer or he's nothing. Eric's a great stage manager, a great prompter, a great one to get the most out of actors at rehearsals, after a director's told him what he wants."

At ten she left the theater, where she really had nothing to do at this time. She rode her bike slowly through town toward the university, where she was to meet Peter and go with him to inspect a house that was a possibility for Wonder Boy and his companion. She grinned, remembering the expression on her uncle's face when she called his find by that name. But it was his fault, she reasoned; he had praised the new director too fulsomely not to evoke some reaction.

Harry Rosen waved at her from his car, on his way to his insurance office, she guessed. She liked Ashland. Everyone she saw who was a resident, not a tourist, smiled at her, waved, spoke, somehow greeted her. She liked that. All her life until she had come here she had lived in one big city after another, one apartment after another, always a stranger among strangers. Here people made her feel welcome and even useful. At least one time each year they asked her to come to the high school to talk to the art students; the Cascade Gallery had invited her to have a show twice now, with her models on display for a week to ten days at a time; if there was an art show, they asked her to be on the jury; she had spoken at the university several times. . . . It was good to belong, to have a community. A town of fifteen thousand was just right.

"Hey, Ginnie! Over here!"

She braked, spinning out her bike on gravel in the driveway of the university-staff parking lot. Peter Ellis covered his face with both hands. He peeked through his fingers.

"Good God!" he said. "Do you always stop like that?"

"Is there another way? No one told me it, if there is."

"Chain the bike and let's go. I have to be back by one. Time to see the house and have lunch. Okay?"

She nodded and very quickly joined him at his car. Peter was six feet tall and fair; he moved as if his joints had not been firmly linked. He was an archaeologist at the university. He had been here for a year working on his Ph.D. dissertation, which he hoped to finish by spring. This quarter was his last here. Then, back to U.C.L.A., dig in and finish the paperwork, he said.

"Tell me something about the house," Ginnie said as he started the car and backed out. "How'd it happen to turn up at this time?"

"Warner and Greta Furness tried to rent it out during the summer, but no luck. They said no actors and no students, and that didn't leave much, I guess. They want a year's lease. They're at Harvard for a year. Yesterday I heard about it and thought of you and your new director and here we go."

Peter was easy to be with, not demanding, and not theater. He seldom even came to the theater to pick her up, or to meet people there. He did not expect her to be any more comfortable with his university friends than he was with her theater friends. In a way, that tended to isolate them when they saw each other, and that, she knew, would not work if things ever started to get more serious. They would have to make some adjustments then, but for now it was fine. They hiked together and looked for good spots for him to dig, went to the coast or the high desert now and again. Sometimes he made dinner for her and sometimes she did it.

The house he took her to was on Alison, up a steep hill, about midway between the university and the theater, half a mile from each. The hill was not as steep as the one that led to her house on West Park Street. Much of Ashland was built on the mountainside, some of the streets so precipitous that she refused to drive on them at all.

"It's beautiful," she said, standing in the driveway. The house had two stories and looked expensive, with carefully sculpted grounds, immaculate paint.

"They'll make a deal. They don't want it empty all winter. Let's go on in."

It was a three-bedroom house, richly furnished, carefully maintained. She nodded. If Wonder Boy didn't like it, let him find his own house.

"Take the key," Peter said. "Show it to them and if they want it, they can get in touch with Warner. Otherwise, just give it back to me sometime. Here's the name and number." He handed her a slip of paper.

"Okay. So I'm a broker or something. Where for lunch? I'm starved."

"You're always starved."

Ginnie had never been able to ride her bicycle all the way up her own hill. But she was getting higher each time, she thought grimly, when she had to get off and walk the rest of the distance that afternoon. Her legs throbbed. At her own house she nodded with satisfaction. It was perfect for her. The yard was messy with uncut grass, dandelions, overgrown bushes, last year's leaves turning a rich brown where they had collected in dips and along the walk, against the foundation of the house. She had dug up the backyard and had sown wildflowers, two pounds of seeds, at twenty-eight dollars a pound. The back was a kaleidoscope of color nine months of the year. She intended to have the front dug in the spring, plant it to wildflowers also.

Her uncle had looked at her with incomprehension when she told him she intended to buy a house. She had the insurance money, she had said firmly, and that was what it was going to go for, her own house.

Inside, she looked at her belongings with the same satisfaction she had felt surveying her yard. Everything in it was hers, things she had chosen herself. It was bright with color—she loved color, none of that neutral, good-taste, decorator stuff for her. The rug in her living room was red, the couch deep forest-green, one chair yellow. A Cherokee wall hanging was red and orange and yellow and blue. . . . There were plants in red and blue ceramic pots. She had caught the startled expression on the faces of visitors now and then, but most people liked it after that first surprise. The colors were carefully chosen, nothing clashed with anything else. She used colors the way they were used in tropical climates, in Indonesia, or Malaysia. It all worked.

She called her uncle and learned that Gray Wilmot and Laura Steubins were due at the theater by four. They had checked into a motel already and were cleaning up, relaxing.

Although she had intended to change her clothes, she forgot, and when she arrived at the theater to meet Wonder Boy, she was still in the jeans and T-shirt she had worn all day. She joined the throng in Ro's office.

William was there, and Eric, Kirby, Anna, Brenda, Bobby . . . most of the actors who had been put through an extra rehearsal for *Dracula*. Everyone wanted to meet the new director. Ro saw her and called, "That's Ginnie. Meet Gray and Laura."

She could not see Laura for the people between them, but Gray was tall enough to spot.

"Hi!" she yelled, and he nodded. Grim, she thought. Probably dead tired from the long drive, and now a mob scene, just what he needed. She ducked to get a glimpse of Laura and grinned at her. Even tireder than he was, apparently.

"Ginnie's located a house you might want to rent," Ro was saying, his voice carrying over the other voices in the office. "Whenever you want to see it, she'll take you."

"Maybe we should do it now," Laura said. "I'd like a nap before dinner. It's been a long day."

He didn't like that, Ginnie thought, watching Gray's expression tighten. And she doesn't like theater people. Like Peter.

"That makes good sense," Ro said heartily. "Ginnie can drop you off at your motel after you see the house. And I'll pick you up at six-thirty for dinner. Okay?"

They made their way through their welcome committee, and she led them out the back to her car. When she opened the door, they both got in the backseat without speaking. She walked around to the driver's side and got in, and realized that they thought she was a gofer, Ro's secretary, or a stagehand or something. She thought cheerfully, well, fuck you, too, Wonder Boy.

2

They had met at a party given by one of Laura's friends. He had looked over the group and withdrawn to a chair near the front window. There were fifteen or sixteen people in the room, all familiar to Laura, some of them friends, most merely acquaintances. Eventually she had found herself in the chair opposite his and they had nodded at each other silently. The music was too loud and the room reeked of pot and spilled wine.

"Having a good time?" he asked with an edge to his voice.

She shrugged. "Typical *Harvey* party."

"Where can you get something to eat at this time of night?" he asked abruptly. "Something not pink, not to go on crackers, not cheese."

She ended up going with him to an all-night restaurant, and she learned about him during the next few hours as they talked and drank coffee. He had had to make the choice, he said, take this part-time job, or hang on in New York hoping for a chance to break in. And in New York, he had added, only he had known he was not just another green pea in a field of peas. He could live on what he made, he had said, and she understood this to mean that perhaps he would be able to pay rent and eat, but perhaps not. There was no screaming demand for new theatrical directors, he said.

"Or anyone else," she said. She had been lucky to get her job with Marianne's new advertising agency and she had it only because she and Marianne had been friends for a long time.

When they parted early in the morning, she knew that something had started. That was in October. Just before Thanksgiving she saw his first play. It was not very good, but the reviews blamed the actors, not him. He had done more than anyone had expected, one reviewer had written, considering what he had to work with.

He was angry and defiant and determined. And he was badly hurt. He made his cast work overtime in rehearsal for the next performance, and by the time the run ended he was exhausted. By Christmas they were living together in her apartment.

She knew from the beginning that he was trying desperately to get a job with any theater, anywhere. He sent résumés, reviews, pictures, wrote long letters, followed up every lead. At times he was jubilant with the possibility of this or that working out; then, when it didn't, he was so low in depression that she was afraid for him.

In March, a very lovely sophomore was in his next production, *Pygmalion*. Watching the rehearsals, Laura wondered how he could not fall in love with the women he worked with. When she mentioned it later, his expression was blank. Then he said, "You look at a marble sculpture and see only the beauty of the finished work, right? How do you think the artist feels about the marble? It's nothing but raw material. That's what the actors are, raw material, and the finished play is the work of art, the raw material forgotten, not important."

She prayed that he truly believed that. She made an effort to still the quiver of jealousy that had presented itself to her as fear.

When he moved in, Marianne had asked, "Whose idea is it?"

She had not been able to answer honestly. She really did not know. When Marianne asked, "Do you love him?" her answer had been immediate and sure. Yes, she loved him and would do whatever it took to keep him.

In September his break came. As soon as she opened the door to their apartment, she knew something good had happened finally. Roses were on the table, the air was fragrant, but it was more than that. The heaviness was gone; it was not like walking into a pressure chamber. Gray yelled from the kitchen and charged into the living room, swept her up, whirled her around, kissing her. "I got it! I got the Ashland job! Ro Cavanaugh was in the audience when *Pygmalion* opened! He loved it!"

At dinner she listened to his excited voice and tried not to think what the words actually meant. Something was ending. After less than a year, something was ending. Gray was thirty-one, two years younger than she was. He was handsome in a classical way, lean and hard of body, thick dark hair, deep blue eyes. He could get a job modeling, she had said once, and he had reacted furiously.

"I don't have to be there until November first," he said, swirling wine in his glass harder and harder. "Six weeks to get everything wrapped up here. We'll drive and use a rented trailer for the stuff we can't sell. It'll take five or six days. A vacation along the way, a little sightseeing." The wine splashed out of his glass and they both laughed.

She finally said, "What about my job? You're assuming I'll go too?"

He nodded. "I was assuming you'd go."

His exuberance had vanished; now he was dark and withdrawn, overwary. Sell what stuff? she thought. He had nothing to sell. He meant for her to sell her furnishings, undo the life she had been building for five years.

"I told them we'd be there a few days early, to catch the last performance or two of this season," he said.

Slowly she nodded. They both knew she would go. Ashland, she thought. Ash land. An image of burned rubble formed in her mind, ashes blowing in the wind, ashes in her mouth, bitter and sharp.

They planned their trip, made changes, planned alternate routes, and they had a garage sale, then another one, and then gave away what they could not sell and would not take. The weeks evaporated too fast, leaving a final frenzy of activity, including a visit to her parents to say good-bye. Her father had said in the beginning that his daughter was welcome in his house anytime, and his daughter and her husband were welcome, but there was one extra bedroom and no unmarried couple could share it. The visit was for one day, uncomfortable for everyone.

Connecticut, Pennsylvania, Ohio, Kansas . . . finally the great Rocky Mountain range, and then the high plateau country. They had stopped at the Craters of the Moon in Idaho, had spent a few hours in the plains of Idaho, crossed the Snake River into Oregon, and were on a road virtually without traffic, with high-desert sagebrush and an occasional juniper tree the only visible life. "What a wasteland," Gray had said, and gone back to his reading.

A few days before they left home, he had received a carton of manuscripts. His first job, he had told her, was to judge a play-writing contest. The winning play would be his first production. Those he found totally hopeless he marked with a red *N* and put aside. Most of the manuscripts were ending up in the reject box. He read while she drove.

Ash land, she kept thinking. They passed more lava fields; the mountains were stark and wind-carved, outcroppings were black volcanic material, foreboding, almost evil.

"Listen," Gray said. He read from the manuscript: " 'Daughter, you must not go out with that no-good Stanley. You know you will end up pregnant and what will your father say?' "

"That's pretty direct," Laura said, laughing. "Are they all like that?"

"No, ma'am, this is one of the better ones." They both laughed.

How easily he picked up whatever accent he heard. He sounded just like the Kansan who had commented on a restaurant with those words. "You could be an actor," she had told him once.

He had nodded. "But they have no power, no control. It's the director who decides what kind of reality will be created on the stage. A good director makes the actors believe in that reality, and they make the audience accept it. But before anything can happen, the director has to step into another world, live in it, know it's real. A good director and a good writer share that world in a way no one else can understand, or enter. The writer sees his world, hears his people, but all he can produce are marks on paper, signs pointing to symbols. The director does magic, moves those symbols through another dimension and creates life with them. The actors are tools, only tools, like models, made to be used. I won't be used," he had finished flatly.

Sometimes it frightened her very much when the thought came unbidden that maybe he was not as good a director as he thought. It frightened her even more when she came to realize that in his world some people were tools to be used, and others were the users of those tools, and she knew that she and Gray were in separate categories.

When she glanced at him again, he was reading another play, this time moving his lips, saying the lines under his breath—a good one finally.

That night she heard her first coyote crying in the distance, lonely, wild, unknowable. She felt a spasm of terror. And that night she roused to see a crack of light from around the bathroom door, dozed, awakened again, then came wide awake when she realized he had been in there for hours.

"Gray?" She called a second time. The light went out and he returned to the bedroom.

"Restless," he said, getting into bed.

In the morning she found the play that had interested him folded in half, pages dog-eared, penciled notes in the margins. She would read it while he drove, she thought, but she put it aside, forgot it.

"You were all over the bed last night," Gray said at breakfast. "Dreams?"

She shook her head, lying. There had been dreams—nightmares, actually; already the details had blurred, only the feeling of terror persisted. She knew that in her dreams wild dogs had fought over her bones, that she had cried out over and over and no one had come.

And she could not tell him. She could not say to him, "I can't go with you to ash land because I'll die there."

3

What perverse or even malign spirit overcame Ginnie she could not have said, but she yielded to it without a struggle and adopted a guide-extraordinaire attitude. "Over there is Lithia Park," she said brightly. "Very pretty. You can walk two miles, maybe three. Great madrone trees, ponderosa pines, beautiful flowers. It leads into the Elizabethan Theater grounds. The Oregon Shakespearean Festival is what brings people here, of course. The Harley simply capitalizes on the overflow. Ninety-three percent attendance each season. Not bad for a town of fifteen thousand. Of course, the university has forty-five hundred students. I don't think they count them in the census. So, twenty thousand. Medford is up the road about twelve miles and that's another forty thousand, and people are scattered all through the valley. It's the Rogue River valley, by the way, wonderful white-water rafting. They've had it on television sports any number of times."

On and on she prattled. When she glanced at them in the rearview mirror, Gray was staring stonily out his side window, Laura gazing just as intently out the other one.

"This is the steep way up to the house," she said, shifting down. "There's another way up that isn't bad at all. I'll take you back that way. And here it is. The view's pretty nice during the day, but at night it's spectacular!" Ginnie parked in the driveway, jumped out, and opened the back door before either Gray or Laura had a chance to.

"Why don't I just give you the key and let you roam by your-selves," she said brightly. "You'll have things to discuss about the house. I'll wait here."

She watched them enter and then turned her attention to the view. It was spectacular day or night, just as the view was from her own house. The mountain dropped down to the valley floor, where the main part of town was, then there was a relatively flat area four or five miles wide, then foothills that rolled exactly the way Delaware countryside did, and beyond that, more mountains. Behind her the mountain continued upward, heavily forested, deep green summer and winter, with firs, pines, spruces, madrones—conifers and broad-leaf evergreens of a rain forest merging with trees of a drier climate. Everything was here together. It was nearly chanterelle time, she thought; she and Peter were going on a great mushroom hunt after a good soaking rain. Any day now it would rain, the start of the new season, but this day was brilliantly clear, the sky gloriously blue, with idealized clouds, the kind that children draw, glowing marshmallow clouds. There would be another breathtaking sunset later.

Inside the house, Gray watched Laura examine the rooms. Too expensive, they both had said on entering, but he wasn't sure. Maybe the owners were desperate to have it occupied during the winter. He would call. And meanwhile he didn't give a damn about room size, or furnishings, or even the view. It was okay, good enough, if they could afford it.

"You going to tell me what's bugging you?" he asked abruptly.

"Nothing." She stiffened with the words in a way that meant: Don't push, not right now, anyway.

He understood her signals, maybe even better than she did. He did not push. He knew part of the problem: as he had become more and more excited and eager, she had become more anxious and withdrawn. What he had seen as the opportunity to meet colleagues, she had seen as the threat of an overwhelming mob. Already he was categorizing the people he had met, and she probably didn't remember a single name, except for Roman Cavanaugh. He understood, but felt impatient with her sudden insecurity. This was his world in a way that the University of Connecticut had never been. Here he would be in charge, in control, not a part-time flunky serving at the whim of a jackass who had tenure. Laura had gone into the kitchen to check on cookware: apparently they would have to buy nothing, it was all in the house, except for linens, and they had packed hers in the trailer. Gray gazed out the window at the view across the valley, and wanted only to get on with it, to start his new job.

Laura returned carrying a notebook. They would have to get the electricity turned on, and the phone, find out about garbage collection. . . . "It's really a nice house," she said uncertainly. It was, but it felt like someone else's house. Wall-to-wall carpeting, soft beige plush, fine furniture, not quite antique, but not Grand Rapids either. A fully equipped kitchen, even a microwave, laundry room equipped . . . The problem was that she kept expecting the owners to enter momentarily and demand an explanation. Gray had walked to the front of the room and was looking out at the street, the driveway. She looked past him and saw the girl who had brought them here. The wind had started to blow, molding her jeans to her long legs, her hair against her cheeks. She glanced from her to Gray and thought clearly, of course, never an actress with her lovely face and body, but someone like that, someone loose-bodied and not beautiful and somehow free.

"Ready?" he asked, turning back to her.

She nodded. She couldn't tell if he had even been looking at the girl in the driveway, but if not now, later, another day. She did not try to rationalize her certainty. It came fully developed bearing its own load of acceptance and dread and inevitability.

Ginnie had the door open for them when they got back to her car. Her cheeks were bright from the wind, her hair tumbled every which way. When she started to drive, she asked, "Do you ski? Mount Ashland is wonderful for skiing, everything from cross-country to beginners' slopes to high-speed downhill."

Neither of them skied. "The wind made me think of it," Ginnie said. "There's been snow up in the mountains already, and the wind smells like warmed-over snow. We hardly ever get any down here, but sometimes you can smell it."

Laura glanced at Gray. He shrugged, paying little attention to their guide, evidently not interested in her or her strange observations about weather.

Ginnie took them down the less-steep way and then on to their motel. She gave Gray the slip of paper with the phone number of Warner Furness and offered her services as chauffeur, guide, whatever they needed in the coming week or so until they got settled in. Gray thanked her politely and distantly; Laura forced a smile, and she left them alone.

"What do you think?" Ro asked her over the phone that night.

"You mean Gray and Laura?"

"You know that's what I mean. He didn't like the production, thought it was too draggy."

"Well, so does Kirby," she pointed out.

"Yeah, I know. Anyway, what do you think?"

"Too soon. Ask me in a couple of weeks. Has he told you the contest winner yet?"

There was a pause, then Ro said, "It's one called *The Climber*. Have you read it?"

"Nope. Didn't read any of them. Do you have a copy?"

"Just the file copy in the office. Juanita will run off some Xeroxes tomorrow. You want to read it in the office?"

She hesitated. Peter had asked her to go to Silver Lake with him over the weekend to a dig that had attracted students from the entire Northwest over the summer. Now that there were only professionals at the site, he was interested. She made up her mind suddenly. "I'll drop in tomorrow and read through it. You don't like it?"

"I don't know," he said peevishly. "It's just not the one I would have picked, I guess. Anyway, read it and tell me what you think. See you tomorrow, honey."

She called Peter and was a little surprised at how disappointed he sounded.

"I've been trying to get you off to myself for weeks," he said, "and you keep dodging. Did Ro know ahead of time that you were considering going away?"

"I'm not sure. Why? What does that mean?"

"I bet he did."

"Come back in time for the party, okay? Between eight and nine?"

He said he would try and she knew he would make it. That was the only condition she had imposed, if she had gone at all, that they be back in time for the big party at the end of the season. Had she mentioned it to Uncle Ro? She thought not, but could not be certain, and even if she had, so what? Uncle Ro was not trying to run her life, she thought emphatically. If anything, he ignored her private life as if it didn't even exist.

If he asked if she was sleeping with Peter, would she tell him? she wondered. Probably. But she knew he would not ask any more than she would question him about his private life.

"Got a cup of coffee?" she called at his office door the next morning. It was raining and she felt smug about not being out camping at Silver Lake. The last time she and Peter had camped out in the rain, both sleeping bags had been soaked and he had caught a cold. She shrugged out of a poncho and held it at arm's length to drip in the hall, not on the office carpet.

"Hang it up somewhere," Ro said, "and come on in. Come on. Such a mooch. Don't you buy any coffee of your own?"

"Hell no. How was dinner with Wonder Boy and the Lady of the Lake?"

He looked pained. "They were both pretty tired. They've taken the house and plan to move in today and he's going to take the trailer to Medford and turn it in and be back here in time for the matinee. Ginnie—" He paused and turned back to the coffee machine, looked at it instead of her. "Why'd you call her that?"

Ginnie had regretted the words as soon as she uttered them. She had not thought of Laura in any particular way since leaving her and Gray at the motel, had not thought about any title or nickname for her. The words had formed themselves in the shadows of the cave of her mind. "I don't know," she said slowly. "I won't do it again."

He nodded. "She's just tired from packing and the long drive, shy with so many strangers all at once. She'll be all right. And so will he."

Ginnie sipped the coffee and knew why those particular words had come tumbling out. Laura had a doomed expression, a sad, aware, and doomed look.

"Well, here's the play," Ro said, handing her a folder. "Take it over there and read through it. Juanita's coming in at ten to pick it up."

His office was twenty feet long, only about ten feet wide. At one end was a mammoth desk, always messy with piles of papers, stacks of manuscripts, letters, a fifteen-inch-tall bronze clown, some pretty paperweights, things no one had touched in years, Ginnie felt certain. His secretary, Juanita Margolis, was forbidden to move anything there, but Ro could shuffle through things and come out with whatever it was he sought practically

ALBUQUERQUE ACADEMY LIBRARY

instantly. Everything else in the office was meticulously neat, as were his apartment, his person, his car, the rest of the theater. Only his desk was a rat's nest.

In the middle of the office, exactly in the way of traffic, there was a round table where Ro often ate lunch. He had not cooked a meal for himself in twenty-five years, except for toast once in a while. There were bookshelves, a neat liquor cabinet that opened to make a bar. At the far end there were comfortable overstuffed chairs covered in green leather and a matching couch. A redwood coffee table with a burl top, six feet by three, several inches thick, made the couch impossible to get to without great determination. There were windows on the outside wall, but Ginnie never had seen them open, or with the red velvet drapes drawn apart. It was always now in Ro's office, never day or night, or any time in particular, just now. It was not quite soundproof, but almost. She could faintly hear the noise of the crew onstage, getting set up for the matinee: *Pal Joey*.

She sat in one of the leather-covered chairs, put her feet on the coffee table, switched on a lamp, and opened the folder. The play had been written on a computer, printed in terrible purple dot matrix. She groaned. "I bet it won't reproduce at all," she called.

He sighed. "We'll see."

She knew what would happen. Juanita would end up retyping the whole damn thing and getting her own copy Xeroxed. Poor Juanita. She wondered what she would give up for Ro. Her arm. Her cats. Her mother. Whatever he demanded. She started to read.

When she finished she looked up to find him regarding her, frowning. "It's a piece of . . . Uncle Ro, it's awful."

He let out a long breath. "I was hoping it was just me, out of touch or something."

"There must have been something better than this. Do you have the other submissions handy?"

"He read them all. He was pretty emphatic about this being his choice."

She dropped the manuscript on the coffee table and stood up. If Gray stuck to it, he would have this one. It was in his contract that he was to judge the contest. "What a stupid thing to agree to ahead of time anyway," she said. "You should rewrite the contest rules. If there's nothing worth producing, nothing gets produced."

"Meanwhile the horse is long gone."

"Who wrote the goddamn thing? Maybe we could send him a mail bomb or something."

"Her. Sunshine. That's all, just Sunshine."

"Yeah, it would be. Boy, what a mess! Think we can talk him out of it?"

"We'll let it ride over the weekend and meet Monday. You, Eric, William, Juanita, Gray, and me. Ten Monday morning. I'll hand out copies tonight or tomorrow. Don't let on that you've read it until then, Ginnie. I don't want any trouble over the weekend. God, I wish I could ask Kirby to come Monday."

She agreed that he could not do that. Kirby was out as of Sunday; this was not his fight. She went to the door. "He must see something in it that we missed. I'll give it another good read over the weekend."

"As I will, I assure you. Thanks, Ginnie. Just thanks."

She grinned at him. "Wonder Boy just might shake things up around here more than you counted on, Uncle Ro." When he had decided on Gray as Kirby's replacement, he had said the group needed new blood, needed a good shake-up. She thought that probably that was exactly what they were going to get.

4

All the rest of Saturday Ginnie worked in the shop, a large Quonset hut where the sets were constructed and stored. It always smelled of paint and newly sawed wood. She was making decisions with William, labeling items to be stored, making notes in her notebook to go in her file. Keep the bay window intact; break down the soda fountain from *Bus Stop;* return the jukebox to the collector who had donated it for the season. . . . The Quonset-hut shop was a jumble of scenery, removed from the stage, brought out from backstage as each show finished now,

each piece demanding a separate decision. Keep this flat, it can be painted a couple more times. That sofa has had it. Tear it down, keep the frame. It was hard work, and dirty work. The wonderful fireplace from *Dracula*—it worked on a revolve. When the secret panel opened, the whole thing turned to reveal the loathsome crypt of the monster. . . . Tear it down.

She made notes. William made notes; Gary Boynton, the shop foreman, made notes, all different, not interchangeable. On Monday the actual work would begin; hoists would lift pieces to the overhead storage areas, the crew would attack other pieces with hammers, crowbars. . . .

The crew began to bring in scenery from *Pal Joey* and Ginnie moved out of the way. Her hands were grimy, her face was dirty, her hair gritty.

"Hi," Gray Wilmot called at the door. "William around?"

William appeared from the rear of the shop. "Afternoon, Mr. Wilmot."

"Please," he said. "Gray. Just wanted to tell you that was a terrific set for *Pal Joey*. Really effective."

"Thanks, but you should be telling Ginnie, not me."

"I thought Ro said you did them."

"Nope. He said I build. Ginnie designs. I just do what I'm told."

Gary Boynton's voice bellowed nearby. "Dammit, Mikey, don't drop it!"

"Better move a bit," William said, and stepped out of the way; Gray followed. Now he could see Ginnie.

"I didn't realize that was your work," he said with a touch of stiffness. "They're both really good. I'm looking forward to working with you. See you later."

He left, and William turned to look at Ginnie when she chuckled. "You baiting him, girl?"

"Now, William, don't be a nag. I've about had it for the day. How about you?" He nodded and she patted his arm. "Give Shannon a kiss for me. See you tomorrow." Shannon was his semi-invalid wife whose heart condition grew steadily worse.

The rain had almost stopped; now it was a patter of isolated showers from stranded clouds that looked lonely in the clearing sky. The air smelled of rain and earth mold and forests and wood smoke. By next month Ashland would smell like a giant wood stove. There was a bite in the air signaling a frost soon, if not this night, then the next, or within a week, probably. Autumn had arrived.

She walked home without haste, stopped to chat a minute with Jarrel Walsh, who owned one of the best restaurants in town, then stopped again to speak with Dancy Corman, who worked in the bookstore that she passed every day. A clump of people stood near the Elizabethan Theater parking lot, actors and Marguerite Demarie, the costumer. Their season was ending, just as the Harley's was, and tomorrow night the party would wend from backstage to backstage as all the theater people in town celebrated another good season. For the diehards, there was Ro's apartment to wrap it all up with a catered breakfast at dawn. She waved; they waved back.

This was what Peter didn't understand, she thought, climbing her hill, hardly feeling the strain in her legs. He thought when she said they were like a family that it was simply show-biz jargon and it wasn't. Any of them could get together at any time and be deep in conversation within seconds and care about the conversation. Right now everyone would be interested in the new director, what he was like, what his routine would be, how he treated actors, stagehands—everything about him, because it could affect any one of them. The actors moved from one theater to the other, stagehands worked both, as did the construction crews. What happened at Harley's echoed through the Shakespeare bunch, the Angus Bowman bunch, all of them. Every rumor made the entire circuit with startling speed.

Peter had tried to convince her that it was just like that at the university, at corporations, everywhere. She didn't believe it. In theater, she had said, every single day you're laying it on the line again, risking everything again. You can't get a reputation and coast on it, not for long. No tenure, no security, no tomorrow; only this show, this run, this performance.

Peter was thirty, and she knew that Gray Wilmot was thirty-one, but he seemed ancient compared to Peter. Theater people all seemed old compared to other people, old and forever young and gullible at the same time. "You can't expect much from a relationship with another theater person," Brenda, the sound technician, had said once over lunch. "You'll be working Toledo while he's in Las Vegas. But you can't expect *anything* from someone from the real world. As soon as they've seen the show once, it's 'What else is new, honey?' "

The only reference her uncle had made to Peter had been oblique. "It's good to know someone from outside now and then, just to remind us what that's like."

She walked up to her door and turned the key in the lock and realized that she was brooding about Peter because this was his last term at school; he would be leaving, and he liked things finished, settled. He didn't like quitting with things undone. Okay, she told herself, so she would have to make a decision, but not right now, not tonight, or tomorrow. All she wanted right now was a shower and food. God, she thought, she was starving.

Everything backstage had been cleared away to make room for tables and chairs, for a twenty-foot buffet. A five-piece band played, and when they took a break, someone put on tapes. Upstage was cleared for dancing. On the buffet there were turkey and ham, shrimp creole, avocados stuffed with crab, chicken breasts in a hot Mexican sauce, potato salad, carrot salad, hearts of palm, mushrooms vinaigrette . . . There were liquor and champagne and red and white wines, and silver urns of coffee.

Ginnie danced until she was soaked through and through. Laura danced with Ro, then William, then with whoever came along and asked. She was a good dancer. Gray did not dance. Peter arrived at ten and Ginnie danced even more with him. One of the actresses, Amanda White, propositioned one of the actors and they left together. Kirby got drunk and wept and declared that he had changed his mind, he did not want to go to Hollywood; he would cancel his contract. Peter and Laura danced a waltz and everyone made room for them and watched and applauded when they were done. Then Ro made a speech and introduced Eric, who handed out awards. There was an award for the most original ad-lib, for the longest pause for a forgotten line, for the cleverest save the night that Eric forgot his prompt-book, for the most athletic entrance or exit. . . .

The Shakespearean crowd arrived; some of the Harley people left, and after that it was impossible to tell them apart. Then it was two in the morning and Ro made a signal to the band. The leader stepped forward with an acoustic guitar; Bobby dimmed the lights and turned a spot on Ginnie. She had protested vehemently against this, but Ro had insisted and finally had agreed to make it a duet with her. Another spot found him. Ginnie's singing voice was too soft for a performer, but there was no sound now except her voice and the plaintive guitar. She sang.

"The party's over / It's time to call it a day . . ." Ro walked to her and they finished the song together; the spots went out, leaving inky blackness for a heartbeat, then the lights came on full and everyone applauded madly and many began to weep. The party was over. The season was over.

Laura was standing near Peter, both suddenly subdued. This was Gray's world, she was thinking, this was what he had been looking for, hungry for, and she would never be part of it. And Peter was thinking that Ro would never let Ginnie go again. Ginnie came up to them, flushed and sweaty.

"Corny, huh? Ro's idea. I told him it was corny."

"It was perfect," Peter said. "The perfect way to end a party. Do you have your car?"

"No. I thought you'd be driving and no point in a parade. Now?"

He nodded and Laura looked away, embarrassed by the sudden sexual tension that seemed to radiate from him. She watched them leave; it took a long time for them to get free of all the people who wanted a last hug, a last word with Ginnie. Gray came to her then.

"Ro said a small group will go to his apartment for a while. You up for that?"

"Do you want to?"

"Yeah. I think so."

She nodded, but what she ached to do was go to their house with him, go to bed with him, make love for hours with him. She felt a rush of jealousy when she thought of Ginnie and Peter, and it was followed swiftly by a feeling of pity for him.

The caterers were starting to clean up and she heard the refrain in her mind: The party's over.

5

At the party, Ro had handed Ginnie a copy of the play—retyped by Juanita, as she had predicted. She had reread it that morning after Peter left, and it was even worse than she had remembered. When she got to Ro's office at ten, the others were already there, and she could tell that it was going to be a stormy meeting. Eric was scowling deeper than usual. He had a permanent frown that was meaningless, but when it deepened this much, so that the lines looked incised with ink, people walked warily. William looked sad, hung over, and he was not a drinker. He looked tired, though, probably stayed as long as the continuation of the party at Ro's house had gone on. Juanita, Ro's secretary, had a carefully held neutral expression, and that in itself was alarming. She was slim, in her late forties, with black hair and very dark eyes; she was so intelligent that people often took whatever problem they had to her, fully expecting her to have answers, no matter if it was physics homework for the college students who worked as stagehands, or a lighting problem, or something to do with costumes—whatever. She was wasted here, Ginnie sometimes thought, but Juanita was not about to go anywhere else. Ginnie suspected that she and Ro had been lovers, and were no longer, although Juanita still loved him. Ro looked exactly the same as always. Late nights, parties, long hours, nothing marked his face. Age was catching up to him so gradually that people who had not seen him in years always felt a jolt of surprise that he was unchanged.

Gray was wearing a sweater and jeans and he seemed completely at ease. It was the first time Ginnie thought he did look at ease.

They all had coffee and arranged themselves in the comfortable furniture around the redwood coffee table. Ginnie did not put her feet up on it.

"There are about three things I want us to get to this morning," Ro started. "General procedural stuff. A schedule. And the contest winner. Want to start with that?"

"A couple of questions," Gray said. "The rules don't say how the winner is to be notified. Do you do that, or am I supposed to? The copy I have doesn't even have a name, you know, just a number. I want to get together with the writer about some revisions."

"We go by number so no one can cry bias," Ro said. "I've got the list. But, Gray, I think we have a problem with the one you chose. What do you think, Eric?"

"It's rotten," he said brusquely. "Amateurish, badly written, juvenile in every way."

Gray flushed and looked from Eric to William.

"I agree," William said.

Gray looked at Ginnie; she shrugged and nodded.

"It's unanimous," Ro said then. "Juanita and I also agree that it's a bad play. Did you read all of them?"

"I read them," Gray said in a hard voice. "I didn't realize that the contest was to be judged by a committee that included builders and secretaries. Why did you have me read them if that's how the winner was going to be chosen?"

Ro regarded him for a long moment; no one else moved. "You're to judge," he finally said. There was no trace of cordiality in his voice. "The contest states that the winner will be notified by phone, a check sent by the first of November. It also states that we have the right to produce it. Not that we're bound to do it."

"It can be interpreted either way. The winner could sue."

"Listen, Gray, and listen carefully. This isn't something I'm likely to say to anyone more than once. This theater is mine. I made it what it is, and by God, I'll preserve what I have here. Contest rules be damned. I don't know what you see in that play. I've been wrong before. I could be wrong this time. We'll see. But, Gray, there isn't a play or a playwright I wouldn't yank if I thought it would harm this theater, these people." He paused, then added, "There isn't a contract I wouldn't break if I had to to keep safe the things I consider important. Do you understand me?"

Gray was very pale, his eyes fierce and unwavering. "And I will do anything I have to to preseve what's important to me, and that's my own integrity. We have a contract, Mr. Cavanaugh, but I would quit, walk out in a second, if I thought I couldn't preserve my independence as a director."

Slowly Ro nodded. "That's fair enough. Why don't you tell us what you see in that play."

Gray opened an envelope and pulled out the folded and written-on manuscript. He turned to a page near the end and read: " 'As you rise, on what live and writhing matter does your foot fall?' " He read well, in a descending tone, and when he finished the line, he waited for a long beat, then folded the play again. "That one line redeems the play," he said. "It turns it into tragedy of the first rank. Until that line Evan has been a besotted, lovesick fool worthy of no consideration, much less sympathy. But all at once, through one brief question, he is revealed as a tragic figure. Because he knows. It becomes tragedy when the victim knows his fate is destruction and he can't turn away from it. When the rabbit falls to the fox, or the steer to the hammer, the dove to the eagle, we experience a lot of different emotions, but not the sense of tragedy. For that there has to be human awareness."

There was a long silence. Ro reached for the coffeepot and poured himself more coffee before he spoke. "That's one line of an hour-long play. I personally think you're reading more into that play than the writer put there, but we agreed that you're the judge. One thing, Gray: I want to see your prompt-books."

Ginnie thought Gray was going to walk out then, but with a visible effort he remained in his chair and nodded. "That's your right," he said evenly.

"Let's get on with the rest of the agenda," Ro said, and they talked about the fall schedule, when and how the other plays would be chosen, the meetings they would have to discuss the rest of the repertoire. "So twice a week we get together and by December we have our lineup," Ro finally said. "Anyone—anything else?"

Now Gray stood up. He looked at Juanita, then at William. "I'm very sorry," he said in a strained voice. "It came as a real surprise to find opposition like that. I reacted very badly and I apologize."

William nodded, ready to get on with the business of theater, but Juanita's eyes were cool, her manner extremely proper and polite. "Of course," she murmured. "Excuse me."

Ro stood up. "Ginnie, want to mooch some lunch?"

"Sorry. I'm going mushrooming. Why don't you come with us? Be good for you to get out in the open air."

"In the woods?" He looked aghast. "Anyway, the woods are full of pot farms and booby traps."

"Those shitheads," Ginnie said with a sniff. "We'll avoid all suspicious clearings, and tonight it's chanterelle omelet! God-damn, I wish they'd leave the fucking time alone! Just remembered daylight saving time is dead. Gotta run."

In half a minute she had done what none of them had been able to do through the past two hours, Ro realized, watching her with great love as she ran from the office. William was grinning, shaking his head; Eric's scowl was hardly noticeable; Gray looked bewildered and much younger; even Juanita had loosened up with a suspicion of a smile at the corners of her mouth. Incongruence, he thought, rising. Ginnie was a model of incongruence, trying to act grown-up by using bad language, dressing like a teenager in ratty jeans and sneakers, moving like a hyper boy, streaking this way and that. He turned to Juanita. "Do you want to have some lunch with me?"

"Muchrooms!" Ginnie said with satisfaction, surveying a mesh bag that was bulging with the red-gold harvest. She and Peter were resting, their backs against a venerable pine tree, their legs outstretched. The woods were deep here, with little undergrowth; the ground was spongy, the silence profound.

"So tell me the story of the play," Peter said lazily.

She had recounted the tense meeting. She took a deep breath and started. "This guy, Evan, is a climber, mountain climber, can't resist the highest peaks, all that stuff. Right? So one day he finds a woman wandering in the woods and he takes her home with him. Bingo, trouble. His wife doesn't like the strange woman. No one likes her except Evan, and he falls for her. She comes out of nowhere, no past, nothing. Suddenly she's there in his life. Things go to hell with the marriage. He's some kind of middle-management mugwump in a corporation. His boss comes and meets the strange woman. Evan gets dumped, of course. Final act shows the wife lying facedown on a bed in their home. Her hand relaxes and a pill bottle falls to the floor. Evan is climbing the highest peak yet and stands on the top, then jumps. And the strange woman is seated at a café table with the boss, laughing, drinking champagne. Curtain down."

"Whew," Peter said. "It doesn't sound so bad."

"Who is that mysterious woman? Why does the wife take the pills? Why does Evan take a jump? Sunshine just says this is how it is, folks." She sighed.

"It's surprising to me that Ro backed down," Peter said after a moment.

"You don't understand him. He's convinced that Gray is really good. He'd hire the devil himself if he was good and fire him if he wasn't. Gray's on the spot with this one. Uncle Ro admires anyone willing to fight, but he'll give him the bum's rush if he thinks he'll hurt the theater."

Peter touched her arm, then pointed off to the side. She squinted and finally saw the creature he was showing her, a chipmunk.

"Golden ground squirrel," he whispered.

The animal was studying them as intently as they were examining it. It craned its neck, reared up high on its haunches, and then with a flicker was gone. Golden, buff, sable, white . . . She automatically sketched it, painted it in her mind, fixing it permanently in her memory.

"We'd better head out," Peter said reluctantly then. They both got up, brushed themselves, and started the long hike back to his car.

Peter had been amazed at her ignorance about the woods, the mountains, the geology of the area, and he had started to teach her. He had instructed her in what she had to carry in her day-pack: a space blanket—such thin Mylar that it had virtually no weight, but might save her life if she got lost and the temperature plummeted. A poncho, nearly as light, a wool sweater or sweatshirt, matches and a candle, toilet paper . . . She had protested that she didn't want to camp out, just walk in the woods, but he had been firm. Most people who get lost planned no more than a stroll in the woods, he had said. She was used to the daypack now and hardly gave it a thought. It was usually packed and ready to snatch up without adding anything except a piece of cheese or fresh fruit. She kept raisins, nuts, chocolate in it.

She watched Peter's strong back and legs as he led the way. Superficially he and Gray were very alike, she realized. The difference came from within them. Peter carried peacefulness and Gray's burden was tension; and that made them so different that few people would even notice the similarities in build. Oh, she corrected herself, casual observers might mistake one for the other, but no one who had been with either of them for more than a minute.

But how much liking made up for a lack of love? she wondered. There seemed no end to the amount of liking she felt for Peter, and there was even love mixed with it, but it wasn't the right sort of love, she was afraid. When she thought these things, she always had to admit that she wasn't even sure of that. Since she was not certain what it was that others called love, she was not certain how it differed from what she felt for him. Or if it did. She knew that thinking about falling in love, marriage, a real commitment to anyone made her anxious, fearful, and she understood that least of all.

At the car Peter rummaged in a bag and brought out two sandwiches, handed her one.

"Why didn't you tell me you had food?" she demanded. "I ate everything I had and I'm still starving!"

"You're always starving." They ate before he started the drive back. They had a narrow log road to follow out of the woods and wanted to be done with it before dark, but Peter seemed unhurried, relaxed. Now he said, "You have your busiest time coming up, don't you?"

She nodded, her mouth full.

"Will you save some time for me? I want to be with you as much as you can stand these next weeks. I feel as if my time is running out. If I can't get my message over soon . . ."

Solemnly she nodded, but she knew there would not be many free hours after the next week or so. As soon as the plays were chosen for the new season, she would have her work—preliminary sketches for the sets, finished drawings, models, detailed

drawings for William to work with, overseeing the lighting, meetings, meetings . . .

Peter studied her face, then he kissed her lightly and turned
on the ignition. "You can finish eating while I drive. I'll cook
the mushrooms when we get back. Do you realize that you hiked
about eight miles today? I expect that any second now you'll
start feeling it."

6

Her real name, Sunshine said, was Elinor Shumaker, but she
had changed it in the sixties, seventies, sometime. She was a
shapeless woman of thirty-five in a long plaid skirt with a petti-
coat showing, hiking boots, a padded jacket over a sweater over
a man's plaid shirt. Her eyes were gentle and vague, pale blue,
her hair vaguely blond. She carried a large quilted shopping bag
with rope handles; it bulged and clunked when she put it down,
rattled and clinked when she picked it up.

Laura glanced at Gray. What were they supposed to do with
her? Sunshine had called from the bus station half an hour ago;
she had arrived, she said, and hung up.

"Do you want some coffee or something?" Gray asked, taking
the shopping bag from her.

"I don't drink coffee," she said softly. "Caffeine's really bad
for you, you know?"

"Uh, yeah, I guess so. Look, Sunshine, do you have any place
to go? Why are you here? I told you we'd mail the check."

She smiled gently. "I thought it'd be neat to watch a play
going into production, might even try out for a part or something, you know? I'll find a room or something. And you said
we have to rewrite it and I thought I should be here for that,
you know?"

"We'd better call Ro, or Ginnie," Laura said, her voice grim.
"We're strangers here, too," she said to the woman. "We don't

have a clue about where to tell you to look for a place to stay."

"I'll get by," Sunshine said, not moving.

"I'll give Ro a call," Gray said in desperation. He left Laura with Sunshine and made the call; in a few minutes Juanita appeared.

"So you're Sunshine," she said without surprise. "Well, come along. There's an apartment building where they take in actors all the time, by the week, month, year, whatever you want. How much can you afford to pay?"

Sunshine smiled at her. "Hundred a month, I guess. More if I have to. But no smokers or drinkers." She turned back to Gray and Laura. "Will we be working in your office or something? I don't have a typewriter, you know?"

"We'll work something out," he said. Sunshine left with Juanita, still smiling, her bag clinking and rattling.

Silently Laura and Gray returned to her car. She got behind the wheel. When they were both settled she said, "She is not to set one foot in our house! You know?"

"Christ," he muttered. "Holy Christ! She's stoned out of her skull."

Laura started to drive. Tightly she asked, "Gray, what exactly am I supposed to do here? You're busy and you'll be busier, but what is there for me to do?" There were no jobs in Ashland, she had learned already.

"Can't you just relax for a few months?"

"Doing what? There's nothing here! Don't you understand? I'm in someone else's house with nothing to do and no one to talk to and nowhere to go."

"We've been here less than a week, for Christ sake! What do you expect?" He said, more quietly, "Look, Ginnie's having Ro, the two of us, and her friend from the university for dinner tomorrow night. Peter can introduce you to a whole new set of people, not theater people."

That was the problem, she admitted to herself. When they first met, he had moved into her circle of friends effortlessly. Over the year she had dropped most of them, but it had been gradual, and there were a few she had kept to the end in Connecticut. He had not moved into the university theater group the way he was doing here. He had known that was a stopgap, temporary, and he had not cared to make the effort then. And she had been busy. There had never been quite enough time there, but when she gazed into the future here, the next months anyway, all she could see was herself alone in a stranger's lovely house where there was nothing for her to do.

She jerked the car when she shifted gears climbing their steep hill. "Goddamn it!" She glanced at Gray; he was looking out his window and seemed very distant, too far to reach.

"Ignore the mess," Ginnie called out when they arrived at her house the next night. "Just step over anything, or kick it out of the way."

She had yelled for them to come on in, and now as they stood in the foyer, she appeared, wiping her hands on a towel. "I sent Peter out for some whipping cream, and Uncle Ro's late. He's always late for dinner at my house. He hates the preliminaries, all that cheese and stuff. Hang up your things in the closet behind you. My hands are sticky." She backed her way into the living room, leading them. "Come on out to the kitchen, okay? I'm up to my elbows in pie crust."

The house was all up and down. Stairs led up to the kitchen, which was large with many cabinets, a handsome oak table with six chairs. Other stairs led to other areas. It seemed too big a house for a single person. On the table in the kitchen there was a blue ceramic platter with Brie and wheat crackers, grapes, and prosciutto, paper-thin, rolled and held with toothpicks. White wine was in a cooler, red wine in a decanter.

"Please help yourselves," Ginnie said, waving to the table. "I have to get this goddamn crust in one piece in the pie pan. . . ." She worked at the counter, muttering under her breath. After a moment, she drew back and surveyed her effort. "To hell with it," she said. "That's why I decided to send Peter for whipping cream. It can hide a multitude of sins."

Ro and Peter arrived almost together and she moved the platter and wine to the living room. Dinner was late.

When it was finally ready, Ginnie brought a casserole to the table and said in awe, "My God, look at it! It's gorgeous!"

It was salmon with shrimp and crab stuffing, and it was beautiful.

"Haven't you made it before?" Laura asked.

"Nope. I always try things out on company. Oh, salad." She jumped up to get the salad from the refrigerator.

"I'm too chicken to experiment like that," Laura said. "What happens is that I try everything out the week of the dinner party, and by the time we have it a second time, I'm bored with it."

"I guess I figure why should I suffer alone if something doesn't work." She looked at her uncle. "William said that Sunshine was in the costumes today. Anna will take her head off for her."

Ro looked unhappy. "I know. We straightened that out. She was just trying on stuff, she said, smiling like an angel. I marched her around the theater, showing her what's off-limits, where she's allowed to go. She wanted to go below and see the trapdoor mechanism. Her words."

Gray shrugged helplessly. "Darned if I know what to do with her."

Ro said, very quietly, "Me too."

And that, Ginnie thought, was known as allowing enough rope.

"We'll work on the play this week, maybe into next week," Gray said. "And then I'll tell her to go back home until late January."

"What trapdoor?" Peter asked suddenly.

"A lot of theaters used to have a single trapdoor on stage," Ginnie said. "They called it the Macbeth Trap, for Banquo's ghost to make his appearance and disappearance."

Ro snorted. "Where'd you hear that? It's the Hamlet Trap. That's where they bury Ophelia."

Ginnie flushed. "I don't believe you. It's the Macbeth Trap. Everything I've ever read about it says that."

"Well, honey, I think you read the wrong things." Ro's voice was easy, he was relaxed, enjoying the evening, the home-cooked meal. Neither he nor anyone else was prepared for the flash of anger that made Ginnie's voice shake when she abruptly left the table.

"Would it ever occur to you that maybe you could be wrong? Why is it always the other person?"

Gray reached for the wine and poured more for himself and for Peter, who was watching Ginnie with a frown. "I've seen it both ways," Gray said. "What I told Sunshine was that there's been a plague of spiders below stage and we had to call in exterminators who used some kind of spray on them. She doesn't go places that have been sprayed."

Ginnie came back with small plates for pie and started to clear the table. "Now you see the magic of whipped cream," she said, but her voice was strained.

As soon as they were all finished, Peter said, "Maybe you'd like to see the house? Would you mind, Ginnie? It's such a great house," he added to Laura. "And her models are terrific."

"Let me," Ro said, and took Gray and Laura off for a tour.

Peter held Ginnie in his arms. "What happened? Are you all right?"

She nodded. "It's . . . I don't know what came over me. It's okay now. Sorry."

Together they filled the dishwasher and prepared the coffee tray. Then the others returned to the kitchen, talking about the models of stage sets that Ginnie had done.

"They're wonderful, just wonderful," Laura said. "What a shame they aren't on permanent display somewhere."

Ro nodded emphatically. "In the lobby. I keep saying we should set up a showcase in the lobby."

Ginnie laughed and shook her head. "Come on. Let's have coffee."

"Gray, how do you feel about musicals, operettas, even opera?" Ro asked suddenly.

Ginnie stopped and looked at Gray, waiting. He nodded, puzzled by the question.

"You see, Ginnie and I tried to talk Kirby into something last year that he really balked at. Never saw him come on so stubborn, but there it was. We had to give it up. What we wanted was *The Threepenny Opera*. Kirby turned it down flat, and if the director says no, you'd better back off or you'll have a mess on your hands."

Gray's eyes had narrowed. "It's a major production. Do you have the singers, the musicians?"

"Some of the best."

Ginnie began to sing in a husky voice: " 'And the shark he has his teeth and / There they are for all to see. / And Macheath he has his knife but / No one knows where it may be—' "

She broke off and laughed. "It has wonderful music!"

She could tell by Gray's attitude that he was hearing the Kurt Weill music in his head. She put the cream on the tray and Peter picked it up to take to the living room. That was when the party ended, Laura later thought, when Gray nodded, and then again, with enthusiasm, and the three of them, Ro, Ginnie, and Gray, forgot Laura and Peter for the next two hours.

They were talking animatedly about the pros and cons of updating it rather than making it a period piece when Peter motioned to Laura and asked, "Did you see Romeo and Juliet in the workroom?"

Laura was certain that none of the others even noticed when she and Peter left.

"Do you know *The Threepenny Opera*?" Peter asked in the workroom.

She shook her head. "I know the song Ginnie sang, or at least it was familiar when she sang it. I couldn't have come up with it by myself."

"Me too. Here's Romeo." He took a tiny doll from a shelf and placed it in one of the sets. It was in scale. "And there's Juliet, hiding as usual." He put her in a different set. Each model set was about fifteen inches high, about that deep, and a little wider. Laura thought one set was for *A Doll's House;* she didn't know the other one. They were not labeled.

"Two different worlds," she said faintly. "They'll never get together that way, will they?"

He moved Romeo to Juliet's world. "How strange to think of all those worlds existing side by side, each one playing out its little drama, none of the people even aware of the other worlds, other people."

Shelves filled one whole wall; the sets were side by side from floor to ceiling, pigeonhole worlds, each cut off from the others, invisible to the others. Laura shivered and drew her sweater closer about her. Romeo and Juliet were together for the present, but she knew what the future held for them.

"It must be fun to make worlds, play with dolls, and call it work," she said.

He nodded. "Speaking of work, Ginnie says you're looking for a job. There's a man at the university, Dr. Lockell, who's looking for a research assistant for a book he's doing. It's his life's work and he's been at it for years and God knows if he'll ever finish it, but he does want an assistant."

"In what field? I've never done anything just like that."

"Paleontology. But it doesn't matter if you know the subject. Believe me, he knows it. He's out to prove his theory in the face of opposition from the establishment that Indians were in the area thirty thousand years ago. The conventional wisdom is that they came twelve thousand years ago, no earlier. He's been amassing data for forty years. Now he's looking for someone to help sort it, to type his notes, organize his findings. He really doesn't want an expert, just someone able to do organizational work. Would you be interested in talking to him about it?"

She nodded. "You got our house, and now you're finding a job for me. How can I thank you?"

With a wry grin he moved Romeo once more, away from Juliet, out of her world. He looked at the two dolls and said, "Maybe, if they can't get together all that much, they need someone else to talk to, someone who understands about all those separate worlds."

Laura wanted to weep, for both of them.

7

Ginnie slumped in a chair in her living room. "It's the damn budget meetings that get me," she groaned. "Gray made Eric fly off the handle by suggesting maybe he wouldn't be able to keep up with all the stage managing, prompting, helping with the directing, and Eric yelled that he could do it, but not with Gray standing over his shoulder all the time. Uncle Ro had to get between them, and then he stirred it all up again by saying he still thinks Sunshine's play should be abandoned, and Sunshine put down a well or something. She's driving everyone crazy." She sighed and accepted the glass Peter held out. It was a rather strong gin and tonic. She drank gratefully.

Peter nodded. Laura had told him that Gray's rewrite of Sunshine's play was driving him, her, and Sunshine all mad. No matter what he did, Sunshine undid it. Her current version would run three hours. Gray had said it would work, and he'd make it work if it killed him. He was up most of the night, night after night with it. As far as she could see, it got no better, just longer.

"Ginnie, is it always like this at this time of the year?" Peter asked.

She shook her head. "Part of it is. This is when they do all the repairs on the theater, painting, cleaning the carpets, plumbing, all that work that gets put off during the season. But the rest of it . . . It's because we have a new director, that makes people nervous; and that woman." She shook her head, drank again. "That helps. Now, let me tell you our program for the year."

He put his finger on her lips. "No more show biz for tonight. Finish your drink, wash your face, and change your clothes. Remember the dinner my department's giving me? It's tonight, one hour from now."

She jumped up. "Oh, damn! I forgot!"

"I know. But I remembered and there's plenty of time."

She looked stricken. "How can you stand it? Why do you put up with me?"

"Because I love you. Now scoot."

There were twelve people at the dinner in Margo's Restaurant, and although Ginnie had met most of them at one time or another, he was certain she did not remember. She charmed them all anew.

"When I was in grade school," she said late in the evening, "I took my collection of rocks for show-and-tell. Remember show-and-tell? It's how they torture children and get away with it. We had to participate. Anyway, I got up and showed my sorry bunch of junk and talked about the Indian heads I had found and they all laughed. I fought at recess with a boy who was built like an ape over it, won, too. It was years later that I realized they were arrowheads."

She told theater stories only when asked. ". . . so she finished her aria and jumped over the balcony," she said. "The stagehands were there with a trampolinelike thing, a fireman's net or something. Well, she hit it wrong, and up came her feet, then a second time, and even a third time. The audience pretended not to notice."

Finally it was over and Peter and Ginnie walked to his car. He put his arm around her shoulders. "You were swell," he said.

"What do you mean?" she asked carefully.

"Ah, Ginnie, I've known you for eight months now, in all kinds of moods. Tonight you were an Oscar candidate. Thanks."

"I'm sorry," she said in a low voice. "They're nice people."

"Shh. No more. Let's go home."

Their lovemaking was almost desperate that night. Ginnie was almost desperate, he thought later, when she was asleep. She knew it was ending, he thought, just as he did. And there wasn't a damn thing either of them could do about it. He had seen Ro in the restaurant when they entered and had pretended not to; Ginnie had not seen him. He had hated the man with an intensity that was alarming at that moment. Ro would win, Peter realized, and not have to lift a finger, say a word. There was nothing he, Peter, could offer her that could compete with what Ro could give her. He thought of her model sets, of Romeo and Juliet in separate worlds. It was a long time before he could sleep.

Ginnie prowled the theater. Outside Gray's office door she paused momentarily. He was shouting, "Damn it, Sunshine, what would a real live man say when he brought home a strange woman? Not, 'This is my angel of destruction.' My God, not that!" Ginnie moved on.

William was directing a crew changing a cable from the overhead grid. She watched for a second, moved on. Bobby was in the light box, playing with his new system. She watched the light sweep across the stage floor, moved on. Anna yelled at a deliveryman not to put it there, goddamn it! Eric and Brenda were arguing about something near the call-board; Brenda stormed away, Eric turned and yelled at a painter. Ginnie left the backstage area, made her way through the dim auditorium, using a penlight now and then in places where the stage lights did not reach, and finally sat down in the last row center. She carried her sketchbooks and pencils in her bag. She stared blankly at the stage, ignoring the men working on it, ignoring the lights that changed with incredible speed. Bobby was having a private light show. After a while she brought out a sketchbook, and her hand flew as she did one sketch after another, hardly even looking at what she was doing, only occasionally shining her light on the pages. After a time she got up and moved to the left of the auditorium, sat down and began to sketch again. She moved several more times, barely aware of when she did so, paying little attention to where she was sitting, never staying long in one place.

She was startled suddenly by Sunshine's voice directly behind her. "Is that how you do it, in the dark? I should have guessed. Your aura's blue, you know?"

Ginnie snapped the book shut. "What are you doing back here, Sunshine? I thought Uncle Ro told you to stay backstage."

"No, that never came up. I can't go in the light box, or below stage, or in any of the offices. He didn't say I can't come sit out here. How can you see what you're doing?"

"I can't." She stuffed the sketchbook and pencil back in the bag and started to get up.

"You want me to read your cards? I read tarot, you know?"

"No, thank you. I have to go now."

"I read them already, you know? I do that, read them first just to make sure there's nothing terrible coming up. If there is, I don't like to talk about it. Yours isn't so terrible. But you have black spots, you know?"

"I don't know what you're talking about. I have to go." She fled.

She found Gray in his office. He looked as tired as she felt. The manuscript was on his desk. Kirby had stripped the room of all but the basic furniture: the desk, two chairs, a filing cabinet. Gray had added nothing of his own. It looked barren and uninhabited.

"I have to talk to you," she said at the door, and waited for his nod. She entered, closed the door behind her, and crossed the room to stand before the desk.

"You've got to get that woman out of the theater. She has to go."

"Sunshine? What's she done now?"

"Never mind specifics. You know how it's been with her. She's . . . she has to be out before auditions start."

He stood up. "I wasn't aware that I was to take orders from you. Is this a new thing, or are you presuming a bit too much?"

"Damn it, Gray! You know how disruptive she is! She's driving people bananas! And for what? Why should anyone have to put up with her?"

He snatched up the play. "This is why. Listen." He read the first page, then the next. He was a very good reader, better than many actors she had heard reading. He slammed the manuscript down again and glared at her. "Say it! It's good and you know it!"

She nodded. "It's good. I'm surprised, but it's good. Your work or hers?"

"Hers! I have to force her to read each line, say each line and then tell me what she wants them to say, and then get that on paper, but it's hers. And it's damn good."

"I don't care! If she were writing a masterpiece, if she were writing *Faustus* I wouldn't care! It isn't worth it to the rest of us!"

"If you can't control your own temperament, maybe it's your problem, not hers!"

The door opened and William stuck his head in. "Private fight, or can anyone get in on it?" Directly behind him was Ro. He gave William a push and they both entered. The office was very crowded suddenly.

"Ah, you know, on this side of the building, the walls are pretty thin," William said apologetically.

"That woman's out there hanging on every word," Ro said in an icy tone.

"Well, let her hear!" Ginnie yelled. "Let everyone hear! What do you think it's going to be like around this place when she starts doing tarot readings for the cast? Can you imagine it? 'I see a catastrophe, a terrible accident. Avoid dark men.' Bullshit!"

She suddenly passed William and Ro and yanked the door open and screamed, "Get the fuck away from this door! Get out of here and let us have some privacy!"

"I wouldn't say anything like that," Sunshine said, smiling gently. "I told you I don't say when things look bad." She smiled at the men vaguely and turned, wandered slowly down the narrow hallway toward the costume room. Her shopping bag clinked and clanged as she moved.

"She minds you," William said doubtfully to Ro. "Order her not to read the cards."

"Then she'd turn up with chicken entrails or a crystal ball or something," Ginnie snapped. "You can't think of all the things you'd have to order her not to do. It's don't-put-beans-up-your-nose time with her."

"Simmer down, honey," Ro said then. "How long do you need with her?" he asked Gray.

"Another week at least. She's doing good work right now. It's just that she has to wander about and think from time to time. Maybe I can keep her confined to the office when she's here."

"Maybe you can make time move backward," Ginnie muttered.

"Maybe you've got some kind of personal problem you're taking out on her," he shot back at her.

"And after you're through writing her play for her, what then? You know damn well she's not going away until it's staged and she plays prima donna at opening night. If you order her to stay out of the theater, she'll hang out at the door smiling at everyone who comes in. My God, she's an albatross!" She pulled the door open. "I'm edgy, and bitchy, and tense, and mean as hell, buster, and it's not because I have a problem. It's because I have work to do and want to do it and this is how I get. I don't need you, or your discovery, to add to any of those things. I'm going home and I won't be back until she's gone. Call me when it's over." She slammed the door behind her.

Gray sank back into his chair and expelled a long breath.

Ro went to the door. His face was composed, his voice flat as he said, "This is your problem, Gray. Solve it before tonight." He left.

"We'd better have a little talk," William said. He pulled a chair around to face the desk and sat down. "There are a couple of things that I don't think you understand yet. One is that Ro won't put up with a lot of hassle where Ginnie's concerned. And less where the theater's concerned. That's just how it is with him. Now what are we going to do about Sunshine?"

Gray shrugged helplessly. "God, I don't know. Laura won't let me take her to the house. We can't work in that room she's renting. I tried and it's hopeless."

"There are several possibilities," William said slowly. "One's here, and that's out. Believe me, Gray, that's really out. Ro knows how Ginnie works. She prowls backstage, out in the auditorium, in the light box, out in the shop, and then she settles somewhere drawing like a maniac. And up again. She walks miles in this stage, and she lied when she said she gets mean. Usually she won't even see you or say a word to anyone. And we've all learned to leave her alone. She's too good to upset, you see, and Ro knows that. He won't let you, or Sunshine, or anyone else upset her. It's not even a choice between her and Sunshine. No choice to it. And I'm afraid that there wouldn't be a choice between you and her, either. Just how it is."

Gray nodded, knowing it also. That meant his house, he realized, and he knew Laura would have to accept it. She had no choice either.

William went on. "And when Ro said by tonight, that's what he meant. He'll want to know exactly how it's been settled, and he'll want to know by tonight. So, it's her room, or your house, or rent an office, or something." He stood up. "I'll talk to my wife about her. Maybe she can stay out at my house during the day until the show opens. Shannon's sick, she might even like having someone in to read the cards, make herb teas, just coddle her generally. I'll see about that."

Gray rose, too. He held out his hand and William shook it. "Thanks. I'll tell Ro I'm getting her out of here, at least until rehearsals."

When Gray told Laura, she stared at him, her eyes wide and frightened. "Don't you see what's happening?" she whispered. "We're acting out her play."

She remembered what he had said about entering another reality, living it, making others accept it. But not me, she wanted to cry out.

"I don't have a choice," Gray said tiredly. "It won't be for long, a week at the most."

Silently she went to the kitchen to start dinner. The next afternoon when Gray returned from the theater to work with Sunshine, he found her reading the cards for Laura.

"What are you doing here? I told you to come at two."

"I didn't want to make you wait for me, so I came early," Sunshine said, smiling her gentle, soft smile.

He looked at Laura. Very brightly she said, "Well, I'm off to the university. I'll work until five or a little after. See you later."

Too bright, too cheerful, he knew, and felt helpless to do anything about it.

It was cold outside, a week before Christmas, and Laura drove instead of walking as she usually did. That had been as silly as she had known it would be, she told herself. Sunshine was mildly crazy, not dangerous certainly, but not quite normal. Auras and tarot cards and prophetic dreams! Silly woman. Still, the words played around and around in her head like a tape loop.

"Danger in water. Money all around. Dreams and illusions, fantasies lead to danger in water, death in water."

8

You want to see it?" Ginnie asked Peter, indicating her large sketch pad.

He joined her in her workroom, stood by her desk. "Okay. The stage is pretty bare for the whole thing. The desk is the symbol of Big Nurse's authority, right? When she's on stage, the light is cold blue, but subliminal, not blatant. There are three levels, one with her desk, one that the inmates use to approach her, the guards use, and so on. That's where they have the sessions. And the lowest level is where the patients talk to each other. When Mac is on stage the light is warm, yellows, reds, again subliminal. The fishing scene has a sky cyc and blue lights running along the floor. Bobby can do amazing things with those lights. The desk is the boat with the men hanging on top of it, one or even two of them on top of it, and the upper platform is gone. They've taken the authority to themselves. Then, for Mac's death, there's only one level. The desk is his bed where Chief kills him. Moonlight comes through the big window here. That's where Chief bends the bars and walks away, into the moonlight."

She looked at him, waiting for his response. His throat felt too tight to speak. Finally he said, "It's terrific, really powerful."

She sighed. She was tired, and by now the idea that had hit her with such force seemed self-indulgent, incomplete.

"I wish you could come with me. I really want to show you off to my folks."

"I know. I wish I could."

"Yeah. Well, remember you promised me New Year's Eve. And the whole week starting on the seventh."

"I didn't either," she said indignantly.

"I know, but you will. Wait and see. I'll be back on the thirtieth. Take care of yourself. Get some rest, okay?"

"I'll be at the airport. Be careful driving. There's new snow on the pass."

He nodded and kissed her and left. Before his car was out of her driveway, she was back at work, humming softly to herself the Moritat from *The Threepenny Opera:* "When the shark has had his dinner / There is blood upon his fins. / But Macheath he has his gloves on: / They say nothing of his sins. . . ."

Ginnie saw Laura and Gray at a party now and then over the holidays, but she did not go to many, and did not stay long when she did, and they did not mention Sunshine, or the rift she had caused briefly. Ginnie knew that Gray was as busy right now as she was; they were the two busiest people of the theater group at the moment. He had all the plays to update, alter, shorten or lengthen, whatever, and she had her preliminary drawings to get done by the first of the year. As soon as he handed copies over to Anna Kaminsky she would hurl herself into work, too, on the costumes, but for now Anna was free, as were most of the others.

Sunshine was going to William's house every day to keep Shannon company. She had decided that she could cure Shannon's defective heart with her herbs and a regimen of vitamins and fruit juices. Shannon, William reported, was thriving on the treatment.

Laura was terrified of Shannon. She had met her only once and made excuses to avoid seeing her again. The only way Shannon could get William's attention even momentarily, she believed, was through illness, and it was frightening to her that a woman would prefer that to being alone. When she mentioned her theory to Gray he looked at her as if she had committed a particularly nasty blasphemy.

For the most part she stayed home and stared at the small Christmas tree she had decorated, did a little work for her employer, who had gone to Indiana for the holidays, and waited for Gray to come home, or for Gray to finish what he was doing and talk to her, or for Gray to get ready to go out to dinner or to a movie with her. Waiting, waiting, she thought, that was her life here in ash land.

Gray had told her about the big fight with Ginnie and Ro over Sunshine, and she often found herself praying that Sunshine's play would be so bad, that she would make such a nuisance of herself, that Gray would get in such trouble over her that Ro would simply fire him and they could go back home and life would be as it had been.

The day after Christmas Ginnie told her uncle that she had given Peter the model for the production of *Major Barbara*.

"You gave it away?" He tried belatedly to keep the surprise and shock out of his voice.

"For Christmas. He really liked that one."

"Ginnie, those models, they aren't for things like that. They belong in the archives, in a collection."

She was sitting in the yellow chair, he was on the couch facing her. She had given him eggnog and cookies, her contribution to the holiday spirit. Slowly she said, "They're mine, Uncle Ro, not theater property. Like my sketches, my notes."

"No, you're wrong. They belong to the theater, not to you, or me, to the theater."

"It's not a body that can own anything. It's a building where we make things happen, but it's nothing in and of itself," she said emphatically.

He shook his head. "That's what it was when I first came to Ashland, a shell, abandoned, in disrepair, ready for the wreckers, but now . . . I hope you'll come to know it's more than that. It really is more than that, Ginnie, or it wouldn't matter about the models. I'd see it burned to the ground before I'd turn it over to a holding company, or a board of directors who saw it only as a way to make a good return on their investment."

"Well, the theater doesn't own me," she said firmly. "You know I've had offers to do sets for other theaters. I can work anywhere, send in my designs, models, finished drawings. I don't have to be there even. I don't have to be here, as far as that goes."

"But you do. I've seen those sets done by a designer in absentia. No heart, no soul. They could get them out of the book. Yours aren't like that."

"You're prejudiced," she said, and bit a cookie in half.

"I noticed that you didn't take any of those offers."

"I'm not ready. I still need to travel, see more and more theater all over the world, see what other people are doing, see how other people live. I didn't say I'd never take on outside work, just not now."

"And where are you planning to travel this year?"

"I've been thinking of South America. Peru maybe." She put the other half of the cookie down; it tasted stale and too dry.

Ro drank his eggnog and for a moment she thought the conversation had ended. Then he said, "Isn't that where Peter is going when he gets his Ph.D.?"

"He says digging in Peru is the greatest," she said with a grin.

He stood up and stretched and then, looking at her narrowly, asked, "Honey, do you love him?"

She hesitated. "I don't know. I'm trying to decide, I guess." She was trying to love him, she wanted to add, but she didn't know how; she was afraid of it.

"Well, I have to get along. You'll have the preliminaries done over the weekend? I'd like to see them before you show them to Gray, if you don't mind. I expect to have his promptbook for that damn play by this weekend. It'd better be decent."

"Are you holding him to showing you all of them?"

"You bet I am. I'm afraid my confidence in him was shaken over this mess with Sunshine. *Sunshine!* for God's sake! More like foul weather, if you ask me. You're looking tired. Pack it up and get some sleep, okay?"

She smiled at him and kissed his cheek. "Nag, nag."

"That's my job," he said and left.

Peter returned for New Year's Eve and they spent the evening at Bellair Inn, where they had dinner, then danced until two.

Peter was packing up his apartment; he already had taken a carload of things to southern California and had left his car there. "I have something to show you," he said mysteriously. "I can't wait. But I'm not willing to do it until you can appreciate it, not while your mind is completely on theater sets."

"Peter, be reasonable. I can't take off a whole week right now."

"You turn in the drawings for Gray to look at on Monday or Tuesday, right? That's what you told me. The following Monday there are auditions and you want to be back by then. But what do you have to do during that week? Even if you make changes, you can't start until after Gray's had a chance to look them over, and you know as well as I do that he's going to love them. You won't work on the models until after the cast is chosen and you've heard the readings. You said that."

"My God! Do you remember every word I've ever said?"

"Yes. I'm going to leave you strictly alone until Friday, when I'll arrive with dinner makings. And detailed plans for our week. Meanwhile, eat. Sleep. I love you."

She could do it, she knew. There was still a lot of work to finish, but by Friday afternoon she could be done. As for a whole week off right now, she was still certain she could not do that, but a few days surely. Four days, five? She went back to work.

There had been rain off and on for a week. Laura sat at the dinette table and talked to her mother, who reported three inches of snow on the ground. They had had a white Christmas, she said. Laura called Marianne next and heard about more snow and parties and how hard it was to get anyone to replace her. She gazed out the window at the dripping trees and found herself weeping. She could not explain it to Marianne; she simply hung up on her friend. She would say the connection was broken somewhere along the line. For a long time she wept. Everything she did was wrong, she kept thinking. She had complained about not having the car and he had put on his raincoat and walked to the theater; Ginnie had driven him home hours later. She complained about not going anywhere and he took her to one of their parties where she was miserable. And tonight, when she wanted him to go to a movie with her, and listen to jazz in a tavern with her, he had to go to a damn high-school play and check out the kids. When he asked her to go with him, she practically screamed no at him. No more plays, no more performances, no more theater, even if it was in a high-school auditorium and the kids were wonderful.

By the time Gray arrived with the car, she was carefully made up, no traces of tears remaining.

"I'll drop you off at the movie," he said. "I'll go on to the school thing and meet you at the bar at nine or nine-thirty. Would that satisfy you? We can stay as long as you want."

She shrugged. The movie house was only two blocks from the tavern and it was a reasonable concession, but she was in no mood even to pretend she was pleased with it. Neither spoke when they left the house.

Peter had brought steaks, salad greens, potatoes. "I knew you would skip food," he said reproachfully. "Look at you, five pounds lighter than last week."

She eyed the steaks hungrily and moved out of his way. It was not that she didn't get hungry when she was working hard, it was only that real meals were a nuisance and she ate whatever she could find that did not require cooking. Cereal, peanut butter, fruit.

"Anyway, I'm done," she said, seated at the table, where he brought her guacamole and tortilla chips. Fattening foods, she thought, and ate gratefully.

"I knew you would be. There's a map on the table. I marked our trip for tomorrow. Want to take a look?"

It was a topographical map with a yellow highlighted line that weaved in and out of the hills to the northwest. "What's there?"

"You'll see when we get there. The woods are wet, remember to bring some extra socks."

"And snowshoes?"

"Nope. We won't be going up. In fact, it's lower than it is here. Eight hundred feet maybe. Now, no more questions."

They would take their first trip and return to her house, he told her over dinner, and on the next day, Sunday, on to the coast, to Whale's Head. There were cottages with fireplaces, overlooking the ocean, and a gourmet restaurant ten minutes from them. . . .

He took her hand. "Okay? I'm not asking for any commitment, not for more than the next week anyway. The rest can wait."

"It isn't fair to you," she said softly.

"It's much better to be me in love with you than to be anyone else on earth," he said. "That's as fair as I expect life to be." He squeezed her hand slightly. "Okay?"

She nodded. "I have to get the sketches to Uncle Ro in the morning, and tell him I'm going."

"Can't you do that tonight? I want us to start without anything hanging over us, just you and me—no work, no problems."

"You win. I'll write him a note and leave it with the drawings at the theater. That's where he'll go first thing in the morning anyway."

"Good. I'll come and we can pick up my gear and be all set to leave at the crack of dawn."

It was raining very hard when they left the house. Ginnie drove down Pioneer Street and turned into the alley by the side of the theater. The rain drummed on the car.

"I'll take the stuff inside," Peter said. "I have to get out at my apartment, anyway. No point in both of us getting soaked."

"You'll need a key, and there's Gray's raincoat on the back-seat. He left it there a few days ago. You know where the office is?"

He nodded and dragged the raincoat over the seat, struggled to get it on and couldn't in the car. He draped it over his head and took the portfolio and key from her.

"Don't put it on his desk," she said. "Just leave it on the table. He's sure to see it first thing there."

"Right." He opened the door and dashed out into the driving rain. Ginnie watched him enter the theater through the stage door, then turned off the windshield wipers and headlights to wait for him. If this kept up into the morning, she thought, it would be one hell of a hike in the woods. Maybe he would call it off, do something more sensible, like curling up in her house before the fireplace and napping all day. She smiled slightly. Peter had had her out in all kinds of weather. He didn't seem to notice if it was raining or not. Like Christopher Robin, she thought, he didn't care what it did just as long as he could be out in it.

She was content, satiated with good food and good wine, warm, and sleepy. Not only did she not eat often or properly when she was working hard, she also did not sleep on schedule.

She tried to remember the past ten days, when and how long she had slept at a time. It was a blur. Not enough, she decided, yawning.

She was not sure how long she had been waiting for Peter when she realized that it was taking him too long. If Spotty had cornered him, she thought, she would be out here waiting forever. She gave him another minute or two, then got out of the car and ran to the stage door. She expected it to be closed and locked, but Peter had not pulled it to, and she pushed it open and went inside. There was a dim light on in the backstage area. It cast a feeble glow down the hallway to Uncle Ro's office, where she could see a brighter light outlining the partly open door. She went down the hall to the office and pushed that door open.

"Peter?" she called, and then she saw him, and she screamed.

9

Gus Chisolm had been the chief of police for eleven years, and during that time there had been murder done, robberies, whatever mayhem people found to commit against other people and property. His first act when he arrived and saw a body was to call the sheriff's office. All murders were handled by that office. He was glad it was like that. Now he surveyed the office from the doorway glumly. Burglar caught in the act? More than likely. One of his men was at the door, another was checking the other entrances of the theater. A search would have to wait for more personnel. He went back to Spotty's room, where Ginnie sat like a marble statue, with just about that much color in her face. She stared straight ahead, exactly as he had left her. She needed a doctor, he thought, and wished the officer he had sent out to find Ro Cavanaugh would hurry on with it before the sheriff's detective got there. He knew Steve Draker would want to question Ginnie right now, and to his eyes she was not fit to answer even one question.

On the table by her chair was the coffee that Spotty had

poured for her, placed in her hands. Gus picked it up and said, "Ginnie, drink some of this. You'll have to answer a few questions."

Obediently she took the cup and sipped from it and returned it to the table.

Gus sighed and pulled a straight chair around to face her and sat in it. "Ginnie, didn't you see anyone at all? Someone come out the door and run, maybe?"

"No."

"Do you remember what happened?"

She nodded.

He wanted to shake her, to make her cry, faint, do something, to make her face stop looking as dead as Peter Ellis was. He patted her arm and stood up. Spotty was watching her with an expression of worry also. Gus motioned to him to step outside the small room.

"Do you know who her doctor is?"

"Jack Warnecke, more than likely. He's Ro's doctor, leastways."

"I think we shouldn't wait for Ro. You'd better go to a phone and call him. Tell him what she's like, what happened here. Tell him to bring something for her." So to hell with Draker, he thought. She needed something. He had known Ginnie first when she was a kid living with Ro, then since she had been back in town working in the theater. He never had seen her like this and he didn't like it. To hell with Draker.

Ro arrived before Draker. He came in with Walt Olien, who reported: "He was at Jake's Place with Jerry Alistair and a couple of other people. They drove over from the high school together."

Gus returned to Spotty's room, where Ro was holding Ginnie, looking almost as pale as she was.

"My God, my God," he said over and over.

There were raindrops on Ro's shoulders and his shoes were wet, Gus saw. But anyone who entered the theater tonight would have wet feet. The alley was awash and a small lake was in front of the stage door. Ginnie was not responding in any way to Ro.

A deputy came to report that the theater was locked up tight, as was the shop out back. He had glanced in various rooms, but had not made a real search. Then Draker arrived with his crew and officially the case was out of Gus's hands.

Gus went with him to the office and waited while he looked over the scene. Peter Ellis was stretched out on the floor with the side of his head caved in from a heavy blow. There was an upset wooden chair that he must have hit on the way down; nothing else seemed out of order, except for a bronze statuette of a clown that was lying by the doorjamb. It was covered with blood on one end. Gus told Draker what he knew about it, damn little. Steve Draker was a thin man of forty with an intense stare that Gus hated. He always looked like he was trying to see clear through you, he thought, when they returned to Spotty's room. He watched Draker make himself comfortable in a straight chair within touching distance of Ginnie. Ro still held her against his chest.

"I have to ask her a few questions," Draker said. "Would you mind stepping over there."

Ro was on his knees in front of Ginnie's chair. He moved to the side and sat on the arm, and held her around the shoulders.

"You're Roman Cavanaugh?" Draker asked. Ro nodded. "The young lady looks perfectly calm to me. If you don't mind moving out of the way . . ."

"I do mind," Ro said. "Can't you see that she's in shock? Her doctor's on his way now. I don't want you to bother her until the doctor says she's all right."

"Miss Braden, do you feel able to answer questions?" Draker asked, turning his penetrating gaze on her. She nodded. "Good. What happened here tonight?"

"He's dead."

"Yes. We know that. Why did he come here?"

"To bring my sketches."

"Were you with him?"

"Yes."

"Who killed him, Miss Braden?"

"I don't know."

"But you said you were with him."

She looked straight ahead without responding.

Ro tightened his grip on her shoulder. His face was darkening with rage. "Damn you," he said. "This can wait for the doctor."

"Mr. Cavanaugh, I have a job to do. Don't interfere, or I'll have you escorted out to wait. Miss Braden, did you see who hit Mr. Ellis?"

"No."

"Where were you? Why didn't you see it happen?"

"I was in the car."

Draker leaned forward. "Just tell me what happened. I don't want to draw it out of you a word at a time."

"I came in and he was dead."

"Why did he come in? Why didn't you bring in the sketches?"

"It was raining. He wore Gray's raincoat. He was closest to the stage door."

"My God," Ro suddenly said in a horrified voice. "What if she had come in first? That could have been her!"

There was a silence in the room for a minute. Gus heard Jack Warnecke's voice raised in argument with one of the sheriff's men. He stepped out of the room and walked the length of the hallway, saw Jack near the door where the argument was going on.

"Gus, will you tell this man I'm Ginnie's doctor? I demand to see her."

"She's back this way," Gus said. He did not know the name of the deputy who was standing in the way. Coolly he added, "I'll take the responsibility. Get out of the way." The deputy hesitated for a moment, then moved, and Jack followed Gus.

"Miss Braden, why were you trying to close the office door when Spotty found you?" Draker asked, just as the two men entered. He scowled at Gus, his eyes very narrow and shadowed.

"I don't know," Ginnie said in the same dead voice.

Jack went to her and held her wrist, looked at her eyes, backed off a step, and said, "That's all. I'm giving her a sedative. Ro, is there someone who can stay with her tonight?"

"I'll call Brenda. After we're through here, I'll go up to her house, too."

"Good. I'll take her home now and wait for Brenda. Come along, Ginnie."

She stood up.

"Just hold on a minute," Draker said furiously. "I'm not through with her yet."

"Yes, you are," Jack said. "If you pursue questioning with her in this shape, I'll file a complaint, and if I have to I'll testify that nothing she says is reliable. She doesn't know what she's saying. Come on, Ginnie."

"For God's sake!" Ro said to Draker, who had moved to block the way. "You know where she lives, where she'll be."

Draker finally nodded. "I want to see her first thing in the morning. Alone."

"With an attorney," Ro snapped.

Jack led Ginnie out. She moved like an automaton.

Laura and Gray were in separate bedrooms. She stared at the ceiling dry-eyed and replayed again and again the furious scene that had led to her stamping out of the living room, to this room. It had been raining when she left the movie; that had started it, she thought now. A cold, miserable rain that had soaked her almost instantly. He had not been in the tavern when she got there. The jazz pianist had packed the place and she had not been able to get a table, or even a place at the bar. She had stood, cold, wet, more unhappy than she had been in years, in a mob of people she neither knew nor wanted to know. And finally he had come, almost as wet as she was. He had surveyed the crowded tavern bitterly.

"This is your idea of fun?"

"Let's go home. I'm freezing."

"And miss the music? And have you complain I won't go anywhere with you? No way. I want a drink. Besides, it's raining."

"I know it's raining, dammit! Look at me! I'm soaked! You had the car. You lost the umbrella. I didn't have a nice big black umbrella, or a poncho, or a raincoat. I want to go home. Give me the car keys. It's my car, remember?"

Silently he turned and stalked out; she followed. The rain was bitterly cold, relentless. Great puddles had formed in every dip. Her toes ached with cold and she was shivering too hard to drive. And she was crying. Only her tears felt warm on her cheeks, burned her eyes, the rest of her was freezing. Neither spoke when they reached the car in the parking lot and he opened her door, walked around to the driver's side, got in. He drove too fast for the terrible visibility. She hoped he would wreck the car, injure her, be sorry . . . Her tears came harder. The rain on the windshield was too much for the wipers to clear off, and between her own tears and the tears of the car she was blinded.

When they were in the living room, he handed her the keys. "You'll have to beg me to drive it in the future," he said in a voice as hard as ice.

"I won't beg you for anything! I supported you! I quit my job for you! I drove you halfway around the world! When have I ever begged for anything, or even asked for anything? You just take and take and take. You use people and never even notice what you're doing!"

"That's what you think? That I used you? All you've done since we came here is bitch. Is that why? Because you think I was using you?"

"Well, didn't you? Don't you? And now I'm not as useful to you as I was. I can have my own car back. You're finished with it. Now the boss's niece can play my part, drive you here and there. Are you just waiting for Peter to leave before you move in on her? Do you think I can't see?"

"I think that," he said flatly, "I'm going to bed."

"So am I. In the other bedroom."

"Good."

"Damn you to hell! Just damn you to hell!"

The next morning she left before Gray was out of the shower. At the university she learned that Peter had been killed; it was all anyone was talking about. She closed her eyes to hide the instant relief that swept her. The doom she had sensed in ash land was not her doom, thank God. Very quickly her relief vanished and she thought of the terrible things she had said to Gray, and she thought, now Ginnie is really free.

Brenda had talked Ro into going home at two in the morning. There was no place for him to sleep, she had pointed out. She was taking the couch in the living room. Reluctantly he left after looking in on Ginnie, who was in a deep drugged sleep. He was back by eight, half an hour before Draker arrived with one of his deputies.

"How is she?" Draker asked.

"I don't know, calm anyway, still shocked, of course. She's in the kitchen." Ro led him through the foyer, up the stairs to the kitchen, where Ginnie was having coffee. Brenda had made breakfast for her, but it was untouched.

"Good morning, Miss Braden. I hope you're feeling better." She nodded.

"Good. Miss Gearhart, Mr. Cavanaugh, would you mind going into the living room." Brenda left. Ro hesitated. "If she wants an attorney present, that's her right," Draker said. "Do you, Miss Braden?"

"No."

"Ginnie, if you want me, just call. I'll hear you." Ro studied her face for an answer. She barely nodded, and he left the kitchen.

The deputy sat down at the table, out of Ginnie's range of sight, and opened a notebook.

"Miss Braden, I want to say first that I'm very sorry. I do sympathize. I found your note to your uncle saying you were going away with Mr. Ellis for a few days. Will you tell me about that?"

"I don't know where he wanted to go. To Whale's Head. I don't know where else."

"Just tell me about your evening with Mr. Ellis, exactly what you did, when you went to the theater."

She moistened her lips. She looked as if she had been sandbagged, he thought, still pale down to her lips, with the staring eyes that he had seen on others who hadn't yet quite faced what had happened. He waited patiently.

Haltingly she told him about dinner, about the sketches that she had to deliver, about Peter's talking her into taking them to the theater on their way to get his things at his apartment so they could get an early start today.

"So it was raining when you left the house here. Do you know what time it was?"

She shook her head.

In her toneless voice she described driving down Park to Pioneer, into the alley on the side of the theater. She stopped again.

"Did you see any lights on? Your uncle's office is on that side of the building. Were there lights?"

"I don't know. I didn't notice. The rain . . ."

"Okay. You drove to the stage door, then what?"

"Peter said he would have to get out at his place anyway, he might as well be the one to take the portfolio in. Gray's raincoat was in the back. He put it over his head, over the portfolio, and went in."

"How did he get in? Did he ring for Spotty?"

"He used my key."

"Okay. Go on."

"I turned off the wipers and headlights, and there was just the rain. After a while I went in and he was dead."

"Let's take it a little slower, Miss Braden. He had your key. The door locks automatically when it closes. How did you get in?"

"It wasn't closed tight. Sometimes it doesn't and you have to push it. It just opened."

After she cried, Draker thought, she'd be all right. She probably was still full of Jack Warnecke's dope, feeling nothing, her voice distant, her eyes not seeing much of anything. He got up and poured her cold coffee out, filled her cup again, and brought it back. "Take some of it," he said and waited until she swallowed a mouthful or two. "Now, you pushed the door opened. What did you see?"

"Nothing. Spotty was in his room. I went down the hall to Uncle Ro's office and he was there, dead."

"How do you know Spotty was in his room?"

"I don't know."

"Was your uncle's door open?"

"A little." She held up her hand to show about three inches. "Go on."

"I opened the door and went in and he was on the floor. He was dead. I don't know what I did then." She shook her head, as if trying to clear a memory, then sighed. "Then you came."

"Did you touch the doorstop?"

She shook her head.

"You must have stepped over it, or put it in the way yourself. Did you see it?"

"No."

"You know which doorstop I'm talking about, made out of bronze, about this high?" He indicated twelve inches or so.

"The clown," she said.

"Yes. It was in the doorway when I got there. Did you move it?"

"I didn't see it."

"After you saw Mr. Ellis, what did you do? Did you touch him to make sure that he was dead?"

"No. He was dead. I knew he was dead."

"What did you do?"

"I don't know," she said faintly. "I can't remember doing anything at all. I was in Spotty's room and Uncle Ro was there and you came."

"You screamed, Miss Braden. Spotty heard you. Where were you when you screamed?"

"I didn't know I screamed."

"And you had to leave the office again because Spotty found you in the hall. Do you remember leaving the office?"

She shook her head.

"Spotty said you were pulling on the doorknob, trying to close the door. The clown doorstop prevented you from closing it."

Her eyes remained blank, almost unfocused, and again she shook her head.

"Were the lights on?"

"I guess they were. I could see."

"Did you see which lights were on?"

"No."

"Did you have to enter the office to see Mr. Ellis?"

"I opened the door and walked in and saw him."

"Did you step over the doorstop?"

"I don't know."

He took her over it again and then came back to several points but got nothing more from her. Finally he motioned to his deputy, who had made notes, and he stood up. "Get some rest, Miss Braden. I may have to ask you some more questions later. We think he must have surprised a burglar. Miss Braden, do you think anyone could have mistaken him for Gray Wilmot?"

"No."

"He was wearing Wilmot's raincoat over his head, is that right?"

"Yes."

"That's a fairly distinctive raincoat. Not many men here wear them at all."

"It wasn't on his head. I saw his head. . . ." She looked at her hands in her lap.

"Yes. Well, it's a possibility, but we think he walked in on a burglary. I'll be going now. Thank you, Miss Braden."

10

She should have gone down to the funeral," Ro said unhappily to Gray, over lunch five days after the murder. The murder was all they thought about, even if no one spoke openly about it. The detectives kept coming around, asking questions, getting in the way, accomplishing nothing except to keep everyone up-tight; he knew they could not continue in that state indefinitely, not and put on plays at the same time.

"Maybe I should ask her to start work on the models now, not wait for the auditions."

Ro shrugged. "Maybe. Not her routine. Doubt that she'd do it."

"I'm tempted to complain about the sketches, pretend I don't like them, have her do some of them over. Might get a rise out of her, jar her out of this mood."

"I don't think we ought to play any games with her," Ro said heavily.

"Yeah, me too." Gray became silent.

After a long time during which they finished their food and had coffee served, Ro said, "I hear that you and Laura are sep-arating. Sorry."

"Good Christ! Where'd you hear that?"

"I don't know. No secrets in this town, I'm afraid. Sunshine found out first, I bet."

"It's been coming for a long time," Gray said. "She doesn't like it here and hates the weather. She'll probably head back East eventually."

They both looked out the café windows at sleeting rain that was falling steadily. The weather forecast was for snow by the weekend.

"Well, some like it fine, others hate it. I asked you to come with me today so we can talk about Sunshine's play. I read it—God, I don't even know when. It's okay. Not great, not what I would have picked, but you did a good job with her on the rewrite."

Gray lifted his coffee cup to hide the small rush of triumph that he knew would show in his expression, but Ro was not looking at him. He was still gazing moodily out the windows, his thoughts on Ginnie.

"Ginnie's mother went crazy, too, when her husband was killed," Sunshine said to Laura. They were in Laura's kitchen drinking rose-hip tea. Laura hated it and wanted coffee, or even a stiff drink, but Sunshine had insisted on brewing her special tea because Laura had a cold and she could cure it, she had said with her gentle smile. "And Ginnie stopped talking for more than a year. So I guess she went crazy, too."

Laura looked at her in disbelief. "How do you know all that?"

"Shannon tells me. She likes to talk about how it used to be. Sick people are like that, you know? It seems the less future they have the more they live in the past."

"How did Ginnie's father die?"

"Their house burned down and he died in the fire. Ginnie nearly died, too. Ro saved her life. He's really crazy about her, you know? Maybe that's why. People like people they help more than others."

Laura sipped the foul tea. Poor Ginnie, she thought. No wonder she was so withdrawn, so . . . absent. Twice in one lifetime to have violence hit like that. No wonder. She glanced at her watch, then asked, "Sunshine, why did you call me? Is there something you want?"

Sunshine smiled. "You're nice to me, not like the others. They don't like me because I scare them too much, but you've been nice. I read your cards again last night. I wanted to tell you."

"They don't dislike you," Laura said without conviction. "They're all just very busy."

"They're scared because of what I might tell them. They're superstitious, all of them."

"Maybe they just don't believe in the cards, that sort of thing. A lot of people don't. I don't. Not really."

Sunshine's smile did not falter; her pale, vague eyes examined Laura, then flicked over the room. "You should go away," she said. "Back home. Real soon."

Laura felt frozen, immobilized. Finally she whispered, "What do you mean? Why?"

Sunshine stood up and started to gather the various garments she had taken off when she entered. A sweatshirt over the plaid shirt, a jacket over that, a poncho . . . "You know," she said with assurance. "The cards said you know, you're the woman of wisdom, and what you know is dangerous unless you go away. I'll leave the tea. Drink some of it every few hours, you know?"

"I don't know what that means," Laura said and heard a thrum of fear in her own voice.

Sunshine looked at her for a moment, then said softly, "You know. Go away, Laura, real soon, you know?" She picked up her shopping bag; it rattled and clanked.

After Sunshine left, Laura continued to sit at the table. Go away, she told herself. Go away now. Pack up your stuff and leave. It's your car and he won't touch it anyway. She got up and poured the tea down the sink and started a pot of coffee. All she could think of was going away, but not without him, not alone. There had to be a way to get him to leave with her, there had to be. She could burn down the theater, she thought, and she shivered, thinking about Ginnie's father dying in a fire. But it would take something that drastic, that final, she knew.

It snowed several inches on Saturday and on Sunday Laura wrecked the car. She was on her way to the drugstore to get something for her cold, which had worsened considerably. She sat helplessly clutching the wheel when the car went out of control on the icy hill and slid sideways into a tree. She was unhurt, but the car had to be towed to a garage and they said it would be a week before it was repaired. Go away, she thought almost desperately, and now she could not, not for a week. As long as it had been her choice to remain in ash land, she had felt some-

how protected, somehow secure, but now with the choice removed, she knew herself to be vulnerable and her fear grew.

On Monday the temperature was sixty-five, the sun was brilliant,
and crocuses were blooming as if by magic. Good sign, William
told Eric, who nodded, and even smiled faintly. The weather
always broke for auditions, Anna Kaminsky told Gray: a good
sign for the coming season. A good sign, Ro told Gary Boynton,
the shop foreman; an omen of better things to come. A great
season was about to begin.

Ginnie wandered into the auditorium to watch the auditions
that morning. She sat alone and watched without movement for
several hours, then left quietly and went back home. She felt as
if she could not get enough sleep anymore. She wanted little to
eat, but she kept wanting to be in bed, to be asleep. Like a baby,
she thought, and yielded to the urge to go back to bed even
though the sun was shining and the air was warm.

She had sent Brenda home the day after, and that night she
had sent Uncle Ro home when he said he wanted to sleep on
her couch. She did not want anyone in her house, did not want
people to bring her things to eat, to try to hold her hand, talk
soothingly to her. She wanted them all to leave her alone, not
say anything to her, not look at her. She pulled the covers up
to her chin and fell instantly into that deep dreamless sleep that
she craved.

For the first time since that night, she came awake again after
a few hours. She was wide awake all at once, and her stomach
ached with hunger. She got up and was surprised to find a big
piece of ham in her refrigerator, and cheese, milk, fruit. Uncle
Ro? Juanita? She could not remember who had shopped for her.
After a few bites of a sandwich, she pushed it aside, but the milk
was good, and the cookies she found on her counter. On the
end of the table there was a stack of unopened mail, and there
was the map that Peter had brought over that night. She drew
it across the table and opened it, traced the highlighted trail with
her finger. He had wanted to show her something.

She did not go back to sleep. She looked in her workroom at
the drawings for the new sets and thought briefly about making
the models, then closed the door and went to the living room,
where she sat in the yellow chair in the dark and watched the

lights of Ashland. There were always a few lights on, and the streetlights were on. Her mind was blank as she watched the pale dawn drown out the artificial lights. It was going to be another perfect day, she thought distantly.

At eight-thirty she stuck her head in Ro's office and asked for a cup of coffee. He bounded to his feet and ran across the room to clasp her against his chest.

"Ginnie! Oh, God, Ginnie girl! Come in, come in!"

She hesitated momentarily, not looking at the floor, unable to look at the floor, afraid to look. Ro had replaced the carpet; there was nothing to see, but she was afraid to look down.

Ro prattled about the auditions, about the new season, how good Gray's promptbooks were, and pretended not to notice her hesitation, her inability to look anywhere except straight ahead. He handed her the coffee and said, "What a mooch!" His voice was hoarse.

She found that she could walk into the office, could drink the coffee, but she had nothing to say, nothing at all. She felt as if she had been gone a long time to a very distant place and needed to become oriented once more. Her uncle did not press her; he talked. And in a few minutes she left him.

She watched the auditions all morning, but without interest, without noticing what they said, how they moved.

Ro asked her to join him and Gray for a sandwich during lunch break and she nodded and sat silently while they discussed the progress of the auditions, talked about one or another of the actors, the musical director.

"Ginnie, come out into the sun for a few minutes," Gray said when it was about time to start the afternoon auditions. "I want to tell you how much I like your drawings. And the sun is fantastic."

They walked out together, out through the parking lot on the side of the shop, onto the sidewalk and around the building, back to the stage door. Gray talked enthusiastically about her work; she listened. Again she could not find anything to say. Back inside, she searched for some response. "Thank you," she said in a low voice.

On the corner of Lithia Way and First Street Laura held on to a parking meter, stunned. She had seen them come out from the parking lot, circle the shop, and turn back in toward the theater. Gray had told her the auditions would go on all day, for most of the week probably. She knew this was just the lunch break. But watching them, she had realized what it was that she knew, and she felt weak suddenly. She was ill, feverish, drawn out by the sun in spite of her cold and chills and headache. And now she knew.

She released her grasp of the parking meter and began to walk again, trying to think, trying to decide what she should do. She walked a block, then turned onto Pioneer toward the theater. A lot of people were heading toward it, actors, Eric, William, the woman from the costume department. . . . As she drew closer to them, one or two spoke to her. Then she saw Ginnie walking toward her. She stopped.

"Ginnie, I wanted to come see you, but Gray said you didn't want company. I wanted to help, at least tell you how sorry I am."

Ginnie looked uncomfortable, at a loss. She began to walk a little faster. Laura turned and walked with her to the corner.

"If there's anything I can do," she said, "please let me." Without thinking she put her hand on Ginnie's arm, then drew it back hurriedly at the look of confused startlement on her face. "I know you've been hurt very much," she said impulsively. "I don't want to hurt you. I can help you."

"Thank you," Ginnie said finally in a stiff, formal tone. She could not soften it; she felt as if she had forgotten how to act with people, how to respond to them, talk to them.

Laura nodded and left her, and Ginnie continued her walk home. All at once it occurred to her that she had to go see what it was that Peter had wanted to show her. She had the map, everything she needed. She had her daypack ready. She walked faster.

Ginnie drove on a well-paved, well-marked road, then one that was potholed with crumbling shoulders, one that had been gravel-covered in some remote past, and finally on a logging road. They all hugged the valleys, wound around creeks, and gradually descended. She was relieved. Going upward would have taken her into a snow zone rather fast. In the valleys it was spring; the creeks were furious white-water torrents with runoff already cascading down the mountains, turning the water gray.

The road was little more than a track; she drove very slowly and began to worry about a spot where she could turn around. It was not a good road to back out on. Peter's map showed the road ending at a waterfall, she reminded herself. He had been here less than a month ago; he had found a place to stop, a place where he could turn his car. She drove on.

All at once she came to the waterfall and a rocky, flat area large enough for several cars. She turned the car to head back out, then switched off the engine. The voice of the waterfall sounded everywhere, echoing from the valley, from the trees, everything at once. It was not very loud, just everywhere, almost intelligible. She walked to the edge and looked down. It was only about eight feet of fall over the rocky outcropping, but the mountainside continued downward steeply here, making a chasm, and across it there was a wall of trees that seemed to rise straight up. She could make out the silver ribbon of another stream tumbling down. It was lost among the trees, then visible again lower, then vanished altogether. The tiny streams were carving away at the mountain, carrying the mountain to the sea grain by grain.

She continued to stand without motion for a long time before she went back to the car and got out the map. Turn left here and go on by foot along the crest of this ridge until it begins to climb, then turn left again, downward. Peter was good with maps, with trails that she could not even distinguish as trails; he had been here within the month, she thought again. The trail was here. She pulled out her daypack and put it on, locked her car, and started to look for the trail. A three-mile hike, he had said. That was nothing. He had had her out on ten-mile hikes, eight-mile hikes, all-day hikes. Three miles was nothing.

Miraculously, the trail was visible, even to her. Not a well-marked trail, not leveled and smoothed, but visible. She wanted nothing more than that. The sound of the waterfall faded so gradually that she did not know how long the woods had been silent when she became aware of the silence. It was a deep silence, as if it had been undisturbed for eons; all the echoes of all past noises here had had time to die. She walked carefully, reluctant to break that silence with rustlings, with snapping of twigs, or even the sound of her breathing. The woods were so thick that no undergrowth survived in the perpetual shadows, the needles so thick that their resiliency made walking almost effortless. The trail was not hard to follow, but she knew that was because she was still on the ridge; when she left it there would be no falling ground on both sides to keep her oriented. He had found the trail, she told herself; it was there. Then she saw where she should turn.

The trail had been level ever since she started on it; now one way led upward, and to her left it went down. Although it started down gently, it soon became steep, and the trees changed. They had been the black firs that made for the darkest forests, with fir branches sweeping gracefully to the ground, and so close together that little light penetrated. Now the trees were the more open ponderosa pines with a scattering of madrones. The madrones were so smooth they looked as if someone had peeled them, sanded them down thoroughly, then polished them until they glowed red. The pine trunks were deeply incised, also reddish. The ambient light became warmer, tinged with pink.

The ground turned rockier; she could not move soundlessly, but it was all right because overhead the madrone leaves were whispering in the wind that was up there and not below. *Stranger in the forest. Who is she? What does she want?* Were they whispers of alarm? Or simply comments? The madrones were broad-leafed evergreens, the wisest trees in the world, Peter had told her. They could live without bark; they could take nitrogen from the air and put it in the soil where other trees could use it; they reclaimed land after fires ravaged it, or loggers. And they talked when there was no apparent wind; perhaps they made the wind, he had said.

There was no way to go except down, even though there was no sign of a trail now, then suddenly the way was level again, and the trees were spread apart as if by a gardener. She started to move forward, then remembered that she should mark her own trail or she would not know where to start up and out of this valley. Carry a good length of twine, Peter had told her when he instructed her about what to keep in her daypack. She got out the twine and cut off a length, tied it to a tree, then went into the parklike setting. And after fifty feet or so, she stopped and caught her breath.

She had been plunged into a valley of giants! The trees were like the sides of buildings, soaring upward to a canopy hundreds of feet over her head. These were ponderosa pines of legends, mammoth, too large to comprehend. Awed, she walked forward slowly, feeling as if she had come upon a holy place, a place where spirits lived. But the spirits were alien, indifferent to her. She touched one of the giant trees; it was warm to her hand. She put her cheek against the trunk, touched it with both hands, and she whispered, "I'm sorry. I'm sorry." She didn't know what she said, or why, only that she had to tell those spirits something, that one thing, and that now it was all right to walk among them.

The trunks had diameters of at least twenty feet, thirty feet. She walked from one to another, touching them, feeling their aliveness, and then she came to a stop again. Rounding one of the giants had brought her out to face the biggest tree she had ever seen, so big it was overwhelming, almost frightening. This tree was twice as big as any of the others. It stood alone in a large circle it had cleared for itself; it glowed in the late afternoon light. She felt its power and found herself moving toward it without volition. When she reached it and put both arms out in an embrace, she looked straight upward and was overcome with vertigo. Slowly she sank to her knees and pressed her cheek against the trunk. She began to weep, silently at first, without any motion, then harder and harder, until she was racked by sobs and her grief shook her entire body.

When the outpouring of grief ended, she sat under the tree with her back against the trunk. Twilight came and soon the darkness deepened. She ate everything she found in her pack and put on her wool sweater, then a poncho and wool cap, mittens. Finally she wrapped herself in the space blanket and lay down on the thick bed of needles.

Sometime in the unrelieved black of night the towering trees she began to whisper. She talked to Peter, to the spirits of the giant trees, to the tree that had to be the god of trees, to the darkness itself. She talked of her childhood, of her mother, of things she had never mentioned to anyone, had not remembered in years. Eventually her voice trailed off and she slept.

In the morning she walked to the end of the small oval valley that had nurtured the giant trees for centuries. It was not more than two miles long, half a mile wide; all around it the mountain rose steeply, hiding this holy place. She returned to the god of the trees, and touched it reverently once more.

"I won't tell," she said softly.

When she found her twine marker, she untied it carefully, then moved away from that trail, not wanting to leave signs, not wanting to make the trail down here more conspicuous than it was now. She started the climb back up to the ridge. She was in no hurry, the going was steeper than she remembered; she rested and looked behind her, but the valley was invisible already, the secret well hidden.

It was after nine when she reached the waterfall once more. She dug in her pack and found matches, and on the rocky ledge she burned the map and dipped water from the creek to wash away the stain of carbon. Satisfied, she got in her car and started the drive back. She was very hungry. She would stop in the first restaurant and have a huge breakfast.

When she got out of her car in her own driveway, a sheriff's deputy appeared from her front stoop and walked toward her.

"Miss Braden, Lieutenant Draker wants a word with you down at the theater."

She stopped. "Why? Can I see him after I have a shower, change my clothes?"

"No, ma'am. He wants you now. I'll take you in."

"But . . ." The deputy touched her arm as if to grasp it, force her; she flinched away from him, turned, and headed toward the car parked on the street. She had not even noticed it when she drove up. Another deputy was inside behind the wheel. "Can you tell me what's happened?" she asked.

"The lieutenant will tell you." He opened the door, and after she got in, he got in beside her. She had her daypack on. When she started to take it off, he helped her, then held on to it.

At the theater the first thing she saw was that auditions were not going on. Eric and William were huddled with Brenda and Anna; Bobby and Amanda White were talking at the stairs to the dressing rooms. Other actors were in a clump before the ward-robe room. She felt a rising panic.

Some of them turned to look at her with open curiosity; William started to move toward her. The deputy waved him back.

"Where is Uncle Ro?" she demanded. "Tell me what happened, dammit!"

"This way, Miss Braden," the deputy said, taking her toward Spotty's room. "The lieutenant wants to talk to you in here."

The room was small, only ten by twelve, cluttered with Spotty's narrow bed, an overstuffed chair, a table with a white Formica top, two straight chairs that went with it. There was a hot plate on the table, dirty cups, a paper doughnut bag. There was a television on a second table and a stack of magazines, more magazines on the end of the bed. Spotty usually straightened up the room before going home; the mess in here now alarmed her even more. She stood in the middle of the room; the deputy stayed by the door.

After a few minutes Draker entered. He surveyed Ginnie with narrow eyes. "Where were you all night?" he asked abruptly.

"Tell me what happened! Is Uncle Ro all right? What's going on here?"

"Miss Braden, we are conducting a preliminary investigation in the death of Laura Steubins. It's my duty to tell you that anything you say may be used in evidence, and it's your right to have counsel present."

Weakly she sat down in one of the straight chairs.

11

The trouble with owning a snowblower, Charlie Meiklejohn thought, wrestling the machine into the garage, was that you felt obligated to use the damn thing instead of being sensible and hiring someone with a tractor to come and dig you out. His face was hot and he was sweating, but his feet were frozen. And that, he thought, was the trouble with the human heating system. Not enough here, too much there. Brutus, the gray tiger-striped cat, stared at him malevolently through slitted yellow eyes. Now Charlie spoke out loud. "I didn't bring the snow. I didn't order it. I don't like it any more than you do, so fuck off."

Brutus flicked his tail and stalked in front of him toward the back porch and the cat door into the kitchen. Brutus hated snow even more than Charlie did. But Brutus hated rain, and fog, and mist, and open country, and company, and a long list of other ills to which he was subjected. What Brutus liked was life in New York City with his own fire escape and his own crowd of night prowlers.

Charlie looked more bearlike than ever, Constance thought when he came into the kitchen. He was dressed in a down parka that seemed to expand his figure outward alarmingly. He put his boots on newspapers to drip and began to peel off garments. His hair was damp, very curly, shiny black, with only an occasional gray hair in no particular pattern. It would go salt and pepper, she often thought, and then silver, and he would be quite distinguished-looking. She timed the process of making Irish coffee so that when he was finished unwrapping, she was ready to place the steaming mug in his hand.

"I'd take you over a whole flock of Saint Bernards any day," he said gratefully.

"I think it's a herd," she said. "Or maybe a school. Or a snarl?"

He grinned at her and sipped the scalding drink. Just right. No whipped cream to muck things up, enough Irish to taste, and coffee thick enough to stand up to the whiskey. Just right.

What she didn't say, he thought, even more gratefully, was that if he hadn't told the Bradens to come on today, he would not have had to clear the driveway; he could have spent the afternoon before the fire with the other two cats who hated snow as much as Brutus did and were smart enough to stay inside and wait it out.

The kitchen was warm and fragrant with the aroma of Swedish limpa bread that was in the stove now. The recipe had been Constance's grandmother's, brought from the old country in her satchel along with her special cookie irons for the fried cookies that Charlie loved and Constance would make only at Christmas because they were not all that good for him. He had to watch his weight. Since he had retired, his tendency was to put on a pound now and then and never take it off again. He envied Constance her long, smooth body that never seemed to change. It was as alluring to him now after twenty-five years of marriage as it had been the first day he met and lusted for her.

They went to the living room, where he opened the fireplace screen and stood with his back to the fire for several minutes. Brutus followed them and went straight to Candy, the orange cat with butterscotch eyes. He sniffed her ear and she jumped up and ran; he took her place on the hearth. Charlie laughed softly.

Constance nodded. The conditioning was textbookish, she thought. At first, when Brutus wanted to torment Candy, or eat her share of the food, or simply raise some hell in general, he had bitten her ears with some ferocity. Candy was a born coward; she ran. Now Brutus simply sniffed her ear and she fled. Any day she expected to see the same outcome if Brutus merely turned his wicked yellow eyes in the direction of her ear.

"That damn cat's too smart for his own good," she said. She sat down in the wing chair; when Charlie sat down it was in his ancient Morris chair with the hand-carved lions on the arms. She sighed with contentment now that he was inside, no longer cursing the snow. She knew it was harder on Charlie living out in the country than he liked to admit. Ostensibly he was writing a handbook on arson and how to detect it, but for several weeks now the snow had marooned them, isolated them, and he had started to pace, absently at first, then with more energy. Like Brutus, she thought, and never said that.

Years ago they had made the down payment on this country house; they had spent summer vacations here, fixing it up, getting it ready. Was it like most dreams, she wondered, hollow when finally achieved? Instantly she denied the idea. It was just the snow and the middle-of-the-winter inactivity that were getting to Charlie. Since retirement, he had taken on investigative work now and then, but for the last few months there had been nothing that had interested him enough to stir out for. Meanwhile, her own book on the comparison of various psychological therapies that had sprung up in the past dozen years was advancing even faster than she had hoped for. Constance was a psychologist; when Charlie retired, she had quit her teaching job at Columbia, sighing a prayer of relief that they both had been able to get out of New York intact. Or almost intact. Charlie had scars that she knew no one else could see. She knew where they were, how painful they could become from time to time. Twenty-five years on the New York City police force left scars of one kind or another.

"The funny thing is," Charlie said suddenly with a touch of surprise, "is that after I'm done with the damn snow again, I feel pretty good."

"Another one?" She suspected the Irish coffee had contributed more than a little to his feeling of ease now.

"Later."

She took both cups to the kitchen and checked on the bread. It was ready to come out. For the next few minutes she was busy, then the doorbell sounded and she returned to the living room in time to see Charlie ushering Dr. Morley Braden and his wife, Louise, into the house.

Charlie introduced her and she helped Mrs. Braden off with her coat, mink. Dr. Braden's coat was vicuña. They were old, Constance thought with surprise, in their seventies at least. Mrs. Braden looked it even more than her husband. He was straight and vigorous with iron-gray hair and steady, clear blue eyes. Mrs. Braden's eyes were hidden behind thick glasses. Cataracts? Constance wondered, and realized that they could not have driven themselves up from New York City. It was a two-hour drive, and in this weather, with snow on the various roads throughout the Northeast, she doubted that they would have started out alone.

"Do you have a driver?" she asked as Charlie led them into the living room.

Dr. Braden studied her with interest. "Yes. I was going to ask if it would be possible for him to come inside and wait."

Charlie went out to bring him in and Constance offered coffee, tea. Courteously they refused. Dr. Braden settled his wife into a chair before he sat down. Charlie returned. The driver was in the kitchen having coffee, he said, and took his chair.

He looked from Dr. Braden to Mrs. Braden. "What can we do for you? I'm surprised you didn't ask me to come into the city for a talk."

"Phil Stern warned me that you probably would refuse," Dr. Braden said. "He also said you were the two people we should talk to. That meant we had to come to you." He took a breath, then said, "We want to hire you both to investigate two murders in Oregon. We are afraid our granddaughter is going to be charged with them."

Charlie glanced at Constance. She looked relaxed, mildly interested. He knew she was content to spend the rest of the winter snowed in, working on her book, planning the spring garden. He knew also how much she hated murder cases.

He said to Dr. Braden, "You'd better tell us what you can about it. If the police are looking into it, ready to bring charges, you may want a lawyer more than another investigator." He was thinking that probably this was not for them, not if it had gone this far. He could not decide if he was sorry or glad.

Phil Stern was a friend from college days, now an independent insurance broker. Charlie and Constance had done a few things for him before. And Phil was jealous as hell, Charlie thought also, because he was still working and Charlie was retired. Phil had called to talk about the Bradens he was sending their way. Dr. Braden, he had said, was not the richest man in the world, but he was not counting pennies either. He had pioneered in microsurgery and, although he no longer did surgery himself, he was still one of the experts in the field, in great demand as a speaker, a seminar guest, workshop leader, all that sort of thing. Phil handled his insurance, and when Dr. Braden had asked for advice about investigators, he had supplied Charlie's name.

Dr. Braden did not speak immediately. He gazed at the fire as he collected his thoughts. "I think I have to start with some past history," he said finally. "Louise and I had one child, Victor. He was intelligent, creative, happy, everything parents always hope for and seldom get in a child. We loved him very much." Mrs. Braden gazed toward the fire with her clouded eyes and nodded slowly. He went on. "He was a student at Stanford, pre-med, when he met a girl, Lucy Cavanaugh. She was pretty, gay, talented, I grant all that. He fell in love with her, and presumably she reciprocated. We tried to talk to him, postpone any decisions until he was finished with his education, but it was hopeless. They ran off together. He dropped out of school and they went to Europe for nearly a year. There were . . . We argued bitterly, I'm afraid, and he didn't write, or call. . . ."

Louise Braden's hands clutched each other. She looked down at her small, pretty shoes.

Dr. Braden's pause was longer this time. Finally he continued. "We didn't know when they returned to the States. They didn't get in touch. I had a detective locate them for me in Ashland, Oregon, and I went there in the summer that their child was three years old. She was a lovely child, very much like Victor as an infant, busy, precocious, charming. I'm afraid I bungled it. I threatened him and his wife when I should have accepted whatever he wanted. I tried to make him agree to give up that life, to return to school, become a doctor. It wasn't too late, I kept saying, and he looked at me as if I were a stranger. It was far too late. Then he said that he was leaving Ashland as soon as the second child was born, in six months. They were going to Paris, where he would study art and architecture, not medicine. A week later he died in a terrible fire. He was twenty-five years old."

His voice did not break; it simply stopped working. He looked at the fire. Charlie got up and added a log, poked at it and sent sparks up the chimney. Brutus protested in a deep voice and moved back a foot or two, then curled up again and tucked his nose under his tail.

"Lucy miscarried that night," Dr. Braden said at last. "Virginia—Ginnie, they called her—was hospitalized for observation. She was in the house. Roman Cavanaugh, Lucy's brother, saved her life. I saw him bring her out; his shirt was on fire, his hair smoldering . . . It was horrible. Horrible."

Now his voice broke. "God help me," he said, "I blamed her, Lucy. Her own suffering, the suffering of her child, my grandchild, Ro's burns, none of that mattered. I blamed her for ruining my boy's life, destroying him. I left Ashland, left them all, and when I came to my senses, months later, she was gone with Ginnie. Out of sight. Ro swore he didn't know where they were, and I guess he was telling the truth. He sent her money through a lawyer, and the lawyer would not reveal her whereabouts. I tried to find her, find our grandchild, and I failed."

His wife touched his arm. She said in a wavering voice, "I made him fire the detective. I was so certain that she had found another man, someone richer than Victor even, married, changed her name and Ginnie's name . . . We were so sure we understood her, it seemed the proper thing to do finally."

Charlie waited for a time, then asked, "Who was Lucy? Ro? Why were you so certain she was after his money?"

"Victor told us about her," Dr. Braden said heavily. "It was sordid. Her father was in radio, an announcer or something, gone most of the time, finally all the time. Her mother had a string of boyfriends. Lucy was twelve years younger than her brother, Ro. When she was about ten, he was gone, going to school and working. One of the boyfriends frightened her. I don't know if he molested her or not, but she ran away, went to her brother, and he kept her with him after that. He took her to the West Coast, cared for her, saw that she went to school, apparently did everything for her. They had no money, except for what he earned, but he was making a name for himself as an actor. Did some commercials, directed a little, things of that sort. The three of them, Victor, Lucy, and Roman Cavanaugh, went to Europe, then to Ashland when Ro went there to buy the theater and rebuild it. When Victor's will was probated, there was only sixty thousand dollars in the bank, and the house that had burned to the ground. But when Victor was twenty-one, he had inherited a million dollars. It was all gone, spent, vanished. I know a million dollars isn't a vast fortune, but still, in five years . . . I blamed her, of course. But I don't know what happened to it. There were no papers, or if there had been, they were destroyed in the fire. Nothing in a safety-deposit box, nothing in a lawyer's office, nothing."

"Did the brother get the money?" Charlie asked bluntly.

Dr. Braden shrugged. "Who can say? He never admitted it if he did."

"Okay, so we have the background. What's happened recently?"

"Yes. Last year I was in San Francisco to give a speech at the AMA meeting there. The hotel had a stack of tourist-attraction pamphlets—wine tastings, shows, things of that sort. There was one about the Oregon Shakespearean Festival in Ashland. It's rather famous, you see. I glanced through it and found a second announcement concerning Ro's theater, Harley's. The announcement said that the sets were by Virginia Braden.

"After I was finished in San Francisco, I went up to Ashland," he said, his voice firm again, his eyes steady. "The sets were marvelous; she's very talented. But she was not in town. I talked to a lawyer there, hired him to inform me when she was home again, to find out everything he could about her past from the time her mother took her away until then. I could have asked anyone, I think now. It seems an open story up there. Her mother was killed in a car wreck when Ginnie was thirteen and Ro has taken care of her since then."

"To the rescue again," Charlie murmured.

Mrs. Braden suddenly said, "Lucy never remarried. She was never involved with another man. All those years we were so wrong about her. So wrong. And then I had to become ill, just when we could have met Ginnie, I had to become ill."

Dr. Braden patted her arm. "Ginnie was back and Louise had to have surgery. We decided to wait until spring and then take a trip to the West Coast, go to Ashland, spend a few weeks getting acquainted with our granddaughter. We planned to go at the end of February, be there for the openings of the new shows of the season." He took a long breath and let it out slowly. "The lawyer I hired called me yesterday. Early this month a man was killed in the theater. Ginnie was present. They were lovers. And Wednesday a woman was killed and Ginnie was gone all night and won't tell anyone where she was. It seems the man and woman had been seeing each other, having lunch, things like that. The circumstantial evidence, according to the lawyer, is damning enough, he thinks, to justify an arrest. But, of course, she didn't do it."

"How do you know that?" Constance asked softly. "You've met her, haven't you?"

Mrs. Braden looked at him sharply and slowly she nodded. "Last summer," she said. "You went back last summer, didn't you?"

"I had to see her," he said, looking at the fire. "I couldn't put us through all that again until I knew. What if she had turned out to be what we thought Lucy was? What if she was mean, hard, greedy, God knows what? I had to know before I told Louise anything about it. I went back. I didn't tell Ginnie who I was. I watched her, talked to her even. She was kind. You know how it is when you get to be our age? People don't want to be bothered if they don't know you. I can give a presentation, hold an audience of thousands, sign books, do all that, and have a waiter snub me because I'm old.''

His voice was too matter-of-fact, Constance thought; he had learned to hide himself thoroughly. Had he appeared brutally cold to his son? Probably.

"Why didn't you tell me?" his wife asked, not looking at him. "After you met her, why didn't you tell me?"

"You were too ill at first," he said slowly. "Later . . . I don't know. I wanted you to meet her for yourself, not spoil that first meeting."

"You were still punishing me for making you stop the search," she murmured, examining her hands, rubbing one of the enlarged veins, then another.

"I've never held you responsible," he said gently.

"What if she actually did it?" Charlie asked coolly then.

"She didn't." He stretched his legs and shifted in his chair. "If they charge her, she'll need an attorney, naturally, but I don't want her to have to go through any of that. I want you to find out who did those murders and spare that girl any more grief. We owe her that much," he added in a lower voice. "God knows, we owe her that much."

"Dr. Braden," Constance asked then, "why did you come to us? What else is there?"

"You tell me something first," he said. "How did you know I'd met her?"

"Your expression when you talked about her. You were seeing her in your mind's eye."

"That's why I want you, too. Phil Stern called you a gifted psychologist; I think you've shown us that his opinion is justified. Ralph Wedekind, he's the lawyer in Ashland, he says they're saying Ginnie's crazy. She needs help, Miss Liedl, your help as well as your husband's."

"Have you been in touch with your granddaughter?" Charlie asked. "Does she know you're hiring us?"

"No."

Constance pursed her lips and Charlie went on. "Do you think that's wise, Dr. Braden? Suppose strangers came up to you and started asking questions about your personal life, your activities?"

For the first time he looked uncertain, grieved. "I'm afraid she might refuse our help," he said faintly. "Please, don't tell her unless it's necessary."

Charlie glanced at Constance and nodded.

Dr. Braden had brought the correspondence from the lawyer, his report on Ginnie and her uncle. Wedekind would arrange accommodations, he said. He was waiting for a call, anytime. He would meet them at the airport in Medford, drive them to Ashland, brief them, do whatever he could to assist them.

The Bradens prepared to leave shortly after that. As Charlie got their coats, Constance asked, "Why are you doing this, Dr. Braden? Hasn't her uncle always taken care of her? Don't you think he'll take care of her now?"

He helped his wife out of her chair and held her arm carefully until she was steady. "He might," he said, "but I want it to be us this time. For once I want us, the two of us, to take care of our own."

"You understand that, don't you?" his wife asked. "After all these years . . . she's all we have now."

"Of course I understand," Constance said, but even as she was saying the words, she wondered if they understood fully, if they were fooling themselves. How hard would they work to eradicate all traces of the trail of guilt they had brought with them from the past?

"Now," Charlie said after they were gone.

"Now what?"

"Now I'll have another Irish coffee. I'll make them."

"If I have a drink now, we won't have dinner until ten. And if you have a drink, I have to. I refuse to let you start being a solitary drinker at this stage in your life."

"What stage is that?"

He started for the kitchen and she followed. "Middle-aged, unemployed, drifting, restless, so bored you're willing to take a very messy case just because it will get you out of the house."

"Hm." He measured coffee beans into the grinder, ran water into the kettle, and placed it on the stove. He then rummaged in the cabinet for the Irish whiskey.

"It's on the counter," she said.

"So you think it's messy," he commented, taking the bottle to the table.

"Murder's messy by definition. And this one's messier than most because there are too many nasty echoes from the past."

"He was an arrogant son of a bitch, I bet, ordering his son into medical school, trying to keep him out of that girl's bed, trying to run his life in every way, I bet."

"He's still an arrogant son of a bitch," Constance said. "Not telling his wife that he met Ginnie. And coming here with a check already made out. He's just learned to hide it better." She watched Charlie pour steaming water over the ground coffee in the filter. "Why did you say yes? You hate this kind of thing as much as I do. What if she really did it? He won't thank us, that's for sure."

Charlie stirred the water and grounds. He thought that made it drip through faster. "You know how long our driveway is?"

She blinked. "Couple of hundred feet. Why?"

"Nope. It's three and a half hours of blowing snow and digging snow. Believe me, I know. I figure a little time in Oregon, which I hear is very nice, then on down to San Francisco, which I know damn well is nice, and from there it's five hours to Hawaii. I want to see a volcano in action. Rivers of fire. Hot sunshine. No snow."

"Have you also thought of who we can get to come out here this time of year?"

"Sure. Cousin Maud and that dumb ox of a husband of hers. So they'll clean out the freezer and drink everything in the house. Let them. We'll be on a blistering beach sipping mai tais. Ah, it's ready." He finished making the Irish coffee. They ended up eating cheese and bread in front of the fire, sipping their drinks. Outside, it had started to snow again.

12

Ralph Wedekind was a powerful-looking man in his middle years. His face was tanned, weathered; many lines converged at the corners of his eyes. He met Charlie and Constance at the Medford airport and drove them to Ashland. His speech was deliberate, without any affectation or accent that Constance could discern.

"What I'd like to do, if it's okay with you folks, is take you to the inn and let you get registered and settled and then come back in an hour and take you to dinner and talk. Would that suit you?"

"Sounds good," Charlie said. He wished it had not suddenly turned dark. Coming in to land, he had seen snow on all the mountains and had felt doomed, trapped wherever he went by winter. The road was clear, but he knew that could be misleading. Snow could be lurking in every shadow, in banks along the secondary roads.

The inn turned out to be a private mansion that had been converted to a bed-and-breakfast hotel. It was spacious and very beautiful, Victorian, impeccably maintained. A broad curving staircase led to their two rooms on the second floor. When Constance looked at Ralph in surprise, he shrugged.

"Dr. Braden said two rooms in the nicest place we have to offer. This is it. Oh, here are car keys. I had a rental car delivered. It's in the driveway. A Buick."

Then he told them he would be back in an hour and left. Mrs. Shiveley, one of the owners, led them upstairs.

"Please, don't bother with the bags," she said pleasantly. "We'll have them brought up in a few minutes." She was plump with greenish eyes and auburn hair in a single braid halfway down her back. She, too, looked as if she spent a lot of time outdoors.

"When you wake up, ring for coffee," she said. "We'll bring

it right away, and breakfast about half an hour afterward, unless you prefer to set a time. We'll serve breakfast in the sitting room. Lunch and dinner are available, but we have to know ahead of time, an hour at least. All right?"

"Fine," Constance said, feeling almost dazed by the treatment Dr. Braden was providing.

Mrs. Shiveley opened the door to their sitting room and ushered them inside. The room was spacious, with wide windows on two sides. The furniture was antique, the rug a Kerman. The bedroom was equally large and well furnished. In the sitting room a bar had been arranged with a bottle of bourbon, an ice bucket, and several glasses. Mrs. Shiveley opened a door on a chest to show them various mixers and several bottles of wine. "If there's anything at all we can do to make your stay more comfortable," she said, "please let us know. Coffee is available from six-thirty in the morning until midnight from the kitchen. If you would like it, we can bring a coffee maker and coffee things up for you to use. And there usually are snacks in the kitchen. Sometimes, if we know our guests will be here in the afternoon, we serve tea, but not unless we know ahead of time." She cast an experienced glance over the room, smiled at them, and left.

"Well," Charlie said, pleased, and headed for the bottle on the table. Constance went back to the bedroom and saw that while they had been in the other room someone had brought up their bags. She was as delighted with the house as Charlie.

"Like it?" Ralph asked when he picked them up later. He was grinning.

"Are you kidding? I may never leave," Charlie said.

"When I told Dr. Braden how much it cost, he didn't even hesitate. He wants you to be comfortable."

The drive to the restaurant was short, mostly uphill. Their table was at a window overlooking the town. It was like a postcard vista.

Ralph called their waiter by his first name, and was called by his. "He's my leader on the rescue team," he said after they had ordered. "Ski rescue," he added. "Do you ski?"

"Some," Constance said. "But probably not on this trip."

"Definitely not on this trip," Charlie said.

Drinks were served and then Ralph said, "Dr. Braden called me last night about the problem of keeping him and his wife out of this. We decided to let me be the one to hire you. You can refer any questions back to me and I'll stonewall as long as I can. If Draker makes noise, I may have to tell. He's the detective on the case out of the sheriff's office."

"Do you know Virginia Braden?" Constance asked. "If she asks you who's paying the bill, then what?"

"Everyone knows everyone in a town like this," Ralph said, glancing around the restaurant. He had nodded to several people as they entered. "I've known Ginnie these last five years, and I knew who she was before she went away to school. I know her uncle much better, of course. We're in several of the same organizations, end up at the same civic-affairs meetings, the same parties. It's a very small town." He had touched his martini to his lips briefly, put it down again, and now moved the glass back and forth an inch or so, obviously not interested in the contents.

"I talked to Ginnie today," he said. "I asked her if she would back me up if I just said I was having someone look into this mess on her behalf. She wanted to know who was paying the bill, naturally, but she accepted that I was not free to tell her. She's not stupid, by the way. She knows she's in trouble."

"How much trouble?" Charlie asked.

"It's bad. You want it now, not after dinner?" Constance and Charlie both nodded. Ralph sipped his martini as sparingly as before. "Okay. The first one, Peter Ellis. He and Ginnie were friends, casual lovers, I think. They were planning to go away for a few days, but she had to deliver sketches at the theater first. They went that night. She waited in the car while he took them inside. He used her key to get in. She watched him unlock the door, then turned off the headlights and didn't see anything else. When she got tired of waiting, she went in and found his body. His head had been smashed with a bronze doorstop. No prints on it. Just smudges. That's her story.

"There's a watchman, Spotty. He got there around eight, as he usually does. He's not due until ten, but he spends his nights there and likes to watch television in the evening. He looked around when he arrived, checked the doors in the shop out back, then in the theater. Everything was locked up. He went to his room and made coffee, turned on the television. He heard

Ginnie scream at nine-eighteen. He looked at his clock when he heard her. He found her in the hallway outside the office where the body was. She was trying to pull the door closed and the doorstop was in the way. She was in severe shock. She has no memory of leaving the office, of seeing the doorstop, or trying to close the door.''

Their waiter brought salads and bread and they were all silent until he left again.

"The theory was that a burglar got in somehow and Ellis surprised him. It was as plausible as anything, I guess. More plausible than believing Ginnie did it. There was another possibility, though. Ellis was wearing the raincoat of the new director that night. It was raining pretty hard and he slipped it over his head, covered the portfolio. Ginnie had given the director a ride a day or two before and he left his coat in her car. Ro raised the possibility that the killer thought it was Gray Wilmot. The coat is black, the only one just like it I've seen around here.''

Charlie cut the bread and they all began to eat their salad. In a few minutes Ralph went on.

"Ginnie was in a really bad state for the next week or longer. Not talking, not eating much, I don't know. Not there, is how someone put it. You know what I mean?''

"Sounds like severe depression,'' Constance said. "Not emotional depression, clinical.''

He nodded. "I guess. Anyway, she was just beginning to show signs of life again when Laura Steubins was killed. And this one is harder because Ginnie won't cooperate and tell us where she was that night. She says only that she spent the night in the woods.''

Charlie looked at him in disbelief. He smiled faintly. "I know it sounds crazy, but it isn't. Not really. People do that around here, even in the winter. I believe that's what Ginnie did, but she has to say where, lead others to the place to see that someone actually did spend a night there, prove it before the next hard rain washes away every trace. She says she doesn't know where the spot is and no one believes that. I don't believe it.''

"What happened to Laura Steubins?'' Constance asked.

"No one knows much. People saw her meet Ginnie outside the theater shortly after noon that day. They walked away together. Ginnie says they parted at the corner; she went on home and put her stuff in her car and took off for the woods. Laura wasn't seen that afternoon. At five she called Gray Wilmot, the director—they were living together, at least in the same house— and told him she wouldn't be home for dinner. He was eating with one of the theater people anyway. She was seen in the restaurant where Ro Cavanaugh was having dinner with a couple of other people. She spoke to Ro and left and no one saw her again. She was found in the river the next morning, her head smashed in. The autopsy put her death at about nine the night before. Ginnie returned to her house at about one in the afternoon, and that's where it is now."

"Motive?" Charlie asked.

Ralph shrugged. "There isn't any. They're saying Ginnie was upset because Ellis was seeing Laura. He got her a job at the university and had lunch with her a couple of times. But he and Ginnie were going out of town together for a few days. Doesn't sound like much of a motive to me. He was in town to clean up some business and spend a few days with Ginnie, then he was going down to California to finish his Ph.D. work. He was crazy about Ginnie."

"You knew him, too?" Constance asked.

"I met him a few times. And I saw them together a couple of times. He was serious. I don't think she was."

"Why are they saying Ginnie is crazy?"

"When Ellis got killed she went into the shock I told you about, wouldn't talk, all that. When they told her Laura Steubins was dead, she went silent again, but this time not from shock. She just won't say where she was and Draker is acting as if he thinks she was pretending before, pretending shock. He's convinced she really is crazy. He thinks her silence proves it."

They ate silently for several minutes.

"That was Wednesday night?" Charlie asked. When Ralph nodded, he continued, "Why the rush? Your Lieutenant Draker seems in an awful rush to settle on any one person this fast."

"Everyone else connected with this mess had an alibi one night or the other, or both. Ginnie was available both times. Draker's been around for seven or eight years. He did a big investigation the year he came, made a tremendous drug bust after a lot of good work, and made a name for himself. He wants to keep up his reputation maybe."

"If he's really settled on Ginnie, that means his investigation will be skewed," Constance commented.

Ralph nodded soberly. "That's how I read it."

Constance was frowning slightly. "That argument seems pretty circular, doesn't it? He's satisfied that she did it; her silence proves both her guilt and that she is crazy. Most people start from the other side: She's crazy, therefore she's the killer." Charlie looked mystified, and she continued, "Well, Ginnie must be passing for sane, as sane as most people, anyway, or he wouldn't have to reach quite so hard to label her crazy. Why does he want the label for her?"

Ralph sighed. "You'll hear this from someone or other, it might as well be me. They say that when her father died she became autistic for over a year. It was only after her mother took her all the way out of here that she began to recover. And they say that she started the fire that killed him, playing with matches. That seems to be enough for Draker. He equates autism with insanity, and as far as he's concerned she was never cured, only in remission until someone crossed her."

Charlie whistled softly. "How old was she?"

"Three." He glanced at his watch. "Well, you've had a long day, and so have I. I have a packet of stuff for you in the car. A map of the town showing where the theater is, where my office is, things like that. My office will be available for you if you want it for anything."

"Just a couple of things," Charlie said. The waiter cleared the table, poured more coffee without being asked. Good waiter. "First," Charlie said when they were alone again, "you said Ginnie has agreed to the investigation, strangers asking questions, all the rest of it. What about the others? Her uncle, for instance?"

Ralph sighed. "I talked to Ro this afternoon. He thinks I'm running scared over nothing. He's clinging to the burglar theory, and he thinks Laura was out with someone who got nasty when she wouldn't play. She wasn't raped or anything."

"Just killed," Constance murmured.

"Yes. Anyway, Ro will cooperate just as long as he isn't too inconvenienced, just as long as his people aren't too distracted from the business. He warned me that they are going into rehearsals in just one more week and there simply won't be time for anything else then." He looked troubled. "I'm afraid Ro isn't going to see anything he doesn't want to see. Having Ginnie accused of murder is one of those things he doesn't want to see."

"And the others?"

"They'll do what Ro tells them to do. And, of course, they're all really fond of Ginnie. Most everyone is. Ro said you can go in and out of the theater when you want to, but you can't interrupt any of the readings or the rehearsals or anything else. Catch people in the halls, I guess." He shrugged helplessly. "They're show people, not quite like anyone else. If Ro ever realizes that Ginnie is in real danger, it'll be a different story, but it might take a baseball bat to drive that into his head."

"Okay. We'll work around that. The other thing: You've said everyone knows everyone here, no secrets. Do you know that they're homing in on Ginnie, or is that a guess? And if you know, how? Do you have sources that are reliable?"

He looked distinctly uncomfortable now. "I know," he said after a pause. "I don't know this detective all that well, but Gus Chisolm, who is our chief of police, is also a good friend of mine. They aren't letting him in on everything, but he hears things. He's reliable."

"Good. And finally, is there a schedule somewhere of when they'll all be in the theater, when we can meet them?"

"I added a schedule to the things in the packet for you. I think there's a nine-o'clock call for readings. What that means I can't tell you," he added dryly.

"So we get to learn how they put on a play," Charlie said easily. He looked at Constance; she shook her head slightly and they were ready to leave the restaurant.

In their sitting room later, Charlie and Constance went through the packet of articles, reports, maps that Ralph had provided. It was very thorough. Ginnie was in good hands, Charlie decided. Dr. Braden had picked a good attorney. They read the many profiles of the theater people with interest and studied their photographs. Ro had been written about most, as was to be expected, since he practically had willed Harley's Theater into existence and prosperity.

Constance left to take a bath, yawning widely; she had little faith in newspaper feature articles, having seen her own words distorted too many times in the past. Charlie continued to read.

She returned in her gown and robe, frowning. She was pink from the hot bath; clinging to her forehead were tendrils of hair so pale that they were invisible until they flashed in the light. "If she's guilty," she said, "I think Dr. Braden sees my role here as providing a case for mental illness. I don't like being used like that."

"Hey, hold on a second. That's a great big leap. You left me too far behind."

"He must have heard the rumor that she started the fire that killed his son. He was on the scene, remember? Now there's a killing spree going on and she might be implicated. She must be crazy. I testify eventually that she's incompetent, was incompetent at the time of the murders; she goes somewhere for a cure. Period. Used."

Charlie grinned at her indignation. "So let's hang the rap on someone else."

"You bet your sweet fanny," she said. "Let's go to bed."

His grin turned into a soft chuckle and he started to flick off lights.

13

Ladies and gentlemen," Gray said, "I want to outline the procedure for the coming week. Each morning at nine I'll read a play, in the order of openings. Starting tomorrow the cast will read in the afternoon. We'll begin with *The Climber* today, and tomorrow at one that cast will gather in this room and read. I don't want you to try to memorize your lines yet. This afternoon, tonight, simply read through the play a few times, think about your character a lot. We may be doing some improvisations, so be prepared."

He looked at the people around the table, then picked up the play. Constance and Charlie had met him and most of the others in Ro's office that morning. Gray was pale and drawn, with dark hollows under his eyes. As haggard as he appeared, however, he looked robust and in perfect health compared to Ginnie. She was ghostly in her pallor and almost gaunt. Everyone was tense except Sunshine. Her eyes were glowing with excitement; it was her play they were going to read, she had whispered to Constance. At the table in rehearsal room A was the cast for the first play of the season. Gray was at the head of the table; at the other end was Eric Hendrickson, the stage manager. In a second tier of chairs were the costumer, the technician, the sound and lights people, others Constance and Charlie had not met. Ro stood by the door, then seated himself next to Ginnie, out of Gray's line of sight. Ginnie sketched as Gray read, paying little or no attention to her hands, turning pages silently, sketching very fast.

"She can draw in the dark," Sunshine had whispered to Constance, who believed it.

Gray read very well. Quite often he stopped reading and talked about the actions, or the dialogue, the characters. His analysis was impressive. Constance watched the expressions on the faces of his attentive audience and knew that his was a god-like position.

When he finished there was applause; he looked surprised. Constance turned to Sunshine and said, "Congratulations. That's very good. You must feel proud."

Sunshine nodded, her smile happy and wide. "I wanted to rewrite it again and he"—she nodded toward Ro—"said he'd wring my neck if I touched it again."

"Are you going to be around all week?" Constance asked. "Perhaps we can talk to you."

"Oh, I'll be here. They said I can watch everything to do with my play. I'm not usually allowed in the theater, you know? They said I was disruptive because Ginnie got mad at me for talking to her, you know?"

"When was that?"

"Oh, a long time ago. She kept moving around out front in the dark and I couldn't believe she was drawing in the dark, you know? I think she was in a trance and if I'd known that I wouldn't have spoken to her. You shouldn't when people are in a trance, you know?"

"You're probably right," Constance said carefully. "When did they let you back in?"

"For auditions, but then he"—she looked toward Ro—"thought I made Ginnie leave that day and threw me out again. He"—this time her gaze stopped on Gray—"said I could come in for the readings and the rehearsals, but I'm not supposed to talk to any of them, you know? Do you want me to read your cards?"

"I'd like that," Constance said. "I'll let you know when I have time, when it's convenient for you. See you later, Sunshine."

Charlie was at the door motioning to her. "There's a meeting in Ro's office," he said when she joined him. "The people with keys who were around when Peter Ellis was killed. Ro says his office is the logical place, probably the only place where no one can overhear."

Ginnie and Gray were already out of the rehearsal room; the actors were gone. A clump of people remained at the table talking. She followed Charlie and the other men to Ro's office.

Charlie took control as soon as everyone was in the office. He would have made a good director, Constance thought with satisfaction. He had Ginnie and Gray on the couch, Ro in one of the easy chairs, Juanita in another one. Eric and William were in straight chairs, as was Constance. Charlie stood before the semicircle they made.

"I know you've all been through hell already," he said matter-of-factly. "I'm afraid I'm going to have to put you through it again. I don't have access to the police records, unfortunately. Now, does anyone else have a key to this building?"

"Spotty," Ro said. "That's all. Kirby Schultz had one but he gave it back to me before he took off."

"Good. Now, let's go through this logically. Someone could have been inside the building earlier and simply stayed after everyone else left." William was shaking his head. "Mr. Tessler?"

"Duane Higgins was overseeing the workmen in the auditorium," he said deliberately. "He checked them out. I did the same backstage."

"I see. But in theory someone else could have slipped in during the day, hung around all evening. We can't prove a negative, you see. It could have happened. It's the sort of straw that defense attorneys cling to. That's one possibility." He turned to

Ginnie. "Did anyone know that you and Mr. Ellis were coming here that night?"

"No. We decided at dinner. I didn't even know it until then."

Charlie nodded. "You see how that goes. If our anonymous stranger did hang around, what for? Not to waylay Mr. Ellis, since he couldn't have known he would show up. Not to steal something, surely, or he would have done it and gone by then. We can't prove that no one was here all that time, but neither do we have to act as if we believe in it. That means that someone with a key entered the theater that night, and if you're certain that only you few people have keys, that means it was one of you. Or the watchman. Did Spotty have a grudge against Mr. Ellis?"

Ginnie shook her head. "He had met him once or twice at the most."

"If Mr. Ellis walked in on Spotty in the office, so what? Is there a safe in the office, Mr. Cavanaugh?"

"No. There's nothing of real value here. During the season there's money in a safe out in the auditorium office, but not off season."

"So again, what if Mr. Ellis had come across Spotty in here? He worked here, belonged here."

"That applies to all of us," Ro said impatiently. "It wouldn't have been a surprise to find any one of us in here."

"That's the point I was coming to," Charlie said softly. "That's exactly my point. Now, what the police have against Miss Braden, Ginnie, is purely circumstantial evidence, or so I've been told. If we can place any other person in this office, that evidence will also be circumstantial unless we can also come up with a motive for murder. I know you've all told the police where you were that night, maybe many times. Will you go through it again, please? Mr. Cavanaugh, will you start?"

"This won't get you anywhere," Ro said sharply. "If they'd been able to put anyone else in here, they would have."

"Did they question you as a group?" Charlie's voice was bland. "Sometimes that shakes a memory; hearing someone else say something reminds you of something you hadn't thought of before."

"They questioned us separately," Ro said with great weariness. "I had dinner alone in a restaurant and at eight went to the high school to see a production. I always see their productions. At nine-fifteen or so I went to Jake's Place, a bar, with several other people, and I was there when the police came looking for me."

"Did you see people at the high school who know you? Did you leave and return?"

Ro glanced at Eric, then Gray. "They were both there. Maybe a dozen other people that I talked to at one time or another that night. I started to leave when Gray did, but it was raining too hard and I didn't have a car or an umbrella or even a raincoat. He was out before I could catch him for a ride. I hung out there until the play ended and got a ride with Jerry Alistair."

"Thank you," Charlie said, and turned to Eric. "Mr. Hendrickson?"

"I stayed at the high school until the play was over and then went straight home. I got there about nine-thirty. My wife was up. We watched television the rest of the evening."

"Now see," Charlie said, beaming at them. "Here's someone who could have been at the theater at the right time."

Angrily Eric said, "I took a friend home that night. He's my next-door neighbor, a teacher at the school in the drama department."

Charlie sighed and looked at Juanita.

"I was in Medford all evening. Dinner with friends, then a movie. I got home at one in the morning."

William had been home with his wife and Sunshine, he said when it was his turn. At eight-thirty Sunshine helped Shannon get ready for bed, then he drove Sunshine home. It was raining but he didn't know what time it was when he dropped her off. He stopped in a convenience store and bought a candy bar, then went home.

"You got out in the rain to buy a candy bar?"

"Yes. Sunshine made dinner that night and it was some godawful mess with rice and parsley and peanuts. I was hungry."

"And you knew the person who waited on you, I suppose?" Charlie's voice was gloomy now.

"Stu Lavelle. He works here as a stagehand during the season."

Charlie sighed again. "Mr. Wilmot?"

"I was at the high school until a few minutes before the play ended. I didn't want to get mixed up with the other cars all trying to leave the lot at the same time. I knew Laura would be waiting for me at the bar. She was there when I arrived. We went home."

"Time?" Charlie asked without much hope.

"I picked her up a little after nine. I don't know exactly what time it was."

Charlie looked at Ro and said softly, "You see how it is, Mr. Cavanaugh? On the basis of circumstantial evidence, they have enough to arrest your niece today."

Ro was pale now. His voice was ragged when he spoke. "You did that to demonstrate something, didn't you? You win, Mr. Meiklejohn. What do you want?"

"Full cooperation from you and all your people here. I'll want to ask a lot of questions and it's going to take time. I don't want you to interfere when I use that time."

Ro nodded. "Whatever it takes." He looked at Ginnie. "It's going to be all right, honey. We're all going to help."

"Aren't you going to ask me?" Ginnie demanded of Charlie.

"We'd like to talk to you at your house," Charlie said. "After lunch, this afternoon."

"That was a gamble," Constance said in the car when they left the theater. "You were lucky."

"I wanted to test the reliability of Ralph's contact, the chief of police. He said they all had alibis for one or both nights, and so far, he's right."

"Not Gray," she commented. "Unless someone else in the bar can confirm his time. And William's alibi isn't all that hot, either. Not unless he drew attention to the time in the store."

"It seemed a good idea to let them all believe we swallowed it whole," Charlie said cheerfully. He was driving along the river that ran through town. On the other side of the street was Lithia Park. The street they were on was lined with parking places, all empty. "This must be about it," he said, and pulled into one of the parking places. "About a mile in. Let's walk a bit."

It was a cool, overcast day with no wind. The river was raging grayish-white and nearly to the top of the banks, only about fifteen feet across, but loud. On a path across it several runners appeared, trotted easily into view and out of sight again without glancing at them. Charlie walked closer to the river and looked at the banks.

The earth was dark and soft-looking, laced with many rocks. Large rocks jutted out of the water, made ripples in it. Charlie found a small stick and tossed it into the water; it was swirled around and carried away quickly.

"The bank was a mess, according to the report," he said. "About a mile from the entrance. Let's see if we can find the spot." They walked slowly and stopped when they came to a roped-off area where the bank was eroded, badly scuffed. Silently they studied it.

The whole area had been trampled a lot, but the place on the bank was only about two and a half feet wide where the earth was gouged out, scraped-looking.

They were twenty feet from the nearest parking spot, a hundred feet from the nearest streetlight. It would be very dark here at night, Constance thought. She looked upriver at a bridge, downriver at another one farther away. Who would have seen anything here, heard anything? And it was only a mile from downtown.

"Someone must have had some pretty muddy shoes," Charlie said absently. His own shoes were already muddy. He backed away from the bank. "Let's walk a minute." There was a footpath between the parking area and the river; in some places trees or bushes hid it from the street. The bridge turned out to be for traffic. All the others they had seen had been footbridges. They walked to the middle of the bridge and looked back at the roped-off area. Their car was not visible from here; none of the parking spots were. The river was very swift and shiny.

Constance was studying the spot they had just left, frowning slightly. Finally she said, "It just doesn't make any sense, does it? Laura came out here with someone, parked. They got out and walked to the bank. Why? You couldn't see anything at night. They fought and she ended up in the river. But why get out of the car at all? And if she was trying to get away from anyone, she would have gone the other way, not toward the river. And it couldn't have been much of a fight, the messed-up spot is too small. People who are fighting move around a little more than that, don't they?"

"Maybe she didn't go in at that spot at all."

Constance looked at him and waited.

"Suppose you want it to look as if you fought on the river-bank. You'd know you had to make a bit of a mess, but remember it was dark and that spot is a good distance from a light. No one would turn on car lights in order to see. He did the best he could in the dark, I'd say."

"But why mess it up at all? What for?"

"To hide the fact that there's no blood, maybe?"

"You think she was killed somewhere else and brought here? Killed in a car? Not with that head wound. A heavy object just behind the right ear. Not easy to do in a car."

"I know. The report suggests that the killer picked up a rock and used that, then tossed it in the river. They didn't find it, obviously, and even if they found a thousand rocks, they'd be pretty well scoured. Try to find a particular one among them. Let's see where this road goes."

They continued across the bridge into the park itself. The road dead-ended at a small maintenance building. There was a turn-around gravel drive. No one was in sight. The trees in the park were magnificent, huge, beautifully shaped madrones, firs, spruces. An almost vertical cliff that paralleled the river was the park boundary. It was covered with trees and bushes; a path or two seemed to go straight up it.

"You could hide an elephant brigade in here," Charlie commented.

He began to poke around in bushes that grew lush on the riverbank. He leaned over and came upright again with a three-foot-long, partly decayed branch in his hand. With a guilty look he went to the bank and started to gouge at the soft, muddy earth. It crumbled at a touch. He nodded and tossed the branch into the water and backed away, then looked at his feet. "I could have done it with hardly a drop of mud getting on me." he said.

They started to walk back to the rented Buick. "Charlie, I really hate this. Why would anyone put the body of a woman in the river? It's . . . it's too crazy. People know that autopsies determine the time of death and cause. No one these days would expect to fool experts into thinking she drowned or anything."

"I don't know why," he said, agreeing with her. Television had educated most people about such things. He looked at his watch. "I have to have something to eat before we tackle Ginnie. How about you?"

14

Ginnie led Constance and Charlie into her living room. Almost before they were seated, she demanded, "Tell me who hired you. I have a right to know."

"Ralph Wedekind," Charlie said. "I thought you did know. He said you did."

"Who hired him? Was it Peter's family? His parents?"

Constance said, "Does it matter so very much? You could ask Ralph for a lawyer-client contract, you know, to be sure he's working in your interests."

Ginnie looked taken aback and abruptly sat down on the yellow chair. Constance and Charlie were on the couch.

"Do they do that?" Ginnie asked. "Write out contracts of that sort?"

"Of course, if you want one. I would, in your position. Why not give him a call and tell him you want it."

"Excuse me," Ginnie muttered and left them. A moment later they could hear her voice from the kitchen; it was too low to understand the words. She came back. "He said he'd have it in the mail today. Thanks. I didn't think of that."

"I understand your concern," Constance said. "For all you know, someone might be trying to close the trap even more."

"At the theater, what you said about one of us . . . Do you believe that?"

"If the key's the deciding factor, it has to be one of the people who have the keys," Charlie said. "May we call you Ginnie? And please call us Charlie and Constance, or else you run into the Mr. Meiklejohn and Ms. Liedl problem. It confuses a hell of a lot of people. They probably all think we're living in sin."

Her smile was not very pronounced, but it was there flashingly. "Okay."

"I know you've told everything a million times," Charlie said. "But not to us. Would you mind going through it all once more?"

She started to speak in a toneless voice and he held up his hand. "You've memorized all that from too much repetition. Let's do it a different way. We'll ask questions, jump about a bit, maybe, and you just say what comes to mind. One word or a paragraph, whatever."

She was gripping her hands together so hard the knuckles were white. Constance signaled Charlie and said, "Ginnie, it relaxes you if you draw while you talk, doesn't it? Why don't you do that?"

Ginnie looked at her hands and sighed. She got up and crossed the room to the paisley bag she always carried and rummaged in it. Suddenly she dumped everything out on the floor and scattered the items—two sketchbooks, half a dozen or more pencils, a penlight, pens, a paperback book . . . "It's gone."

"What's missing?" Charlie asked lazily.

"My other sketchbook, the one I've been using." She picked up one of the two on the floor and returned to her chair. "I must have left it in Uncle Ro's office, or the rehearsal room."

Later, Ginnie could not remember which one of them asked which questions, or even what questions they asked specifically, but she had found herself talking about her life with her mother, about going to college, doing graduate work, moving to Ashland.

"After Mother died, Uncle Ro overreacted. I think he was afraid I'd go into a worse depression than I already was in," she said that afternoon. "He took me to England and France and Italy. He always took me to see big things—cathedrals, Stonehenge, castles, that sort of thing. At first I didn't want to go. I didn't even know him, but he was wise. I know that now. The things he made me look at were all so much bigger than anyone's personal grief. He was wise."

"And your mother hadn't told you about him?"

"No. She never talked about anything in the past. Even when we moved from one city to another, she never talked about the last city. I didn't realize how strange that was until years later. It was what I was used to and I accepted it." A puzzled look crossed her face, left it again. "One time," she said then, "she said something about the theater here, about Uncle Ro. I had forgotten it until this minute. I had a part in a play at school, a Shakespeare play, and she said she had always wanted to play Shakespeare, and he, her brother, hadn't let her. She said she ended up playing Cressida to his Pandarus anyway." She shook her head. "I don't know what she meant and she wouldn't say anything else about it."

"Why wouldn't he let her do Shakespeare, I wonder," Charlie mused.

"Now I understand that part. He'll never do any Shakespeare because of the Oregon Shakespearean Festival. That's their territory and he wouldn't encroach on it for anything."

"And that's the only time she mentioned him, or Ashland, any of this past?"

"I can't remember anything else."

"You and Peter were actually planning on two trips, weren't you? One all-day trip, then back here, and then on to the coast for a few days?"

"Yes."

"Why weren't you planning to camp out overnight and then go on to the coast?"

"It was rainy."

"But you camped out other times in the rain."

She ducked her head and mumbled, "I don't know. He didn't want to this time."

"Did they impound your car when you got home after being in the woods?"

"Impound? You mean take it away?"

Charlie nodded.

"No, but they had a bunch of men in the garage examining it all afternoon. I think they took mud samples. I know they were all through my daypack."

"And they didn't find a map. And that made them believe you knew where you had been well enough that you didn't need a map. Is that right?"

"Yes."

Charlie felt Constance signal and looked at her, waiting for her to pick it up. One time their daughter, Jessica, had demanded to know how he knew when Constance was signaling;

she couldn't see anything, she had said indignantly. Charlie had answered, "She tickles me under the left shoulder blade with invisible fingers." Jessica had flounced out with a disdainful glance. But it was as true as anything else he could have said about it, he thought, watching his wife.

"What would happen," Constance asked gently, "if you led them to this secret place? How would they desecrate it?"

The lead broke on Ginnie's pencil. "I don't know what you mean."

"Not mountains, or canyons; there are too many of both, and even if you found steep mountains or deep canyons, they would be very like all the rest, wouldn't they? Something big. Trees. Giant trees? Was that it? Was that what Peter discovered and wanted to share with you, but not camp out among them, not disturb them with fire and tents?"

"How do you know?" Ginnie whispered in fear.

"Well, as I said, not mountains or valleys or canyons. Not an archaeological site, because that would have to be disturbed in order to investigate it. And he didn't want to camp out there, just go and look and leave it alone again. That's what you did, isn't it?"

"I slept under the tree." Her voice was so low it was almost inaudible; her gaze was riveted on Constance as if she could not look away.

"Did you need a map to find the place?"

"I burned it the next morning when I came out again."

"What would they do to the trees?"

Ginnie finally looked away. "They'd go in with augers and drills and take core samples. Photographers would go in, make a better trail. Maybe they'd make a state park or something, or loggers would take the trees down. People would carve their initials in them, build fires everywhere. . . ."

"We won't tell, but one day you might have to. You understand that? Could you return there if it becomes necessary?"

"I'm not sure. I think so, but I can't be sure. How did you guess?"

"You were healed there, weren't you? Not completely, perhaps, but the process began there and is continuing, the way the cathedrals and Stonehenge started the process when your mother died. Something bigger than anyone's personal grief, bigger than life, awesome. Something holy. Here it would be a tree, or trees."

Constance glanced at Charlie; his turn again. She leaned back in her chair.

"Ginnie, exactly what did Laura say to you that day outside the theater?"

"I told you. She was sorry, she wanted to help. . . ."

Charlie was shaking his head. "Her words. Close your eyes and think of her words. Get the scene back first."

Obediently she closed her eyes and the minutes dragged before she opened them again. She picked up another pencil and began drawing, evidently paying little or no attention to her hand. It looked eerie to see the pencil moving without supervision. "She said, 'I don't want to hurt you. I can help you.' And 'I know you've been hurt very much.' Something else . . . 'If there's anything I can do, please let me.' " She became silent, her brow wrinkled in thought, and finally she said, "I can't think of anything else."

"Did you see Sunshine that day?"

"No."

"Why did you leave at that time?"

She shrugged. "I ate lunch with Uncle Ro and Gray and we walked outside for a minute. Everyone kept talking about how wonderful the weather was, sunny and warm, and I couldn't think of anything to say back to them. I felt as if I had forgotten words, simple everyday words that people use."

"Where did you walk?"

"Just out back, around the shop, and back in through the stage door. It was just a minute or two."

"Could Laura have seen you?"

She looked blank, then shrugged again. "I don't know. If she had been anywhere back there, or even on the corner, I guess so."

"You see the problem, don't you? If she had been going to the theater, why didn't she keep going? Why did she turn around and walk away with you? And where was she all afternoon?"

She looked miserable. She understood what Draker had meant by his questions, implying that she and Laura had spent the rest of the day together, that she had driven Laura to the park and hit her in the head there, pushed her into the river, and then had driven around most of the night terrified.

"Ginnie," Constance asked then, "what did your mother and Ro argue about? Why wouldn't she talk about him?"

"I don't know."

"We have to be going now," Constance said easily. "What you just said reminds me of when I was studying under this bear of a psychology teacher. He hated for the students not to remember word for word every lecture he gave. One day he roared at us: 'You will remember, do you hear me? You will remember, if not in words, then in sounds. If not in sounds, then in pictures. Your hands will remember even if your head doesn't.' " She smiled. "Why don't you keep that sketchbook here? Just so you won't misplace it at the theater. When can we see you tomorrow?"

"I'll be free after Gray's reading," she said in a low voice. "Right after lunch?"

"Fine. We'll see you at the reading, too. Get a good sleep, Ginnie."

In the car Charlie leaned over and kissed Constance. "You're a witch," he murmured. "And I like it."

"Is she really in danger?"

"I wish I thought she isn't. She put that sketchbook in her bag, you know. I saw her do it."

"Me too. I was watching her. It's as close to automatic writing—drawing—as you can get."

Charlie drove cautiously down the steep hill onto the main street. "We're due at Ro's apartment at six-thirty," he said. "And it is now five-ten. What I say is let's have a drink."

"Good thinking. Look, there's Sunshine. Can you endure her for an hour?"

"Might be a good time. Let's nab her and pump her full of liquor and get the lowdown on everyone all at once." He parked the car and they got out and caught up with Sunshine.

"Hi," Charlie said. "We're on our way to have a nice quiet drink. Join us?"

"I don't drink anything with alcohol," she said, smiling. "Or caffeine, you know? You know what alcohol does? It kills liver cells, like radiation.''

"You can have orange juice while we poison our livers," Charlie said.

"They smoke in bars, don't they? I don't go where people smoke, you know? Smoke is worse than alcohol, you know?''

"There's an ice-cream parlor down the block," Constance said, and smiled sweetly at Charlie.

"I am not interested in ice cream," he said emphatically.

Constance took his arm and steered him about. "I wonder how long it's been since I've had a strawberry soda. You know ice cream is full of cholesterol, don't you?" she asked Sunshine.

"They pretend dairy products are bad for you, but they aren't. Not if you exercise. I drink juices and raw milk at home, and herb teas. I can't get raw milk in restaurants. They pretend it's dangerous. Chocolate is bad, but strawberry's all right.''

"I'll have a double chocolate milkshake," Charlie said grumpily.

Constance squeezed his arm. Actually he had a root beer. If he pretended hard enough, he thought, he might even convince himself it was real beer. He failed to pretend hard enough.

"I really like your play," Constance said after sipping her soda. It was as good as she remembered, she thought with surprise. So few things were.

"It's a good play," Sunshine said with her gentle smile in place. "I wanted to write about evil, how it kills everyone it touches, and I had to personify evil in a woman because women are mysterious, you know? Men can be really bad but they aren't mysterious. You always know why they're bad, what they want, but you don't know that about some evil women. You're the High Priestess, you know? And he's the Emperor. I'll read your cards tonight.''

"I'm afraid we won't have time tonight," Constance said.

"That's all right. I always read them first and if there's anything bad I find it and don't talk about it, you know? I sort of talk around it.''

"Have you read for the theater group?"

"Laura. The others are too superstitious. They're afraid I'll read for the actors and actresses and spook them. When the sun came out last week, they were all smiling and saying it was a good sign and then they say they aren't superstitious." She laughed softly.

"What did you read in the cards for Laura?"

She scooped ice cream from the bottom of her glass and looked at it. "I can't tell you. I never tell anyone what someone else's cards say, you know? It would make people nervous."

"I know," Constance said, sighing. "Do you use the Waite pack? I used to read but I had to stop. People acted as if the cards told what would happen, not just say what might happen if they didn't do something. They simply didn't understand that they could change things by taking charge of their own lives."

Sunshine was nodding. "I use that pack, too. That's what I always tell people. I don't believe in determinism, you know? It isn't like you don't have control over your own life. Laura said wrecking her car was a sign that fate was determined to keep her here. She thought the cards agreed with that. But she could have got on a bus. I came here on a bus. She could have walked. Ro walks everywhere practically. She could have ridden a bicycle like Ginnie. But she thought it was fate." Sunshine leaned closer to Constance and said in a near whisper, "She was trying to make up her mind about something and wanted me to read for her. But I didn't have my cards. Ro looked in my bag and saw them one day and threw me out and said if I ever brought them back, he'd burn them. He would do that, you know? He thinks the actors and actresses are little children and he has to take care of them and the cards might upset them. So I didn't have them."

"What day was that?" Constance asked. "Do you want more ice cream?"

She wanted more. They waited until she had a dish of lime sherbet—better for you than real ice cream, she told them. Constance repeated her question.

"The day Ro thought I spooked Ginnie again and threw me out. He's always throwing me out."

"You mean the day Laura was killed?"

"She wasn't killed that day," Sunshine said gently. "She was killed that night, you know?"

"So you met Laura somewhere after you left the theater. Where?"

"William said I could shop for some things that Shannon wanted and take them out to her and be back at the theater by six with his car. William's nice to me. Shannon is, too. I was going to the store and saw Laura and gave her a ride and she said she wanted me to read, that she had a question she needed answered, and I told her I didn't have the cards, but I'd go get them after I took the stuff out to Shannon. She got in the car and went with me. She waited in the car at the store and at Shannon's house. Then we went back to her house and I made her some more rose-hip tea because she had such a bad cold. She didn't like it, you know? Some people don't understand that sometimes the taste isn't the important thing. It would have helped her cold."

Constance nodded thoughtfully, then said, "You haven't told any of this to the police, have you?"

"I don't talk to police. They didn't ask me. You know the criminal mind and the police mind are exactly the same? It's circumstances that turns one into a cop and the other into a crook, you know?"

"I've heard that before," Constance said. She stifled a grunt when Charlie kicked her under the table. He looked sleepy-eyed, as if he might be dozing off and on. "How did Laura's question come out? I've never had any luck answering direct questions about what people should do."

"I told her it doesn't work that way. She finally asked what would be the outcome if she did A. And then what the outcome would be if she did B. Both were very bad."

"Did she seem to make a decision?"

Sunshine shook her head. "She kept going back and forth. Then she thought Gray was coming home and she didn't want to see him until she had more time to think. I told her if William was going to be busy until six, Gray would be, too, but she called him anyway and said she wasn't going to be home and he said he was eating with Eric and didn't care. And she said, 'I'll make you care, goddamn it,' but she already had hung up and he didn't hear her. That's when she decided, you know?"

"It sounds as if you may be right," Constance agreed. "Did she stay there when you left?"

"Oh yes. She was looking for something to drink, something

alcoholic, you know? I don't hang around with people who are poisoning themselves, so I left."

"Sunshine, did she tell you anything to indicate what A and B were? It's very important."

Sunshine shook her head. "Just A and then B. I told her it works better if I don't know. That way I can't read anything into the cards, have any real influence, you know?"

She talked on until Charlie and Constance had to leave for their appointment with Ro. As they put on their coats, Charlie said in his soft and easy voice, his working voice, Constance called it, "Sunshine, thank you for talking to us."

"To her," Sunshine said, nodding at Constance.

"Right. To her. What you've told Constance is vital evidence, Sunshine. You must realize that. I know you're a good woman, a gentle woman with a lot of compassion for other people, a lot of understanding. I wouldn't like to see someone like you hurt because you withheld evidence, but you could find yourself in trouble over it. You have to go to the police, tell them what you've told us—Constance."

She shook her head, smiling gently. "I don't talk to police. I'll read your cards tonight. Good night."

"Well," Constance said after they were alone again. "Are you going to tell?"

"Eventually," he said. "Eventually."

15

Ro Cavanaugh's apartment had enough art to qualify as a museum, Charlie thought when he and Constance were admitted. There was a spacious foyer with a carved Chinese cabinet that held ivory and jade carvings. Above that hung a Chinese silk embroidery of a dragon in a garden. Before they could examine the objects in the foyer, Ro was ushering them into the living room, and it, too, was filled with carvings, paintings, statuettes, plates. . . . A flawless glass-topped coffee table with beveled edges had a pedestal made from a bronze dolphin with a patina that suggested centuries in the sea. A hanging lamp was made of twisted translucent porcelain in pastel colors. There were floor-to-ceiling windows on both end walls that reached up two stories. A balcony on the second floor overlooked the living room; on the wall up there were oversize paintings—Miró, Kandinsky, some Charlie did not recognize. He took a deep breath. He was afraid to touch anything.

"This is very lovely," Constance said, gazing from one object, one painting to another. The couch was covered with ivory velvet; the chairs with red-and-ivory-striped silk. At the far end of the room were a mammoth television receiver and a ten-foot-long cabinet with film cassettes. Around the corner from it was another, equally long cabinet with a stereo, records, and rows of music tapes.

"I pick up things when I travel," Ro said. "These are from Spain." He went to a chest and lifted a carved bull, done in dense black wood. There were other pieces—a matador, a picador. . . . Above them were the two symbols of the theater—the laughing face and the crying face, done in gold, or at least gold-plated. "Those are from England," he said, noticing where Constance was looking. "Irish gold. Now what can I give you to drink?"

"Anything except root beer," Charlie said.

"Martini?"

"That would be very nice," Charlie said.

As Ro started to cross the living room toward the kitchen, Constance asked, "Would you mind if I go up on the balcony and look at the paintings?"

He looked pleased. "Delighted. I'll do the mixing."

She went up the broad stairs from the living room, pausing now and then for another look around; the perspective changed everything again and again. On the balcony she went from one painting to another. Ro and Charlie were out of sight in the kitchen. She opened one of the doors and glanced around the room—his bedroom apparently, as neat and decorated as the downstairs. She did not enter. At the other end of the balcony was the second door. When she reached it, she looked inside that room also. Smaller than the other one, a spare bedroom. The bed was piled high with boxes and books. She was almost relieved that the entire house was not as neat as a showplace. When Charlie and Ro returned to the living room she was standing before the Kandinsky, a dizzying mélange of lines and colors.

"You like that one?" Ro asked from the living room. She nodded and started back down the stairs. "I do, too. The windows are east and west exposures; it changes from morning to night with the different quality of light." He handed Constance a glass when she joined them. "You might as well see the rest of my place."

He took them back through the foyer into a hall that led to his study. On the interior wall there were shelves and a collection of clowns. "This is what Draker wanted to see," Ro said, surveying them with a glum expression. They were molded, cast, carved from all kinds of materials—wood, bronze, silver, glass, china. Some were gaily painted, others not. All were beautiful. He pointed to one of the bronze ones. "That's a mate to the one at the theater, the one the murderer used."

Charlie picked it up. It was very heavy, bronze, fifteen inches tall, a thin, lugubrious clown. A hell of a weapon, he thought, but said nothing.

The desk here had the same cluttered messy look as the one at the theater, with papers in precarious stacks, magazines, some of them open, books with slips of paper sticking out, a road atlas. . . .

Ro led them through the kitchen to complete the tour. He dismissed it with a wave. "Hardly ever use it, except to mix drinks, or breakfast now and then. When Ginnie lived here, I had a housekeeper who cooked and I hated it. She liked things to be on time." He smiled grimly. "I fired her the day Ginnie left for college."

"It must have been hard, having a child on your hands suddenly. I'd be afraid to bring a child in here," Constance said.

"Well, she wasn't a little child," Ro reminded her. "She was thirteen. She was . . . disturbed. We went on a six-month trip and she seemed to mature a lot during that time. I understand that's common, a spurt in maturity about then. Anyway, she was a good kid. I increased my insurance coverage, just in case, but it wasn't necessary. She was a good kid always. And, of course, she was busy with high school and she took dancing lessons and voice, acting. For a time I thought she would become an actress, like her mother, but she decided backstage was more exciting finally. She's a gifted artist, could have gone into fine art, made it as a painter.''

He was keeping an eye on the time, Constance realized. Now he said, "I made a reservation for seven-thirty. It's about a five-minute walk, maybe ten at the most. I'd offer to drive you, but I seem to have a dead battery. Damn cars are nothing but trouble, I just leave it in the carport most of the time.''

"Well, we can drive, or we can walk. If it isn't raining," Charlie said. "You always walk, even if it's raining?''

"Sure. Why not? Only exercise I get, and Ashland's only so big, you know. You can get anywhere in town in ten minutes. If it's raining, I carry an umbrella. Leave them all over town, of course, but umbrellas are cheaper than car repairs and gas.''

"Just wondering how you know you have a dead battery if you never use your car," Charlie said easily.

Ro gave him a shrewd look. "They came looking the day they found Laura. Wanted me to back it out of the carport so they could look it over. They gave up on it right off. Dust all over the windshield and a dead battery. I could have let it roll out of the carport, but then I'd have had to push it back in and I said they needed a warrant or something before I'd do that. They never came back with anything official.''

He drained his glass and put it down. "You want another one? If we're late at the restaurant it won't matter. They'll hold my table all night if they have to. I'm one of their best customers.''

"I need something to eat fairly soon," Constance said.

Ro started for the closet for coats and said abruptly, "That's why I didn't take it seriously, that Ginnie was in trouble with that pissant detective. They've been all over the place asking questions, going away again. Eric, William, Juanita, Gray, it's been the same with all of us. I assumed it was like that with Ginnie.''

Over dinner Ro talked about starting the theater thirty years ago. "I knew the minute I saw it that it was perfect," he said. "Angus Bowmer had already started up the Oregon Shakespearean Festival again. It stopped during the war and then came back stronger than ever. I knew he was right, that you can make a small town into a great theater town, bring in people from all over the world. It's happened here. Over four million people have come to Ashland to see excellent theater. I decided not to touch Shakespeare, that's Bowmer's field, and that just left me everyone else. I wanted a repertory group from the start. I used to say it was all for Lucy, Ginnie's mother, but I was kidding about that. I wanted to run a good theater from the time I first saw a live production. A bunch of amateurs doing *The Cherry Orchard*. They were terrible, the production was lousy, the sets old bed sheets and boards on orange crates, and it was the most exciting thing I had ever seen in my life. I was ten." He laughed at the memory. "Lucy wasn't even born yet and I already knew where I wanted to go, what I wanted to do."

"There must be a theater gene in your family," Constance said. "You, your sister, now Ginnie."

"And my father," he added. "He was in radio. He got me my first acting job on a radio station, back in the days of radio drama. A damn shame that died out. It was a hell of a lot better than anything on television. The sound effects, all those voices. You can make people believe anything with the right sound effects. A hell of a lot better. I made our mother see to it that Lucy got dancing lessons, voice, everything she needed to get a start. Our mother didn't like acting, theater, any of it. She was jealous, I guess, because that was all the rest of us cared about."

He seemed to be looking into the past, a distant expression on his face, dreamy almost. "Lucy was the star in my first production," he said. "She was four and a half. She cried because she was so scared of the audience at first, and then we couldn't drag her behind the curtain later. She wanted to keep bowing. She had learned how to blow kisses with both hands. The audience loved it."

"How old were you?" Constance asked.

Again he smiled. "Sixteen. I wanted to take the show on the road. Mother wouldn't let me. All I asked for was five dollars. I was sure we'd make enough to keep it running forever."

He needed little prompting to continue the story. He had gone to New York University and lived at home until his father left and the boyfriends started. By then he had had many jobs acting on radio and he thought his chances in Hollywood were too good to stay East; he had already made the move out of his mother's apartment and out of her life. He had thought then, and still thought, he admitted, that she had driven their father away.

"Then you and Lucy were reunited," Constance said when he paused. "Was that on the West Coast?"

His face became guarded. "She came out here," he said. "She didn't like living with our mother either by then."

"How old was she?"

"Twelve. Just a kid. Like Ginnie was when she came to live with me."

"Strange that Lucy didn't go to your father."

He shook his head. "She had no reason to trust him. He'd run out on us as far as she was concerned. Besides, I'd given her money and told her that was what it was for. If she ever decided to leave, to take a train and come to me."

Their waiter cleared the table, brought coffee. Charlie added sugar to his, and as he stirred it he said, "She owed you a lot. You provided for her, wanted to make her a star. Yet she moved away, took Ginnie away with her, and never even told Ginnie about you. Why was that, Mr. Cavanaugh?"

"None of that has anything to do with what's happening here now."

"Probably not, but if they try to prove that Ginnie's been disturbed in the past, they won't have to look much beyond the time she came to live with you. No secrets in a town this size, I understand. And that will send them into the more distant past. It'll all come out, whatever it all is. That's the trouble with murder, Mr. Cavanaugh. Nothing that was believed decently buried stays buried. It all gets dragged out and examined again."

Ro drank coffee, his eyes narrowed; he signaled to the waiter. "Just bring the pot, will you, Bill?" He waited, then poured for himself. Finally he said, "I'll tell you about it, Mr. Meiklejohn, but if you bring it up when you don't have to, if you exploit it in any way, I'll come after you. And I'll get you."

Charlie added more sugar to his coffee. "You seem to forget that I'm here to help her."

"I haven't forgotten," Ro said quietly. "I just want to make sure you don't forget that, either. This is ancient history, let's keep it like that. Lucy met Ginnie's father when she was in school. She was nineteen, he was twenty. Kids, both of them.

Vic was crazy in love with her. She was a beautiful girl, talented, wonderful in every way. I didn't blame Vic for falling the way he did. I blamed him for insisting on marriage right off the bat. They were too young. His parents were well off, bound to raise a stink over it. I was on my way to Europe that spring. I'd already found Harley's Theater and knew it was going to be mine, but I had to see other theaters before I made a bid on it. Anyway, they decided to go, too, and the three of us were abroad for almost a year. By then Vic was twenty-one, no longer under his parents' control. They came to Ashland with me. Lucy was excited about the theater, as much as I was. Ginnie was born and then the fire between Vic and Lucy began to dim a little. He began to drink too much. I saw the same pattern there had been with my parents, one of them involved with theater, the other feeling neglected, left out." He sighed. "I blame myself. We were too busy for me to see what I should have seen. I was older than they were, I should have done something about them. We were all too busy. Hanging scenery, painting, taking multiple parts, learning lines, doing everything. All of us."

Constance wanted more coffee, but she was afraid that any motion might interrupt his flow. She waited. Charlie was unmoving; he looked sleepy.

"That day, the day Vic died," Ro went on, "I saw Lucy in town. She had said something about going to the doctor and I knew Ginnie had been sick with a cold. I assumed she had taken Ginnie for that. She passed me in her car and I followed her out to their house, to see how Ginnie was. It wasn't far, ten minutes out of town. The roads were unpaved then. Lucy was driving so slowly that I caught up with her and was right behind her when we turned the last curve and saw the fire. The house was blazing. Lucy jumped out of her car and started to run toward the house. I caught her and threw her to the ground. She was screaming that Ginnie was in there, Vic was in there. I can't remember much of the next few minutes. I was inside, found Ginnie, still in her room, terrified. I wrapped a blanket around her and ran out with her. The blanket was on fire, my hair. Ginnie was screaming hysterically, saying over and over, "I'm sorry. I'm sorry."

His face looked twenty years older than it had minutes before.

Constance now poured the coffee for them all. He lifted his cup and drank without bringing his gaze back from that distant place. "Someone slapped out the fire in my hair. Someone tried to put Ginnie in Lucy's arms and she refused to take her. She was fighting to get free, to run into the house. She was screaming at me, "Why did you bring her out and not Vic? Let me go get him out.""

Suddenly he shook himself. "Ginnie wouldn't say anything at all for the next year. Nothing. Lucy miscarried that night. She was delirious when they put her in the ambulance. She said it was Ginnie's fault, that she had been playing with matches. She had been spanked for playing with matches a week or so before that. Lucy blamed me for luring her to Ashland, for starting Harley's Theater, for everything. She blamed me for not saving Vic. She hung on for almost a year and then left. She said I'd never hear from her again and I didn't. I owed her and Vic money, a hundred thousand dollars. I didn't have that much cash, but I told her I'd send her money every month until it was paid, as long as she needed help, as long as Ginnie needed things. I gave her the name of a lawyer we had used in San Francisco and told her we could go through his office for the payments. She went to a different lawyer and I paid her through him until she was killed in an automobile wreck. Every month I begged the lawyer to ask her if Ginnie was all right, if she had recovered. It was three years before she responded and told him to tell me that Ginnie was well. Other than that I never did hear from her again."

Charlie let out a long breath and looked about for the waiter. He came almost instantly. "Three double cognacs," Charlie said. "Pronto."

No one spoke until they had the drinks. "Ginnie doesn't remember any of that," Constance said then.

"And I don't want her to," Ro said quickly. "You see why I want the past to stay back there where it belongs?" He drank most of his brandy in a large gulp. "When she came to me I thought I was being given another chance, a chance to do things right, not botch it again. She was too quiet, had nothing to say to me. We were strangers. I knew I had to do something, make memories for us to share. That's why I took her on a long trip, so we would have shared memories, something to talk about. Over the years she's become vivacious, happy, and busy. And now this. She's right back where she was then."

"If only she hadn't left town that night," Charlie murmured. "To bring our information up to date, will you tell us about that day and night?"

Ro shrugged. "When I heard that Ginnie had left, and I saw Sunshine, I thought it was her fault again. She bugs Ginnie, bugs everyone. I yelled at her to get the hell out—"

Charlie held up his hand and said apologetically, "Let's do it slower, if you don't mind. When did you last see Ginnie that day?"

"At lunch. She ate with Gray and me in my office. Then Gray talked her into a little walk around the building, to get some sun. It was a glorious day, everyone was up about the weather. Anyway, she went out with him."

Charlie nodded. "And when did you realize she was gone?"

Ro shook his head. "I don't know. An hour later, maybe more. You know what it's like now, people everywhere. I was here and there and quite suddenly realized that she had left again. She had been doing that. Coming in, staying an hour or so, then leaving. I thought that day that maybe she had come out of her withdrawal phase, and it upset me to have her gone again. I looked around for her then, and saw Sunshine in the costume room. She had orders to keep the hell out, but there she was trying on hats. I exploded at her. I was sure she had said something to Ginnie. It was pretty public and ugly, my yelling at Sunshine."

"You didn't try to call Ginnie?"

He shook his head. "I'm afraid I had been hovering too much, getting on her nerves. She asked me and some of the others to please just leave her alone, and I knew she meant it. I didn't call."

"Okay. Did Sunshine leave?"

"Sure. She grabbed that bag of hers and ran, smiling all the time. That woman is a curse." He stopped, then continued in a quieter voice. "I worked until six or so, washed up, met friends here for dinner.

"And that's when you saw Laura? Before or after you had dinner?"

"When I entered the restaurant, she was over there in the lounge. I saw her when I came in at seven-thirty. I said hello to my friends at the table, then went over to speak to her."

"Why?" Charlie asked.

For the first time Ro looked unsure and uncomfortable. He made a slight shrugging motion, then said, "Nosy, maybe. She and Gray were having trouble. She was the outsider, and nothing seemed to make her feel welcome. I don't know why. I didn't stop to ask myself why. I just went over and said hello, asked about her cold. She looked terrible."

"Mr. Cavanaugh," Charlie said slowly, and very directly, "as far as the record goes, you're the last person who spoke with her that night, with the exception of her killer maybe. Let's do this word for word, if you can. You say she looked terrible, but how? Unkempt? Bloodshot eyes? Terrible how?"

For a moment Ro seemed ready to protest, then he sagged back against his chair and drew a deep breath. "It's just that we keep going over the same ground, over and over. She looked ill, feverish even. And she was staring at her glass as if at a crystal ball. When I spoke, she started and nearly knocked her glass over. Nervous, distraught even. That kind of terrible." He was watching Charlie closely; at his nod of encouragement, he went on. "I said I hoped she was feeling better, and she said this medicine was helping. She meant the booze, held up the glass when she said it. And she said she had rose-hip tea. A and B, she called them." He closed his eyes a minute in thought, then went on. "I think that's when she said the rose-hip tea was one of Sunshine's many cures. And then she said did I know Sunshine was rewriting the play yet again." He rubbed his eyes now and shrugged. "I'm afraid I lost the rest of whatever conversation we had at that point. I was seeing red."

Charlie sighed. "I suppose you've tried to recall what else was said."

"I have. It couldn't have been much. All I could think of was that damn woman and her damn play and the trouble she was causing all of us. I cut my dinner short and left the restaurant early, I was so furious. At eight-thirty," he added with a grim laugh. "Trevor, the bartender, noticed the time. He said Laura left at ten after eight."

"So you were home again what, five, ten minutes later?"

Ro shrugged. "I just know I called Gray at a quarter to nine. I asked him if it was true. I didn't tell him where I heard it. I knew he hated for Laura to be chummy with that woman. He said he had threatened mayhem if she even hinted that she wanted to rewrite again. I didn't believe he could handle her. No one had been able to keep her out of our hair yet. Still haven't. She turns up everywhere, always underfoot. Anyway, I called William and Eric and asked them to come over. I wanted contingency plans if we had to yank the play at the last minute, and I was ready to do just that if that woman was driving Ginnie away. William and Eric came and we talked for a couple of hours. I wasn't paying much attention to the time. Eric said he left at eleven-thirty and that's probably about right. I had a nightcap and went to bed."

"And she was killed at about nine," Charlie said. "Do you know for sure what time you were making those phone calls? What time you called Gray?"

"A quarter to nine. I realized when I was dialing that he might not be home yet. He and Eric had dinner together to discuss the auditions. When I got him I knew I'd be able to reach Eric."

Charlie sipped his cognac, his expression unhappy.

"Look," Ro said. "She was in a bar, drinking alone. She was good-looking, lonesome. So someone picked her up and later on they fought. I just don't see the mystery about it."

"And Peter Ellis?"

"He walked in on a burglar, obviously. No one on earth had a reason to kill him."

"You may be right," Charlie said, even unhappier. "But if you are, Ginnie's in for a hell of a time. Unless those two unrelated murderers come forward and confess."

He glanced at Constance, who had been silent and watchful throughout the questioning. She was regarding Ro thoughtfully. "When you were talking to Laura," she said then, "what was her attitude? Was she still staring, looking at you, what? You said she was startled at first. More than you might have expected?"

He nodded. "I hadn't really thought about it, but yes. It was as if she had been so deep in her own thoughts that my voice was a wrench to her. Yes. And then she looked at me almost as if she was studying me, you know the kind of intent look people can assume. That didn't last long. She began to play with her glass, moved it back and forth, back and forth, and didn't look at me again. She might have glanced up when I left. Probably did, but no more than that."

"Moved her glass how?" Constance asked.

Ro glanced at Charlie, who looked as at sea as he felt. Constance watched as he picked up his brandy glass and put it down softly, picked it up and returned it to its original position, then repeated the action several more times. She smiled her thanks and looked at her watch.

"What was that for?" Charlie asked as they drove back to the inn a few minutes later.

"She hadn't made up her mind yet about A and B," Constance said. "It was evident in her earlier remarks about the drink and rose-hip tea, referring to them as A and B. And the glass, back and forth, not making idle circles or just for something to do. Still going from A to B, back to A. What do you think?"

"I think it's funny that Ro keeps threatening to toss Sunshine out on her ear and Sunshine keeps hanging in there. Smiling."

16

Charlie, come look," Constance called. She was in their sitting room before one of the wide windows. The clouds of the day before had left; today the sun was brilliant, and on the hills across the valley the clouds had deposited a dusting of snow. On the higher mountains the snow was dazzling in the oblique rays of the morning sunlight. She turned to look at the mountain behind the inn; there the snow was whiter, deeper-looking, and closer. The evergreen trees were startlingly green; the grassy meadow that was the backyard was summer-green.

Charlie joined her and put his arm around her shoulders. He made a grunting sound of approval at the view.

"Oh," she said softly, and pointed. At the edge of the meadow a deer was grazing.

Charlie squeezed her shoulder and went to the table for coffee. It had been delivered a few minutes earlier and in another few minutes breakfast would follow. They could sit and watch the deer while they ate their own food—rainbow trout, croissants, poached eggs, melon. . . . Too much, Constance thought with contentment. The phone rang.

Charlie answered it. He said uh-huh several times, then, "Have you called Ralph? He'll want to go with you. . . . I'm sure, Ginnie. Don't go alone. Okay? Give us a call later. We'll check in often and call back if we miss it. And, Ginnie, take it easy. We'll see you at the end of the reading." He listened and nodded. "Don't let them scare you, that's the main thing right now."

There was a soft tap on their door and they went into the bedroom while their breakfast was being laid out.

"The detective from the sheriff's office is taking her for a ride right after the reading," Charlie said. "He says maybe retracing her path will make her remember where she went. And just incidentally let him try to find anyone he can who can put her in any definite location at any definite time."

"Poor Ginnie. What will she do?"

He shrugged. "Probably say maybe this way, maybe that way. She'll have to tell eventually. Not that it will make much difference. Out in the wilderness, no witnesses, no alibi. They'll be able to say she saw those trees last month, last summer, sometime."

They returned to the other room and started breakfast. Neither spoke for several minutes until Constance said, "I think we're having some of the best food I've had in years. And the prettiest scenery." The deer had been joined by two does. It was like a picture from a romantic illustration.

"It's okay," Charlie said. "But that damn snow is too close."

She laughed and pushed her plate back a bit.

"You going to finish that fish?"

"Can't."

He slid it off her plate onto his. "I think I'll skip the reading this morning. I want to catch Spotty, and have a chat with the police chief. Want to tag along?"

She shook her head. She knew it would go better without her. Spotty had been a police officer years ago, Gus Chisolm was still a policeman. They would establish credentials, exchange stories a few minutes, test for mutual acquaintances, and then Charlie would ask his questions, and more than likely get full answers. The phone rang again and this time it was Sunshine calling Constance.

"She's read your cards," Charlie said with a grin, his hand over the mouthpiece. He gave the phone to Constance.

"Hi, Sunshine." She listened for a long time, then said, "This morning? I can give you a lift back into town afterward. Okay?"

Charlie had cleaned both plates and now emptied the coffeepot, dividing the coffee equally between the two cups. Yesterday morning they had eaten everything, and this time there had been quite a bit more. Tomorrow would it all be increased again, and then again? He hoped so.

"Well," Constance said thoughtfully after hanging up. "It seems that Shannon Tessler would like to talk to me, alone."

He laughed. "Thank you, Sunshine."

"So, you want to drop me and then pick me up again? Or have me drop you off?"

"I'd better walk," he said with a sigh. "Maybe even run."

Shannon Tessler was in her early sixties, twenty-five pounds overweight, and very pale with black hair that waved softly about her ears in an old-fashioned style that became her. Her eyes were bright blue and lively. Only her unhealthy pallor betrayed her illness. She must have been stunning as a young woman, Constance thought; even now she was quite attractive. There was a dimple high on her cheek.

"I made some blackberry-mint tea," Sunshine said softly. "It's a good spring tonic, you know? Do you want some?"

"No, thanks. I'm just up from the breakfast table. This is a lovely house, Mrs. Tessler."

It was turn-of-the-century clapboard, with high ceilings, lovely mellowed paneling and floors, and crisp white curtains. And not a single reminder of theater to be seen.

"It's too big for us now," Shannon said, "but we're used to it and don't want to move. We just closed doors to rooms that we don't need anymore. Please, sit down. I'd like some of your tea, Sunshine, and then maybe you would leave us alone for a few minutes?"

Constance sat in a high-backed damask-covered chair, Shannon in a straight chair; she sat almost rigidly upright. She did not speak for several moments.

"Sunshine has been a blessing," she said finally. "I really think there may be something to all those herb teas that she serves. And, of course, she's company." She sighed deeply. "We're six miles from town here, but sometimes it feels like the end of the earth."

Sunshine brought a single cup and put it on a table at Shannon's elbow.

"Thank you."

"I'll go upstairs and work on my new play now." She turned to Constance. "My first one's so good I'm going to do a lot of them. I have a lot to write about, you know?"

"I'm sure you do," Constance said.

She left without a sound. Shannon picked up the tea and tasted it, nodded, and sipped. "It's very good. Are you sure?"

Constance smiled and shook her head. "What did you want to see me about, Mrs. Tessler?"

"Please, call me Shannon. Everyone does, always did. When I was a girl they called me Irish and I had to fight a dozen fights to make them stop. Aren't children foolish, fighting over things like that?"

Constance said nothing, waited.

Shannon put down the cup and folded her hands in her lap. "Forgive me," she said. "It's Ginnie. I wanted to tell someone about Ginnie and the fire. I know what the gossip is and it's all a lie, you see. But I didn't know who to tell, or what I should say. It's so difficult to refute gossip, so difficult. And I doubt that anyone would bring it up in any official way, but it influences the way people think about other people."

"Are you talking about the fire that killed Ginnie's father?"

She looked surprised. "Yes, of course. They're saying Ginnie started it and she didn't. The fire started in the kitchen, where Vic died, and she was in bed, nowhere near that end of the house. She was still in bed when Ro ran in and carried her out. They say that she had been playing with matches before and was spanked once, so she must have done it again. But that's wrong."

"How do you know?"

Shannon sighed even deeper. "A week or two before Vic was killed in the fire, the children were out back, here in our yard, and my son Jackie started a fire that almost got out of control in the woods. Everyone around here is terrified of wildfires, naturally. There have been some very dangerous ones from time to time. Lucy was here with Ginnie—they just lived a mile up the road—and together we got the fire put out. We were both very frightened. Four children, Lucy pregnant . . . It was a bad experience. But Jackie was responsible, not Ginnie. He was six."

"How did such a rumor start? Didn't you tell William?"

"No." Her voice was faint. "We were having a bad year, one of several bad years. . . . I hardly ever saw him, and when I did . . . we had little to say to each other."

Constance frowned. "Ginnie's mother must have told her husband, and Ro."

"I know she told Vic. They were both so frightened that they searched the house and threw out every match they found. They didn't smoke and there wasn't any reason to keep matches, so they got rid of them. I don't know if she ever told Ro. They'd had a fight over something and she swore she'd never speak to him again. Vic wasn't talking to him, either." She shook her head. "Those were very bad years in so many ways. That damn theater nearly killed all of us in those years. Every cent, every minute, every thought was for the theater, nothing else."

"What happened to Ginnie afterward? We've heard that she stopped talking."

"Yes. Ro moved her and Lucy into town, rented a house for them, and he brought in one specialist after another for Ginnie. Nothing helped. He was nearly demented himself. Lucy blamed him for everything, everything. She turned on him in a way I wouldn't have thought possible. They had been so close before. At first I thought it was just what he deserved finally, but then even I had to feel sorry for him, the way she turned."

"Why do you say even you? Did you blame him for your problems with William?"

Shannon nodded and let her gaze slide past Constance, out the window. "We all loved him, you see," she said in a low voice. "Every woman he met must have loved him, and he just thought of the theater, Lucy, and Ginnie, in that order. It was all he cared about. He made me feel . . . I thought at first that he cared about me, but I was wrong. I was so wrong. So wrong. I was glad he finally was getting some of it back, some of the hurt, the pain, the loneliness. I was glad at first, but then I had to feel sorry for him, and even sorrier for him when Lucy went away and he really lost them both. But he's so lucky, isn't he? Now he has Ginnie back." She looked at Constance again. Tears were making her eyes glisten. "I was so sorry that Lucy didn't keep in touch. We had become friends, our children were playmates. I thought she would let me hear from her, but she never did. I was with her the night she miscarried, the night of the day Vic died. She was hysterical, out of her mind. She seemed to think that Ginnie had died in the fire, too. She kept saying he's gone and I lost his child and there's nothing left. I was afraid she would try to kill herself that night."

"Was Ginnie actually burned?"

"No. She was treated for smoke inhalation and shock. I saw her, poor little thing, drawn up like a baby, sleeping. I had baby-sat her so many times, she was almost like one of my own children, and she looked as if she had never seen me before, wouldn't say a word. She didn't cry either. I always thought that strange, that she didn't cry."

"I never worked with children," Constance said, "but I've read that shock and grief affect them like that sometimes. Does she know that they say she started the fire?"

"I'm sure not. Not unless it's come up now, since those terrible murders. All that was twenty-six years ago, and until now no one would have thought to bring it up, I'm sure. Hardly anyone around here was even here then."

"I don't want to tire you," Constance said, "but could you tell me how it was when Ginnie came back? Did you see her then?"

She nodded. "I saw her but she didn't know me. She had forgotten everything about Ashland, Ro, all of us. She was silent again. Not completely like before, but almost. She would say yes and no and things like that, but nothing else. No real talk, if you understand what I mean. It was heartbreaking to see her like that again."

"And Ro took her on a long trip," Constance said. "How was she when they got back?"

Shannon smiled. "Almost like a normal girl, not quite, not

that fast, but almost like any thirteen-year-old, fourteen by then, I guess. Ro did a good thing. I've always wondered if he would have done that if the season hadn't already begun, if things hadn't been well started. We'll never know. She comes to visit pretty often, makes me think of Lucy when she was young. Our children are all grown, moved away to big cities. Not a one of them is interested in theater," she added, almost proudly.

"Look, Charlie," Gus Chisolm was saying, "I know Draker's an asshole, but he's a good detective. He doesn't like loose ends and he works to tie off each string thoroughly."

They were in his office; his feet were on his desk, his chair tilted back. Charlie had turned a straight chair around, was astraddle it, resting his chin on the back.

"Suppose you knew for a fact that Ginnie didn't do either one," he said. "Where'd you look then?"

"That's the problem," Gus said. "There isn't anyone else, I'm telling you. The only one of them who could have done it, besides Ginnie, is Gray Wilmot. He left the high school a few minutes after nine and no one knows when he picked up Laura in the bar. Why? There's no reason that anyone's come up with. Because Laura and Ellis were having lunch now and then? It's a laugh. They were splitting. She was getting ready to go back East. What difference would it have made if she'd been having late-night dinners, all-night dates with Ellis? Wilmot didn't seem to give a damn one way or the other. But even if that could work as a motive, there's no way he could have killed Laura in that park. He was on the phone with Ro Cavanaugh just before nine. Now, unless you want two killers instead of one, that lets him out."

"Maybe she wasn't killed in the park," Charlie said.

"Yeah, I thought of that. But that's even worse. How'd he get her body to the river? Their car, or her car, was in the garage being repaired. The only way from their place to the river is through town. I don't think he hauled a body through town that night or any other night."

"And the other alibis check out," Charlie muttered, scowling at the floor.

"They sure do. William was seen dropping off Sunshine, and he was in that store all right. The kid who works there had his girlfriend in visiting, they both back him up. The store closes at nine, he was the last customer, chatted a few minutes. Eric was by his neighbor all night, gave him a ride home. Ro was in the high-school auditorium until he got a ride to Jake's Place."

"Was he with people all night there?"

"No. We have confirmation that he was there during the intermission at eight-thirty; he tried to get a ride with Gray Wilmot a little after nine, and did get a ride with Jerry Alistair at nine twenty-five. As for the night Laura was killed, he was either on the phone or with other people until eleven-thirty. Besides, his car hadn't been out of the carport since before Christmas. Hell, it wouldn't even start."

"And the rain started at ten to nine," Charlie muttered. "Doesn't it rain a lot here? Why were so many people surprised by it? No umbrellas, no boots."

Gus smiled genially. "We don't pay a lot of attention until it's actually coming down. The forecast that night was for clearing. It was a surprise that time. Ro's feet were soaked; Ginnie was soaked, Ellis was. Wilmot and Laura were both soaked. Way it goes. There was a real lake outside the stage door that night. My feet were soaked."

"Okay. Okay. So that leaves Spotty. Why not him?"

"No motive. But let's say he's a nut and doesn't need a motive. We have the same problem with Laura. He doesn't even own a car. And why go to the park with her anyway? Privacy? Hell, they could have danced the jig all night in the theater without anyone knowing."

Charlie glared at the floor. Spotty was incapable of it, he had decided earlier after talking with the watchman for half an hour. Not incapable of murder, but of leaving his job for the time it would have taken to get to the river and back. It kept coming home to those with keys, he brooded. The stage door had been replaced sixteen months ago, the locks changed, and only six keys provided, numbered, registered. Of course, copies could have been made in any big city. No copies had been made in Ashland; Draker had checked. But why? As far as he could tell, people wandered in and out all day long. Who would want to enter at night? And why? And if someone had entered and Ellis surprised him, why murder? Ellis seemed the most unlikely victim he could imagine. No enemies in Ashland, none at the university.

"Was Ellis going in or coming out of the office when he got it?" he asked after a time.

"Looked to me like he was done and coming out again. I've got some pictures from one of my officers in here somewhere." He hunted through a desk drawer and brought out a folder, shoved it across the desk.

The top picture was of Peter Ellis sprawled on the floor of the office. His feet were toward the desk, his head close to the round table. The black raincoat was partially wrapped around his body, clearly wet. There was another picture of his head in a close-up; Charlie did not linger over it. "Where does that door go?" he asked, showing Gus a picture of Ro's desk and a door that was open a crack.

"Little closet and through there to a john."

The hall door opened inward to the office, revealing first the easy chairs and couch. Anyone had to enter entirely to see the desk area. Charlie peered closely at the pictures of the furniture: no coat, no book, nothing to indicate that anyone had entered, had been busy doing anything. The round table was bare; the desk the same kind of mess he had noticed the day before; nothing else seemed disturbed in the slightest.

"And all the lights were on?"

"Every one. Switch by the door turns on the lamps at the ends of the couch, but the desk lamp has to be turned on over there. Ceiling light's got a switch on the wall by the closet."

"How about lights in the closet and bathroom?"

"Closet light was on."

Charlie closed the folder. "So maybe it was a burglar. Why else turn on every damn light?"

"Crazy burglar to do a thing like that. Spotty made checks off and on all night, and Ginnie was sure the office door was open a little. It was dim in the hall and she could see the light from the office as soon as she went in the stage door. Some crazy burglar."

"Yeah. Well, I'm due to meet my wife in a few minutes. Thanks, Gus. Can't say any of this has been really helpful, though. Owe you a beer or something."

"No, you don't, Charlie. If there's any way to get Ginnie off the hook, I'm all for it. I'm just hoping you can find that way. I hate to admit it, but I'm stymied. There just isn't anyone else with enough opportunity both times. Give me a call if you want anything else. And I'd appreciate it if you didn't let on to Draker that I showed you the pictures, stuff like that."

On the sidewalk outside the office, Charlie gazed at the rolling hills across the valley, but it was a long time before he saw that the snow had vanished. The air was brisk, like spring in upper New York, he thought then, and suddenly he wished he and Constance were home with their cats and their fireplace and Irish coffees in front of a sparking fire. Constance had said in the beginning that this was going to be messy, and he was very much afraid that, as usual, she was right.

17

Constance watched Sunshine vanish backstage, merging with the actors and various assistants and workers without effort. She wasn't supposed to be there yet, Sunshine had said, not until one, but as long as Ro didn't see her it would be all right. You know? Constance heard that soft voice in her head and turned away with a twinge of irritation. Sunshine could be trying, she decided. On their way back to town all she had talked about was what she had read in the cards for Constance and Charlie. All accurate enough without being very specific until she had said, "You're the High Priestess because you can see into people and because you're not afraid. Why aren't you afraid, Constance? Most people are, you know?"

"Oh, I'm as afraid as most people, I'm sure," Constance had replied lightly and Sunshine had shaken her head, still smiling.

But she wasn't afraid in the usual way, Constance had realized. She had taken years of training in aikido and that helped, of course. She really was not physically afraid of anyone, and yet she had lived in terror for a long time in New York, especially the last ten years that Charlie had been on the police force. The odds got worse and worse, she had thought then, still thought. Every year he escaped life-threatening injuries made the next year that much more dangerous. Charlie had laughed at her, but had not been able to dissuade her.

The little side trip of thoughts had lasted only a moment, hardly interrupting the conversation. "You're not afraid, either," Constance had said. "It was very brave of you to leave everything and come down here among strangers. Especially a group like this one, so close to each other."

"People don't scare me," Sunshine admitted. "If you watch them, and read their cards and look for signs, for auras, things like that, they aren't so scary. You have to understand the relationships, you know? That's what was wrong with Laura, she didn't understand relationships, didn't even look for them. She just saw herself this way and that way. Like looking at the surface of a pond and not through the water to the bottom. If you can do that, you don't have to be afraid. They're all obsessive, you know? That's why Laura was unhappy. She was obsessive about Gray, and they're all obsessive about the theater."

"Aren't you obsessive about anything? Most people are. Weren't you obsessive about rewriting your play so many times?"

"Up to a point, but that's different. You want things right, you know? As soon as the promptbook was done, I was done. There will be things that come up in rehearsals, maybe, and I'll make little changes, but I'm doing a new play now."

"And you're not afraid of Ro?"

"Not really. As long as I leave Ginnie alone, he won't bother me. That's his obsession, you know? Ginnie is."

"I thought the theater was."

"That too. But mostly it's Ginnie. He thinks I bug her. He's afraid I'll read her cards and scare her."

"I never could read my own cards," Constance said, making a last turn before reaching the theater. She wished the trip could have taken just a bit longer. "Can you read for yourself?"

"Oh, yes. It's hard, though. You're so biased, you know? I'm the child of inspiration on my way to becoming Empress. You know how to read that?"

"I'm not sure," Constance said. "How did you?"

Sunshine laughed gently. "You know how. Thank you for the ride, Constance. See you later."

They had drawn up to the parking lot. Sunshine opened her door and left before Constance drove into the lot to park. Constance watched her for a moment, the awkward-looking bag clanking and jingling as the woman moved swiftly to the rear of the Quonset hut. Well, she thought, the truth was that she did not know how to read that. She didn't know enough about the relationships yet.

She parked, entered the theater, and started for rehearsal room A, where Gray Wilmot was reading. She had just turned the corner of the hall leading to the rehearsal rooms when Ro emerged from one of them.

"Constance, I'm glad you're here. They're almost done, no point in going in there. Come with me, will you? I want you to meet Ginnie's doctor, my doctor. Did you hear that Draker's taking Ginnie for a ride, trying to make her remember where she was last week? Idiot! How can anyone tell one piece of these woods from another?"

Constance went with him to his office. Although he was talking about Draker and Ginnie, she noticed that he was quite aware of everyone they passed, everything going on. For a moment he stiffened, his stride broke, then he continued. Sunshine had slipped into Juanita's office.

"Jack, glad you could come," Ro said brusquely, entering his office.

Dr. Jack Warnecke was in his middle years, tanned, athletic. When Ro made the introduction, his handshake was almost too firm. Constance felt as if her state of health had undergone a complete scrutiny in that instant.

"Constance Leidl. Leidl. Of course, the psychologist! I've read your books. It's a pleasure, Miss Leidl. Or is it Ms.?"

"Or possibly Doctor," she said.

He looked taken aback for a moment, then laughed. "Sorry. Please, call me Jack. Do you like birds? Perhaps you could drop in for a drink, see my birds."

"For God's sake, Jack," Ro cut in. "Not now. Look, you've got to get Draker off Ginnie's back. He wants to drag her off on a wild-goose chase and I won't have it!"

Jack Warnecke raised an eyebrow. "How do you propose I do that, Ro?"

"You took her away from him once. Do it again. She has no business out being interrogated in a car with that man. He's trying to frame her. God knows what she might say while they're driving around."

Jack took a step toward the door. "Ro, that's impossible, and you should know it. She was in shock that other night, but she's fit now. I saw her just a couple of days ago and she's fine."

"She's not fine, goddamn it! She's as disturbed as she was when you said I should take her on that trip! Was she fine then?"

"Ro, you can't direct the world. The police are going to investigate and you can't make them stop. I can't. Sure, she's disturbed; so are you; so is Gray. It would be inhuman if all of you weren't. But she's well enough to be questioned. Tell her to give me a call if she wants to see me." He turned to Constance. "I'm in the apartment next to his. Please do come by. My wife and I would like to show you the birds. Cockatiels, a mackaw, budgies . . . Ro can tell you they're worth seeing. He feeds them when I'm gone. Take it easy, Ro. Just relax, will you? Ginnie's okay. See you later."

"Goddamn fool!" Ro stormed when Jack was gone. "He doesn't understand that she's in danger. You said you're a doctor?"

"Sorry. Ph.D.—psychologist, not a medical doctor. He's right. You can't direct the investigation." She smiled. "I said that just to bring him down a peg. Medical doctors seem incapable of calling anyone else doctor. He's no exception. Does he really have a lot of birds?"

"One whole room's been turned into an aviary. Our leases specify no pets, and spell out cats, dogs, hamsters, but no mention is made of birds, alligators, or rabbits. He decided to make an issue of it and started with birds and got hooked on them. I feed the damn things, all right. Stupid parrot nearly took a finger off once."

Jack had left the door open; now the noise level from backstage increased perceptibly. The reading was over. Ro sat down heavily at the round table and drummed his fingers on it. He looked as if he hadn't slept much the night before. If he had been unaware of Ginnie's danger before, he was making up for his ignorance now, Constance thought.

"I told Charlie to meet me here," she said. "Do you mind if I wait for him?"

"No. No. Make yourselves at home as much as you can, please. Ah, here they are." He stood up as a group entered the office. Ginnie and Gray were in front, then William and Eric, Bobby, the lighting director, others whom Constance had met, some she had not.

"It was a stupendous reading, Gray, really magnificent," one of the women was saying as they entered. "Inspiring, truly inspiring."

Eric was not frowning with his usual intensity and William seemed in deep thought. He nodded as if confirming something in his mind and looked surprised when everyone stopped moving and he was forced to stop also.

Ginnie was too pale, down to her lips. She was clutching her paisley bag in a hard grasp.

"Hi, Ginnie," Constance said. "Did you sleep at all?"

"Oh, hi. I didn't see you. Yes, as a matter of fact, I did sleep. I was a little surprised, but I did. Now I'm off. I'm supposed to be in Ralph's office in a couple of minutes."

"Wait a minute, honey," Ro said. "I'm leaving for lunch, walk down with you." He went to the closet near his desk and brought out a topcoat and put it on.

"Want me to hold on to your bag for you?" Constance asked.

"That's okay," Ginnie said. "I can just leave it here and get it later. You don't have to bother with it."

"No bother," Constance said and took it from her hand. "Remember, give us a call as soon as you're able."

Ginnie nodded and left with Ro. As they were going out, Charlie entered. Constance watched how he searched the room for her, how his expression changed subtly when he spotted her. She always felt as if they had exchanged long messages with that one swift locking of gazes. *Hello. How are you? I'm fine. It's okay. I love you.* And more.

Eric, Gray, and the woman who had been talking when they came in were in a huddle. Now Eric stepped back, nodding. An actress, Constance remembered. She was playing Big Nurse. She was shiny-eyed, gazing at Gray with open invitation in her eyes. He was oblivious of it.

The office was emptying, the backstage noise fading. Charlie waited until Gray was finished with Eric and the actress, then said, "I wonder if we could have a word with you, Mr. Wilmot? In here, maybe?"

Gray looked exhausted and wan. Silently he nodded and the last of the group left, murmuring. Charlie closed the door.

"I understand Ro often orders lunch in here," he said. "Maybe we could do that."

"Not for me," Gray said tiredly and sat at the table.

"Especially for you," Constance said. "Who does he usually call?"

Gray supplied the name of the restaurant and Constance placed the order while Charlie prowled the office. He looked at the bookshelves that lined one wall—all plays; comedies, tragedies, American plays, English, one-act plays. . . . He surveyed the desk but touched nothing on it. He understood the filing system Ro used; it was much like his own. You fish around and bring out what you were after, but if anyone moves anything, all was lost. He nodded at it and opened the door to the closet, peered inside. A couple of jackets, a mackintosh, a pottery umbrella holder with two black umbrellas with crook handles. A smaller door opened to a tiny lavatory. Of course, Ro was always making coffee, he needed a water supply, his own john. A toothbrush, shaving gear, a large bottle of aspirin were in the medicine cabinet. There were fluffy towels on the rack, more folded on a shelf. The soap looked like butterscotch candy. He thought fleetingly of their cats back home. When he rejoined Constance and Gray, she was speaking.

"Why don't you see a doctor? A mild sleeping pill for a few days wouldn't dull you too much for work."

He shook his head. "Drugs and theater, they seem to go together, don't they? Except I can't do drugs of any kind. Wrong reactions to them."

"Mr. Wilmot, would you mind helping me with something?" Charlie asked then.

Gray looked at him expectantly, nodding.

Charlie picked a book from the shelf and handed it to Gray.

He opened the door to the hall and looked out. "What I want you to do is come in, walk to the desk and put the book down and go back out. That's all. When I say 'Start.' "

Gray looked from him to Constance and shrugged. He went to the door and out to the hall, pulled the door closed. Charlie went to the closet and entered it.

"Start," he yelled.

Gray came back into the office with the book in his outstretched hand. It was only a few steps to the desk. He put the book down and turned and was to the door again before Charlie got out of the closet and caught up with him.

"Thanks," Charlie said, and retrieved the book, replaced it on the shelf.

"What was that for?" Gray asked.

"One more little scenario first," Charlie said. "Do you mind?"

"Of course I mind, but let's have it. What this time?"

"I want you to lie down. About here, I think. Your head about here." This time Gray was even more reluctant; he started to shake his head, but Charlie was not looking at him, was studying the floor instead. Gray took a deep breath and got down on the floor. Charlie watched him stretch out rigidly, then said, "Let me fix your arms and legs. . . . That looks about right. Now the chair . . ." Carefully he turned a chair over on its side, then stepped back to survey the scene. Gray's feet were two steps from the desk, one leg partly drawn up under him, one hand outstretched almost to the chair. Charlie opened the door all the way; it cleared Gray by less than an inch. "Okay," he said then. "That's all."

Gray was ashen when he got up and brushed himself. "That's how Peter Ellis was found?"

"Yes. As a director, how would you stage the action that would lead to that final scene?"

Gray looked at the closet, then at the floor where he had lain. A frown creased his forehead as he studied the room considering it. Finally he said, "Not the way I thought it was before. I thought someone was in the closet and got him on the way out. That's what Spotty seems to think. But he would have been farther down the room, nearly out the door, wouldn't he?"

Charlie nodded.

"And why hit him at all in that case?" Gray demanded. "If

someone was in the closet, he was out of sight. Why dash out and kill someone?"

Again Charlie nodded. There was a tap on the door then and Constance admitted the waiter with a tray. He looked at them curiously as he arranged the lunch things. "Ro ain't here?" he finally asked.

"Nope. How much do we owe you?" Charlie replied.

"It goes on the tab," the waiter said and slowly backed out, examining the room as he did so.

"Probably never saw a room where murder has been done," Charlie commented. "Let's eat."

Gray's color was better. Having a problem to solve seemed to improve his circulation, Constance noticed. He ate little, however.

Suddenly he put down his sandwich and said, "Ginnie couldn't have done it, could she? She would have had to come in first, go to the desk and get the statuette and wait for him to turn around and move away one step. What for? Where was he hit?"

Charlie touched his head just behind and slightly above the right ear. Gray said more positively, "She couldn't have done it. He was my height and she's what? Five-six, -seven?"

"It's the kind of thing experts get rich arguing in court," Charlie said. "A bullet track is easier, but even that isn't foolproof. But you were going to tell me how you would stage it."

Gray regarded him steadily for a moment, then turned his gaze to the desk. "The clown was usually on the end of the desk. I never saw it used as a doorstop, anyway." He paused, thinking. "Ellis came in and walked to the desk and put the portfolio down. Since no one could have come leaping out of the closet, picked up the clown, and caught him that fast, he must have seen whoever it was. Maybe even talked to him a minute, while the killer picked up the clown and came around the desk. As soon as Ellis had turned his back, taken a step or two, the killer hit him, sent him sprawling forward. Would he have fallen like that?"

"Probably. Might have clipped the table on his way down, and for certain hit the chair, knocked it over. But go on. Then what?"

Gray swallowed a bite of sandwich and drank coffee, still thoughtful, before he answered. "He must have run, and at the door realized he was carrying the clown and dropped it. Out through the double doors to the shop, I'd say, or Ginnie would have seen light around the stage door when it opened. The doors open from the inside unless they're padlocked, and Spotty doesn't put on the padlocks until after his ten-o'clock check. Once outside, he was home free."

Charlie righted the chair he had turned over and sat in it. "That's how the police will reconstruct it, I'm afraid."

"What's wrong with that reconstruction?"

"Well, it rules out mistaken identity, for one thing. The killer had time to get a good look at him and knew it was Ellis, not you, in that raincoat. And for another, if the killer had been a burglar, would Ellis have turned his back on him?"

Gray finished his sandwich and drained his cup. Constance refilled it for him and he nodded thanks. "Is that what you wanted to see me about? That little demonstration?"

"Actually no. You have to get to the cast reading at one, don't you? That leaves almost an hour. Would you mind filling in a few details for us? We're still trying to get the complete picture for both nights."

"Sure," Gray said with a touch of weariness. "Where do you want me to start?"

"I have a question," Constance said then. "I've been wondering why you didn't go back East for the funeral."

Gray looked startled. "Her family didn't like me. I would have been in the way. I wasn't welcome in their house when Laura was alive. I sure as hell would not have been welcome when she was dead."

"Was she leaving you, going back East?" Constance asked.

"Yeah. Everything blew up when we got here. She didn't like the small town atmosphere, and she couldn't get a job that she felt was right for her."

"Ellis got her the job, is that right? Were the four of you friends?"

"Not really. I met him a couple of times only. He got us our house, too, but because of Ginnie, not us. He would have done anything for her."

Constance glanced at Charlie and leaned back in her chair.

"Why don't you just fill in the details of both those evenings for us," Charlie said easily.

Gray took more coffee and looked at it. "We'd been having a lot of arguments, one after another. That night it was the same thing. Laura got mad when I said I had to go to the high-school play. She wanted me to go to the movie with her, but I seldom go to movies, and I thought it might be important to see the quality of the kids' performance. We get some of our actors from the high school, of course. Anyway, that's what we agreed, that I'd drop her at the movie and see the production, and then meet her in the bar. We had planned to spend an hour or more there listening to jazz, but we were both soaked and she was furious, and we came home."

"Whoa," Charlie said with a grin. "Too fast. Why did you take the car? It was hers, wasn't it?"

"It was hers. I had to drop off the promptbook for Sunshine's play here, and the high school is on the other side of town. It just seemed simpler that way. It's only two and a half blocks from the movie to the bar. In fact, it was her idea that we do it that way, less trouble for both of us. And I'd join her faster that way," he added bitterly.

"So you saw Eric and Ro. When?"

"I got there a few minutes before eight and they were already there. We spoke but didn't have time to talk. I saw Ro again at the intermission at eight-thirty or so. He introduced me to a couple of people. Jerry Alistair, for one. It was hot in the auditorium, people were milling about, going outdoors for cigarettes, things like that. I told him I'd left the promptbook for him. Then we separated and I didn't see him again that night."

Charlie looked at him thoughtfully. "When did you leave?"

"A little after nine. I didn't notice exactly. It was raining and I realized that Laura would be getting wet. The movie got out at nine-ten. I drove right to it, but it was already emptied, and I went on to the bar. I had to park a block away, and by then I was pretty soaked too."

"Where did you sit in the high school?"

Gray looked exasperated. "In the last row, aisle seat, nearest the parking-lot exit. I knew I wanted to get out before it ended."

"When you and Laura met at the bar, what did she say?"

Now Gray's expression was murderous. He stood up and looked at his watch. It was twelve-thirty; he could not plead that he had to get to the cast reading yet. He started to pace. He had good recall and he was a good mimic. He repeated what Laura had said, then added, "I told you we'd been having trouble. We were both bitchy. When we got home it turned into a real fight and she ended up in the second bedroom of the house. She stayed in there from then on."

Charlie stood up and stretched and now Constance also left the table and leaned against the desk watching Gray. He was looking over the shelves of books of plays.

"Gray," Charlie said softly, "was Laura interested in money? Would she have tried to blackmail anyone?"

Gray's reaction was swift. He turned from the shelves and leaped toward Charlie. Constance, almost in slow motion, caught his wrist and he found himself sitting down hard on the floor with a grunt.

Slowly he pulled himself up and sat in one of the chairs at the table. He rubbed his wrist, watching Constance warily.

"Do you know that she wouldn't have tried to blackmail anyone? Really know it?" Charlie asked in the same low, pleasant voice, as if he had not noticed the incident.

Gray shook his head violently. "She wouldn't have done that!" He started to talk about Laura and their relationship, about Laura and Ashland, Laura and Sunshine, Laura and the night they had had dinner at Ginnie's house. He talked rapidly, his voice harsh, his face strained. Suddenly he jumped up and went to the door. "I'm responsible. I know that. She was right about that. It's all my fault. She called me the climber. Maybe I was, maybe I still am. Maybe I saw myself in that damn play. Her father called me, they all know I'm responsible for everything that happened here. I can't deny it. I'm not even trying! I've got to get out of here for a few minutes. Christ, it's almost one!" He left so fast he was almost running.

18

Let's get the hell out of here before Ro comes back from lunch,"
Charlie said. "I've about had it for one day."

"Amen." Constance drew on her coat, collected her purse and
Ginnie's paisley bag, and they left the office in time to see Sunshine enter through the stage door. The cast members for her
play were already gathering backstage. Charlie steered Constance past them all, out through the double doors that opened
onto an alley. Directly across the alley was the shop with open
doors. To the right was the parking lot.

"I parked over there," Constance said.

Charlie nodded and kept walking through the lot onto the
sidewalk, where he stopped and looked up the street in the
direction of Lithia Way.

"Laura was on that corner at exactly the right time to see
someone leave," he said. "The question is, who?"

They retraced their steps to the other alley that led to Pioneer
Street, and again he stopped. "This is where Ginnie parked and
waited for Ellis. No way could she have seen anyone go out that
back door from here. All right, let's beat it."

"You don't think all those alibis will hold up?" Constance
asked as they reached the Buick. Charlie opened the door on
the passenger side for her and went around to get in before he
answered.

"Ro was right about this town," he said as he started to drive.
"You can walk from end to end in ten minutes, and you can
drive in just a couple of minutes. I've been all over it today. I
know. Anyone could have left the high school, driven over here
for something, and met Ellis. Two minutes to get here, a minute
to bash in his head, two minutes to get back. Who'd miss him?
Same with William. Drop off Sunshine, a minute to the theater,
get Ellis, and be in the store less than two minutes later. Even
Sunshine could have hightailed it over after William left her."

"That makes it completely unpremeditated," Constance said slowly. "Not even time for an argument to develop."

He nodded. "That's the hitch. Look, there's Ro's car." He had driven on the street behind the apartment complex. The carports were like stair steps, each one a foot or two higher than the last. The car parked there was a two-seater Fiat. It looked like an antique. Constance told him about Jack Warnecke, Ro's next-door neighbor with the birds. His carport was empty. Charlie drove on and made a left turn at Main Street.

"There's the moviehouse. One block to Lithia Way, another block to Pioneer, half a block to the bar where they met. Three minutes, at the most. Say she took a minute or two to get her coat on and actually leave, that puts her on the corner at about fifteen after nine."

"If she saw Gray . . ." Constance said thoughtfully, "as mad as she was about getting wet, that might have been the last straw. She was jealous of the theater, of course, and everyone connected with it."

"The only one she couldn't have seen was Ginnie."

"Or Juanita. Does her alibi hold up?"

"Definitely. Half a dozen people will swear she was in Medford." He turned again and this time went down Water Street. He nodded toward a restored Victorian house. "That's the boardinghouse where William dropped off Sunshine. Three blocks from the theater." He drove on past a Greek restaurant, past a wooden bridge. The river was no less swift here in the middle of town than up in the park; the banks were steep and rocky. He turned away from it onto a different street. "Let's go home and put our feet up and brood. Okay?"

"Sure. What were you looking for?"

"Some other place where Laura's body could have been put in the river. Not easy. Too many cars, streetlights, no approach to the river by car. No one can tell how far she was carried by the river before she was caught up in the boulders."

As he drove back to the inn she told him about her visit with Shannon. His only question when she finished, as he parked the car at the inn, was "And what did Sunshine say your cards foretell?"

She laughed softly. "Poor Sunshine. No one wants her to read for them except Shannon."

His gaze was on the hills across the valley. "You know what I like? Snow that goes away by itself." The hills were brilliantly green without a trace of snow. He turned to grin at her. She was frowning absently. "What is it?"

"Oh, the town, how accessible everything is to everything, five minutes from here to there, no matter where either point is. People made so much of alibis, remember? What good are any of them in a town that size? Who would miss anyone for five minutes? Even Sunshine. She said she worked on a new play the night Laura was killed, but who's to say if she did or didn't? I bet in a house like that boardinghouse of hers, no one pays any attention to the goings-on of the residents."

"You're right. I asked."

"About Sunshine? I was just making a point. Why would she do it? She didn't even know Peter Ellis, and Laura was about the only person around here to give her the time of day."

"Why would anyone else do it? I'm afraid that Draker's hunt for circumstantial evidence may be the only way to go about all this, and let motive take care of itself. On that basis, of course, the strongest case can be made against Ginnie. Let's go in."

Constance was reading a copy of *Troilus and Cressida,* Charlie gazing out the window. They had been quiet for almost an hour. Suddenly Charlie stood up and said, "I can make a case for just about all of them. Too messy. I don't like it."

Constance put her book down and waited. When he seemed absorbed in the scenery again, she cleared her throat. "Eric?"

"He's easy. He wanted the job that Gray landed. He was next in line, as far as he was concerned, and Ro brings in this young man with practically no experience. He knows that Gray left the promptbook for Sunshine's play at the theater; he overheard Gray tell Ro. He gets bored with the high-school kids and goes to the theater to read the promptbook, maybe with the idea that if it's as bad as they all seemed to think it was, that would be his chance. Ellis comes in with Gray's coat over his head and when he turns to leave, Eric swings, just as Ellis let the coat fall around his shoulders. Too late. He's dead and Eric knows he needs an alibi and hightails it back to the school."

"But everyone agrees that no one would mistake Ellis for Gray," Constance reminded him. "He would have seen his face."

"Maybe not. Everyone's assuming the lights were on when Ellis entered the office, but maybe they weren't. Eric could have turned them on just to make everyone jump to that conclusion."

She considered it, then said, "And Laura? How could he have managed that? He was at Ro's apartment until eleven-thirty, and on the phone to Ro at nine-ten."

"Remember that nine-o'clock time of death is approximate, could be off half an hour, or even more, either way. He leaves for Ro's house and meets Laura and she tells him she saw him the other night and he slugs her. He puts her body in his car and covers her with a rug, a blanket, something, and goes on to Ro's. When he leaves, he drives up the park road, gets rid of her body, and then goes home."

Shuddering, she said, "And Gray? You can see a way he could have done it?"

Charlie picked up the map Ralph Wedekind had provided them. "Look, here's his house, up a pretty steep hill. Everyone says he would have had to go down the hill, through town, up the park road, but that's not quite so. See, he could have stayed on the hill. They could have taken a walk together, talking, ended up on the ridge overlooking the park, here. That park's really in a canyon, with Park Drive winding around the crest over it for several miles. They get to the edge of the cliff and their argument gets worse and he hits her, kills her instantly. She topples over the cliff and goes rolling down the slope. It has dozens of paths up and down it; we saw them, remember? Steep as hell, but obviously used. He goes sliding down after her. She wouldn't have bruised since she was already dead, but she would have been covered with mud, her clothes torn, scratched up, probably. And that's why he puts her in the river and messes up the opposite bank, to make it appear that she went in there. He figures the swift water will tumble her about, account for the shape she's in. Then back up the cliff, the same streets home, and cleanup time."

"Oh, Charlie," she sighed. "We're going to have to talk to that detective, aren't we?" He nodded. "And Ro? Do you see how he might have killed Ellis? He's about the only one who wasn't caught out in the rain that night."

"I'm working on it," he said, and the telephone rang.

It was Ginnie, back from her ride with Draker and Ralph Wedekind. She sounded miserable, Constance reported, as she and Charlie got their coats on again to go to her house.

"Oh, I want to glance through her sketchbook first," Constance said. She started to flip pages, then stopped and examined a page, then another. "Do you remember the scene in *One Flew Over the Cuckoo's Nest* where the Indian kills Mac? Doesn't he smother him with a pillow?"

"In the book he does. Why?"

He looked at the sketch. It was the setting for the play, with the nurse's desk looming large in the background, file cabinets on one side, and in the foreground the figure of a man on the floor, one arm stretched over his head, his legs drawn up. His arm concealed his face.

"She's good," he murmured, and looked at the previous pages. Different views of the same setting, some with figures, some without. There was a sketch of the desk being used as a bed, a man lying on it, someone standing over him holding a pillow. "Here's that scene," he said. He turned more pages— the window with Chief walking away, the boat scene . . . None of the sketches was complete; the details were not the same from one to another, as if she had been trying out this, then that, just to see how well they fitted.

"That isn't the position Peter Ellis was in, was it?" Constance asked, again studying the sketch that was out of place in that play.

"Nope. Not a thing like it. I wonder what's in the missing sketchbook."

"Maybe nothing much. I just told her to remember yesterday. That's why I wanted to snatch this before someone else had a chance to."

Charlie looked at her suspiciously. "When did you tell her to remember?"

"When I told that silly story about a professor yelling at his students. I gave her hands permission to remember even if her head doesn't, and I think it took. Let's go see her."

Charlie thought of the look of wariness that Gray had assumed after Constance put him on the floor, and he sympathized. Gray didn't know the half of it.

He had insisted years ago that she take self-defense classes, and as soon as their daughter was old enough, that she take them also. When Constance protested one day that they were being taught how to kill people, he had said grimly, "If anyone ever touches you or Jessica and you don't take care of him yourself, I'll kill the son of a bitch and that will be murder one, premeditated, cold-blooded murder. If you do it, it's self-defense." He had meant exactly what he said and they both knew it. She had become very good indeed. In the beginning of her lessons she had demonstrated some of her new skills on him, but one day when he invited her to show him what they were practicing, she had said quite kindly that she had better not.

Ginnie admitted them and led the way to the kitchen. "I just put on coffee," she said. "Do you want some?"

"That would be nice," Constance said. "Was it awful?"

"He's such an asshole!" Ginnie muttered. "He really believes I killed Peter and Laura! He believes it!"

She poured coffee and started to arrange a tray. "Let's just have it here at the table," Constance said and sat down. Charlie sat opposite her, leaving space for Ginnie at the end between them. She brought the coffee things to the table and sat also. She was still too pale, but there were spots of color on her cheeks and a glint in her eyes that had not been there before. He had made her angry, Constance thought: a good sign.

"I brought your bag and stuff," she said. "Did the other sketchbook turn up?"

A puzzled look crossed Ginnie's face. "It was on the table in the rehearsal room when I got there. I must have dropped it yesterday. I guess Mrs. Jensen found it when she cleaned this morning."

"That's good. It would have been a shame to lose all that work."

"Oh, it wouldn't have been lost, not really. Sometimes I don't even look in them again. I have the preliminary sets drawn up, and at the readings I might get an idea or two, a nuance I missed, something of that sort. Once I draw it, it seems to stick in my head. For instance, today I realized that I hadn't made the hospital look institutionalized enough, and I added more file cabinets, rows and rows of files. They'll be way in the back and an orderly will go to them now and then as background. People won't consciously notice them, but they'll add to the feeling of bureaucracy an institution has." She opened the paisley bag and pulled out all the sketchbooks; there were four of them.

Constance had looked inside only the one. She wished now that she had examined all of them. "What did you think of yesterday about Sunshine's play? I saw you drawing like mad all through the reading."

"Nothing much." She began to flip through the sketchbook as she spoke. "It's pretty low-budget, not a lot we can do with the sets. Sunshine had action going on in every room of the house and I got that down to the living room only."

Suddenly Charlie felt the invisible fingers on his back and he leaned forward very slightly to look at the page Ginnie had stopped at. The same figure was there in the same position. Ginnie hardly even glanced at it, but turned another page.

"Here it is. I decided to cut away about half of the flats for the living room so that the audience can see through it to the mountains in the background."

She had not seen it, Charlie realized. She had been blind to that intrusive figure. There were sketches of a woman on the couch obviously dying or dead, but that one figure had not been the same. If he had not already seen it in her other book, would he have paid any attention? He could not answer his own question. Constance was idly turning pages in the sketchbook they had looked at earlier. She glanced at the page Ginnie was showing her and nodded.

"That should be very effective. Is that what they call a practical rock?"

"Yes. It's to be about eight feet high, high enough so the actor can actually be seen climbing it. . . ." She talked on, apparently blind to the fact that Constance had placed one of her pencils near her hand.

"Well, these are all so good. You're very talented. I suppose that detective went on about the fact that you're an artist, with fully developed visual memory. It's tempting to think that visual artists must be able to remember everything they've ever seen and reproduce it on demand. I imagine he's still bothered that you didn't see that doorstop in your uncle's office. He might even think you're lying, or something."

"He wanted to know if I studied acting in school," Ginnie said in a low voice. "All drama majors have to."

"I bet he did. I can just imagine him ordering you to remember. 'Of course you can remember!' Just like my professor ordering our hands to remember."

Ginnie was staring at Constance now, nodding.

"Start at the beginning of that trip with him and pick up the pencil and tell us about it," Constance said in her pleasant low voice. Ginnie picked up the pencil without looking at it. Constance slid the sketchbook under her hand, opened to the page with the man's body on the floor. Ginnie apparently did not notice, but as she began to describe her interrogation in detail, her hand began to draw. Charlie exhaled very softly and watched the hand in fascination.

Neither of them interrupted Ginnie as long as her hand kept drawing. When it stopped, Constance laughed and said, "That's enough of that. What a terrible trip that must have been for you." She reached out and took the sketchbook and casually slipped it into her purse. "Charlie, didn't you say you wanted to ask Ginnie something?"

"As a matter of fact," he started, searching for something, anything, to ask, "I wondered if Ro objected to your traveling so much?"

"Not really. You can't do theater work in a vacuum. You have to get out and see other theaters, how other people are doing sets, costumes, all that. He travels a lot himself, that's how he knew about Gray. He saw a production of his last year."

Constance stood up. "Thanks, Ginnie. I know you still have your models to make and we shouldn't keep you any longer. It must be difficult to keep on working right now."

"Thank God I have work to do," Ginnie said fervently. "As long as I'm working I don't think, not really think. It's like coming out of a daydream when I realize it's midnight and I've been working for four or five hours."

"Or a trance?" Constance said. "I've heard artists describe it like that. An altered state of consciousness that is like a trance more than anything else."

"That's right," Ginnie said a little self-consciously. "That's how I'd talk about it with another artist, but not usually with outsiders. They think you're crazy if you talk like that."

Not until they were in the car heading down the hill did Constance ask, "Charlie, did you get a look at the drawing?"

"I sure did," he said grimly.

Ginnie had finished the sketch. The man was stretched out on the floor, an overturned bottle near his hand, a chair upset at his side. There was a kitchen table with a plate that held cheese, a loaf of bread with a knife stuck in it, a very short candle burning on a second plate. A door was open a few inches behind the figure on the floor. A kitchen sink with a pot or pan in it, an open window behind it, part of a refrigerator . . . A typical kitchen, except that there was a body on the floor.

19

There were two messages waiting for them when they got back to the inn. The first was from Lieutenant Draker. Charlie returned his call while Constance hung up their coats and put away papers they had left on the table in the sitting room.

"He's coming over in five minutes," Charlie said. "I don't think he's happy. You want to call Dr. Warnecke?" His was the second call.

She nodded and took his place at the telephone. Jack Warnecke answered at the first ring. "Constance," he said, and she grinned, "could you and your husband join us this afternoon for cocktails? Sandy, my wife, is so eager to meet you both."

She accepted his invitation and called him Jack and was smiling broadly when she hung up. At Charlie's raised eyebrow she shrugged and said, "It's called one-upmanship, played among doctors and other professionals all the time. We're due at his place at five."

"That blows tea again," he said regretfully. "Maybe Mrs. Shiveley could send up coffee now. I used to hate it when people drank beer or booze in front of me when I was on duty and had to say no and be polite and just watch."

"Poor baby," she murmured and called Mrs. Shiveley for coffee.

"You don't understand," he said indignantly. "Suppose it's ninety-five outside, you're covered with sweat right down to your BVDs and this slob in shorts and a tank top is having a frosty glass of beer."

"So you arrested him and tossed him in the slammer," she said, laughing.

"Damn right. Every time."

The coffee and Lieutenant Draker arrived practically together. Mrs. Shiveley was arranging the cups on their table when Draker knocked on the door. Mrs. Shiveley was angry that he had come upstairs alone, unannounced.

"What do you mean coming in here without permission? This is not a public house, young man. Get out this instant." She turned to Constance and Charlie. "I'm very sorry. I'll call my husband and the police instantly."

"I am the police," Draker said icily.

"Where is your identification?"

He showed her his ID and looked past her to Charlie. "Tell her it's all right. Let's not have a stupid scene."

"Are you Lieutenant Draker? We're expecting the sheriff's detective, Mrs. Shiveley. Thanks for your concern. You are Draker, I take it?"

"I'm Draker." His face was flushed a dull red, his eyes nearly closed.

Wired too tight, Charlie thought, and smiled genially at him. "Come on in. We ordered coffee for you. Thanks again, Mrs. Shiveley."

Her gaze that swept the detective was cold and unapproving. Wordlessly she nodded and left, closed the door softly behind her.

"This isn't your average Howard Johnson motel," Charlie said comfortably. "She takes good care of her guests. Sit down, won't you. I'm Charlie Meiklejohn, and this is my wife, Constance Leidl. What can we do for you, Lieutenant?"

Before he could respond, Constance asked brightly, "Cream? Sugar? Look, Charlie, she brought some pastries. They're fresh out of the oven!"

"What a wonder she is!" Charlie said with enthusiasm and popped one of the tiny savories into his mouth. "Mmm."

"She's spoiling us so much, we may never leave," Constance said to the detective, who was still standing in the center of the room. "Please, sit down. Let's all sit here at the table and try the pastries."

What the hell had happened? Draker wondered furiously. Charlie Meiklejohn was sitting down, poking at the plate of biscuits; she was pouring coffee as if they were having a party. Angrily he yanked a third chair back and sat in it and knew instantly it was a mistake. If he looked at Constance, he couldn't see Charlie without turning his head. They both gazed at him with good-natured innocence.

"I don't know what you think you're doing here," he said finally, choosing Charlie as his target. "You're not licensed to practice in Oregon. I checked." He turned to include Constance in time to see a smile on her face.

"Sorry," she said. "You just reminded me of a friend of ours. He won't go to a doctor, he says, until they stop practicing and know what they're doing."

"Try one of these," Charlie said, pushing the plate toward him. "You know, I think they all have different fillings. That woman is a marvel."

Draker ignored the plate and said to Constance, "Let me tell you something about Jackson County. It's a conservative county, one. You might not get that impression if you just hang around Ashland here, because it's a university town, and the theater people are from outside for the most part. But when it comes time to impanel a jury, it's county residents who are sitting in the box, and they don't trust fancy New York psychologists and fancy New York detectives, and they sure don't believe in pleas of incompetency. And number two," he said in a hard voice, "we don't have unsolved crimes hanging over us, and our cases don't drag on for years."

Now he lifted his coffee cup and drank. They both continued to watch him with interest. He looked from one to the other and added deliberately, "And they tend not to trust the word of women who are sleeping with men they haven't got around to marrying yet."

Constance nodded. "Should that be number one, Lieutenant? Would they convict her on that alone?"

"You'll claim that she was crazy, not responsible, and I say that she's putting on an act. They'll decide which of us to believe."

"I can put William Tessler in the theater long enough for him to have done it, and Eric Hendrickson, and Gray Wilmot," Charlie said lazily. "And probably Roman Cavanaugh."

"You can try," Draker said. "But it won't wash with any of them. No motive. And I don't buy coincidence working twice, not with Ellis and then with Laura Steubins."

"You're absolutely right," Charlie said. "I don't either. What crime lab do you use?"

"Oregon State. Why?"

"Just wondering. Isn't that Ernie Stedman's show?"

"Now you tell me you used to work with Stedman. Right?"

"Oh, no," Charlie said very gently. "I taught him. Honey, when did I do that series of workshops in San Francisco? Seven years ago? Eight? It was the same year you gave the keynote address to the international psychologists' meeting in Copenhagen." He looked at Draker and added, "We went by way of Tokyo. I did a couple of workshops there."

He was being laughed at, Draker realized with cold rage. This bastard was patronizing him, laughing at him. Abruptly he stood up, almost upsetting his chair. He caught it before it fell and he felt the way he had as a boy in his aunt's house. Aunt Corinne had always made him feel as if his hands were grimy, his hair uncombed, his knees dirty. She never said anything, but it was in her look of patient resignation, as if she were simply biding her time until he grew up, and meanwhile she could bear his presence only by detaching herself from him at a great distance. He could not remember a visit to her house in which he did not spill something, or drop something, break something, stumble, or in some way make a fool of himself. She had never laughed openly, or even smiled, as her two daughters had done again and again, but her eyes had a way of brightening that he had come to dread. He looked at Constance and saw the same kind of bright interest.

"Lieutenant," she said directly, "Ginnie didn't do either of those murders."

"That's what you're paid to say," he snapped, and started for the door. He looked at Charlie. "You just leave my business to me."

Charlie grinned at him. "You never did actually say what you wanted to see us about, did you?"

Draker felt his stomach muscles tighten in a way that meant heartburn later. "What I came to tell you," he said harshly, "is that when I call for a grand jury hearing, you're going to be subpoenaed and you have no privileges here. None. You'll either testify and repeat what she's told you, or I'll get you for perjury and/or contempt of court." He yanked the door open and slammed it behind him.

Charlie was regarding the plate of savory pastries and now he nodded. "I bet she keeps them made up in the freezer ready to heat in a microwave on demand. How else could she do them?"

"Oh, Charlie."

Although the Warnecke apartment had started out identical to Ro's, it was like entering another country—a tropical rain forest, perhaps. Ten-foot-tall orange trees and an avocado tree nearly that tall pressed greenery against the floor-to-ceiling windows. Hanging pots with vines dangled from stainless-steel rods suspended from a bar across the end of the living room. A four-foot-long aquarium had been turned into a cactus garden, with brilliant fluorescent lights creating the glare of a desert. Two of the cacti were in bloom with flamboyant red flowers.

Sandra Warnecke was in her middle years and comfortable with herself. She was strongly built without being too heavy, and she had a directness that was engaging.

"I've never met private detectives before," she said, surveying them both frankly. "And I must say you two don't look the part. Martinis, wine, a straight slug of something? What can I get you?"

"Martini," Charlie said; Constance nodded.

"But first the birds," Jack Warnecke said. "Come on, come on. Sandy can do the mixing. They're upstairs, except for Pretty Boy, and he's hiding in the orange tree, sizing you up."

The birds were free in the room that in Ro's apartment was a second bedroom. Here, part of the balcony and the room had been done over with plants—in buckets, tubs, redwood planters, on glass shelves at the three windows. A macaw screeched at them; two cockatiels twisted their heads eyeing them; a flock of budgies darted from one tree to another in a spray of blues and greens, chattering as they flew and even more when they landed. A bright yellow finch edged along a branch closer and closer and finally flitted to Jack's shoulder and pecked at the seam of his jacket.

"Dinwiddie," he said, and stroked the bird gently with his forefinger."

"Are they all named?" Constance asked.

"Sure. That's Wallace, and Stan and Ollie over there, and the budgies are Grumpy and Sneezy and so on. I have to confess I can't always tell them apart. Except for Pretty Boy, and he stays in the living room with us. He's the only talker among them, but he tells us everything that's going on."

Half of the balcony had been enclosed with screening; on it there were perches, a swing, feeding dishes, and water. When they started to leave the room, the budgies followed and crowded close together on perches and the swing, chattering.

"They want a treat for good behavior," Jack said, grinning. He pulled a small bag from his pocket and emptied it into a feeding dish. Sunflower seeds, raisins, crushed corn. The budgies swarmed to it and began to eat, scolding each other, elbowing each other out of the way, keeping up a constant barrage of chatter. On the other side of the screen another budgie landed on a perch and said very clearly, "Pretty boy, pretty boy. Hello, Jack."

"I thought that would bring him out of hiding," Jack said. He opened the door to the cage, letting Pretty Boy in, and left the noisy budgies to their treat. Pretty Boy flew to Jack and landed on his shoulder. It stayed there when they went downstairs again.

"They're wonderful," Constance said to Sandy, back in the living room.

"They're all his," she said, looking at Jack with affection. "We had to have an understanding about them the first week. I said I wouldn't feed a damn bunch of birds, clean up after them, or do anything except look at them. He didn't think I meant it, and for a day no one fed them. He gave in. I just look at them."

"Do they have to be fed every day?" Charlie asked. "We can

leave food for our cats for several days. They complain, but that's life."

"Twice a day," Jack said. "Water's even more crucial. They have to have fresh water at all times. That's why I made a deal with Ro. He looks after them when we're gone, and I look after him. Fair trade. I asked him to drop in, by the way."

"We spend Christmas in Honolulu," Sandy said. "Our daughter lives there. Ro takes us to the airport, complaining bitterly about the rain, of course, and almost as soon as we arrive his postcards start to arrive, too. He mails them before we even leave town, from the airport! Things like, Pretty Boy had babies, or Wallace bit the cleaning woman, or something. He's not fond of the birds, he says, but he buys them grapes and pumpkin seeds. He left a tape for Pretty Boy once and taught him four-letter words. We never know when they'll come popping out."

"He says if we ever get another mynah bird he'll teach it Hamlet's soliloquy. We had one that died a few years ago. Now that's a real talking bird!"

Pretty Boy landed on the coffee table and Sandy said, "Scat." Pretty Boy said, "Damn, damn, damn," and flew off, back to the orange tree.

"Before Ro gets here," Charlie said, "I'd like to ask you something, Jack. If you don't want to answer, that's fine. You know why we're here, of course, what our reasons are." Jack nodded. "About Ginnie. When she came back here after her mother died, how disturbed was she?"

Jack glanced at Sandy. She nodded slightly, stood up, and took Charlie's glass to refill. "I'm not a psychiatrist," Jack said slowly, "but 'disturbed' isn't the word I'd use. She was depressed. Maybe severely depressed. She was going through her own puberty crisis, and that made it worse, losing her mother so suddenly. They never had lived in one place more than a year or two, I understand, and she had few real friends, and until she came here and met Ro, she had no other family that she was aware of."

"Did you advise him to take her on a trip?"

"I don't know. His idea, mine. It seemed a good idea. She was a skinny kid with great saucer eyes and nothing to say to anyone. She hung out at the theater a lot, not saying a word, just there. Something had to be done."

"Did you advise counseling, psychiatric help of any kind?"

"No. We talked about it a couple of times, but I felt that she would come around. My God, it was a shock. Anyone would have reacted."

"Thanks," Charlie said, accepting a glass from Sandy. "Just one more thing. How sick is Shannon Tessler? Is she too ill for me to ask her a question or two?"

Constance felt a jolt of surprise and saw the same surprise on the faces of both Jack and Sandy.

Jack lifted his martini and sipped it, thinking. This time he did not consult with his wife. Looking at the olive in his glass, fishing for it with a pick, he said, almost carelessly, "You can ask her anything you want. She's about as ill as I am."

The doorbell rang and he looked relieved. "That's probably Ro. Excuse me." He went to open the door.

Ro looked worn and tired. He was dressed in a blue suede jacket, navy slacks, the best-dressed man in town, but for once his appearance was not dapper and advertisement-perfect. There was a slump to his shoulders now, and his walk was without its usual bounce.

Jack looked at him critically when Sandy handed him a martini. "You sleeping, Ro?"

Ro greeted Charlie and Constance, thanked Sandy, and sat down before he replied. "Hell no. And you wouldn't either if Ginnie was yours. I'm worried about her, Jack. Really worried."

"Well, you're not helping her any by staying awake all night. I'll give you something. I've got some samples upstairs." He left.

Ro looked at Charlie. "Do you think they'll let her go away for a while?"

"I don't know. I doubt it."

"She needs to get away, get some rest. They haven't ordered her not to take a trip."

Jack returned with a small bottle. He handed it to Ro, who slipped it into his pocket without looking at it. "Take a couple of them half an hour before bed."

"Thanks. I'll do that. Right now there's just so damned much to do. . . ."

"If I were you," Charlie said to Ro, "I'd talk it over with Ralph Wedekind before I advised Ginnie about a trip. It could be damaging."

Ro sighed. "You have a daughter, is that right?" Constance nodded. "You know how it is then. When they're small you want to arrange the world for them, and you can almost do it, make things come out all right most of the time. When they're small it's not so hard, is it?"

"It's always tempting to think that when they're grown up you won't have to worry about them anymore," Constance said. "The worries are just different ones."

Pretty Boy flew to Ro's chair and perched, saying, "Hot shit, hot shit." Sandy shooed him away and he left, saying, "Damn, damn, damn."

"And that's your fault," Sandy said with resignation.

Ro grinned. "If he could project just a little bit more, I'd make him a star."

Charlie laughed. "He'd think he had discovered freedom, loose in the theater." He finished his drink and shook his head at Sandy, who reached for his glass. "Mr. Cavanaugh, when you saw Gray Wilmot leave the high-school auditorium, did you notice the time?"

"Not really. I know I started to leave at nine, but it was raining too hard. I growled at it a minute or so, then went back to the auditorium. I was on the opposite side from him. By the time I realized he was leaving and I got back out to the front hall, he was already outside, out of sight. The rain was coming down harder than ever. Five after nine, maybe ten after. Not later than that."

"Maybe the people you had to disturb to get out noticed the time. Did you know any of them?"

"I always take an aisle seat," he said almost apologetically. "I can't stand being a captive audience if the play's really bad. Besides, I didn't sit down again after that. I stood in the back of the auditorium. I was looking for almost anyone I could get a ride with." He fingered his suede jacket and said ruefully, "I wasn't dressed for rain any more than I am right now. I have an aversion to getting wet."

"Don't blame you," Charlie said, and looked at Constance. "We'd better be on our way. Thanks for letting us see the birds, and for the drinks."

In the car Constance asked, "Why do you want to talk to Shannon?"

"Oh, I thought she might know the times that William was in and out both those nights. I noticed that Sunshine doesn't wear a watch. More than that, though. I'm curious about her, about all of them the way they were thirty years ago. Did you know Ginnie would remember what happened the day of the fire?"

"I thought she might. She was reacting to that day, not Peter Ellis's death. I think she wandered into her kitchen that day and saw her father on the floor. Seeing Peter Ellis dead stimulated that memory that had been repressed all these years. She became the three-year-old who had to close the door so no one would see her father like that. So, of course, she had to repress that action, too."

"And if she's lucky, maybe she'll never remember," Charlie said, and started to drive.

20

Rain was pouring down when Charlie and Constance finished dinner and stood in the doorway contemplating the block between them and their Buick.

"An umbrella's in the car," she said morosely. A gust of wind drove rain their way.

"You want to wait while I get the car and come around for you?"

"I think I'd get wet just standing here," she said, drawing her coat collar up. "Let's do it."

They ran to the corner and turned, then Charlie stopped, the rain streaming down his back and off his bare head. He gazed down the street; she realized he was looking at the back of the theater complex, at the shop and sidewalk in front of it. A streetlight on that corner seemed to dance in the driving rain. He took her arm and they walked the rest of the way to the lot where they had parked. They could not get much wetter.

There were few people out on foot, and those who were out were obscured by umbrellas. When they got in the car, the wind drove the rain hard against the windshield. Charlie started the engine, humming softly to himself.

"Aren't you freezing?" she asked, wishing the heater would warm up faster.

"Nope. Rain I can take. It's snow that gets to me. I wonder if Mrs. Shiveley knows about hot rum toddies."

When they got to the inn, it turned out that she knew all about such things, and finally they were back in their rooms, in robes, sipping the steaming drinks and listening to the wind in the trees, the rain pelting the windows. For a long time they sat quietly, glad to be warm and dry again, until finally Charlie opened Ginnie's sketchbook and began to study the sketch Constance had ordered from her. He thought of it that way.

She had been doing the hospital scene, with Big Nurse's desk, the files, but she had drawn over everything as if she had been unaware of it. Now there was the man on the floor, a back door partially open behind him, a cabinet with a large pot of flowers before a window, through which a ray of light spilled into the room; on the other side of the door, a sink, more cabinets that turned the corner, a refrigerator. The table was wooden with matching chairs. A tablecloth had been pulled partly off the table, by the man's fall apparently. One end of it trailed on the floor in the spilled brandy. The bottle had the distinctive shape of a brandy bottle.

He turned his attention to the objects on the table. A loaf of bread, uncut, with a knife stuck in it. Not the way anyone would start to cut bread, he thought. It had been plunged deeply into the loaf. A wedge of cheese was on a plate. A wineglass had been overturned; the spilled wine? brandy? had been drawn in carefully. And that damn candle, he thought in irritation. A stub of a candle burning on another plate, or shallow bowl, a soup bowl? It didn't look like a soup bowl, or like the other plate with the cheese, either. And the candle flame was taller than the candle itself. It was on the dish surrounded with . . . waves? He looked closer and sighed. Waves. What the hell did that mean?

Constance was almost through reading *Troilus and Cressida;* she glanced at Charlie, but he was absorbed in the sketch and she did not interrupt him. She made a note of the page she wanted to read to him and returned to the play. When she looked up again, he was regarding her absently.

"Let me read you this one little speech," she said. "It's Pandarus talking." She found the passage and read: " 'If ever you prove false one to another, since I have taken such pains to bring you together, let all pitiful goers-between be called to the world's end after my name; call them all Pandars; let all constant men be Troiluses, all false women Cressidas, and all brokers-between Pandars!' "

"That's pretty strong stuff," he said after she closed the book.

"It's a strong play. Full of lechery and betrayals and war weariness. It's the most cynical thing Shakespeare ever wrote, I bet."

Charlie drained the last drops from his mug and stood up. "Speaking of lechery," he said with an evil leer.

She laughed softly.

It was still raining the next morning when they drove out to talk to Shannon Tessler. The rain simply made everything greener than ever, but across the valley the hills and mountains had been swallowed by clouds. The small town seemed cut off from the entire world now.

"I thought you might come back," Shannon said to Constance when she opened the door for them. She nodded at Charlie when Constance made the introductions. "Leave your umbrella in the stand," she said, "and you can hang your coats on the tree where they can drip." The coat tree was shaped like a rack of a mammoth buck.

"Thank you for letting us come," Charlie said when she led them into the living room and motioned them to chairs.

"I expected another visit," she said again.

"Yes, I guess you did. Who started the rumor that Ginnie was unstable, Mrs. Tessler?"

"Not me," she said with a faint smile. "Is that what you're thinking? That I did it?"

"Did your husband?"

"No. He never would have thought of such a thing."

"Were you and your husband already living here when Ro first came?"

"Yes. William had a temporary job with the Shakespearean Festival that year. We had a small orchard that was our livelihood, but he was interested in the theater and wanted to work there when he could. Then Ro came with Lucy and Vic. The first year we stayed on the orchard and he was at the beck and call of Ro so much that we never even saw him. We had to get a tenant to run everything finally and we moved to this house. A few years later we sold the orchard."

"What were they like, Lucy, Vic, and Ro?"

"Ro was possessed, as he still is, by the theater. Lucy and Vic were like children. We were older than they were, of course. They were like children, squabbling, fighting, loving, leaving each other, running back. Like children playing at being grown-up, playing house. When they fought, she went home to Ro."

"And then Ginnie was born. Did things change then?"

"For a time. They were children with a living doll for a time."

"And Ro? How was he after Ginnie was born?"

She looked at Charlie, then averted her gaze and looked at the rain in her yard. "He adored her."

"Was Lucy a good actress?"

"She was quite good."

"Did she ever act in the Shakespearean playhouse?"

Again she looked at him with a curious expression, as if she wanted to ask him questions. "He wouldn't let her," she said flatly.

"But she tried? She wanted to play Shakespeare? How did he stop her?"

"I don't know. She never told me. But he stopped her, and after that . . . After that I think she fell in love with Vic. I think she grew up then. And Vic grew up. They were going to leave, go to Europe, but not until the baby was born. She wanted her child born here, in the States."

Charlie regarded her soberly for several moments. "Maybe she didn't tell you, but sometimes we don't have to be told, do we? Roman Cavanaugh came here and rearranged your life, your husband's life; he controlled his sister for years, and her husband. Is he still running everyone's life, Mrs. Tessler?"

"Of course," she said. "He has to. He can't help himself."

"Why don't you tell us why you wanted us to come here again," Charlie said very gently.

When she did not respond, he said, "He started that rumor about Ginnie himself, didn't he?"

"Yes." Her voice was low, hardly audible. "That's how he controls her. She believes she has this instability, this latent insanity. She isn't even aware of how he twists her, how subtly he makes her accept his truths that are lies. She won't let herself fall in love, swears she'll never have children of her own, that her work is all she can handle, all she wants. She's afraid. He has made her afraid to trust herself."

"She seems to love him very honestly," Charlie said when she stopped.

"We all loved him very honestly," she said with great bitterness.

"And he only loved Lucy, his sister," Charlie said.

She became rigid, then shifted in her chair as if it had become uncomfortable. "He loved no one but Lucy," she said harshly.

"Did anyone else know?"

"I don't think so. Not William. I didn't until we moved into this house. Ro used to pass on his way to visit them. The day she drove him out, he came in here, so pale I was afraid he was having a heart attack. And all at once, I knew. That's the day I realized how blind we all were, how stupid. That's the day it ended with them, that Lucy discovered she had a husband who loved her fiercely, a child, money, everything in the world. The day she realized that she no longer needed Ro." Abruptly she stood up. "William knows nothing of any of this. He knew there was someone I cared for, but he thought it was Vic. I let him believe that. It seemed simpler at the time. Now if you'll excuse me . . ."

Silently she led them to the door, watched them put on their coats and retrieve the umbrella. With her hand on the doorknob, she said, "You said he rearranged our lives. That's wrong. He took our lives. He took my husband, took my life. He takes what he wants. Please, don't come back."

She opened the door and let them out. The door closed quietly behind them.

"Well, Christ on a mountain," Charlie muttered, back in the Buick, not starting yet.

"That poor woman," Constance said. "Poor Lucy. Poor Shannon."

"Poor Ginnie," he added. "All this surfaces because we had to find out why Ginnie was trying to close that office door, why she forgot doing it. You were right about this mess. It's a goddamn can of worms stretching back for twenty-six years. Try to look at current events and history smacks you in the face. Try looking at the past, and yesterday, last week is all you can see. I wish to hell Ginnie had left that goddamn door alone."

He turned the key then and they drove back the winding road to the highway, where he made a left turn instead of driving back to Ashland. She did not ask why, but gazed at the green countryside being drowned in the steady rain. He was scowling at the world.

They drove north to the town of Medford, twelve miles from Ashland, and he slowed down, made a turn at a shopping center. "I want to try something," he muttered. "Let's go shopping."

He bought a baking pan, paper plates, and candles. When they were through there, he drove to a liquor store, where he bought brandy.

"I'm done," he said then. "You want anything?"

She shook her head. "Let's go home." For years Charlie had been on the arson squad in New York City, until fire had invaded his dreams, his life at home, his daydreams. He had started to inspect every building they entered, looking for the way out, the hazardous conditions that might lead to a holocaust. He had come awake cursing and shouting from deep sleep, fighting fire. Rags in a corner had become suspect; paper blown against a wall, suspect; faulty wiring, too many plugs in a single socket, suspect; a gas can in the sunlight . . . Everywhere arson was suspected, fire imminent. Finally she had forced him to admit that he had to transfer out of arson, into anything else; he had resisted at first, then agreed, and had gone into homicide.

It had helped, but it wasn't the final answer. The final answer had been his resignation after twenty-five years, his resignation, and enough time to start the healing process that had not yet been finished. She had known he had to resign when the realization hit her with shocking intensity that he no longer distinguished between criminal and victim, when everyone had become a potential murderer or arsonist in his eyes, everyone a potential victim inviting violence.

He had grown up in New York. He said that one day he had

turned east instead of west, otherwise he might have been on the other side. It was that simple. She issued the ultimatum when he shot and killed a drug dealer who had gunned down a pimp, his live-in girlfriend, her two children, and a neighbor child. When Charlie received his last citation for meritorious duty, he had said coldly to the gathered media, "They were just sacrifices, all of them. We need sacrifices, don't we? The kids are better off dead."

"We are leaving the City," she had said. "You're retiring, and so am I. We're getting the hell out before you get killed."

"You're off your rocker!"

"Not me. You're slipping faster and faster and I won't have it! Do you even remember that kid you were? That idealistic kid who thought an honest cop would set an example? Who thought a change here, a little change there, and the whole goddamn system would slowly turn around? Where the hell is he now, Charlie? You're pretending that kid is a casualty, dead, gone, forgotten! I don't believe it. But you don't dare remember him every day, or even once a year, or you'd break down in tears. Admit it, dammit!"

He had stormed out to get drunk, and she had sat with a pencil and notebook and worked with figures. He had walked from their Ninety-eighth Street apartment to the Village and back, and she had figured exactly how much money their two pensions would bring in, how much the royalties from her moderately successful books on popular psychology would continue to bring in, how much money they needed to finish their one daughter's education.

When he returned at three in the morning, she had met him stony-faced and exhausted. He was equally exhausted. Slowly he had nodded, and then she had wept.

And now, she thought miserably, he had that same hard look on his face that he used to get, that same bitter expression. She had known this was a bad case from the start, messy, dark, with a history of evil and meanness to plague the present, to distort the present. That damn fire, she thought. That goddamn fire!

He drove to the theater, although it was at the beginning of the lunch break. Inside, Eric Hendrickson said that Ro and Ginnie had gone out together; Gray was in his office with orders not to be disturbed. Only Juanita Margolis was around. Another superb reading, Eric said on his way out. Actually, to Charlie's eyes it appeared that a mob was in the theater—the morning cast for the reading had not yet dispersed; the cast for the afternoon read-through by the actors had started to assemble; stagehands were doing something to the overhead grid; an electrician was snaking wire through the backstage area. . . . Anna Kaminsky's voice floated over the subdued hubbub. Before they could move away, she appeared with an angry expression.

"They want me to take their word that next month they'll change. Five pounds thinner, ten pounds heavier! Two inches off the waist . . . Hah!" She stamped out.

"Let's take Juanita to lunch," Charlie said, and led the way to her office.

She was eating a sandwich at her desk. A coffeepot on a warming tray was on a table. A cigarette sent smoke curling upward from an overflowing ashtray.

"Sorry," she said when Charlie invited her out with them. "I have to be here for a call from New York. You know, with the three-hour difference, it's a problem. If I leave, by the time I get back, they're off for the day."

What an attractive woman she was, Charlie thought. She had knowing dark eyes, lustrous dark hair, a trim figure, complexion that suggested Chicano, but most of all she was intelligent-looking.

"May we ask you a couple of questions here?"

A look of amusement flashed over her face and she nodded. "I'll even answer between bites."

"Fine. Are you married?"

"Divorced."

"How long have you worked for Ro?"

"About twenty years. And I've been divorced about twenty years." The amusement played with her features, softening her mouth, crinkling the skin at her eyes, making her appear years younger than she looked when she was not smiling.

"That was one of the questions," Charlie admitted. "Another one is, can you prove that you were in Medford the night Ellis was killed? I mean really prove it with witnesses?"

She nodded. "The police are satisfied."

"That's a problem," Charlie said with a sigh. "As soon as they think they know who their culprit is, they stop seeing things that don't fit in. Human nature makes them do it, it's not a conspiracy. We all see what we expect to, and we're all blind to what doesn't fit our scheme of reality."

"I was with a group all evening," she said, still good-naturedly. "One of them held my hand during most of the movie."

"That's nice," Charlie said, pleased with her.

"No, not really. You see, he wants me to move to Medford and I won't do that."

"It's only twelve miles."

"I know." Her tone said that subject was closed now.

"The morning Gray Wilmot announced he had picked Sunshine's play, I understand there was a fight. Will you tell us about it?"

She shrugged slightly. "It wasn't a fight. A disagreement about the play. Gray was furious at first, but it blew over quite fast. He defended the play and Ro accepted it. That was that."

"And were you furious?"

Her eyes lost their sparkle of amusement; she picked up her sandwich and took a large bite and disposed of it before she answered. "I was furious."

"Do Ro and Ginnie fight often?"

For the first time she looked surprised. "Never, as far as I know."

"She had a fight with Gray over Sunshine, didn't she? Wasn't Ro in on that?"

"No. And Ginnie didn't yell at Sunshine until she caught her eavesdropping. She went straight to Gray because everyone thought, still thinks, that Sunshine is his problem. I can't even imagine her going to Ro with something like that."

Before Charlie could go on to something else, Constance asked, "Why not? Isn't the hierarchy such that he's the final authority?"

"Absolutely. He makes all decisions ultimately, and once he's laid down the law, that's it. But Ginnie's been trying so hard to make people accept her as an adult. That's the last thing she'd be likely to do, go running to him like a child when things weren't going right."

Charlie stood up. "Did you drive over to Medford that night?"

"Yes. Do you want the names of the people I was with? I'll happily supply them." A snap had come to her voice, although she did not raise it. She would do, Charlie thought; she would not go running to anyone with her problems, either. He shook his head. "I would like to see the original play of Sunshine's. I understand you had to retype it before you could even copy it. Do you still have the original?"

She looked at Constance, who was equally surprised and bewildered. "Sure. We keep everything here." She went to one of the files and opened it, pulled out a folder, and took the manuscript from it. "I hope your eyes are good. It nearly blinded me." She handed it to Charlie.

"Tell me something about the procedure of making a play," Charlie said. "This is the original, Sunshine's draft. Then what?"

A look of infinite, if somewhat pained, patience crossed Juanita's face. "I retyped it and made copies and handed them out. We had our meeting the first of the following week. Gray defended it and Ro accepted that. The next step was for the rewriting to start. That was between Gray and Sunshine. They worked here, at the theater, for a time, then moved to Gray's house to finish. Gray must have typed the final version. Sunshine's such a poor typist, I don't think she could have done it. Then Gray did the promptbook." At Charlie's blank look, she added, "That's for the director, with his notes, his cues, whatever he feels important. It varies from director to director. At that point the play was finished, except for changes that rehearsals might suggest. You know, things like finding out that a certain actor can't say certain lines as written. That always happens with a new play. You can't know until the actors get their parts. And that's that."

Charlie regarded her for several seconds in thought, then asked, "Miss Margolis, what if the play had still been bad? Would Ro have refused to produce it?"

"Of course."

Her phone rang and she hurried back to the desk. "Hello, Steve? It's about time you called back!" She waved to Charlie and Constance, who went to the door and let themselves out.

"What about the promptbook?" Constance asked in the hall.

"Good question," he said. "The play was done at that time. Why did Laura tell Ro Sunshine was rewriting it again?"

"Or why did Ro say she told him that?" Constance asked.

"Another good question." He took her arm and they started to walk toward the rear of the theater.

21

A gravel truck had pulled up outside the stage door; two men were leveling a pile of gravel where the lake had re-formed under the hard rain. Charlie watched them for a moment, then closed that door and started for the back double doors. Ro and Ginnie were entering, Ro closing a large black umbrella. He gave it a shake or two. "They," he said darkly, nodding toward the stage door, "were supposed to be here last Friday. Charlie, Constance, can I have a word with you?" He patted Ginnie's shoulder, and she nodded at them all and vanished among the many people who were now returning, milling about.

"Won't take more than a minute," Ro said, motioning toward his office. Constance and Charlie followed him.

He let them in and closed the door, then went to his small closet and took off his coat, put the umbrella in the stand, and came back. He glanced curiously at the folder Charlie carried, but asked nothing about it.

"I won't even ask you to sit down," he said. "This is the busiest-possible time for everyone here. Readings, cast readings, rehearsals, conferences . . . It all comes together now or it never comes together. Everything from costume fabrics to upholstery materials, everything needs attention today, this morning, yesterday morning. . . ." He rubbed his eyes, then said more briskly, "I need information. How long does the police routine take? That Draker keeps hinting that he's ready for an arrest, the paper's full of it this morning. When is he likely to do anything?"

"I don't know," Charlie said honestly. "I'd guess not until he gets his lab reports back, and that could be another week, two weeks. It depends on how busy the lab is."

Ro turned to Constance. "I'm really frightened for Ginnie," he said. He sounded near desperation, and looked haggard. "I made her go to lunch with me, but she isn't eating anything. She's a ghost of herself, lost ten pounds at least, nothing to say . . . I'm afraid for her." He took a breath and exhaled the way someone does who is trying consciously to relax. "I want to get her away from here, abroad somewhere."

"What does she say to that?" Constance asked.

"I haven't mentioned it yet. I . . . Will you talk to her? She respects you. She borrowed a book from Jack and read it, your book. That's what she was willing to talk about at lunch," he said bitterly. "Not our problems here, not work, the plays, only your book."

"Ro," Charlie said firmly, "they won't let her leave now. And it would make it look even worse for her if she ducked out."

"For a weekend then! For God's sake, they can't object to just a weekend away. At the coast, down to San Francisco, someplace where people aren't looking at her, wondering, where she won't see it every time she picks up the paper!" His voice was harsh and ragged now. "You didn't know her before. You don't know how she's changed. It terrifies me, that much change in her that fast."

"If she could go away and have it all over when she got back, that might help," Constance said in her no-nonsense voice. "But it won't do her a bit of good to go away and brood about all this, knowing that they might be waiting with a warrant for her on her return."

"You won't help her?" Ro asked in resignation.

"We didn't put her in harm's way," Constance said briskly. "The killer did. And until the killer is found and the police are satisfied, no one is likely to help her. I think she is hanging in there pretty well."

He shook his head. "You don't know how she was before, how she's changed." He moved toward the door. "I won't keep you."

At the door Charlie paused. "I forgot to ask before, but when you found Gray's promptbook for Sunshine's play, where was it?"

Ro looked at the redwood coffee table, then the round table in the middle of the room, and finally at his desk. "God, I don't know. I don't remember. Everything was . . . I can't remember."

"How about the portfolio with Ginnie's sketches?"

"Draker told me he found that on my desk. I had to identify it for him."

"Okay. Thanks. And, Ro, forget about sending her off somewhere. Believe us when we tell you it would do more harm than good."

Ro looked at his watch. "Christ, I've got to get to the cast reading. See you two later."

He opened the door and ushered them out and hurried off down the hallway. From on stage they could hear a concertina playing.

"Listen," Constance said. "It's 'Mack the Knife.' Let's have a look."

They watched from the wing as the musical director, Larry Stein, walked to a young man with the concertina and spoke in a low voice. The man nodded, and when Larry Stein had walked to the front of the stage, he started to play again, this time singing along, "When the shark has had his dinner / There is blood upon his fins. / But Macheath he has his gloves on: / They say nothing of his sins."

Larry Stein approached him again and they walked backstage together. Ginnie appeared and all three stopped as she talked, gesturing with sweeping motions.

"This place is a three-ring circus," Charlie said in wonderment.

"Five," Constance corrected. "They're getting five plays ready all at the same time." She continued to watch Ginnie for another minute. "I don't know how any of them stay sane. Are we leaving now?"

"Let's go home."

"Charlie, aren't you hungry? We haven't had any lunch yet, remember?"

He had forgotten, she knew. She had learned over the years that there were times when she had to put food in front of him, that he then ate with a good appetite, but, without help, might not have anything for days. On their way to the car, when he asked if she had brought any cards in the suitcase, she nodded, and this, too, was part of his system of thinking. He would play solitaire for hours.

That afternoon she watched in fascination as he began to assemble the items he had bought earlier. First he cleared their table and spread newspapers on it. The baking pan went down on them. It was a sheet cake pan, nine by twelve inches. In the center of it he placed a paper plate and surveyed it all. Satisfied, he opened the package of candles, took out one, and laid it down on the paper. He cut off the end of it, a piece about an inch long, and then carved some wax away from the wick. He stood this up in the middle of the paper plate. And, last, he opened the brandy and took a drink from the bottle.

"Good stuff," he said. "Shame to waste it. But here goes." He poured some carefully around the candle on the paper plate. Constance caught her breath sharply, drew back when he struck a match and lighted the candle. "And now we wait," he said. He sounded very tired. She took his hand and held it; his eyes were distant, a stranger's eyes.

They watched the flame in silence. After a moment or two Charlie raised her hand and kissed it, withdrew his hand and pulled out a chair, sat down, his gaze riveted on the steady flame.

Constance sat down opposite him. The flame was hypnotic, burning so steadily, without a waver. In her mind's eye she saw a small child awakening in her room, getting up, thirsty? wanting to go to the bathroom? wanting company? She had been ill, feverish, probably she was thirsty. She called out and no one answered. She looked in the living room, other rooms, finally the kitchen, and saw her father on the floor, sleeping on the floor. And on the table a candle flame that was dancing in the draft the open door suddenly created.

The back door was open, she remembered from the sketch. Opening the other door must have made a draft, made the flame twist and turn, and the child remembered the fire in Shannon's yard, the terror. She backed out, closed the door behind her, frightened. Constance knew this because Ginnie had done the same thing when she found Peter Ellis on the floor. The child had taken over, repeated her other actions, crying out in the only way she could for someone to see, to do something, to understand. She must have got her own drink in the bathroom, used the toilet, gone back to bed, even to sleep again. Ro found her in bed, wrapped her in a blanket, and carried her out with his own hair burning, the blanket smoldering.

Suddenly the candle flame changed, began to twist to one side, sputter a little. She looked quickly at Charlie; his expression did not alter. Nothing was happening that he did not expect, she knew, and watched the flame. It leaned over, straightened, leaned over farther and fell, and in that instant the brandy ignited in a pale blue flame that covered the whole paper plate. In another moment the plate was burning with a yellowish flame. Silently Charlie smothered it with another plate. He looked remote and rigid.

She got up and went to the bar, came back with two glasses. She poured brandy into them and handed one to him.

"Cheers," he said, and drank it down.

"Vic was murdered," she said soberly, "and no one suspected, no one knew."

"Murder," he agreed. "Why else the candle in the middle of the afternoon? But someone knew." He looked at Ginnie's sketchbook, open to the kitchen scene.

He began to clean up the mess he had made and Constance tried to bring something to consciousness, something someone had said. . . . She sipped her brandy, her eyes narrowed in thought. And suddenly she set her glass down hard and sat straight. "Charlie, she thinks Ro did it!"

He waited.

"Remember the argument Gray told us about between Ginnie and Ro, about the name of the trapdoor on stage? She insisted it was the Macbeth trap and he was insistent that it was the Hamlet trap. She became upset, denied it vehemently, according to Gray. Don't you see?" she cried when Charlie showed no sign of understanding. "In *Hamlet,* the uncle kills the father. That's what she was avoiding that night."

He sat down heavily and stared at her. "I was coming at it from a different direction," he said, "but yours works just fine."

She went on. "He told us he thought Lucy had taken Ginnie to the doctor. He went over there prepared to kill Vic because Vic and Lucy were going to leave. He forced them together, forced her to marry Vic, but never planned on her falling in love with him. He did it for Vic's money. He must have needed much more than he had been able to save, more than he could borrow, and Vic had plenty. He must have been horrified when he realized that Ginnie was in the house. . . ."

"Is Ginnie likely to remember this? Really remember it?"

"I don't know. They keep saying how different she is. Maybe all this is struggling to get through to her. Maybe she should remember."

"Maybe, but not right now. That's ancient history. It's a damn shame she's reacting to what happened when she was a baby. That's what bugs Draker; she's not reacting the way she should." He went to the window and stood looking out for several minutes, then cursed fluently and turned back to her. "I knew it! It just had to happen! It's snowing!"

The snow did not last long, and it did not stick; in fact, the sun came out for a few minutes before nightfall, but there had been enough snow to act as a goad, Constance knew. She could almost see his yearning for wide scorching beaches and hot sun, palm trees, and tall sweating drinks.

That night they ate an excellent dinner prepared by Mrs. Shiveley at the inn. Afterward Constance read Sunshine's play while Charlie laid out game after game of solitaire. He never won.

"How was it?" he asked when she put the play down with a sigh.

"Dreadful. I don't blame them all for being upset that he chose it. I wonder what the losers were like."

Charlie gathered up his cards and reached for the play.

"Why did you want it?" she asked.

"Curious. What is there about it that made Gray risk his job right off the bat? The play he read was pretty good, I thought."

"It's as if she planted an acorn and he brought up a wonderful oak tree from it. Magic. Only the kernel is there, nothing else. And the kernel is pretty trite, at that. How an ambitious person can use everyone in sight without a qualm of conscience. But read it. Have fun."

When he finished, he put it down without comment and started to shuffle the cards. Constance got out her notebook and pen. He played solitaire; she asked questions on paper, or doodled, or made lists. . . .

Did Lucy suspect him? she wrote, and studied the question as if someone else had put it there. And, she asked herself and did not write this down, what difference did it make now? Why did Ro start the rumor that Ginnie had caused the fire? To protect himself, obviously, but . . . From what? she added. Who would have suspected him, except Lucy, and Lucy knew that Ginnie had not played with matches. Did Ginnie see or hear him that day? she wrote, and now she put her pen down and left her chair, paced slowly. Charlie looked at her with sympathy and asked nothing. He saw that he had played a red eight on a red nine, and gathered the cards together.

After a few more minutes Constance sat down again. "Charlie? Let me tell you what I think happened."

He put down the cards.

"Ginnie heard Ro and Vic that day. They must have argued violently and one of them stuck the knife in the bread hard, probably Vic, since Ro had other plans. When Ro realized that Ginnie was home, saved her life even, he knew that she was a threat to him. What if she babbled about Uncle Ro fighting with Daddy? He covered himself by suggesting she played with matches. The police accepted that, they always do, don't they."

He started to protest, but he realized she was not looking at him, was not asking him a question.

"Ginnie was so traumatized that she couldn't talk, but it was too late, the rumor was there. And by doing that to her twenty-six years ago, he's responsible for the danger she's in now."

"You think he's as crazy about her as everyone keeps telling us?"

"Oh, yes. He did save her, and he did leave everything here and take her abroad when Lucy died. The way he looks at her, his eyes really do light up, his whole face lights up. That's not a cliché, it actually happens with him. I don't think he's putting on an act. That's why he's so desperate for her safety, I think. He knows he's responsible."

"Let's leave it for tonight. Is it a decent hour for two middle-aged people to go to bed?" He held out his hand for her.

Half an hour later he exclaimed, "My God, where did you learn that?"

"I read a book once," she answered.

"Thank God for literate women," he said fervently.

22

Ginnie carried a model into Ro's office and placed it on the table. It was the set for Sunshine's play: part of a living room on the right, cut-away flats of walls and a window, mountains in the background, and a café table with a red-and-white-striped umbrella over it on the left. The rock they called a practical rock rose up steeply against the mountains. She backed away from the model and sighed.

"One down, four to go," she said.

Ro walked around it and studied it intently. "It's good, honey. Better than the play deserves. You look awfully tired, though. Knock off for the weekend, will you?"

"I'd better not," she said. "With any luck I can finish *Cuckoo's Nest,* and get a good start on *Witness*. And I have clay drying out for the fireplace for the *Inspector General*. They're coming along. Maybe I'll be able to finish them all before they arrest me."

"For God's sake! No one's going to arrest you!"

She made a hopeless gesture. "Charlie says they're just waiting for the lab reports. They're trying to prove that dirt from the inside of my car came from the banks of the river. Maybe some did. I haven't cleaned it in months, and I go there sometimes. I could have tracked dirt back with me."

"Ginnie, go up to Mount Ashland for the weekend. Do a little skiing, will you? Please. You have to get some rest, honey. Damn the models. William doesn't need them."

"Gray ordered them. He needs them."

"Well, I can fix that. You don't have to finish them. Take a day or two off. That's an order."

She shrugged. "I'm better off working."

There was a knock on the door. Ro snapped, "Come on in," and Gray entered with Constance and Charlie.

"Another great reading," Charlie said. "I don't understand how you can do it. Go from one play to another like that, as if each one is the only one on your mind."

Gray had gone to the table and was kneeling before the model, not touching it. "Wonderful," he said. "It's really fine, Ginnie. Just right. Good colors . . . Can you get those colors in fabrics?"

"I'm sure we can. William and I will go scouting Monday. Or he will."

"I'm on the track of file cabinets we can rent," Ro said. "I think there are six of them I can lay my hands on."

Charlie and Constance exchanged glances and hung back listening. Ro, Ginnie, and Gray discussed the different sets, the problems they anticipated, when Ginnie would have the others done. . . .

"Can you come back around three?" Gray asked Ginnie. "Valerie and I want to block off the sets for *The Threepenny Opera*. You could help."

Valerie was the choreographer, and she, like all the others, seemed to be under Gray's direct orders.

Charlie had been watching closely, listening to how everyone responded to Gray, took his suggestions, which he supposed were really orders even if they didn't sound like it. It was impressive. Gray was impressive. He looked hungry, always dressed in jeans and plaid shirts, sweaters, boots. Too pale and haggard-looking. And very impressive.

Ginnie nodded. "I'll come back."

Ro seemed about to speak, but clamped his lips together and looked at his watch.

"Oh, Mr. Cavanaugh," Charlie said, "could you spare us just one minute? Alone," he added, grinning at Ginnie and Gray. They both looked startled, then almost indignant.

"See you later," Ginnie said, and quickly left the office. Gray hesitated only a moment longer, then also left with a vague wave to no one in particular.

"What I'd like," Charlie said, drawing a sketch from his jacket pocket, "is for you to show me about where you think Gray Wilmot was sitting that night in the high-school auditorium. This is a generic high-school auditorium," he said apologetically. "We're on our way over there in a few minutes, but meanwhile maybe this will do." The auditorium he had drawn was idealized past the point of reality. There was a rectangle with a block labeled "stage" at one end, and a few curved lines at the other. "You see, I'm not sure where the doors are, the clock, anything."

Ro examined it with a frown. "The whole end here is made up of doors," he said finally. "I was about here, at the extreme left, and I guess Gray was at the far right. No clock. There's a clock in the hall outside the office. If there's one in the auditorium, it doesn't matter, since it's all dark anyway when they have a production."

Charlie was looking at the drawing thoughtfully; at last he started to fold it again. "How did you know when Gray left? If it was dark, no clock . . ."

"I said before that I didn't know for sure," Ro said patiently. "Just after nine, maybe five minutes, ten. I'm not sure. And I was bored with the play, not paying much attention by then. I was more interested in a ride than the play, I'm afraid." He looked at his watch, pointedly this time.

"Mr. Cavanaugh, if they have you on the witness stand and ask if you can say with any certainty when Gray Wilmot left, what will you answer?" Charlie asked quietly, apparently engrossed in the meticulous folds of the sketch.

Ro hesitated, then said helplessly, "I don't know. I just know it was raining. And that started at ten before nine. It didn't seem important that night to check the time."

Constance was studying the model Ginnie had delivered. "This is lovely," she said. "So detailed. Right down to fabrics. I suppose it's a great help to William Tessler when he starts actually building the sets."

"He's good enough to get by without them," Ro said. "But it's a help in knowing how much room people have to move around in. Gray can visualize all the action much better with models, I'm sure. I always could, I know. It helps the costumers, the lighting crew, everyone."

"I had forgotten that you have been a director," Constance said.

"And a painter, lighting technician, choreographer, prompter, actor . . ." He laughed. "In the early days everyone had to do everything now and then. They still make drama students do it all, just so they know what each job entails."

"We won't keep you," Charlie said then. "Thanks for your help. Actually, I was looking for Sunshine. Has she been around this morning?"

Ro's mouth tightened. "Probably. I haven't seen her, though. She's scared to death of me, I guess. And I like it that way."

"Well, she's a strange woman," Charlie said, "but sometimes people like her notice things. I don't have an idea of what she wants with us this time. If you do see her, will you tell her we're going away for the weekend? We'll catch up with her Monday or Tuesday."

Ro shrugged. "She isn't likely to come to me for information, but I'll pass the word." He opened the door to the hall, then looked at Charlie and Constance worriedly. "You're really going to take off for the weekend? Isn't there something you could be doing, some line you could be following?"

"Sorry," Charlie said lightly. "I guess we're all waiting for the lab reports right now."

Holding the doorknob, poised to leave, Ro asked, "What if they find the same kind of dirt that's in the riverbank in the samples from her car? Then what?"

"I expect they'll arrest her," Charlie said. "As far as circumstantial evidence goes, that's pretty good. People have been arrested and found guilty on less."

Ro's face was the color of putty. He closed his eyes briefly, then nodded. "I have to go," he said in a heavy voice. "Do what you can for her. I think she needs a lawyer. Not Wedekind. God only knows who hired him and why. She needs her own lawyer. I'm making some calls this afternoon."

Charlie looked at Constance. "Let's see if Sunshine is around anywhere, and if she isn't, let's go to the high school and have a look, and then off to Mount Ashland and skiing. Okay?"

Dejectedly Ro said, "I tried to get Ginnie to go skiing this weekend. Anything. She really needs to relax away from here. But she wouldn't."

"Well, the play's the thing, the show must go on," Charlie said. "I guess she got a good dose of that philosophy from her mother and from you."

"Lucy was a pro," he said. "The best Peter Pan I've ever seen. She had those long slender legs, like Ginnie's, and a young freshness in her attitude, the way she moved. . . ." He stopped walking with them and seemed to be looking through the floor to another time, some other place. Abruptly he started to move again. "We've never done *Peter Pan* since that one time," he said. "Never."

When they parted at the door, he waved absently to them and walked away in deep thought. Constance watched him, then turned to Charlie. "And where are we going for the weekend?"

"Home," he said happily. "To the inn, I mean. First, to the high school."

They drove to the school and entered the main door to the office, where they got permission to look at the auditorium. On the way Charlie eyed the lockers with distaste. There were students in the halls, opening, closing lockers, talking, watching the two outsiders with frank curiosity. "Best days of my life," Charlie said, "were not spent in high school. That last year was pure torture. I wasn't sure I'd graduate right up to the last week. God, those lockers! Trying to get all your stuff in that tiny space! Knowing anything of value would be stolen the minute you left it."

There were a few lockers without combination locks. He pulled one open, empty, and examined it, shaking his head.

Constance was thinking: What secrets were in those lockers? Pot, cigarettes, pilfered change or even bills, illicit makeup, not allowed at home, kept in secret in a locker with a combination lock. Pornographic pictures, books, love letters, stolen test answers . . .

"And here we are," Charlie said, and pulled open a door to the auditorium. It was like high-school auditoriums all over the country, they both thought, not very good acoustics, probably, uncomfortable seats that were not raked enough for those in the back to see the stage well. There were four sets of double doors that could be opened but were now closed. And if Ro had sat over there, and Gray over there, Ro could have seen him leave, Constance thought; and there was no clock visible from the back of the room. It was on the back wall, out of sight of the audience unless they turned around to look at it.

They did not linger long. Back in the main hall, they both were startled suddenly by a loud bell and the instant swarm of students that seemed to materialize magically. Charlie took Constance's arm and pushed her toward the nearest exit, two double doors at the front of the building. The auditorium was at the end of the corridor and there were two more doors that led to the parking lot at the side of the building, but that way was blocked almost totally by students in a solid mass.

Charlie was whistling softly when they reached the Buick and got in. He put the key in the ignition, then looked at her. "There's not enough money in the world to pay me to go back to my good old high-school days," he said. "I think every other year or so we should make a pilgrimage to a school just to keep the memory alive."

"I liked high school," she protested. "A lot of people do."

He nodded. "And people like being sick with a cold, or having poison ivy, or freezing their buns at football games. I know. It takes some of us sane folks to keep you crazy folks from hurting yourselves. Let's go to Medford to shop."

"I can't believe what you want isn't in Ashland," she said tartly.

"But if you sneeze in Ashland, good old Dr. Jack comes bustling around before you've had a chance to throw away the Kleenex," he said cheerfully and started to drive.

In Medford he bought an old electric typewriter. The K did not print and the B lost the upper curve of the letter, and the O was out of alignment. "Perfect," he exclaimed to the incredulous shopkeeper. He did not haggle over the price. They went to a stationery store, where he bought a ribbon and a ream of sixteen-pound paper that was grayish and slick.

"All through?" he asked her.

She sighed. "What are you up to?"

"I've had my creative impulses awakened," he said earnestly. "I feel a great restlessness in me, an uneasy feeling of something that needs to be expressed. I have an irresistible urge to write."

They had dinner in the inn that night and immediately afterward returned to their room, where Charlie had already worked for over an hour at the cranky typewriter. He went to the desk, where sheets of paper were facedown, and read them. There were only two.

"When do I get to read it?" Constance asked.

"Right now, if you want. I think I'm bogging down just a little bit with the plot." He handed her the pages.

She suppressed a smile. They looked worse than Sunshine's, with X-ed out words, type-overs, misspellings. The spacing was atrocious, with hardly any margins, and the speakers' names typed in what seemed a random manner. Now and then they were even centered.

She glanced at him; he was watching her closely, feigning an aloof air. "I am a creative artist, not a typist," he said. "You know?"

She grinned and read the beginning of his play. By the time she finished the second page she could no longer stifle her giggle, and once started, it turned into helpless laughter.

"It is not a comedy," he said coldly.

"I know. It's just that . . . that . . ." Her laughter overcame her again and she put the pages down and staggered to the bedroom for tissue.

"You're hysterical," he said when she returned. "After you pull yourself together, maybe you'll show me what's so funny."

She nodded, wiping her eyes. She groped for the play and took several deep breaths, then read: " 'I will render you all asunder just like the butcher's knife rents the bread.' " She could not continue.

He took the play from her and studied it intently.

"Darling, I'm sorry," she began, but it was hopeless. "Where in the name of God does that 'you all' come from? And how can a knife rent bread? Why a butcher's knife? And—"

"I can see that you're not my natural audience," he said stiffly. "Wayne is talking to Virgil about Virgil and Florrie, the woman they both love. I believe 'you all' is quite appropriate in that context."

"Yes, dear," she said. "And 'render asunder' is fine, really fine. Poetic even. And I sort of like renting the bread with a butcher knife. It grows on you, doesn't it?"

"Why don't you just watch a sitcom while I work at my art," he said huffily.

Her mirth was gone now. Somberly she asked, "What are you up to?"

"Making cheese."

"Oh, Lord, I was afraid of that."

"A mousetrap without cheese is like a drama without characters. It won't play in Peoria."

"Have you ever written a play before?"

"Nope. Have you?"

She shook her head.

"Well, we won't worry about that. I doubt if Sunshine ever did either, and she won first place."

"How much do you think you need?"

"Eight pages—ten, if I can get them out. And a synopsis or whatever it is."

"Okay. Let's examine Sunshine's play. Yours is moving too fast. It would all be over in ten minutes at that speed. I'm afraid we've got a lousy weekend coming up."

"But we may discover unplumbed depths of creativity just itching to be set free. We may start a whole new school of playwriting, Hollywood, television, Broadway! There's no limit!"

She did not look up at him. She was making notes, Sunshine's play open on the table before her. "Charlie," she said absently, "shut up, please."

He grinned and went to the bar to mix them both a drink. It was going to be a long weekend, a hard weekend, but a lousy weekend? He did not believe that for a minute.

23

All week Ginnie had worked hard, into the late hours of the night, the early hours of the morning. She was in no mood for a party when Ro called Sunday afternoon asking her over for drinks. Reluctantly she agreed to come when he said that Constance and Charlie were back in town and they would be there. By the time she arrived, Brenda, Bobby, Jack Warnecke and Sandy, half a dozen others were already on hand. Gray was in a corner looking sullen and tired. She nodded to Eric, spoke briefly to William, and then collapsed onto a chair next to Gray.

"He always does this," she said unhappily. "Last party before the final rehearsals start, with no more fun or games until the first opening night."

Gray nodded and sipped his drink, something in a tall glass, not very strong-looking. He glanced at his watch. She knew the signs. As soon as it was polite to leave, he would be gone, back to work. Only at work was it possible not to think, not to worry, not to grieve. She looked at her own glass, mostly tonic water and ice cubes.

In the first half hour there it seemed that everyone in the room drifted over to ask how she was doing, how she felt. Jack Warnecke's glance was piercing, a thorough examination with one swift look, she felt. And Brenda wanted to hover. She watched Constance move about the room easily, speaking pleasantly to one, then another of the guests, as if she were the hostess. She envied Constance, she realized suddenly. She was so self-assured, so calm and poised, so elegant in her high heels and lovely pale blue silk dress with a jacket, discreet pearls. She looked past her to Charlie and found herself nodding. Perfect for Constance; he was strong and capable, with just enough cynicism, just enough idealism to make him intriguing. He had two faces, one for the world, one for his wife. She liked that. And she liked the way Constance looked back at him. That, she imagined, was what it meant to be in love. Would she ever have found that with Peter? Unanswerable. She looked down at her glass to hide the sudden welling of tears. This was what happened when she wasn't working, she thought angrily, and decided she had put in an obligatory appearance, that she could leave now.

Some of the cast members entered the apartment with Larry Stein; they were giddy and loud. When two of the women started to move toward Gray, Ginnie stood up. "Oh, Lord," Gray said. "Here they come. See you later."

She looked at him in surprise. Most men would love to have two lovely women descend at once. He looked grim.

She looked around for her uncle to tell him she was leaving. Constance was on the balcony with Sandy Warnecke, examining the paintings. Charlie and William were in a discussion that seemed to need a lot of arm-waving. Eric and Anna Kaminsky and Bobby were drawing pictures on an envelope, arguing. She saw Constance open the door to the spare bedroom and close it hastily, move on to the last of the paintings. Ginnie suddenly had one of those intense memories that seemed so silly to keep intact. She had come home from school one afternoon to find Uncle Ro and someone unknown hanging a painting up there on the balcony. The sunlight had been at a low angle, but was bright and golden, and for a moment she had been seized with terror. It was as if she had come awake in a strange house, with strangers all around, speaking an unknown language, doing unfathomable things. The same feeling of terror gripped her lower stomach now, caused it to spasm.

"Honey, are you all right?" Ro asked at her elbow, and she started and knocked over her glass, which she had put down on an end table.

"Sorry," she said, near tears. "I was . . . daydreaming, I guess."

Ro picked up ice cubes and wiped up a few wet spots with a napkin. "No harm done," he said easily. "Look, I want to talk to you and Gray tonight. Will you have dinner with me, both of you? Sevenish?"

She started to say no and he caught her arm. "Please, Ginnie. It's important to me. It's about next year's lineup. I want to do *Peter Pan,* and I want to send you off into the world to do some research on flying, but we need to talk."

"Uncle Ro," she said helplessly, "don't you understand I might not even be here? What if they arrest me?"

His face darkened and his grip on her arm was almost painful. "At seven," he said. "Kelly's. I made a reservation, hoping you'd agree. I'll speak to Gray about it. Can you give him a ride? I might be held up a few minutes. I have to wait for Sunshine to bring over the new play she's been working on. That damn woman," he added sourly, shaking his head. "She called and said she'd drop it off a little before seven, but God only knows if she'll be on time. Anyway, I'll get there as soon as I can."

"Ro," Sara Lytton called, "do you mind if I put on the music for *The Threepenny Opera*?" She was holding up an unopened album. She was to be Polly in the production.

"Put it on," he said. "Haven't heard that album myself yet."
He looked back at Ginnie. "Seven. I'll tell Gray you'll pick him
up at about a quarter to. Okay?"

She nodded, thinking what the hell difference did it make?
Uncle Ro wanted this dinner and would have it. She looked
around for Gray and found that he had been backed halfway
across the room by Amanda White.

"You can tell Gray to give me a call if he isn't going or
doesn't want a ride. I'm leaving now. See you in a couple of
hours." The Moritat began and she heard herself singing the
words silently: "And the shark he has his teeth and . . ." Ro
kissed her cheek and she left the party, the music alive in her
head.

"Of course I believe in all kinds of psychic powers," Constance was saying to Jack Warnecke a few moments later when
Ro joined them. "It's the organization of them that charlatans
use that I don't believe in. What if you can have prophetic
dreams, say once a year, and your scientist demands that you
have them on schedule in order to prove they exist? That leads
to real problems, and, I'm afraid, fraudulent reports."

"I thought scientists all dismissed that sort of thing," William
said, studying her curiously.

"You dismiss it if you're willing to discount the evidence of
your own eyes and ears and expunge your own memory peri-
odically."

Jack Warnecke was smiling at her indulgently; he looked as if
he might pat her on the head.

"Take Sunshine," Constance said, including Ro in the conversation now. "She's highly intuitive. She sees things, knows
things that escape most people. Where do you draw the line
between well-developed sensory abilities and psychic phenom-
ena? I think she crosses the line."

Charlie joined the small group and put his arm around her
shoulders. "Tune in tomorrow," he said cheerfully, "and we'll
tell you more. Sunshine's going to read her cards tonight for
Constance. We'll see if there's a tall dark man in the future, or
inherited wealth, or something. And I," he added, suddenly somber, "intend to grill her thoroughly. She was with Laura all afternoon the day she was killed. But Sunshine doesn't talk to
cops." He mimicked her slurred, soft speech. "I'm hoping she'll

talk to Constance, after we win her confidence by letting her read the damned cards."

Ro grimaced. "She drives me nuts," he muttered. "She's as crazy as they come."

"Not really," William started and was interrupted by Gray, who said he was leaving now.

"See you at Kelly's," Ro said, and Gray nodded and left. Ro watched until the door closed after him. He turned to Charlie. "If they don't try to pin all this on Ginnie, they'll go after him, won't they?"

"Sure. He had plenty of time to get from the high school to the theater that night, and if Laura saw something, or guessed something, why didn't she tell? Who else would she have wanted to protect? From everything I've heard, she hated the theater and everyone connected to it."

"Blackmail," William said brusquely. "She was trying to blackmail someone."

Constance shook her head emphatically. "She just wasn't the type, from everything we've heard about her. Evidently she didn't think much about money. All she worried about was losing Gray, either to the theater or to Ginnie."

"But there hasn't been anything between him and Ginnie," Ro said.

"All I'm telling you is what Sunshine told us," Constance said with a shrug. "And she said that Laura told her. Maybe she was looking into the future, anticipating what might happen."

"God, I'll be glad when that woman crawls back into her cave," Ro said bitterly. "She's done nothing but cause trouble from the day she came here."

"Well, we're off," Charlie said, taking Constance's arm. "See you at rehearsals."

Ro walked out with them to the back of the apartment complex where they had parked the rented Buick next to his Fiat.

"Get it running?" Charlie asked.

"Just needed the battery charged. They say that happens if you leave them parked."

"Use it or lose it," Charlie said, and opened the door for Constance.

"You know Gray couldn't have got down to the river the night

Laura was killed there," Ro said, frowning. "How do you suppose they'll account for that if they begin to suspect him?"

"They'll say they walked to the edge of the cliff over the park and he hit her there and followed her body down. I looked; it could work like that."

"Bullshit!"

Charlie shrugged. "They really need a suspect with motive and opportunity. They'll cling to the ones they have."

He got in the driver's side and closed the door. Ro waved to them and went back inside his apartment. When Charlie released the hand brake, the car began to roll down the slight grade to the street. He turned the wheel hard at the street and headed down the hill and did not turn on the key until they approached the cross street.

Constance reached out and put her hand on his thigh. He glanced toward her with a small grin, but he was not really seeing her. She could always tell.

"Where is this restaurant?" Gray asked as Ginnie drove out of town.

"Just past Medford. It's good. Or Uncle Ro wouldn't go there," she added.

"He never eats at home?"

She shook her head, then realized that he was not looking at her, but staring moodily out the window. "He won't cook, and hates to have anyone in the house long enough to do it for him. He wants Mrs. Jensen to get in and clean while he's out, and to do the theater cleaning before he gets there. But why he had to pick one this far beats me."

Gray laughed. "Back East we didn't think anything of going miles away, taking an hour to get to a decent restaurant. What's this one, fifteen minutes?"

"Yeah. I think he wanted to go where people won't give us those looks while we're eating. You know what I mean?"

"I know," he said in a low voice.

Neither spoke again until she had parked in the lot behind the restaurant. Ro had reserved a corner table; the dining room, lighted by candles in red holders, was agreeably dark. No one would stare, Ginnie thought; they couldn't even see them. Ro had said for them to go ahead with drinks. Gray asked for a Gibson, and she ordered white wine.

"You don't drink much, do you?" she asked idly.

"Nope, and I don't do drugs, or sky-dive, or anything else exciting."

"Me too. People think what an exciting life I must have, and really all I want to do is work."

"Laura called it an obsession," he said. "She was probably right."

At Harley's Theater, backstage was almost as dim as the restaurant. Two twenty-five-watt bulbs yielded feeble light and made deep caves of shadows here and there.

The stage door opened and Ro Cavanaugh slipped inside, closed the door softly. He went to his office, not hurrying. In the office he turned on the lights, put down a paper bag, and took off his coat, tossed it over a chair back, and went to the desk, where he sat down and put a tape player on a pile of papers. He turned it on. The music was the Moritat from *The Threepenny Opera*. It was turned high. He picked up the telephone and dialed a number that was written on a slip of paper; when there was an answer he asked to speak to Miss Braden.

Ginnie watched with curiosity when a waiter brought a phone to their table and plugged it in. "Miss Braden? A call for you."

She looked about self-consciously and lifted the receiver, said hello. She moved the earpiece away from her head a little. "I can't hear you," she said. "The music's too loud." Uncle Ro, she mouthed to Gray as she waited for her uncle to turn down the music. When he came back, his voice was clear. She listened, said okay, and hung up. The waiter removed the phone and she frowned at the spot where it had been. "What the hell was that all about?" she muttered.

"What did he want?"

"He's still at home. He said he's waiting ten more minutes for Sunshine and if she doesn't show up, he'll leave. We're supposed to go ahead and order. It'll be half an hour before he can get here."

"Let's get an appetizer or something," he said and reached for a menu.

She moved her own menu and it hit her wineglass, knocked it over. She made a strangled sound and jumped to her feet, staring at it. Again the feeling of terror wrenched her, but this time everything was swirling out of control. Sunlight, candle-light, her father on the floor, Peter . . . She clutched her chair back for support and would have fallen without it. She shook her head violently, trying to clear the merging images.

"No," she moaned. "Oh, God, no!" She snatched her purse and ran from the restaurant.

24

Ro hung up the phone and turned off the tape player and put it in his pocket. He took from his pocket the small container of sleeping pills Jack Warnecke had given him and stared at it for a minute. Then he opened the bag he had been carrying and withdrew a quart bottle of orange juice. It was half full. He opened it and dumped in all the pills and shook the bottle. He put it on the round table, went to the bar and brought out a glass and put that on the table also. He poured Scotch into a second glass but did not touch it again. He looked at his watch, glanced at the table, and left the office, went to the back door and waited. A few seconds later there was a tap; he opened the door and admitted Sunshine.

"Hello, Ro," she said in her soft voice.

"Come to the office. We have to talk." He turned his back on her and she followed him through the dimly lighted hall to the office. They entered and he closed the door.

"How much do you want?" he demanded, standing with his back to the door, watching her move about the room.

"I don't know what you mean," she said.

He went to the table and picked up the glass with Scotch. "I brought juice for you. Help yourself. Sunshine, what exactly do you want now?"

"But I already told you, Ro, you know? Just to be produced,

to have Gray be my director, maybe have Amanda in my next play." She poured juice into the glass and lifted it. "We already agreed to all that, you know?" She put the glass to her lips.

"I wouldn't, if I were you," Charlie said then, rising from behind the chair where he had been crouching. Sunshine screamed and dropped the glass. Ro looked stunned. "Come on out, Gus," Charlie said. Gus Chisolm emerged from the closet, and the door to the hall opened, admitting Constance. "The show's over, folks," Charlie said.

Sunshine was staring in horror at the orange-juice bottle. "He was going to kill me? Like the others?"

"I don't know," Charlie said. "What did you intend, Ro?"

Roman Cavanaugh had not yet moved or made a sound.

"I made a case against you almost immediately," Charlie said. "You left the auditorium the night Ellis was killed. You walked over here and let yourself in and he appeared and said he was taking Ginnie away. You hit him over the head and grabbed an umbrella and hightailed it back to the school. But Laura saw you. No one had missed you and you were covered for the rest of the time. Easy. It explained why the sketches weren't on the table where they should have been. Ellis walked over and handed them to you. Back at the school, you stashed the umbrella in a locker and some kid found it and claimed it. Easy."

Ro was shaking his head in disbelief.

"Laura's death was just as easy," Charlie continued. No one had moved. Constance stood near the door, Gus at the end of the desk, Sunshine by the round table. A tableau, well staged, Charlie thought distantly. "She was blackmailing you, not for money, but to get rid of Gray so he would go home again with her. At the restaurant you agreed to meet at your place as soon as you could leave. You got home and hit her with one of those good solid blunt objects, wrapped her in a sheet or something, and stashed her body in the bedroom until you could make your phone calls, have your meeting, and get rid of your guests. Then you used Jack Warnecke's car to dispose of her body in the river. Again, easy. Problem is I could have done the same kind of thing with almost everyone. And I kept coming up against the same reason not to. Motive. Why?"

"He was afraid Ginnie would leave with her lover, you know? He'd kill to keep Ginnie. I read his cards, you know?"

Charlie shook his head. "He knew Ginnie was obsessed with theater every bit as much as he was. All you have to do is look at William and Shannon to see what happens with a union between one who's obsessed and one who isn't. Or, from what I hear, Gray and Laura. I think he just didn't want Ginnie to suffer too much. Is that right, Ro? In fact, you're apart much of the time as it is, aren't you? One or the other gone for months at a time."

Ro nodded.

"But if he put something in the orange juice and wanted to kill me tonight, it must mean that you were right about him, how he did the other ones. I understand that he doesn't like me, you know? His aura's dark green, you know? I promised I wouldn't read Ginnie's cards or bug her or scare her or anything. There's no reason to try to poison me." She sounded plaintive and hurt, near tears. "I wouldn't have drunk enough to die anyway. I can taste pollution. I would have tasted it and stopped drinking."

Charlie nodded agreement. "What would you have done then, Ro? You made sure Ginnie and Gray were covered. You called Sunshine to meet you here; you must have had something on your mind. He would have done something, Sunshine," he said to her. "You see, he didn't have a motive for Ellis or Laura. He didn't have to kill to keep Ginnie, but he thought he had to kill to protect her."

"From me?" Sunshine asked softly. "I promised not to read for her or hurt her or anything."

"From you," Charlie said. His voice was as soft and easy as hers, as if they were discussing a new herbal brew that was only mildly interesting to him. "You were blackmailing him, Sunshine; Laura wasn't, you see." He looked at Ro again and said kindly, "It's really over, Ro. Today, tomorrow, next week. It'll all be out in the open. You can't hide history."

Finally Ro spoke. "I don't know what you're talking about."

"You do. Did you plan to hang all the killings on her? Make it appear she had gone by way of an overdose, out of remorse, maybe? A tidy way to get rid of the entire problem all at once, get on with the good life? Was that your plan?"

Ro shook his head silently.

"When I smelled blackmail, I thought she must have linked

you to the killings, but it just wouldn't work that way. Oh, you'd kill to keep what you loved, but Ginnie wasn't at risk, at least not because of Ellis." Charlie shook his head, went on. "Imagine Sunshine holed up with Shannon for a few days," he mused. "She would have ferreted out every secret Shannon had by the end of day one. I kept thinking how strange it was that Sunshine really had been afraid of you, by all reports, and then she wasn't afraid anymore. The day Laura died you bawled her out in public and she ran, terrified apparently. But after that she came and went freely, and you glowered, but she stayed. No way to account for that change except by looking for blackmail, and if not for murder, then what? It must have been something she picked up from Shannon, and Shannon's been a recluse for years, so it must have been something from the past. The only way I can see that you're vulnerable is through Ginnie. It didn't have to be hard facts; hints, innuendos, rumors, suggestions, that would have been enough. And Shannon's been hurting to tell someone about the past. All Sunshine needed to do was mention that she had read the cards for Ginnie, that she had seen a terrible catastrophic fire. That would have been plenty."

Ro made a hoarse sound deep in his throat and Charlie went on more briskly. "You made a deal. She could roam the theater if she stayed away from Ginnie, and you would read her plays, produce one now and then. But deals get undone, don't they, Ro? How far can you really trust a blackmailer? She'd tell one way or another, wring you dry, keep you on tenterhooks. You had a taste of it when Laura said she was rewriting the play again. Sunshine told her deliberately, lied about it, knowing Laura would tell you; she was needling you, waiting for you to come to her, knowing this time she would be able to silence you with a word. You had to protect Ginnie or she might go crazy again. Isn't that what you were most afraid of? That she would become insane, catatonic even, maybe not recover? Weren't you willing to pay any price Sunshine demanded to prevent that?"

Ro stared at him dumbly and finally nodded. "But that's all past history. It has nothing to do with what's happening now, with Ellis, or Laura. It doesn't have to be brought into this situation."

Charlie drew in a deep breath. "I hope not. She was black-mailing you, wasn't she?"

"Yes. Just as you said. About something that's very ancient history. Not about now."

Charlie looked at Sunshine and shook his head. "Like I said before, Sunshine, the show's over."

She looked away from him to Constance, then swiftly to Gus Chisolm, who had not made a sound; he was leaning against the desk with his arms folded. "They're trying to frame me or some-thing," she said in a frightened voice. "You heard him. Charlie made him admit something that's a lie. You're a policeman, aren't you? How can they do this?"

"Has she ever been in your office before tonight, Ro?" Charlie asked.

"Never!"

"I thought not. And tonight she's just been in this section, hasn't she? I was behind the chair the whole time, you know."

Ro nodded. He moistened his lips. "What are you getting at? She's been in the center of the room all this time."

"Just wanted to establish that. So if we find her prints in the bathroom, or the closet, or any of the objects on the shelves, they had to have been put there sometime in the past. Right?"

"I've been in here lots of times!" Sunshine cried. "In the bath-room and everywhere. What are you trying to do?"

"You weren't afraid to come in, right into the lion's den?" Charlie murmured. He regarded her. "How can you account for your fingerprints in the promptbook, Sunshine?"

"Gray showed me," she said in a near whisper.

"Uh-uh. He didn't. And even if he had shown you the original, the book he brought here was a Xerox copy. Fingerprints were on that copy."

Ro made a deep sobbing sound. Charlie turned to him with a bleak look. "You were dealing with a blackmailer who just happened to be a killer, Ro, and a killer who didn't give a damn if Ginnie got pegged for it. Didn't you even wonder why she wasn't afraid to come here tonight, to the scene of the first mur-der?"

"No," Sunshine whispered. "It's a lie. I never hurt anyone, you know? I never told them bad things from the cards, or gave them bad things to eat or drink. I don't hurt people. I didn't even know Peter Ellis. And Laura was my friend. I gave her rose-hip tea for her cold.''

"You knew that Gray was bringing the promptbook over here that night and you had to see it for yourself, didn't you? You knew that if he hadn't fixed it sufficiently, Ro would have tossed you out the door. You didn't have anything on him yet and you were desperate. Walking into the theater changed your life. Your genius suddenly had an outlet, didn't it? First-prize money, and a production, people who would finally give you the recognition you deserved. You couldn't bear to lose it after coming so close. You used William's key, didn't you? Slipped it from his pocket, slipped it back the next morning when you saw him. He didn't need it to get in. By the time he got here the place was hum-ming, doors unlocked. He never even missed it. You came over here after he dropped you off. You went to Ro's office to read the promptbook, and Ellis walked in on you. You didn't have to know him; he knew you. And you knew he'd tell he had found you here. You didn't have a motive to kill Ellis. You would have killed anyone who walked in that door that night. It just happened to be him. Everything would be taken away from you again, wouldn't it? You knew damn well that Ro wouldn't tolerate having you in the theater at night, in his of-fice. You hit Ellis and ran out the back door, and Laura saw you. A rainy night, strange town, she didn't even know what she had seen until days later when she saw Ginnie and Gray leave the theater, and suddenly she remembered the other fig-ure she had seen that night. You. Did she actually tell you? Was she that stupid?''

Sunshine was staring wide-eyed at him.

He barely paused for an answer, continued. "It doesn't make much difference now. Poor Laura. A or B. Tell Ro, go to the police with what she had seen, what? Offer to trade with Ro? Save Ginnie in exchange for Gray? The point is that she couldn't do any of those things. She wasn't a blackmailer. And she couldn't bear to go to the police yet, to throw away what she saw as a ticket out of here. You lied about her, told us she had come to a decision the last afternoon that you spent with her. She couldn't decide. A or B. Did she ask for advice? That would have been pitiful, a little ordinary mind like hers trying to manipulate a genius like you. Ro saw her as sick that night, but you knew better. You could read her without even trying, the way you can read all the others. You could see she was ready to break. During the afternoon when you were together, did she try to pump you, hint that she knew? It never even occurred to her, did it, that she might be in danger? All she could think of was getting out of here, taking Gray with her. Obsessed. She couldn't see your pain and humiliation at the public display Ro had put on at your expense, treating you like a bum, a nobody. You told her you were rewriting again, knowing it would get back to Ro, planning the scene when he screamed at you the next time, how you'd slip the knife into him ever so gently, give it a twist, a turn, how you would tame him. Her obsession blinded her to anyone else's pain, blinded her to her danger. They're all obsessed, aren't they? Like children to be read and manipulated and used. Somehow you got her to take a walk with you. Another stroke of genius. You couldn't go to your rooming house, or to her house, or to a bar, or anyplace, really. Just out in the open, in the good clean air. Onto the first footbridge where you hit her and pushed her into the river. Then you had all the time in the world to go up the river farther and pick out a spot to mess up, make it look like she had gone in there. Make it look like someone had driven her there. That was a very good stroke; it really fooled them all."

He stopped, as if waiting for her to comment. She continued to stare, almost unblinking in her fixity of gaze.

"You remember when we met? You called me the Emperor, but you were wrong, weren't you?"

Slowly she nodded. "You're the Magician," she whispered.

"That's right," Charlie said gently. "I'm the Magician who knows all and can do all. I've told you the true story, haven't I?"

"You got some of it wrong."

"Just small details. You write autobiography, don't you? Your play *The Climber* is your story, that's why it's so powerful. It speaks the truth. Gray recognized it. The others did too and were afraid and tried to reject it."

"Yes, they tried that," she agreed. "People are afraid of the truth, you know?"

"I know they are. What did I get wrong in the story?"

"Laura asked me to go walking. She still didn't know who she saw that night, you know? Just a poncho. But I knew they'd make her remember. They can do that. Focus on one detail and everything around it, and then on another, and pretty soon you have the whole picture, you know? Or she would have seen me run sometime and that would have given her another piece of the picture, or something else, you know?"

Constance felt faint from the abrupt release of tension. It had grown almost tangible in that office over the past fifteen minutes or so. Now it vanished. She could sense Gus Chisolm folding mentally, and before her eyes Ro seemed to shrink a little, to relax a pose that had grown unnatural. At the same moment, she became aware of harsh breathing behind her, on the other side of the office door that was still open a few inches. She moved away from it and pulled it open wider. Ginnie and Gray stood there. Ginnie was ashen, and Gray only slightly less pallid.

Ro took a step toward Ginnie, his hand outstretched. She flinched away from his touch.

"I'm calling Draker," Gus Chisolm said hoarsely. As he dialed, he watched Ro Cavanaugh walk from the office out of sight. No one made a motion to stop him.

"Let's all sit down," Constance said wearily. "Sunshine, are you all right?"

"Oh yes. But she—" She nodded toward Ginnie. "She'd better get a drink of water or something, you know?"

Constance glanced at Ginnie and nodded. She was wide-eyed, ghastly pale, staring as if in shock. Constance took her by the arm and moved her to a chair. Ginnie made no resistance.

"Will you tell us about it all?" Charlie asked Sunshine easily. "Starting with Peter Ellis, that night?"

Sunshine gave him a close look and protested gently. "It started with my play, you know? Gray and I produced a masterpiece, you know? I just wanted to look at it that night, read it again. That's when Peter comes into it. He said, 'What are you doing in here alone? Is Ro here?' And he handed me Ginnie's sketchbook." She paused and smiled. "But you'll have to wait and read it in my new play. They'll let me write a play, won't they?"

"I'm sure they will," Constance said, and she released Ginnie's arm. It was going to be a long night, she thought, after leaving Ginnie. She had better put on some coffee or something.

Gus spoke briefly on the phone and hung it up, scowling at Ginnie. "How long were you out there?"

"They just arrived," Charlie said lazily. "I heard them come in. Isn't that right, Gray?"

After a moment Gray nodded. His color was coming back; it seemed almost as if his face had been that of a sleeper and only now he was awakening. He went to stand by Ginnie's chair and put his hand on her shoulder. "That's right. We became alarmed when Ro didn't show up at the restaurant. I thought his battery might be dead again. We checked his apartment and then came over here. Didn't we, Ginnie?"

Ginnie looked at Constance, who was watching her with great kindness and warmth. Her gaze traveled to Charlie, who looked relaxed and even sleepy. He nodded very slightly, or, she wondered, had she imagined a nod? She could feel Gray's hand on her shoulder squeezing too hard, hurting her. She remembered dashing from the restaurant, finding Gray beside her, Gray driving over here. She felt distant, far away from this whole scene, numb. Watching Charlie, as if seeking a clue about what she should do next, she nodded, then moistened her lips and tried to speak. When nothing came out, she nodded again, and lowered her gaze to her hands in her lap. It started with the new play, she told herself. That's when the nightmare began, with Sunshine's new play.

Then people started to move again. Constance began to make coffee. Gus Chisolm muttered something about too damn much coaching. Gray drew the other straight chair close to Ginnie's and sat down. He did not touch her. Charlie relaxed in one of the easy chairs and Sunshine on the couch, where she sat gazing at the ceiling with a dreamy expression. They waited for Draker to arrive. No one spoke until Sunshine said softly, "Amanda White will play the part of the brilliant young playwright."

25

Draker was as furious as Charlie had expected him to be. His thin face was livid; a tic jumped in his cheek, and his hands clenched and sprang open spasmodically. Wired too tight, Charlie decided judiciously. He said, "I borrowed a key from William and asked Gus to come along just to keep it clean. I wanted another look at the layout of the office here. When I heard someone coming, naturally I ducked out of sight."

Draker snapped at Gus. "Where were you? Why'd you get mixed up in it?"

Gus sighed mournfully. "Just like he said. He asked me to come along just in case he stumbled over something, to make it legitimate, so you wouldn't claim he salted the mine while your back was turned. I was in Juanita's office with Constance when we heard the stage door open and close. We waited until Ro came into the office here. When he left again to let Sunshine in, I ducked in here and Constance waited outside the door."

Draker examined Constance's bright-eyed face and turned away in disgust. "And how'd you just happen to be here?" he demanded, trying to pierce Gray with his hard stare.

"Ginnie and I were supposed to meet Ro for dinner. When he didn't show up, I thought his battery had died again. We came back to pick him up."

All according to plan, Constance thought, when Draker sent his deputies to pick up Ro and finally turned to Sunshine. Charlie was the best director yet, she knew. Together they had worked on this particular play all weekend. Now he had given them all their cues and was content to let them take it from there, improvise as much as they had to, as long as they stayed within his guidelines.

"What happened here tonight?" Draker snapped at Sunshine. "Why did you come?"

Sunshine was still looking at nothing in particular with a

dreamy air. "To tell Ro about my new play," she said almost inaudibly. "I'll show you." She got up and moved toward the door. A deputy also moved to block her exit. She ignored him, turned to gaze about the room with a rapt expression. Slowly she walked to the bookshelves, trailed her fingers over some of the books, then went on to the desk. Gus moved out of her way, as he might have done for a sleepwalker.

Sunshine began to speak in her soft, gentle voice. "She knows her books will be there among the others soon. She has reached the first rung and the rest of the steps will be easy now. She sits down to read her own work one more time, and he, the angel of death, enters. He is dressed in black, a black cape, black to the floor, the Shadow of Death. Always there is the Shadow that would drag her back down, but this time she has the courage and the resolve to confront him and to defeat him." She had picked up a sheaf of papers, and put them down again to reach out for an imaginary object. She pantomimed picking it up.

"Lieutenant," Constance said then very firmly, "I think Gray should take Ginnie home."

"By God, so do I!" Gus said heavily.

Brusquely Draker made a motion to his deputy. He did not shift his gaze from Sunshine as Gray and Ginnie left together. Ginnie walked steadily, her back very rigid.

After they were gone, Sunshine acted out the rest of that night when Peter Ellis caught her in Ro's office. She needed little prompting as she went directly to the scene with Laura. "She is looking for the final release, the final freedom. The cards told her: Death in water. Danger in water. Dreams and illusions, fantasies lead to danger in water. Still she seeks her angel of destruction to walk with by the water. 'Ro will make a deal,' she says, feverish, hysterical, wanting only release, the release her angel can offer, no one else. 'I'll tell him I'll swear I saw someone else leave the theater,' she says, throwing little stones into the water. 'He'll have to fire Gray. Not right now, next month. He'll make a deal like that, won't he? Won't he?' Throwing stones into the water, the roar of the water all around, white water racing away with its secrets. 'If he won't,' she says, throwing the stones, 'I'll leave tomorrow. I won't come back. He'll understand the risk to Ginnie, won't he?' Throwing stones, not looking at her angel of destruction. Her finest scene, pale face, drawn, Camille seeking release.''

Sunshine had left the desk, was standing at the end of it, gazing down at the floor as if watching the tumbling, swirling water. She bent down and picked up an invisible rock, raised it over her head, brought it down, and then let it drop.

"And the water takes away the ultimate secret, hissing, roaring, hiding all things.''

She stood with her head bowed, as if waiting for applause. She was an incongruous figure in a long skirt, her slip showing beneath it, her hiking boots, the many layers of shirts, sweatshirts.

For a long time no one moved or spoke. Finally Draker said in a voice thick with anger and disbelief, "You killed her because she saw you leave the theater the night Ellis was killed? You killed him because he found you in here?''

She looked at him with a sad, sweet smile and shook her head. "I am the conduit for the light of truth, you know? A lens that magnifies the truth for others to understand and grasp. Gray understood my play. If she took him away, no one would have defended it, you know? He''—she nodded toward Charlie—"understands a little bit. But not like Gray does. Gray will always be my director, you know?''

Soon after that, Draker sent his deputies away with her, and then he turned on Charlie. "You won't get away with it! This is a setup from beginning to end! You stage-managed this whole charade and you know it and so do I! And you helped him!" He turned on Gus with a furious look.

"All's I know is that that woman just confessed to two murders," Gus said quietly. "Two people threatened her and she killed them both. That's enough for me."

"And you," Draker snarled at Constance, "gave her a couple of lessons in the nut department. It won't work!"

She did not look away, did not make any response, and suddenly he was again reminded of his Aunt Corinne, who also had regarded him as if he were a curious specimen. He broke the gaze.

"Lieutenant," Charlie said, not unkindly, "shut up and I'll tell you what I have. Okay?" Abruptly Draker sat down on one of the straight chairs. "I smelled blackmail from day one," Charlie said. "And Sunshine lied about a number of things. She said Laura had made up her mind about something when Laura was still undecided. She said she was rewriting her play again after it had gone into the promptbook. She said she never told people bad things, when, by God, she was a vulture, a harbinger of evil. She would have killed anyone who walked through that door the night Ellis caught her in here. But there's no proof. And Laura's death. No proof. So I got her over here with Ro just to get them talking. I lured Ro over with a play he believed she had written, and I waited to see if he would call her for a meeting. He did. I wanted to force Ro to admit she was blackmailing him. From blackmail to murder, that's not such a great step, but without that admission from Ro, there was nothing. No place to get a wedge in. And she had to believe I had proof, just to get her talking. She thinks you lifted fingerprints in the bathroom, off the promptbook, here and there around this room. And Ro thinks she wrote the play that was delivered to him this afternoon."

"And not a shred of proof," Draker muttered with bitterness.

"She isn't likely to renege," Constance said. "She's the star of her own play now."

"What does she have on Ro?"

"You'll have to ask him," Charlie said blandly, and they all became silent, thinking, considering. No one made a motion to leave. Not yet, Charlie thought. They were still waiting for Ro.

When Ro walked out of the theater, he paused only a second to look back at the building, then went home. Inside his apartment he took the play from his pocket and began to burn it one page at a time. Now he understood that Sunshine had not written it; Charlie had. Bait, he thought, watching the paper char, the edges curl, then erupt into flames. Bait for him? Or for Sunshine? He was not certain; it no longer mattered.

He waited until the ashes were cold to scatter them; he mounted the stairs and walked the length of the hall, examining each painting in turn. He lingered before the Kandinsky, even touched it lightly, then moved on, making a circuit of his apartment, touching an object here and there, shifting something now and then. Finished, he stood in the doorway and surveyed the living room and nodded. Then he went outside and got in his Fiat. The motor came to life instantly at his touch. Good little car, he thought, in spite of his neglect. He drove slowly through the town, past the Elizabethan Theater which he admired and did not covet, past the wooden bridges in the park, up to Park Drive on the ridge, down past Ginnie's funny little house, and then he headed out of town.

He drove on a dirt road. This was where they used to come for fresh eggs, back a mile or two. Ashland was to his left, perfectly raked up the mountainside, all the lighted eyes watching his performance, center stage, alone on stage. He opened his window all the way, crediting the cold air with the burning in his eyes.

He saw her again, flinching away from his touch, the way Lucy had flinched away. Just like her mother, he thought, just like Lucy. Don't let them bring it all up again, Charlie, he said under his breath. Please let it start with Sunshine and her damn play, with Peter's death. "Please!" For a moment he thought it had started to rain, but then he knew he was weeping. The way she had jerked away from his hand, just like Lucy.

Ashland was almost behind him; soon the road would curve, go under the interstate, loop back to enter it. "Exit right," he said. "Show's over, folks. I gave you your money's worth. I'm sorry," he added in a whisper, and heard Ginnie's voice from the distant past when he carried her from the burning house. "I'm sorry, I'm sorry," she had cried over and over, and then said nothing. Nothing. And now she knew what she had refused to say then, knew what it was she had forgotten all those good years. And flinched away from his hand. He saw her flying down the hill on her bike, her cheeks flushed red, her eyes sparkling, and he smiled. She should put her models on display, they were so very good. People should see them.

There was only a quarter tank of gas. Enough. Enough. He squealed the tires making the turn for the interstate, and again when he entered it, and now the wind was a hurricane carrying him away faster and faster and faster.

The word came a few minutes after the deputies left with Sunshine. Draker talked to another man in the hall outside the office door and then returned with a venomous expression. Icily he said, "Ro Cavanaugh's dead. His car left the interstate doing over a hundred an hour. Are you satisfied? Is that how you planned the grand finale to your show here tonight?"

Charlie looked very tired. "Do you have any more questions for us?"

Draker turned away and shook his head. "Tomorrow. Get out. I'll want a statement tomorrow."

Gus left with them. On the street beside the Buick Gus said, "I was on the phone when Ro walked out, but you could have stopped him." To his surprise it was Constance who replied.

"He knew, I imagine, that one of them had to leave, either he or Ginnie, and perhaps he felt it was his turn this time."

Gus nodded, unhappy with it, but accepting. "See you tomorrow," he said and left them.

Gray watched Ginnie with a growing feeling of hopelessness. She sat at the table in the kitchen in silence, staring ahead, paying no attention to him or anything he said. He had put a sandwich down before her; she had taken a bite and then forgotten about it. He could not tell from observing her how hard she was working.

She remembered the sun slanting through the window, and how, all through her life, now and then a sudden glimpse of sunlight aslant like that had filled her with inexplicable terror. She saw the image of the spilled wine, and tried to remember how many times spilled wine, water, coffee, anything that flowed over a tabletop like that had filled her with the same terror. And the guttering candle. She did not even own a candle, hated candles, in fact. She saw Peter sprawled on the floor and in another lifetime her father sprawled, and now she began to separate the two images, to put them in their own times. They kept merging, and she had to start over with minute details, like the water drops on Peter's raincoat. Gray's raincoat, she corrected. There was nothing that went with the early snapshot image, just her father on the floor, the spilled wine, the curtain blowing in the slanting sunlight. "I'm sorry," she whispered. "I'm sorry." Then she put her head down on her arms on the tabletop and she wept.

When Charlie and Constance arrived, Ginnie was wan, her eyes puffy, and that was how she should look, Constance thought with satisfaction. Completely normal.

"I'm all right," Ginnie said. "Brenda's coming over to stay a day or two. Poor Brenda." She almost smiled.

"I made us sandwiches," Gray said. "We've both eaten. Is there anything else I can do?"

"Sit down," Charlie said. "It's not over yet. Ginnie, your uncle was in a car wreck. He's dead."

"Christ!" Gray muttered. "Jesus Christ!"

Charlie continued speaking to Gray in a practical tone, well aware that Constance was watching over Ginnie, who had gone even whiter than before. "You'll want to see William tonight, and Eric, I suppose, line up a chain of command to keep things moving." Gray nodded as if dazed. "Snap out of it," Charlie said, more brusquely. "All hell's going to break out at the theater if there isn't someone on hand to keep them in line. Who's it going to be?"

"Yeah," Gray said weakly; then he drew himself up straighter, a distant look on his face. "Yeah," he said again, this time without uncertainty. "God, the rehearsals tomorrow! I'd better go." He looked at Ginnie. "Don't worry about things, okay? We'll see to everything for the time being. Just don't worry."

She forced herself to look at him, to hear what he was saying, to return from the great distance she had fled to at Charlie's words. She looked at him, and heard her own voice say, "Yes. But no changes. Everything exactly the way we have it planned. A meeting the day after . . ."

Gray was at the door. He stopped and looked back at her sharply, then shrugged. "Whatever you say." He left.

When he had gone Ginnie turned to Charlie. "It all started with Sunshine and her play, didn't it?"

"I'm almost sure they'll accept that," Charlie answered carefully.

"Before Brenda gets here," Constance said, "we want to tell you who hired us to help you. Let's all sit down a minute or two."

Ginnie looked from Constance to Charlie in disbelief when Constance finished telling about the visit from Dr. Braden and his wife.

"They were right," she said slowly. "I don't want anything from them. My mother didn't and neither do I."

"Your decision," Charlie said. "They'll show up one day and you can run them off or not, as you choose."

"It's another piece of my past," she said. "You've given me back a past I never had. We should know our own pasts, shouldn't we?"

"As much as we can bear," Constance said. "Not all, not always. Ginnie, you had nothing to do with the fire that killed your father. Nothing."

"I know," she said in a whisper. "Now I know. I didn't. For so many years I had bad dreams about fires, about running and screaming trying to escape. I woke up sweating and crying. But I couldn't have helped my father. He was dead already. There wasn't anything I could have done. You let me remember all that. I don't know how, but you did it for me. I owe you a lot." She breathed deeply. "It's better to remember. It really is."

"It isn't all the way over," Constance said gently. "They'll have more questions, of course. Whatever comes up, remember that Ro loved you very, very much, more than he could say."

Ginnie looked at her hands clenched together on the table. After a moment she nodded. "Yes. I know he did. But no one's going to dig up any more of the past now. Sunshine did it, and it started with her play. The nightmare started with her play, we all know that."

Constance nodded. "I don't think Sunshine will want to share billing with you, Ro, anyone else. It's her new production, written, directed, starred in, produced by Sunshine. I think that's how she'll play it, but just in case, be warned."

Constance and Charlie did not linger after Brenda arrived. Charlie drove down the steep hill carefully. He was getting a headache; it was after eleven, and they had not eaten dinner, he realized.

"She doesn't know it all," Constance said sadly. "I hope she never does."

He looked at her hand. "What else is there? She knows damn well that Ro killed Vic and blamed the fire on her to save his skin."

"She doesn't know that Ro was her father."

"Good God!"

"Didn't you guess? Shannon suspects, but I don't think she really is sure. She won't tell. And it explains why Lucy punished him so severely, not even telling him indirectly for three years that Ginnie had recovered. And it explains his terrible feeling of guilt over Ginnie, knowing he was responsible for the trauma of the fire, seeing her relapse when Lucy died, watching it over-whelm her again recently. He knew he was responsible for so much of it, and he loved her more than he could say. He probably believed the theory about children born of incestuous re-lationships. He watched for signs of instability, saw them over and over. Poor Ro. Poor Ginnie."

"You're guessing, aren't you?"

"Of course. The way we both guessed that he took that miss-ing sketchbook. It must have given him a terrible start when he saw that figure on the floor, but she obviously didn't remember, so he returned it, tried to dismiss it, and watched her more closely than ever. I'm guessing, but if I were doing therapy with her, I'd act on all this as if I knew it for a fact."

He grunted, remembering being at the inn, Constance's pro-tests about the trap he was preparing. "We both know Sunshine did it," he had maintained. "I know it for a fact and I don't have a scrap of evidence. Probably there isn't any to be had. If she doesn't confess, they'll nail Ginnie for sure. If she's convinced that I do know it for a fact, I think she'll talk, go all the way. I've seen that happen more times than I want to think about. But I need strong bait for Ro to snap at." He had returned to the end of the synopsis of the play he was writing in Sunshine's name.

What he had written was: "When you start unraveling the past, it doesn't stop until it's all out, back to day one. You can't stop it, all you can do is keep it from starting. If you don't follow my orders, do exactly what I want, I'll tell her who her father really is, tell her why she's so crazy."

He shook his head; the headache was gaining ground. He had not consciously thought about Ro and Ginnie, that he was her father. It had been enough to know that Ro had taken his little sister as lover, enough to know that Ro had killed Vic. He had simply wanted to make the stupid play a compelling reason to make Ro jump. And he had. He had.

Now all he wanted was dinner, a quiet evening with Constance, and two airline tickets for Hawaii. Hot beaches, brilliant sunlight, mai tais in the shade of a palm tree. Constance put her hand on his leg, the way she did when he drove, and he covered it with his hand, the way he did. The fact that she was now feeding ideas directly into his brain did not bother him at all.

Smart House

1

Three things happened that week in April to make Beth Elringer decide to attend her husband Gary's birthday party. The first was losing her job, which came about because of a broken press at the company where she worked as editor. Beth and Margaret Long, her employer, sat opposite each other in a booth at Taco Time. Beth pushed a tamale around on her plate while Margaret talked.

"I just can't take it any longer," Margaret said. She looked exhausted. "We were up all night, and then the damn press went blooey and we have as much chance of meeting our deadline as we have of finding pearls in oysters."

"Why didn't you call me?"

"You know how to fix the damn press? A pulley broke. Three weeks, Mike said, to get a new one installed, if we had the money to do it in the first place."

"What will you do?"

"I wish to God I knew. But, honey, you'd better be thinking of another job. I just don't know if this is the last straw. I have a feeling it could be."

Beth liked her job as editor; she had a book of poetry in the works that she especially liked, by an author who might never get it published if the Long Press went out of business.

The second event came two days later when her brother Larry asked for a loan. She gasped when he told her how much he needed. He had been out on strike; he and his wife had gone into debt and they would lose the house and everything else if he couldn't pay off some bills.

The third thing was finding her cat dead a few nights later. She wept over that. She knew she could get another job, and she had taken out a bank loan to help her brother, but there wasn't a damn thing she could do for the cat. If she had not been so preoccupied with jobs and loans, she would have noticed that it was sick, poisoned maybe; she would have taken it to a vet instead of finding it stiff and cold on her kitchen floor.

That night she examined the agreement she had signed with the Bellringer Company when Gary had given her a share of stock. There were only nine shareholders, and the company was said to be worth millions of dollars. Even one share was worth a fortune, she knew. And she owned one share. The agreement stated that if ever she wanted to dispose of her single share, she must first offer it to Gary without telling anyone else it was for sale. She read the paper twice, then nodded. Gary's party, she decided. That was the time to tell him. He would be in a good mood, happy with a weekend party going on around him, pleased that she was attending. He had predicted that she would be back, had infuriated her with his self-assurance about her penitent return. She read through the agreement one more time. If she and Gary could not agree on a price for her share, she could then present it at the next shareholders' meeting and accept the highest offer that met or exceeded Gary's offer. That would be the day after his weekend party. If still no satisfactory price could be agreed to, an independent accountant would assess the market value of the share, and she would be paid that amount by the company, the payment to be assessed among the shareholders according to percentages of ownership; they would then divide the share. But she knew it would never come to that. Gary would snatch it up. And if he didn't, then his brother Bruce would.

Two weeks later she boarded the small commuter plane in San Francisco on her way to Smart House. The invitation had said simply somewhere on the Oregon coast, and the airplane ticket had been for the town of North Bend. "Don't worry about it," Gary had said on the phone, "we'll meet you." Now Beth stared bitterly out her window at the great expanse of ocean, all gray and frothy near the shore, with deep shadows and gleaming highlights beyond that, and then flat gray to the horizon. She could make out fishing boats, small boats closer in, a large oceangoing cargo ship, all dipping and swaying and passing from sight above and below her tiny window on the world. She could feel her stomach rise and fall in time with them. She clutched the arm of her seat and closed her eyes, but that was even worse. When the plane went down, she wanted to know it. She could not understand why it mattered, but she did not want to plummet into the sea with her eyes closed. The plane was buffeted from side to side, and it rose and fell with an unpredictable motion that did not allow for compensation. Just when she braced for a downward plunge, the plane rose alarmingly, then dropped again.

Damn Gary, she thought over and over. Damn him. Gary had scrawled on the invitation, "You'll love the plane ride. I can't wait to show you Smart House!"

Thirty, she thought morosely. Who would have gambled on Gary's surviving this long? The plane lurched and dropped at the same time. She hung on to the seat and muttered, "Damn him! Goddamn him!" Staying married to Gary Elringer for ten years, she thought, gave her privileges; who had a better right to damn him to hell?

On the ground, waiting for the plane from San Francisco, was Madelaine Elringer, Gary's mother. Maddie was sixty-two, and after fighting plumpness for most of her life, had finally given up the battle, only to find that when she stabilized again she had a new figure, not altogether unpleasing, she thought secretly. She was busty, with a waistline still defined, and shapely legs, nice wrists and ankles. Not bad at all, she had decided, and had colored her hair strawberry blond—pink champagne, the shop called it. She used makeup with a deft hand and bought very nice clothes, all in keeping with her role in life as mother of a millionaire genius. She sat in her BMW smoking cigarette after cigarette waiting for the arrival of her daughter-in-law. A front had come in, bringing erratic winds that were frigid, not at all Maylike; the small terminal was dreary, and she was too worried to be pleasant to the few others who were awaiting the plane. The weekend was a ghastly mistake, she had known that from the start. Bringing together nine of the shareholders, even Beth, and heaven alone knew what was on *her* mind these days, and Bruce being a real shit about the whole thing. She dreaded the shareholders' meeting on Monday more than she had dreaded anything in years, or maybe ever. She lighted another cigarette from the butt of the last one and flicked that one out the window, then felt a start of guilt and looked around hastily to see if anyone had noticed.

At last the plane was down and three passengers appeared on the tarmac; she left the refuge of her car to enter the terminal. To Maddie's eye, Beth looked exactly the same as she had when she and Gary had first met. Boyish, with short dark hair that was instantly windblown, she was too lanky and long-legged to be really pretty, and made no effort to pretend anything else. She was wearing black jeans and a gray sweatshirt, for heaven's sake, Maddie realized. She had not approved of her daughter-in-law, but neither had she caused Beth and Gary trouble, so why did the girl seem to go out of her way always to look just a little wrong? Not quite proper . . .

"Beth, I'm so glad to see you! I'm so glad you changed your mind!" They both stopped advancing simultaneously, suddenly awkward with each other.

"Hello, Maddie. You look great! How are you?"

To the considerable surprise of both women, Maddie burst into tears.

Now Beth closed the gap between them and embraced Maddie; she rubbed her back gently, making soothing nonsense sounds. Maddie fought to regain control, aware of eyes watching her in amazement. People often cried at meeting after a long absence, or at parting with a loved one, she told herself. Let them stare. She took a shuddering breath.

Beth had only her carry-on bag and an oversized canvas purse. They left the small terminal. Beth whistled at the sight of the new automobile and Maddie said almost apologetically that Gary had bought it for her for his birthday. She groped for her keys and sighed when Beth pointed to them in the ignition. "He thinks all children should give their parents presents when it's their birthday, the children's birthday, I mean. To say thank you, I suppose. Bruce was furious about it." She blinked back tears. "Oh dear, I didn't realize I was this upset with it all. Maybe we'd better have a little drink before we go back."

Beth said grimly, "Bruce always was a pain in the ass, even if he is your son. What's going on, Maddie? Why a three-day get-together? What's Gary up to?"

Maddie started to drive jerkily, then jerked even harder when she hit the brake. "A bar, a tavern or something," she said. "We have to talk about it all. Then you can drive. The car hates me."

Maddie drove them to a tavern that also served seafood. The odor of frying fish, rancid oil, and onions was stifling. Beth ordered coffee and listened to Maddie ramble as she gulped bourbon on the rocks. Everyone else was already there, she said. Bruce, her other son, six years older than Gary, the boy genius. Rich, Harry, Laura . . . She did not know what Gary was planning; no one did, but Bruce was trying to organize a palace coup, she said ominously. He would approach Beth, she warned. And he might even have the votes.

Beth listened and tried to rearrange the nearly incoherent information. There were too many bits and pieces, with too much left out. The Bellringer Company, Incorporated, had nine shareholders, but it was Gary's company undisputedly, and he ran it as he saw fit. During the last few years he had been totally preoccupied with creating Smart House, a computerized, automated house that until this weekend no one had seen except those who had worked there.

"I hate it!" Maddie cried. "It knows where you are every minute! It spies on everyone all the time, listens to everything you say, turns the lights on and off, and heats the bathwater and the temperature in the greenhouse. It does everything, and I hate it!"

Beth nodded in sympathy. Bruce had called her months ago, had wanted to meet for lunch, and she had turned him down. She wished now that she had gone. A coup? It did not seem bloody likely, she decided, and tuned Maddie in long enough to know she was still going on about the house. The house must be the rabbit hole where all the money was vanishing, she realized. After Smart House had got under way, the company had stopped showing profits. All the others, except Maddie and now Beth, were also employed by the company, and she had assumed their salaries had been adjusted upward when profits dried up. Now she doubted that such was the case, and it explained Bruce's fury. Enough votes to override Gary? Beth's one share gave her a single vote in whatever came up at the meeting on Monday, hardly worth anyone's while to capture.

She was jolted from her own thoughts suddenly when Maddie put her hand on Beth's and said, "Please promise you won't tell him you want a divorce until after the weekend."

"Who told you I want a divorce?"

Maddie looked about vaguely, as if searching for the informant. "You do, don't you?"

"Has he been spying on me? Have you? Bruce?"

Maddie drained her glass and set it down hard. "Darling, it's not a secret that you aren't living together in any way, And it's not a secret that Gary's a little eccentric. I just want you to wait until after his party, that's all. Don't spoil his birthday party, please."

"Eccentric! Maddie, he's crazy! Your darling boy is a nut!"

Beth drove along a curving road lined with small buildings, shacks, frame houses weathered gray, auto shops, bait stores. . . . Neither spoke now except for the directions Maddie provided from time to time. The ocean was not visible, but its presence was there; the gusty wind off the sea was fresh and cold, bringing news of the East, news of the deeps, of passing ships and whales, shrimps and crabs. The sun made a brightened area in a thick cloud cover, then the woods closed in on the road, and even that timid bright patch was blocked. She turned off this road at Maddie's instructions, onto a much narrower black-top road with no markings, a private drive without shoulders, just woods that came to the edge of the black surface, that met overhead and turned the early evening into night. Still no sea. The road climbed steeply, became more crooked.

She slowed down more when she saw a sign, Stop Ahead. Around a curve there was a mammoth gate that looked like bronze. She came to a stop. No one was in sight; a high chain-link fence vanished among the trees on each side of the gate. A lighted sign asked her to open her window, and as soon as she did, a crisp male voice said, "Please identify yourself and your passenger."

She looked sharply at Maddie, whose face had become pinched.

"Beth Elringer, Madelaine Elringer," she said, raising her voice slightly.

"Thank you." The gate swung open silently; the lighted sign went off.

"See what I mean?" Maddie whispered.

"I see that Gary's being cute," Beth snapped. "Is this what's bugging Bruce? That Gary's sinking company profits into toys?"

"He's spent millions and millions," Maddie said. "I don't think anyone even knows exactly how much. That's what's bothering Bruce, I suppose, that there's no real accounting. A talking gate! Talking doors! An indoor waterfall!" Her voice rose to a near wail.

Someone knew where the money was going, Beth thought, ignoring her mother-in-law again. Milton Sweetwater was the company attorney; he must know. Or Jake Kluge, a whiz kid in business affairs. Or, for heaven's sake, Harry Westerman, the accountant. Someone, maybe all of them, knew. If Bruce didn't, it had to be because Gary did not want to tell him. The road started down, still narrow and as winding as before, but now the greenery looked planned, not the wild growth of the other side of the fence. Landscaping on a macrocosmic scale, she mused, that was her boy, her husband, Gary. Masses of rhododendron in bloom formed immense blotches of scarlet, rose, gold, fringed with lacy ferns that were so deeply green they looked black in the darkening shadows. She made another turn, and finally there was the ocean, a couple of hundred feet down, on three sides of this point that jutted out from the mainland like the prow of a ship. She had to drive another quarter mile before she got a glimpse of Smart House. She gasped and stopped the car in order to gaze at it.

Although the building was tall, apparently it had only two stories, with a gleaming dome on top and walls of glass and redwood and metal broken by a continuous balcony at the second-story level. The building appeared to be curved all the way around the front, with a straight clifflike back wall made of stone. The dome did not cover the entire roof area; there were plants up there, a terrace? She drove on. The house was eclipsed by trees and shrubs; she drove past a tennis court, formal gardens that looked imposing, and finally a broad concrete approach to the house. Apparently every room in it had a vista of ocean. Behind the house a cliff rose almost straight up.

At first the house had appeared almost grotesque, then it had looked like a curious hotel, a resort perhaps, and now close up it loomed monstrously, like a madman's vision. A red-tiled verandah curved out of sight as she and Maddie left the car and approached the front entrance.

"Good afternoon," a pleasant female voice greeted them when they walked across the verandah. "Please identify yourselves."

Beth looked for cameras, but they were hidden too well. Maddie stopped before the high entrance door, intricately carved and polished, and said in a meek voice, "Good afternoon. I'm Madelaine Elringer, and this is Beth Elringer. We're expected."

"Yes. Please come in. If you'll leave your bags, we'll have someone collect them." The door swung open.

Maddie glanced at Beth, as if to say, see?

The foyer was thirty feet by thirty feet, with a curving staircase to the left, and a wall full of museum-quality art on the right. The floor was a continuation of the red tile. There were several black pedestals with statuary. Beth kept thinking that at any moment a uniformed guide would appear and start a spiel.

"I can't actually show you around," Maddie said in her new, subdued voice, with a nervous glance over her shoulder. "I'm supposed to show you your room, that's all. Or you'd never find it." Her voice became shriller, and she caught her breath sharply and clutched Beth's arm. "Up these stairs."

Beth held back a bitter comment. Maddie was acting as if Gary had become Attila the Hun. They went up the stairs. "Do you know what he's planning for the weekend?" she asked.

Maddie shook her head. "No one seems to know yet. He'll tell us after dinner. Drinks in the garden at six, dinner at seven."

They reached the top of the stairs and Beth gasped. Across the corridor was another glass wall, and this one looked onto a jungle. She moved closer and saw that the interior of the house contained a mammoth atrium enclosed in a circular glass wall that was as high as the house. Beyond the glass there were trees, and a swimming pool at the end. The space appeared to be a grotto, with entrances at the second level, stairs that looked like natural rock formations leading down, other entrances at the ground floor; there was a clifflike wall of various rocks behind the pool, with a path, and a waterfall that appeared, vanished, then plummeted down to the swimming pool.

"For God's sake," Beth muttered finally.

"It's . . . just grotesque," Maddie said, and tugged her arm.

She seemed in a hurry now. "Your room's all the way around on the other side."

There were closed doors on one side of the corridor, the glass wall on the other, and as they moved Beth had always-changing glimpses of the scene below. There were rattan tables and chairs, a bar, and half a dozen people standing, sitting, drinking, talking. That must be the garden, she decided. How like Gary to order no tours, to force them to explore the house without a clue. Okay, she thought grimly, she would go along with that; she would not show any more surprise than she had already shown, just accept whatever the damn house had to offer and find a chance to talk alone with her husband. They stopped before one of the closed doors.

"This is your room," Maddie said. "I can tell you this much: No one but you and the staff can open the door. Watch." She put one hand on a panel with the number two on it, and tried to turn the doorknob with the other hand. The door remained closed. "You try. Don't worry, it already knows who you are and what room you've been assigned. And where you are, and what you're doing . . ." She bit her lip and moved aside, her hands twisting together as if with a life of their own now.

Beth put her hand on the panel and turned the knob; the door opened.

"I'll leave you alone to freshen up. We'll all be in the garden. Come down when you get ready." She fled back through the hallway, apparently toward her own room. Beth watched her only a moment, called out her thanks, and entered the room.

She realized that she was moving as quietly as possible, almost holding her breath, and she knew that no one would want to talk in this house, not really. Was it listening, recording everything? She closed the door hard, but it was virtually soundless anyway, and now she saw that her suitcase had been brought up already, just as the house had said it would be.

She spent several minutes exploring her room and bath. The colors were dusty rose and a pale yellow. Twin beds, a good desk with a computer that was on with no visible way to turn it off, some magazines, books obviously from a used-book store— well read, some pages even dog-eared. She picked up a beautiful rose quartz statuette of a mermaid, carefully replaced it on the table; there were two lamps with bases of the same rose quartz, and a massive, matching ashtray. In spite of herself, she was feeling overwhelmed. Angrily she marched into the bathroom, to see an assortment of soaps and shampoos, a blow dryer, many nozzles in the tub/shower, and a panel of push buttons for water temperature, perfume, and bubble bath mixes, all expensive, selected by someone who had known what to buy. And she had to count pennies every day, she thought with fury.

Her room faced south; the outside wall was glass, with a sliding door to the balcony, ceiling-to-floor drapes. She stood gazing at the ocean for a long time. The sun had come out and was low in the western sky at the edge of the vista her room provided. She was startled by the sound of four soft, melodious, clear bell tones, the audible logo of the Bellringer Company. She turned to see the notes displayed on the computer monitor.

"It's six o'clock, Beth," the pleasant female voice said. "Would you like to bathe before dinner? If you will tell me the temperature you prefer, I'll be happy to draw your bath."

"Can I turn off the audio signal of the computer?" Beth asked in a strained voice.

"Yes, Beth. I'll signal if there is a message for you." A message appeared on the monitor: *The audio signal is now off. Please indicate if you wish any service.*

Without moving, Beth said, "Close the drapes." Soundlessly the heavy drapes drew together, shutting out the ocean view. Beth nodded. Her lips were tight as she began to unpack her suitcase, shook out a long skirt and sweater, and yanked off her jeans. No wonder Maddie looked like that. Actually, Maddie had been showing considerable restraint. Beth showered and dressed and left her room to find her way to the garden.

Laura Westerman waved when Beth drew near the small group clustered by the bar in the garden. Laura was in her thirties and very beautiful. She wore a pale green silk dress that showed her perfect figure at its perfect best. She had chestnut hair, tumbled model fashion, and wore makeup so adroitly applied that few people suspected it was even there.

At Laura's elbow was Jake Kluge, over six feet tall, gangly, with limp, straight brown hair. He was the most powerful man in the company, next to Gary, of course. She wondered if Gary had consulted him about Smart House, if he had approved. It used to be that he was the only person Gary even pretended to listen

to. This passed through her mind swiftly as she tried to understand what it was that was so different about Jake. Then it came
to her. He used to wear oversized glasses that magnified his pale
blue eyes eerily, but now he seemed to have gone to contacts
and looked younger than when she had last seen him. She knew
he was five or six years older than Gary. He came to meet her
with his hands outstretched.

"How are you?" He gripped her hands firmly and examined
her face, then kissed her on the forehead.

"I'm fine," she said, wishing he were not quite so earnest all
the time, wishing he would not show concern for her, for Gary,
for everyone he came across. She pulled loose and looked beyond him at Milton Sweetwater, the handsome lawyer who
groomed himself to look like a lawyer, or like Gregory Peck playing the role of a lawyer. She had always felt a great reserve concerning him, never certain what he thought of her, if he actually
disapproved. He was too well mannered to let anything except
civility show. But then, she thought, he would never mention it
if Gary had a limp either. Suddenly she felt as if she were Gary's
limp that Milton Sweetwater was too polite to notice. She nodded to him and went to the bar, then hesitated. Automated,
damn it, she thought in disgust.

"Let me," Milton said, joining her. "I take it that you feel as
uncomfortable as I do talking to a machine."

"You take it just right," she admitted. "Is there wine? If I drink
anything harder than that, I might pass out. It's been a long time
since breakfast." She glanced around as he opened a refrigerator
and brought out a bottle of white wine. "Where's . . . everyone
else?"

"Inspecting the marvels of the new age of electronics, I think.
In the basement."

He handed her the wine. "It's all something else, isn't it?"

She nodded. The wine was excellent. "Forty-eight degrees, I
bet," she said, holding the glass up. "Bet?"

He laughed. "It's good to see you. How long has it been?
Four, five years? You look exactly the same. Wonderful."

"You too," she said, and she felt as if something had clicked
off, or perhaps on. When she first met him, ten years ago, he
had awed her with his impeccable manners, his expensive
clothes, an obviously superior education—his elegance, she

summed it up now. She had been timid, almost tongue-tied, in his presence because she could not see past the highly civilized facade he presented; she never once had glimpsed the person behind the smile. For the first time she felt at ease with him. Not that she would be able to talk to him, even now, but it no longer mattered. Back in San Francisco he had an elegant wife and two superior teenage children going to superior schools and making superior grades. She wondered what people like that talked about. Laura sauntered to the bar.

"Are there ice cubes, Milton, darling?" Her voice was the caress that Beth remembered. Laura turned to her and smiled. "I heard what he said, and it's true, dear. You do look very nice. I always did like that skirt."

Beth gripped her glass harder and nodded, then looked past Laura at the garden and did not speak. At first glance she had assumed that they had brought in loads of dirt and dumped it to make a hill, but she saw now that all the greenery was in planters arranged in a semicircle on wide stairs that rose to the second floor, where there was a balcony. The illusion of being at the bottom of a hill was magical, and although she had been able to see into the garden, she could not see out. The illusion was that it went on and on. There were banana plants and palm trees and climbing philodendrons with leaves three feet long. There were orchids hanging from trees, growing in baskets, growing on trunks of trees. There were blooming orange trees and lemon trees scenting the air, but overriding all the other fragrances was the smell of the swimming pool, a tinge of chlorine; the air was heavy and humid, junglelike, and always there was the sound of the waterfall splashing into the pool.

Then at the far end of the atrium Gary and Bruce Elringer appeared. Tweedledum and Tweedledee, she thought distantly. The brothers were arguing, their voices loud and carrying, neither listening to the other, neither intelligible because of the other. They both had dark curly hair and blue eyes; Bruce was an inch or so taller than Gary. Both were chubby with legs a little too short for their torsos.

"What a lovely sight," Laura Westerman drawled.

"Shut up," Harry Westerman said.

Beth looked around in surprise; she had not seen Harry enter, but suddenly he was at Laura's side. More startling to Beth was the expression that crossed Laura's face; she became rigid, and even looked afraid for a moment before her customary mask reappeared. Beth looked from her to her husband. Harry Westerman was hard all over, wiry gray hair, wiry hard body, hard black eyes. He was not a large man—both Jake Kluge and Milton were taller and broader—but Harry gave the impression of great strength. He looked like a pole vaulter in the instant before a leap; he had that kind of tension about him, a furious energy that was being consciously suppressed. It was said of him that he never saw a mountain he didn't covet and eventually climb. If he saw Beth, he did not acknowledge her in any way, but kept his gaze on the approaching brothers, watching them with a remote, unreadable look.

Beth turned to watch them also; their voices were still raised in argument. She could make out some of the words, but before they made sense—going over budget, going broke, going for broke, whatever—Gary spotted her and abruptly cut off what he had been saying. He hurried to her and seized her arms, shook her.

"It's about time you came back," he said. "You know I want your input. My wife belongs at home."

2

If it had not been for Laura Westerman, Beth might have hit him, but she knew it would vastly amuse Laura. She gritted her teeth and yanked away, spilling her wine on him in the process. He wiped at it halfheartedly and turned to Laura.

"Come up with any ideas about the campaign yet?"

"Gary, darling, you put it in my lap two hours ago! Come on!"

"Okay, okay. But, listen: Alice in Wonderland, how about that? A ballet dancer exploring Wonderland, Smart House." He took

Laura's hand and pulled her toward a table, at the same time drawing a notebook from his pocket. "Greatest character in English lit exploring the greatest house ever built . . ."

Beth realized that Milton was taking her wineglass from her hand, and she breathed deeply. She was shaking. The others drifted in, chatting or talking with intense concentration, or maintaining a sullen silence, and she paid hardly any attention. She sipped wine, grateful to Milton, and decided to leave the next day. It had been stupid to come in the first place, to have expected any changes in Gary. She would get a lawyer to handle the entire matter, including a divorce, she thought with surprise. Actually she had not come around to that decision until just now, but having arrived at it, she knew it was part of her reason for being here this weekend.

At dinner she was seated with Alexander Randall on one side and Jake Kluge on the other. Alexander was twenty-seven, painfully shy, painfully thin, so adolescent in every way that it was an ordeal to have to spend any time at all with him. His fingernails were bitten off, his fingers red and sore. He was terrified of women. When the talk wound back to computers, as it did repeatedly, he became statue-still listening, then withdrew again when any other subject was raised. He ate with furious energy, barely glancing away from the food before him. Jake Kluge appeared to be preoccupied, either in deep thought or else totally absorbed in the conversation at the far end of the table, where Gary was going on about his plans for advertising Smart House. TV, of course, national magazines, tours. Jake's gaze was on Gary, but Beth didn't really believe he was listening any more than she was. She felt almost a malicious satisfaction seeing Laura squirm as Gary demolished her one reason for being in the company at all. If he took on advertising, along with every other phase of company business that he had already assumed, Laura would be as valuable an asset to the company as Maddie was. And that was zilch.

Beth paid no attention to the food, or the two middle-aged people who served it—husband and wife presumably, Mexicans maybe. She was vaguely aware that the food was good, the service excellent. She was thinking: They would finish dinner by nine; she would follow Gary and speak to him about her share of stock, if he would listen. If he would not listen, she would still follow him out, wish him a happy birthday, and tell him she was leaving first thing in the morning. He would have a tantrum, and Maddie would cry again, but she no longer cared. Coming here had been a mistake, staying would be a bigger mistake; she knew with certainty that if he manhandled her ever again, she would hit him. Clobber him, she amended.

Across the table from her Bruce suddenly threw down his spoon. "What the fuck makes you think you'll have another million or two for advertising, you asshole?" he yelled at Gary.

Maddie cried, "Bruce, behave yourself!"

Milton said coldly, "This is hardly the time or place for a scene."

Others said other things, but at the end of the table Gary laughed. His laughter always had been too loud, a braying, animal-like noise. Beth flinched at the familiar sound. "We can pour our own coffee," he said to the man servant. "Take it and cups and stuff to the living room and then you and Juanita beat it as soon as you clean up here." He stood up and walked out.

The rest of them began pushing chairs back, and in an awkward silence they trailed out after Gary.

The room they entered was as big as a hotel lobby; and like every other room so far, beautifully decorated. In here the colors were a deep rich maroon and pale blue with gold accents. There were several groupings of couches and comfortable chairs and low tables. Gary was already in an armchair before the window wall. The woman servant was arranging a tray with coffee and cups and the man was busy with another tray with pastries. They finished and left soundlessly before the shareholders were all settled. Maddie stationed herself at the coffee service and started to pour, a nervous, if very proper, hostess.

"By Monday, I'll have the votes," Bruce said. He sounded less angry now, more in control, but his eyes were cold and fierce. He accepted coffee and sat down with it.

Gary smiled. One by one they all were served by Maddie, and seated themselves on the twin couches, the various chairs that made up a semicircle before the window wall. The sun had set, the sky was now deep violet; the sea a leaden gray with white-capped waves rolling in. Crashing, Beth thought, but the house admitted no sound from outside.

"By Monday," Gary said as soon as they were all seated,

"you'll have seen Smart House in operation. It won't matter who has how many votes by then. And, in fact," he went on, regarding them all with the smile that seemed too amused, too superior, as if he were looking at idiots at play, "to show you how sure I am of your confidence on Monday, I have planned a little entertainment for this weekend." No one moved. "A game," he said, "called Assassin."

Maddie clattered a spoon on the table; it was the only sound. Gary laughed and put his cup down. "The rules are very simple. I'll state them briefly, and if you want to study them, they're on the computer in your room. The idea of the game is to kill off a designated victim in front of a single witness, record your kill with the computer, and get a new victim. Each player starts with one vote that his killer will gain. If a victim already has collected other votes, his killer gets them too."

"You're crazy," Bruce said harshly.

"It's just a game," Gary said with a shrug. "A way to force everyone to experience Smart House. As I said before, by Monday I don't think it will make any difference who does or doesn't have the votes. You'll all see Smart House my way by then, but someone could pick up a few extra votes and swing things his way on Monday. Of course, if you don't dare risk anything, you don't have to play."

But he did have to play, Beth thought, chilled through and through. They all had to play. When Gary said eat, they ate; when he said walk, they walked. Now he had said play, and they would all play.

"Gary, this is ridiculous," Maddie said nervously. "Grown-up people don't play such childish games. This is a game for children. I read about it. Teenagers play it."

He looked sullen. "Kids play a lot of things that work for grown-ups. I never had a chance to try most of their games, remember. I want to catch up. One vote each. The weapons will be in the showroom downstairs. You can only have one weapon at a time, and you have to register it with the computer or your kill won't count. The computer will keep score, and its decisions are final."

"What weapons?" Milton Sweetwater demanded.

"Squirt guns, poison darts, poison capsules, poison gas balloons, things like that. Key in *Weapons* on your computer. It'll show you what's available. They all are down in the showroom in a case with a computer lock. After you use a weapon you can't use it again, even if you don't make a killing with it the first time. You have to turn it in and get a different one. And you can't tell anyone anything, not who your victim is, or what weapon you have, or if you've been killed yet. Nothing!"

Maddie was shaking her head. She stood up. "No, Gary. I won't have anything to do with this."

"Then your vote can go to Laura. She's the only one with nothing to lose." He looked at his watch. "The game starts now and will end Sunday night at ten. You all know already that no one can enter your rooms except you. Those are safe places, the only perfectly safe places unless you invite your killer in. Remember, you need one witness—anyone, dead or alive, playing the game can witness, but no more than one. And as soon as you make a killing, you and the victim and the witness have to report in to the computer. It will instruct you further."

He stood up and looked them over. No one voiced an objection. Abruptly he laughed his insane laughter, too unexpected, too loud, then cut off so totally that it was as if it were controlled by an on/off toggle, not an emotion. He walked from the room.

"He's really crazy," Bruce said in an intense, low voice. "I mean certifiable!"

Milton Sweetwater turned to Alexander Randall. "Is this what he's been up to? Programming a damn game?"

Alexander fidgeted. "I didn't know anything about it until right now. He was afraid that no one would really give Smart House a chance. I guess it's like he said; if you play the game, you'll know what it can do."

"You already know, you little jerk," Harry Westerman snapped. He glared at Alexander, then at Rich Schoen. "And you. What do you know about all this?"

Rich Schoen was the architect. He and Alexander and Gary had lived in the house for months, had worked on it together from the beginning. Beth had met Rich only one other time, and he had been distant, abstracted then. He seemed just as distant and abstracted now. He was a heavily built man, thick through the chest, with large hands, big wrist bones, an especially large head that was nearly bald. His wife and daughter had been killed in an accident a few years before he went to work for Gary on the house. Very calmly he regarded Harry and said, "I never heard of this game before tonight. You don't like it, don't play."

Watching him, Beth thought, that was what he would do if he didn't want to play. He would say no. He had nothing more to lose. What she had regarded as abstraction and distance had been the veneer over emptiness. Gary had told her that for Rich there was nothing on earth except work, and God help anyone who got between him and his work. She watched silently as he stood up and left the room without a backward glance.

"He's going to look up weapons and get one," Laura said, and stood up. "And so am I." She left the room also.

With some embarrassment, some hesitation, the others began to get up, to mill about, and gradually to leave the spacious room.

In her pink and yellow room again, Beth paced for a long time. Was Gary really crazy? At length she had to conclude that she did not believe that. She suspected that he had told the exact truth: He had not had time to play as a child, then as a teenager, and he wanted to catch up. What did he mean *experience* Smart House? She glanced at the computer monitor and was not at all surprised to see a menu displayed. *Rules, Weapons, Victims, To register a point, Layout of Smart House, Kitchen.* She sat down and selected the first item on the menu and read through the rules of the game. Gary had stated them succinctly, without any obvious omissions or additions, as far as she could tell. Next she examined the weapons, each one displayed on the screen, with a brief text about its use. *Water gun. Range of four feet. Will not fire through glass or through any solid material such as a door or wall.* There was a section of plastic rope. She read: *Electrical line, assumed to be plugged into a power source. May be used any way that a real electrical line could be used.* There was a self-sticking dagger made out of soft plastic. Three "poison" capsules, quarter-sized discs the color of chocolate. A ribbon with Velcro on both ends—a garrote. It had to be secured to the victim's neck, the Velcro fastened, to count. An open-weave net bag to be used as if it were plastic film. She went down the entire assortment of weapons, and then selected the house layout. When the basement level was displayed, she asked if there was a printout. She typed the question.

In the top desk drawer there is a printout, the computer responded on screen.

What else was it programmed to serve up? she wondered, but did not pursue the question. She took the printout and spread it on the desk to study. Beautifully executed house plans. Rich's work? Probably. There was an elevator, and two flights of stairs, front and back, to all levels, and there was a terrace surrounding the dome on the roof; it could be reached by elevator or stairs.

After looking over the house plans, she reluctantly returned to the menu and selected *Victims*. The computer displayed: *Your first victim is Rich Schoen. Good luck*. The message vanished and she was back in the menu again. She bit her lip. One of the others had just done that, she thought, and her name had come up. One of them would be selecting a weapon, making plans. She blinked when the computer flashed a new message. *Would you like to see the weapons displayed again?*

"No," she snapped. "Do you know where Gary is?"

Yes, Beth.

"Where?"

I'm sorry. I am not allowed to give out that information.

"Fuck you," she muttered, and turned toward the door, belatedly realizing that she had been talking with the damn machine, not going through the keyboard. Okay, she thought, so Gary had a genius computer on the job, one that understood spoken language that had not been programmed in. She realized this was one of the things he wanted them to experience for themselves. What else?

She opened her door and started to leave her room, just in time to see someone on the far side of the curving corridor duck back inside a room. She had not been able to identify the person. Unexpectedly she felt a jolt in her stomach—fear, anxiety, nerves, something. "For God's sake," she muttered, "it's just a game!" But in that moment she knew that others might be playing the game seriously, with every intention of winning, of garnering points in order to sway decisions at the business meeting on Monday. For the first time since the founding of the company, her one vote was important to someone, important enough to "kill" for. For the first time she was perceived as a menace to someone else. She felt a giggle start to rise, and drew in a deep breath. Damn Gary, she thought again, as she had so many times over the years. Damn him.

She wandered for a while but did not find Gary. She tried the elevator, looked at the terrace on the roof, glanced into the kitchen, and finally she found the basement showroom with the case of weapons on display. Silly water guns shaped like dragons, a pea shooter and pellets, the "poison" discs. . . . Each weapon was in a section that obviously was under observation by the computer, otherwise how could the computer keep up with who took what? She could not locate cameras. She turned away from the display case and looked over the rest of the room. Here were all the Bellringer computers, from the first one—it now looked tacky, more like a toy than a working machine—to the most recent one, which cost over a hundred thousand dollars and looked it. Each system was set up on a flawless acrylic pedestal. Hanging on the walls were pictures of silicon chips magnified, blown up to four by six feet; they were very beautiful.

"Impressive, isn't it?"

She whirled to see Harry and Laura Westerman at the doorway. Neither was carrying a visible weapon. Then she saw Alexander behind them and released the breath she had drawn in. One witness only, she remembered. They would be safe in groups of four or more.

Laura laughed. "We decided to roam in packs. It's like finding a fourth for bridge. Have you picked your weapon?"

Beth shrugged. "Maybe. Have you?"

Alexander shuffled his feet and looked from Laura to Beth to Harry Westerman. "There's four of us now, so let's get the weapons and then I'm taking off. Things I want to get done tonight."

Beth stared at him, then at Laura and Harry. They were all going along with it! Helplessly she nodded, and she and Alexander moved to the door, where they stood facing the basement playroom. The central portion of the basement had been given over to Ping-Pong, pool tables, electronic games, hockey, pinball machines. . . . Gary really was making up for a lost childhood, she thought bitterly. No one was in sight among the many amusements. Behind her she could hear Laura tell Harry to turn his back, not to peek; then the computer voice said, "Thank you, Laura. Your weapon is registered." The process was repeated with Harry. She and Alexander moved inside the room once more when the other two were finished.

Alexander waved her ahead and turned his back when she approached the display case. She could not tell what was missing. There had been multiples of everything she had noticed before; there still were. Since she had not made a selection on the computer in her room, she was not even certain she would be allowed to take anything now. After a moment's hesitation she lifted the lid of the display case and picked up one of the balloons. The voice thanked her by name, as it had done all the others. When she closed the lid, she tried to lift it again; it did not budge. Okay, she thought. She stuffed the balloon in her skirt pocket.

"Your turn," she muttered to Alexander. He was fidgeting with impatience.

"Later," he said. "I'll pick out something later. Look, I really have work to do . . ."

Laura laughed her throaty laughter again. "Hold it a second, will you? Give us a minute to get out of here. I want the dessert we missed before. Coming, Harry?"

Two were safe, Beth thought distantly, or four, but not three. She stood with Alexander until Laura and Harry had vanished, and then Alexander was galvanized and nearly sprinted across the game room, to disappear in a corridor on the far side. Slowly Beth made her way to the stairs and the first floor again. The balloon felt like lead in her pocket.

On the first floor a cluster of people had gathered in the hall near the kitchen door. As Beth drew near, Milton nodded to her, and Maddie said she had taken the tray of cakes to the kitchen. She was carrying a glass of ice cubes. She waved vaguely when Laura invited her to join them. "Watching a movie," she said. "Good movie." She wandered into the atrium, leaving the door open after her. The smell of chlorine drifted into the corridor. With a scowl Laura pulled the sliding glass door shut again. She looked at Milton and Beth and held up four fingers. Harry looked disgusted and entered the kitchen ahead of them.

The kitchen had a fifteen-foot oak worktable, a double-doored refrigerator, a walk-in freezer, the biggest microwave Beth had ever seen, and on and on. Wearily she stopped examining it all and turned to the table for a cookie. Laura demonstrated a cleaning robot that detached itself from the wall to wipe up milk she had deliberately spilled. Milton watched her intently, nodding now and then; Harry ignored her and went to the refrigerator for ice cubes. Self-cleaning windows throughout, Laura said, munching a cookie. You want coffee? Press a button. Milk? Another button. Harry poured himself a drink from a decanter on a sideboard.

"I'm taking this up to our room," he said.

Laura jumped up. "You know I won't stay here with two others," she said. Then she laughed. No one laughed with her.

"A whole damn weekend of this," Beth muttered, watching them leave. "I wish I could find Gary. I have to talk with him."

"He could be anywhere," Milton said with a slight shrug. "Swimming, in the Jacuzzi, working, sleeping, watching the movie with Maddie, killing someone, getting killed. He thinks you're here to demand a divorce, you know. He asked me if there's any way he can prevent it."

Beth drew in a deep breath. "What did you tell him?"

"That it's not my field. But you should have an attorney represent you, Beth. Don't take him on alone." He went to the door. "See you tomorrow. Good night."

Beth finished her milk, thinking about Milton and the disquieting feeling that he was not at all concerned about her, but that he simply did not want a scene this weekend when he was part of the captive audience. Nothing had changed, she thought wearily; they were all still afraid of Gary and his tantrums. She put the glass in the dishwasher. Gary was still up, she knew. He never went to bed until two or even three in the morning. He never got up until after noon and was barely human until 2 P.M.; if she did not talk to him that night, she would not see him until late in the day tomorrow. She felt tired enough to fall asleep standing up. Five minutes, she told herself. If she didn't find him in five minutes, she would give up and go on to bed. But if she found him, they would have it out. She smiled grimly; she and Rich, she thought, the only two with nothing to lose.

She left the kitchen and headed for the television room. Before she reached it, she heard Maddie's voice raised angrily.

"I told you to count me out! I meant it! Leave me alone!"

Beth stopped at the door to look inside. The room was lighted by an oversized screen where Ginger Rogers and Fred Astaire were dancing; the sound was off.

"You saw it! I got him and you know it!" Gary yelled. Bruce shoved him out of the way and stamped to the door; Beth moved aside. He continued, with Gary at his heels. "You son of a bitch! Don't you walk away from me! I got you!"

"Gary!" his mother wailed.

"You got nothing, you asshole!" Bruce's voice rose to a screech.

Beth clamped her hands over her ears, turned, and fled to her room. By the time she got inside it with the door closed she was shaking, not with fear, but with a rage she hadn't known she was capable of.

3

Beth could not sleep until she draped a towel over the computer monitor, and even then she fantasized that she heard footsteps for a long time, first on the balcony, then in the corridor, in the room next to hers. She knew all this was due to an imagination working overtime, but she strained to hear again and again. When she woke up shortly after seven, she was headachey and sore. She emerged from the shower to hear the four notes of the Bellringer Company, and snatched the towel away from the monitor. There was a message: *Good morning, Beth. Breakfast will be served in your room in a few moments. The highlighted items have been chosen for you. If you would like to make changes, please select from the menu.*

She was looking over the menu when the drapes opened behind her; she whirled around. It was a sunny morning, with a bank of fog or low clouds out to sea. Closer, the ocean was brilliantly blue and appeared calm. "What's the forecast for today?" she asked aloud.

Do you want me to use the audio mode today, Beth?

"No." Just testing, she thought, and turned to look at the

monitor. It was showing the forecast—sunny with late-afternoon clouds, high sixty-eight, low forty-five, wind out of the northwest at ten miles an hour, gusting to twenty. She turned back to the window; when she glanced at the screen again, it was cleared. Watching, she thought. It was watching, recording every motion. She decided to eat and get out, and stay until afternoon.

It was after one when she returned to Smart House. Her face was windburned, and she was ravenous. She washed and followed the sounds of voices to the dining room, where a buffet was laid for lunch: salads, sliced meats and cheeses, a chafing dish with something steaming. . . . Rich Schoen and Alexander Randall were at the table eating, Jake Kluge was serving himself. Everyone looked up when Beth entered; there was a momentary lapse in the talk; then Rich shook his head and speared a bit of ham on his plate.

"Not a good weekend for ulcers," he said. A large roll of blueprints was on the table; he moved it closer to him as if to make room for someone else.

"Sorry," Beth muttered, joining Jake at the buffet. She was instantly aware of his size again; she tended to forget it when he was seated, or standing across a room. He was over six feet, broad through the shoulders, with a deep chest, but he didn't use his size as a weapon, she realized suddenly. That made the difference. She felt a little confusion about what it meant to think that, and couldn't sort it out at the moment, but it was important, she knew. God, what if Gary had size like that to go along with his ego? The thought alone was enough to bring a shudder.

Jake grinned at her, made room, and then looked over his shoulder at Rich and resumed speaking. "At least four modes, so far. It's pretty damn impressive. Security. Housekeeping. Maintenance. Plants? Sure, why not? Automatic watering, fertilizing, creating a dozen different microclimates. Rich, Alexander, my God! Hat's off!"

Rich was grinning widely and Alexander was twitching with embarrassment and pleasure. Jake could do that to people, Beth thought. He was lavish with praise and apparently did not have a trace of jealousy concerning the accomplishments of others. She had watched the end of a chess game between him and Gary once. Gary had won, and crowed over his victory until it had been ugly, but Jake had reconstructed the last ten moves to show her the beauty of the final trap. Naturally he would go along with the insane game and find it exciting and fun, just like Gary, but she realized, watching him, his exhilaration now was over Smart House. Again she was struck by how much younger he appeared with contacts than with the thick glasses she had become used to. That change and his excited animation made her feel almost as if he had become a stranger, no longer the avuncular guest who never quite saw her. His excitement and pleasure enveloped Alexander and Rich now, and she felt out of place, unable to share it with them.

They were all experiencing Smart House, in their own peculiar ways, just as she was, Beth realized, making a sandwich, listening but paying little attention to the words.

"So," Jake was going on, as he joined the other two men at the table, "you have to have both boards in tandem. The good old BOS and the new arsenoid celsium, and that costs a mint, but my God, it's worth every million!" His laughter was genuine, unaffected. Rich chuckled in a low rumble.

Beth finished assembling her own lunch and left them talking. At the door she glanced back, trying to tell by looking if any of them had been killed yet. Not Rich, she knew. She had his name, and upstairs in her skirt pocket she had a murder weapon, a balloon.

For a moment she stood uncertainly in the corridor, then went into the atrium to eat. It was peaceful there, and coffee was available at the bar. She took her lunch to a small table off to one side.

Now she could appreciate the glass dome on top of the building. It allowed the sunlight to enter and light up the stone wall behind the pool. The stones were varied, some gray, some black, obsidian she guessed, a pink that might have been sandstone. . . . Mosses and lichen grew on the rocks, and the waterfall trickled, vanished, reappeared to make the plunge into the pool. She finished eating and stretched out on the chaise, watching the shifting light at the far side of the atrium.

She had slept, she realized, and felt disoriented, unsure where she was. Then she heard a man's deep chuckle and a curse. Gary's curse.

"I think your computer called this a blunt instrument. You're dead. Harry? Witness?" It was Rich speaking.

"Sure thing," Harry said. "We can use the computer at the bar."

They moved into her line of sight. Gary was scowling. One by one they keyed in something on the computer; it thanked them by name.

"Now, off to collect a new victim, new weapon. Fun game, Gary. See you guys."

Rich sauntered toward the rear door. Harry followed after a moment, and Gary began to move in Beth's direction. He stopped when he saw her.

"I want to talk to you," she said, joining him near the bar.

"Next week."

"Now, Gary. Let's sit down a minute and talk. You're out of the game."

He shook his head. "The only thing that matters is that you came home again. I knew you would. They'll all be gone again by Monday evening. We'll have all the time you want then."

"I'll be gone, too, Gary. I'm not staying. We have to talk!"

"Not now!" he yelled shrilly. "Why do you do this to me? You won't be gone, damn you! Haven't you looked around Smart House? Don't you understand what I've done here, you idiot? I'm putting you to work. Everyone's going to be working from now on. No more free lunches for you or anyone else. Monday!" He wheeled and left.

She leaned against the bar weakly. Her hands were clenched, her entire body felt clenched. Suddenly something was wrapped around her throat and she clutched at it reflexively.

"Sorry, Beth. I'm afraid you're dead."

Her heart was crushing thunder in her chest; her knees were giving. If she had not been supported by the bar, she would have fallen. The thing at her throat was taken away again, and she turned to see Jake Kluge looking at her anxiously. He held up a ribbon with Velcro at both ends. "Garrote," he said. "Harry?"

"You got her," Harry said in a voice charged with irritation and even anger.

Beth had not heard them enter. She felt her neck, then nodded. "My God," she whispered, "this is an insane game!"

Jake nodded, at first glance apparently as upset and unhappy with the game as she was, but then she realized that his face was too rigidly set and that behind his show of concern, he was laughing. He was having fun with the crazy game. She looked at Harry; at least his anger and impatience were visible and honest. For the first time since she had met him, she felt more allied with him than with any of the others in the company. Jake moved around her to the other side of the bar and keyed in information to the computer. When he motioned to her, she went to the keyboard silently and confirmed that he had strangled her with the garrote. Harry confirmed the kill. The computer thanked them all in the nice low female voice. It congratulated Jake and told Beth it was sorry she had become a victim. All of them by name.

She read in her room until she was too restless to sit still. She had explored the entire house and had no wish to meet any of the others, and she felt too wind-scoured to go down to the beach again. Finally she left by way of the balcony and made her way to the greenhouse. When she entered, Jake and Gary scurried out the other end.

The greenhouse was forty by sixty feet with rows and rows of vegetables, strawberries and melons, ornamentals. There were glass-walled rooms within the structure that simply baffled her. Little greenhouses inside a big greenhouse? Why not? No one else was there now. Slowly she wandered up and down the aisles. Summer fruits, ripening tomatoes, cucumbers. A room without a season, controlled in every way. She spotted a misty area and went to investigate. Watercress in a tray of circulating water.

Dinner was a dismal affair that night. Everyone was edgy, even the dead ones, Beth realized. Gary snapped at Maddie and Bruce, and Harry told Laura to shut up when she laughed and started to say something. Gary glowered at Beth. Bruce muttered to Jake and Rich and ignored everyone else. Milton looked pained, as if there were at least a million other places he would rather be; he said nothing and ate little. Maddie was drinking steadily. Even Laura became subdued and her stunning beauty suddenly seemed painted on, and not a very good paint job at that. She would look old suddenly, Beth thought, studying her.

The lines would start, the flesh sag, and it would happen all at once. She was that type. Beth poked her food around on the plate with no interest and was relieved when Gary jumped up and left the dining room abruptly. No one else lingered after that.

"Some of us are watching movies," Maddie announced. "We'll have coffee in the television room."

"What movie?" Laura asked.

"Who cares?" Maddie said with a shrug. She took her glass out with her when she left.

And that was right, Beth knew. No one cared. If they could get through this evening, all day tomorrow, it would be over. Anything on the screen would serve.

The problem was that no one could sit quietly and watch a movie, no matter what it was, she thought a while later. They had argued at first about *Yellow Submarine* or *Topper*. They would watch both, they decided, but then people kept getting up and going to the bar at the end of the room, or leaving altogether and returning. One of the times it was Laura who left her chair, and Beth heard her stifle a scream, then laugh too shrilly. Killed, she thought. Another victim bites the dust. She did not turn to see anything going on behind her. Maddie left and came back. Rich drifted in, then drifted out. Beth went to her room and paced a few minutes. When restlessness drove her out again, she saw Jake closing his own door, and she hesitated a moment. He appeared as self-conscious as she felt, and apparently had as little to say as he caught up with her and they went down the stairs side by side in an awkward silence. She was relieved when they parted in the wide corridor and she returned to the television room. Bruce muttered something that she did not catch, and she looked away from him, closed her eyes. A moment later she heard Gary's laughter and a vacuumlike silence when he stopped. There was the odor of chlorine and popcorn, she thought without wonder. Why not? Press a button, *voilà* popcorn! She wandered to the kitchen for no real reason and got a drink of water that she did not want.

When the Beatles came on singing, Maddie left again. "Save my chair," she said in a loud voice. "I'll be back, just not soon. Maybe they'll get that out of their system. I didn't know it was cartoons!"

Maddie heard Laura say something unintelligible as she walked out, no doubt something snide or crude. She was tired, tired of them all, of the silly game, of Gary's tantrums and Bruce's sulks. Just tired, she thought. Getting old maybe. Used to be able to stay up as long as anyone, drink as much as anyone, joke, laugh, tease. But this was a hellish weekend and she was plain tired. She waited for the elevator. Lie down a little while, rest. Too early to actually go to bed, but rest a little, that would be nice. The door slid open silently, and she started to enter the elevator, then stopped.

"For heaven's sake!" she muttered. That damn game! That goddamn game! Rich Schoen was lying on the floor, taking it too far, too damn far. "Rich, get up. Stop that." Then she knew. She took a halting step backward, another, and she screamed again and again and again.

Things happened, too many for Beth to track. He couldn't be dead, she wanted to explain to anyone who would listen. That thing on his head was an open weave net bag; it couldn't hurt him, not really. Milton told them all to go to the living room and stay and no one argued with him, and that would make Gary furious, she thought. He couldn't bear for anyone else to give orders. That was his prerogative, no one else's. Bruce took Maddie to her room because Maddie would not stop yelling, and that was silly. It was a game, Beth thought at her, just a game. Rich was playing the game. Then someone was shaking her slightly and she focused her eyes to see Jake.

"Hold on, kid," he said. "Just hold on. Okay?"

She nodded, and she was okay suddenly. His face was ridged, with hard lines down both sides of his cheeks, like a wood carving, she thought, as if he had put on a mask. "Is there something we should do?" she asked then. "Call the police? An ambulance? Where is everyone else?"

"Milton's trying to find everyone now. He called the sheriff's office already. Can you help me get some coffee? I'm afraid we're in for a long night."

She nodded. Laura was on one of the couches looking like a zombie. Bruce was there, and Harry.

"We're going to get coffee," Jake said to them. "Milton wants everyone to wait here. We'll bring it back when it's ready."

Milton Sweetwater was the company attorney, Beth thought distantly. Perry Mason taking charge. She followed Jake from the room. They had barely got started searching for the coffee when Milton appeared at the kitchen door and asked them to come back to the living room.

"We can't find Gary," he said. He was pale and so somber it was like another mask. They all had masks, Beth thought almost wildly. Milton turned to Alexander and said, "Get on that computer and unlock his door."

Alexander Randall was biting his fingernails as he faced Milton. "He'll kill me if I unlock his door," he protested.

"And I'll kill you if you don't."

Alexander looked at the others beseechingly, then seated himself at the computer terminal in the living room and started to key in something. He stopped and looked up at Milton. "There's a better way, through security. At least I can find out if he went to his room."

They all watched the screen as Alexander typed in instructions. No one moved. Finally Milton said, "In the Jacuzzi."

They started out together and, without volition on her part, Beth followed. They went around the atrium, to a narrow hallway backed by obsidian, through another short hall to a closed door. It opened at a touch. The insulating cover was over the Jacuzzi pool. The room was hot, the air foul with chlorine, dense with steam, more like a steam bath than a Jacuzzi room. For a moment no one moved, then Milton found a control panel on the wall and studied it for a moment; he pushed a button. The cover of the pool slid open, releasing clouds of steam, and there in the water, face down, was the fully clothed body of Gary Elringer.

4

Charlie Meiklejohn brooded about the weather. The end of August, two more weeks of hell before they could expect real relief. And what the devil caused the haze that hung between the trees and followed the contours of the hill out back like a London fog? Not rain. The grass was browning nicely and he'd be damned if he would water it. There was too much. Constance watered a patch surrounding the terrace behind the house, but that was because it bordered her flowers, and no drought would be allowed to detract from the riot of colors. They had a green backdrop, and then the grass turned brown. So much the better. It might not need mowing again this season, and if there was anything Charlie disliked more than shoveling snow, it was mowing grass. You water it, and fertilize it, and then you cut it down, he thought, and shook his head. Dumb.

"Dead cat," Constance murmured, joining him on the back terrace, shaded by purple clematis and wisteria. She pointed to Brutus, on his back under the lilac bush, his head twisted to one side, his feet splayed out in what looked like a joint-breaking position.

"We should put in air conditioning," Charlie said in a grumbling way. It wasn't fair, he thought aggrievedly; Constance always looked cool. She was ivory pale and never looked flushed, never tanned very dark, and always seemed to have the right sort of thing to put on for whatever weather they were having. Now she wore a loose cottony dress that touched her at the shoulders and nowhere else and was exactly the color of her eyes, light blue, cool blue. She was slender, with long legs the color of honey, just enough color to be interesting. Charlie was dark, with unruly black hair speckled with gray, and he was thickly built, heavy in the chest, thick arms and legs. He was very muscular, but he knew he could lose ten, fifteen pounds and maybe take the heat better for it. Thin people didn't know what it was to suffer from the heat, he decided, and it wasn't fair.

Constance smiled and sat down in a chaise longue. She did not say, "Yes, dear," about the air conditioning, but her look said it almost as clearly as words. They had talked about it last summer, and the summer before that. They had talked about it years ago when they bought this place in upstate New York, while they were still living in New York City and could only make it up here on weekends and holidays. And they would talk about it next summer, she knew. Her smile was contented. They had a window unit in the bedroom, and a fan that they moved from living room to kitchen to dining room. Always before when they talked about it, when they had reached the point of actually doing something about it, a cold front had come through bringing cooling rains, or autumn had come along, or they had had to leave for something or other.

"Those poor bastards," Charlie sighed, and she knew he was thinking of people in the city.

"Rather be here," she said.

If it had not been so hot, he would have turned to give her one of his looks, but he didn't bother. That's what came of living together so long, he thought. They could speak in code by now, speak by number and have perfect understanding. Sometimes he missed the city. He had lived there all his life until retiring after twenty-five years of service, first with the fire department, later as a city police detective. Constance had taught psychology at Columbia for most of those years. On days like this they used to meet after work, both of them exhausted and wan, and plan for the time when they could chuck it all, move to the country, where it was cool and fresh. Hah! But he knew what it was like in the city now. His memory of Manhattan during an August heat wave was clear in his mind—hot buildings, hot pavement, hot metal smells, hot tempers. God, those tenements! He stirred restlessly, willing the memories away. He did not miss New York in August.

"After what's-his-name leaves, let's go to Spirelli's and eat."

"Maybe we should talk out here," she said. "It's better than inside."

He nodded. "Probably won't take long. Look." He pointed. Another cat, Ashcan, had spotted Brutus playing dead and was sneaking up on him. Brutus would slaughter him, Charlie thought. But Brutus opened his yellow eyes when Ashcan got close, glared at the meeker gray cat, and closed his eyes again. Ashcan began to clean his tail.

"Have you read through all that stuff he sent?"

"There's not that much. A computerized house went bananas and killed a couple of people. Case closed. Evidently the house is guilty as hell."

And Milton Sweetwater had asked for an appointment to discuss it, she thought, and almost felt sorry for Mr. Sweetwater, although he was a stranger. Where computers were concerned, Charlie was a hanging judge; sentence first, questions later, if ever. For two weeks Charlie had been doing battle with the telephone company over an error in their billing. "Let me talk to a person!" he had yelled into the telephone finally. Then he had banged down the phone and turned a stricken face to her.

"What happened?"

"It was a computer pretending to be a person," he said in a near whisper. "By God, it was passing itself off as human!"

Milton Sweetwater did not hesitate a second about taking off his jacket. He handed it to Constance with gratitude, followed her to the terrace, and shook hands with Charlie in the ritualistic manner of men, eyeing each other carefully. He accepted a beer and sat down. Very handsome, she thought. Movie star looks, like Gregory Peck. And he was obviously studying both her and Charlie as much as she was studying him. Charlie, she also thought, was not being helpful.

"Hot day for driving," Charlie said; Milton Sweetwater agreed, and now there was silence.

Abruptly Milton Sweetwater laughed and leaned back in his chair, obviously relaxing. Until that moment Constance had not realized that he had been tense.

"I got your names from Ralph Wedekind," he said and drank his beer thirstily. His glass was covered with condensation, so heavy that it dripped like a shower when he moved it. "Actually I have three names. I already talked to someone else and didn't like him. You're the second. If you turn us down, there's another man in New York that I'll talk to. I was ready to reject you for making me drive out to your place, instead of your coming in to the city, but after a couple days in New York, I'd be the first to admit you'd be crazy to live there. And the last thing we need at Smart House is a crazy detective."

"Why a New York detective?" Charlie asked lazily.

"We don't care where our person is from, as long as he's good, with good references. Wedekind gave you his highest recommendation. So I'm here."

"Did the computer kill those two men?" Charlie asked, but without any real interest.

"Of course not. But the shareholders are in a bind. We've had three meetings so far and no one knows exactly where to go next, what to do next. The company's in a tailspin financially and the management is in a tailspin psychologically. Beth Elringer is crying murder, and her brother-in-law is screaming for action. It's a real mess."

Charlie sighed and poured himself more beer. "I read the news stories you sent. What else is there to know? Were the stories accurate?"

"To a point," Milton Sweetwater said after a pause that was hardly noticeable, as if in that brief moment he had come to a decision. "Can we all accept that our conference today is confidential whether or not you take on our problem?"

Charlie waved his hand. "That's the way we play it."

Milton Sweetwater leaned forward. "There's a major part of that weekend that we decided not to talk about with the press or the police. I don't think it has a bearing, but at our last meeting, we decided to tell a detective all of it and go on from there."

Charlie nodded, then regarded the cats under the lilac bush again. The leaves of the bush were drooping dispiritedly; the cats looked dead; he felt wrung out.

"You should know something about Gary Elringer and the company or that weekend won't make a bit of sense," Milton began. "Gary was a prodigy. I guess the news stories went into that. He built his own computer before he was ten, went to Stanford at fifteen, Ph.D. by twenty, with half a dozen innovations or outright inventions or discoveries under his belt already. He had a couple dozen patents before he could legally take a drink. He also had a difficult personality. Spoiled rotten as a kid, spoiled as an adult. He was chubby and had the social graces of a polecat, snarling, taking what he wanted, and generally making people miserable. In college he met Beth MacNair, shy and very bright, and undeveloped physically. Somehow they hit it off and got married. That was ten years ago. Bruce Elringer, Gary's brother, meanwhile had come up with a program to write music on a computer, some kind of breakthrough, and they decided to start the Bellringer Company. They had a new computer— hardware—and a lot of software to go with it. Gary had already made a lot of money—not enough, but a lot. They rounded up a few others, including me, and we launched the Bellringer Company, Incorporated. It was a spectacular success from the start. That was eight years ago."

He finished his beer and lifted the bottle to read the label.

"Local company," Charlie said. He went inside and returned with two more bottles. Constance was having iced tea. She drank beer with Mexican food. He began to think of Mexican food— pork with green sauce, chicken breasts with chilies in a creamy sauce·. . .

"Well," Milton went on after pouring more beer, drinking again. "The company was Gary's from the start. He kept con- trolling interest. And no one objected. We all knew that without him there wouldn't be a company. Even after he started handing out shares to buy loyalty, he kept control, no doubt about it." He went on at length explaining the articles of incorporation, the shares that had been distributed, how the company func- tioned. "And until three years ago it didn't make a lot of differ- ence who had control," he said presently. "In the first years there weren't any profits to go to shareholders; we were all on salary. Then there were profits to parcel out, but when Gary started Smart House, the profits vanished."

Charlie didn't actually yawn. He wasn't that much of a boor, he told himself, but neither could he work up any interest in the corporate structure that the lawyer was going on about. Mex- ican or Italian, he deliberated. Hot, spicy food was said to be more cooling than nonspicy food in the long run. And a pitcher of margaritas. He was leaning more in that direction. Maybe Mil- ton Sweetwater would finish in another few minutes and go away, and he and Constance could discuss the matter of food until it was time to go eat the food.

"You have to understand some of the background or you'll never understand why we all went along with Gary's game of murder," Milton said then, not at all unaware of the effect his words would have.

Charlie blinked at him. "Tell me about it."

By the time Milton had finished describing the game, Charlie was regarding him with disbelief, and Constance was looking at him with horror.

"You're a lawyer and you went along with that?" she asked.

He shrugged. "You had to know Gary. It would have been worse if we hadn't gone along with it. I decided that it was relatively harmless, and it did exactly what he predicted: It made each of us find out for ourselves what a marvel Smart House really is."

"Such a marvel that it wanted to play, too," Charlie muttered. "Go on. I take it this is what your game players failed to tell the cops."

"Exactly. We just didn't see the point. Think how it would have looked all over the newspapers, the tabloids. And the game had nothing to do with what happened. It might have been any game, or no game at all. What difference could it make to their investigation?"

"I don't know," Charlie said. "You tell me. What difference did it make?"

The lawyer looked uncomfortable now. "For one thing everyone became paranoid. It seems incredible now, but we were all paranoid almost instantly when the game started. The other thing is that because of the game we knew that the house, the computer, I should say, appeared responsible for both deaths. You see, it kept track of everyone's movements all that weekend, and when that portion of the program was displayed, it clearly showed that Rich had been alone in the elevator, and that Gary had gone into the Jacuzzi alone. The police determined that there were glitches in the program, as we all agreed; after all, this was its test run, the weekend, I mean. And no one came forth with any information to contradict that, so although the case wasn't officially closed, it's at a standstill, a dead end. An unfortunate accident—two of them. And Bellringer makes killer computers," he added bitterly.

Charlie was shaking his head. "The police had more than a lousy program with glitches. What else?"

"Yes," Milton admitted. "There was more. You see, the way

the game was set up, and everyone so paranoid, no one was staying for any length of time with just one other person. For the most part we were all staying in groups of four or more, and keeping a sharp eye out for each other. If you were with one other person, a third person might join you looking for his victim, you see. One victim, one witness, one killer. I think we all had our suspicions about who had been killed already and who hadn't, but even an apparently nonchalant attitude could have been an act." He spread his hands in a curiously helpless gesture. "Anyway, we knew Rich was alone, not with just one other person, and we knew he wasn't in a group of four."

Very patiently Charlie asked, "Exactly how did you know that?"

Milton looked more uncomfortable than ever. Sheepishly he said, "I was stalking Laura Westerman. She was in a group watching a movie. There was a bar set up in the room, and she was drinking. I thought it was just a matter of time before she wanted to refill her glass, so I waited near the bar. Sure enough, she came back. Rich was near there, too, and I spoke to him, to get his attention, so he would be my witness. When Laura got within range, I shot her with a pea shooter." He did not look at Charlie or Constance, but frowned into the distance. "It was listed as a poison dart, an instant kill."

Charlie watched his glass sweat and Constance swirled her ice in her tall glass. Finally Milton glanced at her, then at Charlie, and continued.

"I motioned Laura and Rich to come out of the room where others were watching the movie. We stepped into the next room, the library, where I used the computer to register the kill. Rich witnessed, and Laura confirmed it. She and I both saw him leave alone. I suspected that he needed to report in to the computer in his room to get a new victim, or else go downstairs for a weapon. That's how we were all thinking. I kept a close watch on him because for all I knew, he had my name. That was the last time anyone saw him alive."

"No wonder you didn't want to discuss this with the police, or reporters either," Charlie muttered. "Of all the goddamn foolishness! What time was that?"

"Ten to eleven. He was found at eleven-forty, and they estimated that he had died between eleven and eleven-thirty."

"The story I read mentioned a net bag over his head," Charlie said. "Another deadly weapon?"

"Yes. I think he went down in the elevator to collect his next weapon and that was it."

"A net bag?"

"It was supposed to be a plastic bag, like a laundry bag, I guess, the kind with the warnings not to place them over your head. Anyway, it was supposed to suffocate the victim. It was loosely woven, soft cotton netting."

"That suffocated him," Charlie said dryly. "Did the police even try to explain why it was on his head?"

Milton shrugged. "How could they? They think the automatic vacuum system came on while he was in the elevator, that it sucked out the air, and he collapsed before he realized what was happening. Maybe the elevator locked and wouldn't open. Anyway, since he was alone, and he died of suffocation, that was all they could come up with. There weren't any marks on his neck, no marks at all to indicate otherwise. None of us could come up with anything better," he added.

"Okay. How about Gary Elringer? What's the story on his death?"

"No one saw him after dinner. A couple of people watching the movie heard him laughing at one point, but no one even noticed what time it was then. The police say he walked through the Jacuzzi room for some reason and fell in, and the computer closed the cover on him. It had overheated the water drastically; why not also cover it by mistake?"

"Nothing was in the news story about overheating. How hot?"

"By the time anyone thought to check the thermometer, it was one thirty-five, but I think it had been quite a bit hotter. Clouds of steam rolled out when we opened it. The heat made it impossible to tell exactly when he died. Maybe even before Rich. His death was attributed to drowning."

Constance shivered in the August heat.

"And you say the computer had tracked both of them all evening? It can do that?"

"I tell you it's a true marvel. I've never seen anything like it. It kept track of everyone in the house, by name, from the time of arrival until Alexander stopped the program. According to the display, Gary went into the Jacuzzi room alone. No one else went in until the search party entered."

Charlie regarded the lawyer morosely, then turned away to observe the third cat, the fluffy orange and white Candy, wend her way through the dying grass. She walked with her tail straight up, twitching at the end. Some hunter, signaling by semaphore to any prey within range, *Here I come*. Her eyes were the color of butterscotch. Ashcan gathered his legs under him in a spring-ready position; Candy ignored him, and he became interested in something moving in the grass, pounced at that. Candy continued toward the terrace until she spotted a stranger; she stopped, her fur rose along her spine, her ears flattened, and she yelled obscenities at Constance and Charlie in a hoarse, raucous voice. Ashcan fled in terror and Brutus heaved himself to his feet and stalked away in disgust. Finally Charlie brought his gaze back to Milton Sweetwater.

"What did the computer do to convince the police that it had really gone berserk?"

Milton drew in a long breath and nodded, as if to say, *good for you*. "Not a word of this was in those news articles, but you're right, of course. They had been there an hour perhaps when lights here and there went off or came on. Doors that had opened at a touch were locked; other doors opened. Alexander Randall was beside himself. Then, the final touch: An insecticide was released in the greenhouse, enough to have killed anyone exposed to it, I gather. It set off an alarm. Fortunately no one was inside the building at the time. I think that was what convinced them that the house is a killer."

"Uh-huh. And you. What do you think?"

"It can't be," Milton said without hesitation. "If it is, we're ruined."

Charlie raised an eyebrow at him and reached for the bottle of beer that had very little remaining in it. "What do you want? Why are you here?"

"Right. That's the scenario we're working with, pretty much as I've outlined it for you. After the funeral, after the formalities, things were supposed to get back to normal, as normal as possible, with reorganization and replanning for the future, and so on. Suddenly Beth Elringer, the widow, started to voice objections. And Bruce Elringer backed her. Well, by now there's a schism as broad and deep as the one that parted the Red Sea. No one has enough votes to do anything at this point. The company will go under if it doesn't move forward. That's the way it is in the computer industry. No one can simply stand still. We had a shareholders' meeting last Thursday and everyone screamed at everyone else for three hours, until finally I said we should bring in an independent investigator to clear the air. Bruce has another idea, and in the end, we decided to work with both."

"Bruce Elringer? What's his scenario?"

"He thinks Beth killed her husband."

Charlie whistled softly.

"It's ugly as hell," Milton said with some bitterness. "Anyway, Bruce has invited everyone back to Smart House next weekend, to reenact the last day, to demonstrate that Beth had the opportunity to murder Rich and Gary. He's talking about her motive, and circumstantial evidence, and so on. Enough of us protested that he had to allow for you, or someone like you, to be there also. And that's why I'm here now." He took a deep breath.

Silently Charlie left, returned with two more bottles of beer. Constance poured herself the rest of the tea, and for a long time no one spoke.

At last Charlie said thoughtfully, "If we go to Spirelli's we won't be able to talk because that damn accordian player starts at eight. I say it's El Gordo's and margaritas. How about you two?" He added, almost kindly, to Milton, "I have a hell of a lot of questions to ask, I'm afraid."

5

Late that night Charlie and Constance talked in the cool bedroom, both of them propped up on pillows, the television on, the sound off. Outside the bedroom door, Brutus screamed for admittance. The cats hated it when they closed the door all the way, and with the air conditioner on, they kept it closed.

"If I let him in, he'll prowl around five minutes and then yell to get outside again," Charlie said. "Pretend you don't hear him. What do you think of Sweetwater?"

"Awfully slick, and smart. Charming. He looks like Gregory Peck, and, unfortunately, he knows it. Your turn."

"He's a computer nut," Charlie said as if that defined his entire impression.

"From what he said, they all are."

"I know," he grumbled. Brutus raised his voice, and Charlie cursed him. For a moment there was silence, then Ashcan screeched, and cats galloped through the hallway. With a sigh Charlie left the bed and went out into the hall. He could hear Constance's soft chuckle behind him.

He led the three cats to the sliding glass door to the terrace and shooed them all out, then stood outside for a minute. Lightning played with clouds in the west, too distant for the thunder to reach this far. The air felt heavy, ominous, and too damn hot, he decided. Then thunder rumbled closer, the lightning flashed to the ground, and thunder boomed.

"All right!" he said, and went back inside to call Constance. Three times that summer they had had electrical storms that had taken out the lights. One of the neighbors, the Mitchum family, had had a television and an electric stove ruined by a power surge.

They went through the house together pulling plugs and then sat on the terrace waiting for the storm to drive them inside. A fitful wind was rising. The temperature seemed to go up, and the air smelled of ozone. Charlie hoped it would be a good storm, a freshening change of weather, an end to the heat wave that was turning him into jelly day after day.

"If the house, or the computer in the house, actually did kill two people, don't you think it might be a dangerous place?" Constance asked between two rolls of thunder. Moving away, she thought with regret.

"We'll stay out of elevators and away from the Jacuzzi. Nervous about it?"

"Not really. It just occurred to me. It also seems that if they were all that disturbed because of a game before, just imagine what they'll be like this time when they get together. Now they know there's a killer house, or else a human killer among them."

"Damn storm's going to stay south of us," he said, disgruntled. "At least it'll be cool on the Oregon coast."

For a moment she had the distinct feeling that he had agreed to look into this insane affair simply to escape the heat wave. She opened her mouth to protest, then closed it again. If those people were as bothered as she would be in their situation, he might wish he were back here very quickly.

"Charlie, after talking to Milton, reading the material he gave us, do you think the computer is to blame?"

"You know, when a guy wants to kill someone, usually he reaches for a weapon he's familiar with—a gun, a club, a brick, poison, whatever it might be. Or else he grabs what's at hand, a skillet say, a dandy weapon. Good old black skillet meets head, head gives. But an open mesh bag? Drowning a guy in a whirlpool? Well, like I told Milton Sweetwater, we'll have a looksee, keep an open mind as long as possible, and hang the computer in the end. Let's go to bed. No storm here tonight. It's hotter than it was an hour ago."

People on the coast went inland to warm up in the summer, the gas station attendant had told Beth that morning, a few miles south of Bandon, Oregon. The day was misty, gray, and cool. Earlier, there had been dense fog, but it had lifted by the time she reached this area. From there to Smart House had been less than an hour.

Crazy, she told herself, shivering when she drove up to the house, suffering from déjà vu, her stomach in a hard knot that she could not relax no matter how many deep breaths she sucked in. Crazy, crazy, crazy.

The front door opened before she had her suitcase out of the car. Jake strode out to meet her. He stopped short of actually touching her this time, but examined her face closely, then nodded. "Why didn't you return any of my calls?"

"I don't know. There didn't seem much point, I guess."

She turned from his searching gaze and opened the back door and now he moved past her and brought her suitcase out. Silently they entered Smart House. Neither suggested taking the elevator up. As they mounted the stairs from the foyer, the house seemed uncannily quiet. In the upper hallway she looked down into the atrium, as beautiful as before, with no one in it. The waterfall was working, the splash of water reflected one of the hanging lights, sparkled, and broke the sparkles in an endless kaleidoscope effect. Someone must have left open one of the doors, she thought distantly; the unpleasant odor of chlorine was everywhere. She had forgotten how it filled the house when the doors were left open.

She wished that someone other than Jake had met her, or no one at all. She could manage her one suitcase. It was true, he had called quite a few times, and she had listened to his voice on her machine, and turned it off each time. What was the point? she repeated to herself. They reached her door.

"Is . . . is the computer turned on?" she asked, hesitating now.

"No," he said brusquely. "That damn thing's off for good." He reached past her and turned the doorknob. "There's a lock inside, a plain, old-fashioned mechanical chain lock. I installed it a while ago."

"I'll have to open my own drapes and regulate my own bath—" Beth started. At the sound of laughter she became rigid and felt the world going out of focus—Gary's laughter. She clutched the door frame.

"Take it easy," Jake said; he held her arm in a firm grip. "He's been practicing."

Bruce yelled from the elevator at the end of the hall, "It's about time you got here! We're having a family meeting in the garden in five minutes."

"Oh, my God!" Beth breathed, staring at Bruce. Always before he had stressed the small differences between himself and Gary: He had worn suits, Gary sweaters; he had worn polished shoes, Gary sneakers; his hair had been relatively neat, Gary's unruly, a mop of curly hair that he had cut only when it got down to his eyes. Today, Bruce was in a sweater and slacks, untied sneakers, his hair wild and bushy.

Even the words, she thought, he even remembered what Gary had said the last time.

"As I said," Jake muttered savagely, "he's been practicing." He carried her suitcase on into the room; she followed and stood by the door.

Now Jake looked awkward. She moved aside for him to pass, but he didn't move yet. "Beth, don't let him get to you. Okay? You've got friends in the company, you know. Milton, me. Bruce is being ugly, but he doesn't have any power, and he knows it. He can't actually do anything. So take it easy."

She nodded. "Thanks, Jake. I appreciate that."

"Yeah. I'll see you later." He left swiftly.

Beth closed the door, and after a moment she put the chain lock on, and only then advanced into the room, the same pink and yellow room she had had the last time. She opened the drapes and gazed at the sea. There was no horizon, just the gray sea and the gray sky that became one. No escape there, she thought. You could sail out that way only so far and then you would be sent back by way of the sky. She turned away from the ocean and found herself gazing at the computer, silent and blank. She was shivering. Walking quickly she went to the bathroom and got a towel, brought it out with her, and draped it over the monitor. *There,* she breathed at it. In no hurry, she unpacked, washed her face and hands, and pulled on a sweatshirt, not sure if her chill was due to cold or to an internal malfunction. It didn't matter; she was freezing.

Maddie and Bruce were in the atrium garden at the lowest level near the bar when she arrived. It was hot and humid here. Something new must have come into bloom, she found herself thinking, something heavy and too sweet. Gardenias? She embraced Maddie, who looked glassy-eyed, tranquilized, and smelled of gin and tonic. A coffeepot and cups were on the bar counter. She nodded briefly at Bruce and poured herself coffee.

"All right," Bruce said. "Here's the program. The company's

in a hell of a spot. We've got to raise money enough to pay for forty-five shares of stock, and frankly, there's no way on earth we can do it. The others are going to opt for a sellout, naturally, take ten cents on the dollar and be done with it."

"Bruce, stop it!" Maddie cried. "We agreed not to have a business meeting unless everyone is present."

Bruce went on as if he had not heard. "Milton says we have to reorganize first, before any decisions can be made. You know who will take over if we go along with that! Jake. And then Milton will get in line and they'll vote to sell out. So we have two choices. We can serve up the murderer, clear the computer of all charges, and then the shares go a different direction. Mom and I split them and we both waive payment for now. Or you can defer payment for an indefinite period," he added, glaring at Beth. "Deferred payment is acceptable, Milton said."

"What are you talking about?" Beth demanded.

"A murderer can't benefit financially from her crime," he said almost petulantly. "You know that. I checked it with Milton. That means that Mom and I will split Gary's estate. The money stays in the company and we'll start showing Smart House—"

Beth felt distant, an observer of a scenario she had no understanding of, with no means of arriving at an understanding. She stood up.

"Sit down!" Bruce yelled at her. "I'm giving you a choice, goddamn it! You sign a waiver about payment for now and we let it rest there. I don't say a word about what I know."

She felt herself moving before she realized she had willed motion. She walked blindly toward the sliding door to the hall, hearing the shouts and curses behind her as if Bruce were on a stage rehearsing for a production she had no interest in.

"You'll do what I tell you! Or it's your ass!" Bruce screamed.

Because she was walking in the direction of the foyer when she left the atrium, that was where she found herself a moment later, and she kept going to the front door, and on outside. She did not see the man and woman approaching until she nearly bumped into them.

"Hi," Charlie said, "I'm Charles Meiklejohn, and this is my wife, Constance Leidl. Who are you?"

"You're the detective?" she said, and blinked several times.

"He is," Constance said briskly. "And from Milton Sweetwa-

ter's description, I'd guess you're Beth Elringer." Beth nodded.
"Look, we were just debating whether or not lunch would be
possible inside. Arriving at this time of day is a little awkward,
isn't it? We said we'd arrive in the afternoon, and, of course,
officially it is after noon. About one, isn't it? But still, we did not
say we would come for lunch. Will you have lunch with us somewhere? Maybe you could direct us."

Charlie raised his eyebrows at her, but she was already taking
the young woman's arm, steering her toward the rental car they
had just driven up in. Lying like a trooper, he thought happily
about Constance, and took Beth's other arm; the three of them
went to the car and got in.

"I'd better go somewhere," Beth said, between them on the
front seat. "If I go back inside right now, I might kill Bruce, and
that would really look bad for me, wouldn't it?"

"That would look bad," Constance agreed. "What on earth
did Bruce do?"

"He accused me of killing Gary."

"Did you?"

"No."

"I thought they all said the house killed both men," Constance said.

"They said it, but I don't believe it. I guess Bruce must have
done it, after all."

"You thought he did, and then you changed your mind, and
now you think it again," Constance said thoughtfully, as if they
had discussed this before.

"Yes. I couldn't think of a reason before, but he just gave a
reason, only he didn't seem to realize it. Actually I don't know
this area," she said then, looking at Charlie. "I don't know
where there are restaurants or anything else."

"That's all right," Constance said reassuringly. "We passed a
lot of them on our way in. Charlie knows where to go. What was
the reason Bruce just revealed?"

She would get away with it, Charlie knew. She had moved in
when Beth was practically in a state of shock; she had said and
done exactly the right things at the right time, and this poor kid
had no more resistance to her than he himself did. No sound
escaped, but he was humming under his breath, listening to
every word, and searching for a restaurant.

"It's pretty complicated," Beth said after a brief hesitation. "I thought I understood it just a minute ago, and now it seems confused again. It has to do with the company and the way it's set up." She lapsed into a troubled silence.

"I never studied economics enough to get a decent grasp of business affairs," Constance said. "That's a closed corporation, isn't it?"

"That's it," Beth said, and now her words came in a rush. "When they started it all, Bruce was still married to Binny. They got divorced a couple of years ago. Two kids, perfectly awful little monsters, all whining and smeary and clinging. It's sad for Maddie, her only two grandchildren turning out to be monsters. Anyway, Gary couldn't stand Binny, and no one else could either as far as I could tell, except Bruce, and that didn't last. She isn't very smart, doesn't know anything about computers, or anything else, I guess. So when Gary was starting the company, he had Milton write up the articles of incorporation in such a way that no stock could be inherited in the case of death of the share-holder. He was terrified of letting someone like Binny get any shares, having any voice, input, he called it. You can't just sell a share, either," she added in an aggrieved voice.

"So the shares of the deceased revert back to the company, which has to pay the estate the market value of them and then divide them up using a formula based on the percentage of shares they already own. The company has to buy back Gary's shares, and Rich's, now and redistribute them."

"But weren't you named his primary heir?"

Beth looked at Constance, puzzled, then nodded. "I don't get the shares, that's the point. They have to pay me their value, and they don't have enough money. I think the courts will force a sale, or something of that sort. That's my motive, according to Bruce." She no longer seemed able to get from that to the reason she had found for Bruce to have done it. She frowned in thought.

Charlie slowed down and clicked on the turn signal. He glanced at Constance; she grinned back, her look telling him she had known all along that he knew perfectly well where a good restaurant was. He parked and they all got out in front of Ray's Clam Chowder and Other Fine Food restaurant. Charlie took a deep breath of the cool, misty sea air. Back home it was closing in on a hundred degrees, he thought with satisfaction.

The restaurant was small, with only two other parties in booths. They seated themselves in a booth overlooking the parking lot and consulted the menu, and suddenly Beth said, "Oh, yes. That's it."

"First we order," Charlie said firmly. "You two can have the other fine food. I want chowder."

They all did, and as soon as the waiter left them alone, Beth said, "If he can convict me of murder, I can't inherit. The stock still goes back to the company, but he and his mother will inherit the estate. They will be owed for the shares. He'll make Maddie accept a deferred payment plan, and he will too, and the company won't have to raise millions of dollars to pay for Gary's shares. And the company won't be under the cloud, either, of having a crazy computer that kills people." She nodded. "That's his motive."

"Is the company really broke?" Charlie asked.

"Practically. A cash flow problem, as they say. I guess there's operating money, money due on back orders, and so on, but nothing more than that. Gary sank every cent he got his hands on into Smart House. If they can clear the Smart House computer, they have a new gold mine, of course. God alone knows how much they'll make when they start selling the advanced programming, the computer systems, everything to do with Smart House."

Charlie was studying her thoughtfully. "It seems to me that if there is a human killer, he cut his own throat by casting suspicion on the computer. Everyone there is involved with the company, even if you do say 'they' when you talk about it."

She blushed and ducked her head. "I guess I never thought of any of it as having anything real to do with me," she mumbled. "It was always Gary's, and theirs, not mine."

"How long were you married to him?" Constance asked, and although that was not the question Charlie would have put to her then, he leaned back to see where Constance was heading now.

"Ten years," Beth said in a low voice.

"You were both children," Constance said, also softly, with great sympathy.

"Yes. We were nineteen when we met. He was getting his doctorate already, and he was so shy and funny looking and awkward. I was the only girl he ever went out with. And I didn't have any social life either, until he came along. In my own way I was just as funny looking and awkward and shy. Two misfits. We got along somehow. No one understood what either of us saw in the other, and now I don't either, but then . . . All those years, for the first seven years, I did exactly what he wanted. He was hardworking, determined to make his mark in the world of computers, full of ideas, some of them wild, some simply wonderful, and he made his mark. He really did. He wanted to re-design the architecture of the machine so that he could develop half a dozen software packages that would be totally compatible and require a minimum of available memory. He did it, too."

The waiter came with their chowder. His frank appraisal of Beth was oddly reassuring. He was young, probably younger than she was, but interested. She was oblivious. Constance watched her eat a few bites, and as soon as she seemed to lose interest in the food, Constance asked, "You could work with him on computers at that depth? I'm awed. All I know about computers is that you plug them in, insert a program, and hope for the best."

Beth laughed politely. "Actually I only worked with him for the first few years. I took my degree then, and four years ago I told him I wanted to go back for my master's in English. For the first year that I was back in school, I kept working with him, but it was too much and gradually I gave it up. Three years ago I moved all the way out to go to Berkeley. I had an apartment, and after that I saw very little of him. I don't know how far he moved during those four years; pretty far, I guess."

"Did he object?" Charlie asked. "Did you fight over leaving him for school?"

She pushed her spoon around with one finger and shook her head. "We never fought," she said. "Never. He said at first that going back to school was a good idea, and later he said he didn't really have time for me anyway, not then. He was too immersed in the work on Smart House. He agreed to help me financially, of course, until the money ran out anyway. We never were sep-arated the way people thought we were. We just weren't together. He believed right up to the end that one day I'd be fed up with trying to support myself, and I'd be back."

"And you? Did you think that?" Charlie asked, baffled by her in a way he could not fathom. Didn't she know she was a damn good looking young woman? And smart as hell?

She looked at him candidly and sighed. "I don't know. Probably I would have gone back eventually, if he insisted. Once he said that he knew computers would do anything you wanted them to—the trick was to find the right language, the right method and sequence of commands to tell them what you wanted. He believed that about people, too. And he was right, at least about people. They always did exactly what he wanted them to. Always."

Charlie shook his head at her gravely. "One of them didn't, Beth. Either a computer or a person did not do exactly what he wanted at the end."

6

Dessert," Charlie announced, "is loganberry pie, and I intend to have it. Ladies?" They both shook their heads. "Good. I eat. You, Beth, talk. Thumbnail sketches of the players at Smart House."

She looked toward Constance, as if for help, and got only an encouraging smile. Did this mean they trusted her, or that they were testing her? She felt her confusion rise and shook her head, but Charlie was motioning the waiter over, and Constance was watching him. He finished with the waiter and turned expectantly to Beth.

"First, the brother, Bruce," he prompted, when she did not speak immediately.

"Bruce," she said after a lengthy pause, "seems to equate genius with insanity, but he's acting. Gary wasn't crazy," she added hurriedly, not certain why she was defending him even now. She stopped in confusion, then said carefully, "He wasn't aware of what he did to the rest of us . . . them." She had to stop again, because that wasn't right, either. Charlie made a noncommittal noise, and Constance simply waited; Beth tried again. "His priorities were different," she said finally. "Anything to do with problems, puzzles, games, anything intellectual, I guess, came first, people second." She thought a moment, then nodded. "Look, it wasn't that he was unaware of people, it was rather that he had a way of delegating importance that left them behind other things. Once," she hurried, wondering again why she was trying so hard to make them understand Gary, since it no longer mattered, "when Jake was still married, his wife gave him an ultimatum. He could keep working eighteen-hour days forever, or he could be married to her, but he couldn't do both. Gary understood exactly what was happening, and he gave Jake even more work. He tested him. In full awareness of the consequences, the cost to Jake, his wife. It was another problem, nothing more than that. He had a good understanding of human problems, but he filed them under a different category than most people."

The waiter brought coffee, and they were silent until he left again. Then Charlie said, "Harry."

Beth blinked and regathered her thoughts, tried to encapsulate Harry. "He's driven," she said slowly. "It's as if he got a glimpse of something he never used to believe was attainable, and suddenly began to believe he could have it. Like a mountain peak," she added, and looked from Charlie to Constance. "You know, he climbs mountains. I mean, almost obsessively." Charlie nodded. "Sometimes I get the feeling that he's climbing a mountain all the time, even if he's on level ground just like the rest of us. I wouldn't want to get in his way. He'd push anyone out of his way, and if you fell over the side, tough."

"Even Gary?"

She shook her head. "You don't understand. Gary was at the peak already, urging him on, encouraging him. He was the role model, the goal. Probably no one admired him more than Harry did."

"Poor Gary," Constance murmured, when Beth lapsed into silence again. "Didn't anyone care for him as a person?"

Beth flushed and ducked her head, watched her spoon whip the coffee in her cup into a whirlpool. "Maddie did, of course, and I did, a long time ago. Jake cared for him."

The vortex in her cup spun higher and higher until it reached the rim and sloshed over the side in a torrent. She was remembering the day of Gary's funeral. They had all gone back to Maddie's house to find it full of people, curious people, friends, strangers, some malicious, some caring, some huddled, held together by whispers, some wanting to touch, to pat, soothe, feel. She had fled upstairs to Maddie's tiny office, where she stood with her back to the room, head bowed, both hands pressed hard against the door as if the mourners might follow and try to gain admittance.

She stiffened at a touch on her shoulder, spun around, and found herself being gathered into the arms of Jake Kluge. He held her and stroked her hair as if she were a child, and she had been overcome by guilt, guilt at not feeling bereaved, at not suffering, at not caring; guilt that she was alive and Gary dead and maybe she was even glad he was dead; guilt because she did not know what she should be feeling and was as empty as the guests downstairs, as cold as ice. Jake murmured nonsense words and she wept, not for Gary, but for herself and the ruins of her life. The guilt doubled, redoubled, until she shoved Jake away, unable to bear his touch. He was wearing his glasses, so thick they distorted his pale eyes but did not hide the reddened eyelids. His very real grief made her more ashamed.

She had run from him, all the way out of the house, to her car, had driven for hours. After that, when he called, she had listened to his voice on her machine and turned it off, turned him off. She had understood that he wanted to share her grief, assuage their mutual grief, and she had none, unless for the girl she had been ages ago.

She looked up from the mess in her saucer, and now on the tabletop as well, and put her spoon down. "They'll be wondering where I am," she said quietly. "We should go now."

When they drove back to Smart House, Charlie had Beth show him where she had stopped to wait at the massive bronze gates, which were standing open now. He drove on, and waited for her to go through the motions she had gone through the day of her arrival. He looked for the camera eyes just as she had done that day, and with as much effect. They were hidden too well.

He rang the bell then and the four clear notes of the Bellringer Company sounded. Seconds later the ornate door opened and a middle-aged woman stepped aside.

"This is Mr. Meiklejohn and Ms. Leidl," Beth said. "Mrs. Ramos."

She was a handsome, sturdily built woman, graying hair in a soft chignon, no makeup, no jewelry, not even a watch. Charlie remembered that she and her husband had been on a long-distance call from a few minutes after eleven until nearly eleven-thirty the night of the deaths. Mrs. Ramos was a new grandmother. She inclined her head fractionally. "I will show you to your room. Do you have bags? If you will please leave your car keys, we will bring up your bags and park the car in the garage. Mr. Sweetwater asked to be notified on your arrival." Her voice was very pleasant, musical even; she had no trace of an accent.

Beth said, "If I see Milton, I'll tell him. See you later." She waved and went around them, through the spacious foyer.

"Would you like to take the elevator up?" Mrs. Ramos asked.

"Yes indeed," Charlie said, and she led them into the wide corridor with the glass wall of the atrium. Charlie whistled.

"We can go that way," Mrs. Ramos said. "Most people do. It's the shortest way through the house."

They examined the garden, the pool, the arrangements of chairs, tables, the bar, the way the room was built up to resemble a rocky hill covered with jungle greenery. The air was heavy.

"You know why we're here?" Charlie asked, pausing to study the rock wall where the water plunged down into the pool.

"They told me."

"I feel like I'm in some damn pasha's palace," he said, and started to walk again. "Will you be here all weekend? We'll want to talk to you at some point. You and your husband."

"Of course," she said. "We are in a cottage on the property. Whenever it's convenient."

The unflusterable, perfect housekeeper, Charlie thought, and wondered what lay behind the serenity of her expression, the wise black eyes. She stopped again almost immediately on leaving the atrium.

"The elevator," she said.

The elevator was at the end of the corridor, with a narrower hallway leading directly away from the pool area. The doors to the elevator were bifold, open. They stepped inside. On the wall next to the doors the control panel was a music staff with notes, the controls flush with the wall. Gold metal strips divided the walls into random sections, each a different pastel—blue, green, yellow. . . . Rich burgundy carpeting underfoot seemed almost too deep. The ceiling was ivory colored, luminescent, the light source. The cage was eleven feet deep, five feet wide, with a ceiling eight feet high, Charlie knew from the reports he had read.

"Where's the automatic vacuum?" he asked Mrs. Ramos.

"The center panel on the rear wall," she said, nodding toward it. "I can't show you on this floor. It only operates on the basement level. These are the floor indicators," she said then and touched one of the notes. "The first one shuts the doors," she said. The doors closed soundlessly. "The next one opens them, and of course the rising notes are for the floors. We're on one, and your room is on two." She touched another note. There was no sensation of motion. "When the computer is operating, there's no need to remember to press any buttons, you just tell it what you want. It's automatic."

She led them into the hallway on the second floor, the glass wall on one side, the bedroom doors on the other between long expanses of wall with very nice art, each picture illuminated with its own light above it. They passed several closed doors before she stopped and opened one. She did not enter, but held the door for them. "I hope you will be comfortable. Number six on the phone rings in the kitchen, if you want anything. And I'll make certain that Mr. Sweetwater knows you have arrived."

Throughout the minitour and minilectures Constance had remained silent and watchful. Now she asked, "Did you work for Gary Elringer?"

"No. I work for the company. Sometimes he was here, sometimes not; I work in the house for the company."

"Do you like it, Mrs. Ramos? Smart House, I mean, the computer controlling things?"

For an instant there was something other than the pleasant well-trained-housekeeper face, an expression stony and cold; it was so fleeting it might not have been noticeable if Constance had not been watching closely.

"The computer is turned off; it isn't running anything anymore." She glanced inside the room in a professional way, then turned and left them.

While Constance crossed the room to open the drapes, Charlie examined the door lock and the numbered panel on the outside and tried to fathom how the thing worked when the computer was operating. He could not understand it, he decided, and closed the door, looked for a lock that he did understand, and failed to find that, too.

"This isn't a house!" Constance exclaimed, standing at the wall of windows. There was an ocean view, misty and gray and beautiful. The room was decorated in orchid, lavender, and navy blue, with exquisite cloisonné objects here and there—lamps, a statuette of a crane, an ashtray. "This is like one of the four-star hotels you read about."

Twin beds, a desk with a computer, a television, chests of drawers, large closet, extravagantly fitted bathroom, like an expensive hotel, Charlie agreed, after looking through it all. Except there was no way to lock the door. He knew he would use the old chair-under-the-doorknob trick.

When they left their room, it was to find Beth in the corridor. "I'll take you to the living room," she said. "Milton's waiting for you. And Bruce and a couple of the others." She looked gloomy as she motioned down the hall. "No elevator. I wouldn't get near that thing again." She led them down the back stairs.

"You really need a guide." Constance said.

"They handed out floor plans last time. There must be some around still. Milton will know."

They entered the living room and she introduced them: Alexander Randall looked nervous and uncertain of what to do with his hands. Milton nodded to them. He was carrying a large manila envelope. Maddie Elringer nodded to them both and did not speak. Her makeup was a mess: too much lipstick not very well applied, and her mascara had run and had not been repaired, as if she had not looked at herself in a mirror since morning. She was holding a tall drink and every sign said that it was not her first although it was then only four in the afternoon.

As soon as the introductions were over Milton Sweetwater held out the envelope to Charlie. "I managed to get everything you asked for, and Alexander here worked on the house from the start. Anything you want to ask about the place, he should be able to fill in."

"Thanks." Charlie tucked the envelope under his arm.

From behind him a new voice demanded harshly, "What did you give him? Dossiers on all of us?"

"That's Bruce," Beth said wearily.

"And that's not an answer," Bruce said in a truculent tone. He joined the group near the window, looking over Charlie, ignoring Constance. "I know who you are. What I want to know is what he told you we hired you to do."

"Bruce, you're making a fool of yourself," Milton snapped. "I told him exactly what we discussed at our last meeting, and I supplied him with the forensic reports, the police reports, the articles of incorporation, the terms of Gary's will, a summary of the company's financial statement of the past year, a floor plan of the house, and perhaps one or two other documents, a list of which I can and will supply at our next meeting."

Constance was watching with an interest that was nearly clinical. Maddie's hands had started to shake so hard she had to put down her glass, and now each hand gripped the other so tightly that the ends of her fingers were scarlet, the knuckles white. Alexander was edging toward the door, ready to bolt.

"I already told them what you're accusing me of!" Beth said coldly, looking at Bruce with icy disdain.

He made a grab for her arm and she twisted out of reach.

"Don't you touch me!" Her voice was choked with fury.

"Stay and listen to me tell it. I don't want you accusing me of saying anything behind your back. I was watching her," he said to Charlie. "We heard Gary laughing. I was watching her. She heard it, just like I did. And she got up and went out after him. She'd been trying to get him to talk to her all day, and that was her chance, while everyone else was watching the movie. He was going to make her work for some of the dough he was shelling out on her, and she wanted a divorce and a fat settlement. I know the signs, by God! That night I saw her go after him. Who else would he let anywhere near him in the Jacuzzi? Who else could turn off the computer so it wouldn't track them into the Jacuzzi? He was mad because she didn't show any interest in his new toys. He would have shown it to her; he wanted to show off to her. He turned them both off the tracking program and said he'd talk to her and they went into the Jacuzzi. She got her hands on it." He raised his voice to a falsetto and went on, "Oh, Gary, let me see it. How clever of you."

Beth made a strangled noise and shook her head. "You're insane!"

"Then you shoved him in the pool and pushed the button to cover it. He never had a chance! And you had the control computer in your hand. You could go anywhere without any record. He wouldn't have let anyone else touch it, just you!"

"What do you mean, a control computer? How big was it?" Charlie asked.

"Little. Like a pack of cigarettes."

"How do you know?" Alexander asked in wonder. "He said he wasn't going to show anyone until our meeting on Monday."

Bruce looked at him in contempt. "Everyone knew, you asshole. You think he could resist showing off?"

"I didn't know," Milton said slowly, shaking his head. "I don't think anyone did. It would have come out before now."

"Neither did I," Beth said.

Bruce looked from one to another in disbelief. Maddie was near tears, raising her glass again, her hand trembling visibly. "You all knew," Bruce said harshly. "Nothing else made any sense. I figured it out and so did all of you. What are you trying to pull off? A frame? It won't take! She did it! No one else had a reason except her!"

"Did you people tell the police about this little gadget?" Charlie asked blandly.

Alexander shook his head. "I thought I was the only one who knew, and I couldn't find it later. I didn't even think of it at the time because Gary was playing the game, same as everyone else. He wouldn't have used it during the game. He was going to demonstrate it on Monday. The whole house was on a trial run that weekend, a demonstration. Everyone here was a Beta tester for the weekend, even if they didn't know it. Anyway, that was just a safety device, a backup in case something went wrong, a door stuck or something like that, and nothing did. Go wrong, I mean. I never gave it a thought until later."

Charlie said easily, "I wonder if you would mind giving Constance and me a guided tour, explain things about the house as we go, since you're the one with the most complete knowledge of what it can and can't do."

Alexander moistened his lips, glanced at Bruce, at Milton, back to Charlie, and nodded.

Bruce glared at the others in the room, then stamped out, yelling over his shoulder, "Any hacker in the world would have figured out that he had such a device. You all knew!"

They started in the lowest level—computer laboratories, offices, the playroom with billiards, pool, and arcade games, and finally the showroom with the glass case that had held the toy weapons used in the game. Charlie gazed at it with brooding eyes. The case was empty now.

"How did it work?" he asked finally. "Beth said it wouldn't open unless you were due a weapon, and then it thanked you by name. How?"

Alexander shifted uncomfortably and mumbled, "By visual identification and the original visual scan at the entrance, and the weight of the object itself. It was pretty good, but not perfect, not yet. We were still working on it."

"So I approach the case and I'm recognized by the computer." At Alexander's nod, Charlie moved to the case and stopped. "I could open the top now?"

Alexander went to his side and pointed toward the ceiling. "There's a scanner up there, and one on this side," he said. Neither showed even though he was directing Charlie's attention to them. "It's up there," he said. "And outside the bedroom doors, and the front door, and at the gate. By the time you get inside the house there are two pictures of you, and at the front door and the bedroom door your weight is registered. The carpet runners in the halls are wired, of course, but not the interiors of any rooms, except the elevator. After that it's a matter of matching data, that's all."

"The toy weapons were on a scale of some sort?"

Alexander nodded. "They were registered by number, and as soon as one was lifted, it was recorded. Then the case wouldn't open again until someone else tried, or you registered a kill and could take another weapon. That part was simple."

Charlie and Constance exchanged glances. Hers said, *Simple as any magic*.

As Alexander led them through the corridor, Constance asked almost meekly, "What's a Beta tester?"

Alexander looked at her suspiciously, as if he thought she was teasing him. "End-user tests," he mumbled. "Someone who's not supposed to know how the program works, just if it does."

She nodded gravely. The next room they entered was Gary's former office and laboratory. A maze of wiring, computers without cases, some wholly encased, test boards, extra keyboards, disk drives, and monitors appeared arranged haphazardly, but obviously there had to be a method, Charlie assumed, without being able to discern it. On the back wall were shelves, a filing cabinet, a workbench with what looked like more testing equipment . . .

"What's behind that wall?" he asked after surveying the room a few moments.

"A fruit cellar. You can get to it from the pantry upstairs."

"Onward," Charlie muttered. "I want to see how the vacuum system works in the elevator."

Alexander explained that it was simplicity itself, one of the best features of the house, as far as marketing was concerned. The units fitted into the walls of every room. Each room had a control, or they could be put on a timer, individually or as a complete system. He touched the control button, a small bar under the musical staff that had looked merely decorative. At his touch the back panel detached itself and slid to the floor on casters that were hidden by the body of the machine. The whole unit was only a few inches high, about twelve inches by sixteen; the top was the same material as the elevator walls, a pastel blue plastic with a soft sheen. It began to move along the floor of the elevator; when it reached the end of the wall, it made a right-angled turn, continued, and repeated this at the next corner, humming softly.

On the wall that had housed it were two strips of metal to guide it back into place, and a round hole. Charlie nodded toward the housing. "It's emptied there?"

Alexander reached down and picked up the humming vacuum cleaner and turned it over. It stopped its operation. There was a brush visible, and the four ball-bearing-type wheels, and a round hole for the dirt to enter. Part of the mechanism was hidden by a metal plate. "See," Alexander said, pointing. "When it's cleaning, this hole is opened; the cover slides over it to expose the other one when it's in place to be emptied into the system. Here are the air vents to assist the suction phase."

The vents were almost invisible along the metal strips that edged the machine on both sides. Charlie studied the whole machine dubiously. "They actually think enough air could have been pulled through there to cause anoxia?"

Alexander put it down and touched the bar button again. The vacuum moved silently to the wall and slid back into place. The humming increased for a few seconds and then died out.

"That's how it should work," he said. "They had people measure the elevator and calculate the cubic feet of airspace and how much air can be pumped out in a minute, all that, and they said it could have happened, if the machine malfunctioned."

"And the man simply waited and died."

"They said that's what happened."

"You don't agree, I take it."

Alexander Randall bit his thumbnail and shifted on his feet, glanced at Constance, at Charlie, at the vacuum cleaner, and back at his thumb. "I don't know," he said at last.

"Okay. Can we get to the back of the elevator, the pipes, whatever?"

He looked relieved. "Sure. Best way is through the heating plant." They went back through the game room to the other side of the basement, into another large area.

They passed an oil-burning furnace, an equally large air conditioner, other oversized machines. There were rows of tanks on one side of the wall, with pipes from them vanishing behind panels. Chlorine, algaecide, other pool chemicals, carbon dioxide.

Charlie looked from the last tank to Alexander. "What's that for?"

"The root cellar, cold storage for apples, grapes, things like that. Carbon dioxide helps keep them longer. And some goes to the greenhouse. One part per thousand increase raises the yield by some incredible number. I don't know much about that. Rich knew, and there's a horticulturist working on the greenhouse."

Charlie's expression was murderous. "A man dies of anoxia,

you have tanks of carbon dioxide handy, and no one thinks to mention it! Why not?"

"The police tried to make a connection and couldn't," Alexander said, his nervousness making his voice almost shrill. "No one could see how it got from here to the elevator, or anywhere else. There's no way."

"I bet. Where do the pipes go?"

Alexander led them from the room into a narrow passage between the back of the house and the concrete wall of the swimming pool. The wall was a maze of pipes and ducts. The carbon dioxide pipe was thin stainless steel tubing near the top. In the center of the passage a steep flight of stairs went up; the pipes continued straight ahead. The largest duct stopped at the back of the elevator wall; other pipes went on through the end of the passageway.

"And that?" Charlie said, pointing to the end. "What's behind there?"

"The cold-storage room. You can't get to it from down here, only from the pantry off the kitchen."

Charlie examined the tubing again and could find no way the gas could have got from it to the elevator. It was unbroken, without a valve, without a seam. He turned and led the way now, up the narrow, steep stairs that took them to the back of the house near an entrance to the rear garden. Opposite the stairs was the door to the Jacuzzi room.

The whirlpool was ten feet long, six feet wide. There was a taut plastic cover over it, a roller at one end, grooves along the sides where the plastic cover was secured.

"Open it," Charlie ordered, and watched the unhappy young man go to the wall with a control panel. He touched a button and the cover slid back, rolled itself up, and vanished.

"Close it again." Charlie grunted, his eyes narrow as he watched the cover slide over the pool. Although it moved fast, it was not fast enough to keep anyone in who wanted out. But once in place, it would be almost impossible for anyone under it to move the cover out of the way. Less than an inch of space separated the cover and the surface of the water. He looked closely at the groove and tested the cover, and finally said with a scowl, "Let's move on."

"The cold-storage room?" Alexander asked. He had started to

chew on the other thumbnail. The rest of his nails were bitten to the quick.

"Naturally." Charlie took Constance's hand and squeezed it a little, reassuringly, he hoped. She had not said a word since their tour started, but she had seen everything he had, he knew, and later they would talk about it, compare notes. Her hand was cool in his.

They passed a dressing room and a lavatory, then found themselves in the corridor by the elevator doors again. Another hall led to an outside door. Alexander went down that one. Near the end of this passage there were doors on both sides, one to the kitchen, one to the pantry, which he opened. Just inside the pantry was another very heavy, insulated door. A draft of cold air flowed from below when he opened this one.

"It's really a refrigerator," Alexander said, leading the way down. "Gary called it a root cellar, but it's a refrigerator."

It was like entering an ice cave. The room was so heavily insulated that no sound penetrated; the walls were stainless steel, the floor plastic. Bins lined one wall, shelves the other. Two fluorescent ceiling fixtures cast a bluish light. Constance shivered and hugged her arms about herself. At the far end of the room were two stainless steel carts on wheels and another door, this one only about five feet high. Charlie spotted the steel tubing; it dipped down in this room and went behind the bins.

"Explain all this," he said brusquely, waving at the bins, the other door, the room in general.

"It's Rich's experiment," Alexander said. "The room is a low-oxygen, high-CO_2 environment. Not dangerous," he added hastily. "Fifteen percent oxygen, one percent carbon dioxide, it won't hurt you, at least not very fast. The bins are meant to hold special produce—grapes, pears, whatever, each in its own environment most ideally suited for long keeping. The bins are airtight, and the carbon dioxide mixture is controlled by the computer."

Charlie reached for one of the bins, and Alexander caught his arm.

"Don't do that. Look." There was a panel with symbols that meant nothing to Charlie. "That says this bin has a concentration of twelve percent carbon dioxide, and the temperature is forty-two. You don't want to open it until you exhaust the gas, you see."

Charlie examined other bins with other panels, all slightly different, all containing carbon dioxide. He pointed at the end door. "And that?"

"A dumbwaiter up to the pantry. The idea is that you can hang a side of beef down here, or bushels of fruits, stuff too heavy to lug down the stairs. So there's a dumbwaiter."

Charlie was looking at him with incredulity. "I hope we can open that," he said.

"Oh, sure. I know what you're thinking, Mr. Meiklejohn. I really do. But the police swarmed over this room and the bins and everything, and they couldn't figure out a way to make it add up. Look, this bin is empty." He pulled it open. It was about two feet deep and just as wide, narrowing at the bottom. He closed it again and went to the back of the room and opened the door to the dumbwaiter, a stainless steel box, two by three feet, about five feet high. The control here was simple: one black button for up, one for down. There was a bar handle on the outside of the door; the inside space was completely smooth without controls or handle.

Charlie was glaring at Alexander by now. "Let's have a look at it from upstairs," he growled. They left the cold-storage room gladly. Constance was shivering, and Charlie felt chilled through and through. The dumbwaiter in the pantry was behind another insulated door, and there were two control buttons on the wall. Alexander started to reach for one and Charlie shook his head. "In a second." He pulled the door open and examined the space. There were vents in the ceiling of the enclosure. He looked at Alexander questioningly.

"A duct leads to outside. In case of a leak, you know. Carbon dioxide is heavier than air, so it wouldn't go out the door at the top of the stairs, but it could flow into the dumbwaiter. If the dumbwaiter gets up here with any carbon dioxide inside it, it's automatically vented out before the door will open. At least, that's how it works when the computer's controlling it." He pointed to what looked like a thermometer without mercury on the side of the up and down buttons. "A safety backup sensor," he said. "It determines if there's carbon dioxide in the cage."

Charlie nodded and pushed the up button. Nothing happened.

"It won't work with the door open."

Charlie closed the door and tried again. The mechanism was soundless. In a moment the box had arrived; the door opened.

7

Neither Charlie nor Constance objected when Alexander began to hurry to finish the rest of the tour. He showed them how each doorway had been under observation during the game, and where the sensors in the floor were concealed under the carpeting so that no one could enter any of the rooms without being registered.

"It's sure to revolutionize security systems," the earnest young man said.

"Big Brother is alive and well," Charlie said sourly.

"If you have to have security, you might as well have good systems. Gary's room was upstairs. You want to see that?" He sounded defensive and a little belligerent.

"Is it stripped?" Charlie asked.

"You mean his personal things? Yes, but the furnishings are just like they were, and the computers he used are still there. It's not locked or anything."

"We'll manage by ourselves, but before you vanish, tell me something about the gadget Bruce was talking about, the control computer. He said as big as a cigarette pack. Is that about right? Exactly what could he do with such a small device?"

Alexander brightened again. "There were several of them, actually, each a dedicated computer." He looked from Constance to Charlie, as if testing if they could follow, then looked despairing again. "You know garage door openers? The hand-held signaling device that opens and closes them? That's a dedicated machine. Made to do one thing only. That's sort of like the hand-held computers for Smart House. Suppose someone fell down in one of the bedrooms and couldn't get to the door, or there was a fire, or any number of emergencies arose. One of the hand-held computers worked sort of like a master key, a skeleton key. It could open doors. Any of them. Another one could intercept, alter, or add to some of the basic functions of Smart House, like if the lights were timed to go off at eleven and you wanted them to stay on until later, you could do that. The basic instructions would still be functional, and the program would revert back to them, but temporarily you could control some things."

"What besides the lights?" Charlie asked patiently when Alexander's voice trailed off.

With a vague gesture Alexander indicated the entire house. "Just basic things like lights and the climate-control system, bath-water temperatures, things like that."

"Swimming pool temperature? Jacuzzi temperature?" Charlie asked softly.

Alexander fidgeted, his glance darting all around them. They were standing at the foot of the stairs, the glass wall behind him, Charlie and Constance facing it. Nervously he glanced over his shoulder. When he spoke again, his voice was nearly a whisper. "Mr. Meiklejohn, I honestly don't know what all he programmed into them. There were three of them, and I haven't been able to find a single one. They were always kept in the office downstairs, but after Gary decided to play the game, he kept them in his bedroom, and I haven't even seen them since last spring some-time. He could have added features, macros, I don't know any-thing about, or he could have put them somewhere and forgot about them. I just don't know. But no one else could have used them, sir. I mean, our program is unique, and each of them was programmed in a language that is brand-new. No one else here could have used them."

Charlie studied him with great curiosity. He could not decide yet whether this young man was simply ingenuous or extremely clever. "We'll talk more later, Alexander," he said then. "Right now I don't know enough to ask many questions. I'm sure I'll think of some."

"One question," Constance said as the young man turned away in evident relief. "First, you said he could have pro-grammed in features or macros. Would you explain those terms?"

Alexander shifted as if in agony. After a pause he said, "Let me describe one of the things we programmed in, to give you an idea. Suppose someone in room number three is a smoker. In each room there's a smoke alarm, of course, but they're all set to register minute amounts of smoke—cigarette smoke or pipes, whatever. We put in a conditional macro that says in effect that if the smoke detector is activated at a certain minimum level, then certain other steps are taken. I mean the air conditioner is reprogrammed to exhaust smoke, and change the air more often, things like that. That's a feature activated by a macro—it's a string of commands in a permanent file that is started by a signal, in this case the smoke detector. Of course, smoke from a real fire would cause other things to happen—the fire alarm, sprinkler system to start, things of that sort. But any string of commands can be activated by a key, or combination of keys, or any signal you program in. That's what the hand-held computers could do, send the signal."

Constance nodded thoughtfully. "I see. So the little computer could have been used to erase someone playing the game, just as Bruce suggested?"

He shrugged his thin shoulders. "Sure. That's the point. Gary could have programmed that in, or a number of other things. I don't know if he did, but he could have."

"Thanks for being our guide," Charlie said, taking Constance's arm. "Onward and upward. See you later."

Alexander darted away, and they went upstairs without speaking. At the top Constance said, "Charlie, you know carbon dioxide poisoning isn't the same as anoxia."

He grinned. "I thought I would have to explain that to you."

"But why did you go on about it down there?"

He put his finger on her lips. "I want them all to talk as freely as possible. If our killer needed inside info, who's a better bet than Alexander? Good God, he must have chips instead of gray matter in that skull of his. Look, there's someone new. More than one, in fact."

He was looking down into the atrium. Constance joined him and saw Milton with three people they had not met, two men and a woman. The woman was very beautiful.

"Let's take a quick look at Gary's room, and a quick look at the roof, and then go meet the newcomers."

Gary's suite was a disappointment. Without his possessions it was just another luxurious hotel suite. There were two rooms: a small office with two computers, and his bedroom. There was a walk-in closet, and a bathroom twice the size of the one in the room Charlie and Constance had. Charlie gazed around with dissatisfaction. "We'll get back to it," he said. "Now the roof."

This was a disappointment also. The mist had grown so dense that the ocean had vanished into it. Little of the grounds was visible. The dome was glass, the flooring plastic, and, Charlie realized, it was constructed of solar collectors. A small redwood building housed the elevator and held many outdoor collapsible chairs and several small tables. It was cold and wet up there; they did not linger.

They took the elevator back to the ground floor and entered the atrium, where a small group had gathered and was having drinks at the bar. The odor of chlorine and gardenias and blooming orange and lemon trees made the room stifling to Constance. As they approached the bar, she realized that she hated Smart House. As beautiful as it was, as modern and comfortable and convenient, it was also too inhuman in scale, in expertly selected furnishings and colors, and in spy eyes everywhere that might or might not be watching.

"Constance, Charlie," Milton Sweetwater greeted them. "Laura and Harry Westerman, and Jake Kluge, and now you've met us all."

It used to be, Charlie thought almost aggrievedly as they all shook hands and made quick, mutual assessments, that businessmen going into middle age had certain similarities, a bit of a paunch for example, or a receding hairline, or something. Here were two more healthy specimens—Jake Kluge was gangly and strong, with straight brown hair that could stand cutting and was a bit limp. His eyes were pale blue behind contact lenses. Harry Westerman was a mountain climber, according to Milton, and he looked it. He was rock hard all over, wiry, with the sort of muscularity that never turned to flab because there was absolutely no fat coating the muscles and underlying the skin. His eyes were piercing and dark, and now looked irritable and impatient. And Laura Westerman was a knockout. She kept his hand less than a second too long, but he knew it and she knew it. He had seen her, or women who could pass for her, for years in New York, usually carrying hatboxes, makeup bags, hurrying to meet this photographer, or make that modeling event, denying themselves any calories more than an allotted number carefully arrived at with the aid of a nutritionist. And he had seen the husbands, he thought soberly; either they were eaten alive by jealousy, or they were so involved in their own endless affairs that they were oblivious to the fact that their wives were saying yes to every man they met.

"You aren't afraid of the house, I hope," Jake Kluge said to Constance. "We agreed at our last meeting that except for basic systems that we're all familiar with, nothing would be turned on this weekend. There's no more to worry about than the elevator in any building in Manhattan."

Before Constance could reassure him, Charlie said, "That's a damn shame, in a way. I'd love to see this joint in operation."

Harry Westerman turned abruptly and went behind the bar. "We're having martinis. What would you like?"

"That sounds fine," Charlie said, after glancing at Constance, who nodded. He looked about the garden and waved at it all. "How about the lights in here? On a timer, or do you have to go around and flick them on and off?"

"There's a light switching board," Milton Sweetwater said, glancing uneasily at Harry, who was shaking the drinks. "Or you could do them individually."

Harry poured two more drinks and put them on the bar counter. "Usually they're under the control of Smart House," he said. "Like everything else." Charlie handed a glass to Constance, lifted his own, and sipped, and Harry asked in a voice as hard as everything else about him, "Exactly what do you think you can learn in a weekend, Mr. Meiklejohn? The police held us here for days, and they've been coming around ever since. I voted against bringing you in, you should know."

"I already know some things the police weren't told," Charlie said easily. "I know about the game, and I know about the handheld computers that could override the main system. And now I know that the decision wasn't unanimous to open yet another investigation. I'd say I'm making a certain amount of progress."

Harry's expression darkened, his eyes narrowed, and Laura laughed softly. "Harry did come around," she said. "By the time we thrashed it all out, he agreed along with everyone else."

Harry motioned for her to stop, and Charlie filed away the fact that in spite of her feigned disregard for him, she seemed uncommonly aware of his gestures, his frowns.

"What hand-held computer are you talking about?" Harry demanded.

Charlie looked from him to Jake, who shook his head. "Gary didn't demonstrate one for either of you?" He looked at Laura. "Or you?"

Her laughter was brittle this time. She moved to stand by Harry behind the bar and began to look over bottles there. "You might as well add something else to what you know that we didn't mention to the police. Gary loved secrecy more than anything else in life. If he had such a toy, he would have guarded it very jealously, at least until he was ready for the big production, which was to take place on Monday. Isn't that about right, darling?" she said to Harry mockingly.

"All I know is that he didn't tell me about it."

"I'll be damned," Jake Kluge murmured. "Of course he would have had such a thing, a number of them. Where are they? Have you seen them? Does Alexander have them?"

Charlie shook his head. " 'Fraid not. Alexander says he can't find them. Why do you say, of course?"

"We should have figured it out," Jake said. "Obviously you'd have an override control. Another ace in the hole for Gary. But they must be around somewhere. Did Alexander search for them?"

"He said he couldn't find them. Why are they important, Mr. Kluge?"

Jake started, then grinned. "Jake," he said. "And you're Charlie, and she's Constance. Okay? You've brought us something already, Charlie. You see, some things the damn house was doing we haven't been able to figure out, and this could explain why. If he was overriding the main system, he could have made it perform in certain ways. Harry, let's go find Alexander. Thanks, Charlie."

Harry came out from the bar and they started to walk out together.

"Before you take off," Charlie said. "Just one thing. You

weren't eager to open this can of worms, I take it. Either of you. Why did you change your minds?"

Jake shrugged. "I never said I was against it."

"But weren't you?"

He regarded Charlie curiously for a moment, then nodded. "I think we just want to put it behind us, get on with company business. And, as Harry said, we have little faith in anything coming of a new investigation."

"Did the house do it?" Charlie asked very softly.

"For Christ's sake!" Harry snapped. He started to move again, but Jake caught his arm.

"Wait a minute," Jake said. "We hired him. The company hired him to ask questions, and we agreed to answer them. No, Charlie, not in the way you imply by your question. The house couldn't have intended to kill anyone."

"I didn't bring up intentions," Charlie murmured. "But, Jake, Harry, if the house didn't do it, then a person did. You want to put that behind you, too? Leave it alone if we determine that a person killed two men?"

Harry looked murderously at Milton Sweetwater, as if the lawyer had been responsible for making him change his mind. "Bellringer could go under," he said sharply. "I don't give a damn who did it. I just want it settled for once and for all so we can get on with things. Does that satisfy you?"

Charlie nodded. "Yes indeed. Jake?"

"You didn't bring up intentions, but neither did you bring up accidental deaths. That is the third alternative."

"I'll keep it in mind," Charlie said agreeably. "And if we decide it was a person? What will that do to the company's outlook?"

Jake shook his head. "I don't know. None of us knows. We could all be ruined one way or the other, but we do know that if we don't clear up this mess, we'll certainly be ruined. We'll cooperate, Charlie. Is that the real question?"

"Partly. Partly. See you later." He turned to Constance. "Let's go unpack and wash our hands."

Milton mentioned that dinner would be at seven, and Laura watched Charlie take Constance's hand with a slight smile. She looked at him and wiggled her fingers in farewell.

Going up the stairs, Constance chuckled softly and Charlie

made a snorting sound. "You won't think it's funny when I sling her over my shoulder and take off for Mexico."

"No, dear," she said.

In their room again, she unpacked while Charlie went through the contents of the envelope Milton had provided. He studied the beautifully drawn floor plans for a long time. The articles of incorporation looked intimidating, and the forensics reports chilled him too much to dwell on before dinner. He pursed his lips over the list of toys that had been designated murder weapons, then folded that paper and put it in his pocket. When he looked up from the papers on the desk, Constance was standing at the window gazing out at heavy fog that rose and fell, revealed, concealed, teased. He joined her and put his arm around her waist.

"What do you think?" she asked.

"They're like passengers on a ship that was being tossed in a storm with a mad captain. Any of them might have wanted Gary overboard, I guess. Milton must want the company to be as stable as IBM or Ma Bell; he doesn't like disorder. Jake is in line for power, money, prestige, whatever goes along with being head honcho now. Harry could be hiding a case of terminal jealousy under that Mount Rushmore exterior. Bruce? A nut, also jealous for other reasons, in debt. Beth wanted out from slavery. Laura? We'll see. I don't have a doubt in the world that she had a case, too." He squeezed her shoulder. "How'm I doing?"

She laughed softly. "A-plus. They're a strange group," she said thoughtfully. "I don't think they would do a thing about either death if it weren't for company profits."

"Want to bet that one of them will bring up the possibility that a stranger got in that night, and at least two of the others will back up the idea?"

"You know very well that I am morally opposed to gambling," she said primly. "Besides, I already picked Bruce to raise the possibility, and his mother to back it. Charlie, don't you think it's strange that Alexander didn't mention the little computers before? Of the three men who really worked on the house and understood the entire system, he's the only one left. He probably can make the computers do whatever they're capable of doing without any effort at all. Don't you think so?"

"I think," he said grimly, "the only way you're going to get anything out of that twerp is by nailing him down and poking him with a sharp stick from time to time. Well, ready for another go-round with them all?"

Bruce said at dinner, "You know, it's quite possible that some- one actually got in that night, someone not invited, I mean."

Maddie nodded emphatically. "Of course, it's possible. I never believed in that total security system."

Constance looked at Charlie brightly; he sighed.

"Jake, Harry? Would it have been possible?" he asked, pre- tending to be unaware that Alexander had stopped his fork mid- way to his mouth, that he had started to speak.

Jake shook his head. "I doubt it. The police spent hours trying out the system, first at the gate on the hill, then at the various entrances to Smart House proper. You just couldn't get in and out unregistered. There's a log of every entrance and exit that was made. They tried to get around it, just to see if anyone could have done so."

"How about the roof?" Bruce demanded.

"The balconies," Maddie said. "All those balconies! Anyone could walk in!"

This time Alexander spoke before Charlie could interfere. "No way! That's one of the systems we were ready to market, prac- tically."

"Practically?" Charlie asked. "You mean it wasn't complete?"

"It was still too specific," Alexander muttered. "We were in the process of generalizing it before we actually showed it. A few more months, that's all it needed. It was working back in May for the specific conditions, though."

"That's the hitch," Harry said angrily. "It would have to be custom tailored for each individual or company, and that means time and expense. A few months? I think a year or more."

"Do you think it might have failed to register an intruder that night?" Charlie asked him.

"Sure. Especially since Gary had the override system. He could have turned the whole thing off. We're talking about a system that controls this whole house, the grounds, the green- house, everything, and whatever the main system can do, the hand-held computer can start or stop."

"Someone could have come up from the beach," Maddie said with a touch of desperation in her voice.

"Maddie, stop it!" Milton said, but his voice was gentle. "We all know no one got in here that night!"

"Why not from the beach?" Charlie asked thoughtfully.

"Because we're on a headland here, and at high tide you can't get around it," Milton said. "There's a cove with rocky cliffs on the both ends, completely cut off at high tide. The police looked into that."

Charlie turned to Bruce. "You said the roof. How could anyone get up there?"

Bruce glanced at Harry, who collected mountains, then away quickly. "I examined that rock wall today. It's climbable. A good climber could go right up the back wall to the roof."

Harry nodded. "That's true. I looked at it too, from a different angle, of course. Not just a good climber. Anyone who wanted to go up could do it. But once on top, Bruce, you still have to pass through a scanner and a sensor in the floor." His voice was vicious. "Okay, Gary or Rich, or someone else, could have turned off security, but they didn't. There's a record of movements that would show an intruder. And don't even pretend an outsider could have got his hands on the system, and not just that, but have time to learn the system and reprogram it."

"It's been my experience," Charlie said comfortably then, "that practically every action made by people in close quarters is noticed by someone, even in a house as big as this."

"We were taken over that whole evening by the police several times," Laura snapped. "I am sick to death of thinking about it all, who was where, when. No one saw anything!"

"I think people saw more than they realized then. The police accepted your statements because they had not been let in on the fact of the game, and I have been. You were all watching each other closely, I'll bet. In fact, if you had admitted how closely to the police, it might have appeared suspicious. Now you can all admit it freely. What I propose is that you reenact the game as it developed back in May. Going through the movements probably will stimulate memories in a way that just talking didn't do."

"No!" Maddie said, and she started to get to her feet. She groped for the table and knocked over her glass of wine and sank down again staring at it in horror. "Look what I've done. Look what you made me do!"

Gently Constance said to her, "You didn't play the game then and you certainly don't have to play it this time."

"No one has to play it," Laura Westerman said. "If that damn computer is turned on again, I'm going home." She glared at her husband. "I'm not even a shareholder. I don't have to agree to anything."

"But we need you," Charlie protested. "You have to take Mrs. Elringer's one vote. Isn't that what you did before?"

"Gary insisted," she said sharply. "He didn't give anyone a choice, and another thing you might as well know is that no one here dared cross him in any way. No one! He wanted to play his insane game and everyone said good, let's kill each other for fun! If I had turned him down, Harry would have bitched for months! Does that satisfy you? You, I'm afraid, don't have that kind of power over us."

"Of course not," Charlie said in a placating way. "I wouldn't want that kind of power." He regarded them all broodingly. "I confess I'm still trying to figure out why you all went along with it, why you all played for votes."

There was a lengthy silence. Finally Jake cleared his throat. "It was an important meeting. Gary and Rich, and Alexander, of course, and a few others in the company were researching artificial intelligence in their computer systems in Smart House. Making some real breakthroughs, apparently. But others among us saw it as a black hole that would suck the company dry in no time. It's the sort of research that needs government grant money, big money, not a small company like ours to back it. It was an important meeting. The idea of gaining enough votes to have an influence was irresistible to many of us."

"He was willing to risk so much?" Charlie asked. "Would he have gone along with a negative vote? One that forced him to stop his line of research?"

"It wasn't a risk!" Alexander cried. "He knew that if they all just gave it a chance, they'd see what he had accomplished here. He had done most of the things he had set out to do, and that weekend would have proven he was on the right track. Whoever makes the breakthrough in linking a digital computer with an analog computer in a comprehensive, parallel system that is both logic-directed and goal-directed will be the intellectual hero of the century. Gary was doing it!''

"That sounds like big bucks," Charlie murmured.

Jake laughed suddenly and tossed his napkin down on the table. "Charlie," he said, "that must be the understatement of the century. And that's why we never seriously considered that any of us could have murdered him. That's what you're talking about, of course. Murder. By one of us. But he was the goose who could produce the golden eggs, you see. And while the rest of us don't match him in intellectual capacity, neither is there an idiot at this table. We're in the process now of reviewing all the work he did here, trying to debug some of it with Alexander's help, and the help of others who came in very skeptical and are true believers now. If we can stay afloat, the systems in this damn house right now will mean big bucks, very big bucks, and there wasn't a one of us who didn't know that by midafternoon of that Saturday, many hours before Gary died. That's our dilemma, Charlie, in a nutshell.''

"Then there shouldn't be any real objection to going through the motions of playing the game again, just to see if someone spots something not quite in line with what memory serves up."

Bruce shoved his chair back. "Okay. Now we go to the living room for coffee and hear the game rules, just like we did then. You going to chicken out, Laura?''

She raked him with a contemptuous look. "I meant it. If that computer is turned on, I leave."

"We won't use the game program," Charlie said. "What I propose, actually, is that I'll take the part of the computer. Coffee, you said? In the living room? I'll tell you what I have in mind over coffee.''

8

The coffee service was on a sideboard in the living room; this time they all helped themselves. Charlie waited until they were settled and then said, "I asked Mrs. Ramos to bring out the conference notebooks and pencils, and here they are." A stack of yellow legal pads and a pewter mug of pencils were on an end table. He picked them all up and began to hand them out. As he moved along, he asked pleasantly, "Whose idea was it to erase the game from disk, by the way?" No one spoke. "Let's try it this way," he said. "Was it before the cops came, during, or after?"

"After," Alexander said. "They were gone by then."

"I see. So while they were here, you simply kept mum about the game and the record of movements." He finished giving out the note pads and sat in a deep chair the color of midnight; it was so soft, so comfortable, it was almost too sensuous. He resisted the impulse to stroke the arm. "Where were you when the decision was made to erase everything having to do with the game?"

"The library," Alexander said. "They said they would send someone down from Portland, a special detective, and we should all stay here until he came and asked questions. We had a meeting. We didn't know where we stood legally, the company and all, I mean."

Charlie nodded sympathetically. "I can imagine. So you were at the long conference table. Where Mrs. Ramos got the note pads, I understand. And someone said, let's get rid of evidence of any game. Is that how it was?"

"You know it wasn't like that!" Laura Westerman cried shrilly. "No one thought of it as evidence of anything except stupidity. I said we'd be on every front page of every tabloid in the country. They'd make us all look utterly ridiculous."

"So they would," Charlie agreed, and waited.

Jake shrugged. "I could have been the first to voice the suggestion. I simply don't remember. I do remember that suddenly we were all talking about it. The police had the disk with our movements, remember, from the Smart House security program, a totally different system. But we all thought all our movements were on it. At least," he added flatly, "that's what I thought. And, at our meeting concerning you, we agreed to provide you with a printout of the record the police took." He looked questioningly at Milton, who nodded.

"I have it," Charlie admitted. "But if Gary had an override system, I wonder how accurate it can be. Anyway, to get to our reenactment of the game, what I want you to do is try to retrace your movements that had anything to do with the game. When you found out who your victim was, when you got your weapon, what it was, when and if you used it."

"Starting when?" Harry demanded. "I for one can't provide you with a minute-by-minute account of my movements for the whole twenty-four hours. Who could?"

"Just the highlights for now," Charlie said soothingly. "Victim, witness, weapon, time. You'll be surprised how much you recall once you actually start something like this."

"What difference does it make?" Harry insisted. "This is more damn nonsense!"

Charlie regarded him soberly. "Someone was playing the game for very high stakes. Someone found out about the override gadgets and used them. Do you know who that was, Harry? One of you knows for sure, and others know more than you realize. If there was a murderer here, someone, or more than one of you, saw enough to point at that person."

"My God!" Beth said with a moan. "We were paranoid then, but this . . . this is monstrous!"

"Murder is monstrous," Charlie agreed. He surveyed them coldly. Maddie's face was chalky, her hands shaking too hard to hold the pencil, coffee, anything else. At Charlie's words Laura had put her hand on her husband's arm, and Harry had shrugged it off again and was contemplating his shoes with a distant hard look. Jake was watching Charlie closely, his expression remote and unreadable. Alexander twisted his pencil, bit the eraser, twisted it again and again. Only Milton Sweetwater looked resigned. He broke the silence.

"Charlie, what do you suspect? What do you know already?" he asked.

"I know that something's wonky with the printout of movements starting with the opening gambit. If you hadn't withheld evidence from the police, they would know it, too. Gary had you all in here Friday evening and outlined the game rules, then he left. The printout shows him going up in the elevator, then into his room. It does not show him leaving it again that night, and yet I know he was on the first floor later, playing the game, trying to kill Bruce." He laughed harshly. "A magic act. The printout shows him entering his room a second time that night." He looked them all over again. No one had moved. "Unless you people have secret clones that you haven't bothered to tell me about yet, either the system didn't register all his movements, or else he pulled off an impossible stunt. Didn't the police ask to see the entire printout?"

Alexander shook his head. Suddenly the pencil snapped in his fingers, making a cracking sound that was too loud. He cleared his throat. "I didn't look at the entire printout a single time. No one thought of going back to Friday. What for? The police wanted it from Saturday from after dinner until they arrived. No one asked about any movements before that evening. Why would anyone?"

"Exactly," Charlie said dryly.

Harry jumped to his feet, flung down his note pad, and glared at Jake. "The whole thing's a fucking lie! That record doesn't mean a goddamn thing! Proving that no one was on the elevator with Rich, that no one went into the Jacuzzi with Gary! All a fucking lie! See what keeping our mouths shut about the goddamn game got us!"

"The program's full of bugs," Bruce said murderously. "I knew it! That bastard! That goddamn bastard! All that money down the drain! You can't trust any of it! I knew it from the start."

"It isn't!" Alexander yelled and leaped to his feet, his hands clenched. "If Gary turned it off, that's one thing, but the program didn't make a mistake or lie. It works, damn it!" His voice was shrill.

Constance was watching them all. When Maddie took a deep breath and got up, she stood up also.

"I don't feel very well," Maddie said faintly. "I'll just go lie down a bit."

"Let me go with you," Constance said. "I want to go up for a few minutes, too."

The voices continued to shout as they left the room. As Laura's high-pitched voice chimed in, Constance wondered if Charlie had pushed them too hard. She had flashed him a message— she would try to get Maddie to talk—and had been acknowledged by such a brief, tiny nod that it would have passed unnoticed by anyone else, she knew. All those geniuses, she thought then, had performed exactly as Charlie had planned, and now he would sit back and watch and listen and when the time was right, he would prod them again. And one of them would say something meaningful. At the stairs Maddie turned without hesitation and started up. No one appeared to want to take the elevator in this house.

Halfway up the stairs, out of sight and hearing of the others, Constance said, "Mrs. Elringer, you can stop acting now."

Maddie paused and looked at her sharply.

"I mean the drinking act," Constance said, and took her arm. They started up again. "I've been watching you all evening. You haven't had as much alcohol as I've had, I'd say."

"They all keep wanting me to take sides," Maddie said in a low voice. "Gary's been dead for under three months, and they're fighting like dogs. Like dogs."

Constance nodded. "As long as they think you're feeling the alcohol, they leave you alone, is that it?"

"I guess so," Maddie admitted.

"Can we talk a few minutes?"

"I really am tired," she said. They stopped outside a door; she reached for the knob.

"And you're terrified, too," Constance said gently. "Perhaps you should talk a little."

Maddie's face crinkled and tears welled in her eyes. Constance leaned past her to open the door and they went inside the bedroom.

"He should have been an only child," Maddie said a few minutes later. She had gone to the bathroom and washed her face and was in one of the chairs at the table before the windows. Constance was seated in the opposite chair. The drapes were drawn, the room lighted only by a dim wall lamp. "He was a difficult child. Very difficult. So precocious, of course, but Bruce . . . He was only six and didn't understand. A bad age to bring in a new baby, they tell me. He had been the baby of the family so long, and he was brilliant, of course, but suddenly there was someone new who was even more brilliant. There wasn't a thing Bruce could do that Gary couldn't do better, from the time he was three or four. He was Bruce's equal at first, and then surpassed him. In all ways. They fought so much. Car trips were hellish, staying home with them was worse." She shook her head, her eyes closed, her forehead furrowed.

"He didn't realize how much he could hurt people," she said. "His father, me, Bruce, then Beth, everyone eventually. It wasn't malice. He wasn't evil. He just didn't know. He took what he needed from people and when he had all there was, he turned his back on them without another thought."

She sighed deeply and became still now, wrapped in memories that twisted her face in pain. After a moment, Constance said, "Yet you all remained loyal to him. You all went into business with him, kept protecting him even after he was grown up."

"He was always so vulnerable," Maddie said. "He just didn't know what effect he had on people. That night when he talked about the game, he was sincere. To him it was a game. I had a premonition," she said nearly in a whisper. "I don't even believe in premonitions, but suddenly I knew there would be a tragedy because of the game. I just knew it. Everyone had so much hurt, I just knew they'd all want Gary to be their victim. But it was more than that. I had the feeling of horror. I said I wouldn't have anything to do with it. I wouldn't. Tonight when your husband began talking about the game again, it came back, that awful feeling of horror, of terror."

When Constance went down to the living room again, Charlie looked up at her questioningly.

"She's resting."

His look said, you did fine; hers asked how it was going. He nodded slightly and she went to the sideboard for coffee. Apparently no one else had left yet. There were sheets of the yellow notepads on tables, on the floor by chairs, several on the coffee table Charlie was using as a work surface. It did not surprise her at all to find them doing it Charlie's way.

"Okay," he said, consulting his own notes. "It's after one. Gary has just tried to kill you, but your mother can't witness since she's not in the game. Right?"

Bruce's expression was petulant, his voice a whine when he said that was right. Constance watched him, wondered if he had developed that attitude in reaction to a genius brother. Was this the real Bruce, or the man who shouted and cursed and screamed obscenities almost randomly?

"Jake didn't cooperate," Bruce went on. "He ducked out when he saw what Gary was up to."

Jake nodded at his account and made a note on his paper. Beth wrote briefly on hers. Bruce finished writing something and they all handed the sheets to Charlie, who added them to the growing stack.

"Anyone else?" When no one spoke, he asked Jake, "Why didn't you witness for Gary?"

"By then I'd begun to get a feeling about the magnitude of his accomplishment in Smart House and I wanted to talk to him, but seriously, not with the game in the way. I thought we were heading for a talk, but at the door to the television room, he said something like 'Gotcha' when he saw Bruce. I realized I'd be witness, and, frankly, I decided not to help Gary win the game if I could help it. I ducked out."

"Where did you go?"

"To the garden for a nightcap, then up to my room with my drink."

"You didn't see him again that night?"

Jake shook his head.

Charlie turned to Bruce again. "Where did you go?"

"I was going to go to the kitchen for a snack, but he kept following me, yelling, and I got on the elevator instead and went up to my room and stayed. I think he turned and went on into the kitchen."

Charlie frowned at the printout he had opened on the table. He tapped his eraser on it absently and said, "According to the official printout, Gary went into his room on the second floor at ten-ten Friday night and never came out again. And he went into the kitchen at one-twenty-five and never came out of it again, either. Maybe the rules he had were different from the ones the rest of you were using."

"How about when he got that damn dagger?" Bruce demanded and got up to look at the printout over Charlie's shoulder.

Charlie shook his head. "Nothing." He looked at Alexander thoughtfully. "Could he have programmed the computer to erase selected activities and still allow him to open doors?"

Miserably Alexander said yes.

"All right. Could he have programmed it not to record his movements when he was with another person? Jake here, for example."

Alexander nodded.

"I doubt that," Jake protested. "I mean, even if he'd been able to do it, why? It was a game, for God's sake! You just don't understand about him and games! What in God's name would be the point in programming a game like that and then cheating?"

"Don't know," Charlie said. "Could someone else have programmed in the same instructions, Alexander?"

The young man blanched, then flushed brightly. "I could have done it, or Rich. No one else knew the system yet. No one here, anyway. There were a couple of others back in Palo Alto who worked on it and could have done it."

"Okay," Charlie said then in his most pleasant voice, the voice that sometimes gave Constance a chill. What had he just learned? she wondered. "So you're all safely inside your rooms now. We don't know where Gary was. What came next?"

"Are you really going to make us go through every minute?" Laura asked in disbelief. "This is crazy. What possible difference can it make?"

"Don't know that either," Charlie said easily. "You get the picture of what I'm doing, you could shorten all this by trying to fill in the time before we drag it out second by second. When and where you got killed, who you killed, and who witnessed it; then backtrack, and go forward. If there wasn't any more activity that night, let's move on. Now, it's morning."

Minute by minute, encounter by encounter, he took them through the day. Now and then he stopped someone to ask a question, but for most of it, he simply listened. When Beth mentioned the blueprints she had seen at Rich Schoen's elbow on Saturday, he stopped her.

"I guess Rich carried the foam club rolled up in them," she said. "That's the weapon he used on Gary later."

"Where are the blueprints now?"

They all glanced at each other, and then Milton Sweetwater shrugged. "In one of the offices, presumably."

"Rich brought them up from the Palo Alto office," Alexander said. "He was going to show them at the meeting on Monday. Usually they'd be down there, not in Smart House any longer. I don't know where they are."

Charlie nodded and let them continue describing the afternoon.

He stopped them again later. "So far no one has reported an encounter with Gary. Would that have been normal? It's nearly three in the afternoon."

Beth nodded. "He stayed up most of the night and never got up before twelve or one, and he liked being alone then for breakfast. I didn't give it a thought not to see him around."

"That's why we eat dinner at seven," Laura said with a malicious smile. "Gary wanted it over and done with by nine so he could go to work."

They went on recounting their adventures as killers and victims up to the time they gathered for cocktails, when Charlie stopped them.

"Let's call it a day," he said. "Papers, please, if you have any notes of times, observations, anything else. We'll finish this tomorrow." It was nearly midnight.

9

Beth stared at him in dismay. Leave it now? She looked around at the others. Jake and Milton were in a huddle whispering. Bruce hovered nearby as Charlie gathered up the loose sheets of paper. Laura had started to go out, apparently realized that no one else was leaving, and was now standing near Harry at the sideboard. Harry looked so tightly wound that a touch would make him explode; Laura did not get close enough to touch him.

Charlie glanced at them all and shuffled papers. Constance had not moved from her chair.

Abruptly Jake and Milton finished their dialogue and approached Charlie. Milton spoke in a commanding voice. "Charlie, it's obvious, to me at least, that you've decided murder was committed; those two deaths weren't accidental." No one else moved. "If you're up to continuing tonight, I strongly urge that we do so. If anything is going to come out of all this, it would be better to have it out tonight. If we have a murderer here, and if anyone did see him do anything suspicious, that person may be in danger. I, for one, intend to secure my door somehow tonight."

"I agree absolutely," Jake said. "You've managed to scare some of us to death," he said levelly. "I'm not willing to leave it here."

Charlie held up his hands. "Fine with me. Objections anyone?" No one moved. "Let's take a break, say twenty minutes. We could use some fresh coffee, maybe some sandwiches. During the break maybe you could all just jot down the next game killings, who the victim was, the weapon, witness, the next victim, time, whatever is appropriate. It will save time. And meanwhile, Alexander, would you mind showing us where Rich Schoen worked here? Did he have his own office?"

Alexander jumped up, evidently relieved to be able to do something. Before he could speak, Harry said, "We all know damn well that Rich wouldn't have let himself be suffocated in that elevator. And this surprise that one of us might be a murderer, bullshit! We've known that too. We've always known it," he said harshly, "and we chose to pretend not to." He scowled at Jake with bitterness. "But there is a place where the air can be exhausted in seconds. Those growing chambers in the greenhouse. They were designed airtight, with an exhaust system, a gas-pumping system."

"I thought of that," Jake said with disgust. "It's the same problem. Why would Rich stay there while someone went over and turned the knob, or punched keys in the computer, or any other damn thing? He designed it! He knew what it could do!"

"But if the killer had the hand-held computer, he could have controlled everything in the greenhouse, too. A push of a button would have done it," Harry said. "Remember, later that night a pesticide was released in there. Things got smashed up. I think the killer did that to cover his trail. Maybe Rich did struggle and something got broken earlier. No one could have known after things got so messed up."

Charlie turned to Alexander.

The young man nodded unhappily. "It could have been programmed to do anything like that," he said, and then added almost pleadingly, "but it would take time. Time to learn the system, the language, the program for that function. It wouldn't be like turning a light on or off."

Softly Harry said, "For Gary it would have been exactly like that. Who had more time than he to program whatever he wanted into it? Who else would Rich have gone into the chamber for?"

"Oh, God!" Beth whispered. "Gary? Why?"

"I don't know why. But who else could have set things up in advance? Just one of those three, Rich, Gary, or Alexander."

Alexander looked helplessly from Harry to Charlie. His face crinkled as if he might burst into tears. He shook his head. "We didn't. Wreck our one dream? Ruin everything we planned for?" He shook his head harder.

"And then our heroic, athletic Gary picked up Rich and moved him to the house, down the hall, hoping all the time that no one noticed that he was carrying a hundred-ninety-pound dead man, of course," Jake said with heavy sarcasm. "He put him in the elevator, and went to the Jacuzzi and threw himself in out of remorse, and conveniently covered it so the sight would not be offensive to anyone. And somewhere along the way, he disposed of the little computers, just to muddy the issue." He started to move toward the door. "I volunteer to make coffee and sandwiches, but I want a witness, to make sure I don't add arsenic to the sugar bowl."

"That's not funny!" Laura screamed at him. "Do you have a better idea of what happened? At least Harry's trying."

Harry didn't even look at her when he snapped, "Just shut the fuck up!"

Charlie motioned toward the door and Constance got up and walked out with him and Alexander.

"This is awful," Alexander said glumly. "Worse than I thought it could get."

"You think so?" Charlie asked in surprise. "I thought it was going pretty well myself." He was grinning.

Alexander looked at him in shocked disapproval. So young, Constance thought. So bright and so ignorant.

"I'll help with coffee," Beth said. "If we can find it."

"I'll go, too," Laura said. "I know where it is."

"I think you know too much about Smart House," Bruce said suddenly. "You did last spring, too. You'd been here before, hadn't you? You finally got around to Gary, didn't you?"

The look Laura gave him was venomous. Before she could respond, Milton took her arm, not very gently, and turned her away from Bruce. "I want a word with you," he said.

Beth found herself studying Harry; he looked metallic. Even his eyes. He did that where Laura was concerned, she thought, with a chill. Somehow he made himself absent; he became iron or some other cold dark metal that reflected nothing of what he was feeling. Bruce glared at Laura and Milton, swung around as if seeking a new target for his anger, and Harry turned his granite face toward him. Bruce stopped all movements and, after a moment, stalked silently from the living room. Again Beth examined Harry and knew that if he looked at her with that expression she would flee also. It wasn't even that he looked particularly threatening, she thought; it was worse than that. He looked inhuman.

Beth realized in surprise that she felt sorry for Harry. She had never liked him—he had always seemed too brusque, too single-minded—but now she sympathized. No one should be forced into inhumanity. She found herself wondering what he was like when he was happy, when he was nearing the peak of a new mountain, maybe, and knew he had won. She never had seen that side of him.

Then Jake touched her arm, and she went out with him.

"A lot of unpleasant things are going to be brought up the next day or so," Jake said in a low voice as they drew near the kitchen. "I understand the necessity, and it has to be, I suppose, but I'm sorry that came out like that."

She shook her head. "It's all right. I knew." She had known, just not the details, like when it started or how long it lasted. But she had known. Then she said, "You're right, though. Things will come out now. We'll all remember things we'd forgotten, see them in a new light. Charlie is a bit scary, isn't he?"

"Smart. He knows what he's doing."

They had stopped outside the kitchen door. She glanced at him and said almost apologetically, "While we were recalling the game, I remembered how angry with you I was, not that you killed me, but that you were enjoying the game."

He looked somber and troubled now. "You were right about it. You, Maddie, even Harry. That night, when we met in the upstairs hall and went down together, I was as tongue-tied as a junior-high-school boy. I thought you were still sore with me, and I was full to bursting with excitement about the house, having fun with the game."

She smiled faintly, also remembering how stilted and awkward that brief encounter had been, how relieved she had been when he left her in the wide corridor near the television room.

"And then Gary laughed," he said in a harsher voice. "Come on, let's get coffee and stuff."

"Talk about Rich," Charlie had said to Alexander on the way to Rich's office. It had been painful, but eventually Alexander told them a little, in stumbling, halting, even agonized phrases. He told them about the team within a team that Gary had started to assemble more than five years ago. Constance glanced at him sharply and he shrugged. "I was still in school," he said. "Any-way, Gary had this vision of Smart House, an integrated system using both kinds of computers—"

"No more computer talk," Charlie interrupted. "He put to-gether a team. Go on."

"Okay. But that's the basic idea . . . Okay. Rich was a leading developer of a particular CAD—a computer-assisted drawing and drafting program for architects," he added hastily. "He was writ-ten up in the journals. So Gary gave him a call and they met and talked, and Rich joined the team. Gary even gave him a per-centage of his shares because he knew the money would get tight down the road, and he wanted to make certain Rich was in to stay if things got rough. That wasn't even necessary, but Gary did things like that. He gave me shares when I came in. He told me it was because when the others knew what he was up to, they might try to oust us, the team, and this way they really couldn't."

"Right. So now the house was about finished, Rich's work about done. What was he going to do next?"

Alexander's pain increased. His voice dropped to a near mum-ble. "That was a problem." He led them through the basement, past the garish arcade games, the pool table, toys. His hand trailed over the glossy surfaces as he passed them, but he did not give any of them a glance. "At first the plan was to build Smart House and start showing it to hotel people, resort people, developers, building management people. They could buy the whole system, or just a part of it. Rich was going to manage all that, package the separate programs, or integrate them, what-ever. But Gary kept changing things. He hated the idea of having groups come for demonstrations. He decided Beth could be the hostess for demonstrations, when it came to that. He hated peo-ple he didn't know, and didn't want any part of that aspect. But he liked working here with his own projects. He seemed to think he could keep doing that and just avoid everyone."

"And you? You were after the artificial intelligence aspect of it, too, weren't you?"

"Yeah. Gary and me." He waved toward a door. "That's where Rich had his office."

They went inside. It was another spacious room complete with several computers, drawing tables, deep shelves for blueprints, vertical bins for drafting materials. One of the biggest printers Constance had ever seen was hooked up to one of the computers. Everything was scrupulously neat, as if it had not been touched in months, as was probably the case, Constance thought, surveying it. There was nothing of Rich's visible, nothing human visible. It might be a display room itself, the perfect workplace for an architect. She glanced at Charlie. "I'll start over there," she said, indicating the right wall covered with many shelves of neatly stacked graph paper.

Alexander looked bewildered for a moment, then nodded. "You're looking for the blueprints?"

"You got it," Charlie said.

"I don't think they're in here."

"Neither do I. But why don't you?"

"A lawyer came for his things. You know, to settle the estate. If the blueprints had been in here, I would have found them. They would have got sent back to Palo Alto, the main office where the other blueprints are kept. We didn't find them. Of course, we weren't looking for them specifically. I never gave them a thought. I mean, who needs blueprints after the house is built? Besides, there must be a dozen copies."

"Good point," Charlie said, and took Alexander's arm, steered him back to the door. "Thanks again for guiding us, and now you go on back up. Okay? We'll be up in a few minutes." He did not actually say "run along now," but the inflection was there. Alexander flushed and left quickly. As soon as the door was closed after him, Charlie took Constance into his arms and nuzzled her fragrant hair. "Missed you," he said. "Get anything out of Mom?"

She laughed softly and pushed him away. "Dirty, scheming old man. I thought that was a show of affection."

He drew her to him again and kissed her. "Who said love and business don't mix? He lied. Tell me."

She grinned. "As we say in the trade, right."

When they got back to the living room, there was a platter of sandwiches on a low table, the coffee urn filled again. Charlie surveyed the various guests of Smart House. Maddie had returned. She was pale, her face scrubbed, but she was composed and watchful. Most of the others were helping themselves to the food, coffee, or booze. He waited until they were settled once more.

His voice was brisk when he spoke. "Okay. It's cocktail time Saturday evening. What next?" No one volunteered. He said, "Safety in numbers. Right. So on through dinner. Then what?"

Bruce cleared his throat. He looked more disheveled than he had earlier, as if he had purposely tousled his curly hair to make it stand out wildly; his sweater sleeves were stretched out at the cuffs, one pulled above his elbow, the other down to his fingertips. His mouth was pouty. "I was probably next," he muttered. "Rich got me with a poison snake in the ice bucket in the garden bar. Milton was the witness."

"Time?"

"About ten," Milton said. "We recorded it, and I went on to the library."

Charlie turned to Bruce. "You stayed there with Rich?"

"For a few minutes. Then he left, I assumed to go to his room to check out his next victim, and then get another weapon. I finished my drink, went down to talk to Alexander in the basement awhile, and then went to the kitchen."

"Next," Charlie said.

"Me, I suppose," Milton said after a brief pause. "I took the elevator to the basement to get a weapon at ten after ten. I heard Rich and Jake, and the door to Gary's office closed when I got near it. I went on past the door to the showroom, and when I went back out, Rich was at the elevator door. I looked in to make sure no one else was there, and we went up together."

Charlie looked at Jake. "And where did you go then?"

Jake glanced at the notes he had made, then spoke briskly. "I waited until they were both on their way up, and then I left and went up the stairs to my room. I realized that Milton must have been getting a weapon and I didn't even know who my next victim was supposed to be." He spread his hands expressively and said, "It turned out to be Rich."

"How did Rich open the office door? Wasn't it computer-locked the way the others were?"

Jake looked puzzled and slowly shook his head. "I didn't give it a thought. Maybe it was, and it was programmed to open for him."

Alexander said hurriedly. "It wasn't. Gary said he was the only one who could go in. The program was being run by the computer in there. I couldn't even get in."

Jake looked more puzzled and shrugged. "I don't know. He just opened it."

Charlie nodded. "Okay." He turned to Bruce, and said mildly, "You left Rich and went to the basement to talk to Alexander. Right?"

"Yeah," Bruce said sullenly. "I wanted information. With Gary keeping out of sight, I thought he might be running things from his office, not the computer doing it all." He turned his venomous glare toward Alexander, who squirmed unhappily.

"Gary warned me that Bruce would try to quiz me," Alexander said in a rush. "He told me not to tell him anything. I was just doing what Gary told me."

"He didn't even want me in his fucking lab," Bruce said furiously. "They were telling the others everything, but me they didn't even want in the offices! He kept trying to hustle me out the door, down the hall. He even walked to the stairs with me, looking for Gary or Rich or someone to save him. It was ten to eleven and I knew Gary would be making his damn popcorn pretty soon, so I went on up to the kitchen to wait for him, but he was in there already getting the stuff together, the popcorn maker, popcorn, salt. He said how did I like his playhouse, and was I having fun, and stuff like that, and when I told him what I thought, he laughed and took the popcorn maker and stuff out, laughing."

Charlie held up his hand. "You were in the basement at ten to eleven? And you used the stairs? Say another minute went by. How long did you and Gary talk?"

"Two minutes, three. We didn't talk. He laughed at me, mocked me. That's not talking. He was having the time of his life, a real birthday party."

"What door did he leave by?"

"What the fuck difference does it make?" he yelled. He glanced at the others watching him stonily.

"It'd be nice to understand why no one else saw him that night," Charlie mused. "That main hallway is like a fishbowl."

"I got between him and the door to the main hall, and he laughed harder and walked out the other door to the back hall. He walked on his own two feet, under his own power!" With a

visible effort he controlled himself and went on. "I decided to
see what else my money had bought and I was looking around
the kitchen when Mom came in to raise hell with me. By then
I'd about had enough of the bullshit and I just left her there
yelling, out the door to the back hall, to the elevator. I was ready
to go to bed, but the fucking elevator didn't come, and I went
to the john by the dressing room, got a drink in the garden bar,
and then . . ." He rubbed his eyes and shook his head. "I don't
know. The breakfast room. The library. Harry came in right after
me. I didn't want to talk and left again. TV room. Gary was laughing in the garden, and it went right through me. I said something
to Beth and she ran out, and I couldn't stand the stupid movie.
The Beatles. I went back to the library. Milton was there, and
Jake came in." For the first time he looked at the sheet of paper
covered with childish-looking handwriting, ran his finger down
the page, and then tossed it down on the floor. "That's it."

Charlie nodded. "Thanks."

Alexander was folding and refolding his sheet of paper, as if
trying to see how small a package he could make of it. "Bruce
came down," he said, "and later on Harry came down, and I
didn't see anyone else and I didn't go upstairs all night. I had
too much work to do. I was in my lab all that night."

"All night?" Charlie murmured. "But you went to the stairs
with Bruce, didn't you?"

"Yes, but I didn't go up. We stayed at the bottom of the stairs
a few minutes. He wouldn't go away and leave me alone. I had
to go with him that far or he wasn't going to get out of my lab.
Then I went back and stayed there." His paper had been re-
duced to the size of a flattened straw. In a few minutes he would
start shredding it, Charlie thought, and turned his attention to
Jake.

"Let's back up. How long did you stay in the office after Rich
left?"

Jake held up his paper. It had a single line of neat script. "It
didn't exactly overwork my brain to recall," he said dryly. "I
waited until the elevator door closed and I knew no one was
around, a minute, maybe. I wasn't paying much attention to the
time. I went to my room for a while. I consulted the computer
and learned that my new victim was Rich, and I decided to go
hunting. I was just leaving my room when Beth came out of hers,

and we went down the stairs together. She went to the television room and I headed for the library. When I heard Gary laughing, I figured Rich would be around somewhere, too, and the library was as good a place as any to start looking. I sat where I could keep an eye on the door figuring that he'd either come in or pass by eventually. He didn't. I was still there when Maddie found his body.''

"Did you notice the time you went to the library?''

Jake nodded. "Eleven-fifteen. I looked at my watch and thought I'd give him until midnight and then go to bed if he didn't show up.''

"Good,'' Charlie said. "Nice and succinct. Milton, you took the elevator up with Rich on your way to find Laura. Right?''

Milton looked very much the somber attorney considering a worthy client. "Exactly right. I knew she had been watching the movies, and I went there to wait for her. It was ten-forty-five when I got her, and Rich was the witness. We retired to the library to record the kill. Rich left immediately afterward. I had the impression that he was in a hurry. Laura and I talked for a few seconds.'' He cleared his throat and looked at Laura and said quietly, "We agreed to meet on the roof at eleven. I remained in the library until it was time to go up, and then used the stairs and met her going up. We talked on the roof for about ten minutes. The elevator was in use then and we walked back down. She went back to the television room and I returned to the library and remained there the rest of the evening.''

Laura looked incredibly bored. Harry watched her broodingly.

"Laura?'' Charlie said.

She swept a contemptuous glance over him and shrugged. "I haven't the slightest idea. Here and there all evening. I wasn't paying much attention.''

Charlie regarded her without expression for another moment, then turned to Harry with raised eyebrows.

Harry unfolded the sheet of paper he had written on and read from it. "In our bedroom. Down the elevator to breakfast room. Couldn't work. Maddie and Bruce fighting. Downstairs to Alexander's lab, five minutes. Stairs to first floor, to garden for drink. Started back up to our room, saw Laura going up, and went to library instead. When Milton returned, I left, looked in TV room, then upstairs to our room and stayed.''

"Did you notice any times?"

"No."

"How did you go up the last time, elevator? Stairs?"

"The elevator was tied up. I used the stairs." His voice was so toneless it sounded mechanical.

"Did you hear Gary laughing?"

"No."

If Charlie was disappointed by his dry account, he gave no sign of it; he turned to Beth, but before he could ask her to begin, Harry spoke again.

"I forgot. I was ready to come down when Beth came up. I pulled the door closed for a minute, and when I opened it again and actually went out, she had gone into her room." He shrugged. "If it helps."

Charlie nodded gravely. "Everything might help. Beth?"

"That's who it was," she said in a soft voice. "Charlie, you just don't realize what it was like that night. Everyone ducking out of sight, doors opening and closing, people vanishing."

"I'm beginning to get the picture," he said. "You were in the TV room, and then what?"

She glanced at her paper; the words were scrawled so badly she could hardly read them. She recounted her night, watching the movies, up to her room, back down. She finished: "I was in the television room when Bruce came in and then we heard Gary laughing and smelled the popcorn and chlorine. I went to the kitchen for a drink of water and then back to the movies."

Charlie looked around at the others. "Anyone else smell popcorn or chlorine in the television room, or the library? Anywhere?"

"You could smell it throughout the hall outside the atrium. You know how the odor of popcorn carries," Jake said with an edge to his voice. "He made popcorn every night."

"Milton, did you smell it?" Charlie asked.

"Yes. He left the door open to the garden, apparently. If it's open even a minute the smell of chlorine drifts out, and that night it was mixed with popcorn." He sounded a touch impatient, but then straightened in his chair. "It was after eleven— ten, fifteen after at least. I was back down in the library by then." He looked at Charlie shrewdly. "That didn't come out before."

Charlie had already turned to Maddie. "You're the last one," he said kindly, "and then we can all get some rest."

She shook her head. "Not until you find my son's murderer. Then we can rest." She had drawn herself up very straight and looked almost regal. "I won't take long. I was lying down in my room for half an hour or so, and then went down on the elevator. I talked to Bruce in the kitchen. We certainly were not fighting or making loud noises." She looked at Harry severely.

"I heard what he was calling you," Harry said with a touch of anger. "Want me to repeat the conversation I caught before I got disgusted and left?"

She held her head a bit higher. "My mother said you cannot believe a word an eavesdropper reports. We were not fighting." To Charlie, she said, "From the kitchen I returned to the television room to watch the movie. I became fatigued and decided to go to bed. And you know what I found when I summoned the elevator."

"Yes, I do," he said. Then very briskly he started to gather up papers. "Thank you all, and please let me have your notes. You may find that this discussion stimulates memories of other things you simply haven't thought of before. If you do, please tell me. I'll want to talk to you all again, of course, but singly from now on."

10

They straggled out, not talking to each other now, avoiding each other's eyes. Alexander vanished swiftly. Harry and Laura went up the stairs together, not speaking, not touching. No one took the elevator.

On the second floor, Charlie and Constance stopped to look down again at the atrium, where the soft lights were glowing, the trees and blooming plants Edenlike, the pool glimmering with underwater lights in pale blue. The waterfall made a geyser, gleaming spray rising, flashing, settling without end. Milton appeared and vanished in the shadows behind the pool; in a moment the pool lights went off; he reappeared, glanced around, and left the atrium. Here and there dim lights remained on; the shadows deepened, but the room took on a new dimension, seemed to expand, to become what they called it—a garden. Charlie made a low noise in his throat and took Constance by the arm. They went on to their room.

Constance kicked off her shoes as Charlie added his papers to the ones he had already stacked on the desk. He frowned at the messy pile.

"Charlie?"

"Hm?"

"Why would anyone bother to steal one set of blueprints when there are so many of them altogether?"

"Don't know."

"Not fingerprints. Anyone might have handled them and left prints. A bloodstain or something like that?"

"Two bloodless deaths," he said morosely. He picked up a chair and crossed the room with it, wedged it under the doorknob, and stepped back to regard it with an unhappy expression. "Know what I hate? Hotel rooms without locks on the doors."

"I don't like Smart House," Constance said. She went to the sliding glass door to the balcony and made certain it was latched. There wasn't a lock on it, but she knew that if anyone tried to force the latch, both she and Charlie would hear it in this abnormally quiet house. The building was so solidly constructed that no sound of the sea penetrated, and beyond the balcony the fog was so deep that nothing showed, no lights, nothing. She shivered, and turned to find Charlie at her side. He put his arm around her and drew her close.

"I'm still wide awake. How about you?"

She nodded. "What are you up to?"

"A little prowling. Let's give them fifteen minutes to get settled first."

During the next few minutes he sorted through the papers he was accumulating, studied the floor plans for several minutes, then gathered up most of the papers and put them in one of the suitcases. He locked it and returned it to the closet. Constance had put her shoes back on and found a penlight. Charlie arranged the remaining papers, most of them in a heap, a few scattered, and regarded them for a moment. With a sigh he turned to Constance and she meekly bowed her head. He plucked a single hair and went back to the desk with it and lifted the top sheet of paper, placed the pale hair on the next one, where it seemed to disappear, and covered it again with the top piece.

"Did you know polar bears have hollow hairs?" he asked then. "Transparent."

"You should work with a polar bear," she said agreeably.

He shook his head. "Too bad-tempered. And they can't cook."

He took the chair away from the door, flicked off the lights, and they stepped out into the wide hallway that curved away from them in both directions. Ahead, the glass wall of the atrium gleamed. He took her hand and positioned her next to the glass.

"I want to find out just how visible people are coming and going in there," he said softly, nodding toward the pool, the atrium in general. "You watch while I prowl a little. Okay?"

He brushed her cheek with his lips and left her. He vanished around the curved hallway in a few steps, and then appeared again on the other side of the glass wall. He had entered the second level of the atrium. Almost instantly he was out of sight again.

Charlie ducked behind some kind of plant and then another. He could still see Constance, but from the way she was looking around, he could tell that she had lost him. He kept behind plants and trees and made his way down the broad stairs that looked like natural terracing. At the first level he paused again and no longer could see her through the glass wall. He went on to the bar and tables. The illusion of being in a jungle was nearly complete now. The dim lights were like moonlight filtered through a hazy cloud cover. He stepped behind another planter containing a banana plant with eight-foot-long leaves; he did not linger, but made his way to the pool, around it to the corridor that led to the Jacuzzi and the dressing rooms. The light control box was on the wall here. He turned on the pool lights, crossed to the Jacuzzi room and looked inside, recrossed the hall to glance inside the dressing room, then stepped out to walk around the pool to the exit nearest the elevator. He felt very exposed and vulnerable, bathed in the pale blue light that seemed brighter than he remembered. At the door he stopped and waved to her, motioned for her to join him. He could not be certain he was visible to her; he could see nothing through the glass wall.

Constance watched him appear and vanish, then appear again after the pool lights came on. When he waved to her to come down, she drew in a long breath and only then realized that she had been breathing guardedly, unwilling to make a sound. She left her place at the window and started down the hallway. When she reached the stairs she turned to descend without even considering the elevator at the far end of the hall.

Something, she was thinking. There was something . . .

Charlie walked toward her in the hall and she said under her breath, "Of course!"

When he reached her, he put his arms around her shoulders and could not account for the feeling of relief that washed through him. "Well?" he asked.

"Wait a minute. How did it seem to you?"

"Like you were watching my every movement. How much did you see?"

"That's how they all felt during the game. As if every movement was being watched. And not just during the game. It's this damn house," she said, and waved her hand. "Right now, I feel as if a thousand eyes are on me."

"Honey," he said patiently, steering her into the kitchen, "tell me." A dim light had been left on here. He found the switch and turned on brighter lights.

"Oh, that. Not much. I saw you at the bar, and again after the lights came on, when you walked along the edge of the pool and went to the door. But, Charlie, there's something else . . ." Her thoughts raced as he pulled out chairs at the long oak worktable and seated her, then himself very close to her. He did not nudge, did not ask anything else. He waited, his gaze fixed on her.

"It has to do with Gary," she said at last, her voice very low. "Even now, knowing the computer is off, listen to me," she said with a wry smile. "There's nearly an irresistible urge to whisper, to look around to make sure no one's watching, listening. It's this house. How big? Ten thousand square feet, more? And wide open. No privacy anywhere. You feel as if it's watching you every minute, as if all the others can see everything you do. It's all that glass, the arrangement of the rooms, everything about it. A giant fishbowl. And Gary was emotionally childlike. That's what they all keep telling us, he was like a small boy with secrets, loving games and surprises and secrets. Charlie, he had the money to play with, he would have had a secret way to move around without being seen. I know he would!"

"The missing blueprints," he breathed. He looked at her with an expression that was close to awe. "You've hit on it."

"It might not have anything to do with the murders," she said thoughtfully. "If he saw Rich carrying them around, he could have hidden them himself, to keep his secret until he was ready to reveal it."

Charlie nodded. He was reconstructing Gary's bedroom suite and his office. His mental maps were very accurate. Some people called it uncanny, his ability to reproduce drawings of buildings, rooms, halls, staircases, closets, electrical systems, everything about them, but he knew it was simply training. Exacting, painstaking training as a fireman had forced him to develop this skill, and he had used it for many years as an arson investigator in New York, before he quit that department to become a police detective. Now he was placing light fixtures and plumbing in Gary's rooms, and he knew where the extra space had to be. He stood up.

"Let's go have a look," he said, his voice as soft as hers.

A few minutes later Constance stood out of the way while Charlie examined the walk-in closet in the room that had been Gary Elringer's. A large sliding door opened to the closet, which was paneled with fragrant cedar; it was bare now, with only a few wooden hangers on one of the rods. There were shelves and drawers on one wall, two clothes rods, a ceiling light. Charlie was feeling the wood along the end wall. He finished inside, and examined the wall on the bedroom side just as minutely. He stepped back finally and nodded.

"Three by three," he said, still speaking very softly. "Either a ladder or an elevator. My money's on another elevator, side by side with the big one on the other side of that wall."

"Can you open it?"

"Nope. I can't even find the damn door, but it's there. Probably computer-operated." He took her arm. "Let's trace it all the way. His office next."

"Fruit cellar," he murmured in Gary's office, pacing off the space. Behind the wall was the refrigerator room, the bins for long storage of fruits and vegetables, and then the dumbwaiter. He measured it off and was left with three feet unaccounted for. He was humming under his breath. Again nothing showed to indicate a door; the office was paneled in a golden-hued wood, expensive wood, exotic. Although Charlie could not identify it, he nodded at it approvingly. "Onward," he said at last. "First floor, pantry. We'll save the roof for daylight." He was very cheerful.

The dumbwaiter was next to a freezer in the pantry, and there was the same three feet of space tucked away between them and the big elevator. The paneling hid the door in the office; the sliding closet door masked it in the bedroom. On the first floor that wall had wainscoting, white and dark wood, perfect disguise again. He turned off the hall light and was ready now to find a snack and then go on to bed. Good night's work, he thought; suddenly Constance's fingers dug into his arm.

"*Shh,*" she whispered, and turned toward the atrium. The swimming pool lights illuminated this end of the area, leaving the rest in murky darkness with small pale spots here and there. Someone was there, moving about.

They froze in place, trying to see past the glass wall, past the pools of pale light. Cautiously, after a moment, Charlie edged closer to the main hallway. Too many exits from the atrium, he was thinking. Four or six on this level, at least four on the bedroom level. A shadow passed between him and one of the light spots.

"Keep an eye out for him," he whispered. "And stay here."

He raced back down the hall to the kitchen, through it to the dining room, and out into the main corridor again, this time at the foot of the wide stairs. He ran up the stairs and stopped at the top, hugging the wall. Here, too, a few lights had been left on, dim, unevenly spaced. He waited a moment to catch his breath, and then edged out into the hall, ducked in order not to eclipse a wall light, and stopped to peer down into the atrium, knowing no one there would be able to see him. At the same moment he caught a motion across the expanse of the atrium, on the far side of the upstairs hall, and he cursed under his breath. The other prowler had beat him upstairs. He trotted down the curved hall; empty. But someone had been there, probably had entered one of the two last rooms, or had gone down the front stairs. He kneeled at the door of the second-to-last room and put his ear against the door, listening. Nothing. He passed the front stairs to the foyer and listened at the last door just as futilely. He had one hand on the carpet in front of the door and slowly he raised it, examined his fingers, and then the carpet. Dirt. Potting soil. Soundlessly he drew out his wallet and extracted a stiff credit card and used it to scrape the soil together and lift it. There wasn't much, a teaspoonful, moist, crumbly, with bits of grainy stuff, little pellets of planting medium. And now he could smell chlorine.

He found the door to the second floor of the atrium and slipped through, pulled the sliding door shut, and made his way down the broad stairs. He could not see Constance, and he thought she probably could not see him either. The cover of greenery was dense.

When Charlie emerged on the first level of the garden, approaching her, Constance left her position and joined him in the hall. "Did you get a glimpse of him?"

"Nope. You?"

"Just a glimpse. About halfway up. Not enough to tell anything. What do you have?"

"Dirt. Let's see if we can find a plastic bag or something in the kitchen. And a couple of spoons maybe."

They returned to the kitchen, where Constance found the drawer that held plastic wrap, aluminum foil, plastic bags. Together they gazed at the soil before Charlie carefully slid it off the card into a bag and secured it with a fastener. He replaced his card and put the bag in his pocket. "Spoons," he said.

Constance looked doubtful. "There are an awful lot of plants in containers in there."

"I know," he said unhappily. "If we don't find something in a couple of minutes, we'll let it go until tomorrow and have the gardener do his stuff. Let's give it a try now, though."

At the door to the garden, Constance paused again. "You know where the lights are for the whole place?"

He did. He went behind the pool to the light panel in the hallway and tried several switches before he found the one that turned on every light in the garden. It was like sunrise. His unhappiness increased. It was a damn jungle. There were pots and containers of every conceivable size and shape—some long troughs, some like half barrels, some simple round pots. Sphagnum moss was everywhere, in between the containers, piled on top the soil in them. At first he had thought it would be simple to find where the prowler had been digging, just by looking at the tops of the things, but he realized now that such was not the case.

"Well," he said, "he dropped dirt upstairs, maybe he did it more than once."

She nodded, surveying the pots through narrowed eyes. "He must have been putting something in, not taking it out, and depending on the size of the object, there could be dirt left over."

"Why not digging something out?"

"Just wouldn't make much sense. These are all portable, repotted often, I imagine, moved around. The gardener would have found anything left in them more than a few days, I imagine. The big ones are on casters. I expect they all spend part of the time in a greenhouse, maybe get rotated on a regular basis. They do better in a greenhouse," she added, almost absently, not moving yet, considering the task before them.

Charlie began to mount the stone stairs, studying each one before he put his foot on it, searching for more loose dirt. Each riser was on a slant, not really noticeable unless he examined them closely, and there were drainage channels along the rear of each one, and, he cursed, even an automatic watering system, the kind people installed in lawns, with pipes that would emerge and spray water and then sink back out of sight. He was not quite certain why it infuriated him, but it did. Then he knew. If they didn't find the right pot, the system might come on at dawn and wash away every trace, just as the little vacuum cleaners would pop out of the wall and clean up any dirt in the carpet.

He mounted another step, then another. A heavy perfume was cloying; white flowers and pink, then a bigger pot with a climbing vine, and a palm tree. . . . He grunted softly and squatted. Dirt.

Constance joined him and they looked at the scattering of dirt, then turned their attention to the pots. The gardenias were in bloom, with many buds that had not opened yet. Verbenas crowded them, and a dainty trailing lobelia covered with blue flowers. Charlie began to move the sphagnum moss out of the way. The soil in the first pots he uncovered looked untouched. But the dirt came from somewhere, he thought morosely, and reached out to take away more moss.

"Wait a second," Constance said. She picked up a pot of gardenias and grasped the plant, tilted the pot, and was holding the plant, roots in a tight ball. She replaced it and lifted the next one. Charlie stared. He never had seen a pot-bound plant, she realized. "They like to fill the pot before they make buds," she said, and turned the next pot over. And the next. He moved ahead of her to uncover the big pot that held the palm tree. That at least had room to dig in, he was thinking, when he heard her soft exclamation. "Charlie! Look."

She was holding a plant in one hand, the pot in the other, and when he looked inside it he saw an object that might have been a calculator, but that he knew was the hand-held computer control. He lifted it out carefully, holding it by the narrow edge.

"What the fuck are you doing?"

They both looked up to see Bruce and Jake coming down the wide stone stairs. Jake was in his robe and slippers, Bruce in the disarray of clothing he had been wearing all night, the misshapen sweater, untied sneakers, jeans.

"Is this the gadget you were talking about before?" Charlie asked pleasantly, as he watched them both walk through the dirt on the stairs to join him and Constance.

Jake whistled and nodded. Bruce reached for it, but that, Charlie thought, was going too far. He drew it back. Now Jake looked down at the pots, the sphagnum moss that had been tossed out of the way. He frowned. "It was in the plants? How did you find it?"

"Wild guess. Let's go to the kitchen. I can use a wash."

"Is there just one? Maybe . . ." Jake looked over the nearby pots, then gazed around the room, and finally shrugged. "If there are more, they could be anywhere," he said.

"If so, they'll keep until tomorrow," Charlie said. He waited until Constance returned the gardenia to its pot, and then led the way down and out of the garden.

In the kitchen Constance got another plastic bag out and they all watched Charlie put the computer control in it and fasten it.

"Shit!" Bruce cried. "Just like in the movies! You're actually going to look for fingerprints? Don't you think a smart killer would have wiped them all off?"

"What makes you think he's smart?" Charlie asked as if he were really interested in a new and strange idea. He slipped the second bag into his pocket and went to the sink where Constance had already started to wash her hands.

"Up until today, everyone in this house was smart," Bruce said.

Charlie nodded and grinned. "You both just happened to be up guarding the pool room?"

"I wasn't up," Jake said, and he yawned. "I heard someone on the balcony. I looked, of course, but didn't see anything. I was good and awake by then, so I decided a drink was in order. Met him up in the hall. He was watching you and Constance."

"That's a damn lie!" Bruce yelled. "You can't hear anything on the balcony from inside. I was on my way down to get something to eat. I thought we had burglars. You're lucky I didn't go back and get a gun."

Jake nearly choked. "My God!" he said incredulously. "*You* have a gun?" A shudder passed over him and he averted his face.

"Yeah! And I'm a damn good shot! So just be careful, you asshole!"

Jake faced round again, and it became apparent that he was laughing. He shook his head. "I'm getting that drink I came down for. There must be something in the kitchen. I certainly don't intend to go to the bar in the garden, not until someone makes a search anyway." He began to open cabinets, grinning widely now. He found a bottle of bourbon. "Charlie? Constance?"

Bruce began to rummage in the refrigerator. Jake poured drinks for Charlie and Constance and himself and went to the door with his. He raised it in a semi-salute, "Cheers. See you tomorrow. And, Bruce, you do know which end shoots, I hope." He left.

Bruce's mouth was more pouty than ever when he took out a plastic-wrapped platter of sliced ham and started to make a sandwich. Charlie joined him and picked up a piece of the meat. It was very good.

"Did you handle the computer control when your brother showed it to you?" he asked.

"No. No way would he let me get my hands on it. Mustard," he said, and returned to the refrigerator.

"I'm just trying to get an idea of what it could do," Charlie said. "Did he demonstrate it?"

Bruce looked at him with contempt. "You don't know a goddamn thing about computers, do you?"

"Nope." Charlie was being inhumanly cheerful and pleasant. Constance sat at the table and watched them both.

"Okay. Okay. Look, the main computer has the program, and the control is really like a radio signal that it can pick up. You looked at it? There's a keyboard, and numbers. Say you program it to turn on lights when you press A. A signal goes to the main computer and it takes the command and carries it out. You don't really program the little one to do anything except send a signal." His voice had lost its petulance; there was the same underlying patience that Charlie himself could assume when he explained something to a naive student. "What that means," Bruce went on, "is that you can use all the letters, the numbers, any combination of them to make it send the right signal, up to the limit of the main computer's memory, anyway. So it can do whatever the main computer can do, if you programmed it in in advance."

"Seems kind of risky," Charlie said thoughtfully. "What if you touched the A accidentally?"

Bruce took a bite of his sandwich and shook his head. "You'd activate it first, some sequence of letters to tell the main computer you were going on line with it." He talked with his mouth full; the words came out muffled.

Charlie reached for another piece of ham. "How long would it take to reprogram something once it was in the computer?"

Bruce shrugged. "Depends. The whole thing, a couple of minutes. One or two commands, seconds, if you knew the program to start with. None of us did, remember. That would make it a little longer."

Charlie looked surprised. "You mean you could do it even though you didn't know the program, the language, whatever?"

"You can't keep a good hacker out of any program. Look, you know anything about music?"

"I can tell Wagner from Verdi," Charlie said cautiously. "Why?" But from the blank expression on Bruce's face, he knew the names were the wrong ones.

"Let's pretend you know music," Bruce said. "Like you recognize the style if it's Springsteen. Or Simon. Or anyone. The good ones have a style you hear; you know who's playing. Right? Same with programmers. The good ones have a style you get to recognize. They do the same things over and over. Maybe one's succinct, someone else is wordy, someone else uses shortcuts that get familiar. Alexander's maybe the best. And he's got style that stands out. And he was the group leader for programming, see. So someone who knows his style knows what to look for, what he's likely to do next. Anyone here with computer smarts could crack his software, anyone. And, like I said, until today everyone in this house was pretty damn smart."

Charlie nodded absently. "I wonder," he said, "why no one's mentioned that before."

Bruce shrugged and took more ham.

"If it was that easy, I wonder why your brother didn't reprogram the computer to take your mother out of the game."

Bruce wiped his hands on his jeans.

"Or if he didn't do that, why he thought he could get her to confirm his killing you, if she had said she wouldn't play." He glanced at Bruce, who had become very still; his mouth was sullen again, his eyes narrowed.

"What does that mean?" he demanded. "What are you getting at?"

"Damned if I know. Didn't you think it was curious at the time that he'd make such a big thing of it when he knew she wasn't in the game?"

"He was an asshole."

"Did he rig the game to get you for his first victim?"

"Probably. It would have been like him."

"But then you knew he had your name, even if the first attempt wasn't recorded, didn't you? Seems you might have tried to avoid him after that try. When did he show you the control computer?"

Bruce's face went slack, then it wrinkled, like the face of a child about to throw a tantrum. Charlie remembered how he had treated his daughter Jessica when she was small and her face changed that way. "Storm front moving south," he would say then, and she always had turned suspicious eyes on him, scowled, and most often refused to weep simply because it was expected. The memory was very sharp. How like Constance she was, more so every day. He blinked and focused on Bruce.

"He didn't tell me," Bruce muttered. "I overheard him telling someone else."

Charlie raised both eyebrows and said nothing.

"I thought he was going around telling everyone but me. That's why I . . . Anyway I thought everyone else knew. I was looking over the stuff in the basement, the automatic pool stuff, the vacuum systems, all that. I went behind the elevator to look at the vacuum intake and exhaust, and I heard him. On the elevator, I thought. Must have been for me to have heard him. Anyway, I don't know who was with him. I didn't see them, and the other one didn't say anything. Gary laughed and said, 'Don't be stupid. Of course, I have a safety backup system. In my pocket. Look.' And I knew what it had to be, and about how big it was. Nothing else made any sense. And it would have been stupid not to have a control."

Charlie nodded. "Then?"

"Then nothing. They stopped talking, or the elevator went up, or they left it. I went up the back stairs, the ones that go to the Jacuzzi area, the outside door."

"That's the space where all the pipes are, the wires, tubing to the greenhouse and the cold-storage room?"

Bruce shrugged. "You'd need access to all that stuff. I figured that out and went back there to examine the system."

"What time did you hear them?"

"How the fuck do I know? Sometime in the afternoon. If I'd known it was going to be a federal case, I'd have made notes! I'm going to bed."

He stamped out of the kitchen, and now Constance left the table and joined Charlie at the counter where he was picking at

the ham absently. She moved it out of reach. "You'll have nightmares."

"Probably. What do you make of him?"

"Being eaten alive by jealousy. If it's this bad now with his
brother dead, what must it have been when he was still alive?
That poor man."

"Remember, that 'poor man' has a gun, and he's something
of a nut."

She looked at him in surprise. "You believed it about the
gun?"

"You didn't?"

"Of course not. It was a typical, my father's-bigger-than-your-
father kind of little-boy threat. It never occurred to me to take
it as literal truth."

And it had not occurred to him, Charlie thought darkly, not
to accept it as true. "Where are you taking that?"

Constance had picked up the platter of ham. "To the refrigerator. And then I'm taking you to bed. You know, the more of
all these other men I see, the better you keep looking."

"And you," he said, "are a proper sort of wife."

11

The next morning the fog swirled outside the window wall, was
lifted by the offshore breeze, dissipated, then formed again.
Charlie watched it broodingly as he and Constance waited for
their breakfast.

"Problems?" Constance asked.

He nodded. "Time problems. Not enough at the right time.
Look, let's place people and set them in time as if they were
cherries being plopped in whipped cream. First, we know Rich
was alive at ten-forty-five, and we can assume he was alive at
eleven when Maddie used the elevator. And Gary was alive at
eleven-ten or eleven-fifteen. But by then everyone's pretty much
accounted for. We have to make another assumption, that Rich

died first, simply because the others were all together from eleven-fifteen on. See what I mean by not enough time at the right time?"

Constance raised her eyebrows questioningly, but he was gazing at the restless fog. "Around eleven," he said unhappily, "Harry hears Bruce and Maddie fighting in the kitchen, and the elevator is clear. Rich must be alive somewhere. Harry goes to chat with Alexander. Milton and Laura take off for the roof. Maddie and Beth watch the movie until Beth goes to her room. Bruce is alone, wandering about. Then at ten after eleven, Milton and Laura rejoin others either in the television room or the library. Beth and Jake come downstairs together. Bruce is with others in the TV room when they all hear Gary laugh, and smell popcorn. Meanwhile Harry has gone upstairs. So he's free now, but he wasn't free earlier. So it seems that almost anyone could have found time to get Rich, but not Gary. He's a problem."

She said in a low voice, "Alexander was alone from the time Harry left him until after the body was found in the elevator."

"Yeah," he said gloomily. "And he's probably the only one who really needed to keep Gary and Rich, and the project, alive and well and funded."

"And," Constance added thoughtfully, "we really only have Harry's word for it that he looked in on the people watching the movie before he went upstairs after talking with Alexander. It's possible that he was free from then on, too."

"Milton saw him," Charlie said. He sounded disgusted. "He didn't mention it, but it's in his notes of his own movements. Harry looked in seconds after Milton got down from the roof rendezvous. It's not the sort of thing he would be likely to want to talk about, I guess, but he did make a note of it."

"But that still left him time . . ."

Charlie was shaking his head. "There's the problem of Rich, though. And damn, I don't want to think about two killers, a conspiracy—" He stopped when Mrs. Ramos entered with the breakfast tray.

While she was placing soft-boiled eggs before Constance, and then pancakes and eggs for him, he asked, "When Gary made popcorn at night, what did he use? An automatic gadget, a pan, what?"

She raised her eyebrows a fraction of an inch; her idea of a surprised expression, he assumed.

"A popper. Automatic."

"Did he have a special bowl he used?"

"Yes. A stainless steel bowl."

"And the day after his death, after the police had gone, where did you find the bowl?"

She finished serving them and paused thoughtfully. "In the cupboard where we always keep it. But the popcorn popper was in the garden, the pool room."

"Had it been used?"

She studied Charlie for a lengthy moment, then nodded. "It was filled with popped corn."

He asked her about the blueprints and the hand-held computers and drew a blank. Then Laura and Harry Westerman joined them and Mrs. Ramos left.

Laura's gaze swept over Constance; she nodded slightly and inspected Charlie more leisurely with a hint of a smile, as if they shared a secret. Reflex, he thought; was she even aware of it? He grinned at her and Harry. He was wearing a sweatshirt and pants. "You've been running?"

"Yes." Harry poured coffee for himself. Laura poured her own, and neither of them looked at the other. He tasted his, set his cup down hard, and asked bluntly, "What the hell is going on in the garden?"

Charlie shrugged, but did not explain. He had caught Mrs. Ramos before seven, had spoken with her husband a few minutes later, and now Ramos and a helper were searching pots. It didn't surprise him, he reflected, that Harry had been out running. He didn't keep that muscular physique sitting all day in an office adding up columns of figures. Ignoring the question, he commented, "I noticed, during the recital of killers and victims last night, you weren't a very active player."

Harry drank his coffee. When he spoke again, his voice was frigid, "You noticed right. Damn stupid game. I did not participate."

"Oh? But you took a weapon, and you were witness to two murders. What weapon did you choose, by the way?"

"A water gun. A plastic water gun. And the day after the deaths, the real deaths, I went to the edge of the point out there and I heaved it as far as I could into the ocean. I never even put water in it."

"Why did you take it if you didn't intend to play?"

Harry finished his coffee, poured more, and did not answer.

"We didn't have much choice," Laura said. "Gary had it in his head that we'd play the game, and we had to go along, or risk having him in a tantrum all weekend. He could have done that, stormed around for days, you know. Others were doing it too, going along with him just to keep him happy. Taking weapons, tossing them. We were talking about it last night while you were out with Alexander. Bruce found a pea shooter at the bar in the garden, Milton picked up a water gun on the roof when we were up there, I found two balloons in the television room. We had to take them but we didn't have to use them."

"And you thought Gary would be able to check up on all of you? Cheat?"

She tilted her head and her smile deepened. "Wouldn't you have thought so? I mean, he made the rules, provided the weapons, programmed it all in; of course, we assumed he'd supervise."

Charlie nodded. "What weapon did you take?"

"The garrote. A pretty blue ribbon with Velcro on the ends."

"And did you toss your weapon out into the ocean, too?"

"I don't have an idea about what happened to it. I never gave it another thought," she said with elaborate disinterest.

Charlie turned back to her husband, aware suddenly of the amusement in Constance's eyes that to anyone else might simply look bright with interest. "Can you tell me exactly what happened when Rich Schoen killed Gary? In the game, of course."

Mrs. Ramos appeared with their breakfasts before Harry could speak. She put half a grapefruit down for Laura, and a bowl of what looked like straw before Harry. Charlie stared at it. Shredded wheat, he thought in astonishment. He had not seen shredded wheat in more than twenty years.

After Mrs. Ramos was gone again, Harry said, "I was talking to Rich, about Smart House, of course. That's what we were all doing, finding out as much about it as possible. He spotted Gary and motioned for me to go with him. In the garden, by the bar, he unrolled the blueprints he was carrying and pulled out a foam bat of some sort and touched Gary with it. It counted as a kill.

We went to the computer around the bar and recorded it and had it confirmed. Rich left, and I followed him. I didn't want to hang around with Gary mad, and he was mad. He was not a good loser."

Charlie held up his hand. "Slower. What about the bat? The blueprints?"

He munched on his straw, frowning. "I don't know. He put the blueprints down on one of those tables in there. Maybe he put the bat on the counter at the bar. I didn't pay any attention. Beth came up while we were recording the kill. Ask her."

"Okay. You left with Rich, but then you went back, and this time you witnessed Jake murdering Beth. Why'd you go back?"

Harry sighed in an exaggerated manner. "Look, try to get the picture of that goddamn weekend. We were not happy, none of us. It was a stupid game, and we had serious business. Okay, the house is a miracle of innovations, but it's a black hole, too. And Gary was being childish. No one knew when he'd blow hot or cold. I was fed up with him, with the goddamn game, with his tantrums, just about the whole damn show. Even this hideaway. Stuck out here for a whole weekend. He never gave a thought to how inconvenient it would be for us, for prospective clients, for staff, everyone. I sure as hell wasn't planning out every step, keeping track of every minute. Most of us were simply trying to learn what we could, and keep out of Gary's path. I didn't have a reason to go back. I just did it."

"Why did he build the house here? Why not down in California?" Charlie asked when Harry paused.

"Because he was a goddamn maniac!"

Laura said coldly, "Because he knew the industry was full of spies. He told me the reason. He had a contract with a private airline to bring him and his crew up here, and actually it's only a couple of hours out of Palo Alto. And he knew no spy could get in."

Charlie nodded. "Did you fly up when you came to visit?"

If he had wanted to shake her, he did not succeed. She shrugged. "A couple of times."

He turned back to Harry. "The day of the game, when you went back to the garden, was Jake already there?"

"Jesus Christ!" He rubbed his hand over his eyes. "Yeah, I think so. I just wandered in. He motioned for me to come with him. Beth was standing by the bar. We weren't even trying to keep quiet, just walking, and she didn't notice. She'd been fighting with Gary, obviously. She spent the whole weekend in a rage. She wanted a divorce; that's all that was on her mind apparently, and he, for God knows what reason, wasn't letting go. Ego, I guess."

"Not just that," Laura said coldly. "He was going to make use of her, let her be his hostess in this place. He liked to use people he knew."

"Everyone seems to be aware that she wanted a divorce even before she had made up her mind about it," Charlie said. "Did Gary mention it to you two?"

"He told me," Laura said, and suddenly her voice was hard and bitter, her face strained.

Harry looked at her with surprise, then deliberately stared at his cereal again.

"You were Rich's last victim, weren't you?" Charlie asked.

"I don't know," Harry replied. "The rules stated that no one tell anyone things like that. How the hell would I know?"

"Oh yes. I forgot. But if Bruce had your name, and he did, and if Rich killed him, then Rich inherited you."

"You've got a good memory," Harry said in a tight voice.

"Just fair to middling," Charlie said modestly.

"Well, remember this. Whoever had that goddamn hand-held computer could get a weapon any time he wanted one. That's one of the things it could have done without any trouble at all."

Charlie glanced at Constance. She appeared to be so placid, so removed and distant, that she might have been off in her own reverie. She felt the look and came back, and her own glance at him said *wait a second*.

She looked at Harry and said, "You knew Gary for a long time, didn't you? Why do you think he insisted on a game like this at that particular time?"

Harry put his spoon down and poured coffee, watching his own motions, as if considering if he would even bother to answer, or considering what kind of answer would satisfy—or, she thought, perhaps he had not asked himself the question until this moment.

Finally he said, "I think he intended to keep us apart as much as possible, and still make us switch our position, those of us opposed to sinking more money into this project. He and Rich were working on Jake, getting his support, most of Saturday. If they had lived, I would have been next to be won over. I think every single move had been planned in advance."

"Were you won over by the house itself?"

"No. Remember, I'm the company treasurer. I knew better than anyone what it was costing, what it would continue to cost." His voice had gone very flat again. He picked up his spoon, but did not use it; this time he examined it. "Sterling," he said in that flat hard voice, and tossed it down.

"I see," Constance said thoughtfully. "I can understand why a tall man like Jake would choose a garrote for a shorter woman like Beth. Did you see the ribbon?" she asked Harry, who was regarding her with dislike, possibly even contempt. Charlie blinked at the sudden change of direction.

"No. He had it palmed, and then her hands went up to it the way people would do if they're being strangled."

"Oh, of course. That's a reflex, isn't it?"

Charlie was watching her closely. God help the guy who tries to strangle her, he thought. She was a black belt in aikido, had given demonstrations for years. Her hands would go to places and do things a would-be killer would not like.

"Did you learn who your victims were before you picked weapons?" Constance asked.

Laura and Harry exchanged irritated glances. Laura looked at her watch and said, "Either way. I don't know about the others, but I did. What are you getting at?"

"Just curious," Constance said brightly. "A garrote is such a strange weapon for a woman to pick when her victim is so much larger than she is. You're what, five seven, five eight? And Jake is six one at least, isn't he? I just wondered if you tried to use the weapon and failed, if you gave him the idea of using it on Beth later."

"I couldn't even find him all day!" Laura said furiously. "He kept himself holed up with Rich or Gary or Alexander all day long."

Harry jerked his chair away from the table. "If you two are finished," he said roughly, "I have some work to take care of." He stalked from the room.

Constance turned back to Laura, who was glaring at her.

"I planned to sneak up on him when he was sitting down. I never had a chance to get behind him."

"How long have you and Harry been married?"

Charlie blinked again, and Laura flushed an angry red; her lips tightened.

"That's none of your damn business!"

"Of course not," Constance said pleasantly. She held Laura's gaze with her own clear-eyed, cool look, the unanswered question hanging between them until Laura jumped up and ran out of the room.

"What the hell was that all about?" Charlie said softly, impressed that she had been able to rattle Laura's cage so effectively. His own attempts had been water on the proverbial duck.

"Just curious. I wondered if they were sleeping together. They aren't."

"How do you know?" He peered at her through narrowed eyes.

"I just do," she said. "I guess he's impotent. No pheromones at all."

"Good Christ!"

"Now, Charlie," she said kindly. "All the signs are there, you know. The way he talks about Beth, looks at her, the way he looks at me, the way he treats Laura. I thought at first maybe homosexual, but I don't think so. Asexual is more like it. She plays the field and he knows it and doesn't do anything about it. She rather taunts him with it, like bringing up again the fact that she and Milton met up on the roof, and deliberately choosing a weapon that meant close physical contact with Jake. If he tried to get rid of her, the threat is that she'll tell and he'd rather die than have it known. All those mountains, you know." She sighed. "Poor Harry. And she might have flown up in the company plane, but Gary ended their little affair, not her."

Charlie sputtered on his coffee, and she looked surprised. "Well, it's obvious. He held people by giving them shares of stock, didn't he? And he never gave her any. And she's rather mean-spirited about the way Gary treated her, considering her own actions, I mean. I believe he told her there was a divorce in the works soon, and then he told her of his plans to use Beth for his hostess, a role ideally suited for Laura but never for Beth. Oh, she's angry. And of course she wouldn't try to sneak up on a man from behind. She would have gone up to Jake openly, put her arms around his neck, and then said, 'Gotcha!' Don't you think so?"

"You said no pheromones," he said darkly. "Literally? How do you know?"

"You know, the green cloud of buzzes that most people carry around with them, a little shock here, there, a tingle in your toes when you get near them. Some are pink, of course, or blue, but green is common, too. His are missing. Laura's cloud is puce, and very dense."

Charlie had been listening seriously, intently. He began to laugh, his face crinkling the way it did, taking off many years. "That'll teach her to give me the glad eye in front of you."

Constance looked innocent.

The air was almost too cool when they walked out on their way to the greenhouse. Mist was still snagged in the tops of trees, still hid the horizon and lingered on the hills behind the house. The grass sparkled with droplets; even as they walked among them the rhododendrons seemed to shrug away the last of their burden of overnight moisture and straighten up for a new day.

"Nice," Constance murmured. The rumble of ocean, the crash of an occasional breaker, the sharp sea air, it was all very nice, a perfect morning.

Mr. Ramos met them at the open doors of the greenhouse, a building large enough and with enough plants to pass for a commercial enterprise. Charlie whistled softly. No wonder the shareholders were griping about money down the tube, he thought. Gary had done things in a big way indeed.

Mr. Ramos was wiry and sharp-faced. His muscles and sinews and bones all were of a piece, all alike, sharp. He was in his fifties, his hair gray, his eyes nearly black and too small. When he smiled, his teeth gleamed white, with gold inlays that flashed. He smiled at Charlie's awe.

"Good greenhouse," he said. "You want to see it?"

"Sure do. You finish going through the plants?"

"All that's been inside. Nothing. They haven't been bothered. This here's an experimental special environment room." He pointed to one of the small glass-enclosed rooms within the big glass structure. There were six of the small rooms altogether, each with an assortment of plants, many in flower or fruiting. "We can keep different temperatures in them," Ramos said. "And mix different air for them, more carbon dioxide, or not so much, things like that. Some like more oxygen than others. That's the propagating room back there."

They walked through the building with him as he explained the various areas. When he got to a maze of pipes, Charlie stopped him. The pesticides were stored in a separate room on the end of the garage; the carbon dioxide came through a pipe from the house. Water and fertilizer came through other pipes, and the whole could be run by the computer. "Except for now," Ramos added, flashing his gold-edged smile. "Now we just do it the old-fashioned way, by guess and by God."

"And the night of the deaths, insecticide was released in here," Charlie murmured. "I'd think you'd be pretty happy to have the computer out of the picture."

"Told the police, and I tell you now. Computer didn't do it. Took a hand to open that valve, not a computer giving orders."

"Show me," Charlie said.

Ramos led them to the end of the wall with the spaghetti tangle of pipes. "See that one," he said, pointing to a narrow steel pipe. "Goes to the malathion in the storage shed. From the unit it goes to a mixer and then gets mixed with water and pressurized and comes out like a spray. I turned it off early that day because we were out of malathion and had to install a new unit. Didn't need the stuff right away and never got around to opening the valve again. Told the police that, too. They chose not to believe me, I guess. Thought I might have forgotten."

"Which valve opens and closes that pipe?"

Ramos pointed again. One valve among dozens. "The idea is that they stay open all the time and the computer regulates what goes through them. But when something runs out, I'm in charge. Me or one of the boys. Bring in more fungicide and set it up, or more pesticide, fertilizer. And when we run out, we shut the valve, or it messes up the readings, pressure, that sort of thing. Stuff might be forced through the wrong way, or not enough of whatever would get sprayed. I don't forget stuff like that."

"Who would have known about it?" Charlie asked, trying to follow the network of tubing that spread throughout the large greenhouse. It was futile; he couldn't do it.

"Mr. Schoen or Dr. McDowd, the horticulturist. He's a consultant, comes in two, three times a week now. Me. One of my men. He wasn't here that weekend, though."

"Gary Elringer?"

"Not to my knowledge. Not his department. Didn't care to know what went on in here."

"How did you get rid of the poison once it was in the air?"

"We can exhaust the air in here in four minutes flat. Just about all of it. Takes just a couple of seconds for the experimental rooms. That's what the police wanted to hear about, not the valve."

Charlie studied him curiously. "They thought Rich Schoen might have been suffocated in here and moved?"

"Course, they didn't tell me what they thought, but they sure looked over the experimental rooms and asked questions about how we could exhaust the atmosphere in them."

"Was any other valve turned the wrong way? Off or on?"

"Nope, not that I could see. The alarm went off and some damn idiot broke the glass to let the air out. By the time I got here and got things organized, the exhaust system working, there was glass everywhere, and they broke the water pipe somehow, so there was water underfoot. A mess! They sure made a mess."

"They all trooped out here?"

Ramos looked toward the big house and shrugged. "They must have had a dozen or more cops up there. The computer flashed the alert about poison, and Alexander and Bruce Elringer led the whole pack out here. Bruce, I guess, was the one who began banging away on the glass with a spade."

They continued the tour, Charlie feeling more and more frustrated. Too many ways it could have been done, he thought grumpily. The cold-storage room, in here, the vacuum system in the elevator, God alone knew what else. They paused when a tractor with a grader blade started up. It was moving a pile of bark mulch; two men shoveled the stuff into big plastic bags.

"Buy it by the truckload," Ramos said over the noise of the machine. "Some of the plants don't like sphagnum. We dress them up with bark mulch." He looked at Charlie shrewdly then. "The police wanted to see the wheelbarrows, the garden cart."

Almost helplessly, Charlie nodded. "I might as well see whatever interested them."

Two wheelbarrows, one large-wheeled cart that was piled with sphagnum moss in burlap sacks. Charlie regarded them, feeling nothing but blank, and then took Constance by the arm. "Thank you, Mr. Ramos. You've been helpful."

"Be damned if I have," Ramos said.

12

Looking for Alexander they found Beth instead. She was pale and nearly in tears. "I just can't stand much more," she said wearily. "They're all driving me batty." She had a sweatshirt over her arm, and was dressed in jeans, a plaid shirt, and sneakers. "I'm going down to the beach."

"What happened?" Constance asked.

At the concern in her voice, Beth nearly wept. She shook her head dumbly.

"Have you eaten anything yet? Come on, let's get something in you before you go out. It's pretty cool, and everything's still wet from the fog. I'll catch up with you, Charlie."

He watched her lead the young woman into the breakfast room, and continued on his way to find Alexander. Whatever was bugging Beth, Constance would learn within five minutes, he thought, and he would have bet on it if there had been anyone around to steal money from.

Charlie had turned toward the basement stairs when he saw Harry and Bruce in the wide corridor outside the library door. They seemed to be arguing. Abruptly Harry took Bruce's arm and steered him to the nearest garden door and they entered. Charlie changed his goal and trotted up the stairs to the hall, on around the curve, and entered the garden on the upper level, moving quietly now. He knew that no one below could see through the greenery to this area. It's a jungle out there, he thought, and began to make his way around the garden cautiously, ducking when he had to keep out of sight in case one of them happened to look up.

He had gone two-thirds of the way around before their voices floated up to him. They were at the bar, one on each side of it. Now he could see the tops of their heads. Moving with even more caution, he edged his way down the steps closest to the bar until the blur of their voices cleared enough to catch the words, and then he stopped moving altogether. A luxuriant banana plant screened him from them. A large red protuberance indicated that the plant was going to bear fruit. It looked strangely obscene. He listened.

Bruce had been cursing steadily for nearly a minute already, a monotone of filthy words; Harry hit the bar top with a hard slap.

"Just stow it, for Christ's sake, and listen. There's no time for that now. Can you get her in line?"

"I told you already. Sure. I'll get Mom on it. Don't worry."

"Don't worry! Right. I'll remember that. Look, we need to float a rumor. I want the word out that BOS and BOS Two make UNIX look like a child's game. And that we'll announce in the fall and show in the spring. That's all."

"Fuck you! We never went for vapor ware before!"

"Will you shut up! Grollier would be good to start the leak. Who can we get to spill it?"

"Not Beth, even if we had her already. She knows too much to spill, and Grollier knows that. One of Alexander's team?"

"No. Same reason."

"But why vapor ware? Why now? What the fuck are you digging in that shit for?"

"Christ!" Harry moaned in a despairing voice. "Use your head! We need cash, lots of it, and we need it soon. Or it's bottom's up for us. We can't go for DOD money, but what if they come to us? Our terms? They all know what Gary was working on. Good Christ, the whole world knows what he was after. Now a rumor that says he did it. They come to us. You have to keep Beth in line, keep her trap shut, don't rock the boat for the next three, four months at least. That'll give us time for the rumor to come back home to roost. And then, fuck her!"

"It's too vague," Bruce said after a pause. "BOS they know, but they'll see BOS Two as a series boost, no more than that."

"Wrong," Harry said. "We want this leak phrased very carefully; that's why it has to be someone who isn't aware of the significance. That's why Beth wouldn't do. BOS 3.7 and BOS Two 2.4, say. That should do it, don't you think?"

There was a longer pause and then Bruce spoke again, his voice more guarded now. "It wouldn't have to be Grollier. There are a couple of others who'd work out just as well. Sal Vinton, for example. Laura could do it, Harry. With Sal Vinton Laura would do great."

Charlie had been content just to hear the voices; now he wished he could see the two men as well. He moved the branch in front of his face slightly, and caught another movement from the corner of his eye. He looked harder and saw Jake eavesdropping exactly as he was, from the upper level, hidden by foliage. Jake obviously had been aware of Charlie for some time. He nodded slightly and made no other motion, made no sound.

"The next item is when," Harry said finally, without a change in his voice at all. "As soon as possible. This weekend will be a bust, naturally. Monday she can get it started. Two weeks, three should be time enough . . ."

Jake was moving now, easing himself back up the steps. He made his way to the nearest sliding door and pushed it open, then stepped before it, as if he had only then entered the atrium. He called out, "Beth, are you in here?"

Charlie watched the two heads below as Bruce and Harry quickly left the bar, and then the garden altogether. He turned to Jake. "Thanks. I was getting a lesson in computer ethics, I think."

"If we wanted to save souls, we'd have joined the ministry," Jake said sharply; he turned and went through the doorway.

Beth had felt too awkward to ask Mrs. Ramos for breakfast, and too much in the way to go to the kitchen and make something for herself. Now she admired how matter-of-factly Constance asked for scrambled eggs, toast, and fresh coffee for her. "It's the idea of so much money," she said suddenly, and felt as if she had only then learned something important. But that was it.

The money was turning everyone into a stranger, and she was a stranger to herself. "I just blew up at Maddie," she said in a small voice. "Funny. All the years I was with Gary, all the times when I might have found excuses to blow up at her, I never did, but now . . ."

"What does she want you to do?"

"Be nicer to Bruce, for one thing," she said bitterly. "It's like saying be nice to a rattlesnake."

Mrs. Ramos brought in dishes and coffee and left again without a sound. Constance poured for them both, although she felt afloat in coffee already. Somehow, she thought, sharing coffee, sharing food made conversation easier. Made self-revelation easier, she corrected herself.

"She's treading awfully close to hysteria," Constance said when Beth seemed disinclined to continue. "People in that state do and say things they might not ordinarily."

"I suppose. We never had money before. My family never did. My family worked for the state government; my mother was a nurse for a time and quit as soon as we were in college. My brother and me, I mean. We had scholarships, but he dropped out. Too rough financially for him, and he wanted to get married. Even when Gary began making money, we didn't really have money. You know what I mean? He would get a check for a thousand dollars and spend it on something that cost two thousand, instantly. Then the company came along and everyone was on salary, and we still didn't have money. Always a bigger or better something to be bought, more workspace to rent, more help to be hired. On and on. It was just starting to get better when I went back to school. I really thought all the scrimping was over with by then. I think they all thought so. None of them had real money, either. Ideas, schemes, dreams, hopes, but no cash. Except Milton, I guess. But not the rest of us."

All this was beside the point, Constance realized. This was not what Beth and Maddie had fought about. She waited. When the door handle started to move, she got up and very pleasantly took the tray from Mrs. Ramos, murmured something, and returned to the table with it. Beth was still gazing out the window, oblivious.

"She's saying if I had been nicer to Gary, if I hadn't walked out on him, none of this would have happened. He turned mean because of me. And now everyone's being so terrible to Bruce that he'll be hurt, he'll turn mean or something. She wants me to be nicer to him, tell him I don't want any money for the shares of stock, that I'll wait until it's convenient, until the trouble here blows over."

"Eat your breakfast," Constance said when she fell silent again.

Beth took a bite, then another, without looking at the food. Then she put her fork down and drank more coffee. "She said Bruce agreed to awful settlement terms with his wife. His ex-wife. Because he thought there would be money. If I'd been with Gary he wouldn't have thought of that stupid game. Grown men skulking around with balloons, water guns, brother against brother. All my fault! If I'd stayed with him and we'd had children, he wouldn't have got involved with Smart House!" Her chin was quivering again, and her eyes were glassy with unshed tears.

Constance put her hand on Beth's arm and said firmly, "Beth, she's very frightened, you know. Why is she so frightened?"

"Her world's ending. Gary dead. Bruce a . . . She thinks Bruce killed his brother, I suppose. Gary was the sun, Bruce is the moon, and that's all she ever had. It scares her to death."

Charlie and Alexander were in Gary's suite. Charlie was in the chair before the computer, hating it fiercely; Alexander was in a second chair at his side.

"You don't have to know how I know," Charlie said murderously. "He had a separate set of commands, or something, that he could get to through this damn machine. Take my word for it. You knew him. Put yourself in his head. If you had a secret room, for instance, how would you open and close the door?"

Alexander chewed his fingers and looked here and there nervously and refused to put himself in Gary's head for even a second. "Anything. He could have programmed in anything he wanted. How should I know?"

Charlie sucked in his breath. "Okay. Okay. Let's play a game. We can talk to the main computer through this machine. Right?"

Alexander nodded warily.

"Let's pretend I want to lock that door and I don't want to get up to do it. What could I do instead?"

"Go through security. It's a separate program. Under *security*. Just type it in."

"Good. He'd use regular words like that? No secret codes or anything?"

"It depends on what he was doing."

Charlie muttered a curse under his breath and faced the young man. "Would he have a record of a secret code, if that's what he used?"

"I don't know."

"You do know!" Charlie yelled at him. Alexander looked as if he might bolt for the door, and Charlie got up and grabbed his arm, pulled him to the chair before the keyboard. "You know, and you're going to find it for me. Not security. Anyone could find it in the main computer that way. A different program? A signal? An access code or command? What would it have been?"

Alexander looked terrified. He shook his head.

"You're not getting up until you give it to me. You hear that?"

Miserably Alexander tapped the keys. He was a two-finger typist. He watched the monitor as text began to scroll. He did something to clear it, and typed again, and then again, and again. He looked up with hope a few minutes later when there was a knock on the door.

"Don't you move!" Charlie opened the door a few inches, saw Constance, and admitted her.

She looked past him to Alexander, back to Charlie with questions in her eyes. He was scowling ferociously.

"Alexander is searching for the code Gary used," he said darkly.

"It's no use," Alexander said, appealing now to Constance. "He can't make me tell something I don't even know."

"What about the directory?" she asked.

"I know all the items on it. He thinks there's something in addition to those things."

Constance nodded. If Charlie thought so, there probably was. "Maybe not in addition to, but buried in one of the files you know about?"

"That's what I'm trying to check out," he said miserably.

Constance watched him for several seconds and then said, "What was he least interested in? The greenhouse? Kitchen? Something out of the house? The garage?"

Alexander shot a fearful glance at Charlie and keyed in a new command. Another. He was scrolling inventories of various rooms, the music room, library, and had just touched the key for kitchen, when suddenly he started at the sound of Charlie's voice, this time as soft and low and soothing as a fond parent's. "That's enough, Alexander. You may go now. I know you have work of your own to do."

He glanced from Charlie to Constance and then jumped up and nearly ran from the room.

"Did you see?" Charlie asked. She nodded, and he sat down at the keyboard and typed in: *TV Room*. A whole new screen appeared, with subcategories of furnishings, and then video cassettes. This list had caught his eye, and hers also. The first item listed was *Sesame*. Charlie moved the cursor to it and pressed Enter. Constance made a low noise, and they both turned and watched as a piece of the wall moved to reveal a door.

"I knew the son of a bitch could do it," Charlie muttered. Constance grinned.

He began to hum, a low droning sound that was more like a cat's purr than a human noise. He did not touch the door, but leaned forward to examine it, and then returned to the desk and picked up a pencil. He pressed the eraser against the first of three dots on the door facing. The door opened. They were looking at another elevator, this one no more than three feet by three, and on the floor there was a roll of blueprints and two of the hand-held computer controls, exactly like the one they had recovered from the gardenia pot.

"Well, well," Charlie said softly, very pleased. "Now, how about that!"

Beth stood at the top of the long trail that led to the beach two hundred feet down. The day was calm now, and even warm, a rarity for the Oregon coast. In the distance she could see tide pools left by the receding tide; no one else was in sight. She started down. The trail had been carved into the rock in places, paved in some places with a black topping, stairs added where the trail was too steep for safety, a railing here and there. Going down was simple, she had learned the last time she had been here; coming up again was not. Ever since talking to Constance in the breakfast room she had felt curiously blank, empty, and what thoughts had come had fled again too fast to consider. Yet she knew she had to think through the various things Maddie had babbled about that morning. It wasn't fair, she found herself thinking again and again, and this time she seized the thought and went forward and back with it. If she agreed to a deferred payment for her share of stock, she would stay broke for months, years even, and that certainly wasn't fair. But if she demanded her rights now, they would have to sell the company at less than market value, and that wasn't fair either. And she had left Gary's bed and board because of what he had become; he hadn't become that because she'd walked away. It wasn't fair! Bruce wasn't her responsibility. Nor Maddie.

What she really wanted, she thought then, was to collect some of the money the company owed her. Owed her, she repeated. Invest in Margaret Long's small press, go back to editing the kinds of books no commercial publisher would touch. No one even considered that she had her own dreams, her own ambitions, she thought miserably.

She slipped and grabbed the railing. There was a shady area of the path that was wet; a trickle of water crept across it, vanished in the tough dune grasses that went down to the high-water mark. The tide was lower than it had been the other time she had come down; the beach was wider than she had realized it would get. To the north another headland made one boundary, and the cliff that held Smart House made the other, but today she could get over the rocks in either direction, keep going for hours. She thought again: It isn't fair, and bit her lip in exasperation. Then she made the last turn off the trail and waded through sand to the hard-packed beach where walking was easier.

In the tide pools there were pink and purple starfish, and multicolored anemones that closed when she touched them, bubbling angrily, she thought. Small pink crabs scurried in their unreasonable sideways motion. She sat on the edge of a rock and stirred the water in a tide pool and watched the frightened creatures until she became ashamed of herself, and then she walked again.

At the northern boundary as she clambered over the newly exposed basalt prominence she stopped to gaze at the next crescent beach, as deserted as this one, with another rocky barrier at the far end. She turned and went back the way she had come. It wasn't fair. Going back, she did not pause at the many tide pools, some already brimming over with the incoming tide; she strode briskly, trying to think, trying to define what her responsibility actually was. She reached the southern prominence and stopped again. This cliff rose almost straight up and was broken into massive blocks and boulders only for the bottom twenty feet or so. From above one could look straight down into crashing surf when the tide was high. Now it was possible to climb over the tumble at the base of the cliff and go on, and on, and on. To California? To Mexico? Forever.

She started to climb over the fragmented rocks, and stopped again, this time frozen, mouth open, but no scream issuing. She was too frightened, too stunned to scream.

Wedged in the rocks was the body of a man in a dark suit coat, one hand hanging almost to the surface of a pool captured ten feet above sea level. He wore a gold watch. She could see the back of his head, the upper part of his back, his shoulders, one arm and hand. Hung out to dry, she thought, draped over the rocks because he was wet. The gold watch gleamed in the sunlight. His other hand and arm were not visible. Broken off when he fell, she thought clearly, and suddenly she vomited.

She had no memory of scrambling back up the trail, or of getting back to Smart House, but once inside, it seemed they were all there, and suddenly Charlie was giving orders in a crisp and even reassuring way. It was good he was there to take charge, she thought, because Milton was dead. Then she wept.

Charlie sent Constance and Bruce to the cliff top overlooking the headland. "No one's to go near it," he said. "Alexander, call the sheriff and the special investigator from the attorney general's office. Tell them we won't touch him if he's dead, unless the tide starts to move in too fast. I want the sheriff's homicide crew as fast as they can make it. Jake, Harry, come with me."

"You're assuming he's dead?" Jake asked as they trotted to the beginning of the trail.

"I don't know. But that damn tide has turned and I want a crew here before it reaches him. If he's alive, we'll call back."

They would haul him to high ground if he were alive, but Charlie knew he wasn't. Beth knew it, too.

On the beach, Charlie and Jake watched Harry climb up the face of the black basalt to the level of the pool, the rock that had broken Milton Sweetwater's fall into the sea. Harry climbed carefully and very surely. He skirted the pool and reached out to touch Milton, to feel for a pulse in his neck. He yanked his hand back fast, and now he hesitated, clinging to the rocks. He began to work his way back down.

"Jesus," Jake said in a low voice and turned away to gaze out at the ocean. He was hunched, his hands thrust deep into his pockets, as if he were very cold.

Charlie was remembering that the last time he had seen Milton Sweetwater he had been going around turning off lights. When Harry rejoined them, his face was gray. He shook his head.

"Someone has to stay here and make sure he doesn't get swept away by the tide," Charlie said brusquely. "Both of you. Don't go up there again, and don't let anyone else go up, either. If the water gets to him, give a yell and we'll get him off that rock."

He did not wait for agreement or questions, but left Jake and Harry on the beach and started back up the trail. The sheriff would be there soon, and he had a few things he wanted to do before that. The first thing was to have a look at the top of the cliff.

He sent Bruce back to the house, and as soon as he was gone, he turned to Constance. "Anything?"

"No. He wanted to go closer, but I stopped him. I wanted to get closer, too. Doubt that it means anything. He's dead?"

"Yeah." Charlie looked at the immense house against the cliff. The greenhouse was visible from here, and two cottages, the servants' quarters. The red tile terrace circled the house, then down a couple of steps to the landscaped grounds, paths surfaced with bark mulch, some with tiles or bricks. Nothing high grew between the house and the edge of the cliff, nothing to obstruct the view; he and Constance would be perfectly visible to anyone looking out. He turned his back on the house and studied the ground. Here the lawn had yielded to the basalt, and the basalt ended in a cliff. No fence, no guardrail. But why would there be? This was not a family residence; it was a showcase for business people who presumably would have enough sense not to fall off the cliff.

He walked toward the edge slowly, looking for anything. He stopped and got down on one knee to examine brown spots, dull against the basalt that had a surface shine. He looked until he found three more of the brown spots, skirted them carefully, and moved on.

"Is it blood?" Constance asked, keeping back.

"Probably." Two small areas, four spots, about a foot from the edge of the cliff. He took one step closer to the dropoff and felt a catch in his stomach, a tremor of fear in his bowels, the way he always did when he first approached a high place with no rail. It passed, and he looked down. Almost straight down here, to the jumble of broken rocks where the land and sea were slugging it out. Harry and Jake were standing where he had left them, both of them turned to face the sea. No one else was in sight, except Milton Sweetwater.

"He could have fallen," Constance said.

"Or jumped."

"But you don't think so."

"Do you?"

"No."

He put his arm around her shoulders. "We might as well go in with the others. I just wanted a look."

The sheriff arrived soon after they reentered the house. He took two deputies down to the beach, with Charlie tagging along behind them. No one spoke to him. The three investigators surveyed the body, consulted, and two of them went back up the trail. Jake, Harry, and Charlie followed. The sheriff was in his fifties, weathered with deep furrows in his face, his skin shiny and hard. He looked like a farmer, or a fisherman, Charlie thought, watching him work. He went straight to the telephone, still not speaking to anyone in the house, and he called for a helicopter, the Coast Guard rescue team. Then he hung up and regarded Charlie with unhappy eyes.

"There's what looks like blood on the edge of the cliff out there," Charlie said.

"I'm not on this case," the sheriff said. "State investigator is. But the tide's moving in pretty fast. If it wasn't, I'd just post a guard and wait it out." He looked beyond Charlie at the others, who had spaced themselves as far as they could get from each other and still be in the same room. The sheriff surveyed them with disgust. "No one's to go anywhere until Dwight gets here." He stalked from the room.

And that solved his own dilemma, Charlie decided. He didn't have to tell the sheriff about the little elevator. The question before had been when to tell him, and the answer was never. Dwight, he thought, Dwight Ericson, the state attorney general's man. He sat down to wait for him.

13

For the next hour they waited. Now and then someone got up to go to the bathroom, or to get a drink or get coffee, and was accompanied by a sheriff's deputy, right to the door, anyway. They spoke in monosyllables when they spoke at all. Maddie picked up a book and put it down repeatedly. Bruce paced, sat, got up, and paced again. Alexander twitched and fidgeted. Laura sketched, flipped pages, and sketched again. Harry and Jake were both quiet, subdued, and each one seemed wound so tight that no spring could hold such tension.

Charlie played solitaire and watched them all. They were staying as far apart as the room allowed, as if each recognized that a touch, a look, might be enough to set off an explosion. The helicopter had come, and they all had watched from the wide windows as it circled, hovered, then dipped down out of sight in a crescendo of noise, and departed again. Now they waited for the special investigator. One of the deputies stood at the window, looking out. And no one had had a chance to ask Charlie if he intended to talk about the game. He gathered up the cards and shuffled, dealt again.

Finally there was a soft rustling in the room, almost like a collective sigh of relief, and two state police officers in uniform entered with a third man not in uniform. He wore a khaki jacket over a T-shirt, and denim jeans. Harry and Jake both got up, and were silenced by his icy survey of the various members of the group. His gaze lingered on Constance and lingered longer on Charlie, who had leaned back in his chair to watch.

"You know the rest of us," Jake said then. "This is Charles Meiklejohn and his wife Constance Leidl. They're . . . consultants. Captain Dwight Ericson," he finished.

Looking at the newcomer, Constance realized that Dwight Ericson could well have played the part of the younger brother she never had. How pleased her father would have been with such a son. Her father had never even hinted at disappointment over not having a son, but he had taught his tall daughters to ski and shoot, ride horses and milk cows, and had insisted on college and professional careers for them. He would have liked a son who turned out like Dwight Ericson. He was not yet forty, large—over six feet tall—and broad in the chest, narrow through the hips. His hair was as blond as Constance's, his eyes the same shade of pale blue. She sat and watched as he and Charlie sniffed and circled like two stray dogs even though neither of them moved; she suppressed a smile.

"A consultant?" Ericson said, not quite voicing his utter disbelief.

Charlie nodded. "You're a special investigator?" His tone said Dwight Ericson was too green, too young, too naive for his position. He stood up lazily. "You know all about the fun and games that went on here last spring, no doubt. No point in going into all that again. But now there's a third body to consider. Shot?"

Ericson's eyes narrowed and he nodded.

"I think we'd better talk," Charlie said.

Ericson hesitated only a second, then turned and led the way out, into the library. One of the state policemen stayed behind, one went with him. The sheriff's deputy left. Charlie and Constance followed Ericson. Constance knew every eye in the room was on Charlie; everyone wanted to ask how much he would tell of the stupid game of murder they had agreed to months ago. There was no way to reassure them that he had decided not to talk about it; he had told them already, if they had just been listening.

In the library Ericson stopped at a long table and seemed to be considering it. Then he turned and looked at Charlie and

Constance more closely. "Meiklejohn. You were in on that Ashland murder case, weren't you?"

Charlie nodded.

"They brought you in to look into those other two deaths in
May?"

"To be precise, Milton Sweetwater came to see us and
brought us in." He pulled a chair closer to the table for Constance and another one for himself. "Ericson, we can work together, or I can poke around on my own, but one way or the
other, I'm afraid I'm in."

Dwight Ericson sat down and rubbed his eyes. "I'm not fighting you. You know the population of the state of Oregon? About
three million. And it covers an awful lot of territory. And I'm *the*
special investigator. I'm it. Frankly, Mr. Meiklejohn, if you can
help, believe me, I'll accept it."

Charlie's nod was sympathetic. "Doesn't matter, three million, thirty million, you're always shorthanded. I can show you
how Gary Elringer, and maybe others, moved around this damn
house on the night of the other murders without being seen."

"They lied about the computer keeping track of their movements?" He looked offended, like a little boy who had just been
told the tooth fairy was a myth.

"To a point. At least some of them have lied."

"What about the shooting? How did you know Sweetwater
was shot?"

"Didn't," Charlie admitted. "But it was a logical guess. I told
the sheriff about the blood on top the cliff. And I sure didn't see
a weapon of any kind. He was a vigorous man, in good shape.
Didn't seem reasonable to assume someone just pushed him off,
or that he fell or jumped. The blood didn't fit those scenarios.
Not much left except a gun."

"Right. Okay, how did they get around without the computer
tracking them?"

"Best way to see our find," Charlie said then, "is from Gary's
office, I think. It was Constance's idea. She figured out that Gary
Elringer would have had a private way to get in and out." They
went down the stairs to the basement.

"See," Charlie said in Gary's office a few seconds later. "You
call up the television room directory on the computer, and use
the secret code and watch!" Ericson made a soft noise in his

throat. "We just got here yesterday," Charlie said, almost apologetically, without a trace of mockery. "Haven't really had time yet to start digging, but this seems a pretty good beginning." He pushed the open button with the eraser as he had done before and they gazed into the small elevator with the blueprints and the computers on the floor.

Ericson stepped closer, then snapped, "Have you touched anything yet?"

"Nope. We just found it when Beth came in after spotting Milton Sweetwater's body. Didn't really have much time to investigate. But there's a back door," he added softly, "and the only place you can use it is on the first floor, exit behind the big walk-in freezer, into the small hallway behind the john and the dressing room. From there it's a straight shot to the Jacuzzi, or outside through a door in that hall."

Ericson motioned to the uniformed officer. "I want prints, fast. Everything in there."

He turned back to Charlie and Constance, and now he paid as much attention to her as to Charlie. "You just figured this out? Or did someone tell you?"

"I think most of them will be surprised by this," she said thoughtfully.

They moved aside as a second officer came in and the two men went to work on the elevator.

"No one knows yet that we found it," Charlie said. "I told you we had something for you. There's this, too. You might want to look for prints." He took the third computer from his pocket, handling it carefully by the top of the plastic bag. He described finding it and explained what the hand-held computers could do.

Suddenly Ericson grinned, and he looked many years younger. "Okay. What else?"

"Your turn," Charlie said gravely. "Was either man moved, dragged, dumped? You know what I mean."

They were playing a game they both understood, Constance knew, neither of them yielding an inch yet, still feeling each other out, gauging how far to go.

"No," Ericson said.

"Can you be certain?" she asked.

"Oh yes. You look for scuff marks, disarranged clothing,

marks on the floor or carpet, shoe polish, bits of thread, things like that." He glanced at Charlie, but did not go on. "We thought of that, naturally."

Charlie nodded. "Naturally."

"And you just figured out how that gizmo works, too?" Ericson asked, pointing to the computer in the plastic bag.

"They talked about it last night," Charlie said. "Bruce Elringer assumed everyone else knew about it, and they pretty much admitted that they did know, or should have known, but it slipped their minds."

Ericson made a rasping sound in his throat, as much like an animal growl as a person could make. "What happened last night?"

"I asked questions. They answered some of them. Then everyone split to go to bed. Constance and I could have been the last ones who saw Milton Sweetwater. We watched him turn off the lights. I doubt you'll get much more than that from any of them. No point in driving too hard until we have a time of death, is there?"

It was a question, but also a suggestion, very nearly an order. Dwight Ericson considered him another moment, then shrugged. "We'll do what we can." He started for the door, paused again. "You want to sit in on it?"

Charlie shook his head. "Thanks. Rain check? What I bet they'll tell you now is that they went to sleep, those we didn't meet again anyway, and no one heard or saw a thing."

"Yeah. Bruce Elringer and Jake Kluge were up and prowling. And Bruce claimed he had a gun." Ericson took a breath and started to leave again. "Bet it's missing."

Charlie grinned. "Mind if I do a little prowling of my own?"

"Help yourself. When I'm done upstairs, maybe we can sit down somewhere and have a cup of coffee? See you later."

Charlie chuckled. Not quite a question, more like a suggestion or even an order. He decided Dwight Ericson was okay. He took Constance by the arm. "Let's go to the roof for a breath of air."

They left the office and walked to the main elevator at the end of the corridor, eighteen feet, twenty feet away, but side by side with the secret one. The arrangement on the second floor was like the basement setup: Gary's suite with the elevator door in the closet was as far from the main elevator as it was here. And on the roof, they were right next to each other, he knew. He wanted to look at the two doors, at the concealment provided there. He had not yet examined that. The housing was a redwood structure on the roof. Charlie walked around it slowly, then entered the storage section. There was the pile of outdoor furniture, several small tables, lounges. From the inside it was not at all obvious that a second elevator had been provided for. From outside, the little elevator was just as invisible, the door perfectly hidden in the redwood siding.

"Are you looking for something in particular?" Constance asked after a moment. Charlie was on his knees examining the wood.

"Damned if I know," he muttered. "We'll have to wait for Ericson's men to finish with it, I guess. Are you getting hungry?"

"Yes. It's after two."

"How about we continue this search in the kitchen."

Mrs. Ramos was heaping turkey and ham and cheeses on platters under the supervision of another uniformed officer. Her composure wavered momentarily when Charlie and Constance entered.

"Wonderful!" Charlie said. "What we'll do, Mrs. Ramos, is make up a few sandwiches and take them into the breakfast room. If that's okay with you."

"Or even if it isn't," she said and went on arranging a tray with onion rings, pickles, and lettuce.

Charlie nodded pleasantly and began to make sandwiches. Silently Mrs. Ramos brought a tray for him, and napkins, coffee cups. She filled a small pot with coffee from an urn and put it on the tray, then went back to the big one she had been working on. In a few moments Charlie was satisfied; he picked up the tray and started out.

"Will you tell the captain I have a sandwich for him in the breakfast room?" he asked the officer who was eyeing the tray hungrily. In a low voice he added, "She can't stand to see anyone go hungry. Go sniff the ham a time or two." The officer was already moving toward the worktable before Charlie reached the small hall that separated the kitchen from the breakfast room.

They were just finishing their sandwiches when Dwight Ericson joined them and sat down with a grunt. He stared out the wide glass expanse at the sea where fog was forming again in the distance. Closer, the ocean sparkled.

"Nothing?" Charlie asked, and there was the note of sympathy in his voice that had been there earlier.

Dwight Ericson shrugged. "I wasn't pushing too hard yet. Not until we get the time of death and the weapon." He faced Charlie and grinned slightly. "Bruce Elringer says he never owned a gun in his life. His mother backs him up, naturally. Harry Westerman says that Milton Sweetwater always took a gun with him on trips. A thirty-eight. We haven't found it."

Charlie glanced at Constance, who very definitely did not say I told you so.

She said, "We could probably find a thirty-eight and shoot it over there and see how much sound carries to the bedrooms. But it would be better to wait for the fog to move in, don't you think?"

Dwight Ericson looked from her to Charlie, who raised one eyebrow and said in a kind voice, "You should have something to eat." He stopped there, although he might have added, "She does that, you see, picks the words out of your mind and says them before you quite get around to it. And puts others in your mind." But he didn't say any of this, not with the captain looking at her so warily.

Ericson picked up a sandwich. "It was pretty much the way you called it. Jake Kluge says he was in bed, almost asleep when he heard a noise, he thought, on the balcony. A door closing hard, something falling; he can't say. He couldn't go to sleep then and eventually got up and wandered down in time to see Bruce watching you. After he got his drink, he went back up and to bed and fell asleep right away. Period. Bruce says he was up working and got hungry and saw you two in the garden area and stopped to see what you were up to. Period. He didn't hear anything. No one else heard anything, and no one else was up wandering around. All sound asleep."

"But those two both managed to get some of that dirt on their feet while I watched," Charlie said. He picked up another half sandwich. "That end room is Bruce's."

"Yes. I didn't tell him you found dirt outside his door before he walked through it in front of you."

"Where are they all now?" Constance asked. The house was eerily quiet again. She very decidedly did not like Smart House.

"I asked them to stay in the dining room until we've made a search for the gun. They aren't happy, but they're staying put for the moment. All hell's going to break loose when the reporters start popping in."

"Right. You sure as God don't have to be clairvoyant to see the headlines: Smart House Claims Third Victim." Charlie finished his coffee and leaned back to brood at the sparkly ocean and the approaching fog.

"Did your people find any fingerprints on the little computers or the blueprints?" Constance asked, but without hope. The people in Smart House were also smart, too smart to leave prints. She felt something that refused to be more than a stir of uneasiness.

"Clean as a whistle," Ericson said.

"And that means that neither Gary nor Rich put them there, more than likely," she murmured, wishing the stir would come back with some definition the next time. Dwight Ericson was looking at her with a question in his eyes and she added, "Either of them had a reason to handle the blueprints and the computers, but the killer didn't, so he had to get rid of all prints in order to be able to deny he knew about the secret way to get around, or about the way to erase his record from the main computer."

"If your guys are finished with the little elevator, I'd like to have a look at it," Charlie said.

Ericson nodded, drank his coffee too fast, and stood up. "Me too."

In Gary's office a young officer saluted snappily and stepped aside for Charlie and Dwight Ericson to approach the elevator.

"I made measurements, sir," he said, looking at Charlie. He sounded like an adolescent at summer camp. "Two and a half by two and a half and seven feet high. But there's ventilation holes in the roof, and the doors don't really make a seal—the inside doors don't. I figured he might have suffocated in there and got moved, but it's too big, and too ventilated . . . sir," he added, and blushed furiously. He set his face deadpan and looked past Ericson, who regarded him sourly for a moment, then continued on to the elevator.

"Thank you, Howie," Ericson said. "Go get a sandwich in the kitchen."

The young officer nearly raced from the room. Ericson glanced at Charlie and said, "We've all heard of you, apparently."

But Charlie was paying no attention. He stood in the elevator and looked at it, turning slowly to examine each wall; they looked like quilted aluminum. Both doors were made of the same material, to keep the weight down, he imagined. He reached out to touch the wall and nodded. Cold. The fruit cellar/refrigerator room was on the other side. This wall was backed up by the dumbwaiter, and the second door that was still closed was on the wall in the fruit cellar, the space where the carts were stored. Satisfied, he nodded again, and turned to examine the open door more closely. The young officer had been right; it did not make a seal at the bottom, nor did the other one. There was a crack less than an eighth of an inch, but there it was. He sighed and looked upward. The ventilation holes were very small, but there was a ventilation fan in the light fixture. But, he reminded himself, Rich had died in the big elevator, so it didn't matter. He sighed more deeply.

A small handle on each door, the control buttons, up, down, open door, close door, none of it held him much longer. The second door did not budge when he tried the handle. Locked because there was no rear exit on this floor. He moved out and let Ericson enter and stood with his hands in his pockets scowling at the elevator that had become nothing more than the repository for the hand-held computers and the blueprints.

"Let's try one more thing," he said when Ericson finished his examination of the space. "How does the light come on? And the fan?"

"The computer's turned off," Ericson said. "Maybe it won't work without it."

"The computer opened it," Charlie reminded him. "But what are the buttons for if you can't run it manually?"

"Go ahead," Ericson said.

Charlie tried the buttons without effect until he closed the door, and then the ceiling light came on. On the other side of the door Constance gasped when the wall slid back into place and the elevator vanished. Ericson stifled a curse and moved in to examine the wall that appeared completely intact. There was a slight noise from behind it, and then it started to move again, and in a moment the door was visible and then swung open. Charlie looked strained.

"Claustrophobic," he said. "The fan must come on when it's in motion."

"My turn," Ericson said. "Meet you on the first floor, back door."

This time Charlie watched the wall slide into place silently, and just as silently he led the way from the office, down the corridor to the main elevator, and entered with Constance at his side. They listened for a sound from the small elevator next to this one, but there was nothing. On the first floor they hurried around to the back of the house; when they got to the rear of the main elevator, Ericson was already there, the elevator door opened behind him. Here they were in the narrow hallway that ended at the back of the large walk-in freezer in the pantry.

"The front door doesn't open on this floor," Ericson said. "I'll get back in and let you see how the wall works, and then I'll watch it."

Now Constance said, "You can both watch. I'll push buttons this time. And then what, on up to the bedroom suite?"

"Might as well," Charlie said glumly.

As soon as she closed the door, she wished she had not volunteered. The elevator was cold and she shivered, but also she had a feeling she did not identify, uneasy. Claustrophobia? Perhaps. The ride was very smooth, starting and stopping without a bump, the fan operating without a sound, and the feeling intensified until she could identify it. Dread. As soon as the motion ceased, she hit the button to open the door; when nothing happened, the dread threatened to become panic. She remembered that on this floor the other door opened and she quickly turned and hit the button on that side. The door opened as silently as all the other mechanisms. She left the cage exactly as Dwight Ericson had done on the first floor, unwilling to spend even a second in there in there that was not necessary.

It took Charlie and Dwight at least a minute to reach the bedroom. By then she was breathing normally. Obligingly she stepped back inside once more and closed the door to let them see it work here, and then went to the roof. By the time she left the cage and breathed in the good cool sea air, she knew she would never willingly ride in that thing again. This time she had to wait a bit longer for Charlie and Dwight Ericson to catch up with her.

Charlie looked as strained as he had when he had been the one inside, and she thought, of course; if she was uneasy, so was he. It just worked out that way.

"Try one more thing?" he asked her, his arm around her shoulders.

"Or a dozen," she said, managing a light tone, wanting to ease that tightness in his face now.

"Just one," he said. "Promise. I'd like to know if you can hear people talk if they're inside. Dwight?"

The captain nodded and Charlie and Constance stepped inside one more time. It was a tight squeeze. He closed the door and put his arms around her, kissed her, and then drew back and said in a normal conversational tone, "You are my good and true friend. Let's get the hell out of here."

She laughed and opened the door and they faced Dwight, who was shaking his head. "Nothing. Not a single sound."

"Now to see how you close it when no one's inside," Charlie said then and surveyed the open door, the redwood siding that had moved out of the way. "Here goes." He pushed the door to and felt it click into place, and at the same moment the siding began to move. It was so well constructed that by the time it was restored there was no sign that a section could move.

Dwight was looking sour again. "It blows to smithereens the alibis the computer record gave them," he said. "Whoever knew about that could go anywhere he wanted a damn sight faster than anyone on the main elevator or stairs and not leave a trace." He glanced at his watch and got in the big elevator. "Enough fun and games; back to searches and missing guns and noises in the night."

14

Charlie and Constance walked the grounds, the garden area behind the house, where the stone wall rose straight up like a fortress. Charlie regarded it with brooding eyes. "Maddie thinks a burglar scaled the wall to gain entrance," he muttered. "Fat chance."

"She doesn't really think it," Constance reminded him. "She'll probably make up a story about how Milton was out for a stroll and came across the same burglar, with a gun this time. It's comforting to her."

"I know." He linked arms with her and they continued to walk among the rhododendrons. The back garden was too shaded, with the house wall on the west and the cliff on the east, for much sunlight to penetrate. It was pleasantly cool and moist. The paths were bark mulch.

"You couldn't get a cart through here and into the house without some of it clinging to the wheels, leaving tracks," Constance said, finishing the thought he had abandoned. "Of course, if they both died where they were found, it wouldn't matter anyway." She paused and he looked at her expectantly. "I want one of those garden carts," she said with a nod, thinking of their apple harvest. "You can haul really heavy stuff in them easily."

He took her arm in a firm grasp and steered her around the front of the house. The vista there was of tennis courts, and a formal flower garden with masses of roses and lilies and flowers he never had seen before. Men were searching among them. The fog had moved in closer, lower, truncating the cliffs to the north and south; the sun looked pale and deformed already. Soon it would be completely obscured and this would become another foggy, misty day on the coast.

"Let's take a walk on the beach," Charlie said, and they veered seaward, only to stop again at the top of the cliff, where Dwight

Ericson joined them. Several men were gathered above the high-water mark, waiting for the tide to run out all the way. Two men were clinging to the basalt formation where Milton's body had come to rest.

At Charlie's questioning look, Dwight shrugged. "Nothing. They're using metal detectors on the potted plants in the house. But it's a big ocean. A good toss can get rid of a lot of stuff out there. Especially heavy stuff."

They watched in silence as one of the men searching among the rocks slipped and caught himself and did not move again for a time. When he did, Constance exhaled.

"You're sure Harry Westerman didn't have a chance to pick it up?" Dwight asked.

"Sure. Or put anything down, either. I was watching."

"Yeah. Well, I'm holding them here as material witnesses until we get a prelim on the death and time, through the rest of today, at least. But I can't keep holding them longer than that."

One of his men appeared and spoke quietly to him. He nodded. "Maybe that's the preliminary report on Sweetwater. See you later."

Neither Constance nor Charlie mentioned the walk on the beach now, as they continued to watch the men on the treacherous rocks below. Even in retreat the ocean hissed and crashed; the men were getting soaked. The fog had completely covered the sky, the temperature dropped, and Charlie shivered and found himself thinking longingly of the hot sunshine at home. Jake and Beth appeared then.

Beth looked very tired and pale, and Jake was still too tight, too tense.

"They said we can go anywhere we want as long as we don't leave the grounds, or go down on the beach, or into the atrium, or—" Beth stopped as her voice became shrill. She looked down at the men on the rocks, then let her gaze go beyond them to the visible ocean, all gray and foamy white. "They're still looking for the gun? They'll never find it."

"You're probably right," Charlie agreed unhappily. He glanced at Jake, who was watching the men below. "How smart is Bruce, would you say?"

Jake appeared startled by the question. "Plenty damn smart," he said after a moment. "I know he hasn't been showing it, but

he was a hair's breadth behind Gary, that's all." Beth started to
say something; he took her hand and held it. "Wait a minute.
This needs saying. Gary made mental or emotional cripples out
of everyone he came in contact with." Beth pulled her hand but
he continued to hold it. "I observed you with him all those
years," he said. "I'm not blind. He turned Maddie into a slav-
ering idiot. Maddie's smart, too, you know. Her husband worked
on ENIAC years ago, and she worked with him. She's kept up,
but Gary turned her into a *Saturday Evening Post* mom with
flour on her cheeks and apple pie in the oven. That was the
mother he wanted; that's what she became for him. Rich, Alexander? They worked on Smart House *for* Gary, not really with
him. We all worked for him. And we're all pretty much okay,
but, Charlie, he was a genius, a bona fide genius, and we all
knew it. We stayed."

Beth had been tugging at her hand. Jake turned to look at her
directly, and the expression on his face was no longer tight and
frozen in tension, but rather puzzled, even hurt; a muscle
twitched in his cheek. "Why didn't you leave him? Really leave
him, divorce him?"

Abruptly she stopped trying to free her hand. Confusion
crossed her face as she stared back at him. He released her and
jammed his hands into his pockets.

"Sorry," he said. "That was uncalled for." He glanced at Charlie and then turned to look out over the ocean. "The point is
that I did know what was going on, we all did, and no one left.
No one could leave. One way or another he held each of us.
Sometimes, being with him was like being caught in a blizzard
of ideas, a white-out of ideas. Not pie-in-the-sky spitballing, but
things that would work, that you could see happening, and you
knew that never in a million years would you have thought of
them. That was the attraction for some of us. He was stimulating
and challenging and he made us be more than we are, more
than we thought we could be. But no matter how good we were,
he was so far out in front, we knew we'd never catch up—and
that was the attraction, just knowing we were in the same circle,
that big things were happening, bigger things would happen. He
made us do the impossible, and by God, that was the attraction!
And if he wrecked our lives along the way, we let him."

His words had started out measured and calm but they began

to tumble and his voice became low with intensity. He was nearly whispering now. "If I ever met another man like him, I'd run like hell away from him. If Gary came back to life today, knowing the dreams he had, the plans he had, the ideas he hadn't even started to work out—" He was facing out to sea, his face bleak and haggard when he stopped talking abruptly. "We'd all be exactly where we were before," he finished in a flat voice.

"Right back in the dream," Beth whispered.

He shook himself and looked at her, then nodded. "Right back in the dream, and loving and hating every minute of it. Let's take that walk."

She nodded, and silently, without glancing again at Constance or Charlie, they walked away, side by side but not touching.

"Well, well," Charlie said, then fell silent as a uniformed officer approached them. It was Howie, the one who had reported to Charlie in the office earlier.

He started to salute, blushed, and stopped the motion before it was completed. "The captain said I should tell you we're going to shoot in a couple of minutes and see if anyone inside can hear the noise." Almost unwillingly, he finished, "Sir."

Charlie nodded gravely, and Constance suppressed her smile, and hand in hand they walked back to Smart House.

"What I thought we might do," Dwight Ericson said when they entered, "is have people in several different rooms and see what happens. With the draperies closed, doors closed, as much like last night as possible. Okay?" He did not wait for an okay. "I already told them what we'll be doing. They were supposed to leave their doors open."

Charlie ended up in Laura and Harry's room. He glanced inside the bathroom; it was almost identical to the one he and Constance had, but the bedroom was quite different. There were the two beds, and a desk, and comfortable chairs, but also a bookcase with very nice books inside, and crystal bookends. A crystal ashtray held paperclips and two cigarette butts. Laura's, he knew; Harry wouldn't risk his health that way. The usual clutter of hairbrushes and toilet articles, and two fine crystal-based lamps, were on the dressing table. It looked rich. His and Constance's room had articles in cloisonné, a bird, an ashtray, lamps. Each room had been decorated with care, with handsome accessories, apparently all different. Black hole, he thought. The term was taking on more and more meaning. He checked the sliding glass door, pulled the drapes together the final inch or so, and waited for the sound of a gunshot. A minute later he heard a tap on the door and when Constance entered, they both shook their heads.

She glanced about the room, nodded her approval, and they went out to the corridor to wait for Dwight Ericson. He looked disgusted when he joined them.

"Anything taken from Milton's room yet?" Charlie asked.

"No. Want a look?" He led the way down the corridor to the room numbered three, beside Beth's room, which was next to the stairs. On the other side of the stairs was Gary's suite. They entered the room; a uniformed officer rose from a straight chair and looked at Dwight Ericson for orders. Dwight waved him back down. This room was different again, the walls ivory, rich dark mahogany touches here and there, forest green carpeting, paler green bedspreads on the two beds. The accessories were gleaming copper. One bed had been turned down; white silk pajamas and a matching dressing gown were precisely arranged at the foot of it. The white fabric gleamed against the green spread. A briefcase was on the other bed, and papers were on the table. In the midst of them sat a copper ashtray with a half-smoked cigar and ashes in it. A glass with half an inch of what looked like water was also on the table, and an assortment of pens and pencils. Some papers were in neat stacks, others spread out as if Milton had been going back and forth among them. An almost military neatness was displayed by two brushes and a comb carefully lined up on the dressing table; the same neatness was repeated in the bathroom, the closet. A fastidious, precise man who had treated his possessions with respect, who liked order, smoked little, drank little, looked like a movie star and knew it, and died too young. Charlie sighed.

"How I felt when I was done with it," Dwight said with a last glance around. "Exactly nothing. He hadn't gone to bed yet, was working, and went outside to get himself shot and tossed into the ocean. Someone must have tapped on his door, or maybe someone was taken by surprise on the cliff by his late-night walk, or maybe he had a date out there. But why the edge of the cliff?"

"How did you get in? He said he intended to secure his door. I used a chair in our room."

"Never got around to it, I guess. We just walked in. You're assuming he went out through the balcony door?"

"At this moment, I don't think I'm assuming a damn thing," Charlie muttered. He could feel Constance's invisible fingers between his shoulder blades, and he looked at her. She was standing at the door, out of reach, but that didn't matter; he had felt her touch.

She shook her head slightly, bothered as he was by something not quite right but not immediately identifiable either. "Have you taken fingerprints in here?" she asked slowly.

"What for?" Dwight Ericson asked. "Even if we found prints, what would that mean? They could have trooped in and out of each other's rooms all day."

"Things look too clean," Constance said. "Cleaner even than our room. Would he have been likely to go around and shine things? What if there aren't any fingerprints at all?"

Dwight motioned to the officer stationed in the room. "Get Petey up here." As soon as the man was gone, he asked Constance, "What makes you think there might not be any?" He glared at the room as if it offended him.

"I don't know," Constance said. "It just looks obsessively neat, and I didn't think Milton Sweetwater was an obsessive man. I could be altogether wrong, of course. About the room. About him."

Half an hour later Dwight was regarding Constance with something like awe, and Charlie with resignation. "That couldn't have been just a guess," Dwight said.

No fingerprints had been found on the desk or the dressing table, on the lamps or light switch or any of the shiny copper accessories. The glass had yielded good prints, as had various surfaces in the bathroom.

"Get pictures first and then strip it," Dwight said to the technicians at work searching for fingerprints. "Everything portable to the lab. You can leave the furniture here. Come on," he said to Charlie and Constance.

In the wide hall outside the room, Charlie held up his hand. "I don't know about anyone else, but I intend to head for the bar and get a drink."

"Wish I could," Dwight said in a growly way. "Later."

"Speaking of later," Charlie said, "are you going back to Portland when you wrap it up here?"

"My office is there, but I'm setting up shop for a couple of days in Coos Bay. Why?"

"Dinner. We pump you. You pump us. The company pays. Deal?"

"Sure sounds like it might beat McDonald's." He glanced at his watch and grimaced. "Seven-thirty? I'll pick you up."

Apparently the police had finished their search of the atrium garden. When Charlie and Constance entered, Bruce waved at them from the bar, and Maddie nodded. A tray of cheese, tiny sausages, and crackers was on the bar. Charlie headed for the bar and motioned Constance to the table.

"I'll be waiter," he said cheerfully. "What'll it be, lady?"

"Wine, please. Are they letting people down on the beach yet?" she asked Maddie, who held a martini but seemed not to be drinking it; she merely touched the glass to her lips and put it down again.

"I think so." Maddie's voice was that of a very old woman, throaty, rough, quavering. "They didn't find anything, according to Harry. I think they're still on the grounds somewhere."

Charlie brought the wine and a plate of snacks, took a sausage, and returned to the bar. Constance helped herself to cheese, a very good creamy Brie that she spread on a wheat cracker. "Good," she said, and to her surprise she found herself thinking of one of their cats, Brutus. He had come in off the streets in New York City and was a street-smart beast. His favorite food was Brie, or any other cheese that Charlie had. For years she had tried to break Charlie of the habit of leaving a plate of cheese in the living room. In New York it was an invitation to untold millions of uninvited guests, and she had got in the habit of picking up his plate and taking it to the kitchen herself. Then Brutus came into their lives and within a week Charlie was retrained.

It was the damnable house, she realized, making her want to go home, back to the heat, the awful cats, everything that meant home, and no chlorine smell permeating everything all the time, no cloying gardenias and orange trees . . .

"Well, this must be where the party is," Laura said then in a too loud voice. She walked to the bar. "If there's a way to turn on some music, I'll furnish the quarter."

"And we," Charlie said, "are heading for the beach. I've been trying to get in a walk since morning. Maybe now." He held up his glass and surveyed the contents. "This goes with me. Ready?" He stood up and extended his hand for Constance.

"Yes indeed." She glanced at Maddie. "We won't be here for dinner, by the way. I guess we'd better stop by the kitchen and tell Mrs. Ramos."

"I'll tell her," Maddie said in her new old voice.

"You'll need sweaters," Laura called after them as they left the atrium. "Oregon summer! Hah!"

When they left the trail down to the beach they saw Beth and Jake walking toward them slowly. Beth's head was bowed, her hands in her pockets; Jake was several feet from her on the ocean side, kicking at froth and ocean detritus as he moved. He looked up and waved first, and then Beth waved and picked up her pace a bit.

"Relax," Charlie said as they drew near. "We're out for a walk, nothing more exciting than that." He looked around approvingly. "Nice down here." They all pretended not to notice that two men were still searching the jumbled rocks as the retreating tide uncovered them more and more.

Jake nodded. "About a mile to the next rock pile. Run up there and back and you've put in your two miles, a good workout for the day."

"I should hope so," Charlie said with a slight shudder. "I think we'll dawdle and poke." He had the firm conviction that an adult should run away from a menace, or run to a treasure, and walk in between. Children ran simply because they could.

"We've been finding agates," Beth said almost awkwardly. "But there aren't that many in the summer. It's best after a winter storm." She looked embarrassed, and said briskly, "Well, I need a shower. I'm gritty all over."

She and Jake started to walk again, then he stopped to say, "If you go past the rocks, keep an eye on the tide or you could be stranded. It comes in pretty fast."

"Thanks," Constance said. "We'll be careful. See you later." She and Charlie headed on up the coast.

"A mile," he said dubiously. "Doesn't look that far, does it?"

The cove was a perfect crescent between the two rocky arms that stretched into the sea and ended in twin jumbles of broken rock fingers. Now, with the tide still running out, the beach was two or even three hundred feet wide at the center of the curve, but the high-water mark indicated that most of it vanished when the tide was high. Against the mass of the cliff there were piles and heaps of water-borne, water-discarded logs, some of them over seventy feet long, three or four feet thick. Charlie regarded them with respect. A log that size tumbling in the surf would be a killer. An entire tree, skeleton-white, rose from the sand with the root mass higher than the branches that remained. The spread of the roots was twelve feet high, each root ending in a water-sharpened daggerlike tip.

They walked slowly and stopped now and again to pick up something for closer examination, then return it to the sand. More and more tide pools came into existence, each with its busy inhabitants, each needing study—purple starfish, gaudy anemones that closed with a disapproving snap at their approach, darting fish, and mixed-up crabs scurrying through life sideways. They covered the mile quickly after all and clambered up on the rocky outcrop to survey the next cove, identical to this one, just as isolated, just as protected. The rocks continued out to sea with waves breaking over them, foaming, crashing with eruptions of spray, like miniature rainstorms. They did not go farther.

There were the cliffs, sandstone with black basalt exposed like the substructure of the earth itself, the pale sand that looked silver in the fog shroud, the ocean silver and gray and foaming white. On top of the cliff was a black fringe of trees, and nowhere another person. Charlie slipped his arm about Constance's waist as they walked back; her arm slipped around him and they matched their steps.

"Know what I'd change about my life, if I could do it over?" he said after a few moments.

"Tell me."

"I'd marry you earlier. Think of all those years we weren't married. Wasted. Just wasted."

"Charlie, we were practically children when we got married, just out of school!"

"You might have been too young," he said judiciously, "but I was a mature, responsible, horny male." He ignored her chuckle and added, "Beth and Jake look good together, don't they? Something going on there?"

"If there is, they haven't got used to the idea yet. They looked like kids caught in a back seat." She tightened her arm about his waist and asked in a lower voice, "What's wrong? What did you hear or see or do or think?"

He stopped walking and stood still, facing the ocean, and told her about the conversation between Bruce and Harry that both he and Jake had overheard in the garden.

A shiver ran through her, and this time his arm tightened. Finally she said, "Harry sent Laura here to find out what Gary was up to, didn't he? Now this . . ."

"Doubt that either of them would admit it," he said, "but I'd bet on it. They're playing real-life chess, using each other, mating . . ."

She nodded. "That explains something else. She was so bitter, remember, because Gary talked about divorce and then so obviously sent her packing. He must have known what she was up to; he was playing their game, too."

"I think it's a miracle that he lived to reach his thirtieth birthday," Charlie said. They started to walk again. After a moment, he said aggrievedly, "You know, when they talk computers, I don't understand a thing they're saying. And they're not even really talking nuts-and-bolts computers, but the business end, the wheeling and dealing part, and even that is like a foreign language. I take it they're planning to get the government to force them to accept development money. Damn, I should have made notes so I can get in the money line myself someday."

When they got back to their room, Constance said she was gritty and salty and went into the shower, where Charlie joined her. She pointed out that there was time for two showers, and he pointed out that he had other things on his mind, and by the time Dwight Ericson arrived to pick them up, they were both fragrant and moist and shiny eyed.

The restaurant Dwight took them to was too elegant, Charlie decided after they were seated and the waiter confided that his name was George and implied that he had been born to serve them and make their dinner a happy occasion. Charlie sighed and looked at Constance, who was studiously absorbed in the elaborate menu, her mouth twitching with either hunger or amusement. He looked over the menu and thought with regret of the buckets of steamed clams he and Constance had shared the last time they had been on the Oregon coast. Here the food was overpriced, overwhelmed with sauces, and served by George.

When the drinks came, perfectly composed, perfectly chilled, he felt considerably more cheerful. They ordered their dinners, and then Charlie looked severely at the young waiter.

"George," he said, "I am a cranky old man, very, very set in my ways. In exactly twenty minutes, I want another Gibson exactly like this one to appear on this table, unaccompanied by conversation. And she will have another daiquiri at that time, and he will have another Scotch and water. And meanwhile I do not want any food to appear, nothing. No salads. No bread. Nothing. Got that?"

George looked more frightened than offended; he ducked his head and scurried away. Charlie sipped his drink appreciatively, then said to Dwight, "We may have twenty minutes of peace and quiet. Anything?"

"Something," Dwight said, and leaned forward. "And it makes about as much sense as anything else in this cockeyed affair. The preliminary report has it that Sweetwater was killed by the fall. He was plenty smashed up, cause of death a head injury. Also he was shot in the head, but the wound didn't bleed. He was already dead. Charlie, it looks like someone followed him down to the rocks and shot him after he took the tumble. Or else, someone hit him with a rock or something and then shot him and pushed him over the cliff. It doesn't make any sense either way."

"Good Christ!" Charlie drank the rest of his Gibson and thought he had been premature in saying the next one should appear after such a long time.

"Yeah," Dwight said with a bit too much satisfaction. "The only way I can make it work is that he was out there with someone and they argued. The other person picked up a rock and let him have it, one of those smooth, decorator rocks up there, and then he took Sweetwater's gun and shot him, thinking, I guess, that he might not be dead yet. That explains why there's so little blood on the cliff. Sometimes the good old-fashioned blunt instrument does the job without a lot of blood being spilled. Then the killer rolled him over the edge and threw the gun out as far as he could. Low tide's at six-forty in the morning. I have a couple of divers lined up to search for that damn gun. What do you think?"

"I think it's a goddamn mess," Charlie said glumly.

"But the tide was in," Constance said then. "It really doesn't make any sense. He was dead, but even if the killer didn't know that for certain, he was surely not moving, obviously unconscious. There couldn't have been any doubt about that part. Why not just roll him off the cliff and let the ocean finish it? It might even have passed for an accidental death that way. A man walking in the fog slips, falls into the surf among those dangerous rocks. At least, no one could have proved murder in that situation."

"I know," Dwight said with a deep sigh. "I know."

No one spoke for the next few minutes. George appeared with a new tray of drinks and timidly removed glasses, replaced them, stole away again without a sound. Dwight lifted his and stared into it.

"I'll tell you what else I think," he said with a touch of anger. "They're all lying in their teeth, protecting each other, protecting Bruce Elringer, protecting the company. Sweetwater finally came to his senses, brought you in, threatened to blow the whistle—that's why he had to be taken care of. And now they think they can close ranks again the way they did before."

"Bruce?" Charlie murmured thoughtfully.

"Bruce." His face was grim now. "I've known since spring that he killed his brother and Rich Schoen, and I couldn't put together a shred of proof because they're all lying up and down the line. If there's any way to tie him to that gun, I've got him this time."

15

Their food arrived and as they ate, Dwight talked. "The key for me was Rich Schoen," he said. "Why kill him? I can see why they'd all want to get Gary off their backs. From all indications he was a real monster, controlled his family and everyone at work with some kind of insane power that they all bowed to. Everyone who knew him must have had a motive to kill Gary Elringer at one time or another, while that bunch up there hardly even knew Rich Schoen. But who had the *most* cause to commit murder? Bruce Elringer. His brother had made life hell for him apparently, and he's in debt that makes the federal deficit look reasonable. His ex-wife took him to the cleaners, and it's been downhill since. So he had a real motive. Now *he* controls the women in the family, and they control the stock and the money, and he makes out okay. And who else had a real motive? Rich Schoen."

George sneaked up to the table and asked hesitantly if everything was all right. Dwight looked down at his plate as if he had to remind himself and then said, "Fine, fine." Charlie nodded. "Fine, just not clams." Constance laughed and coughed at the same time and had to drink wine to keep from choking. Dwight looked from her to Charlie in bewilderment and she said, "Never mind. Go on." George tiptoed away again.

"Okay. You know about the setup at the house, Smart House? It's some kind of miracle, to hear them tell it. And Rich Schoen's job was finished. He wanted to start showing it, to be the head honcho of the next step, raking in the dough. And Gary wanted to play genius inventor or something. They were split down the middle about it, I guess. And the company was going broke. So Rich and Bruce huddle and decide to get Gary out of the picture. Maybe it was Bruce's idea, maybe Rich's. Maybe Bruce will tell us one of these days. Anyway, it would take two to get Gary to the Jacuzzi, hold him under long enough to drown. We looked for bruises, anything to indicate he went in unconscious, that he was slugged first, or doped, and nothing. Hardly enough alcohol to measure. Nothing else. It's not easy to hold a grown man under water if he's conscious. He fights. I think they both were in the Jacuzzi, stripped, and got him in and held him, and when it was done, they got out and dressed, covered the pool, turned up the heat to confuse the picture, and got the hell out of there.''

"That's pretty damn impressive," Charlie said when Dwight paused. "I never thought of that."

"I've been on it a long time," Dwight said, pleased. He took several more bites while they considered his scenario.

Finally Charlie asked, "And you figured out how he killed Rich in the elevator?"

"Yeah. You know there was a big to-do in the greenhouse, poison released, things smashed, water and dirt everywhere. I kept coming back to that. What in hell was that all about? Then I saw those big plastic bags the gardeners use to shovel bark mulch in, dirt for the atrium plants, all kinds of things. And I realized that that kind of bag would work just like a thin plastic film bag, better even. Bruce could get hold of one without any trouble—folded up they don't take much room, and there are three different sizes they use in the greenhouse. So he gets Rich in the elevator and pulls the plastic bag down over his head. It wouldn't take long, Charlie," he said soberly. "And the reflexive reaction would be to grab at the bag, not the one holding it. Too tough for him to break, or even scrape his fingernails in and leave a trace. A couple of minutes and he's out cold, another minute or two and he's dead. Bruce probably put the mesh bag on him to hide any possible mark he left. There were a couple of very small bruises on one cheek, actually. Then he had to get rid of the plastic bag he had used, so he staged the mayhem in the greenhouse and ditched it when everyone was milling about." He stopped and leaned back in his chair watching Charlie.

Charlie was deep in thought as he finished his dinner and then was surprised to find everything gone. "Not bad," he said almost grudgingly. "Coffee?" He didn't have to raise his finger to get George, who appeared and deftly began to clear the table without a word.

"Coffee for three," Charlie said absently. "And please bring a pot."

George looked startled, but he said, "Yes sir," and was quickly gone again. It seemed only seconds until he was back with a coffeepot and cups, poured for them all, and retreated once more.

Now Charlie regarded Dwight and nodded. "You've covered the bases. Why didn't you go after him?"

"That goddamn computer security printout," Dwight said with poorly concealed fury. "They snowed me, all of them. Alexander demonstrated it and we tried to get around it and couldn't. It tracked every step and kept a record, and no one peeped about the hand-held controls, or about the little elevator that let him get around without anyone seeing him. Not a single peep."

"And you think the others would lie to protect Bruce?"

Dwight shook his head. "They hate him, maybe even more than they hated Gary. But they'd sure lie to protect that company. And when that didn't work, and the company kept on the slippery slide, they decided they had to end it, even if it meant Bruce's skin. Sweetwater must have realized it, being a lawyer you'd think he'd have known it from the start, but anyway, eventually he did. Maybe he even had the proof and confronted Bruce with it last night. Plead insanity, something like that probably would have been his pitch. Get the company off the hook, let them go back to making money, but by then Bruce was off on his own course. He wants the company for himself. Charlie, that company is big bucks, really big bucks. Multimillion neighborhood."

Charlie poured more coffee for them all.

"Dwight," Constance asked, "isn't there a test you can make to see if anyone has fired a gun recently?"

"We did it. Nothing. But we found a pair of gardener's gloves tossed in the shrubbery under the balcony. Under Bruce's window, in fact. We're running the test on them. Want to make a bet he wore them when he shot Sweetwater?"

"I never bet," she said. "But that makes it more complicated, doesn't it? I mean, he either planned it and took the gloves with him and knew the gun would be on Milton, or else he hit him with the rock and went back for the gun and gloves, and that is truly insane. Isn't it?"

"Maybe he's a nut," Dwight said slowly. "That might be his best plea. And if they all decide to go along, they'll provide anecdotal evidence to support such a plea. So could I," he added, "because he is a nut."

Constance looked at Charlie, who raised his eyebrows and shook his head. "Could be," he said. "I sure as hell can't come up with anything better."

There was another long pause, then Charlie said, "It's circumstantial as hell. I don't think you can tie him to the first two in a way that'll satisfy a jury."

"I don't need to. If I get him for Milton Sweetwater, I'll be satisfied. One murder, or three, he'll be out of circulation a long time." His voice flattened and his face hardened as he added, "I'm afraid you'll have to appear as material witness."

Charlie sighed. "I thought you were being pretty free with information. Let's see. The gadget in the flower pot. What else?"

"You heard him admit he knew about the gadgets in the first place, while everyone else was still denying any knowledge of them. And he's the one who brought up the subject of a gun. It was on his mind, obviously. The dirt outside his door, before he had a chance to get it on his shoes in front of a witness. I may think of another question or two before we're done here. Tomorrow we use divers and see if we can't locate that damn gun."

"What if you don't find it?" Constance asked.

"It's there someplace, if not in the water, then on the grounds. No one's taken it anywhere. We'll hold them all until it turns up."

"It's a big beach," Charlie said thoughtfully, remembering the heaps and piles of mammoth driftwood, all the crannies and crevices among the logs, the arm of rocks at the northern end of the beach, with more beach north and south, on and on and on. He shook his head. "I don't envy you the search."

"I don't think we have to pay much attention to the beach," Dwight said with a touch of triumph. "I thought of that, and had the guys look over the various bedrooms, the clothes in the closets, to see who had tracked in sand. You know you can't go to the beach and not track in sand, no matter how careful you are.

Even if you take off your shoes, sand seems to cling to you somewhere, to your clothes. Most of them were down there, but not
him. Not Maddie Elringer, either, but somehow I just can't see
her committing murder.''

Constance was looking at him with admiration. "You've been
very thorough. I'm really impressed. If the gun doesn't turn up,
maybe you should consider the possibility that he got one of the
others to hide it up the beach for him. I mean, if he got Rich to
help get rid of Gary, that's possible, isn't it?''

"Well," Dwight said dubiously, "considering how they all feel
about him, I don't think it's likely.''

As he continued to explain why he did not accept that theory,
Constance watched him in rapt attention, and Charlie ducked
his head and began to fumble among his credit cards. When they
left the restaurant a minute or two later, Dwight was in the lead
looking pleased, Constance in the middle, and Charlie last. Charlie pinched his wife, who jumped, but did not look back at him,
and George watched them all from a distance.

Back at Smart House, they stood on the verandah as the lights
of Dwight's car turned into a hazy red glow, and then a patch
of pink in the fog, and then vanished. "Dinner was very good,"
Constance said.

"And that was a mean trick you pulled on the poor guy.''
She laughed softly.
"Don't giggle about it. It was mean.''
"Charlie, he was trying so hard to impress you I felt sorry for
him. One of us had to be impressed. And I don't giggle.''
He opened the door and they entered. "You giggled very dis-
tinctly. I heard you. Want to bet the gun doesn't turn up under
the cliff?''
"How much and which side do you want?''
"It's my bet. I say it won't turn up. Ten bucks.''
"That's the side I'd want, that is, if I gambled at all.''
They were in the spacious foyer, where they could hear
Bruce's braying laughter from one of the closer rooms. Charlie
scowled and motioned toward the stairs, and they went up and
to their own room.
"Paperwork," Charlie said in a disgruntled way. "I've barely
even skimmed the stuff Milton put together for us. Okay?''

She nodded. "I want to make a timetable of sorts before I lose it all."

Together they cleared the table and pulled chairs closer to it, then seated themselves, Charlie to start reading the material that made a considerable stack by now, and Constance to try to decipher the various notes people had made about their movements the night Gary Elringer and Rich Schoen had been murdered.

When Charlie looked up again, she was staring at nothing in particular, a slight frown on her face. "What?" he asked.

She slid the sheet of paper she had been working on in his direction. "The timetable," she said with a sigh. "They keep turning up together all evening. But also, at least four of them tried to use the elevator after Maddie went down at about eleven, and it was busy each time. Or locked in place somewhere."

"That's one of my good questions," he said, scanning her timetable. "Why didn't it come when it was called?"

"Ghost or no ghost," she murmured.

Charlie groaned. "Rich could have been aboard, dead, or alive and chatting with a killer, or a chair could have propped it open, or a computer glitch could have done the same. Or they're all lying and alibiing each other like crazy."

"But if they aren't all lying, and if those men were both killed after eleven-fifteen, there are only two real suspects in this group, or else an outsider got in somehow," she added slowly.

"Right. Tell me something. Harry says he tossed his water gun out into the ocean, and Laura says that Milton picked up a water gun on the roof that night. What the hell does that mean? Would she try to implicate Harry on purpose?"

Constance looked troubled; slowly she shook her head. "I really don't think so. It's a relationship that most people would reject, but in a way they are mutually dependent. Each protects the other. There's real need in a relationship like theirs. If it was his water gun that Milton found, what difference does it make? Oh, he would have been lying about going to the roof that night." She paused, and asked again, "But what difference does *that* make?"

He shrugged. "I wish I knew. Let's go to bed. I feel like suddenly I'm on West Coast time and it's bedtime." It kept coming back to the same problem, he thought grumpily. At least two of them had the opportunity, and probably all of them the motive. But how the devil had anyone managed to kill two vigorous, strong men without a hell of a fight?

She began to stack the papers again as he got up and stretched, then pulled the bedspread off the bed and tossed it on a chair. He was unbuttoning his shirt when she whispered, "That's it!"

"That's what?"

She was eyeing the bed narrowly. "I knew there was something else wrong in Milton's room, more than just all that shiny copper stuff. Look at what you just did." She pointed to the spread. "That's the normal way to get a bed ready for use. Pull the spread off, or fold it down and take it off if you're fairly neat. But Milton's spread was still in place, turned down with the blanket and sheet. Remember how white his pajamas looked against the spread? Why were they even there? How do you get ready for bed?"

He blinked. "I give up."

"Your robe is still in the closet and even if you had got it out, you wouldn't lay it out neatly on top of the bedspread because that has to come off. Maybe in the winter in a really cold room you would leave the spread on, but not in this house, not in summer, not with a blanket on the bed. It would be stifling. And Milton was too neat, too orderly to have left his pajamas and robe out on the bed all day. I don't think he would have got them out until he was ready to put them on, and, remember, he didn't put a chair under his doorknob, or secure the door in any way. He must not have had time. The killer must have gone to his room, or he must have left it almost instantly. I don't think he would have turned down the bed with the spread in place. I think he would have folded it very neatly and put it on the chair, if he had had time to do it at all. Charlie, someone else turned down that bed, not Milton."

"And then wiped off fingerprints from everything in the bedroom. Laura?"

"Why would she? She didn't seem to care who knew what she did before."

"Harry, to protect her? Maybe. Beth? Her room is next to his and she says she didn't hear a sound. Beth?"

She had no answer. A few minutes later, he watched her fold down the bedspread on the second twin bed and remove it in a neat bundle, the way she did every night.

16

From the top of the cliff Charlie watched the men below swarming over the rocks, and Dwight Ericson prowling at the edge of the black jumble, where erratic waves now and again splashed on him. The tide was lower than Charlie had yet seen it. The morning was cool and still; the sun in the east had not cleared the cliff behind Smart House.

Jake Kluge appeared on the trail, coming up from the beach, wearing running shorts and a sleeveless shirt. He was very muscular and fit, and his loose-jointedness seemed appropriate now. He was not breathing hard after his run and the climb up from the beach. He waved but continued on to the house. Only a moment ago, Harry had gone down to start his morning run.

Charlie thought about how much he disliked men who showed off muscular legs in shorts, who made a ritual of running at dawn. At last he turned to the house again and saw Constance on the wide verandah waiting for him. He walked to her with dignified, sedate moderation as befitting his position in life, and they entered to have breakfast.

Bruce was standing at the door of the breakfast room glowering at Alexander. He yelled, "I don't give a fuck about that! I want that list! I have a right!"

"I'll make another copy for you," Alexander said. "I'll make copies for everyone. After breakfast."

"Be sure you do!" Bruce stamped out and slammed the door.

Alexander began to inch toward the door after him; he looked terrified, more of Charlie than of Bruce.

"Well, the boy's in a snit this morning," Charlie said cheerfully and drew out a chair for Constance, another for himself. "Sit down, Alexander."

Miserably he perched on the edge of a chair.

"This thing you will copy for him, what is it?"

"It's nothing, really. A list of things the police took from Milton's room, that's all. But Bruce is trying to make an inventory of the house, the contents. Afraid someone's stealing stuff."

If he looked any guiltier, they'd haul him away and hang him, Charlie thought.

Constance said, "I'll copy it for him." Alexander hesitated in confusion; she held out her hand and said firmly, "I'm sure you have more important things to do."

His indecision, while brief, was painful to watch. Finally he drew a sheet of paper from his pocket and handed it to her. He looked instantly relieved. "How long will they keep all of us? What are they waiting for?"

Charlie shrugged. "They're looking for the gun. As soon as they find it, they'll probably release everyone."

"If they don't let us go soon . . ." Alexander started, then shook his head. "They have to let us go. They don't realize the strain, the tension, tempers. We all have work to do. They don't understand."

"Oh, I think they do," Charlie said dryly. "I'm sure they do."

"Alexander, how well do you people know each other? Off the job, I mean?" Constance asked idly.

"Some more than others," he mumbled. "I don't know."

"Does anyone here know any of the martial arts, do you suppose?"

He stared at her as if she had uttered an obscenity, or was speaking Swahili. Charlie found that his patience with this skittish young man was wearing very thin. Alexander shook his head and mumbled something inaudible; he got up and sidled toward the door. Neither of them tried to stop him this time, and, close to the door, he turned from them and darted out.

"We can probably find out," Charlie said thoughtfully, "but why?"

"I was thinking of Gary. I could put someone in that whirlpool, winded, without a bruise. I wonder if anyone else here could."

Upstairs at that moment Beth was leaning against the frame of the sliding glass door in Maddie's room. She felt heavy, leaden all over, even her brain; she could not seem to comprehend what it was that Maddie was suggesting. All night she had twisted and turned and stared into darkness, and twice had started upright, holding her breath, listening. Finally she had turned on the light in her bathroom and left the door open a crack, and then she had been able to doze off, but fitfully.

Maddie had started out by asking if the detective intended to drag them all through the mud over the stupid game, but she had left that very quickly, and what she was saying now made no sense to Beth.

Maddie's eyes were red, her lids swollen, her face puffy. She kept looking past Beth, out the glass at the sea below, lifting and putting down her cup repeatedly without drinking from it. Her breakfast was on the table before her, untouched.

"You owe us something," she said. "You could have prevented all of it. All of it. He needed you always, and you knew that. You destroyed him and now you'll wreck Bruce's life, too, and mine."

"I don't know what you're talking about!"

"You do. You do. You drove him to that woman! He despised her. He told me over and over, and you drove him to her. And now you'll have the money and Bruce will be ruined. You owe us something!"

"What do you want from me?" Beth demanded, determined not to cry, not to scream at this woman who appeared insane to her now.

"You come home with me. Bruce is coming with me, too. We'll be a family again, the three of us. Bruce needs someone he can trust, someone to help him now. There will be enough money; you don't need it all, no one does. Not the money Gary made out of nothing. You owe us . . ."

"Stop it! Just stop it! I don't owe you anything! Not you, not Bruce. My God, he would have me hanged if he could!"

Maddie apparently had not even heard her. "He wanted a family. I know he did, a real family with you, children, a real home. He would have been happy then, contented. You took that away from him, from me. How can you be so heartless now? There's enough money. You don't have to destroy Bruce, too.

How can you do it? Be nicer to us, Beth. Please don't hurt us any more."

Beth jammed her hands over her ears. "I won't listen to this! Maddie, you know what it was like, living with Gary. You do know, goddamn it!"

"How he worked," Maddie said, and started to weep again. "All his life, just work, and you. The only two things—"

With an inarticulate cry, Beth ran to the door and out, to stand shaking in the wide corridor. She was startled by the sound of Jake's voice calling her.

"Are you all right?" he asked, approaching her with a worried expression.

"Fine," she said. "I've been talking to Maddie. Before breakfast yet. That's a mistake."

"I knocked on your door," he said, and suddenly he sounded awkward. "I thought we might have breakfast together. But after yesterday, maybe you'd rather not. Beth, I'm sorry. I shouldn't have dumped on you. Me yesterday, now Maddie."

"But you didn't," she said. "I mean, it wasn't what I'd call dumping." And now, she realized, she sounded just as awkward as he did. She took a deep breath and attempted a smile. "Anyway, I'm glad you talked to me a little."

"A little! Just my life history."

They walked to the stairs, where he stopped her with his hand on her arm, and now he looked at her steadily. "Listen, Beth, you let everyone take advantage of you. Me included. Now Maddie. Whatever it is she wants, she isn't your worry. She doesn't need to tie you in knots. Any more than I do. Last night, a bad night," he added grimly, "I kept thinking how I went on about Gary yesterday, and about my hopes, my plans, my concerns, and I realized all at once that that's how we all treat you and always have. I used to come over to your place, yours and Gary's, and watch you now and then and wonder how and why you put up with him and his pettiness, his constant demands, and last night I realized that I had put you in exactly that same position. I'm sorry." Suddenly he grinned and took her arm, started to propel her down the stairs. "There. I was sure I wouldn't be able to get through that, and I rehearsed it over and over when I was running this morning."

As Constance and Charlie ate ham and eggs and biscuits, Constance glanced over the list of items the police had taken for laboratory examination. She started to speak, then handed the list over instead, pointing to one of the items. "That's strange."

He read the line: *3 sheets, 2 blankets, 2 bedspreads*. The door started to open and hastily he folded the paper and put it in his pocket. Beth and Jake entered the breakfast room.

Beth looked from Charlie to Constance and blurted, "Have you talked to the police yet about—you know?"

"No, I don't," Charlie said.

And Constance said, "Oh, you mean the game?"

"Yes. Have you? Maddie thinks you have, and I was sure you wouldn't, not without telling us. Have you?"

"Why does she think we have?"

"Something Bruce said to her. The police accused him of keeping something back, lying to them. That captain practically accused all of us of lying."

"We haven't mentioned it, Beth," Charlie said. "But, Jesus, he has a point. All of you have been lying to him."

She bit her lip and looked down at the coffee cup at her place, moved the cup around on the saucer until it scritched like fingernails on a blackboard. Jake took her hand from it. "I told Maddie I'd try to find out for her. We should tell them, shouldn't we?" she whispered, not yet looking up. "Maybe it would help their investigation if we tell them."

"Has it helped you, Charlie?" Jake asked.

"Don't know yet. But, Beth, if it seems necessary to tell them, I will. You do understand that, don't you?"

She nodded.

"How stable is Maddie right now?" Charlie asked.

"She's not going to pieces, but she's close," Beth said. She glanced at Jake, who nodded. "I think she's had just about all she can handle. Why?"

"What would it do to her if they accuse Bruce of murder? Could she handle that?"

"Oh, God! Are they going to?"

"I think they might. In any case—" He stopped when Mrs. Ramos appeared with a tray and watched her until she finished and went back through the doorway. Suddenly he stood up.

"Excuse me. Right back." He followed Mrs. Ramos to the kitchen.

Beth stared after him, then turned bewildered eyes to Constance, who shrugged. Slowly Beth started to eat, but after only a bite she put her fork down again. "She'll take it really hard," she said soberly. "She thinks she failed Bruce over the years, and he knows it and reinforces that feeling every chance he gets. Last night, it was just awful. He kept laughing the way Gary always did, and she kept shaking. It was awful."

"Did he always try to mimic his brother?"

"Not really. I think this is part of the reversed Turing test they were playing with several years ago. He's perfected his imitation since then."

Constance shook her head, smiling. "Would you mind backing up a bit? What's a reversed Turning test?"

"Turing," Jake said. "After the mathematician. He came up with the original test. The subject sits at a computer terminal and types in questions and tries to determine which answers come from a computer, which from a person in another room. It's a forerunner of the research going on now with artificial intelligence. Gary's idea was to make voice prints and program the computer with them, plus pertinent data about each person being used, and then try to perfect it to the point where even a professional mimic couldn't fool the computer. So, a reversed Turing test, trying to fool the computer instead of a person." He added dryly, "The computer never misses anymore."

"My goodness," Constance said softly. "People do all the time, don't they? You hear a voice and think it's someone you know and turn around to see a stranger. Can it pick out voices in a crowd? I'd think the intelligence services would be after it."

Suddenly the silence was strained as Beth and Jake exchanged glances. Constance felt as if she had stumbled onto forbidden territory.

"That's one of the reasons for the isolation of this place," Jake said after a moment. "Gary wanted complete secrecy until he was ready to disclose the entire package he was developing. I wormed that much out of Alexander finally."

"Good heavens," Constance said then. "If it was tracking people by voice the night Gary and Rich were killed, it must have overheard the killer with them." She realized with a chill that she was talking about it as if it were a person.

"It wasn't a tape recorder," Jake protested.

"But it was," Beth said quickly. "Remember the first program Bruce wrote that was successful? It was a music program," she explained to Constance. "He could synthesize music, any instrument, and play back a complete symphony, every instrument with its own part, every instrument unique. That's how they could work with voices, any number of voices treated as instruments, to be played back."

And that explained Bruce's appreciation of Alexander's accomplishments as a programmer, Constance thought suddenly; Bruce would recognize exactly what it was that Alexander was doing, what it meant.

"Bruce . . ." Beth whispered then. "If Maddie thinks she's likely to lose him—"

Jake took her hand. "Beth," he said firmly, "remember what we were saying? They aren't your problem, none of them." He was gazing at her steadily, with concentration, as if trying to force her away from her thoughts. He did not relax until she finally nodded and lifted her fork again. "After breakfast, let's take a walk and then drop in on Maddie and see how she's doing. She likes to play bridge. We'll get Laura to play, too. Maybe it would help all of us to play cards for a while today."

Constance watched him with great interest. He could have gone into counseling, or the ministry, or anything having to do with an intense dialogue. He had the gift of focusing that was one of the requirements. She felt that during this short interlude he had forgotten her altogether. Now that the moment had passed, he once again could include her, and, in fact, did include her, invited her to play bridge with them in a polite way that meant her refusal was taken for granted. She refused.

When Charlie returned only a minute or two later, Constance was surprised that neither Beth nor Jake reacted to the new charge in the air. She could feel it almost like an electric current. She pushed her plate back slightly and stood up. "I think it's time for our walk," she said. He nodded and she joined him at the door. "See you later," she said over her shoulder and went out with Charlie.

"What did you find?" she asked as soon as they were in the hall.

"*Shh*. Outside."

On the verandah she tried again. "What are you up to?"

"I want Dwight Ericson to get his ass up here and get his men to work for me."

"Charlie."

"I looked at the popcorn popper. It's exactly like our old one that Jessica stole when she went to school."

He had never forgotten that their daughter had taken the popcorn maker away with her when she left for college. Having a new one come into their house had done nothing to dim the memory, the feeling of being suddenly bereft that he had complained bitterly about. Constance dug him in the ribs with her elbow. "Charlie!"

"And I found out that Mrs. Ramos had two sheets on every single bed in that house. She thought I was insane to ask."

"Ah. Well. You should have known."

He chuckled and put his arm about her shoulders and steered her toward the cliff. They went down the trail to meet Dwight at the bottom. He looked disgusted and tired. Seeing him next to Charlie gave Constance a little jolt as she realized that this was how she and Charlie must appear to others: one tall and lean and very, very blond, the other chunkier and shorter and very dark. She liked the way it presented itself to her mind's eye.

"Nothing," Dwight said, responding to Charlie's question.

"Not even a sheet?" When Charlie sounded that innocent, Constance always feared that someone might hit him.

"What now?" Dwight asked.

Charlie told him. "So one missing sheet. Maybe the gun's wrapped up in it and they're both at the bottom of the ocean."

Dwight chewed his lip scowling at the horizon. "You think he was killed in his room?"

"Maybe. The bed was funny, prints wiped off too many things. Maybe."

"And was wrapped in a sheet and moved to the cliff? Jesus Christ!"

"Maybe. If I had a crew of men, I'd have them search for bloodstains, and a burn mark maybe."

"Burn?"

"Picture the ashtray," Charlie said dreamily. "Half-smoked cigar, and a smidgen of ash. Where was the rest of it? Suppose Milton was smoking it when he was gonged. It would fall, obviously. Not in wet grass or weeds, or it would have gone out, and in that fog just about everything was good and wet, but the cigar was still lighted when it was put down in the ashtray. You could see the dead ash on the end where it burned itself out. And that means it was still lighted when it was picked up and replaced there, and that could mean a burn mark. Or someone relighted it, and somehow that sounds too damn macabre even for this bunch."

"Damn it, Charlie, that's reaching too far. He could have partly smoked that cigar anytime, anyplace that evening and put it down to let it burn out."

"And when did someone wipe the prints off the ashtray? Picture it. You've got a half-smoked cigar, and you have to get your prints off the ashtray for God knows what reason. You put the cigar down on the edge of the table or something and clean the ashtray and put the cigar back and let it burn without disturbing it again. That's one scenario. Another one is that Milton got bashed somewhere other than in his room, dropped the cigar, and the killer tidily returned it to its proper resting place after wiping off fingerprints. So a little ash is in the ashtray and there's dead ash on the end of the thing. Undisturbed until the police move it."

"In that case, why mess around with the fingerprints?"

"I wish to God I knew."

Dwight was very gloomy now. "You know what's going on over in Jordan Valley? Three, four hundred miles away from here, near the Nevada border, a rancher got beaten to death last night. That's the sort of thing I usually get called in to see about. Round up his work crew, the foreman, ask a few questions, maybe start the search for a poacher, get it over with pretty damn fast. Sheriff could do it, but chances are he's got cousins or brothers or sons working for the rancher; might be biased, they say." He was watching his men scrambling out of the way of fast-moving waves; the tide was rushing in. "Well, this is a bust." He grimaced. "The last time I asked a few questions about the carts, the wheelbarrows, and then found out no body had been moved. This time I didn't bother. God almighty, what a mess."

They walked up the beach after Dwight and his men left. "Not bad," Constance said, patting Charlie's arm. She did not mean the scenery, as he well understood.

"They haven't proved anything yet," he said.

She waved her hand, dismissing that. "They will." She told him about the reversed Turing test and the voice prints. "I'm getting a better picture of what Gary was actually pulling off," she said slowly. "I think that computer must have been able to understand anything said to it and respond exactly the way a person might. It's scary."

"*Hmf,*" he said, the grunt more eloquent than anything else he might have thought of at the moment. "How about *I'm buffaloed?* Think it would get that?"

She nodded gravely. "Or *fly by night.*"

"*Chinese boat drill.*"

She laughed. *"Wolf in sheep's clothing."*

"Wow!" he said, stopping. A particularly large wave crashed against the cliffs ahead of them. The rocks that reached into the sea at the northern end of the crescent were being covered rapidly by the encroaching tide. Waves smashed into them, sending spray and foam high into the air. "When the tide comes in here, it doesn't fool around," he muttered, and they started to walk again.

"It's damn hard to move a dead body," he said after a moment. "That expression *deadweight* came from the real world. Why kill him and then push his body off the cliff? Why wipe the prints? It's true, anyone might have been in and out of that room earlier. The killer could have bluffed it out. Why shoot him in the head after he was a goner?"

"Maybe he wanted to make certain that no one even pretended to believe this one was an accidental death."

Charlie came to an abrupt stop, his fingers hard on her arm. "Jesus! That's it!"

Startled, she turned to see him staring fixedly at the waves smashing into the black rocks.

He came back. "Enough walking. Walking, running, bad for the joints, bad for the knees. Let's go."

They returned briskly; now and then Charlie muttered something under his breath, and in between he hummed almost inaudibly. They had a never-stated rule in their house that anyone was allowed to mutter without interruption. Sometimes, when it was not entirely clear if it was a mutter or merely conversation too low to catch, it was permissible to ask, "Are you muttering?" Constance recognized what he was doing now very definitely as a mutter; she did not interrupt.

They met Beth on the red tile verandah. "Hi," Constance said. "No bridge game yet?"

Beth shuffled her feet. "Maddie doesn't seem to care one way or the other, and I can't seem to concentrate on cards today. They're searching again. We can't even go to our rooms now. What are they doing?"

Before Constance could speak, Charlie's fingers tightened briefly on her arm, then withdrew. "I'll see if I can find out," he said. "Good-bye, ladies." He sauntered off.

"Of course it would be hard to concentrate now," Constance said. "I'll tell you a story. Once upon a time there was a beautiful princess whose parents both died quite suddenly and left her an orphan." She ignored Beth's incredulous stare and said with a smile, "Sorry, but that's how these stories always start: They get right down to the point without any shilly-shallying. So the princess's fairy godmother came to the grieving girl and said, 'You must go live with your eldest uncle until you come of age.' Thus it was that the girl went to live with her uncle."

As she continued the story, Constance appeared unaware of Beth's disbelief and even alarm, as if Beth was convinced that she was in the company of a madwoman.

"From the first day the uncle beat the girl if she was too noisy, or too quiet. If she wept, or did not weep for her parents. If she ate too much or too little. And gradually she came to know what he expected, and always did that before he could beat her. When her fairy godmother came to see how she was, she found the child cowering in a corner watching her uncle, trying to anticipate what might arouse his wrath next. And the fairy godmother spirited the child from that house and took her to the second eldest uncle instead. 'Here you must remain until you come of age,' she said, as before, and left her there.

"This uncle was married to a woman who said on seeing the

child, 'Oh, you are so young and strong, and I am old and weak and soon I must die.' When the girl laughed, her aunt said, 'Oh, you are happy and gay, and I am careworn and sad and soon I must die.' When the girl ran, she said, 'Oh, you are straight and full of life, and I am tired and in pain and soon I must die.' This time when the fairy godmother returned, she found the girl with her hair tied in a tight knot, and wearing a voluminous gown that concealed her young limbs, walking with a bent, hunched position, rubbing her eyes often to make them red and watery. Of course, she removed her at once.''

Beth found herself strolling the length of the verandah with Constance, listening to the silly story, strangely unwilling now to pull away and run inside.

"In the next house, her aunt wept bitterly when the girl erred. 'How you wound me who loves you with such complete love.' And in the next, her uncle found her so pleasing that he could not bear to be apart from her for even a moment, and when she walked, he walked also, and became red in the face and held his heart and drew in long, choking breaths, but never complained. And when she ate a sweet, he ate the same, and suffered spasms of the chest and stomach, but never complained.

"In the next house her aunt promised every day that if she did well, then tomorrow she might have this or that, and tomorrow was as long in coming as the sun on a gray winter day."

They had walked the length of the verandah two times when Beth stopped. "The story doesn't have an ending, does it?"

"Each listener determines when it should end," Constance said.

"You left out duty and shame and love and a few other things."

"Not left out, just not reached yet."

"It's a very good story. Thank you."

"You're welcome. I think I'll see if I can find out what Charlie's up to."

For another moment they faced each other gravely, and then Beth nodded. "A good story. I'll see you later." She walked away.

Charlie was at the table in the breakfast room watching Dwight Ericson take Bruce Elringer over the house inventory item by item. They had finished the dinnerware and were on pictures, statuary. Bruce was sullen and mean, his face flushed dark.

Dwight was being extremely patient. And he might as well be, Charlie thought, since it was taking his men forever to make their new search. This was the part of police work he had hated when he was a New York cop, he remembered: detail work, searching, looking for one particular straw in a broom factory. He sympathized with Bruce when he considered the amounts of money that Gary had spent on Smart House: seventeen thousand for china, another three thousand for porcelain, nine thousand for silverware, on and on. Four dozen sheets at twenty bucks apiece. He shook his head and listened.

"Okay, okay," Dwight was saying. "The original inventory shows fifteen pictures, and there are still fifteen. Pass on. The statues in the foyer. None's missing, right?"

"Not yet," Bruce snapped.

"Okay, Mr. Elringer. You weren't able to update your inventory in the bedrooms, so I guess that about does it. I'd like a copy of what you have there."

Bruce clutched his notebook.

"Howie, go with Mr. Elringer to the basement office and get copies of what he has," Dwight said, still patient, but it was wearing thin.

"I'll make the copies," Bruce said quickly. "He can watch if he wants."

"He wants," Dwight said.

"Bruce," Charlie asked. "Exactly why did you start your own inventory? You did it last May, didn't you?"

"You know it. Because I don't trust the one Rich put together. Don't trust the people who've been free to come and go in this place. Five-hundred-dollar ashtrays, three-hundred-dollar lamps, thousand-dollar knickknacks! Someone's got to keep a list, keep track." He stood up, still clutching his notebook. "You know how much has walked out already? Thousands! My money, and it just walks out the door!"

"Yes. So you said before. But exactly what walked out the door? I mean, was there something specific, or just a general suspicion?"

Bruce leaned forward and nearly spat the words. "A blue malachite whale, about this long." He held out his hands to indicate ten or twelve inches. "Seven hundred dollars! What the fuck for? Who needs stuff like that in bedrooms?"

"When was it gone?" Charlie asked. "How did you know it was missing already last May?"

Bruce glared at him, then at Dwight. "You fuckers, you'll try to pin that on me, too, won't you? It won't work! That's why I began the inventory, to prove that someone here has sticky fingers. It was in my room in May when we first came here, and I looked at it and looked at the price on the inventory and I knew the sucker would tempt someone. So I started the list. Every fucking room has something like that. Portable, pricey, tempting. What the fuck for?"

"When did you realize it was gone?" Charlie asked again, as patient as Dwight, but with an edge to his voice also.

"How the fuck do I know? June, July. When I came back in the summer sometime. It's gone, all right. Who the fuck knows what else is missing by now?"

"And did you update your inventory back then when you returned?"

"You bet your ass I did! And again this time!"

"Wonderful," Charlie murmured and relaxed back in his chair, finished.

One of Dwight Ericson's men entered the room as Bruce and Howie left. The newcomer was another of the earnest uniformed officers. He saluted, and Dwight glanced at Charlie with a look of embarrassment.

"I think we might have found the burn mark," the young officer said, and Dwight and Charlie both stood up fast. "At least, there's a burn up on the balcony, and it might be fresh. No way of knowing, I guess."

"Oh, sweet fanny," Charlie breathed. "Don't let anyone touch it! Are they all still in the library or television room?"

The officer acted as if a stranger asked questions and gave orders routinely. Without hesitation he said they were.

"Make sure they stay there," Dwight said. "Let's go look."

The mark was hardly visible, a dark smudge against the redwood plank on the balcony. When Dwight started to get too close to it, Charlie automatically motioned him back.

"You're an expert on burns?" Dwight asked, irritated enough finally for sarcasm to overtake the patient voice he had been able to maintain before.

"Oh yes," Charlie said softly. "Oh my, yes." He surveyed the area, a foot in from the edge of the balcony, at the place where the floor was cut away for the stairs to the grounds below. The railing was waist high, with a middle bar; the balcony was fifteen feet wide, narrower at both ends where the stairs began. Ten feet here, five for the stairs. The closest window was to the suite that had been Gary Elringer's. Satisfied with the general survey, he now dropped to one knee and studied the burn mark more intently, and then he bent lower and sniffed it. He stood up and looked at Dwight.

"This is where he got bashed in the head and dropped his cigar. I think you'll be able to get enough ash from the wood to cinch it. There's a bit caught in the grain."

Dwight was regarding him with a very blank expression. "You are an expert on fires, aren't you? I read about that."

Charlie nodded. "For a lot of years. An awful lot of years." He turned away and gazed out at the ocean, the smell of rotten smoke in his nose, too many memories surging now, too many rotten fires blazing before his mind's eye. "Can your tech men deal with that?"

"Yeah. We'll cut out the section, but first we'll use a vacuum on it." He began to give orders to his men.

Gazing at the brilliant ocean, Charlie thought of the many smells of fire. The blazing fire without added water or chemicals, almost a clean smell, an autumnal smell; then the filthy odor of plastics and fibers and chemicals, wet wood and paint and insulation . . . A cold fire was worst. No more blazing, no more heat, but somehow smoldering still, emitting a poisonous vapor, that was the worst stink in the world. Then the builders came in and sealed it, and that was yet a different odor, almost corruption-sweet, and the glare of the sealant, a sickly blue-white with a high gloss . . .

"Let's have a look below," Dwight said at his elbow.

Charlie followed him down silently, thinking: They would find wheel marks that would now take on a significance they had not had this morning, and maybe a broken plant or two that had gone unnoticed before, with any luck a smear of blood. And so it was. They found the wheel marks and the broken plant, and even a very small smear that could have been blood. Lab tests would decide.

17

Before Charlie left Dwight to oversee the removal of a section of the planking, he said, "The gun will turn up. I'd have them go through Maddie Elringer's room and car again." A glint of satisfaction showed for a moment in Dwight's pale eyes.

"Yeah. He could have moved it more than once. See you in a little while, Charlie."

Charlie walked slowly along the verandah to the sliding door where Constance was waiting for him. She took his hand when he entered.

"Coffee in the garden bar," she said. "With maybe a slug of something more potent than caffeine. Sound good?"

"Where are they all?"

"In the television room or the library. Seething. I stopped in and left again. Too turbulent for me."

"Garden bar," he said emphatically. He indicated the verandah. "You saw?"

"Enough to guess what I didn't see. But it's insane, isn't it?"

They went to the bar, where she had coffee and cups waiting. She poured while Charlie scowled at the turquoise pool at the distant end. The waterfall splashed and glittered in the sunlight that came through the dome on the roof; the air smelled of gardenias and chlorine and felt too heavy. She rummaged among bottles and came up with Cognac, added a therapeutic dose and a spoon of sugar to Charlie's coffee, tasted it, and then slid it across the bar to him.

For many minutes they sat in silence until he grunted. "Milton's in his room shuffling papers, smoking his cigar. There's a tap on the window and he opens the door to admit the killer. Milton knows something, probably doesn't realize that he knows it. The killer talks to him a short time, then coughs on the smoke and suggests they step out on the balcony to continue their conversation. He picks up something heavy in the room and carries it out with him. He says how about we walk down away from the other doors. Beth's room is next door, she might hear us. They walk to the stairwell and he hits Milton over the head, kills him instantly. The cigar falls, but he doesn't notice it yet. He runs back and yanks a sheet off the bed, returns to the body and manages to get it wrapped more or less, and drags it off the balcony to the landing, out of sight. It's foggy; no one's likely to be out strolling, or if anyone does take a walk on the balcony, there's nothing to be seen. So far, so good."

He tasted his coffee for the first time and looked surprised. "You make a mean brew," he said with appreciation, and drank more of it. "So now he goes back up and sees the damn cigar and picks it up. He could just toss it, but he takes it back with him instead. He's staging a show, and this is one of the props." He paused, his eyes narrowed in thought, and sipped his coffee again. "We'll come back to that," he said finally. "So there he is, the bed a mess. He makes the bed, the one with a sheet missing now, and puts Milton's briefcase on it, and turns down the other one, and goofs. He leaves the spread on it, and you spot the mistake. That's okay, it works. The prints," he said. "The fingerprints. He shouldn't have left many, not on the lamps, the ashtray, all the copper stuff. Why clean all that stuff?" He became silent, finally exhaled softly, and said, "He had to wipe them because Milton's prints weren't there on any of that stuff."

He became silent again, this time immobile, staring blindly. Constance poured more coffee for them both and waited. There was no point in her asking anything yet, she knew; he was asking and answering questions in his mind, probably the same ones she would have asked.

At last he spoke again. "It was the ashtray," he said with conviction. "The murder weapon must have been the ashtray. Either he had already wrapped it with the body, or he carried it back and realized that it would be obvious that it had been used. Blood, or hair, something. Maybe he cracked it. That's why he had to get a different ashtray and wipe off his own prints, and that meant he had to switch the other stuff, too. Lamps, book-ends, all that matching stuff, and not a piece of it with Milton's fingerprints. So, it wasn't to hide his prints, it was to hide the fact that none of that stuff belonged there. All right!" He smiled at her and finished his coffee, and then gazed about the mammoth atrium with pleasure. "Not bad," he said.

"Charlie, cut it out. Finish."

"Oh well," he said airily. "The rest is child's play. He gets the gun, then goes around to the greenhouse and gets the cart and parks it under the landing at the stairs. The landing's only four feet above the ground level; the cart bed is a couple feet high; no big deal to roll the body off the landing into the cart and trundle it down to the edge of the cliff, where he shoots Milton in the head and rolls him over the side." He paused again and added, "It wouldn't take a lot of strength, either, not with that garden cart we saw. It can carry a horse, make it possible for anyone to carry a horse."

"I'll roll you off that chair if you don't fill in the details. First of all, why? It would be no less a case of murder if Milton had been found on the balcony with his head smashed in."

"But he didn't dare fire the gun that close to the bedrooms. They would have heard, no matter how tight that house is."

Constance changed her position slightly, a change that was very subtle, but one that Charlie recognized. He had insisted that she study aikido in the beginning, had even urged her to show him personally what she was learning, but the time had come when she regarded him kindly and said that perhaps she should not demonstrate the new movements her class was studying.

Hastily he said, "Milton was not a small man. We all jumped to the same conclusion, remember? He would not have stood still for someone to push him off the cliff, but a shot? That's different. There weren't any powder burns, and that seemed to indicate some distance. Actually the killer was probably real close. When they find the sheet, they'll find the burns. But, most important, it had to be on the books as murder, and there has to be a weapon to implicate someone most decidedly, and then the rest of them will be out from under. Not another mysterious fatal accident, a possible fall from a balcony, or even from the cliff, but a deliberate murder with a gun."

She was still considering this when Dwight joined them, his lean face ridged and set. "We found the gun," he said. "Under Maddie Elringer's mattress. It wasn't there yesterday."

"Do you want coffee?" Constance asked.

He ignored her and continued to regard Charlie with hard eyes. They had become even paler, almost colorless. "I'm beginning to wonder if you don't know too much."

Charlie shrugged and looked lazy as he leaned back against the bar counter. "How's that, Dwight?"

"You're calling the shots, aren't you? Leading us where you want us to go, holding back until you get ready to give a little. What are you up to? You're working for that crowd all the way, aren't you?"

Charlie grinned mockingly. "Well, you know I'm not here on vacation, and the state of Oregon sure hasn't hired me."

"You knew damn well that gun would turn up in his mother's room!"

"Wrong. I didn't know it. Let's say I would have been surprised if it hadn't. He's being framed, Dwight." The captain flushed slightly, but before he could interrupt, Charlie went on meditatively, "Either that, or he's smart enough to mock up a frame-up." He raised his eyebrows at the wording he had produced.

Dwight turned to Constance. "Is it hot?"

"Oh yes." She poured out another cup of coffee.

He sat behind the bar and studied Charlie bitterly. "Okay. I'm the village idiot. The role fits. Explain."

"The problem is we're dealing with extremely clever people. They like puzzles and traps and countertraps. That's how they earn their bread, solving puzzles. Computer puzzles, but the principle's the same. Anyway, suppose Bruce is our killer and he's smart enough to grasp early that he's the prime suspect, just because of who and what he is. Okay, he goes along with that and puts on his Gary act and generally makes an ass out of himself. Offensive, but not a hanging offense, you see. Then he goes further and plants evidence that is all clumsy and amateurish. Like the dirt outside his door." He glanced at Constance, who had made a soft noise, an exhalation or a sigh, at his words.

"Ah," she said, "that's what I thought of when we found the computer in the flowerpot. Anyone smart enough to know how to uproot the plant and hide it there wouldn't have scattered dirt around to track to his door. It didn't make sense. Then I forgot it again. But the point is that when you examine plants that way, you don't usually scatter dirt at all. I didn't when I showed you how pot-bound the gardenia was."

"See?" Charlie said. "That's exactly the kind of thing I'm talking about. The gun was a cinch, either way. He hid it himself knowing a good lawyer would make mincemeat of your case, or else someone else is framing him. Mom hides murder weapon for killer son. Not very good. Clumsy. Interesting, either way."

"Charlie, you and I both know that pretty clever people do some god-awful dumb things when it comes to trying to beat a murder one. I say if it walks like a duck, and quacks like a duck, and swims like a duck, then by God it's time for the orange sauce."

"They won't even indict him if you can't tie him to the other two deaths in a more convincing way than you tried before. Can you?"

"No. Can you?"

"I'm working on it. No sheet yet?"

"No. Where do you suggest we go pick it up?"

Charlie smiled good-humoredly. "It's a big beach, a lot of ocean. When's low tide again?"

"If it was in that damn rock pile, they would have found it."

"Maybe they've been looking in the wrong rock pile."

For a period that stretched into a long time Dwight studied him bitterly. Abruptly he got up and headed out of the atrium.

When they were alone again, Constance said, "It was high tide when Milton was killed. The killer must have hidden the sheet somewhere until low tide and then tossed it, or it would have been exposed when the tide ran out. Down there in the driftwood? Who would spot it before he got back?"

"That's how I see it working," Charlie agreed. "He probably wrapped rocks in it to weight it down, maybe included the ashtray, and around dawn at low tide he could get out to the end of the rocks and give it a good toss." He sighed. "If he did, they might never find it, depending on currents, deep holes, how good an arm he had, a lot of things." He looked at his watch; it was after one. "Getting hungry? Let's see what plans Mrs. Ramos has for lunch."

Mrs. Ramos was busily preparing another buffet, hurrying

back and forth between the kitchen and the dining room. Ten minutes, she told them brusquely.

"Enough time for another look at that cold-storage room," Charlie said, and led the way through the kitchen, out the back door into the narrow rear hall, and across it to the door of the room Gary had called the root cellar. Charlie opened the door and switched on the lights and they entered.

The air was cold and dank, oppressive; the lights were the fluorescent sort that turned lips purple and skin a sickly greenish-yellow. Constance shivered and hugged her arms about herself. It hadn't affected her this way the first time, she remembered, but now it seemed the very air carried a new menace. And that, she knew, was because the murderer was in this house now. Charlie quickened his pace down the stairs, across the room to the dumbwaiter, and she thought he must be feeling the oppression that she felt. He examined the door to the dumbwaiter, then opened it and examined the interior of the cage: a stainless steel cubicle without markings, revealing nothing. He dropped to his knee and felt the floor and wall joints, and then backed away from it, frowning.

"What are you looking for?" she asked, shivering.

"Not sure. If I send it up, the door locks automatically. I wonder . . ." He took out his pocketknife, opened it, and held it in the door frame with one hand, pushed the close button with the other. The door closed on the knife blade and he could not force it open again. He muttered under his breath and looked around. "Bring one of those carts over, will you? I think I've got the sensor here."

She brought the cart. He pressed the open button and the door swung open smoothly; he withdrew his knife blade. "Now, let's see if I can fool it," he said. He turned the cart on its side with the stainless steel handlebar along the edge of the door frame, then positioned himself on the side of it and pressed hard. "Try the close button and then send it up, if it'll go." He wedged himself firmly and held a steady pressure against the cart. The mechanism clicked, and then the dumbwaiter cage moved upward.

"All right," he muttered. "It might come down again when I let go. Let's see if we can let go and push the cart under the floor at the same time. At the count of three. One, two, three.

Now." He let go and she gave the cart a strong push that sent it into the shaft. The cage did not start descending, and if it did come down, the cart might not hold it, but it would slow it down, Charlie decided, satisfied. He grinned at Constance and fished for his penlight, then got down to his knee again to look at the interior of the elevator shaft.

His satisfaction increased as he examined the side walls, and then edged inward a bit to look more closely at the back wall, the one that abutted the secret elevator. He had thought that elevator was an afterthought, and now he was certain of it. This wall had been replaced, redone. It didn't match the sidewalls in finish work, in craftsmanship; there was even a gap at the bottom. Shoddy, shoddy. And it was damn cold. He knew now that it had bothered him to find a cold wall the first time he had examined the secret elevator. In a house as well built as this one, that had been wrong, and he had been dumb not to follow up. He heard himself repeating silently, *Dumb, dumb,* and realized he was staring at his fingers, which seemed unable to hold the light steady enough. His fingers felt detached, too large. He tried to look at his hand to see if something was wrong with it, but that seemed to require too much effort. His eyes were detached, he thought, bemused at the idea.

Constance had been leaning over trying to see what he was looking at, but the effort became too great; her head was getting too heavy, she realized, and thought it might become so heavy that it would topple her over, and how would that look to be sprawled out on the floor of the cold-storage room, getting colder and colder second by second, maybe frozen stiff before anyone got around to finding her, and the—

Abruptly she stood upright and drew in a breath of air. She was dizzy, her eyes not focusing properly.

"Charlie!" she cried. "Charlie!"

How strange, he was thinking, the way the little spot of light drifted around and did not settle anywhere. He heard her call as if from a long way off and thought that was strange also, and then the light made a track down the wall and his fingers were so far removed that he no longer could use them to pick it up, even if he had wanted to do so. He wanted only to put his head down and rest at the moment. He heard the call again, frantic and shrill, and he roused.

She was tugging at him and he was trying to back out of the elevator shaft, but he was so leaden that each movement was tortured, in slow motion, and the cart was in the way. He finally got out in a tangle with the cart and Constance was pulling him upright. He wobbled and the room tilted, but he took a breath and another. Then they were pulling each other to the stairs, upward. Each step took them into better air; by the time they got to the top, they were both drawing in long shuddering breaths, very frightened and pale.

Constance reached for the doorknob, tried to turn it; nothing happened. She tried again, and then with both hands. Charlie pushed past her and tried.

"We're locked in," she whispered. "My God, we're locked in!"

"*Shhh. Shhh.*" He looked past her. The door was solid, with only the brass knob on this side. No lock. On the other side was a bolt, to keep anyone from opening the door accidentally in case they wanted to purge the air inside. He did not waste time trying to force the door now, but looked back at the room. Stainless steel walls, shelves, bins, a counter, the upended cart and another one at the far wall, the open door of the dumbwaiter, the shaft behind it, and the dumbwaiter itself on the floor above. Even if he knew which pipe was feeding in carbon dioxide, there was no way in here to turn it off again.

"Don't move," he said then. "I'm going up in the dumbwaiter and I'll come around to open the door. The air's okay near the ceiling here, so just don't move."

She did not argue. Her pale eyes were wide and very frightened, and she was the color of snow, right down to her lips. She touched his cheek and closed her eyes for a second, a blessing, transferring all the love a touch could carry, and then he took a long breath and, holding it, started down the stairs. He had not broken anything, he told himself, the mechanism would work okay. He pushed the cart aside, but on second thought dragged it back, then he pushed the down button. He had to close the door first, he realized, cursing himself for an idiot. He closed the door and pushed the down button again and stepped on the cart to keep his head as high in the air as possible. He could not remember that the infernal thing had been so slow before, but now it seemed to creak at dinosaur speed. He exhaled the air in his lungs and took a shallow breath, not certain how good it was here, then certain that he had to breathe it in, no matter good or bad. The dumbwaiter finally came and he pushed the open button, and now he had to abandon his place on the cart, lean down to enter the cage, hold himself in a bent-over position because it was not quite five feet high, and at last it began to ascend in slow motion.

At the top of the stairs Constance had taken off her shoe and was pounding on the door with it. They both knew it was a futile gesture. This room was too well insulated.

He held his breath in the dumbwaiter, certain it was filled with dangerous air. By the time the cage came to a stop, his lungs were afire, his head pounding; he could see veins in his own eyes with each beat. When the door opened, he lurched out, staggering and reeling, and tried to race through the pantry to the door at the end, into the hall. His gait was like that of a drunken man; he crashed into a wall, veered off it, and made his way to the door of the cold-storage room and fumbled with the bolt. Constance fell into his arms when he opened the door.

18

There had been times when Constance had glimpsed an anger in Charlie so intense that it had been frightening. The time that Stan Walinowski's wife had been beaten severely, so badly that she had lost an eye, Charlie had turned to stone. He and Stan had worked together, and following the beating suffered by Wanda Walinowski both men had worked overtime, weekends, after hours, until one day Charlie had come home with a pinched look, a haunted look in his eyes, and that night he had made love to her passionately. The following day he had insisted that she learn self-defense because, he had said, if anyone ever laid a hand on her, he would kill the son of a bitch. There had been no doubt then, or ever, that he meant exactly that. He and Stan had gone back to regular hours, and no one ever brought up the subject of the vicious attack or the guilty person. And, God help her, Constance thought, neither had she. She had been afraid to.

That afternoon Charlie had turned to stone again, she thought, and instantly corrected herself. Ice. He had turned to ice. Dwight had found them on the steps of the verandah, leaning against each other, simply breathing.

"What's up?" he asked.

Charlie did not speak, and Constance told him what had happened.

"Jesus! Are you all right?"

At her nod, he turned and hurried off with Howie in tow. He returned a few minutes later. "No prints," he said in disgust. "Oxygen turned all the way down, carbon dioxide all the way up."

Charlie did not even look at him.

"When did they all leave the library and television room?" Constance asked.

"Right after I left you two. Mrs. Ramos was making lunch. There didn't seem much point in keeping them locked up after we found the gun."

Constance shook her head at him gently. "Of course not. It wasn't your fault, Dwight. We know that." What a nice younger brother he would have made, she thought, so concerned, so . . . She realized with a start that the look on his face was awareness, and it was directed at Charlie. Another shared man thing, she thought distantly. He knew that Charlie had turned to ice and why.

"Why don't I bring out a tray of sandwiches," he said, a touch too eagerly. "You haven't eaten and neither have I."

"You go ahead," Constance said. "I want to go up to our room. I need to wash. I feel filthy."

Charlie was on his feet before she finished, and she knew this would be part of it; he would not leave her alone a second until they were well away from Smart House.

Constance took his hand; it was icy. "Well, it wasn't really a serious attempt," she said. "Not with the dumbwaiter as an escape hatch. It must have been meant to frighten us."

Dwight looked uncomfortable, glanced from her to Charlie and back, and said slowly, "It was serious. It looks like someone tried to jimmy open the dumbwaiter door in the pantry. If he'd managed to do it, the door in the cold-storage room wouldn't have opened. If Charlie hadn't already forced that one and held it open it would have worked."

Charlie's hand tightened painfully on hers.

Still Dwight hesitated. "Charlie, take it easy, okay? Don't do anything stupid, old buddy."

Finally Charlie really looked at him and grinned. "Do something stupid in Smart House? They'd toss me out on my can. Are you bringing the divers back?"

"Yeah. Six-thirty."

"Good. Let's go wash up." He tugged her hand and they went back inside, up to their room.

Constance showered and tried to scrub away the feeling of violation. This was how people said it felt to be burglarized, she thought, scrubbing, scrubbing. And rape victims. She shut her eyes hard and let the steaming water hit her face, her head. Violated. Someone had wanted her dead, had wanted Charlie dead. If either of them had fallen, no doubt that one would be dead, maybe both of them, drowned in the incoming tide of carbon dioxide that would pool near the floor, gradually accumulate to fill the room. She shook her head angrily, determined to stop thinking about it, and saw instead how Charlie had been leaning over, low to the floor, his face in the pool of poison.

He met her at the bathroom door and held her, nuzzling her wet hair. "You're as shriveled as a raisin," he said finally, stepping back to examine her. "Okay?"

"About what you'd expect from a raisin. What are you doing?"

Their suitcases were on the bed, one on each, and a few garments had been folded inexpertly and put inside. Other things were in a heap.

"We strike our tent and decamp," he said and looked ruefully at the mess he had made. "No more sleeping in Smart House. We're heading for a hotel or motel or something."

How could his eyes do that, she wondered. At times they seemed to become flat, lusterless, like smooth rocks. "All right," she said without argument. "I'll pack, but on one condition. We get something to eat first."

"Not here." Bad policy to eat in the house of anyone who was trying to kill you, he thought. "Get some clothes on and we'll hop in the car and go find a place that knows about steamer clams and beer and civilized things of that sort." He looked at the papers on the desk. "It's actually a good idea to get the hell out of here for a while. I'll take that stuff and we won't come back until six-thirty."

They met Dwight in the downstairs hall, and he told them about a restaurant that knew all about clams, gave them directions, and said if they were still there in a couple of hours he'd join them. Five-thirty or a few minutes later.

The clams were exactly right, Charlie announced with satisfaction after the second bucket was emptied. And the booth was exactly right, with a good view of the ocean, and, more important, good lighting. A pleasant-faced middle-aged woman had served them and now returned with coffee and the dessert menu, which was the same menu they had scanned earlier. Charlie asked if anyone cared if they used the table for a spell and she looked surprised and asked why anyone would. And so they had a well-lighted table and coffee and he began to spread out the papers again.

Constance read the ones Charlie already had finished with: the corporate structure, the forensics reports on Gary and Rich, financial forecasts . . . She wished they had the inventory that Bruce had compiled, and then muttered, "Damn."

"I agree, but why?"

"Bruce has covered any missing object from his room, hasn't he? The blue whale that he says is gone."

" 'Fraid so. That inventory gives anyone else an out, too. Suppose a cast-iron sea lion is missing. Our guy would say, 'I don't know what you're talking about. Never laid eyes on it.' Who could prove otherwise?"

"But why go to the trouble of switching things like that? Why not just let the object be from Milton's room?" She stopped, then said, "Oh, I see. You're right. It must have been the ashtray. We know Milton used that. It would be missed even if another object wouldn't be."

Charlie grinned at her look of annoyance. Food had done wonders for his disposition, and distance from Smart House had helped, he knew. He turned once more to the timetable they had made up for the time of the game, the night of the two first deaths.

She gazed at the sparkling water that rose and fell, rose and fell forever. The trouble was, she thought, anyone could have killed Milton and tidied up afterward, and no one could have killed Gary and Rich. She nodded to herself. That was the problem. Why hadn't Rich Schoen put up a fight, struggled to save himself? Why had Gary let someone push him into the Jacuzzi without taking the other person in with him, at the very least? Maybe Dwight's scenario was the only way it could have been done, with two people working together. Or maybe both men had been moved, after all. Milton had been moved, perhaps they had been also. The police work might have been ineptly done, a mistake made. She frowned at the blue Pacific Ocean. No matter how inept, no one would mistake death by drowning for anything else. She muttered another *damn*, under her breath this time, and Charlie's hand covered hers on the table.

"Let's take a walk on the beach out there," he said. "We'll come back by five-thirty to meet Dwight." His voice was very low, very quiet; he sounded weary.

"Charlie! You know!"

"Not yet. Not yet. I want to think about it. Let's walk."

She knew he did not see anything of the beach as they walked side by side without speaking. He could walk tirelessly in this stage, or play endless games of solitaire, or drive hundreds of miles. What he could not do was sit and do nothing. It was as if he had to give his body a task and turn it loose on it as if that controlling part of his brain might otherwise interfere with his thoughts at these times. That part of his brain needed something to occupy it just to keep it out of the way.

Here, children were playing in the sand, racing back and forth with pails of water, building forts, castles. A few teenagers were in the water, splashing happily, but no one was really swimming. The waves, even though the tide was receding, were too unruly, the water too cold, even though it was August. The air had a fresh ozone smell, good, clean air, and it was pleasantly cool, even though the sun was hot. So many contrasts, contradictions, she thought. Other strollers smiled, nodded, spoke, and she responded, although Charlie was oblivious. Runners overtook them, passed them, leaving deep prints in the wet sand, and she thought about how Sherlock Holmes could tell the height and weight of a person by examining such prints, or know if he had been carrying something, or someone.

They got back to the restaurant only minutes before Dwight arrived, tired, irritable, hungry. They had come back thirsty and already had ordered beers, and now Charlie was sketching rapidly on a napkin as Dwight ordered a sandwich and beer.

"Still nothing?" Constance asked Dwight.

He shook his head. "Oh, there's something," he said with great bitterness. "Harry Westerman and his wife have been in touch with their lawyer, who spoke to me and ordered me to get my crew out of there, to let those poor people go home. And so the bloody damn on."

"Tough," Charlie muttered without conviction. He finished his sketch and eyed it a moment, then turned it so that Dwight could see.

"Look," Charlie said, pointing to three rectangles. "This big job here is the main elevator, and next to it is the private elevator, and the last little shaft is for the dumbwaiter. Granddaddy, Poppa, and little John, all side by side."

He was so pleased with himself, he was intolerable at the moment, Constance thought, glancing from him to Dwight Ericson, whose face was a mask.

"Now," Charlie went on, "at the bottom here we have the cold-storage room. And in the cold-storage room there is a controlled atmosphere. Fifteen percent oxygen, one percent carbon dioxide, and so on, all appropriately monitored with alarms and exhausts if things get out of hand. But the low oxygen and high carbon dioxide are givens; they don't trigger alarms. And here," he said, drawing in some hash marks, "we have leakage from the little-John shaft to the Poppa-elevator shaft, an inch gap at the bottom of the wall. That whole shaft becomes part of the closed system practically."

Dwight Ericson was shaking his head. "We've done the figures, Charlie. It would take too long to build up enough carbon dioxide or exhaust the oxygen in a space that big. No one was missing long enough. And what do you think they did in there, just fold their hands and wait an hour or two to die? They would have raised a ruckus, and you know it. Someone would have heard them pounding on the walls or yelling."

Serenely Charlie continued. "I did the figures, too. If that cage were hermetically sealed it would take two men about half an hour to die of carbon dioxide poisoning. Drowning in their own waste, so to speak. But they didn't die of carbon dioxide poisoning, you see. And besides, the cage isn't hermetically sealed: There is that leakage through the bottom, and ventilation holes in the top. So, let's say the cage is up here on the second floor when they enter for whatever reason and close the door. The cage is filled with warm air, of course. As soon as they start to descend, the fan comes on and the nice warm air is replaced with cool air from the shaft, and the nice warm air starts to rise, taking its nice oxygen with it. We all felt the same thing, dank, cold, oppressive, but we opened the door and got out. Anyway, by the time the cage gets to the basement level, the air has been changed a few times—good air out, bad air in. Normally that wouldn't even be noticeable because you open the door and in comes more good air. But this time, let's say, the door doesn't open. And the cage comes to rest in a pocket of air that is very bad, very concentrated carbon dioxide, low oxygen. You know about carbon dioxide, pockets of stale air, poisonous air that collects?"

Dwight's expression had changed. He no longer looked impatient or bored or forbearing. His eyes narrowed and he nodded. "Yeah. Miners, divers, cave explorers, they all know about coming across pockets like that."

"And firemen," Charlie added darkly. "You go in a big building in any city and if the sub-subbasements haven't been used for a spell, you know. Anyway, that's what would collect in that shaft. Carbon dioxide on the bottom, because it's heavy, the lighter elements above, all of it bad."

"Dear God," Constance said softly. "Those poor men!"

"Right," Charlie said, almost brusquely. "So there they are. Their own body heat would create an updraft of air, enough to make the ventilation holes practically useless, a menace in fact, because the heavy carbon dioxide mix would be pulled in at the bottom while the better air escaped out the top. And every minute they are consuming about seven hundred cubic centimeters of oxygen, and they're producing five to six hundred cubic centimeters of carbon dioxide." His voice had become very flat now, a machine voice. "You learn things like that so you know what you're dealing with in fire situations. Are people still alive in pockets of air, breathing? Is the good air exhausted yet?" He stopped abruptly, then went on. "Anyway, by the time Gary and Rich realized they could die, it was probably too late to do anything about it. First, in only a couple of minutes, discomfort, headaches, then a condition that, I've been told, and can now attest to, is like almost waking up from a nightmare, knowing you have to move, but you can't seem to locate your body parts and do it. Five minutes at the most. By then it was too late. Collapse, unconsciousness, it happens fast."

Dwight started to speak, subsided, as if aware that Charlie should not be interrupted right now, that he was looking at something not quite visible to anyone else.

The silence endured until Charlie shrugged slightly, and said, "But, as you say, they didn't die there and get moved to their final resting places. They weren't dumped as corpses anywhere. And they sure as God didn't walk alone. The damn house was responsible for their deaths, but the final act was somewhere else. In that state, when the door opened, they both had to be alive still. Whoever found them must have had the hell shocked out of him. And instantly he knew they had to be taken somewhere else, or the house would be blamed. Maybe at that time they could have been revived, could have recovered, but if even one of them died, the house would be the killer and there goes the company. Either or both might have been brain damaged. If one did recover, he might implicate whoever closed the door on them. The killer couldn't risk any of those things. So he probably sent the elevator up to the roof, and he took the main one up. That's the only place both elevators are side by side. His first thought must have been to get them both the hell away from the secret elevator, away from the office or Gary's room, where walls might be tapped, the secret elevator might be found. Or maybe he was already on the roof when he called up the elevator and opened it to find them both dying. Anyway, the next act must have been up there, someplace where he could go from one elevator to the other with little risk of being seen. I think he must have got Rich to his feet first, walked him to the big elevator, and finished him off there. Maybe Rich actually collapsed and that's how he bruised his face, on the carpeted floor. But the human killer finished him off, all right. Anything at all over his face at that moment would have been enough. He was incapable of fighting back. Maybe he marked his face and used the mesh bag to hide the marks, but probably he used it just to make certain the police didn't settle for an accidental death. Then back to Gary. Down to the first floor with him, out the rear of the elevator, and through the back hall. Gary might have been reviving by then; opening the door would have flushed out the bad air, brought in breathable air. He could walk; the original printout showed that he did walk into the Jacuzzi room, but he was dazed, stuporous; that's how victims of anoxia are, before they actually die. The killer walked him through the dark back hall, to the Jacuzzi, and tipped him in and covered the pool. He was trying hard to make certain the police would look for a murderer, not label either death accidental. But his very cleverness made him botch it. Too many directions, too many false clues pointing every which way.

"He had to have a few minutes free just to tidy up, and neither body would be found too soon. The hand-held computer would lock the elevator wherever he left it, and Gary was out of sight. He put the other control computers and the blueprints in the elevator. He didn't want anyone finding that secret elevator just then. He made popcorn and imitated Gary's wild laughter so everyone would assume Gary was alive and he would be provided with an alibi. Then, unlock the big elevator, rejoin the party, and wait."

Dwight had been eating his sandwich mechanically. He chewed for several minutes. At last he shook his head. "It's plausible, I grant you that. There are messy areas, like why did he move Gary somewhere else instead of leaving him in the big elevator too?"

"What if he was interrupted?" Charlie said. "Actually a couple of people went up to the roof at exactly the wrong time for the killer. If Gary was reviving in the cold fresh air, he would be a risk. He might start making noise. So our guy had to close the big elevator and lock it, close himself in with Gary in the secret elevator and take him someplace where he could finish what he had set out to do, and that was to clear Smart House."

Dwight sighed, still doubtful, still not accepting. "And what's that about the popcorn? How in hell do you figure that?"

"Gary took the popcorn maker from the kitchen before eleven," Charlie said. "He went out the back kitchen door, on his way, no doubt, to his little elevator that would deliver him either to his office or his bedroom. Customarily he had popcorn every night in his office. So why did he then not make it there? Why carry the stuff around with him for fifteen or twenty minutes? He wasn't in the garden during that period; too many others wandered in and out to miss him. No, he went from the kitchen to somewhere else and put the stuff down, and later the killer must have seen the perfect way to establish that Gary was still alive and hungry at eleven-fifteen. When he got the blueprints and computers to stash away in the elevator, he got them from Gary's office; the popcorn maker was probably there, and he saw his chance and took it."

"It could work," Dwight said after another thoughtful pause. "And the good Lord knows I want something that could, but there's no way on this earth to prove any of it."

Charlie spread his hands. "Neither Rich nor Gary was drugged or drunk. They probably weren't hypnotized into lying down and dying, voodoo cursed into it, or talked into it with promises of candy. You can't order a man to lie down and stop breathing, even at gunpoint. They had to have been in a stupor of some sort, incapable of resisting whatever was being done, but capable of walking with help. Anoxia stupor. Not forced on them by having their heads held in fruit bins, or by being urged to enter one of those experimental growing structures in the greenhouse. Someplace close by, accessible. A place that didn't alarm either of them enough to put up a fight. I came up with the elevator. You're right. No proof. But what else is new at this point?" He leaned back in the booth with his arm along the seat back and his hand on Constance's shoulder. "Besides," he said, "I knew from the beginning the damn house was guilty as hell."

"And I suppose you know who took a chance like that just to clear the house?"

"Sure," Charlie said. "But it's going to be tricky to prove it."

19

It was nearly eight, and Charlie had just finished loading the suitcases into the rented car when Beth and Jake found him. Beth was deathly pale, her eyes very big and frightened. Jake seemed more concerned for her than for the fact that Charlie obviously was planning to leave.

"Alexander said you're going away!" Beth cried on the verandah as Charlie approached. "Why? What are they doing? Why did they rip up part of the balcony? Charlie, what's happening?"

He took her arm and steered her into the foyer. "Calm down. Take it easy. We would have found you to say good-bye. Where's Alexander now? Where are all the others? I thought you'd all be eating and we didn't want to disturb your dinner."

"Who can eat?" she cried.

"They're in the dining room going through the motions," Jake said soberly. "What's up?"

Charlie looked at his watch and said resignedly, "Beth, will you tell Constance I'll be in the garden bar? Let's get a drink," he said, turning to Jake.

Beth bit her lip, then darted up the stairs. "I'll be right back."

"Drink," Charlie muttered, and led the way through the corridor into the atrium, where he went behind the bar and began to look over the assortment of bottles; Jake sat on a stool opposite him. The sun was very low now, but still came through the dome on the roof, lighted up the rock wall at the far end of the room where the waterfall sparkled in its plunge. That end of the room was bright; shadows had gathered at the bar end. Charlie hummed tunelessly as he poked among the bottles and came up with Drambuie. Regretfully he put it down again and settled for bourbon on ice. Jake shook his head when Charlie offered him the same.

"I was going to meet the group in a group," Charlie said after taking a sip. "But this might be better. I think your story should be that you and Milton struggled. He said nasty things and pulled the gun on you and you hit him. When you wrested the gun away, it went off and a bullet grazed his head. And then you panicked and tried to cover up. It isn't neat, and it leaves a lot of questions, but between you and me, there are always a lot of questions without answers."

"You've gone mad!" Jake said coldly.

"Not a bad story, all things considered," Charlie went on, as if he had not heard. "Temporarily out of your mind, that usually works. That way I don't have to mention the secret elevator, or the carbon dioxide in the basement, or the unattended popcorn in the garden here, or the gun on the roof. Or even the reversed Turing test and how all of you practiced being each other to fool the computer. Of course, people will assume that you were responsible for Gary's and Rich's deaths, but they won't be able to prove anything, and in a way that would be good. Smart House is cleared in the minds of the people who count, and you still own the lion's share of a prosperous company. You'll need it, no doubt. Defense comes in costly packages. Did you know attorneys charge for every phone call, every minute they even think about your case, even if they're on the can?"

"You son of a bitch, you're trying to frame me and blackmail me!"

"You don't have much time," Charlie said easily. "When the captain calls it off for the day, I'll tell him my story, make my report to your colleagues, and take off. Did I mention where the divers are working now? The north end of the beach. If they don't find the ashtray and sheet today, then tomorrow they'll bring in a logging helicopter and start playing jackstraws with all that driftwood, and maybe the divers will go on to the next rock pile, and then the next one. I have to admire that captain. He's got gumption. He'll stick with it until he finds something— sheet, ashtray, pair of slacks, shirt, something. But I want to get the hell out of here. So I'll tell him a story, and I don't give a damn which version it is, one that involves fun and games and foolishness, secret elevators and a killer house, or one that starts and stops with Milton's death."

"This is extortion and you know it, you bastard! I'll get you for this, so help me God!"

"You almost did," Charlie said mildly.

"Next time you won't be so lucky. Have you told any of the others any of this?"

"Nope. Haven't talked to the shareholders. I decided to let you pick the story you like best first."

Jake looked around desperately, as if searching for a weapon, a rock, a bottle, a gun, anything. His hands were white on the countertop. Charlie was out of reach on the other side. Jake flexed his fingers and said, "You're close to what happened." His voice was hard, tight, the words clipped. "I was taking a walk on the balcony when Milton went mad and attacked me. He had a gun. I hit him in self-defense and he fell hard and struck his head. It was an accident, but I blacked out in a panic." His face was white, his expression murderous.

"It might work," Charlie said judiciously, "if the others co-operate. But after trying to frame Bruce, you lost him, and probably lost Maddie, and when Beth realizes that you were trying to win her over for her shares, I don't know. One or the other might even remember that you were out of sight when they heard that laughing they assumed was Gary."

"Beth will believe what I tell her, and the others don't matter." He leaned forward and said in an intense, low voice, "When it's over, Charlie, I'm coming for you. I'll have resources, more than you've ever dreamed of."

"Number four," Charlie murmured. "What about Laura? She saw Milton pick up your water gun on the roof. One day she might connect that to Rich's killer."

"You can speculate all you want, but you can't prove anything about Gary and Rich, and you know it, or you wouldn't want to make a deal."

"Just how far gone were they when you found them?" Charlie asked.

For a moment he thought Jake wouldn't answer, but then he drew a deep breath and said in a hoarse whisper, "Like zombies, both of them. They were dying. I know about brain damage. You can't understand, no one can, what that would have meant to a man like Gary. To see a mind like his gone, destroyed. Maybe they could have been revived, but they were dead; they would have existed maybe, but not as men with minds. Gary . . ." His voice dropped even lower until it was nearly inaudible. "He was a devil, and the other side of that is that he was a god, and I worshipped him. I did what I had to, what he would have wanted if he had been conscious enough to say so."

Charlie shook his head. "People have pulled through after accidents like that."

He might not have heard. His face was agonized, his expression black. "I opened the door, holding the water gun, aimed at where I thought Rich would be. They were out, both of them, Rich in front. I got him to his feet, to the big elevator. I was going to take him down, get help, and he collapsed. Unconscious. Gary was in the little elevator, unconscious, moaning. They were too far gone! I didn't want to finish them, but I had to or we would have been ruined, all of us, and they were already dead men, still breathing a little, but dead. Past saving."

His eyes were staring, not through space, but as if through time, back to that night. His voice was thick and low when he continued. "Rich fell down and I could see how it would work out, step by step—Smart House blamed, all the work destroyed, the dream gone, everything shattered. It couldn't appear to be accidental. I saw that before I touched him, before I even knew what I had to do. Gary would have wanted me to save the company, at any cost. Any cost. Save Smart House. His dream . . . I tried to make the police understand that the computer couldn't have done it. Anyone who knows computers would know it couldn't have done all that—the insecticide, the lights going off, the pool cover. No computer could have done it, but the fools didn't understand, no matter what we all said."

"You were too clever for them," Charlie murmured. "So that's going to be your story—two accidental deaths and self-defense when Milton attacked you. It might fly."

With a start Jake brought his gaze back to Charlie. He shook his head. "I don't know a goddman thing about how Gary and Rich died. That's my story. And Milton pulled a gun on me. He must have killed them and thought I was onto him. That's my story and it'll work. I'm good at details, Charlie, remember? It'll work. I'll make it work. They'll buy it."

Tiredly Charlie said, "Dwight, is that enough yet? I'm getting rather bored."

The lights came on and Dwight Ericson stepped out from the storage area behind the bar. Two other men came from the shadows; they were carrying guns.

"You goddamn son of a bitch!" Jake cried in disbelief, incredulous. "You lied!"

Charlie shrugged. "And you tried to kill my wife." He set his glass down and the musical computer voice said, "Thank you, Charlie. Would you like another drink at this time?" He looked at Jake. "We've been broadcasting ever since we came into the bar. It's all on tape; they've been listening in the dining room. The voice prints, they tell me, never make a mistake. If you claim this one is wrong, you blow the whole security package, don't you?"

For a moment there was a glint in Jake's eyes, almost of recognition of a good endgame, Charlie thought, appreciation maybe. But probably not, he decided.

Now the sun was setting, the western sky a red-streaked blaze, the ocean azure fringed with white. Charlie and Constance were in the living room with the group, Charlie at the window looking at the panorama of sea and sky, Constance in a straight chair near him. Very nice, he decided, very nice. He turned to look at the others, who were still arranging themselves: Beth in a white high-backed chair that dwarfed her and bleached the color from her face; Laura and Harry Westerman at opposite ends of a sofa; Maddie in a chair drawn close to Bruce. He was ignoring her. Bruce was sprawled, his clothes a mess, his hair a mess, sneakers untied. Alexander had not yet lighted on anything, but paced around the room jerkily as if seeking a special perch. Dwight Ericson and his men were gone. Jake was gone, too.

"Alexander, if you will come to rest someplace, I'd like to get this over with," Charlie said.

"Sorry, sorry," Alexander said, as flighty as a hummingbird, and sat on the edge of the nearest chair.

Charlie nodded. "By now you've all seen that little elevator, and you know about the hand-held computers that could control just about everything in this house, including the secret elevator. I'll keep this as brief as I can. From the beginning there were several questions that seemed to need answers. Playing the assassin game, why didn't Jake kill Rich when he had a chance, several chances, in fact? He inherited him as victim early in the afternoon when he got Beth and did nothing about it the rest of the day and evening. Then, why would Gary cheat in his own game, when he tried to get Maddie to witness after she was out of it? Why did Gary laugh in the garden that night? At whom? Everyone was accounted for and no one was with him, apparently. Why didn't Gary make popcorn in his room or his office? Why didn't the main elevator work after eleven o'clock that night? Those questions all came up when you told me about the game and your movements."

They were all looking blank. He shrugged. "There were other questions that came up over Milton's murder. Why did anyone pick that night to hide the little computer? Why scatter dirt and leave a pile at Bruce's door? Why was Jake wearing his contact lenses if he had been in bed asleep? If he hadn't been in bed, why the pajamas? Why did anyone wipe prints off all the accessories in Milton's room? Why did Bruce mention a gun that night?

"We'll have to go back to the game for this," Charlie said apologetically. "Milton Sweetwater has gone down to the basement for a new weapon. He hears Jake and Rich, and sees the office door close. Minutes later he returns to the elevator to see Rich alone, and they ride up together. The problem is that Jake had Rich's name, and made no effort to get him either time, although when Milton came down he could have been a witness. Why not? He says that he didn't know his next victim, that he kept forgetting to check. Maybe. And remember that curious scene when Gary had a tantrum because his mother would not witness his killing Bruce. Very strange. What was that all about? Everyone insisted that Gary loved games, that he wouldn't have cheated, and yet, that was clearly an illegal move. And in front of Jake. Picture it: Gary and Jake enter a room where Bruce and his mother are and Gary uses the plastic knife to stab Bruce, but his mother won't play, and Jake has left by then. Gary has a royal tantrum. Why? Because Maddie refused to play, something he already knew, or because Jake left prematurely? What would have happened if he had entered the kill in the computer and Maddie had witnessed?" He looked at Alexander and waited.

Alexander fidgeted, embarrassed again, and shook his head. "It would not have been allowed, not if Maddie had been taken out of the game."

"But exactly what would have happened?" Charlie persisted.

"The computer would have said something to the effect that

nonplayers wouldn't be allowed to participate in any way, that Gary was out of line, and he could not make another attempt at murder with that particular dagger. Depending on who made the mistake, it might have added a penalty. Because it was Gary, it probably would have given Bruce a twelve- or twenty-four-hour reprieve, a time that Gary could not attack again. That's all."

Charlie nodded gravely. "And how unusual would it have been, to have a computer respond in that way?"

Alexander looked infinitely relieved now. He brightened, his eyes gleamed. "You just don't know! That's what I've been trying to tell you. That's reasoning! Human reasoning, not just number crunching! Jake would have been plenty impressed! Plenty!" He stopped abruptly and looked panic-stricken.

"Exactly," Charlie said. "I've been listening, Alexander. I really have been." He turned to Beth. "That day after Jake killed you in the garden, you wandered down to the greenhouse, didn't you?" She nodded, her gaze fastened on him as if hypnotized. "Which door did you enter by?"

She moistened her lips and swallowed, then said, "I walked around and went in the end door."

"So Gary and Jake were at the end nearest the house. And they both ran out when you entered. I wonder why. Jake had killed you; he knew you were no threat. And Gary knew you had overheard his murder; again, no threat. Why did they duck out? What were they carrying, Beth?"

"I never said they—"

Charlie was smiling gently at her. "It's all right, Beth. I know you never said they were, but close your eyes and see that scene in your mind's eye. They were carrying something, weren't they? One of them, or both of them, Beth?"

She blinked finally, then closed her eyes. After a moment, she cried, "Both of them. I thought books, but they weren't books, were they? The little computers! It must have been the computers!" Her eyes opened. "I thought it was just the paranoia, everyone afraid of everyone else. And they had no reason to be afraid of me, neither of them. That's what I focused on. That's what was so awful. I never even gave a thought to anything in their hands. How did you know?"

"It had to be something they had that made them dodge you that way. As you said, neither of them had a cause to fear you.

But a private demonstration of the computers, that was different. That was serious business that Gary wasn't ready to share with anyone but Jake yet. I suspect that sometime during that day or evening Gary programmed in a command either to keep Jake from getting a new weapon or from learning his next victim, or even both, and Jake knew it and didn't even try, and that's why he didn't go for Rich when he had a chance. You were his last victim, in the game anyway. From all accounts he was an avid game player, just like Gary. It didn't add up."

Beth was nodding. "They had been down there by all the valves and gauges and things. Holding the computers."

"And later, to add a bit of confusion, Jake used the computer again to release poison in the greenhouse. Not to hurt anyone; he chose his time, after all, but to lead the police there, to the demonstration rooms, the little experimental atmosphere-controlled rooms where people could be suffocated. He was trying hard to force them to look for a human killer. He was doing all he could to keep Smart House out of it."

"You jumped to that conclusion just because Jake didn't try to get Rich when he had a chance?" Harry looked angry and sounded disbelieving. "For Christ's sake! I never got a victim all weekend!"

"But you weren't reported closeted with either Gary or Rich all afternoon and evening the way Jake was. From late afternoon on, he seemed to be with one or the other every time anyone reported his presence. They were showing him everything, together, and separately, each with his own game plan, no doubt. Rich wanted to start showing the house to potential buyers, and Gary wanted to continue researching artificial intelligence. Meanwhile, Jake was the largest shareholder after Gary; he was the one to convince. When Rich went up in the elevator with Milton, Jake stayed behind in the office. And no one saw him again until he came back down with Beth at eleven-ten or a little after. During that time, he found the key to the main computer and began trying it out. Beth, you told us he could recreate up to ten chess moves; he had a phenomenal memory for details, and during the day he had seen many computer operations, remember. We know Gary kept the little computers in his office, and Bruce overheard him demonstrating them to someone. And Gary had made use of the secret elevator, no doubt about that, but he must have used the manual controls. Why not? It wasn't computer locked, the way the bedrooms were. Why would it have been? No one knew about it yet except Gary and Rich and Jake. So the little computers were in the office and Jake was in the office.

"And now things changed. Jake could unlock the weapons cabinet and get his new weapon. Remember, he wasn't planning murder or anything else at that time; he was playing the game."

Charlie turned to Laura. "After Rich witnessed for Milton, you all went to the library to record the kill, right? And Rich seemed to be in a hurry?"

"Yes."

"He knew Jake was in the office. So he went back, and Gary showed up with his popcorn maker and popcorn and oil, and in the next few minutes Jake managed to get Rich and Gary in the little elevator together and locked them in with computer control. He must not have had a weapon yet or he could have taken Rich out the second Gary joined them, but he didn't. So he put them both on hold and went out for a weapon. And he probably was taking his time, in no rush because he knew where his victim was, along with a witness. He locked the elevator at the basement level so that no one would be likely to hear if they got mad and pounded on the walls. This is the crucial time period. Everyone is accounted for except Jake. I told you people notice each other more than they realize, and they did. But Jake was out of sight for half an hour or longer. Anyway, he got his squirt gun and then went up the stairs to the roof. We know that because the main elevator was in use about then, Maddie was coming down. It takes a little time to get up three flights and he was in no particular hurry. Five or six minutes after he closed the little elevator door and locked it at the basement level, he called it up there and opened it to find two dying men."

Maddie lost her control then and began to sob. She buried her face in her hands and rocked back and forth.

Harry stood up abruptly. "This is pure fantasy. You don't have a shred of proof. Horseshit! Why not in Gary's office, if he had the computer? Or the bedroom? Any other room?"

"If anyone saw him entering the office or Gary's room, the game would be up. Remember the computer-locked doors. He wasn't supposed to be able to open either room. And people were milling about all over the place, potential witnesses. The first floor? He would have had to go through the garden room, behind the pool, around the back hallway, and, again, too many people. He liked fun and games as much as Gary did, I take it. He wouldn't want to give away the secret elevator any more than Gary did at that point, and he didn't want to risk having someone tag along and upset his plan to get Rich as soon as the door opened. One witness, Gary, was all he wanted on hand, because he was playing the game. He had outwitted Gary, solved the computer puzzle, got his weapon, locked them in. He must have been feeling pretty triumphant. He opened the door and found two dying men in the little elevator." He stopped and rubbed his eyes absently. His voice was tired when he resumed.

"You heard what he said about that part. He tried to revive Rich, couldn't, and finished them both off in a way that he thought would make the police go after a human killer, not link the house and computer to the deaths." He paused, then went on briskly. "And Laura and Milton came up before he was finished. He had dropped the water gun without a thought, no doubt. Milton picked it up; as soon as he mentioned it, he was tagged the next victim. This time it was a deliberate decision."

Charlie stopped and looked at Maddie. She was sitting rigidly upright watching him fixedly.

"So, now they were both dead, and Jake had to move fast. He started the automatic popcorn maker to establish that Gary was still alive at approximately eleven-fifteen, hurried back to the secret elevator and got the blueprints from Gary's office, and put them and two of the little computers in the elevator. He let himself out of Gary's bedroom on the second floor and raced to his own door and pretended to be leaving just as Beth was coming out of her room. They went down the stairs together, and he left her on the first floor long enough to go uncover the popcorn maker, to let out the aroma, and open one of the sliding doors. He imitated Gary's laughter, and went into the library where he remained until the first body turned up."

"You couldn't have proved any of this," Harry said. "If the fool had kept his head, he would have been home free. That goddamn fool!"

Charlie shrugged. "He framed Bruce, you know. And I suppose he had plans for an untimely death for Laura, just in case she ever began to piece it together. She did see Milton pick up that water gun on the roof. If the fool had kept his head he might have ended up sole owner of the Bellringer Company eventually."

Beth flushed and ducked her head.

"Anyway, we don't have to prove any of it. He's tagged for Milton's murder, and that's plenty."

Harry took a deep breath. "That goddamn fool! You might as well finish this. How did you guess?"

Charlie looked aggrieved. "I deduced it," he said. "Jake killed Milton on the balcony, wrapped him in a sheet, and trundled him to the cliff, where he shot him and then rolled him over the edge. But it all raised questions. Why pick that night to hide the little computer? There hadn't been any need before there was another death, more searches in store. He could have kept it forever, except for that. Suddenly it was a liability. He could have stashed it in the little elevator, but he needed a victim to frame. So he planted the computer in a pot and made a mess generally with the dirt, left some outside Bruce's door. He was to be the goat. By then Milton had to be dead, you see. Jake knew Bruce was up all hours, and it was a good bet that he'd be down in the garden before the night was over, to get dirt on his shoes. He was watching to make certain, and when Bruce did go down, he followed in time to see Constance and me in there, too. That made it even better. But then Bruce said something about a gun, and that got a very strange reaction from Jake. He laughed, for him a wild laugh, in fact, because he was shaken by the mention of a gun. He passed it off rather well, but still I had to wonder. And I wondered why he had his contacts in if he really had been sleeping. No one puts in contacts just to get up and get a drink, they simply put on glasses. But if he hadn't yet been sleeping, why lie about it? And why the pajamas if he hadn't been in bed yet? What if, I thought, he somehow had messed up the clothes he had worn earlier? Whoever wrestled Milton off the balcony, down to the cliff might well have messed up his clothes. Changing clothes in the middle of the night would have been like pointing a finger at him, so the pajamas and robe, but he forgot about the contacts. Sure enough, his gray slacks are missing, the ones he wore yesterday. And Bruce mentioned the gun, not because he had one, but because he had heard a shot and had not consciously identified it as a shot, but part of his brain knew. By the time we met them both in the garden, Milton was already dead.

"So there it is," Charlie said with an air of finality. "He switched stuff from his room to Milton's room and wiped off his prints, but his ashtray is missing, a heavy mahogany ashtray with a crystal bottom. Mrs. Ramos assures us that the inventory about which accessories were in the various rooms is correct. Eventually she might have noticed the switch, but no one asked her. I expect that Dwight Ericson will find the sheet, Jake's slacks, and the ashtray off the rocks at the north end of the beach." He glanced around at them all and added without expression, "No one knows about that stupid game of murder. I'll send you a written copy of my report, and God help you all. Satisfied?"

Harry closed his eyes briefly, then glared at Charlie. "He could have beaten it. A good lawyer would have got him off."

"And left Bruce holding the bag," Charlie said dryly. He held out his hand to Constance. "Let's hit the road."

"Beth, don't leave yet," Harry said sharply when she stood up also, a look of revulsion on her face. "There's the company to consider, our plans for the future . . ."

"Go to hell," she said. "You can talk to my lawyer as soon as I sign one on."

"He killed my son," Maddie said suddenly in a cold, furious voice. "I intend to cooperate with the police in any way I can to have him found guilty, even if it means talking about that insane game." She stood up and walked out.

Bruce began to laugh.

At the door of the room Constance glanced back once. Harry was seated on the deep couch, scowling at nothing in particular; Laura was across the couch from him, frozen faced. Behind them both the immensity of the Pacific Ocean stretched out forever, and for the first time Smart House looked small, insignificant. The shareholders of Bellringer Company looked like motes against that infinity. Constance took Charlie's hand and they walked out to their car.

Beth was waiting for them. She held out her hand, first to Charlie, then to Constance. "Thanks." She looked past them at Smart House. "Gary, Rich, Milton, Jake. They were the real brains of the company. It's over and done with now. All of it."

She stepped closer and swiftly kissed Charlie on the cheek, and then said gravely to Constance, "I won't forget you. I owe you a lot." She turned and ran to her car, got in, and drove off fast.

"There goes a potential millionaire. Millionairess? Anyway, thirty, eligible, rich, pretty."

Constance held his hand firmly. "Free," she said. "None of the rest matters very much." They went to the rented car and got in, started out the wide driveway, up the hill. "I'm just glad to be away from that place," she murmured when they made the curve that took Smart House out of view.

"I knew it was a killer the minute I set eyes on it," Charlie said, and started to hum in the tuneless way he did.

"Before you set eyes on it," she said lazily, and rested her hand on his thigh the way she did.

"Right. You know the trouble with geniuses?"

"Tell me."

"They think they're so damn smart."

He looked at her sharply, because in his head he heard her soft voice saying, *Yes, dear, but I forgive you.* She was gazing out the window at the sculptured grounds, smiling slightly.

Seven Kinds of Death

1

Bob Sherwood simply kept out of the way while the two white-coated attendants got the girl in the cast aboard car seventeen. They had brought their own wheelchair, and a ramp, but, even so, all three people had worked up a good sweat before they had her settled. Her cast went up out of sight under a full skirt; she was the color of skim milk when they wheeled her past him, and by the time they were all finished, and he looked in on her, there was a green tinge under the white of her face.

"I'll come around just as soon as we're under way," he said. "Won't be long."

She nodded. They had put her on the bench that would become her bed later on; her leg in the cast was straight out in front of her. There was one big suitcase, a carry-on type of bag, a paper sack, her purse, and, leaning against the bench, a pair of crutches. The little room looked very crowded.

"You okay? You going to be okay until I get back?"

"Fine," she muttered. "Lovely."

He hesitated only a moment, then swung around to go meet the other passengers booked for car seventeen. One of the guys who had brought her aboard was waiting for him at the outside door. He thrust two twenty-dollar bills at Bob Sherwood. "Look after her," he said—something Bob Sherwood would have done in any event.

Now they were coming: a couple with too many bags; a family with two kids—whiners, shriekers, already in good voice; two women who would inspect the silverware and peer under the beds, and ask for one more pillow or blanket. . . . There was a lot of excitement—there always was for a cross-country trip—as well as a touch of boredom for a few of the passengers who had done it all before, manic behavior from some youngsters who couldn't wait to start roaming . . .

"I called you," Toni Townsend said when he got back to her. "Didn't you hear me?" She looked very near tears. "They didn't bring my bag of books!"

The green had left her skin; there was even a touch of pink in her cheeks; she looked to be twenty-five at the most, with straight, shoulder-length brown hair, no makeup, brown eyes that were quite nice. He glanced at the suitcase, the carry-on, the paper sack. "You sure? Maybe they're in one of the suitcases."

"I had a stack of books in a paper bag, and they must have left it in the station wagon. I called you," she said again, plaintively. "Four days! When's the first stop, long enough to buy something to read?"

"Well, there's Salt Lake City, around five-thirty or so in the morning, and tomorrow night around eight-thirty we'll be in Denver . . ."

She groaned and turned to the window, ignoring him completely as he moved her bags out of the way so she could get to the little sink and toilet across the room. He always left the curtain open long enough for the occupant to get the idea, but then he closed it out of discretion.

"Now, there's anything you want, you just pull the button, day or night. Something to drink, eat. I'll see if I can find you something to read, and I'll pick up your meal vouchers and bring your food . . ."

She kept her face averted, fighting tears, until he left again. Four days, she kept thinking, in prison, solitary confinement. She thought of the prankster god who had been playing with her and laughing at her for the past three weeks, and she cursed that god. Three weeks ago she had received the long-distance call from a California firm inviting her to appear for an interview. They liked her résumé and the work she had submitted; they would pay for her trip and a hotel at that end for two days. Her roommate had shrieked with joy, and awakened the god, Toni now half believed. And that god was getting even. The interview had gone well, and then, as she had left the company grounds, her taxi and a delivery truck had collided, and she had ended up in the hospital with a broken leg. Try us again in a year or two, the company goon had said, even as he was making arrangements for her return to New York.

And the goons had kept her books. Nothing to read, nothing to see. Beyond the window heavy fog lay over the fields; the Sacramento Valley was fogged in from side to side, top to bottom.

Then she heard a knock on her door and it was pushed open; a tall slender woman stood there with a friendly grin on her face, a shopping bag in her hand. "Hi," she said. "I'm Victoria Leeds. The car attendant mentioned your problem with books and I came to the rescue." She drew near and put down the shopping bag where Toni could see; it appeared to be filled with books.

In the dining car a little later, Victoria Leeds was sitting next to an obese man, opposite his wife and her sister, who was also very fat. The wife seemed quite normal. The man was saying: "You know, I always thought I could write, if I had the time, I mean. I tell you we've had some adventures out on the farm, haven't we, honey?" His wife smiled and nodded.

Their waiter brought soup, which Victoria began to eat with apparent concentration, but actually she was thinking: It was evident why this trio had chosen the train, not a flight; she wondered if it was even possible for them to fly. He filled three quarters of the seat they shared. And Toni Townsend obviously couldn't fly with her leg in the cast straight out like that. The families with several children would find it difficult, of course.

"Remember that poem Freddy wrote back in high school?" the man was saying to his wife. "Got it published in the Davis newspapers, he did."

Across the table his wife smiled and nodded. He talked on and on. "Always thought it was knowing the right people, being in the right place at the right time. Know what I mean?"

Victoria picked at her salad. The train was getting near Davis. As soon as it stopped, she decided, she would escape. Waiters dodged passengers who passed back and forth through the diner; a child paused at her table to eye her disconcertingly, its expression as alien as a wild animal's. She watched the woman across the table bite into her chicken sandwich, and half listened to the man next to her suggest that if Freddy just knew one editor who was interested in him, he might really make it, know what I mean? She drew out two dollar bills from her purse and put them under her plate as the train slowed for the Davis station.

"You going on in to Chicago?" the man asked.

"Yes."

"Well, we'll see you again in the next day or two. Nice talking to you."

She fled. She made her way through the two cars separating her own from the diner before the train started to move again. In her tiny compartment she drew the curtain across the door, sat down, and closed her eyes. Across the hallway, down a room or two, a child was screaming lustily. She envied it.

"Why are you traveling by train?" Toni asked later that afternoon.

Victoria had been talking about her luncheon companions, the others in the diner. She shrugged. "Time out. I just wanted a little time out. Do you like that book?"

"It's okay," Toni said. "Do you get a lot of that when people find out you're an editor? Wanting you to look at Freddy's poems, their stories, stuff like that?"

Laughing, Victoria held up her hand. "First, I have a question. Are you now, or have you ever been a card-carrying aspiring writer?"

Toni laughed with her and shook her head.

"Okay. Sure we do, all of us do, I guess. And in a way that guy in the diner is right, partly it is a matter of luck, being in the right place, and so on. If they persist, I give them my card and say send your stuff in to the office."

"Do you ever accept anything that comes in like that?"

"Hardly ever," Victoria said slowly. "We deal almost exclusively through agents. As I said, he was more right than he knows."

Later, in her own compartment again, Victoria wondered at the pinched look that had crossed Toni's face. All right, she thought, Toni had a problem. Who didn't? Determinedly she watched the passing scenery; the Sierra mountains now. Then, there would be darkness, the wasteland of Nevada, the desert of Utah. . . . Soon she would think about Paul Volte, she told herself. Not this minute, but soon. For that was why she had taken the train, why she was spending four days that she could not really spare, time out, in order to think seriously of herself and Paul Volte. But not just yet.

During the next day the train wound through spectacularly beautiful river valleys and gorges, the canyons cut by the Colorado River through the Rocky Mountains. Victoria visited with Toni several times during the day; they chatted about books, movies, music, New York, but most of the time they simply gazed at the view beyond the window.

As she neared Toni's room late in the afternoon, she saw the car attendant, Bob Sherwood, blocking the doorway.

"You made this?" he said, the wonder in his voice undisguised. "I'll be damned! How'd you do that?"

More faintly Toni's voice floated out, "I don't know. I never know. My hands know what they're doing, but they don't talk to me much."

Victoria felt as if the train had lurched violently, although it had not; she felt as if she were falling, although she was unmoving. She held on to the metal of the bathroom door waiting for the vertigo to pass, and when it was over, Bob Sherwood was talking again, this time turned to include her.

"Did you know she's an artist? A real artist. Just look at this."

It was a plasticine bas-relief head, Bob Sherwood's head, rising from a smooth base no more than four inches square. Even without studying it closely, Victoria could see that Toni had caught his broad face, the widely spaced eyes, the thick nose and narrow lips. The expression was of intelligent patience, exactly right.

He held it out for her to look at, but his hand was protective, cupping the piece; he was not inviting her to touch it. When a call button sounded, he looked resigned. "She gave it to me," he said to Victoria, then turned back to the room. "I'll bring your dinner between six-thirty and seven. Okay? You want anything before that?" Her response was inaudible. "Okay. You take it easy. And, Ms. Townsend, thanks. Just thank you very much."

After he had left, Victoria entered the little room, studying Toni as if for the first time. "What was that job you interviewed for? You said a computer company?"

Toni was on the window bench that opened to make a bed. She nodded. "In the graphics department."

"Oh," Victoria said. "Designing software packages, something like that?"

Toni lifted her chin almost defiantly. "It had something to do with art, anyway. The first job possibility that did."

"What will you do now?"

"I don't know," Toni said miserably. "Back to my job washing dishes, I guess. I'm a very artistic dishwasher."

"You have a lawyer, I hope," Victoria said. "Have you signed anything yet?"

Toni shook her head. "I was too mad."

"Good. Don't. Not until you see a lawyer." Abruptly she stood up. "I've got a bottle of wine in my room. And a book you might want to read. I'll be right back."

In her room she picked up the page proofs of Paul Volte's book, *With These Hands,* and for a moment she stood holding it tightly. She could have opened it and found a passage almost identical to Toni's words, almost as if she had been reading from the text: *I never know. My hands know what they're doing.* She retrieved the wine from her bag, and returned to Toni's room.

"Do you know his column?" she asked, handing over the book. It had an orange cover, and the stamped message, *Uncorrected Page Proofs.* It was very thick.

Toni examined it curiously, shaking her head.

"Too bad," Victoria said dryly. "His column on art and architecture appears every month in our magazine. This is his third full-length book, and it's going to be a best-seller. Due out at the end of the month." She began to work with the cork in the wine. Her little corkscrew was sometimes uncooperative and crumbled the cork instead of lifting it neatly.

"How do you know it'll be a best-seller?"

Victoria was turning the corkscrew slowly. "Oh, two book clubs have taken it, and advance reviews have been dynamite. And it ran as a three-parter in the magazine last winter. I was the editor for the piece," she said, even more dryly than before. She glanced at Toni in time to see a flush cover her face. The cork came out smoothly and she nodded at it in satisfaction. She poured the wine into little plastic glasses and handed one to Toni. "Cheers," she said. "Now let's talk about you and your accident and broken leg and lawyers and your future. And cabbages and kings, if they seem pertinent." Toni looked mystified and Victoria drank all her wine and poured herself a second glass.

At two in the morning Victoria finally brought her thoughts to the problem that had made her take the train. There had been far less thinking time than she had anticipated. The train was crowded and noisy. A child down the corridor from her room was unhappy and vocal about it. Intermittently the loudspeaker brayed announcements about meals, about a bingo game or something like that, about a trivia game, about movies to be shown in the lounge car, about happy-hour prices, about snacks. And, of course, there had been all that scenery.

She sat up in her bed with the curtain open to the black night with not a sign of human activity out there on the prairie, nothing to distract her. "All right," she said under her breath. "All right."

In three months she would be forty-two years old. Sometimes she looked it, most often not, but she knew. She knew. She had been married for seven years, a long time ago, so long ago she thought of that period as if it concerned someone other than her. She had a good job, with the offer of a better job waiting for her decision. And she had to face the fact that although she and Paul were a "thing," had a relationship, were ideal for each other, loved each other, nothing was going to happen between them that hadn't already happened.

"All right," she said again. "Them's the facts. Now what?"

You have to bring it out into the open, discuss it with him, her counselor had said nearly two years ago. Two years, she repeated to herself. Yes. Right. Bring it out, talk to the wind, throw the words on the waves. He wouldn't discuss it. He wouldn't go to a counselor. She had dropped counseling when the question surfaced: what are your choices then? She didn't need to pay anyone to tell her the choices. Don't rock the boat, go on with everything exactly the way it is, or get out.

Out, she thought clearly, and yanked the curtain closed. She felt as if the decision had been there for more than two years, but she had not found the words to tell herself what it was until that moment. Now it seemed so simple. One word, that was all. Out. Dawn light edged the curtain when she finally fell asleep.

"He's wonderful," Toni said the next day. "You said best-seller and I kept thinking of those other books you loaned me, you know, best-sellers. But this is different."

"I know."

"He understands everything," Toni went on, oblivious. "He knew how to put the questions, the answers he was after. He knew."

Victoria watched her, the sparkle that had come to her eyes, the animation in her face; she listened to the excitement in her voice as long as she could bear it, and then said, "Come to the office before the end of April and I'll introduce you to him. It has to be before the end of April. Will you be on your feet by then?"

Toni counted quickly, then nodded. "Five weeks. Oh, yes! Victoria, how can I thank you?"

"For what, for heaven's sake? It's an introduction, not a betrothal."

"It's more than an introduction," Toni said in a low voice. "It's more than that. You know what you said about that fat man in the dining car? He was right. Being in the right place at the right time, meeting the right person, something arranges things like that. Fate. Karma. Whatever." She almost added, or a prankster god toying with you. She still felt herself to be on a string, pulled this way and that, with no choices, but now it felt wonderful, even if a little eerie. She said, "If I hadn't had the accident, I wouldn't have taken the train. If I had got the job, I'd be in San Francisco right now. But I wasn't meant to be there. We had to meet, and now I have to meet him. That's what Paul Volte understands. That's what he gets people talking about, and you feel as if, as if . . . it's as if someone managed to look into your head, into your heart, your soul even. Talking with all those other people, he could have been talking with me, making me say things I never dreamed of saying out loud. Things that are just right. I can't explain it, but he knows what it's like."

"Possession," Victoria said. "That's what he was talking about in the book all the way through. Fanaticism. Absolute egomania. An acceptance that the artist is the tool without choice." When she became aware of the anger in her voice, she stopped speaking.

Silently Toni nodded. Her face had become set in a curious

expression, withdrawn, distant. For a moment her exhilaration was like an adrenaline rush of fear; for this moment she felt she could choose after all. Right now, this instant, she felt, she could still say no.

Victoria stood up, shaking her head. "You'll meet him. Give me a call at the office before the end of April." What she had not added, something Paul's book said distinctly, was that the truly gifted artist was owned by a jealous muse that would give success with one hand and snatch away happiness with the other. He had written it, she thought then, but did he believe what he had written? She did not know, and not knowing, and having no way of learning the truth made her more determined than she had been the night before. Out, she said to herself again. Out!

At lunch the next day, gazing moodily at the flooded fields of Iowa, gray and unquiet water in every hollow, every flat place as far as she could see, and if not standing water, then mud, drowned shrubs and trees, she realized that she had done what she had to do; she had made her decision. Now she could leave the train in Chicago and fly home.

She went to Toni's room to tell her good-bye, and made her a present of all the books, even Paul's. Later, in Chicago, she took a cab to O'Hare and by ten that night she was in her own apartment.

It was Friday of the last week in April when Toni walked haltingly into the anteroom of *New World Magazine* at four in the afternoon. She was approaching the reception desk, carrying a large canvas bag that she managed awkwardly; it was heavier than she had realized, the walk was longer, her leg weaker. Then she saw Victoria coming toward her.

"Hi. Good to see you on your own feet," Victoria said. She waved to the woman behind the desk, took Toni's arm, and reached for the bag. "Let me. Hey, what's in there? This way." She led Toni around the reception desk, through a doorway, into a narrow hall. Everything looked old and threadbare, as if the building had been decorated back in the thirties and not touched again since. Carpeting on the floor was worn, with holes before some of the doors; molding that was almost to Toni's shoulders was chipped here and there, with an undercoating of brown paint showing through the top layer of tan.

They passed an open door beyond which was a room that looked to Toni like chaos: long tables were piled high with papers, several people were talking in loud voices, one woman was holding up an oversized color print. Victoria continued to lead her to an elevator that creaked and groaned its way to the fourth floor; they went down another corridor as shabby as the first one, and finally into a small office, barely big enough for both women. Victoria left the door open and moved behind the desk, leaving room for Toni on the other side. In here were cartons, most of them taped closed, a few not quite filled, stacks of papers, manuscripts in piles, a wall of shelves, nearly empty, and on a narrow window sill three pots of pink geraniums.

"Home," Victoria said. She put the heavy bag on the desk on top of some papers, and surveyed Toni with a critical eye. "You look fine. How's it going?"

"Wonderfully," Toni said. "I got a lawyer, and he'll get me enough to live on for a year, he says. Maybe he will. And two different insurance companies are paying my bills, the doctors and everything. I . . . I have something for you." She opened the bag and, using both hands, carefully removed an object wrapped in a dish towel. She set it down and took the towel away. Another bas-relief, this one life-sized, of Victoria's face. It was done in a streaky blue-green soapstone.

"Good God!" Victoria breathed. "It's . . . it's very beautiful. Too beautiful." She touched the stone, then let her fingers trail over the surface, over the cheek, the forehead. The stone eyes were downcast, the expression introspective, somehow sad. Her fingers lingered over the smooth face that was pleasantly cool. "Toni, it's wonderful. Thank you."

Toni nodded mutely. Too idealized, she knew. Too beautiful. Not quite right, but she didn't know how to make it more right. Suddenly, perversely, she wished she had not brought it, not yet, not until she was better, until she knew how to get it right. Her hands were clenched painfully; she wanted to weep because it wasn't right yet.

"Well, come on. I'll bring this. Paul's office is on this floor, not far." Victoria picked up the stone carefully and they went down the corridor. She stopped before a partly open door, took a breath, then called, "I've got the artist I wanted you to meet. Are you decent?"

The door was pulled open and Paul Volte moved aside to admit them. He was tall and almost too thin, like a marathoner; his hair was gray, and his eyes a bright, sparkling blue. Although he glanced at Toni, and at the stone, Victoria was the one he looked at with a yearning so visible, so unconcealed, it was painful to witness. Victoria made the introduction.

He shook Toni's hand, and looked more carefully at the bas-relief when Victoria put it down on his desk, then nodded. "Nice," he said. "Very nice."

Toni's eyes burned more fiercely than before.

"Well, I'll leave you two to get acquainted," Victoria said. She had not looked directly at Paul, and did not now. She lifted the bas-relief and turned toward the door. "I'll give you a call in a couple of weeks," she said to Toni. "This is my last day here at the magazine, then off for a little vacation, and back to a new job. Busy time. Toni, this is one of the nicest presents I've ever had. Thank you so very much." She left the office.

Toni started to follow her. "I'm sorry," she said without any clear idea of what she meant.

Paul Volte was staring at the empty doorway. Abruptly he looked at Toni. "Can you make another one? Just like it. I'll buy it." The sparkle had left his eyes; he looked old; his voice had become harsh.

Slowly Toni nodded. She had read and reread his book many times; she had even bought a copy and read that to see if there were differences. She could quote long passages. In her head she quoted one now: *People think of it as a gift, and they're wrong. It isn't like that. A gift implies something freely given with no thought of reciprocation, nothing is asked in return. This is not a gift; it is a trade. It's as if this something promises success but at a price. With the first success, the death of a pet. Then of a parent perhaps, or a lover. On and on until you don't dare love again. You don't dare.*

2

As soon as Toni arrived at Marion Olsen's house in the lush countryside of Montgomery County, Maryland, she knew she would not stay more than politeness demanded. Since Paul Volte had acted as if this were Mecca or something, and she felt obligated to him, she had to do this much. If he was trying to help her, and believed that Marion Olsen could help her, she would be able to say she had tried it. The problem was that Marion Olsen was about the ugliest woman she had ever seen, the coarsest, almost brutal, with a harsh, husky voice, and a peremptory manner that made Toni cringe. Toni was afraid of her.

"Is it Antoinette?" Marion demanded, surveying her as she got out of her car. She had come off a porch to meet Toni.

"Antonia," Toni said, taken aback. Marion Olsen was a large woman, looming over her like a dream menace, with ropy muscles in her arms, hands like a stevedore's; she was dressed in black sweatpants and an oversized black T-shirt that reached nearly to her knees. She wore sandals, no socks: her feet were dirty. Her hair was long, streaked with gray, tried back with a string. She glanced inside the car, at the boxes of artwork that Toni had crammed in beside her suitcases, and other boxes of her personal things. A mistake, Toni knew; she should have brought only enough for one night.

"I'd be Toni, too," Marion said. "Antonia ended up with what, nine, ten kids, living in a hole in the ground? So much for that. Come on in." They started to walk toward the house, and she asked, "What's wrong with your leg? Can you do any work?"

Toni bit her lip, then answered in a measured voice, "I am quite capable. I broke it, but it's almost healed now."

"Well, I hope it is. You'll sleep upstairs, and there's always garden stuff that needs doing. This used to be a little farmhouse," Marion said. "We've been adding to it right along." They entered by a side door that opened directly into a very large workroom with a smaller studio angled off it. Several people were in the studio working, men and women in jeans, one woman lying on the floor with her feet on a chair, hands behind her head, a man sitting cross-legged on a cushion playing a mouth organ badly. Marion did not introduce anyone, but waved and led Toni on through to a hall, past a bathroom, another room that might have been a breakfast nook but was actually an office, she said, although it looked like a dinette. Kitchen, pantry, dining room several halls that just made it all more confusing. At the other end of the original core of the house a huge living room with a fireplace big enough to walk into had been added; a library or television or music room adjoined it. That room seemed to serve all purposes. The additions attested to various levels of skill of the builders, none of them as good as the people who had constructed the original building. The floors of the additions were wide planks; the original floors were lovely oak. The new walls were drywall with inept taping that was peeling here and there; the original walls were well plastered. It was like that throughout. Some windows had leaded glass, others did not quite close because they did not hang perfectly straight.

But everywhere there was artwork: stone sculptures, wood pieces, bronze, iron, copper. . . . They were on every flat surface, on the floor against the walls—abstract pieces, representational pieces, some that reached the ceilings, others no bigger than her hand. Every shelf was jammed with art, every table, the top of the piano in the television room; pieces lined the staircase, mobiles hung before windows . . .

Upstairs, Marion said, were six bedrooms; Toni would share a room with Janet Cuprillo, who was out somewhere or other right now. Abruptly she left Toni and started to talk to a young-ish man about a statuette he was holding. She appeared to forget Toni completely.

"Look at that line," Marion said. "Get one of the girls to model for you. You just don't contort muscles like that. You need the tension in her as a whole-body, whole-person tension, not in particular muscles. . . . What the hell? Looks like she's got grapes under her skin." They walked away, leaving Toni in the hall.

At dinner Toni did not say a word. She made no attempt to remember anyone's name, since she planned to leave again the following day. Tommy, Hal, Janet . . . it didn't matter. They were talking excitedly about a trip that most of them were taking in ten days—to Italy for six months or longer. Toni didn't try to sort that out, either.

As soon as dinner was over, Marion said, "I had Willy put your pieces in the office. Let's go have a look."

She didn't wait for Toni's response, but started out the door, and after a moment Toni followed. One of the other women in the room winked at her, but it didn't really help. She wanted to turn and run the other way; her legs felt leaden, her stomach suddenly ached, and curiously she was freezing and sweating at the same time. She should have locked the car, she thought, but rejected the notion; Marion would have got the pieces out somehow.

In the office there was a green Formica-topped dinette table and several matching chairs with splits in the plastic, stuffing turned brown poking out. One wall had floor-to-ceiling unfinished wood shelves, all filled with more art objects, with boxes, glasses, a Barbie doll, a rubber frog, a wind-up bear, a mason jar filled with chopsticks. . . . Toni's few pieces were on the table: her bas-relief faces, several full-figure statuettes, some wood pieces she had done years before in art school, one studded with bits of colored glass.

Marion walked back and forth examining the pieces carefully; Toni gazed past her out the windows, which were grimy. This wasn't real country, she thought, not farming country; but countryside that had freed itself from the burden of crops, and now was reverting back to forest as quickly as possible. The country she had driven through that afternoon had appeared almost empty of people; even the developments, the projects, the subdivisions without end had seemed devoid of people and preternaturally quiet. All the people had been in cars driving on the roads. And she had lost them all, she thought then. From the interstate, to the state road, to the county road, then on to a dirt road where her car was the only thing that moved. She felt as if she had journeyed to the end of the world.

Twilight had come while they were at dinner, and the shadowless world was still, the tender May leaves that had been whipping in the wind an hour earlier were quiet, as if waiting, just as she was. Not that it mattered, she told herself fiercely.

Marion touched one of the pieces of cherry wood, carved, abstract, with such a high gloss finish it could have been metal. "How long a period from this," she asked, "to this?" Her hand went unerringly to the last piece Toni had done before Victoria's, the face of an elderly woman who lived in her apartment building in New York.

"Eight years," Toni said. Her voice came out as a whisper.

"Yes. You can stay as long as you like. You have the hands and skill. But do you have eyes? I don't know yet."

Toni swallowed painfully. "Thank you, Ms. Olsen, but I think I've already decided that this isn't my sort of thing. I don't think I would fit in."

Marion smiled. "All right. I would never try to talk anyone into going into art seriously, never. In fact, I usually advise people to keep it as a hobby, something they can enjoy doing without pain. I advise you to do that, let it be your hobby. Amuse yourself and your friends with it. You may even sell a piece, the faces especially. That saintly woman would like that on her living room wall, don't you think?"

Toni watched Marion's long hard finger trace the chin of the woman's face. The stone was a gray soapstone, very cool, very smooth. The image was exactly like her neighbor who had offered her a hundred dollars for it, a hundred dollars she certainly could not afford to part with.

"What's wrong with it?" Toni demanded.

"Nothing. Your hands did exactly what your eyes reported. It's your eyes that lied. I wonder if anyone ever suspected that she killed her first husband," Marion mused, regarding the face.

Toni gasped. "She didn't!"

"Maybe not. It was her child born without the benefit of a wedding first or a doctor, back alley stuff. She drowned it. Or maybe it was just kittens she drowned."

"What are you talking about? You don't even know her!"

Marion looked from the face to Toni and shrugged. "Neither do you. She isn't real to you. People generally aren't very real for you, are they? You invent them and your clever hands create the image you require to keep yourself safe. Stay or go, I don't care which. If you stay, you'll work very hard, and you'll learn to see. It may be that you won't like what you see and you'll wish you had left. But until you can believe that people are real, and stop inventing them, I don't know if you can create good art or not. You don't have to tell me your decision. If I keep seeing you around, I'll assume you're staying. Janet can help you stake out studio space, if you want it. And you can put these things in your room or your car, or in your space. Or just leave them where they are." She pulled at her black shirt and added, "I've got to get out of these mucky rags before Max gets home."

"Why did you say I could come?" Toni asked as Marion started to leave.

"You know as well as I do," Marion said. "Paul told me to. If he saw talent, no doubt it's there. No one has a better eye than he does." She left the room and closed the door behind her.

Toni sank down on one of the ratty chairs and stared at the gray stone face. She couldn't remember her name. Mrs. Franklin? Mrs. Frankel? She shook her head. All her life she had pretended, and at this first meeting, within seconds, she thought wildly, Marion Olsen had seen through her pretense. People weren't real. She had come to understand that very early. Her mother was a face on television telling everyone what had happened that day. Her teeth were capped, her hair tinted, her figure controlled by a careful diet and more carefully chosen clothes, and at home she did not look or sound like the television person. At home she had always been extremely busy, but that had not mattered since she had not been home very much. Unreal. Toni had not seen her for five years. Her father had managed a print shop until he left them when Toni was twelve. He had been three or four different people—a loving stranger with presents; a strange man with beer on his breath; a furious, swearing, cruel stranger; a pitiful, weepy, red-eyed stranger. She didn't believe in him, either. She hadn't seen him since she was twelve.

She remembered Victoria's words, *too beautiful*, and Paul's, *nice, very nice*. Paul had bought the bas-relief she had made, not because the art was all that good, she understood now, but because she had created a Victoria who was lovely and not quite real, the way he wanted her to be, the way Toni had seen her. Had invented her, she corrected herself under her breath. Victoria was not real, nor was Paul. The face of the stranger from her apartment building now looked like someone she never had seen before in her life; the woman's name was gone, she was gone, hardly even a memory of her remained. An unreal woman.

She tried to conjure up Marion's face, the way she always did before starting to mold the plasticine; nothing came. She could say the words that described Marion: too large a nose, a mouth too wide, deep-set dark eyes, heavy eyebrows, long graying hair. No image came with the words. She shivered. Marion refused to be created, imagined, idealized. Marion was too real already. Whenever she thought of what Marion had said, that Paul had told her to invite Toni, she shied away from all the possible reasons she could think of for Marion's being that compliant. As far as Toni could tell, Marion was not that manipulable with anyone else.

Day by day she delayed her departure. Tomorrow, she told herself. Tomorrow. She watched the others work, although she did no work of her own. She listened intently when Marion critiqued a piece of work; everyone listened intently. She hung back at the group discussions. Tomorrow, she told herself again. Tomorrow.

Those heading for Italy left, and now she and Janet had private rooms; two of the men remained behind also, but still they had the group sessions, and with so few people, she felt pressured to contribute to the session both with her own work, and her critiques. The pressure did not come from Marion. She did not pressure anyone about anything. You did things or not; she never asked what you were working on, or to see what you were doing, or if you had plans for next week, next month, or next year. She was a hard critic, merciless and radiant. When she talked about a piece, Toni found herself thinking, of course, she should have seen that; it was so obvious now. Marion illuminated art in a way no one had done for Toni, and her language was earthy, never elevated, never obscure or abstract, always to the point.

Toni did only small things in clay. The others critiqued her work seriously and listened to her with concentration. But it was Marion they all wanted to hear. And Marion's face eluded her. She watched her as she spoke, the animation that changed her from second to second, from youthful, even pretty, to ancient and cruel. She memorized the coarse features, big nose, heavy eyebrows, a slight crookedness in her grin, up on the left, down on the right side . . . but as soon as she was away from Marion, the face vanished from her mind and she was left with the words instead of the image.

There was a fancy party in Washington in Spence Dwyers's gallery, to celebrate Marion's coming touring show. The young people did not attend that one, the real party would be here at the house, and to this private party she invited Paul Volte.

Now Toni started saying to herself that she would leave after the party. She wanted to see Paul again, to thank him again, but not to show him what she was doing. What she was doing was crap, she told herself, just as it always had been. She stared at her hands with hatred. All they could produce was crap.

Claud Palance from nearby Bellarmine College brought a couple of graduate students and began to teach the others how to crate artwork for a touring show. They worked in the big barn on the property across a narrow dirt road. The barn was another studio, bigger and dirtier than the one in the house. Massive pieces of granite were strewn about; what appeared to be whole trees stripped of branches and roots were behind the barn. A kiln was back there. Inside, all the work for the tour had been gathered together; only the major piece *Seven Kinds of Death* was missing. It was in the center of the living room floor, the focus for the real party, Marion said with satisfaction when the movers safely positioned it.

"You don't think it's a bit in the way?" Johnny Buell asked that afternoon, walking around it. Johnny was Marion's stepson. He was six feet tall and weighed two hundred pounds and was not fat. His dark brown hair had a nice wave; he had deep-set blue eyes, like his father's. But his eyes did not sparkle with amusement the way Max Buell's eyes did.

Marion raised her unkempt eyebrows at Johnny. "It's supposed to be in the way, damn it," she said. "That's what death's all about, for God's sake. We can't keep pussyfooting around it forever. Let it come out into the open, get in the way for a change. No one's going to trip over it, for Christ's sake!" Since the piece was five feet tall and massive at the base, with shiny metal here and there, and several kinds of wood here and there, it was unlikely that anyone would trip over it.

Toni and Janet Cuprillo had entered the house in time to hear this exchange. Janet had been Toni's roommate in the beginning. She was very pretty, with short black hair shingled in the back; her brown eyes were almond shaped and beautiful, with long, long lashes. She was extremely talented, everyone agreed, but within days Toni had come to realize that words were not the same for Janet as for other people. She liked some more than others for the way they sounded, or the way they looked, and she rarely gave a lot of thought to what they meant.

She had summed up John Buell for Toni during her first week here. Johnny took the world seriously. Living was a serious matter with him. Like a saint with arrows sticking out all over, he bled a lot. Toni had looked at her with incomprehension. "You know," Janet said, "he has a mission, and if he has to suffer for it, that's fine with him. That's what a serious person does, suffers and bleeds if he has to, but he gets his mission done."

"A mission?" Toni had echoed.

"Like missionary? A message to give. In his case buildings to build."

This was the day that Toni had come to realize that Janet took a lot of interpreting. Mission, message? Buildings as message? She wasn't sure what Janet had meant, but the gist of her comments was clear enough. Johnny was a serious young man with an important job. He took work seriously, took Marion seriously. The Max Buell Company was building a multimillion-dollar condominium complex a mile away from Marion's house, and Johnny took that most seriously of all. Then, Janet had added dreamily, if he weren't already engaged, she'd go for him. But as it was she was indivisible, and so was Toni.

Invisible, Toni decided, and that was fine with her. As far as she was concerned, Johnny's attitude was no more false and unreal than his father's: Max Buell seemed to find everything amusing, and took nothing seriously; Johnny found nothing amusing and everything was serious. He was unreal, and Janet, who was only twenty-one, was almost as unreal as Johnny.

Toni and Janet had stayed back out of the way while the movers strained getting *Seven Kinds of Death* in place; both young women were grimy with sweat and caked dust from the work in the barn, Janet nursing a splinter in her finger, and anxious to go give it a soak. After the movers left, they started up the stairs, but stepped aside once more as Max Buell came down. Unlike his son, he saw not only them but everything about them, every smudge, every scrape, every speck of dirt. He grinned as he passed them on his way to the living room.

"Message for you," he said to Marion. "Your friend Paul Volte is bringing a lady friend with him." Max was as tall as his son, and heavier, thicker in the shoulders and chest. His face was weathered dark brown, and there were crinkly lines at his eyes. He walked to the piece in the center of the room and whistled. "Hey, that looks like hot shit there! Marion, I think it's just dandy!"

"He's bringing someone," Marion said in a grating voice. "I don't suppose we know if the lady friend will want a separate bedroom, do we? My God, I'm going mad! I've rearranged sleeping accommodations a dozen times already! Why didn't he tell me weeks ago? That bastard! He didn't even tell me he was coming. What does he think, I'm running a goddam hotel or something?"

Max chuckled. "I don't think you need worry about it. It's that lady editor, and from what little I know about things like that, I think you could call them real friendly."

At the doorway Toni gasped and clutched the framework to steady herself. Not Victoria! He wouldn't! She was aware that they were all watching her as she turned and fled upstairs.

3

Later, Charlie would be able to pinpoint the exact moment when he wandered innocently into the trap, and then the exact moment when it was sprung, but that morning in early June he had no intimation of hazardous moments ahead. Things had been peachy, he thought later, recapitulating that morning. He had done a little job for Phil Stern that had put a little money in the bank, and, more, had been entertaining in its own way, culminating in a little joust with a very good arsonist who had had very bad luck and cursed his date of birth for it. Good clean fun. The guy probably would beat the rap in court, but that wasn't Charlie's problem. And the car had not needed the overhaul he had been dreading. The sun was shining, the weather strange, but rather nice. The whole world had had strange weather that spring, but few places had it as nice as upper New York in early June.

He and Constance had corralled the cats inside and she had taken them out to the patio one by one to dose them with ear drops. Ashcan had ear mites, but you don't treat only one cat. Brutus had to be first always; he had an elephantine memory, and the sniff of medicine was enough to alert him that it was hiding time. Charlie admired Constance's ability to snag a cat, hold it in a grip that made the cat look as if rigor mortis was well advanced, and then do whatever was needed. Afterward, Brutus streaked off shaking his head, flinging medicine to the wind in both directions; he would not return until supper, and by then it would be time for another treatment. Candy complained in her scratchy voice when it was her turn, and Ashcan, who was the bearer of evil tidings this time, tried to crawl under the doormat.

Then Charlie had gone out for the mail. Constance was drying her hands when he returned and sorted it at the kitchen table. Very little, very dull looking. He was browsing through a catalogue with high-tech fishing gear that featured things like a computerized casting outfit that you attached to a box that told you what was biting, what bait to use, how to use it. Maybe if your Aunt Ethel was coming for a visit, he was thinking, grinning, when the trap opened.

"For goodness' sake," Constance murmured. "Do you want to go to a send-off party for a gallery tour that Marion Olsen is having?"

"Nope," he said, and turned a page. At the time he did not hear a clash of metal, did not hear the door bang, but later he knew that was the moment. That *Nope* was the magic word. Without looking up, he asked, "Who's Marion What's-it?"

"Oh, Charlie," Constance said in that particular tone of voice that held such a mixture of exasperation and patience that it was hard to tell which was uppermost. "You remember her. We went to some of her shows. I grew up with her. We saw her all the time in New York when we were all just out of school, before she moved down near Washington. We exchange notes and Christmas cards every single year." She sounded like a saintly teacher struggling with an overgrown student who couldn't quite grasp Dick and Jane.

"Oh," he said. "You mean Tootles."

"I mean Marion Olsen," she said coldly. "She's finally surfacing again as a sculptor, after all these years. A fifteen-gallery touring show. Good for her. I'm so glad."

"She did that thing she called the *Seven Kinds of Death*, right?"

"You know very well she did."

"And she asked you if you really had married a fireman, and then she said, 'A terrible waste.' "

"Charlie, I've told you a dozen times, she didn't say that. You misheard her."

"Maybe," he admitted. "It could have been 'What terrible taste.' And everyone at that last party was a kook of one kind or another, including sister Babar."

Constance's look this time was withering. "Her sister's name is Beatrice. When she was a very small child they called her Ba Ba."

"She was never a very small child," he said. "And she's a nut. Your pal Tootles has a knack for nuts."

Constance opened another envelope, a bill, and he said, "Anyway, her husband was making passes at you right in front of me. Now is that a kook or isn't it?"

Constance ignored him. She crossed the kitchen to throw away the junk mail and envelopes.

"And you know damn well Tootles was making passes at me. You thought it was funny!" *He* had been indignant.

Constance was heading toward the hall. She paused. "Maybe she wanted to see what kind of equipment a fireman had. I did marry a fireman, you know."

"And was it a terrible waste?"

She walked from the room carrying her mail and the bill with her. Charlie was grinning again when he went back to the fishing-gear catalogue. Later, he knew if she had phrased the question differently, he would have said sure, let's do it. The way you ask a question is important, he would have said. There was no doubt that he didn't want to go, and that was the question she had asked, after all. A yes or no answer was required, and a yes would have been a lie. If she had said she wanted to go, he would have agreed without question, maybe with a few jabs at Tootles, but without real argument. If she had brought it up again in any way, he would have said he had intended to go with her all along, just teasing a little that morning. If she had left the invitation lying about, he would have picked it up and said something like *Why not?* None of those things happened, and neither of them mentioned Tootles or Babar again until two weeks later, when he found Constance poring over a road map.

"What's up?" he asked. He had mowed the lawn and carried the fragrance of newly cut grass with him into the house, which already was perfumed with roses in just about every room. Mowing his own lawn always made him feel virtuous; shoveling snow did also, although he complained about both chores.

"I thought I might drive down," Constance said. "The flights are awful, with changes at La Guardia or Philadelphia or somewhere. Or else the shuttle and then rent a car. And the train's even worse. Three hours in Penn Station."

"Down where? Are we going on a trip?"

"I am. Marion's party. I'll leave on Thursday, get there that night and start home on Sunday. If I'm too tired, I might stop at a motel Sunday night. Depends on what time I get away."

"You'll drive more than three hundred miles for a party?" He heard the incredulity in his own voice.

She looked up at him and said yes. Her pale blue eyes were glinty.

It was that damn Viking blood surfacing, he thought then, a streak of stubbornness, a fierce loyalty that verged on insanity, a perverse determination. . . . If she thought he would yield just like that, he also thought, she was wrong. Why didn't she come right out and ask him nicely to drive down with her? Make a little vacation out of the affair.

It wasn't that they never did things apart. He did little investigative jobs for Phil Stern's insurance company from time to time. They both did other investigative jobs now and then that took him to one place, her to another. She had presented a paper at a psychology conference just a few months before and had been gone almost a week. He went fishing now and then, and had done some workshops in the past year on techniques of arson investigations. It wasn't that they would be separated for a few days, it was the glint in her eyes, the too-cool, too-aloof expression on her face that made this different.

"Watch out for the husband," he said coldly.

"I think I'm a little old for such a warning, but thank you. You needn't worry, that one's been gone a long time. Actually, she's married again, to a millionaire, a fact I've mentioned more than once—when it happened, and again this past Christmas, as I recall. I sometimes worry about your memory, or is it that you didn't want to hear anything about Marion? Anyway, she probably will keep her eye on the current husband."

The fact that Tootles could snag four or five husbands, and her looking like a horse, meant to him that Constance could have had a dozen, if she had chosen that route.

To *his* eyes Constance was the best-looking woman he had ever seen; she had been the most beautiful girl he had ever seen back when they were both students in Columbia, and the years had been loving and kind to her. Her platinum hair had never darkened, and now that it was starting to turn gray, it looked no different from all the years he had known her. She moved with the grace of a dancer, and her slender body had not changed that much. The little bit of weight she had picked up over the years was a plus, he thought. Back when Tootles either had said what a waste, or hadn't—he really wasn't all that certain—he had been cut sharply, because he had believed it. Constance was wasted on anyone but a god, he had thought then. He knew the theory that the passion of youth matured and became companionship, if the couple was lucky, and he knew that if he were a religious man he would thank God that the theory was baloney. They had the companionship and the mutual respect their maturity demanded, and they still had the passion. But also they were individuals, not a matched set, and by God, he thought then, she was the one who had to give a little; just a fraction of an inch would have been sufficient, but it had to come from her.

If he had said any of those things at that moment, if he had simply kissed her, he thought later, they probably would have gone to the party together. But he said, "Send me a postcard," and stalked from the room.

Constance knew almost precisely what had gone on in Charlie's head during those few moments, not the word-by-word struggle, but the essence. She knew far better than he did if he gained or lost a pound; she knew to the day when the first gray hair had appeared in his crinkly black curls. She knew the way the light came into his eyes and then left them flat and hard black, the way his face softened or turned to stone, the way the muscles on his jaws worked, and each nuance spoke multiple meanings for her. The words had formed in her mouth, "Oh, Charlie," meaning, this time, we're having such a silly quarrel. Her hand had nearly spasmed when she restrained its motion toward him. The moment passed that could have ended all this.

The day the invitation came, she had been dismayed by his instant reaction, his instant refusal to go to the party, but after no more than a second or two, she had decided he was right and probably he should not go. Actually, she did not want him to go with her. When Charlie first met Tootles—she bit her lip in exasperation with herself, but that had been her name from the time they both wore diapers and it was hard to remember it was no longer appropriate. When Charlie first met Tootles, she started again, he had been deeply offended. Charlie, so faithful and steadfast, so young, had not approved of promiscuity, and Tootles was promiscuous. Honest and truthful, he had not approved of lying, and Tootles sometimes seemed to make little or no distinction. He suspected that people who talked of their work as art, always with a capital A, had to be phonies of some sort, and Tootles had talked of her WORK as ART, and of little else in those days. Charlie, unstinting in his own generosity, was suspicious of people who were born to be takers, and Tootles, he had said, was a saltwater sponge.

Those first impressions had endured for more than twenty-five years and nothing else about Tootles had stayed with him, although they had been with her subsequently half a dozen times at least. He had failed to see the three or four other artists Tootles always maintained because they were even hungrier than she was. He found no virtue in her real appreciation of the work of others. He never had seen her working with a child, a teenager, any talented novice.

Constance began to fold the map. She had not shown the invitation to Charlie, had not left it lying on the table for him to see because Tootles had written a message on the bottom in her scrawly script. *Please, Constance, please come. I am in desperate trouble. I have to talk to someone I can trust. Please.*

The message would have confirmed his worst feelings about Tootles and the little spat would have been blown out of proportion because he would have tried to prevent Constance's going. He believed Tootles was never happier than when she had created a maelstrom, when she had her stick in the waters muddying them more and more, involving everyone possible.

Aware of all this, Constance had phoned Tootles, whose voice had been husky with desperation. "I have to talk to someone," Tootles had whispered. "I have to! I'm in so much trouble. You know me, Constance. You know the good and the bad, all of it. You can tell me what to do if anyone can. And if there's no way out, I'll just kill myself!"

4

By Friday afternoon Constance was wishing she had stayed home with Charlie. At first she thought she could never admit that to him, but then she knew she would. *You were right, darling,* she would say as airily as she could manage. *Tootles is a basket case, and Ba Ba is a kook.* Babar was wrong, though. She was more like a great sleek seal, with dark, almost black hair beautifully styled; she was expensively gowned, manicured, painted and powdered, bedecked with jewelry, but still a nut.

"It *is* you!" she had exclaimed, when Constance arrived. "I always said there was something fey about you. You have the gift and you tried to tame it by studying science, but the gift is there, I can see it in your eyes." She said over her shoulder to the room in general, "She's clairvoyant, you know. You can see the aura, feel the power of her gift coiled, ready to spring. You don't change, that's the other side of the gift, you know," Ba Ba was going on, and would continue to run on as long as anyone was in range, Constance had remembered belatedly. She had passed her to find the living room filled with people.

She had kissed Tootles and met Max Buell and his son Johnny, and the two young women students, and two male students who were taken away by a man called Claud Palance, an art teacher, she gathered, but it was difficult to be certain because too many people were talking at once, and most of them were Ba Ba.

Claud Palance was on his way out with the young men. "We'll come back Monday to finish up the crating. Have a good party." They left.

"Well," Tootles said, "that does relieve the bedroom pressure, I guess. Men hate parties," she added to no one in particular. She was in black sweatpants and black T-shirt, and sandals that revealed dirty feet. "God, I need a drink or three. Constance, have you had any dinner? I can get you a sandwich or something."

And from that moment until after lunch the next day Constance had not had a second alone with Tootles, who, in fact, was apparently avoiding her. On the very few occasions that they might have talked for just a moment, Tootles remembered something that had to be done instantly and dashed off. Ba Ba, on the other hand, was everywhere all the time. Constance had escaped her by taking walks; Ba Ba did not walk much, she had said positively. It was easier to imagine her sliding through water with hardly a motion of her hands or feet than to see her in walking shoes making her way through woods. Constance roamed through the back of the property where an unkempt garden seemed extraordinarily productive, through a grove of massive oak trees, down to a tiny brook. Across the dirt road in front of the house, she wandered into the barn where the show pieces were being crated. There were still a few things to be boxed up, but many crates were already secured with screws. The big barn doors had been closed, making it dark and airless inside. In the gloom she could see that people had been working in here with very big pieces of stone and wood. She already had gone through the studio in the house; it did not surprise her to find another bigger one here.

She left the barn by a small door, walked around it, and found a path through the woods. She had been here years before and was pleased to find that she remembered the property rather better than she had realized. The woods had grown up thicker than she recalled, but that was the only difference as far as she could tell. Up half a mile or so, she knew she would come across a small stone building, a one-room house from some distant past, Tootles's retreat. She smiled, remembering the story Tootles had told about it: a Civil War romance, Northern woman, Southern man, trysting place, death from a broken heart.

But eventually she always had to return to the main house, where chaos was developing rapidly. Caterers were unloading equipment and food; kitchen help had appeared; someone was going upstairs with an armload of fresh towels, and Tootles was running around barefoot, giving orders, getting in the way. Constance retreated to the living room, where she regarded the work called *Seven Kinds of Death,* and she was struck by a very vivid memory of the evening when she and Charlie had seen it together, when it was first installed in the National Gallery seventeen years ago. They had overheard a group of people walking around it, pointing. "I can see at least five kinds of death in it," a narrow-faced young man had been saying. "There's death of a forest, obviously, and death of innocence, and death by war, and death by starvation, and this could be death . . ."

At that moment Charlie had whispered in her ear, "Death by boredom."

She was still there when Johnny Buell arrived and asked Ba Ba, "Has he come yet? Paul Volte?"

They entered the living room together, Ba Ba talking about Paul Volte; Tootles, close behind them, said to Constance, "He and Max made me invite him. Paul, I mean. You remember Paul, don't you? That's all Johnny is thinking about. Paul Volte. Maybe he'll do an article about the condos. Not bloody likely. They made me ask him."

The two girls followed her into the room. Constance thought of them as Toni-sad-eyes, and Janet-the-manic, who bounced a lot. They reminded her of her own daughter, and that made her think again of Charlie and how much she would rather be home with him than here with these people.

Moments later Paul Volte and Victoria Leeds arrived. Each carried a small overnight bag; she had a book and a sweater, and her purse. They put everything down in the foyer and entered the living room to be introduced. Johnny Buell turned shy and left, muttering he'd meet them later. And Paul made it clear almost instantly that not only were he and Victoria not sleeping together, they were hardly even speaking. He called her Ms. Leeds, and did not look directly at her, but thanked Tootles for permitting him to bring a friend. Victoria Leeds did not look at him, and also thanked Tootles. But the most interesting thing, Constance thought, watching, was how the expression on Toni's face changed. From a deep-seated sadness, or even fear, or a clinical depressive withdrawal, she became almost as manic as Janet. She hugged and kissed Victoria and Paul both, and smiled broadly even as Tootles groaned and cursed.

"What the hell am I supposed to do about beds? I thought it was all fixed!"

Victoria said she would go to a motel in the village, and Paul said they would both go to a motel, and Toni said Victoria could have her bed and she would sleep in the studio in her sleeping bag, and Janet said no, she would do that. Since Victoria was Toni's friend they should share the room . . .

Ba Ba said maybe one of the twin beds from her room could be moved somewhere. Then Tootles was shaking Paul's arm and saying he did this on purpose, and he was a son of a bitch for not calling to explain the situation. By now Victoria had drawn apart and was merely watching with a trace of a smile on her lips. Constance moved forward and took Tootles's hand.

"Calm down," she said. "Janet can have the second bed in my room. Toni and Victoria can share a room, and Paul can have the room you meant him to have."

"Victoria, do you mind?" Toni asked anxiously. "I can sleep in the studio if you want a private room."

"I think it's all been arranged very nicely," Victoria said. She smiled at Constance.

"Well, I'll just move some things off the other bed," Constance said to Janet, who was watching it all, very bright-eyed, apparently breathless. "And you can move in whenever you like."

Toni led the way upstairs to show them the rooms, and Constance followed. At the top of the steps when she turned one way, and Paul, Victoria, and Toni went the other, she heard Victoria murmur, "You didn't warn me that it was a madhouse, Paul." Constance laughed softly to herself.

Charlie always said people were either coaster-carrying types, or wet-glass-and-hardly-a-second-look types. He put his wet glass down where it was convenient, sometimes remembering a napkin or even a coaster under it, but not usually. From what little she had seen of Victoria, Constance decided, she was another wet-glass type, while Paul without a doubt was a coaster carrier. She imagined that his house, apartment, wherever he lived, would be like a museum. First impressions, she knew, could be misleading, but there they were. Victoria found the world interesting, the people in it more interesting; her bright eyes and little smile of acceptance said as much. And Paul was a sufferer who suffered most especially at Victoria's hands. Why? Constance wondered. And why did it amuse Victoria, as she felt certain it did, to see him in pain? She shrugged and began to move her things in the bedroom to make space for Janet.

A little later Constance was saying to Max, "I saw your fence when I drove in. An impressive fence."

He laughed delightedly. "Isn't it, though? And tomorrow you get a tour behind the fence—the first building is ready for a grand unveiling." He raised his voice a bit. "Paul, Victoria, you want to see inside the condo tomorrow? A grand tour."

Paul and Victoria had been trailing after Janet, who was putting names to the various pieces of art in the living room. It appeared that most students who ever had passed through here had left pieces behind. When Constance glanced in their direction she saw that Johnny Buell was at the doorway and had come to a complete stop with the question.

"I'd love to see inside the fence," Victoria said, and Paul shrugged.

Johnny Buell entered the room and joined Victoria and Paul; Janet introduced him, and soon they were all laughing as they drifted into the hall, out of sight. It was not yet four-thirty; Toni and Ba Ba had taken Tootles upstairs to get ready for the party. Toni was good with hair, Tootles had said vaguely. Victoria had not changed yet from her jeans, nor had Paul, and Johnny was in tan slacks and a matching shirt, his working clothes. Constance assumed they would all drift apart now and adorn themselves properly. The cocktail party was scheduled from five to seven, and then, Tootles had said emphatically, she intended to vanish until eight, or else the guests would never leave, and they had to eat a real dinner, didn't they?

Constance had decided to go up to change when Max said, "I suppose you shouldn't ask an art critic to write up something, should you? Her show, I mean. Or the condos either, far as that goes."

"Let me tell you about a client who consulted with me once," Constance said. "He was a poet, and quite good, according to his reviews. The problem was his lover. This was what brought him to me for advice: He said that every time he became really involved with a woman, it ended when he asked for an honest opinion about his work. He was afraid to ask the current lover, and he couldn't stand not knowing exactly what she thought. He respected her opinion, of course."

Max laughed. "Old rock-and-hard-place choice. What did you tell him to do?"

Constance said gravely, "I told him that when the current affair ended, to find himself a woman who was illiterate in English." She left Max chuckling.

Cocktail parties, Charlie always grumbled, meant funny food that you never would make for yourself or order in a restaurant, and standing up too much being polite to people you didn't know or give a damn about. If numbers meant anything this was a smashing success of a party. There was a crush of people in every room. Now and then Constance glimpsed Janet bopping around explaining the art pieces; apparently that was her role. And Toni appeared looking anxious, casting an eye at the tables, the drinks left on tables, just checking on things; her role was to be responsible.

Constance found herself standing next to Max once. He was beaming, to all appearances having a remarkably good time. He looked past her and his face changed subtly; the pleasure was still there, but he looked softer, and very proud. Constance glanced in the direction he was looking to see Tootles arm in arm with two men, holding a drink in one hand, laughing. Apparently she was teaching them a dance step. Toni had done her hair in a chignon that was very flattering; she was wearing a long green skirt and a gold top tied at the shoulders, leaving her arms bare. Although she was more muscular than most women, she looked very handsome that night.

"Isn't she wonderful," Max Buell said in a soft voice.

"Yes," Constance said. "She really is."

He smiled at her then. "I'm glad you came. Have you met Spence Dwyers?"

A man had joined them. "Hello, Spence," Constance said.

"My God! It is you! I thought I recognized you. Constance Leidl, isn't it?"

A long time ago, when Tootles's first husband died suddenly in a car wreck, Spence had rallied about, as he put it. He had married her and they had stayed together for several years before the slow drift apart started, or fast split, or whatever it had been. Constance never had been told, but whatever had happened, it had not changed one important aspect of their relationship. Spence Dwyers owned the gallery where Tootles had shown her work then, and he had arranged the tour they were celebrating now. Throughout the years he had been her most steadfast patron.

He looked like a boxer, which he had been in his youth, with a thick chest and heavily muscled arms. His nose had been broken and retained a crook, and he wore heavy, thick glasses, almost bottle-glass lenses. When he smiled it was like looking into a gold mine.

Max left them chatting about the old days; the party shifted this way and that; groups formed, broke up, reformed. Constance looked at her watch often, counting the minutes until seven. Once she saw Toni whispering urgently to Max, and they left together heading toward the porch. Champagne running short, Constance assumed, and smiled at a woman whose name she had not learned. She met Johnny's fiancée, Debra Saltzman, and was not surprised that she turned out to be a most expensively casual young woman, a bit bland and pretty with long, blond, permed hair that looked windblown, and would always look windblown. She said, wasn't it *exciting* that Marion's work was going on tour; it was so *exciting* to know a famous artist.

Constance drifted over to Paul Volte and congratulated him on the success of his latest book. He nodded in an abstracted way, and she realized that he was searching the room. He held a highball glass that was nearly full, twisted it around and around as he studied the shifting patterns the guests made.

"Have you seen Victoria?" he asked, refocusing his eyes on her. It was obvious that he had heard nothing of what she had been saying.

She thought a moment and realized that she had not seen Victoria a single time that evening. She had meant to speak with her, in fact, because she had been so attracted to her. She told him no and abruptly he walked away. It was five minutes before seven.

Then it was over. Tootles was gone, and Johnny and Debra were telling Max good-bye, Johnny speaking in a voice loud enough to carry. They left with another young couple. Right on cue, Constance thought with amusement.

"Constance," Ba Ba said at her elbow, wheezing slightly, "have you heard yet? No one can find Victoria Leeds. She isn't in the house and she never changed her clothes or anything."

Constance and Toni looked through the upstairs bedrooms and closets, the three bathrooms. When they returned to the first floor, Paul was entering from the back of the house. Toni's fingers dug into Constance's arm. The young woman was staring at Paul, her expression a mixture of anguish and fear; she was ashen. She turned and ran.

"Would she have walked to town, to take a taxi back to Washington, perhaps?" Constance asked Paul.

He shook his head. "I called the two taxi companies and asked. I called the train station and the bus depot. No sign of her." He glanced beyond Constance; a few guests were still partying, no more than five or six. "We need to organize a real search," he said. "Why don't they clear out?"

Spence joined them. "She's not on this side of the property, I'd swear to it. Did she even know there was the rest of it across the road?" His voice was gravelly; a frown etched deeply into his forehead.

"She never came out here before, but someone could have told her. Let's start over there." Paul Volte was nearly as pale as Toni.

Constance saw again the look of terror that had come to

Toni's face, and although she had no idea of why these people were all assuming the worst, their fear became her fear. She said slowly, "Paul, perhaps we should call the sheriff's office. Two or three people can't really search the woods thoroughly." It was fifteen minutes before eight.

Later, when Charlie asked Constance exactly how she got rid of the lingering guests, she said simply, "I told them to go away." It wasn't quite that abrupt, but very nearly. Max called the sheriff, and Spence and Paul left to search the woods across the road.

Ba Ba came up to Constance to complain about the summary dismissal of guests and Constance didn't really tell her to shut up, just something like that, and then Tootles appeared again, coming from across the road. She had found time to change into her black pants and shirt.

"What's happening?" she demanded. "I met Paul and Spence and they practically ordered me to get my butt over here."

"And she's ordering everyone in sight," Ba Ba said aggrievedly, glowering at Constance. "All I said was that I was still having a conversation with Susan Walters, and here she comes and—"

"Ba Ba, shut up," Tootles said and asked Max, "What's wrong?"

"It seems that Victoria Leeds is missing," he said with a shrug. "Personally, I think she must have decided to take a powder and just forgot to mention it to anyone. I called the sheriff."

Tootles's eyes widened, then narrowed to slits. "Good Christ! Not Paul!"

The sheriff's deputy arrived a minute or two after that, and he called back to his office for help for a real search of the woods before it got too dark. It was nearly eight-thirty.

Dinner was a buffet; since the cook had no clear idea of how many people she would be feeding that night, it had seemed the simplest way to go, Ba Ba explained, and then started to explain again. This time Max told her to shut up. They picked at food that was very good. Paul and Spence had returned, and Paul didn't even attempt to eat. He sat in the living room with his eyes closed and started at every sound from outside the house.

The deputy returned at nine-thirty. It was still day-bright outside; he was sweating heavily. He was a florid-faced man in his twenties, blond, blue-eyed; his shape was somehow not right, too narrow in the shoulders and chest, too wide in the hips. "What's in the big boxes in the barn, Mr. Buell?" the deputy asked, standing in the doorway to the living room.

"Artwork, pieces going on tour," Max said.

Everyone had stood up, and as if managed by a choreographer, they all began to move toward the door. The deputy looked surprised, but did not object, and the group went outside, across the porch, through the front yard that was several hundred feet deep, across the dirt road, and finally into the barn. The big double doors had been opened, and interior lights had been turned on. The crates were in the center of the building; leading to one of them were red spots.

Janet screamed shrilly and Toni grabbed her; they stood with their arms around each other.

"Hey, take it easy," the deputy said. "It's just paint. But it looks to me like someone's opened a couple of the boxes, and didn't take the time to close them again, not like the others, anyway."

Constance moved closer and saw what he meant. Some of the screws had been removed evidently and replaced, but were no longer in all the way.

"Open it," Tootles said in a croaking voice. "For God's sake, just open it!" She flew at the crate and tried to rip the front off. Max drew her back and nodded to the deputy, who began to take out the screws. Max held Tootles against him until the box was opened.

Constance was aware that Janet screamed again, and Tootles made deep, hurt-animal sounds against Max's chest. There were other sounds of incredulity, of fury, anguish. . . . Inside the crate was a wooden sculpture about three feet high, two feet in diameter, securely fastened to the crate with straps, and covered with red paint. The paint had splashed against the wood of the box, turning the interior into a grotesque red stage.

Wordlessly Spence went to a worktable and came back with another screwdriver. He opened another crate. More paint. A piece of wood had been broken off the sculpture and was lying on the bottom of the box.

Janet was keening, her voice rising and falling. Constance

moved to Toni, who was holding the younger woman. "Take her back to the house, will you? And stay with her. And Max, you should take Tootles back." Ba Ba, stunned into silence, left with Max and Tootles. Toni pulled Janet out the door. The deputy and Spence opened more crates. Paul had found another screwdriver and was opening crates also.

Out of fourteen sculptures that were already crated up, eleven were paint-daubed, or broken. There were five pieces yet to be boxed; none of them had been damaged.

When they finished, the three men gazed at the spoiled pieces, and finally Spence said, "Why in God's name did she do it?"

"Who?" the deputy asked.

"The missing woman, Victoria Leeds, obviously. She must have come over here, and destroyed a lifetime of work. For God's sake, why? Is she crazy?"

For a second or two Constance thought Paul was going to hit Spence Dwyers. Paul's muscles tensed; his face became set in a grimace of hatred, but then he relaxed. And she could think of the expression that replaced the hatred only as one of hope. She thought then that nothing she had seen or heard since all this started made a bit of sense, including Tootles's original note to her and the mysterious words she had uttered over the phone.

5

When Constance returned to the house, Ba Ba was talking shrilly: "Well, he shouldn't have brought her out just to fight with her! They could fight back in New York."

Tootles and Max were on one of the sofas, his arm around her shoulders; she looked dazed. Ba Ba was sitting near them, leaning forward speaking into Tootles's face. Janet was huddled on another sofa looking terrified, and Toni, only slightly less frightened, was sitting close to her. Ignoring Ba Ba, who had glanced up without interrupting her stream of words, Constance went over to the young women.

"Why don't you rearrange things one more time," Constance said to them. "Both of you take my room, and I'll move into Toni's room for the night."

"Would you?" Janet asked. Her voice was tremulous.

"No problem," Constance said, but she wished she knew the girl better, knew how close to the edge she really was. Too close, she thought. "Let's go up and do it." They had to walk around *Seven Kinds of Death* in order to leave the room. At least, Constance thought, the best of the lot had been safe, under the eyes of sixty or more guests all evening.

"Why she had to carry the fight beyond Paul is more than I can see . . ." Ba Ba's voice floated out with them. In the room Constance had used, Toni said they'd do it themselves, if that was all right, and Constance left them moving bedding and clothes.

The search was called off when it became dark enough to justify abandoning the effort to find a woman who apparently was missing only because she chose to absent herself. The deputy clearly was no longer interested in searching for Victoria. Paul looked murderous, and he paced the entire downstairs jerkily. He would be exhausted, Constance knew; his muscles were so tight, and all that walking with so much anger or worry would exact a high cost physically. Spence slouched in a deep chair and scowled at the floor.

Two women from the village who had cooked and served and cleaned up were gone, and the house felt eerily quiet after so much commotion. Ba Ba was talking steadily; she seemed quite unaware that no one listened, no one responded. She was talking about her premonition about the weekend.

"No show," Tootles said to Spence during that evening.

"We'll assess the damage tomorrow," he said. "I think everything can be put together again, cleaned up. We'll see tomorrow."

She shook her head; she appeared to have aged ten years or more since the party. "No show," she said again, and put her head on Max's chest. He stroked her hair.

"I knew something evil would happen, you see, just not what it was. That's how it works for me so much of the time . . ." Ba Ba talked on and the others drifted away to go to bed.

The next morning Constance talked to Janet and to Toni, and she talked to Paul, and to Spence, and began to think she was learning much more about all these people than she needed to know, or even wanted to know. But she did not talk with Tootles, who had a headache and was staying in her room. And she talked as little as possible with Ba Ba. Actually she talked not at all to Ba Ba, and she tried to avoid listening.

Victoria had not returned to her New York address: she had not shown up anywhere.

"Well, I don't think it's fair for her to spoil the weekend for all of us," Ba Ba said at lunch. It was not at all clear to whom she was addressing her complaints. "I mean we have only until Monday, and today we're supposed to get a peek at the condo that will be home for Max and Marion any day now." So she wasn't talking to Tootles, Constance thought. The air? Was that her audience, just that simple: the air? ". . . and tomorrow we're having brunch in that nice old inn, aren't we? They used to have Bay clams, remember? They did them in a champagne sauce. I wonder if they still do that. That means out until late in the afternoon . . ."

Wearily Tootles said, "Ba Ba, for God's sake, stop. We'll go look at the condo. Let's walk over. I feel as if I'm going stir crazy!"

"I'll meet you," Ba Ba said hastily. "I'll drive."

"Good, you drive. I'll walk. Paul, Spence, Constance, who else wants a walk through the woods?"

So even this walk would be semipublic, Constance realized, and she also heard herself making plans to start for home as soon as they got back from inspecting the condo. Say she left at two, she was calculating, she could make it home before midnight without pushing too hard. And before she left, she had already decided, she would give Tootles what-ho for alarming her with talk of desperation and suicide.

Max drove over with Ba Ba; Toni and Janet, who had already seen the condos, chose to stay behind, still huddling together, still wary around Paul. Whatever had been bothering Toni seemed to have infected Janet, who now regarded Paul with fear also. He ignored them both. Constance doubted that he had even noticed their fear. He was very pale, and his hands trembled; a tic jerked in his cheek over and over. He seemed unaware of it. Constance walked next to Spence, with Tootles and Paul leading the way, talking in low voices. Tootles strode along briskly; he walked with a hunched shuffle like that of an old man. The day was heating up; it would be very hot before evening; already the woods felt close and too still, with no air in motion.

"Have you had a chance to assess the damage yet?" Constance asked Spence.

"Yeah. Son of a bitch, what a mess. It can be cleaned up, most of it, but it's going to take patience, and she doesn't have the heart for it right now."

The stretch of woods covered uneven ground that rose and fell, rose again. The path was the only sign of any usage here; on both sides the undergrowth was dense and wild. There were many brambles with blackberries starting to turn color, the brilliant red giving way to black.

Then they reached the tiny stone structure, a one-room house built of gray fieldstones; Tootles led the way around it, to the right and downhill twenty or thirty feet. Across a train track, and the state road that ran parallel to it, they could see the high construction fence and the tops of several condos. Only one of them was finished, Constance understood, but there were six in all being built more or less at the same time. It looked like an alien city rising from behind the wide-board fence.

Max had already arrived with Ba Ba; they had driven over in Tootles's ancient station wagon and were standing by it; Johnny had borrowed Max's Continental, Constance remembered, and Ba Ba was not a likely candidate to ride in a Corvette. In the compound, enough landscaping had been done to be impressively pretty, if artificial looking—too institutional.

Ba Ba appeared to be the only one in the group who had any interest in the condo. Spence and Paul were both impatient, and Constance, thinking now of driving home, was eager to be on her way. The building they entered had a wall of handsome, dark, carved doors, each with a smoked glass oval insert, most of them numbered: 6, 5, 4. . . . The numbers were eight or ten inches high, in brass, very rococo. Max inserted a computer card at 6. The oval window lighted up, and the door opened. It was more like a small foyer than an elevator; there was a mirror on

one wall, and a shelf nearly overwhelmed with a large arrangement of roses. Their perfume was cloying in the small space. A
small helium balloon floated over them with *Congratulations*
printed on it.

"Hey!" Max exclaimed. He peered at the card and then turned
to Tootles. "You did this?" His voice was husky.

Tootles looked embarrassed; she shrugged, but when Max
took her hand and held it, she did not try to pull away.

There was no sense of motion whatever after the door closed,
and then a moment later a door opposite the entrance swung
open. Dedicated elevators, Constance realized, and this really
was a foyer, of a piece with the bigger foyer that they now entered. A blast of frigid air hit them; the air conditioner apparently
was super efficient, and set far too low.

Straight ahead was a wide hall, bright with sunlight. A door
to the left was partly open to the kitchen area. Max was smiling
broadly, and Ba Ba was praising everything, even the sunlight.
They paused while she exclaimed over a curved hallway, broad
enough to permit bookcases on one whole wall. Then they took
the few remaining steps toward the living room. Spence and Max
were in front now, Ba Ba close behind them, Constance, Paul
and Tootles trailing. And Ba Ba screamed.

Constance darted away from Paul and Tootles, passed Ba Ba,
and caught Spence's arm just as he reached out toward Victoria
Leeds, who was on the floor. She was lying on her stomach, with
half her face visible; both arms were outstretched, one hand
clutching a tarpaulin partially dragged off a table. Around her
throat was a piece of rope buried in the swollen flesh; only the
ends could be seen. Her face was grotesquely swollen and dis-
colored, her eye wide open and blind.

"Don't touch that," Constance said in a low voice to Spence,
who was reaching for a slip of paper. He was as white as the
newly painted walls, his eyes seemed not to be focusing properly. Constance looked back at the group still in the doorway,
and realized that Ba Ba was still screaming, over and over. She
said sharply to Max, "Get them out of here and call the police."
He nodded and just then Paul Volte started to move toward
Constance and toward Victoria. He walked like a man in a trance.
Constance caught Spence's arm, pulled him back a step from the

body, and said in a very brusque voice, "Get Paul out of here. Take care of him."

Spence looked at the body, at Constance, and ran his hands down his face; then he seemed to focus his eyes again, and he moved toward Paul and took him by the arms. Max had already herded the others out the doorway. "Come on, old buddy," Spence said. "Can't do anything for her now. Come on. Let's go." Slowly he got Paul turned around, moving in the opposite direction. Constance doubted that Paul would remember any of this. Without touching the body on the floor or anything else, she also moved to the door, where she stood studying the room.

A conference table and chairs were in the center, covered with tarpaulins. Opposite the door was floor-to-ceiling glass, with a balcony beyond it. No drapes or curtains were at the windows. She could see into another room with another long table with blueprints and a typewriter on it. A temporary office apparently. It looked as though more tarps were on the floor in that room, and now she could smell the paint, and she could smell death. She turned and followed the others into the foyer, back into the elevator, and down to the lobby to wait for the police.

This time the sheriff came with the deputies. Bill Gruenwald, he said, examining them all very carefully and quickly. He looked like a man who took good care of himself; he was muscular and trim, in his early forties, with a brush mustache and short brown hair neatly cut.

Ba Ba had stopped screaming to take up moaning. Gruenwald turned his gaze to her, and she said, "I knew it would happen. I knew it would. I had a premonition of evil. I usually listen, but my own sister called me to come, and I did. But—"

"Ba Ba, shut up," Tootles snapped. "Sheriff, can we please go back to the house?"

He sent a deputy to follow them, and they all rode in the station wagon.

"I have to tell Toni," Tootles said when they entered the house. "My God, just my God!" She started to walk toward the studio; the deputy made a motion as if to stop her, and she looked at him in a way that made him flinch and move aside. She went on, and in less than a minute Janet screamed, and she and Toni ran from the studio, up the stairs, and banged a door closed.

Johnny Buell arrived only seconds after that; he shook his head in disbelief when Max told him Victoria was dead.

"Murdered? Why? How did anyone get in the building? That unit? I was over there at seven, I took Debra and Phil and Sunny, and got my briefcase. A little after seven. And I locked up, but anyway Pierce was working by then. We saw him. How did she get in?"

He stopped abruptly. He had looked stunned, disbelieving, but now a different expression crossed his face. He suddenly looked sick. "I have to call people," he said dully. "How long will it be before we can get into Six, clean it up, make it accessible again?"

Max glared at him, and Paul left the living room abruptly. After a moment, Johnny walked out.

When the sheriff finally came to the house, he was met by his deputy, who talked to him in a low voice on the porch.

Sheriff Gruenwald looked particularly grim when he entered the living room, grim and angry.

"John Buell?" He looked at Johnny, who had come from the studio area when the car drove up. Johnny nodded. "You went to the condo last night with some other people?"

"That's right. We left here right after seven and drove over there. We went up to Six and I got my briefcase, and we went down again. The watchman came over and we talked a minute or two. I remember that it was ten after seven when I went up to check out the other units, to make sure the painters hadn't left anything. That couldn't have taken more than a minute or two, and then we drove into Washington."

"We who?"

Johnny gave him Debra Saltzman's name and address, and the names of her friends whose addresses he did not know. Gruenwald looked very unhappy. "Our report from yesterday says no one saw Ms. Leeds after about four-forty." He looked them all over again, as carefully as he had done before; Toni and Janet had come down, and his gaze rested on them.

"Ms. Cuprillo?"

Janet nodded.

"Right. You were still talking to Ms. Leeds, I understand, after the others left to change their clothes. Is that right?"

She nodded again. Her eyes were very large.

"Fine. Did she say anything about meeting anyone? Did she mention an appointment or anything of that sort?"

"No," Janet whispered.

Toni looked from her to Paul. "She got a letter, remember?" she asked Paul. She said to the sheriff, "I showed them their rooms and there was a letter for her, in Paul's room."

Patiently Sheriff Gruenwald asked Toni to elaborate. When she led them into Paul's room, there had been a letter propped up on one of the pillows, addressed to V. Leeds, typed. She and Victoria had not gone into the room with Paul. He found the note and brought it to the door and handed it over. Toni didn't remember what he had done then, only that Victoria had opened it, glanced at it, crumpled it, and put it in her pocket as they walked toward the room she was to have used.

"Okay, Ms. Townsend. Did you get a glimpse of it? Handwritten, typed? Half a page of type, full page, a few lines? What did you see?"

She hesitated, thinking. "Not much. A few lines, typed, I guess."

"Good. Was there a signature? Ink? Blue? Black? Felt tip? What did you see? Could there have been a map of the area?"

Constance watched this with admiration. He was very good, but Toni could add no more to what she had already told him. If there had been a signature, she had not seen that, either. She had gone up with Tootles and Ba Ba before four-thirty to do Tootles's hair, and she had not seen Victoria again.

"When did you miss her?"

Toni looked at her hands, tightly squeezed together in her lap. Her voice was nearly inaudible. "Not until after six. I was so busy. And I didn't look in the bedroom and see that she hadn't even unpacked until after that, six-thirty maybe, when Paul told me he couldn't find her."

"I see. Thank you."

He took them back over their movements of yesterday. Constance had gone up while the group was still talking and laughing, about four-thirty, she said. Johnny had left right after he saw Constance go upstairs; he had gone back to the condos to send home a few guys who were still painting in the sub-basement and to shower and change his clothes. Then at five, he had gone to meet Debra's train and they had come to the party.

"Did you set the air conditioner at the minimum setting?" Constance asked. "It was freezing in the apartment," she added to the sheriff.

Johnny shook his head. "We keep it around eighty," he said, shrugging. "I didn't touch it."

Sheriff Gruenwald had looked surprised at her question, but he nodded very slightly, as if to say message received. Fingerprints, she wanted to suggest, might be on the controls. He turned to Paul Volte.

Paul said he had gone up soon after Johnny left, leaving Janet and Victoria.

"She said she wanted to step outside for a cigarette," Janet said. "I didn't see her again. I had my other clothes in the studio and I went in there to change."

Paul said, "She quit smoking three years ago."

"You're sure that's what she said?" Sheriff Gruenwald asked Janet. She nodded. "Okay. We didn't find any cigarettes in her purse, you see," he said almost apologetically.

"Oh!" Janet said then. "Something else. She said he," she nodded at Paul, "was being worn down by his ironic pose. She seemed worried because he was tired and sick."

The sheriff narrowed his eyes at her. "I don't get it," he said. "She said what?"

Janet repeated her words and then shook her head. "I didn't understand either," she said. "But I felt funny asking her what she meant. I pretended it made sense."

Sheriff Gruenwald studied her for another moment, then turned back to Paul. "Does that mean anything to you?"

Paul shook his head.

"You handed her the letter you found on the bed. Did you see the contents? Could there have been a map of the property, do you suppose?"

Paul shook his head. "She didn't open it in the room. I didn't see it."

Sheriff Gruenwald said then, "How it looks at the moment is that the lady went out to meet someone, and on her way she could have stopped in the barn and made the mess you folks found last night. That could account for the missing time. We know she was still alive at ten past seven when John Buell and his friends were in the building. What I'll need now is to find out where everyone was, starting at seven-ten and for the next few hours last night."

"We were all right here, saying good-bye to the party guests!" Ba Ba cried. "We had a party, you know, dozens and dozens of people were leaving from seven on and we were talking and saying good-bye. And then we were all out looking for her."

He waited for her to wind down, and then asked softly, "All of you were here? All the time?"

"Yes! Yes, of course," Ba Ba said shrilly. "You have to tell your party guests good-bye. Haven't you ever given a cocktail party to celebrate something? Haven't you ever gone to one? Doesn't someone tell you good-bye and I'm happy that you came and—"

"Ba Ba, shut up," Tootles said. "I wasn't here," she said to the sheriff. "I went to the little stone house at the end of the property and stayed there until nearly eight."

He let out a long breath and nodded.

6

The sheriff asked questions, he talked to Paul alone, and then Tootles alone. Although this all took several hours, Constance knew it was not yet a serious interrogation. They didn't have the time of death yet, the exact cause of death. . . . All the routine things would take a few days, and then they would come back and start the serious interrogation.

"I know some of you are from out of town," Sheriff Gruenwald said to the group that afternoon. "I'll want statements from each of you before you leave again. We can do it in the morning, nine o'clock. If that isn't possible, tell me."

No one moved or spoke. They were all in the living room, where *Seven Kinds of Death* now looked obscene. He nodded

at them generally, and told them he would return in the morning, and then he left.

No one moved except for Johnny, who was chewing on a
fingernail and looking at his watch. He jumped up suddenly and
said, "I've got calls to make." He ran from the room.

Paul said to Marion, "The sheriff thinks you invited her out.
I told him she didn't know you."

Tootles shook her head. "I know. He was asking me the same
thing: did I ask her, why? Paul, just when the hell did she decide
to come along? How the fuck did she know about the party if
you didn't tell her?"

"I don't know," Paul said miserably. "Last week she called
me, the first time we've talked in several months." He looked at
Toni. "Since the day I met you, in fact." He rubbed his hand
over his face, over his eyes, and stood up. "She knew about the
party, and said she'd like to come along with me. I didn't ask
how she knew. I thought . . . I thought we might be getting back
together again, that maybe this was her way to come back." He
laughed with great bitterness. "We said hello in the taxi, and sat
together on the airplane. I asked her how she was doing, and
she asked me the same, and that's all we had to say to each
other. I thought during the weekend there would be a chance.
I didn't press it." He looked at Spence. "I'm going to walk to
the village. You want a beer?" Spence nodded and the two men
left together, one looking like a tired pugilist, the other like a
half-starved art critic.

Janet had watched and listened, as motionless as a carving;
when she moved she was as jerky as a badly managed puppet.
And Toni was only slightly less rigid; whenever Paul was within
sight, she did not shift her gaze from him.

Once more Ba Ba started to describe exactly how Victoria had
looked. With a cry Janet leaped up and ran from the room, tore
up the stairs; Toni was close behind her.

"For God's sake," Tootles exclaimed, "Ba Ba, can't you stop
just for a while?"

"I can't get over how her face was so swollen—"

"If you don't cork it," Tootles snapped, "I'm going to hit you
in the head with something hard and maybe lethal."

"Well, if that's how you feel," Ba Ba cried. "I'll just go home,
now. This minute!"

"You can't leave until tomorrow," Max said quietly. "And you do have to stop babbling."

Ba Ba drew in a sharp breath, and walked from the room with her chin quivering.

"Tootles," Constance said, "I want to talk to you before I leave tomorrow."

"Yes, of course," Tootles said. "I mean, you came all the way from wherever you live now and we haven't had a second together."

Then Janet came back, red-eyed, jumpy, and nearly in tears. "Johnny's still talking," she wailed. "I have to make a call. I have to call my mother."

Max strode from the room; in a minute he returned and nodded to Janet. Johnny was at his heels. "But make it quick," Johnny snapped. Then he softened his voice, and looked contrite, even ashamed. "Sorry." Janet was already out of the room, running toward the office.

"I'll go to town and finish," Johnny said abruptly. "I'll come back when I'm done. God, I haven't been able to reach Stein yet. I'll be back." He hurried out, and soon they heard his car throwing gravel.

In another minute or two, Janet said from the doorway, "I called my mom. And I have a reservation for tomorrow at twelve." She drew in a quick breath and added in a rush, "I have to get out of here. I have to get out! I have to!"

Tootles had been on the sofa; she got up and went to Janet. "Come along upstairs," she said quietly. "We can talk, and I'll help you pack. Of course, you have to go home for a while. Come along." She put her arm around Janet's shoulders and walked out with her.

After they were gone Max said reflectively to Constance, "You called her Tootles. I like that. From her childhood?"

She nodded.

"Right after we acquired the land for the condos," he said, walking to a sideboard where there was a bar setup, "I took a stroll over this way to meet the artist and her crew. I'd been warned that it was an unconventional bunch over here. They were all out in the front wrestling a tall wooden figure, eight feet, nine feet, into a truck. It wasn't even her work, but Marion was right there with the kids, all of them filthy, sweaty. I pitched in and helped, too." He poured a glass of mineral water and sipped it. "Next thing I knew she was asking me if I'd had dinner yet, and we all came in to eat chili and homemade bread. Marion's bread; one of the kids made the chili. I don't think they had a cent between them, her or the kids. It was the best food I'd had in years." He drank the water and said, "I wish I'd known her when she was Tootles."

Constance wanted to tell him that would have been a mistake. Before Ed Holbein, or after? Before Spence Dwyers, or after? Before Walter Buckman, or after? None of that really mattered, she understood, not to Tootles, possibly not to Max.

"You're going to live in the condo?" she asked.

"Yes. I'm out here about half the time, in downtown Washington the other half, and this is better. I'm ready to slow down a little, and, of course, she wants to be close to the work, to the kids."

"I'm just surprised you got her to agree to go even that far," Constance said. Then she added, "Max, I think you should talk to a lawyer, you and Tootles, maybe before the sheriff asks any more questions."

His face became very still, the smile frozen in place. "You think it's going to come to needing an attorney?"

She nodded. "It could. Maybe I can get to the telephone now." She went into the dinette-turned-into-office and dialed, only to get the answering machine at the other end. She frowned and said that she would be delayed, please call her, and gave the number. Then she cursed under her breath.

That afternoon Constance mounted outside stairs that led up to a sun deck that ran the length of the house, facing south. Her bedroom, which Toni and Janet now shared, opened to it, as did a number of other rooms. Up here there were lounges, chairs, pillows, tables; Toni and Janet were sunbathing on mats.

"Hi," Constance said as she approached them. "Toni, I wonder if I might borrow Paul's book. I noticed it in your room earlier, but it isn't there now."

"Oh," Toni said. "Marion has a copy."

"She doesn't know where," Constance said.

"I'll look for mine," Toni said after a moment. "I'm not sure where I put it."

"It's on the table by your bed, the bottom shelf," Janet said. "I remember seeing it there."

Toni stood up finally; she was in a bikini that revealed a beautiful body evenly tanned all over. She pulled on a terry shirt that reached to her knees, and went to the bedroom window, where a screen had been removed and propped against the house. She stepped over the sill to enter the room. Constance sat in a chair near Janet.

"Yesterday, when Victoria and Paul came downstairs, you introduced them to Johnny Buell, and then you were all laughing. Remember that? It seemed such a lively and pleasant little group, telling jokes so soon, having a good time."

Janet raised her head from the mat in order to look at Constance. "I know. And then . . ." She buried her face in the mat again.

"What was the joke?" Constance asked, ignoring the young woman's distress.

"I don't know," Janet said, her voice muffled. "Something about opposites attracting."

"Ah," Constance said thoughtfully. "Like Max and Marion. Or Spence and Marion in the distant past."

"Yeah, just like that. I was thinking of Spence and Marion, in fact. You know, how crazy he is about her and all. Victoria said jocks often were attracted to artists, like that. And, how often real ladies seem to love prizefighters. Spence used to be a fighter. Victoria said she got a proposal from a jock recently. That's why she came out here, to get away from him or something." She had raised her head to speak, and now lowered it again. "It doesn't sound a bit funny now, but it did then." Her voice became muffled again.

"Then Johnny left," Constance said. "Did she say anything then? Maybe something to you and Paul?"

Janet shook her head. "Next thing she said was when Paul left, how his ironic pose was wearing him down." Janet scowled at Constance. "It sounds so dumb, but I can't help it. She said it, I didn't. Then she said she was going to check out a smoke. And she went out to have a cigarette. That's all she said."

"Check out a smoke?" Constance repeated. "Were those her words?"

"I don't know," Janet cried. "It's how I remember them. I don't know!"

And apparently her memory was all they had to go on, since Paul would have missed whatever Victoria had said about smoke, and whatever she said about his ironic pose. Constance studied the young woman in silence for a time, until Toni stepped through the open window again carrying Paul's book. "I couldn't find my copy," she said. "But I remembered where I saw Marion's down in the music room. This is hers." Her face was sweat-shiny and her breaths were coming hard and fast. She had been running.

Constance stood up to take the book, and then started back toward the stairs. "Thanks," she said. "See you later." Toni lay down again, her head turned so that she could watch Constance.

The deck had been added by inept carpenters; the floor was not level, and the slope was toward the house, not away from it. At the far end where the steps had been built, there was a walkway that led toward the rear of the house. Constance followed it to an outside door that opened to a very narrow hall, then to the central hall of the upper floor, and on to her own room that overlooked the back of the property, the kitchen garden area, the ancient oak trees in the distance, shrubs that needed pruning. It was very quiet out there today. She sat at a window in her room with the book in her lap, wondering why Toni did not want to lend her copy. She must have written in it, Constance decided, underlined passages, highlighted it, annotated it in some way. And by now probably no one would be able to find it without a prolonged search. She opened the copy she held and began to read.

Alice Weber, the woman from town who had made lunch, returned to cook dinner. Ba Ba joined her in the kitchen and their voices rose and fell, rose and fell. Spence and Paul returned from the village; Paul looked as if he had been sleep-deprived for a week; his eyes were red-rimmed, bloodshot, and sunken deep in the sockets. Spence went straight to the little bar. Johnny came back and talked in a low voice with Max for a few minutes, exactly like a child checking in, making a report. Afterward, he said to Tootles, "I had to leave this number for calls to be returned. You can't find anyone on a Saturday afternoon." It sounded almost like an apology, but not quite; it was too sullen for that. He glanced at his father as if to say, okay, I did it. Max's expression was unreadable. Tootles shrugged.

Dinner dragged interminably. No one except Ba Ba had anything to say, and no one paid any attention to her flow of words. As soon as possible Constance went up to her room to finish Paul's book, only to find that after she was done with it, she was too restless to settle down. What did he believe? She saw again his haggard face, his trembling hands, and realized that she did not have even a clue about the man behind the appearance. She knew his column, read it with some regularity, in fact. He was witty writing about art, with a dry humor that was lacking in personal exchanges, as far as she could tell, and that wasn't a fair judgment, she knew, not under the circumstances. And, of course, he was so knowledgeable, recognized as a world authority. But what did he believe? Possession? A jealous muse? A price that must be paid for every success? What did he believe? And more important at the moment, what had happened between him and Victoria Leeds? Tomorrow, she thought, she would find an opportunity to have a little conversation with Paul Volte, not more than that. Just a little talk to satisfy her own curiosity before she started for home. She finally went to bed and was lulled to sleep by the music of crickets, tree toads, a frog chorus.

When she woke up, it was fifteen minutes past eight. She started to roll over, to pull the sheet over her head, to go back to sleep, but she remembered that today she was going home, that she had packing to do, and she forced herself out of the bed, to her feet.

Spence was in the kitchen drinking coffee, reading the *Washington Post*. He had already been down to the village. He grinned his crooked grin at her silently and she was just as silent. What a homely man, she was thinking, and such a charming man. Years ago she had not seen the charm, or had it developed with maturity? He seemed to have traded in a certain belligerence for a great dollop of charm. A fair exchange, she thought, a fine trade. She poured coffee, sat opposite him, and started to read another section of the paper. Yesterday Toni and Janet had made breakfast; Alice Weber had come in to fix lunch, and again later to make dinner. Whatever the arrangements were between the young people and Tootles, teacher and students, hostess and not-quite-guests, boss and slaves, chief and Indians, it seemed to include a bit of work on their part, and they seemed to find that perfectly acceptable. Constance found it perfectly acceptable also.

The others were drifting down, helping themselves to coffee, no one talking much that morning. Spence got up to make another pot of coffee. "Don't touch that paper," he said over his shoulder from the sink. He had left it open to the editorials. Max was homing in on the newspaper. He looked sheepish and drew back.

Toni appeared, looking for coffee for herself and for Janet, who was packing. Ba Ba came in and said she would make breakfast if people would just get out of the way, and she began to talk about the stacks of pancakes and fried eggs they used to have when she was a girl. . . . The sheriff walked in then, along with one of his deputies and a woman he introduced as a stenographer, and by now the kitchen was quite full, with several people talking at once.

Then another voice cut through it all: "Of course, I'm coming in. I'm looking for my wife."

Constance had never been so glad to hear that voice in her life.

7

When Charlie heard the message from Constance on the answering machine he had tried to call back; the line had been busy. When he heard on the evening news that Victoria Leeds had been murdered while attending Marion Olsen's house party, he had tried to call repeatedly. The line had stayed busy. Finally he had called the airport instead, and at five that morning he had flown into La Guardia; at seven he had boarded the shuttle, and by nine he was at Tootles's house, where, it seemed to him, they were having a party.

At that moment Mrs. Weber arrived carrying a large bag of pastries. She looked at everyone with astonishment, and without argument they all left the kitchen to her. Charlie held Constance's hand and permitted himself to be led to the living room, where dominating everything was the monstrosity that Tootles had named *Seven Kinds of Death*. Charlie had hated it when it was first unveiled; he saw no reason today to change his opinion about it.

"I'd like a room where we can take statements," the sheriff said to Max Buell. Max nodded and they walked out together. At the same time, others came downstairs and introductions were made all around. Everyone was up, in the living room, waiting for the sheriff, waiting for breakfast, just waiting. Ba Ba was talking about how many calories were in doughnuts compared to whole wheat toast. Doughnuts won. Charlie and Constance crossed the room to the far side; his gaze remained on the work, *Seven Kinds of Death*, as Constance filled him in rapidly and concisely in a very low voice. When she paused, he shook his head.

"What?" she asked.

"Craziness," he murmured. "If Tootles found Victoria Leeds destroying her art, why go all the way over to the condo to do her in? The Tootles I used to know would have picked up the nearest blunt instrument and finished her off on the spot, yelling bloody murder all the while."

They stopped talking when Sheriff Gruenwald and Max returned.

"Sheriff," Johnny Buell asked then, "when will your men be done with the condo? Can the guys get in tomorrow to finish up?"

"Yes, I think so. We'll probably clear out by evening."

"And can I go home?" Ba Ba asked shrilly. "I want to leave here now. Today. I knew I should have stayed home. Larry said I should stay home and he was right. He's my husband and for once he was right. He wouldn't come, and he said I shouldn't either."

Sheriff Gruenwald waited patiently until she paused. "We

have no intention of holding anyone here longer than absolutely necessary."

"And Victoria? Her body? When will you release her?" Paul asked. He had trouble with the words; his voice broke and he had to swallow before he could finish the question. "Have you been in touch with her folks?"

"Yes. We'll ship her remains to her family in Michigan just as soon as the autopsy is completed." He went to the door. "I'm expecting the state investigators to arrive any minute now. Meanwhile we'll begin. Ms. Cuprillo, this way please."

"Well," Charlie said. "Is there coffee left in that pot?" He went to the sideboard where sweet rolls and coffee had been arranged, and poured himself a cup, then one for Constance.

"I'll stay if you want me to," Ba Ba said to Tootles. "I didn't mean to run out on you if you need me. You know I wouldn't do that. Larry didn't mean you were the reason he didn't want to come. It was business really, but if you want me to, I'll call him . . ."

Tootles didn't even glance at her. She was looking straight ahead with a distant expression. "He thinks I did it," she said in a low, very hoarse voice. "My God, that man thinks I did it! Did you see how he looked at me?"

Max made a comforting sound and put his hand on Tootles's shoulder. She shrugged it off and jumped up and swung around to glare at Constance. "You told Max I should get a lawyer before I answer any more questions. You think I did it, too! Don't you? Don't you?" Her voice rose until she was shouting.

"No," Constance said without hesitation. "That isn't what I think."

Tootles jammed her hands down in her pockets and began to stride back and forth through the room.

In a few minutes the sheriff returned and nodded to Constance. "Ms. Leidl, please. I'd like to ask you a few questions."

Charlie stood up. For a moment he and the sheriff regarded one another without expression. The sheriff shrugged slightly, turned, and walked out; Constance and Charlie followed him. The sheriff motioned the stenographer away in the hall. She nodded and went out to the porch.

"You're private investigators," the sheriff said in the little breakfast room that he had turned into an office. He stood at the table; Constance sat in one of the old wrecked chairs and Charlie wandered around the room looking at the various objects. His gaze lingered on the Barbie doll. "I just got some stuff on you, Meiklejohn, and I remembered your name. Are you working on this case? Have you been hired?"

Charlie raise his eyebrow in surprise. "Nope. I just got here, remember."

"*She's* been here several days."

Charlie shrugged.

"I've known Marion Olsen all my life," Constance said. "We grew up together."

Gruenwald sat down heavily and regarded her for a few moments.

Charlie picked up the windup bear and turned the key a few times. The bear danced. "You have a time of death yet on Leeds?" he asked, his back to the table and the sheriff.

"Why, if you're not working?"

"Curious," Charlie said.

After another moment of silence Gruenwald said, "As soon after seven as we can put her in the apartment. It's going to be tough to pin down. The air conditioner was set nearly to freezing."

"Ah," Charlie said. "I see. Quarter after seven? I suppose Tootles is in pretty good shape, isn't she? She could have sprinted over there in a few minutes, waited for the Buell crew to depart, waited for the watchman to hie himself off on the rounds, got herself up to Six, and accomplished the foul deed. Then, of course, she had to reverse every action, dash back down, out, through the woods, and so on. Doesn't leave her much time to discover the damaged art, though, does it? And without that knowledge, it's hard to imagine a motive for her. Of course, she could have stumbled across Leeds in the process of closing crates up again, and chased her through the woods, into the condo complex, and so on. But who unlocked doors, if that's the case? Leeds? Not bloody likely, is it? And why would Leeds take it on herself to be the ultimate critic? Good luck, Gruenwald. You're going to need it."

Gruenwald nodded. "I know. Yesterday, I would have bet you anything we could put a tramp in that room, something like that. Nothing pretty, but neat. No way. Watchman was on duty from

six on; the building was locked when he got to work. John Buell
locked it up at five-fifteen, and unlocked it when he took in his
group at a couple minutes past seven."

Charlie shrugged. "Hard to fit a tramp in, all right. Same old
story. Spot a likely suspect and the hunt ends. Bingo. She won't
be convicted, you know."

"Maybe, maybe not. But it won't be in my hands." His voice
changed subtly. Now he sounded as if he were talking to the
chamber of commerce about a highway project that didn't interest him very much. "The state is taking over the investigation
almost immediately."

Charlie knew about things like that, too. A small-town killing,
domestic murder, break-in and death at a convenience store, all
that the sheriff would be expected to handle. But this had turned
into a big-town killing; big-time builder involved, with his backers; New York editor as victim; some of the party guests, no
doubt, wanted this all taken care of pronto. He knew about
things like that very well.

Gruenwald said, "The state investigator is named Belmont;
he'll want it closed as soon as possible. And he doesn't know
Marion Olsen."

Charlie studied him thoughtfully for a moment, then asked
softly. "And you do know her?"

"Yes. But even if I didn't, I'm not in the habit of railroading
anyone. I just wanted you to know."

"Why?" Charlie asked in honest curiosity.

Sheriff Gruenwald flushed a shade or two, and muttered, "I've
studied some of your cases, the arson cases in particular. They're
good."

For a second or two Charlie was speechless. Then he said
kindly, "Sit down, Sheriff. Let's talk." He pulled a chair around
to sit down also. "First, the note you found is probably a fake."
The sheriff started to say something, refrained. "She told me,"
Charlie said, nodding at Constance. "She saw it. The note Leeds
got when she arrived was in an envelope; she took it out, crumpled it and stuck it in her pocket. The note in the condo was
smooth, not wrinkled. Right?" He didn't wait for an answer. "So
you have a fake note that you will claim puts Tootles at the
scene. Maybe it does and maybe not. How did Victoria Leeds get
into the condo? She couldn't have gone in on her own, could

she? I suspect most of the building is under a security system that needs special keys, computer cards, something of the sort." The sheriff hesitated a moment, then nodded. "Yes. So someone had to be there to let the victim enter, or she had to enter with her killer. Since the watchman was around at seven-fifteen, after the Buell gang took off, we have to have our pair wait behind a tree or something while the watchman closed and locked the fence gate, right? It starts to get a little weird, doesn't it? Or else the killer and victim were both already in the building, maybe in the apartment before Buell and gang arrived, but that means someone other than Tootles. She couldn't have got there before seven-ten even in a car. At seven she went up and changed her clothes, a matter of several minutes at least, and then she took off into the woods on foot. Guests were leaving; she couldn't have driven off without being seen, and anyway I bet her car was in the garage, hemmed in by a dozen others. We could make her run a mile and time her, I guess, to prove it one way or the other. She must have collected Leeds somewhere along the way." He shook his head. "Weird. Where was Leeds from before five until then? Smashing and splashing paint on art?" He frowned at the Formica tabletop, and began to run his finger in a circle, around and around. "It just refuses to make much sense, doesn't it?"

He stood up. "Well, I doubt you'll be able to get enough on Tootles to make it stick. With what you have right now, I know I couldn't."

"But it's early," Gruenwald said. "Lots of time to dig around and see what turns up."

They all turned toward the front of the house. Cars were throwing gravel; brakes screeched. The state investigators had arrived, Charlie decided. The sheriff went to the door with them and pulled it open. "Don't wander away," he said. "They'll want to talk to you."

Charlie nodded; he knew the game rules very well. "I suppose we can get some air," he said. The sheriff shrugged and started to walk toward the front door. Charlie took Constance by the arm. "Let's take a walk." They went out the back door.

8

As soon as they were away from the house Charlie stopped walking to take Constance into his arms and kiss her in a way he had not been willing to do in front of others. "There, now," he said when he drew back finally. "That's better."

"I'll say," she murmured. "And it was only three days."

He grinned and took her hand. "We don't count by days," he said. "Onward. Let's mosey down to the little creek. I remember when Ed Holbein called it his private trout stream."

"Poor Ed. Remember how happy he and Tootles were? I wonder if she's been that happy with anyone else since?"

"How about Max?"

"He's fine. I like him a lot, but it's different. He adores her apparently. And from what little I've seen, she appears content. I never thought that was a word that could be applied to Tootles."

He nodded. Tootles content was an oxymoron as far as he was concerned.

"You think she's really in for it, don't you?" Constance said a moment later. They were walking under the giant oak trees; they could hear the soft rush of water over stones.

"She's in for it," he said. "Trouble is they just don't have anyone else. Could anyone else have left the party, stayed out at least half an hour, starting at seven?"

She shook her head. "Not the overnight guests. I've tried and tried to make any of them work, but they won't. People were either paired up looking for her, or in plain sight telling other guests good-bye. It could be," she added, "that it really was an outsider we know nothing about. Or someone she knew in the area and was in touch with. We just don't know enough."

He spread his hands. Neither of them believed an outsider had entered the house before Victoria's arrival in order to leave a note for her on Paul's bed. They had reached the little brook that was only six or eight feet across and inches deep. It had a pleasant singing voice, he thought in approval. Unpretentious, nice. And if trout ever had been present in those waters, it was back in prehistoric times. It was at least ten degrees cooler here by the running water in the deep shade.

He looked around for rocks or logs to sit on, and had to give that up and lean against a tree instead; grasses and weeds grew right down to the edge of the water. "You don't think Tootles did it," he murmured. "Why? Just because you've known her all your life?"

"I don't think it's that." She considered it with her head cocked, accepting that bias could be a factor, accepting that if it was, she could do nothing about it. "But you said it before. If she had found anyone messing up her work, she would have thrown a fit on the spot. She isn't devious, not that way. Action/reaction are never very far apart with her. Deviousness and a cold-bloodedness just aren't her style." She drew in a deep breath and went on to tell him about Tootles's note, and the phone call.

Charlie scowled at her. "Good God, that's all the cops need," he said. "She says she's in desperate trouble and someone gets killed! Think she'll blab about it?"

"Of course not." And it went without saying, they both knew, that neither would Constance. "But I can't believe it had anything to do with Victoria Leeds. I'd bet a lot that they didn't know each other before Victoria showed up here. Paul said that, and so did Tootles, and I believe it; I was watching when Paul introduced them."

Charlie knew that if Constance was willing to put up money, it meant she was certain, not that anything was at risk. He grunted as he pushed off from the tree; there simply wasn't anyone else, he told himself again. It was Tootles or a stranger. And he didn't believe in strangers wandering in through locked doors to commit murder that apparently had nothing to do with robbery or rape.

"The sheriff's pretty good," Constance said a moment later, but without much conviction. "The old Sherlock truism comes in just about here, doesn't it? If you rule out all that just won't work, you're forced to take whatever is left. I'm so afraid that's how his mind will work, and apparently he's very much afraid the state investigators will take Tootles with even less struggle than he's having."

She watched a monarch butterfly pose against an umbel of Queen Anne's lace, and then rise without effort to catch a ray of slanting light that made it glow like a magical creature. It drifted away, and if she blinked, or if it did a vanishing act so fast she could not follow, she could not have said; the butterfly was there, then gone.

"Charlie," she said, "you keep calling Tootles a nut, and Ba Ba, of course. But why? I mean, Ba Ba talks incessantly, but does that really make her a nut? And what is it about Tootles?"

She kept her gaze on the spot where the butterfly had vanished; it must have fallen through a hole in space, she thought distantly.

The silence that followed her question had become too long, too intense, so that no matter now how it was broken, there would be that interval when her question hung between them. Charlie squatted and picked up a handful of stones that he began to toss into the fast little stream.

"It was a long time ago," he said at last.

"I know. We were all little more than children."

Not Tootles, he thought; she had never been a child. The funny thing, he also thought, was that he had been invited in, but had not entered, and yet the guilt he had felt then had made it seem that he might as well have yielded. Now he could admit that the cloud of pheromones that Tootles had moved in was almost more than a fellow could resist, but in those days he had been terrified. He and Constance had only recently married, and he could not have been less interested in another woman; and that state had endured. But there were all those pheromones calling, beckoning. The spell had been there; he had been targeted more than once, and he knew that others, including Babar, probably believed he had taken that next step. Over the years he had met other women like Tootles, and men also, who exuded sex appeal the way the Greeks in the deli he had grown up near had exuded the aroma of garlic and olive oil. But sex appeal alone did not qualify anyone for nuthood, he also knew.

Slowly he said, "When we were all still living in New York, Babar and Tootles had that rattrap apartment down on Twenty-second. Remember? Just before they moved down here, the last place they had in the city, I guess." He remembered clearly a series of ratty apartments that he associated with Tootles and Babar, all firetraps, walk-ups, infested with vermin, and all vibrating with a feeling of excitement nearly uncontainable.

That last day, he had gone to their apartment late in the afternoon, planning to meet Constance there after she finished a class she was teaching; then half a dozen or more of them were going to go eat Chinese food—cheap, abundant, good. None of them had money for restaurants; he had started his career as a fireman by then, but Constance was still in school, working on her doctorate, teaching. A long time ago, he thought again.

"Anyway, there I was, dead tired from coming off the four-day stint. Remember, four days on, four off?" She nodded. "I conked out on the floor, out like a light, and when I came awake enough to hear anything, they were having a go with that damn Ouija board they used to play around with. But this time it was different. I think Babar was in a deep trance, or something, and she scared the shit out of me. And Tootles, too, I'm sure."

Constance turned to look at him with an expression of bewilderment. "You were afraid? They used to do that back when we were just kids. What was frightening?"

He shook his head. "I was half asleep, just waking up, and Babar was going on about a spirit she had summoned, and damned if I didn't see something like a cloud form behind Tootles, and then settle over her, and disappear. Okay," he said hurriedly, lifting his hand palms out, "I admit I was groggy from missing sleep. But that wasn't even the scary part. It was what Babar was saying, and how she was saying it, and how Tootles was reacting. I think they both believed every word. And that was scary, their belief, their acceptance. Talking to the air as if it held a genie with wishes to hand out, payments to exact, you know, cutting a deal. I was wide awake by then and made noises and broke it up. They were both really sore, especially Babar. Apparently this was the most successful trance she had achieved, the best spirit she had called up, or some damn thing. Anyway, they were furious with me, and kicked me out, just like that. Both of them were like . . ." He shrugged then. "Nuts," he said. "Two nut cases if I ever saw any."

"Oh, Charlie," she said in a soft voice. "You never even mentioned any of that. I thought . . . I don't know what I thought. That Tootles had really tried to seduce you, I guess."

"You were willing to pal around with her thinking that?"

"It didn't matter," Constance said. "I knew you wouldn't, and she didn't mean anything by it. She was never out to hurt anyone, just to give everything a try. She gave spiritualism a try, and Catholicism, and Zen, and TM. Heaven alone knows what all she's tried over the years."

"Especially men," he said darkly.

Constance nodded. "I know. Especially men. And as for the fortune-telling, they used the I Ching, various kinds of cards, including the Tarot, the Ouija board, maybe even entrails. I bet right now Ba Ba has a drawer full of crystals, talismans, fetishes of all sorts. . . . She's intrigued by the occult and always was, and yes, maybe a bit of a nut where the supernatural is concerned. I just never realized that you had seen them going at it. I wish you had mentioned it years ago."

Even thinking about mentioning it at a time when it would have been meaningful brought back the memory of near terror he had felt that day. He had been incapable of talking about it then; he couldn't have explained the fear he had felt, couldn't have justified his aversion to both women after that day and for years to come. Over the next ten years they had attended a Marion Olsen opening or two, they had gone to a show or two, had come out to the farm twice, neither time staying more than a few hours, and in his mind Tootles and Babar were still the nuts he had come across nearly thirty years ago. That had not changed a bit with time.

Constance was frowning thoughtfully at the stream; she nodded, as if reaching a decision. "Tootles has left all that far behind, I'm certain," she said. "Ba Ba is still interested in the occult. Not that it matters; it doesn't have a thing to do with what's going on now. Information, data. Just sorting out things."

"Let's walk," he said, and for the next few minutes neither of them spoke. They had nearly reached the house when Charlie stopped and put his hand on her arm.

"Honey, you know, don't you, that they won't just let us walk away from this one? I think there are times when I can look into the future without a crystal ball or the Tarot cards, or any other damn gimmick. One of them will ask us to take this on, prove Tootles didn't do it, find out who did. Bet?"

She shook her head emphatically. "You know I don't. Ever."

He laughed. "Okay. Want to make book on who will ask? Max?"

"Maybe," she said cautiously. "Or maybe Paul Volte." He looked surprised, and they continued to walk toward the back door of the house. "But, Charlie," she added, "we can say no. You can say no. You don't have to hang around and ask questions, or do anything else about this mess."

That should have been an option, he knew, but it wasn't, not really. They would manage to hang this one on Tootles if someone didn't do something to prevent that, and no one else could be expected to have this deep belief in her innocence—as far as this murder was concerned, he had to add to himself. No, if he believed in fate, karma, any of that stuff, he would have to accept that this was the trap that had opened weeks earlier; finally it was shutting all the way.

"Check," he said. "One thing, though. I don't want to stay in the house even if we hung out for a day or two. Agreed?"

She nodded. He would have to throttle Ba Ba, and that could be serious. Or she might decide to throttle the woman. "We probably can get a motel room, or a hotel in the village, or something."

He snapped his fingers in irritation then. "Damn," he muttered. "Forgot about that car." He glowered toward the driveway, where a rental car was parked next to their Volvo. "How much would you say it's worth not to have to drive in to National?"

"That bad, hm?"

"Tourist season," he said. "You wouldn't believe downtown Washington in the summer."

She eyed him curiously. "Why were you downtown?"

"Never mind," he said. "Just a little wrong turn, that sort of thing that can happen to anyone at all."

"Fifty dollars? Forty? Whatever the kid you ask says he'll charge," she said.

He knew she was right. Some things he refused to bargain over. They both stopped again when Janet appeared with a deputy and got into a taxi. The driver put her suitcase in, and drove off. Janet had looked infinitely relieved; standing in the drive watching the taxi vanish down the road, Toni looked forlorn and miserable. She ducked her head and slouched back into the house.

Two hours later the state investigator, Lieutenant Belmont, told Constance she was free to go.

Constance found Charlie on the back porch. "Done," she said wearily. "Statement accepted, signed, tucked away where maybe no human eye will ever spot it again."

"Rubber hoses and all?"

"On both sides, and bright lights, the works."

"Let's scram. Onward to the village green. You hungry or anything?"

He drove down the gravel road, crossed the railroad tracks, and came to the state road, where he turned left. He was watching the odometer closely. It was nine-tenths of a mile to the gate of the construction fence at the condominium complex. He slowed there and pulled to the side of the road, surveying the fence, the railroad tracks a few hundred feet away, parallel to the road, and beyond the tracks the stand of trees that was Tootles's property.

"Problems," he said then. "This is pretty exposed, wouldn't you say?" From here he could see that there was the big gate, double doors that could admit trucks, cranes, whatever equipment the job required. Next to it was a door no more than three feet wide. Both were closed now. The gate was at the corner of the fence, a car length off the road; to one side the undergrowth was cleared away, no place to hide there. On the other side of the gate a parking lot had been bulldozed and covered with gravel. The fence on that side appeared to go back to the river bank. "No lurking space at all," he said morosely. "You'd have to stay all the way over there in the woods."

"And then cross the tracks and hope no car came while you were in the open," Constance added. "It doesn't work very well, does it?"

He made a grunting noise and started the car again, put it in reverse and backed into the parking lot, where he surveyed the length of the fence. There was no other gate in it, just the two entrances at this corner. He drove out of the lot and very slowly along the frontage of the condominium property. The fence was unbroken after they left that first corner.

"Okay," he said then and pressed the accelerator.

The village of Maryville had a population of twelve thousand two hundred residents; there were three motels within a few minutes of downtown, and a hotel in the center of town, but there was no vacancy in any of them.

"Tourists," Charlie said with resignation, joining Constance at the car. She had gone in with him the first two times, before accepting defeat.

When they got back to Tootles's place, all the police cars were gone. Paul Volte was standing on the back porch, his arms crossed over his chest, a deep frown on his face.

He watched Constance and Charlie without speaking until they were within touching distance, and then he said in a low voice, "I think that idiotic lieutenant plans to arrest Marion!"

"What's been happening?" Charlie asked.

"The questions he asked me all kept leading back to Marion. How did Victoria know about the party? Was she interested in Marion for literary reasons? Planning a book or something about her. Like that."

Charlie nodded in sympathy. "Way it works," he said. "You find a good likely suspect and work and work with it, just to see how long it takes to shake it apart. If it doesn't come apart, you begin to think you've got the answer. So far, everyone keeps coming apart, except for Tootles. They'll keep at her until they make a case, or she falls apart before their eyes like everyone else is doing."

"Christ!" Paul said. "It's the most ridiculous thing I can imagine!"

"Paul, exactly when did Victoria tell you she wanted to come to the party?" Constance asked. "Could there have been a news item about it?"

He shook his head. "What for? Marion's not really a hot news item, you know. Victoria called me on the fifteenth, one week before we actually came. She said she understood there would be a party for Marion, and that I was invited, and would I mind if she tagged along. Would I give Marion a call and make sure it was all right? I said why didn't she call for herself, and she said she didn't even know Marion Olsen, who might not accept a call from a stranger, and a party crasher. So I made the call, and a week later we got together and came by plane and rented a car at the airport to drive the rest of the way." He had said all this so often it now was singsong. He ran his hand over his face and closed his eyes wearily.

"Would you have considered an article about Marion's touring show?" Constance asked.

He looked at her in surprise and shook his head. "No. *Seven Kinds of Death* is the best thing she's ever done, and it's eighteen or nineteen years old. I wouldn't have written about her, and she didn't think for a second I would. I wouldn't have written about the condominiums, either," he added. "The International Style passed through the corridors of the Chicago School, interpreted by Le Corbusier, diluted by Howe and then translated into binary by a hacker, who invariably selected the worst features he could find to produce a CAD program. For fifty dollars extra you can get variations."

His contempt was so blatant that for a time no one spoke. Constance gazed at a willow tree fluttering gently, and finally Charlie said, "We have no authority to ask questions, no reason to expect anyone to answer them, but for what it's worth, I don't believe Tootles killed Victoria Leeds. I've known her for more than twenty-five years, and I just can't see her doing it. For what it's worth. And I could be wrong, natch."

"What do you want to know?" Paul Volte asked. The animation that his scorn had enlivened vanished and weariness settled over him again like a miasma.

Constance had already told Charlie about Paul's relationship with Victoria, and with Toni; there seemed little point in rehashing any of it now. "You asked Tootles to invite Victoria Leeds?" Charlie asked, and Paul said not exactly. When he called, Max had answered, not Tootles. Charlie sat down on the top step of the porch; Paul left the rail he was leaning against to sit down also. Constance pulled a lounge chair closer and stretched out on it.

"This is all meaningless," Paul said. He sounded dispirited and despairing; his voice was monotone. "I called here and got Max," he said in a flat voice. "I said I'd like to bring a friend,

Victoria Leeds, and would that be convenient. And he said he would be delighted to meet Ms. Leeds. That was all."

He said he had not paid much attention the day he and Victoria arrived and Johnny Buell joined them for a few minutes. Janet and Victoria had been laughing at something, but he didn't know what; he had not heard the joke. He had, he admitted, taken a dislike to Johnny Buell when he realized that he was the one who had been responsible for his, Paul's, invitation. Just two weeks before the party, he had received the invitation, and he would not have come if Victoria had not called him. Inviting him was obviously an afterthought, he said bitterly. Johnny had read his book, had been flattering about it, but it was obvious that he was looking for a free lunch.

"Did you notice what time it was when you realized you hadn't seen Victoria at the party?" Charlie asked.

"I came back down a little after five-thirty, and I sort of looked around for her, but there was a crush already. It must have been close to six-thirty before I started to worry about it." He described the half-hearted search at first and then the real search, and finally calling the police. A little after seven when the party was officially over, they finally had crossed the road to search the barn. He had not paid any attention to the crates. "It probably wouldn't have meant anything to me even if I had seen the loosened screws. I hadn't seen them before and hadn't worked on crating up, so I doubt I would have noticed anything out of ordinary there. We were looking for a woman, remember."

"That was near seven?" Charlie asked.

"A little after. Johnny and his friends had left already; most of the guests had left, I think. Seven-fifteen, something like that."

"And as far as you can say, the crates had been opened by then?"

"I don't know," he said. "I just don't know."

Charlie glanced at him unhappily. "Can you think of anyone who might have wanted to kill Victoria Leeds? Or a reason?"

Paul shook his head. "There isn't anyone, and there isn't a reason in the world. I've tried and tried to come up with anything, and there's nothing." He caught his breath in sharply, closed his eyes, and then added, "She was one of the kindest, gentlest, most understanding people I've ever known. No one could have had a reason.'' His eyes gleamed with unshed tears.

There was a silence following this. Paul gazed blindly past Charlie, who felt almost embarrassed. Constance broke the silence.

"I understand that you recommended Toni to Tootles,'' she said. "Is that something you do often? Recommend young artists to study here?''

He shrugged. "This was the first time. Victoria asked me to do something for her, and when I saw the relief Toni did of Victoria, I agreed that she would benefit.''

"Is she exceptionally talented?'' Constance asked.

He shrugged, but now he looked more alive than he had only a moment earlier. "She's good. There's talent. We'll have to wait and see.''

Charlie stood up and stretched. "You leaving today?'' he asked.

"I don't know, but in any case not until I've had a chance to talk to Max and Marion. I can't believe that policeman intends to saddle Marion with this. It's the craziest thing I've ever heard of!'' His respite from grief, guilt, whatever it was, had been short-lived; he looked miserable again. He had got to his feet as he spoke, and now he started to walk toward the door of the house. He hesitated before opening it. "What about you? Are you leaving?''

"Haven't decided,'' Charlie said.

"Hang around if you can,'' Paul said suddenly. "Are you free to take on an investigation now? Would you be interested? I have to talk to Max and Marion first, but if they agree, would you be interested?''

"Mr. Volte,'' Charlie said softly, "do you know anything about me, about us?''

Paul nodded. "I called my lawyer yesterday and briefed him about what was going on here. Your name came up because of her.'' He nodded toward Constance. "I believe my lawyer would approve if we hired you. And if that lieutenant really tries to hang this on Marion, we'll want to hire you, I'm certain.''

He reached for the handle of the screen door but stopped again when Constance asked, "Paul, why do Toni and Janet think you had something to do with Victoria's death?''

He hunched his shoulders for a second as if to ward off a

blow, then he said, "Because I'm responsible. Not for the act itself. I didn't do it, or hire anyone to do it. But I'm responsible. If it weren't for me, she'd be alive now." Abruptly he yanked the door open and hurried inside.

9

Whatever Charlie had intended to say next, he forgot because Spence Dwyers came shambling around the corner of the house. He spotted Charlie and Constance on the back porch and headed toward them, straightening his back, raising his head, as if his awareness that he was being watched had pushed a button. Charlie had sparred with Spence once many years ago, and had been trounced, but not hurt. He remembered how careful Spence had been not to hurt him.

"Charlie!" Spence said as he drew near them. "Thank God you're here! Has Paul spoken to you? Or Max? We want to hire you to get to the bottom of this mess. My God, I can't stand seeing Marion like this!"

"What happened?" Charlie demanded. "Is Belmont giving her a hard time? Doesn't she know she doesn't have to say a word without a lawyer at her elbow?"

"No. No. It isn't anything like that. They haven't come down hard yet. But she's . . . I think she's shrinking right in front of our eyes! It's awful, the way she looks."

"Are they through with you?"

"Yes, they told me I could leave. But who could leave now? With her like that? We have to talk, make plans."

"Sit down," Charlie said, indicating the top step. He waited until Spence sat down, and then sat beside him. "Did you know Victoria Leeds before she showed up here?"

Spence shook his head. "I never even met her. I got here after the party started, and she never put in an appearance. I don't think any of us knew her, except for Paul and Toni. You know about that? How they met and all?"

"Yes, we know," Charlie said morosely. "Spence," he went on, gazing out through the trees, "if we take this on, we're going to need all the help we can get. You understand? I mean no holding out, no half truths. It's not going to be a snap, and we may not be able to take the heat off Tootles, but I'll try."

Spence nodded. "Yeah, Charlie, goes without saying."

Charlie became aware that Constance wanted to ask something. There was nothing he could have pointed to; he was certain she had not cleared her throat, or shifted her position, or touched him. But he knew just as surely as if she had run her hand down his back.

And she knew he was pausing to allow her question. She asked, "Why did you arrange a touring show for Tootles at this late date in her career?"

Charlie continued to look out over the trees, but he was fully aware of the rigidity that had come over Spence Dwyers; the man hardly seemed to breathe for what seemed much too long a time. Charlie waited, mulling over the question.

"It's never too late," Spence said finally. "She has some very good pieces, after all. A lot of them I've had in my gallery over the years. Nice work. She can use a little appreciation, we all can, no matter what stage we're at."

Constance said, "Hm," and Charlie said, "Knock it off. Whose idea was the traveling circus? Yours or hers?"

Again the silence stretched too long. Pay dirt, Charlie thought then, and he hadn't even known what they were scratching for this time. He got up and brushed off his trousers. Very slowly Spence stood up; he didn't look at Charlie or Constance. "Damn it," he said finally, "her work, the show, it's got nothing to do with the Leeds woman. She was just someone Paul knew. Let's let it go at that."

"Can't," Charlie said with regret. "We'll come back to it."

For a second or two Spence hesitated with a curious look on his face, partly embarrassment, partly surprise. "Jesus," he said in a low voice, "the way we're talking about her, Victoria Leeds, as if she didn't matter. Me, I mean. The way I was talking about her. Jesus. It's just that I didn't know her, and I do know Tootles."

"Paul's certainly taking it hard," Constance murmured.

"Yeah. I know he is."

"Too hard?" Constance asked in a low voice. "I understand Victoria Leeds wanted to marry and he wouldn't do it. She left him months ago apparently."

Spence nodded. "That's what I heard, too. So now he's having all the guilt in the world settle down around his shoulders. Way it goes. Anyway, I don't know anything about their private lives, you understand. I only met him a few times over the years, not like a bosom buddy, you know."

Constance nodded and said *of course,* and now Charlie asked, "You know of a place where we can get a room, an apartment, anything for a day or two?"

"Out here, or in town?"

"Here."

"Not offhand. Let me give it a little thought. I'll ask Max. There's got to be something."

Constance now asked, "Spence, is Toni any good? Is she going to make it?"

He looked surprised, then shrugged. "Who knows? She's clever, smart, good with her hands. More than that? Not yet. But she's pretty young. Give her a few years, see what develops." He grinned lopsidedly, "Tootles wouldn't have invited her to stay if she hadn't thought the kid will make it eventually." Shaking his head, he repeated, "Tootles. I haven't called her that in thirty years. Tootles. Still fits, doesn't it?" He sobered again quickly. He glanced at his watch, then started to move toward the door. "I'll make some calls, see if I can find you a place to stay. And, Charlie, later, this evening, let's get together again with that other question. Okay? Just need a little time first, that's all."

"Sure," Charlie said. "Sure, Spence."

One by one the others drifted out to wander around in confusion; no one seemed in a hurry to leave now, not even Ba Ba. She appeared, hesitated, turned and reentered the house. Spence came back and handed Charlie a piece of paper with the name of a motel and directions—ten minutes away, he said, no more than that. Then Toni appeared and said there was a phone call for Charlie. "I think it's the sheriff," she said, leading them to the telephone in the office. She watched Charlie as he lifted the receiver. He returned her gaze pointedly and did not speak until she flushed crimson, turned, and walked away with her head very high, her back very stiff. She pulled the door closed behind her unnecessarily hard.

"Meiklejohn," he said then, grinning at Constance.

"Mr. Buell said they might hire you," Gruenwald said. "You working now?"

"Not yet."

"Want to go with me to talk to the guy who was crating up the artwork? He's due back around nine. Thought we might like a word with him."

"I'd like that," Charlie said. "We'll be staying at"—he glanced at the paper Spence had given him—"Lakeside Inn."

"Know where it is," Gruenwald said. "Pick you up around eight forty-five. Okay?"

Charlie said okay and added, "You understand that I might be working by then," he said.

"I know. See you later."

Constance was watching him with a slight frown as he told her about the invitation. "But if the state police are handling the investigation, why is he doing this? And why ask us to go with him?"

"Good questions," Charlie said. "Let's ask him."

He looked past her at the hall door, and then went to open it to listen to voices raised somewhere around the front of the house. He motioned, and they walked quietly down the hallway toward the foyer.

"I don't give a shit!" Tootles was yelling. "That pipsqueak can't come and go like that, give orders to stay put like that. Who does he think he is?"

"He's the law," Spence said.

Paul's voice was lower. "Marion, just don't let him get to you. Talk to your lawyer first thing in the morning."

Max said, "He isn't after you, Marion. I'm sure he isn't."

"And you're wrong," Ba Ba cried. "Of course, he's after her. I knew it would happen! I read the cards and they were full of death omens, catastrophes . . ."

A strange voice said, "Mrs. Buell, you want lunch in the dining room? I can put out sandwich stuff, and salad. I wasn't sure what to do, what with all those men hanging around . . ."

Max said, "The dining room's fine. Fine. We need coffee, and something to eat. Sandwiches are fine, aren't they, Marion?"

"You're hungry? How can you be?" Tootles cried. "I can't stand this! Food. Coffee. Let's all pretend nothing's happened, nothing's going to happen. That man plans to arrest me, for chrissake!"

Charlie took the next step or two into the foyer and Tootles ran to him, caught his arm. "You will help, won't you? You can find out who killed Victoria Leeds. Charlie, someone has to help me!"

He looked at her in wonder. She could still do it, he realized. The hormones, the appeal was still there in this coarse, not at all handsome woman with unkempt graying hair, unkempt, not-very-clean clothes, dirty feet . . . He pried her fingers loose from his arm, and took her by the shoulders, moved her back a foot or two. "Let's make one thing clear," he said. "If I take this on, you don't lie to me. Is that a deal?"

She looked bewildered. "Of course. Why would I lie to you?"

He sighed and looked past her to where Constance was standing, watching all this with a very bright look. Probably no one else would recognize it as amusement, but he knew that expression. He scowled at her.

"I thought he was a fireman," Ba Ba said.

"And you'll all cooperate," Charlie said to them all generally.

"What difference does it make, if he's a fireman?" Ba Ba asked. "We haven't had any fire, thank heavens. At least, we've been spared—"

"Babar, shut up," Charlie said. Count the small blessings, he thought with relief; when you told her to shut up, she did. For a few minutes. And she didn't seem to hold a grudge. She assumed a pout now and pointedly looked out the window as if she had suddenly gone deaf. "I'll want to ask you as a group about the night of the party. I'll want to ask some of you questions not in a group. And I'll want to have a look at that condo. Can we get in yet?" he asked Max.

Max glanced at Johnny, who shrugged and said, "The lieutenant said they'd clear out by four at the latest."

Charlie nodded. "Four it is. And right now, I want a sandwich." They all followed him meekly enough into the dining room. It was nearly three already.

Asking questions of the group was a bust, he decided later. Nothing turned up that he had not already heard. Constance went upstairs to gather the few things she had unpacked, and now it was going on four, and they were ready to leave.

Johnny Buell met them at the door. Although he looked serious, there was also an underlying eagerness in his expression, his attitude, like a Boy Scout after another merit badge. "Now what?"

"Exactly the same as it was the other night. You said good-bye to everyone, and your group went outside. Where were you parked?"

"Across the road," Johnny said. "I knew we'd want to leave promptly at seven and I didn't want to get blocked. I had moved the car over there already. Dad's car," he added. "Mine's a Corvette, a two-seater."

"Good," Charlie said. He looked at his watch. "Let's pretend it's about three minutes after seven. We've said good-bye, and it's time to leave. Let's go."

Johnny would have hurried them through the yard, but Constance did not permit it. "I noticed Debra's shoes," she explained. "High heels, sandals. And this is rough ground."

They reached Max's Continental, and got in. Johnny drove fast, but not dangerously so, and probably at his usual speed, to the condominium fence. No one spoke until he stopped. "I had to get out and open the gate," he said, opening his door. He unlocked the gate and swung it back, returned to the car and drove on through, to the first of the buildings. An iron-grille gate closed the driveway outside the building itself. He touched a signal button on a box on the dashboard and the gate swung up; he drove in and down a long ramp. "Basement," he said. "This will all be parking space for the occupants." They drove past some elevators and stairs. The parking spaces were marked by pale green lines painted on the floor. He drove slowly to the far end of the basement and made a partial turn, touched the signal button again, and the second grillwork gate opened.

"We got out here," he said.

"You opened the gate there before you left the car and went upstairs?"

Johnny nodded with a crestfallen look. "I don't know why, no reason. I just did. I know. Someone could have entered the building while we were upstairs."

Charlie nodded and opened the car door. The wall to his right housed many elevators, a staircase, and two or three unmarked doors that he assumed were maintenance closets. All the doors were the same dark green as the walls. Stenciled on panels on the elevator doors were oversized numbers on one side and the letter A on the other in the same pale green as the floor stripes. The numbers and the stripes seemed to glow against the dark green; easy to spot late at night, after a hard day, Charlie thought. Johnny went to Six A and pushed the button. He had to use a computer lock card to open the elevator door; they entered the small foyer that looked almost exactly as it had when Constance had ridden it up before. Now the roses on the shelf were dying and their fragrance had turned to a musty odor.

No one spoke until they reached the sixth-floor apartment and entered. Charlie said, "Seven-ten. Was the timing about the same as the other night?"

Johnny moistened his lips and nodded. His subdued eagerness had vanished; he looked apprehensive and seemed reluctant to leave the foyer and advance into the apartment until Charlie realized the cause of his nervousness. "She's gone," he said kindly. "Believe me, it's all right."

They walked through the hall into the spacious living room, where even the chalked outline of Victoria Leeds had been cleaned up. The tarps were back on the furniture.

"Now what?" Charlie asked.

"I went on through to the dining room. I had left my briefcase in there. The others didn't move from the doorway. No one wanted to get paint on their clothes. It smelled pretty strong, you know, wet paint. The walls, the door facings . . ." He hurried across the room to the dining room, went in, came back out and rejoined Charlie and Constance at the door. "Then we went down."

They reentered the foyer/elevator and rode to the basement, where they got back in the car, and Johnny drove out of the building and touched the button to close the gate after him. "I stopped here," he said, pulling on the hand brake. The iron gate had already closed. "I began to wonder if there were tarps, the heavy odor of paint in the other units, and I knew I wouldn't rest unless I checked them out. This was a big weekend," he added. "You know about the two tours through the buildings we had planned?"

Charlie nodded. "Let's go in and go through the exact same movements you made before. Honey, you want to chat with the watchman?" Johnny looked around in bewilderment; there was no watchman in sight.

"Oh," he said, and then led the way back into the building; they were now on the first floor; here the elevators had the big brass numbers that Constance had seen on her tour. "I went up to Five A," he said, and held up a wallet with computer lock cards. He used one to open the elevator to Five A and they entered it. "I used the stairs to go to the other floors. Each elevator is dedicated to its own unit at this end of the building." He glanced at Charlie, who nodded in understanding. They arrived at the foyer on five, and glanced inside the unit without entering, went to the end of the hall and down the stairs to four, and repeated the inspection, then to three, two, and finally they were back on the first floor. It had taken no more than five minutes in all. The apartments all appeared to be identical. Only Six A still showed the evidence of recent painting activity. Six A and Five A had both been outfitted with a conference table and chairs in the large living room. In Five A coffee service had been added. Probably they would have had doughnuts, Charlie thought, for the money men. This side of the building had the biggest apartments, the most expensive, the only ones with their own elevators.

"The watchman was here when I came out," Johnny said on the first floor, walking toward Constance and the car. "I didn't talk more than a few seconds with him. Then we left. Pierce, the watchman, followed us to the construction gate and closed it after us."

He started to open the car door, and Charlie said, "Hold it just a second. What about the briefcase?"

Johnny looked blankly at his hands, as if trying to remember. Then he said, "Yeah, I tossed it inside the trunk." He went back around the car and opened the trunk and made the motion of throwing in the briefcase, and then they all got inside the Continental again, and he drove to the gate.

Charlie looked at his watch, more unhappily than before. Fifteen minutes, at the very least, and eighteen was more likely.

"Okay," Charlie said. "Back to the house. Thanks. You were over here earlier, weren't you?"

"I'm over here every day," Johnny said. "It's our job, I'm riding herd on it."

"I see. But you came over Friday and sent some workers home, and told them to come back Saturday and finish up? Is that right?"

"Yes. I came back to change clothes, and they were doing the stripes on the floor or something. I told them it could wait until the next morning, and I locked up when I left to pick up Debra and her friends at the train station in Maryville. I don't know what time that was. I had to wait a few minutes at the station, not long. The train comes in at five-thirty."

"Um," Charlie said. "What I really wanted to know is did the men return Saturday morning and finish? Would they have been likely to go up to Six A to clean up their stuff?"

"No," Johnny said. "I told them I'd pull the tarps off and put them in one of the closets sometime Saturday afternoon. All they had to do was finish up in the basement and clear out the brushes and cans and stuff. They did that. At least the stuff is all gone now. This is the first time I've been back over," he added, disgruntled. "They wouldn't let me back into Six A at all to get those tarps out and look around."

"Then you and your friends drove into Washington and you didn't come back here until afternoon on Saturday. Is that right?"

Johnny's voice was hard and tight when he said, "I drove to the city and we had dinner, and I was with Debra Saltzman until after two-thirty in the morning. I slept until noon on Saturday, and after I showered and ate, I came out here, and have stayed on since then. Is there anything else?"

Charlie looked at him in surprise. "Okay," he said. "Take it easy. Were you able to reach everyone about canceling the tour?"

"Finally," Johnny said. "Sorry I jumped on you like that. This is my first . . . investigation of this sort. Edgy."

They had reached the house again; this time he pulled into the driveway and drove through until they were even with the back door. "I'll go park," he said. "You can get out here if you want."

They got out and he continued to drive toward the garage. "Did you find anything new?" Constance asked as soon as the car left them.

"Hm, not sure. Look," he said, and pointed. At the far side of the yard Paul Volte and Toni were walking together, her hand on his arm, his head bowed as if listening to her.

"Looks like she's over her fear of him," Charlie said. He continued to face their direction, but he was no longer seeing them. Something, he thought, something about the crates. "You saw those boxes before and after they were opened," he said slowly. "Was there anything on them to identify them, stenciled addresses, names, contents listed, anything?"

She had to concentrate on visualizing how the crates had looked. No marks. No names. No contents. Nothing to identify the contents to anyone who hadn't already known. She described them and said, "Oh." But someone could have told Victoria about them, she thought swiftly then. From inside the house Ba Ba's voice screeched suddenly, and Tootles yelled something at her, and then they were both yelling.

Charlie took Constance by the arm and turned her toward their car. "You know what would be nice along about now?"

"Tell me."

"A nice quiet room, eventually a nice tall drink, and no Babar, no Tootles, no Johnny."

"You say eventually?"

"Well, I always say first things first. Let's wrap it up here and scram, kiddo. Show you some interesting etchings, or something."

He loved the way she laughed then, and later in their room he knew he would love the way she would agree that first things should be first.

10

Claud Palance lived in an apartment near Bellarmine College; about ten miles from Maryville. That's how this part of the world was, Charlie brooded. You think you're out in the country, and then there's another bedroom community, another town, another complex of apartments, schools, shopping centers. He thought gloomily of a megalopolis stretching from above New York City down to the Keys, one bedroom community, one city center, one parking lot after another all the way. He shuddered. To get to country, real country, you would have to turn inland and even then it wouldn't start for another fifty miles, a hundred miles. At *their* place in upper New York State real country began at their door.

Sheriff Bill Gruenwald drove five miles over the speed limit in his unmarked green Ford. He appeared to be in deep thought and was silent for the fifteen-minute drive. He had called ahead; Palance was watching for them and met them at the door of his apartment before they had time to ring. His rooms were at ground level, spartan, obsessively neat, the sort of place where you asked permission to move a paper or chair, maybe to breathe. He led the sheriff, Charlie and Constance out the back door to a shared courtyard with several grills, comfortable chairs, and a small swimming pool. The young men he had banished to camping in the wilderness were now taking turns tending sausages at the grill, plunging into the pool, returning to stand dripping once again at the grill.

Claud Palance was in his early forties, with thinning light-colored hair, smooth-faced, with watery pale blue eyes. They had camped near the Appalachian Trail at a lake, hiked in seven miles to it. They had heard no news, he added. He mentioned the name of the lake they had camped by and Sheriff Gruenwald nodded. No news out that way, he agreed, and proceeded to give a concise rundown of the events of the weekend. Palance was stunned and speechless over it. It seemed difficult for him to make sense of the questions the sheriff asked; he had to go inside and get a Diet Coke first, and then he did a few breathing exercises before he began to describe the boxes of artwork for Tootles's show.

"Do you know without a doubt that the crates had not been tampered with Thursday night?" Gruenwald asked.

"Yes, at least up to the time we left. We worked until dinnertime on the project. Six maybe. After we ate I reminded Marion that I planned to take the boys away for the weekend. We left then, but they were okay at that time."

"Do all of them stay over at Marion Olsen's?" Gruenwald asked, indicating the boys, who were splashing each other vigorously; they looked like high-school kids.

"Two of them do," Palance said. He pointed them out. The other three were his students, or had been, and all of them had worked on crating up the pieces at one time or another.

"Why?" Charlie asked then. "Why you and your students? Did she hire you to do it?"

Claud Palance looked startled at the question. "No, of course not," he said. "When it came up, I just said we'd do it. She didn't know how and neither did the kids at her place. I did. It's that simple."

Charlie was studying him curiously. "But that doesn't really get to the question of why, does it? Volunteer work? I take it that it was dirty, time-consuming, exacting. You were over there a couple of weeks already?"

"Yes. Each piece requires its own unique box, its own straps or braces, supports, whatever. You don't just pack up art with newspapers and hope for the best. You need to crate each piece in such a way that the gallery people, or museum people who are going to show it can uncrate it and then box it again when the show comes down. They aren't expected to reinvent the wheel, but simply follow instructions, and that means the instructions must be exact. Crating up a show that size might take weeks if you're using novice labor, as I was, teaching them as I went."

Sheriff Gruenwald was following this with narrowed eyes. "How long would it have taken to open twelve of them, slap paint on them, break a piece here and there, and then close up the boxes again?"

Claud Palance hesitated. "It really would depend on how careful the person was, how hard he was trying to hide what he had done. Couple of hours probably. Maybe more. Did he open one and destroy that one and close it up again and then go on to the next, or open them all at once and then have to find the screws again to close them? If you want fast and malicious damage, why bother to close them up again afterward?"

And that, thought Charlie, was one of the best questions yet. Another good question, he realized, was why not mess up all the pieces? Why leave two untouched? It sounded to him as if the guy had run out of time.

"Did Marion Olsen help with the crating?" the sheriff asked.

"Once or twice." He grinned, and something about his musculature made his ears stand out, almost pop out. Charlie tried not to stare. "It went much, much faster when she didn't help," Palance said, the grin fading away.

Across the apartment complex a young woman appeared with two small children in tow. They all hesitated at the sight of the college boys playing in the pool. Claud Palance called, "Hey, Ron, settle down, okay?" One of the boys looked at him, glanced at the woman and children, and nodded. All the boys climbed out and sat on the grass.

"You know Marion Olsen at all?" Claud Palance asked the sheriff then; he glanced at Charlie and Constance as if inviting them to answer or not.

"Some," the sheriff said cautiously.

"Well, let me tell you something you'll run into. People either love her and will do anything on earth for her, or else they want her driven out of the state. I don't want her driven out of the state."

"That's a school over there?" Charlie asked. "She's running an art school?"

"A one-woman art academy," Palance said. "No credentials, no diploma, no grades, nothing to show for it except some of the best instruction you can find in sculpting. That's what she does, and as far as I know she's never charged a cent. Some of them pay, if they can, whatever they can, but they don't have to.

And I don't know anyone in the business who wouldn't trade years at any accredited school for a year under her tutelage. I would be her student like a shot if I could be."

"Why aren't you?" Charlie asked.

"Because I'm not good enough. She knows it and so do I."

The sheriff drove them back to their motel. He had to pass through Maryville, out the other side, and on for another few miles. They were all silent during the drive. It was deep twilight now, the countryside very still.

"There's a coffee shop, isn't there? At the motel. Or a bar or something?" Gruenwald asked.

"Yep. Nice little lounge. You knew pretty much what Palance was going to say, didn't you?" Charlie commented; it wasn't really a question.

"Yeah. Some of it." He slowed down as he neared a congested area, and then turned off the highway and stopped at their motel. Lights from the building turned his face pink and green. He glanced at Charlie. "You working yet?"

"I'm working," Charlie said.

"Come on. I could use a beer or something."

The lounge was almost deserted; a man and woman were having a quiet talk at one side, and at the other the bartender watched a television screen with the sound turned way down. They took a booth; the bartender came quickly and they ordered, beers and wine.

"Charlie," Gruenwald said then, "let me tell you about the first time I saw Marion Olsen." He sprawled back in the seat on his side of the booth, his arm across the top of the backrest, gazing away from Charlie and Constance. "About seven years ago," he said, then shook his head. "Exactly seven years ago in May. There's a children's hospital not far from Bellarmine College. For what they call special children, exceptional children in some places." He stopped when the bartender came with a tray, and then he took a long drink from his glass of beer before he continued. "Okay, special children. I had reason to be in the hospital seven years ago, and I saw this woman come in and head straight to one of the activity rooms. That's what they call them, activity rooms. She had a big box of stuff that she lugged in. I was curious and followed. The room she went in already had about eight or ten kids in it. Not doing much of anything, hanging out. Little kids, five years old, six. So Marion Olsen goes to a long table in there and begins to unload her box. It's full of partly made clay things, some you could tell what was intended, but mostly not. One little statuette could have been a horse, I guess. Hard to tell. Without a word she starts to mold that clay they use, plasticine. And pretty soon one of the little kids comes over and picks up one of the other pieces, whatever it was, and begins to squeeze it, change it. It was hers, apparently. And it was like that. Marion never said a word, and neither did the kids, but before long nearly all of them were working on something or other, purposefully working." He drank again and put down his glass hard. "For some of those kids this might have been the first time they did anything with any purpose. I asked about Marion. She showed up one day with her box and said if she could have space, maybe some of the kids would play with her. Just like that. At first they said no way. Only trained personnel allowed. She threw a fit, and they gave her space just to shut her up and prove you can't reach those kids with anything not analyzed and planned and presented by a shrink of some kind. That was seven years ago that I saw her, and she'd been doing her thing for three or four years by then, and she still does it once a week."

They were all silent for several seconds until Constance asked gently, "Is your child any better now?"

He nodded. "Not much, a little. A girl, Nancy. She's thirteen."

Charlie signaled the bartender, who came over with two more beers, another glass of wine. No one spoke until he was gone again.

Then Gruenwald said, "That place of hers, what Palance calls a one-woman art academy? She doesn't dare call it a school or the county would close her down. Firetrap, they call it. A few people complained; they go around and inspect it regularly, but what the hell, it's a private residence. She doesn't do anything by the books, get the right credentials, stuff like that. She'll take in anyone she damn well pleases, and if there's any formal education or training, it's kept a secret. She's turned down some people who've made a royal stink about her and her place that she won't call a school. And she's taken in some that have made people hereabouts want to scream. Blacks, gays, weirdos of every make you can imagine. But no one can prevent anyone having guests. As long as they don't pay her, she doesn't call it a school, she can do what she damn well pleases. She does and it drives a lot of folks nuts."

"You love her or want to run her out of the state," Charlie said.

"I don't want to run her out of the state," Gruenwald said deliberately. "I don't want anyone to hang a murder charge on her, either."

Charlie nodded. "They hired me today. I've known some of them for more than twenty years. It's possible one or another of them might tell us something they wouldn't tell you. Just possible. So far no one has told us diddly. What was in the note you found by Leeds?"

"I think it's a fake, like you suggested, but still there it is. It was typed on the machine in the condo apartment, in the dining room. It said *Meet me at the condo, Six A, at seven-thirty*. Signed M. Typed M, no handwriting anywhere. No prints recoverable. Paper and envelope from the house. There's a drawer with stationery in the office. The state lab has all that stuff now, but I don't think they'll come up with more than that."

"No map or directions?"

"No. Just that."

"Too pat," Charlie said after a second. "And it would make her out to be too dumb, to leave it in plain sight like that. But those who want to run her out of the state will buy it. A jury could be talked into buying it."

"I know," Gruenwald said. He lifted his glass and drained it. "I'll be around tomorrow. You going to stay here at the motel for a while?"

"Couple of days. Then New York City. Why did Victoria Leeds invite herself to the party, that's the question, isn't it? Without an answer to that, we're stuck exactly where we are right now."

Gruenwald nodded. "You might want to do it again, but I checked out the group that went over to the condo Friday night. Debra Saltzman, Phil Michelson, Sandra Door. They call her Sunny. Good upstanding types, with fathers in Congress or counting their millions, that sort of thing. They confirm John Buell's story. No body was in that apartment at ten past seven."

"Right," Charlie said gloomily. "The way it stands now, the artwork was okay Thursday evening. Friday night it was a mess. Victoria Leeds vanished a little before five Friday, and is unaccounted for for the next two hours. Where the hell was she? Smashing art? Why? Everyone who was an overnight guest or regular in that house, except Tootles, is covered by nearly everyone else from seven onwards. Have you talked with the watchman yet?"

"Pierce? Sure. He got there at six Friday; gate was closed, locked. He made the rounds, everything locked up tight. Nothing out of ordinary. They are being careful because there were a couple of accidents earlier on, one was fatal. So they're being very careful."

"Accidents?" Charlie asked, perking up.

Gruenwald shook his head. "Nothing for us. Some kids got in the grounds when they were still digging holes, and one of them had a fall, broke his ankle. That was over a year ago. This spring a guy fell from the roof of one of the buildings. Died instantly. Insurance company got antsy, I think, and now they're super cautious. Both good and bad for us. But Pierce says the gate was closed and locked when he got there at six. Then Buell and his crowd came in a few minutes after seven, left ten minutes later, and he locked up again. No one came in after that. The buildings that have doors were all locked, and he checked the others. Nothing. He's a pretty good guy. He's sure. And like I said, they're being careful."

"Someone else got in," Charlie said darkly. "The delivery man with the flowers?"

Gruenwald shook his head again. "Nope. Pierce met him when he arrived for work and carried the flowers inside himself; that's when he checked out the building."

"And those young people, they really went in far enough to be certain no one was there?"

Constance made a slight noise, then said. "You couldn't have missed seeing her. Even if they had stayed in the foyer. Johnny had to pass within two feet of where her body was."

"They all say they went through the hallway to the living room doorway," the sheriff said with finality. "They would have seen her. When Buell went back to check the other units, it took five minutes probably. They agree on that. Pierce had joined them by then and confirms that Johnny was gone just about long enough to glance into the rooms, but not a minute longer."

Charlie's gloom deepened as he considered this. It could be a conspiracy, he thought, and mocked himself for the thought. Pierce, the son and daughters of public figures, Johnny Buell, all in a conspiracy to hide the fact that Victoria and her killer had to have entered those grounds, that building, that particular room at the same time that they were all coming and going without seeing a thing.

Slowly he said, "Suppose Johnny goes to the dining room and sees Victoria Leeds hiding, or even just there. He says, stay put and I'll be right back. He gets rid of the other young people, returns with the rope and kills her."

Sheriff Gruenwald waited him out patiently. "How did she get in? Where did the rope come from? Was he expecting her? What would his motive have been? Why was she hiding? Why didn't she just say *hi* to the gang?" He looked apologetically at Constance and added, "Besides, it wasn't really a clean kill. She was trying to crawl away apparently, grabbing at the tarps; the killer held her with his knee in her back, used some weight to hold her, bruised her pretty bad, and it took a few minutes. I'm not saying your scenario is totally impossible, only that I don't believe a word of it. I doubt that anyone who isn't a real psycho could have killed her and then appeared normal immediately. Psycho, hired hit man, there's some that could, but we don't have them around here, far's I know. Just don't believe it."

Nor did he, Charlie had to admit to himself. "That still leaves the time that Buell took his friends up to Six A and left the gate open. She and her killer could have got in then. At least that gets them inside, instead of lurking behind a tree somewhere."

Gruenwald nodded. "That might be the only scenario that will work, and it brings in an outsider." He looked very unhappy about it. "Belmont doesn't like outsiders wandering into locked buildings with so many people milling about. Can't say I blame him." He took a deep breath, shook his head, and went on. "We're checking the guests who drove past the condo that evening. It will take time. That's a long guest list. But maybe someone saw something." He did not sound hopeful. "Well, I better be on my way."

Charlie motioned the bartender over, signed the tab and showed their room key, and, when the bartender left again, Gruenwald stood up. "I've got to get home and get some sleep." He glanced at Constance, then at Charlie. "You know that I'm off the case officially? I mean, anything I do now is just because I'm interested. A responsible citizen, that's me."

Constance nodded and Charlie walked partway out with him. She watched the two men go through the ritual of shaking hands; she listened to the words, *keep in touch, take care, I'll let you know*, but she was brooding over the many men who felt the great urge, the need even, to help and protect Tootles. Charlie returned.

"You want anything else?"

She shook her head.

Slowly, hand in hand they left the lounge and walked through the lobby to the elevator to ride up to the seventh floor, where they had a minisuite. They had spent some time in the room earlier; she had remade the bed more or less, and she had unpacked for both of them while Charlie showered. Now he moved back and forth from bedroom to bathroom, yawning widely often. But she was not at all sleepy yet; she picked up Paul Volte's book. There were a few things she wanted to reread before going to bed.

It was hard to remember, she thought much later, that a writer like Paul Volte was a true artist, as much as any poet, or playwright, or novelist. His craft was as demanding, and his knowledge of people possibly even more so; he could not make it up, only report and interpret what was. His prose was lucid and beautifully rhythmic, very precise. A true artist, she repeated to herself, deserving of the various awards he had gathered over the years. Coming from a background of art history, art appreciation, criticism, he had developed a superb talent for spotting what was wrong with a piece of art, or, more important, possibly, what was right about it. His word was the word of God in that world, enough to make or break, to send the artist to the heights, or bring him or her down to the gutter. Yet, talking to him, observing him, thin, hungry-looking, abstracted, it was hard to discern any self-awareness in him of the power he wielded. Until you looked closer, she added, remembering the small glint of satisfaction he had revealed when she asked about Toni's talent.

Was Tootles as unconcerned about his opinion as she appeared? What had the students thought of him? Filled with fear and awe? Toni had shown both, and then, curiously, had dropped both attitudes to show something else, a demanding persistence about something that overrode her earlier fear of him. And Johnny Buell? Had he really thought Paul would write about the condos? What a coup for him that would have been. Worth conniving to get Paul to appear and take the tour. There was little doubt that a good word in Paul's column, or a paragraph in his next book would send Johnny's stock off the chart. The people Paul had chosen to write about were all doing extremely well, she had read. The kiss of an angel, his words had been called.

But the wild current that ran all through his book was the common acceptance of possession that surfaced again and again in artist after artist. The artist as one possessed, helplessly yielding to the power possessing him or her, or giving up art, that was the subtext that had turned the book into a best-seller, she was certain. That mysterious power to possess, to demand, to exact a terrible price for success, that was what people had wanted to read about; that was what people wanted to believe, did believe, and he had handled it with such conviction, such delicacy and even humor that to the believers, it must be like an *ex cathedra* pronouncement from the Pope himself, while to the nonbelievers, it was just another one of those superstitions that artists professed to believe in, no more powerful than the old wives' admonitions: no hat on the bed, salt over the shoulder, no open umbrella in the house . . . all very *in* right now, very much New Age. But she heard her own voice arguing: Just because something had become acceptable that had been scorned by so many for so long, didn't mean it couldn't be true. Popularity didn't automatically make it false.

She yawned and stood up then, stretched, and got ready for bed, disturbed by something she could not quite define about Paul and his book. She got into bed beside Charlie, and he turned in his sleep, his hand seeking her the way it did if he was asleep or awake. She settled in close to him, their bodies touching here and there, their breath mingling, and she began the long slide into sleep.

He believed it, she felt almost certain, Paul believed all that he had written; of course, a good writer must believe, but when had he started to believe it? Before or after writing the book? Could he have written that particular book without first knowing what he had to ask, what he was looking for? She could not think now why the question was important, why this entire line of thought was important. The slide was moving her faster and faster downward, her thoughts becoming more and more jumbled, surreal even. She imagined, then saw, Paul Volte digging a hole that looked very much like a grave. A line of people stretched out of sight over the horizon, each person carrying something—a basket with a kitten, a St. Bernard dog, a tin of muffins, an old woman in a pail, a case of leather-bound books. . . . When they reached the hole that Paul was digging furiously they tossed in whatever the burden was, and then trudged away with bowed heads, downcast eyes. The line did not diminish.

11

All right," Charlie said, after finishing his second cup of coffee the next morning. Breakfast had been decent—not good, not bad—decent, and filling. He did not expect much more than that from motel restaurants; decent was a plus, in fact.

"So, all right," Constance said, watching him. She liked Charlie in the morning. He always woke up so chipper, ready for anything, eager. Youthful, she thought with surprise. Charlie in the morning was very much like the youthful Charlie she had married; as the hours passed, he grew up and matured all over again, day after day. She knew he had seen too much, had been through too much with a big-city fire department, then the arson squad, then as a city detective in homicide. Just too bloody much. You can take the boy out of the city, she went on, but

you can't take away the synapse tracks, the traces, the imprint-
ing, the knowledge, the memories of what he had done, and
what he had not done, what others had done. . . .

"What I'd like," Charlie said, gazing past her innocently, "is
to tackle Tootles, but she would close like a clam if I attempted
it, so that's your department. I'll put in some time at the condo,
and inspect that fence and do other pretty important things like
that."

"Charlie," she asked in wonder, "how can you take on a job
to save the life of a woman you can't even bear to spend five
minutes with?"

"But I thought I explained," he said, and began to search for
the bill.

"You already signed, remember?"

"Oh, yeah, I forgot. Anyway, it's not Tootles so much as Babar.
My God, she's worse than ever."

They walked from the restaurant. "I thought she'd be gone
by now," Constance said, heading for the Volvo. "Oh, dear, we
have to do something about that rental car today."

"Babar won't leave until the excitement is over," Charlie said,
"and God knows how long it's going to take to reach that point.
Poor old Larry will just have to rough it alone. I hope he's eating
all right with her gone."

Constance frowned at him. "All right, darling," she said
coldly. "I'll talk to Tootles. You've made the point, don't try to
stretch it too far."

He looked at her with renewed innocence.

"Tootles, this is ridiculous, and you know it!" Constance was
saying a bit later. They were in the office in the main house;
sounds of hammering, pounding, banging echoed from within
the nearby studio.

"I don't have an idea in the world what you're talking about,"
Tootles said, but with an absent look, as if she were paying little
attention to her own or Constance's words.

"For heaven's sake, what are they doing in there?" Constance
asked then, as the hammering noise increased.

"Roger, one of the boys who stays here, is making a birdhouse, a memorial. His way of reaffirming life, I guess."

Constance bit back a retort, and drew in a deep breath. "Let's go someplace quieter. I have to ask you some questions, and you have to answer them. Do you grasp the danger you're in?"

"Don't be silly," Tootles said with a quick laugh. "But it's quieter in the other side of the house. Let's go to the music room."

It would be the music room for her, Constance realized; Tootles played the piano with gusto and not a trace of talent. Today she was wearing faded blue jeans, and a handsome silk-screened T-shirt with a panorama of butterflies and flowers front and back. Dressed up for the reporters, she had said grimly; they had been snooping all morning, and they would be back. Tomorrow she would wear her T-shirt with dragons.

Constance followed her to the living room, on through to the adjacent room where Ba Ba was watching television with headphones on. Constance glowered at Tootles, who, she was certain, had known they would find Ba Ba in here. She took Tootles by the arm and turned her, marched her out of the room again. "Out to the porch," she said with grim determination.

The front porch had a pair of wooden benches and several bentwood chairs. Constance did not release Tootles until they reached the furniture, where she almost shoved the other woman into a chair and then dragged a second one closer.

"Now, you just listen to me," she said crisply, her anger as evident in the coldness of her voice as in the stiffness of her posture. She made no effort to conceal it; she wanted Tootles to see how furious she was. "You're the only one from this house who could have found time to get over to the condo and kill Victoria Leeds. That's for openers. Someone, possibly Victoria Leeds, made a mess of your art, providing you a very fine motive for getting even. How much more does it take to convince you that this is serious trouble?"

"But what makes you think I doubt it's serious? I didn't do anything, that's all there is to that. And what good would it do for me to scream and cry and wring my hands and come on like some poor damn bedeviled ingenue? I don't even know the fucking words! I sure as hell couldn't improvise that role with any conviction."

"Why did you ask me to come here? What's the crisis you claimed threatened you? Why that note on my invitation?"

"Constance! What a dumb-ass question! To share my success,

to celebrate with us. To have someone from home witness this
crowning achievement. All the above. Emergency? Of course, my
very first touring show! Ruined. Maybe I had a premonition.
Maybe it rubbed off from Ba Ba."

"Stop it, Tootles! I mean it, stop or I'll just walk out and take
Charlie with me!"

Tootles shrugged eloquently. "I threw myself on his mercy,
and he agreed to help. I think he's more a gentleman than you
give him credit for."

Now Constance laughed, without guile, a pure laugh of real
amusement. "Do you really think he'd stay if I said I wanted to
leave?"

For a long time Tootles examined her with narrowed eyes,
the way she might have looked at a piece of work one of her
students had presented for judgment. She shook her head and
leaned back in her chair. "I asked you because I was afraid the
weekend would be too much for me. I wanted to lash out and
hit Johnny for topping my party with his own viewing of the
condo, even trying to get a write-up about it, and then assuming
I would play hostess for him without so much as 'if you please,
ma'am.' He ordered flowers in my name and told me I was supposed to pour the coffee for the financiers! He suggested I might
even wear a nice dress, or at least a nice pantsuit! And have my
hair done. The little shit! As if I give a goddam about the fucking
condos or his long-range goals! My instinct was to wear the
crummiest sweats I have, and show up barefoot! And I couldn't.
I didn't know what it would do to Max if I lashed out at Johnny.
Or poured scalding coffee down the crotches of a bunch of fat
bankers. Johnny wants the company to become another Bechtel,
you know. He has plans, five-year plans, ten-year plans. Christ,
he has plans for the next century! All this mess probably set his
plans back five years. I hope to hell it does."

And she was lying in her teeth, Constance thought distantly.
Everything she said could be true, it sounded plausible if a bit
weak, and it didn't really sound like a lie, but it had nothing to
do with why Tootles had begged her to come. This was how
Tootles had been as a child, a teenager: once she started on a
plausible story she could keep spinning it out interminably, until
her questioners forgot the original question and simply gave up
in fatigue. Constance had watched this kind of performance

many times. The beauty of Tootles's stories was that they were always based on a foundation of truth that appeared strong enough to support whatever she constructed on it. No doubt she really had resented Johnny's topping her party with his own. No doubt she had hated being dragged in in any capacity. Tootles playing hostess to businessmen who were not *her* businessmen was a ludicrous idea.

Constance finally put her hand on Tootles's arm to stop her. "Do you have the computer card key for Six A?"

Tootles had to blink several times to return to the real world. "Sure. It's going to be our new home."

"Where is it?"

Tootles shrugged and looked blank. "I don't know. Usually it's in my purse. In my wallet. It's sort of flimsy, like a cheapo credit card. They're made that way because, according to Johnny, they're supposed to be changed every month or so. You know how that works? They key in an order for a random number or something and that's your lock number and the printer issues a card that gets laminated and if you lose it, presto change-o, a new random number."

"You weren't carrying a purse or a wallet Friday night when you returned," Constance said, interrupting her. "Were you?"

Tootles shook her head, then suddenly brightened and sat up straighter. "That's right! I knew you could do it, you and that gorgeous man of yours. I just knew it! Maybe this is why I asked you, and I just couldn't explain it ahead of time. Ba Ba's right, after all! We're in touch with more than we can explain, more than we know. Constance, that's so smart!"

Constance watched her silently. A datum, she thought; that was all that was, another datum, not a reprieve.

"Tootles, knock it off," she said after another moment. "Why does Paul Volte accept any responsibility for Victoria's death? Does he believe that superstition? That each success must be paid for?"

Tootles became very quiet, as if she had fallen into a deep sleep with her eyes open. She seemed not to breathe, even.

"It's all through his book," Constance said impatiently. "He can't deny the book. But how strongly does he believe in what he wrote? Does Toni believe it? Do you?"

With a jerky motion Tootles jumped up and went to the porch

rail and stood holding it with both hands. Constance followed her to lean against the rail at her side. "Tell me about it," she said in a low voice. She glanced at Tootles, then turned her gaze away, toward the trees, the sky, anywhere but the woman holding the porch together, possibly holding her own world together with white-knuckled fingers.

"You remember how it was in the sixties?" Tootles said in a rush. "How poor we all were? At the beginning, how poor we were. But did you know that a few of my things had already been well received, well reviewed? It wasn't much, no money involved, there seldom is in art. At least, I never expected money from it. That didn't matter, I was on my way." Her voice had dropped lower and lower, and had become hoarse, almost a whisper. "I had the gift," she said. "Ba Ba knows; she was there when it happened. I had it, and I was on my way. I didn't know what the price would be. Ed and I got married and came down here. Remember? My God, Ed was the only man I've ever loved like that, with innocence and passion in equal amounts, and enough awareness to know what you're doing! My first real love. You can't have it twice, can you? He was a beautiful man, beautiful." She stopped speaking, gazing straight ahead, her hands white on the rail, the muscles in her forearms like knotted ropes.

"Then Ed died. My first show was up in Spence's gallery. My first real success, something else you can have only once." She laughed harshly. "That's when I learned the price. Ed got killed in a stupid wreck. Later that year I married Spence. Remember? Everyone was so shocked that my grief didn't last longer. It was a marriage of convenience, as the saying goes. I would be safe with a man I didn't love. Or more to the point *he* would be safe. He was great in bed, maybe the best fuck I've had—something to be said about doing it without love, I mean if there's a real interest there. Anyway, I could go on making things, doing good work, and we'd both be safe; no one would be at risk. What a deal!

"Spence was good for me," she said after a moment, much quieter. "He was a good guide, a good critic for me. But he began to notice that he was the one doing all the loving." She shrugged again and turned to look at Constance. At that moment she looked to be a hundred years old.

"I began to see other men," she said deliberately. "And along in there I met Paul and a friend of his, Gray Axton. They came down together the first time. Gray Axton," she repeated. Tiredly she thrust her hands in her pockets and walked back to the chairs and sat down, her legs sprawled out, her chin sunken against her collarbone, scowling into the distance. Constance trailed after her and resumed her seat. "Gray was the second Ed for me, the second chance at love, all that mushy stuff," Tootles said; her voice had gone very flat. "It wasn't the same, not the thing I'd had with Ed, nothing could have matched that, but I fell hard, and so did he. He was a painter, and damn good. Spence was excited about his work. And Spence never made a fuss about him and me, or anything else. He just moved out, back to his Washington place. After a few months with Gray I finished *Seven Kinds of Death,* and he went to Vietnam. Back in 1972, winter. My piece made the National Gallery, and Gray was killed."

She ended it in such an uninflected tone that it was another few seconds before Constance realized that without prodding Tootles would stop there. Constance leaned forward. "You believe, that's what the point of the story is, I take it." She kept all compassion out of her voice, all warmth, allowed only an intellectual curiosity to come through.

Tootles looked at her with dull anger now. "Yes, damn it! I believe! You stick your damn hand in the fire once and you learn something about pain; do it again and learn something about idiocy. Ed was the first one that I knew about, knew I was responsible for. Poor Mitch Phillips was the first, before Ed even. But I thought he just died; people did now and then. We were eighteen, and he died the same week I was accepted as a student by the New School of Fine Art in New York. I didn't make the connection, not until years later. I made it right away with Ed, and with Gray. Yes, damn you, I believe! So does Paul. As for Toni, ask her!"

"Hm, I don't understand," Constance said after a moment. "If you had it at eighteen, why didn't Ba Ba know it and make it clear then? Why didn't you understand for years?"

Tootles sighed theatrically. "She developed her gift later. I mean, for God's sake, when I was eighteen, she was just fifteen! She got in touch with . . . with whatever it is after she came to live with me in New York. She was eighteen by then. And Mitch had been dead for years. It just didn't come up. I mean, there were other men, but . . . you know what was going on in the early sixties. It didn't mean much."

"Hm," Constance hmmed again. "So after Gray, there was Walter. Is that right? Where's Walter now?"

"God knows. But let's get this straight. After Gray there were a lot of guys. A whole lot. And none of them meant shit to me. Now, we can move on to Walter. It was fun with him. You know he dug for gold back by the brook? And he built onto the house as if he thought he was Noah, and this was the Ark, and the water was rising. We learned to hang glide together. Fun. That was Walt. Just plain old fun. He sort of drifted away after a while. No surprise; we both knew he would one day."

"And now there's Max," Constance said quietly. "He really cares for you."

"I know," Tootles said, and then she threw her head back and laughed as raucously as a teenage boy. "You know what he said to me? Bastard. He said it turned him on to see a woman my age with dirty feet. The first time we met, I guess I had dirty feet. I don't remember." Her voice was affectionate, and her face had become soft; almost instantly she had shed the years that pain had put on her face just moments earlier. "He said he never had met anyone like me before. I bet the bastard didn't."

Constance nodded. "Did you ever even consider that the deaths might all have been simple coincidence?"

Tootles sounded mocking now when she said, "Isn't that the first explanation a sane person would consider? Sure I did. And Paul has done the same thing. Everyone does."

"Why are you afraid for Max?" Constance asked, still quietly, still being a professional, not the life-long personal friend who might have yielded to sympathy or impatience by now. "In spite of yourself, did you come to care for him?"

Tootles was startled by the question apparently. She snapped her head around to glare at Constance. "Don't be stupid," she snapped. "You don't know what you're talking about."

"I know. That's why I asked. If you really believe in the curse, or gift, whatever you call it, you must be afraid to love him. Afraid you'll lose him maybe. You begged me to come here for something; is that it? To get you out from under this curse? Are you afraid for Max?"

"I'm not afraid of anything. Period." She stood up.

"Just one more thing," Constance said, standing up also. She was taller than Tootles. As a professional psychologist she rarely would have put herself in a position where she would actually look down on a client or a patient; a few minutes earlier she had leaned against the rail in order to maintain equal eye height, but now she drew herself very straight and tall quite deliberately, forcing Tootles to look up. "When you left the party, what did you do? Minute by minute."

Tootles made an impatient gesture, as if she would sweep the question aside if she could. "I've told it over and over. I went up and changed my clothes and went out on the upper deck, down the outside stairs, up the driveway to the road, across the road to the path, and on to the little house, where I sat down for a few minutes, and then walked home again."

Constance was following this with her head tilted, frowning slightly. "I just don't see why," she murmured, as if to herself. "You wanted to be alone, that I can understand, but why so far? Altogether that's a two-mile walk. Why? You could have gone down to the brook. Or you could have just stayed on the sun roof. Or in your room."

"Aren't you leaving out one of the other things I could have done?" Tootles snapped. "I could have hurried over to the condo to kill Victoria Leeds."

Constance shook her head. "No. I don't think so. I mean, I don't know who killed her, but I don't think you could have got over there that quickly and then back again by eight. Do you have a dirt bike, something like that that you could ride through the woods?"

"Jesus! No!"

"Where did you go?" Constance asked, just as if they had agreed that Tootles would now answer. "Not the retreat a mile away. Where?"

"I told you," Tootles said harshly, breathing too fast, too shallowly. "I told everyone. I have things to see to. So long, Constance." She wheeled and reentered the house, nearly running.

Constance watched her go; she hoped Charlie was having more success at the condo than she was having.

————

Twice, at least, Charlie had hoped the same thing about her, that she was getting something worthwhile from Tootles, because he wasn't getting a thing.

In a few minutes he had an appointment with the construction superintendent, Thomas Ditmar, who was in a trailer office near Building C. Someone could have climbed over the fence, Charlie was thinking moodily. No marks, no grappling lines, no indentations of ladder feet, nothing to show that they did, but it was still possible. Someone could have come up from the river, he went on, scowling now. No mud, no messed-up banks, no trace of mud found in the building, but it was possible. Someone could have been dropped in by an eagle, he thought then. Right.

He had talked to the painters, who confirmed Johnny's story; he had sent them home a little after four-thirty. They had come back to finish up on Saturday. They had put the panels on the elevator doors, finished the stripes on the floor for parking spaces. They had not gone up to Six A; what for? They had washed up their brushes, gathered the buckets and stuff and put everything away in the sub-basement, and they were done.

Charlie looked at the sub-basement, full of heating equipment and plumbing, and individual storage compartments for the tenants. The brushes were there, dry and clean: rollers, small finish brushes, large ones. The paint was there, and tarps. Stencils for the door numbers and for the numbers on the storage compartments that were as big as commercial ministorage units. Like them, these compartments were metal, rows of them, with four-foot aisles between them, all neatly numbered.

He inspected the scene of the death again. She had entered the living room, he decided, had gone in several feet and had been attacked from behind. The killer had been there already, he thought, waiting for her. You need a little bit of distance to reach out and put a rope around someone's neck; if they had come in together, it would have been hard, unless the killer had hung back, let her get to the right distance. Someone could have said, go have a look out the windows. Great view. Then the rope over her head, jerked tight, no time for her to try to run or even to try to turn around. He remembered what Bill Gruenwald had said: she had tried to crawl away.

He walked through the apartment, dissatisfied. The police had taken the typewriter, but some tarps were still on the long table, still in the dining room, on the floor and on the table there. The police had taken the one she had grabbed and pulled partway off the table. He went to the window and looked out over the river and the woods. It seemed a wilderness out there. Finally, still dissatisfied, he left the apartment.

"Thomas Ditmar," the man said, in the doorway of the trailer. He was built like an elephant, thick in every dimension, very powerful looking. His hair was sandy colored and fine, his eyes clear, pale brown, his skin weathered to a deep brown.

They shook hands and he stepped aside for Charlie to enter the room he was using as an office.

"Max says you're hired on to clear up this goddam mess," Thomas Ditmar said. "I hope to God you do, and do it quick. We had goddam reporters messing around this morning. Reporters!"

The trailer was small for a mobile home, but large enough for a comfortable office. A coffeemaker on a counter was nearly full; half a dozen mugs were upside down on paper towels near it. A gray corduroy sofa, two small matching chairs, a table, and a desk with a computer were the furnishings. The table was covered with blueprints and pencils, pens in a mug, note pads, drafting paper. . . . The tiny kitchen was super efficient, it seemed, with everything built in and nothing used, from all appearances, except the sink, where more mugs were draining.

Ditmar poured coffee for them both and sat down on the sofa, cradling his mug in both hands. "Max says you'll ask questions. I'll answer. Your turn."

Charlie laughed and took one of the small chairs; to his surprise it was very comfortable. "That makes it sound pretty neat," he said. "Like erecting a building. Get the plans, the site, the materials, and up it goes. No problems."

Ditmar grunted and shook his head. "Always problems. That's what life's all about, solving them. But my problems usually have solutions. Think this one does?"

Charlie shrugged. "Always a solution, sometimes you just don't find it. History corrects the mistake you made, sometimes. Been with Max long?"

"Ever since he went into this business, twenty-eight years."

"So you're the last one to ask what's wrong with him," Charlie murmured.

"Nothing is," Ditmar said matter-of-factly.

"What I mean," Charlie said. "Know his wife?"

"Yep. Best thing ever happened to Max."

"Knew his previous wife, too?"

"Yep. A very good lady, very, very good lady. Gone to her just rewards in heaven, at God's right elbow, no doubt." Nothing at all changed in his voice; his eyes did not sparkle with amusement, no laugh lines deepened, but it was there.

"Making sure he stays on the straight and narrow?" Charlie asked lazily. Ditmar nodded, and finally a gleam of amusement lighted his eyes. "What about Johnny Buell?" Charlie asked.

"Learning the business the way he should. Not half the man his father is, but Max wasn't half the man at that age, either. He'll be all right."

"Will you keep on with the company if Max retires, turns it over to Johnny?"

"Nope."

"Look, Mr. Ditmar," Charlie said then, "I don't know what the hell I'm after. Just talk, okay? I mean, I could ask you simple questions all afternoon and get nowhere, because I don't know where I want to go yet. For instance, what's with you and Johnny?"

Thomas Ditmar regarded him for several seconds in silence. At last he said, "You retired, from the New York police department, something like that? Isn't that right?"

"Yep."

Ditmar grinned and nodded. "Okay, then you know. You do things one way all your life, a pretty good way it looks to be, and then someone comes along and says that's hokey, from now on we do it this way. No harm intended, you understand, just different ways. You must have seen it in your field. I know damn well doctors know what I mean. When Max wraps it up, so will I. Tired, ready to retire, hit the road off-season, leave winter behind a couple of years, head for mountains when it gets hot, do things like that, things I never could do before. Not ready to learn my trade all over again. There's plenty others ready and able to step in and run with it."

"How bad is it with Johnny?" Charlie asked. He understood exactly what Ditmar was talking about.

"Not bad at all. Max is still in charge. It's a good company, one of the best, some of the best construction anywhere around, never lost a penny of anyone's money, good times or bad, but things change. That's all. Things change. You ever try to draw building plans on a computer?" Charlie shook his head; Ditmar did, too. "And I don't aim to learn now. Max never wanted a company so big he couldn't oversee everything personally; Johnny's already planning to expand, get managers, go public maybe. Max never would have thought of trying to get a big write-up, not without paying for it. You know, advertising. Different philosophies, that's all. Max leaves, so do I."

"Is Max planning to leave?"

For a second or two Ditmar regarded him without expression. Then he shrugged. "Eventually. Won't we all?"

"This is his last job maybe?" Charlie had no idea about this; a random shot, he thought, no more than that.

"If you already know that, there's not much more I can add," Ditmar said. "It'll take close to a year to finish up here, and then . . . let Johnny diaper the baby, I guess." He shrugged. "This is his solo flight, with the instructor in the next seat, but next time out, no copilot, just him, if he's ready." He examined Charlie closely. "Let me ask something, Mr. Meiklejohn. This have anything to do with the killing?"

Charlie had to admit probably not. "What I really need is a way to get someone in that building and out again past your watchman, Pierce. And so far, no dice."

"What times you looking for?"

"Between seven-ten and about seven-thirty."

Ditmar shook his head. "Johnny and his gang, then Pierce was on this side, closing the gate, things like that. I left the party with my wife and a friend of ours at ten after seven. Johnny pulled out of the complex in front of us, and I turned in at the parking lot over there and we had a little discussion about looking around. Decided not to, not until another building is finished, but we were there until twenty after seven probably, maybe a little longer if you count the time we had to wait for traffic to clear so's I could enter the road again. Lots of folks were leaving the party along about then, you know. Fifteen, twenty cars must have gone by while we sat there."

Charlie stared at him, aghast. "Jesus Christ! Have you told the sheriff?"

"Nope. Haven't been asked."

Charlie thought of the two scenarios he had come up with so far: one in which Victoria and her killer entered the building while Johnny and his group were all up on six. That one didn't explain how they had got into the apartment on six, but at least they were in the building. And the other was the little scenario in which Johnny left his friends for five minutes in order to return to Six A to kill Victoria Leeds (who had obligingly set herself up for him without a sound), and then drove his girlfriend and her pals back to Washington to have dinner, and do a little screwing, he added darkly.

At this moment one or the other seemed to be the only one that would work at all.

12

Charlie had walked to the condos from Tootles's house, and now as he left the trailer/office to start the trek back, he saw Johnny Buell coming forward to meet him. Johnny was wearing good-looking tan work pants, a matching shirt, and a hardhat. He could have been dressed for an ad for an expensive liquor, or a sports car. He looked a lot like the boss's son.

"How's it going?" he asked, falling into step with Charlie.

"About what you expect this early. How many people have keys to the gate?"

Johnny looked startled, then thoughtful. Finally he said, "Damned if I know. Various foremen, Ditmar, of course. Dad. I do. Maybe Marion, but I sort of doubt that. Why would she? Pierce. Half a dozen, a dozen at the most."

"How about the computer card keys?"

"Maybe the same list, with a few additions. I know Marion

has one to the sixth-floor unit. She's been in and out, picking out colors, drapes, that sort of thing. Ditmar has them all, and I do. I guess Dad does, too. A few others."

In other words, a bust, Charlie thought regretfully. Too many people with access. They had come to Building A. One of the workmen had already explained the building designation: A is for Applegate, first in the row. B is for Birmingham, upscale, don't you know? C is for Carlton, Rich, rich, rich, rich; D is for Davenport, a son of a bitch. E is for Ethridge, first among peers. F is for Farmington, or maybe for fears. Charlie thought the workers did not take the project quite as seriously as Johnny did.

He paused at the grillwork gate to the below-ground parking section. The gate was open now. "When you drove out on Friday, did you close both gates?"

"Sure. The system's electronic. Going in, the thing closed after me, and coming out I just touched the button and it slid down when I drove up to the street level. I went back inside on the first floor."

Charlie walked into the lobby at street level; the dedicated elevators with brass numbers lined the wall to his left, flanked by the door to the stairwell, broom closets, whatever. . . . He walked to the center of the building and gazed down the long corridor, with another bank of regular elevators at the far end, and apartment doors in between. "Are the rooms all kept locked?" he asked Johnny, who had remained at the entrance.

Johnny said they were, and Charlie sighed and shrugged. So it would take more computer card keys to enter them. He walked back to the front of the building. "Okay. See you later. Thanks." He continued to walk toward the gate. It was open during working hours; trucks came and went, workmen came and left, there was a steady flow of traffic in and out. It had been open on Friday until Johnny closed it when he left to pick up Debra Saltzman and her friends, five-thirty or thereabouts. The train had arrived at five-forty and Johnny was waiting for it. So, he followed the thought, Victoria Leeds could have entered the grounds before five-thirty without being seen. All right, he mocked himself. Now tell us why, Mr. Bones. Step one, and then step two, he told himself firmly.

He went through the gate and came to a stop at the edge of

the road; a movement across the train tracks near the woods caught his eye. When he looked more carefully, the scowl on his forehead vanished and he smiled broadly. It was purely reflexive. Constance had stepped from behind the trees, and was walking toward him. Seeing her unexpectedly usually gave him a jolt of pleasure like this. He quickened his steps to meet her on the other side of the train tracks.

She held out both hands to him, and he kissed her lightly before they turned toward the woods. "Anything?" he asked.

She shrugged. "I was trying to put myself in Tootles's place," she said. They had reached the trees, where she stopped to look back at the road. "It's Friday evening, and I am tired of the party, and want people to go home. I go upstairs and change my clothes, go out by way of the sun deck, dodging anyone who might be outside smoking or something. Across the road, and then through the woods to the little retreat. So far, okay. It's fifteen, twenty minutes after seven. I can get this far, but then I'm stumped, why didn't someone see me?" She eyed the train tracks, the road, the condos across the road. "There's just no cover at all. And people certainly were driving by at that time."

They stood together looking at the clearing maintained by the railway, twenty feet on both sides of the tracks at least, then the state road with the cleared shoulders, and then the condo complex. No cover. He told her about Ditmar. "He sat there waiting to enter the road until twenty-five after seven probably. They were still coming out of the dirt road when he finally took off. I'm just glad that's not our chore—to interview all the guests and find out if anyone saw anything." He sounded glum and not at all hopeful.

They started to walk through the woods now, holding hands. It was very warm, no wind stirred, and the humidity was climbing. Summer had arrived without fanfare, simply heating everything, sweating everything. The woods seemed unnaturally quiet.

"I think it's time to look beyond our little circle of old buddies," Charlie said.

"New York," she said unhappily. "Charlie, I don't have a thing to wear for New York. And from the glimpse I got of your suitcase, neither do you."

He laughed. "When we lived in the city, you would go out

dressed exactly like you are now and think nothing of it. I think you look great." She was wearing tan slacks and a pale blue shirt, a red belt, red sandals. She looked wonderful to him. No matter what came up, what they did, she was always dressed exactly right for it.

"That's different," she said patiently. "If you live there you can dress casually, do whatever you want, but if you go there from outside you have to dress differently."

"Why?"

"Because."

"Okay," Charlie said later; after half a dozen phone calls he was now driving the rental car in to Washington. "I'll go to the precinct house and go through the stuff they hauled in from the publishing office. Since the BB's have the case, no problem there." The BB's were Bergdorf and Beckman; Charlie had known them for many years. "And while I'm doing that, you can talk to the people at Magnum Publishing. How's that sound?" She hated the precinct stations. "Then we meet at Phil's, do something about dinner, and crash. And tomorrow go together to see her apartment."

"Not okay. Not quite. First I go shopping. A power suit, maybe," she said with a thoughtful expression. "And a shirt for you. Anything else?"

"You might pick up a toothbrush for me," he said, paying close attention to a semi that wanted to pass, but not enough to go ahead and do it.

"You forgot your toothbrush?" There was a note of disbelief in her voice.

"It's okay," he said quickly. The truck driver had given up and was back doing a sedate seventy-five. "I've been using yours."

"Charlie! You haven't!"

He looked at her, startled. "All right. I haven't."

"But you have, haven't you?"

"Which do you want, yes or no?"

She turned to look at the passing scenery. If she had turned any further, he thought, she would have broken her neck.

At four that afternoon Constance walked into the office of Lewis Goldstein at Magnum Publishers. "It was good of you to see me on such short notice," she said, shaking his hand. "I appreciate it."

"Not at all. Not at all. Please, sit down. Poor Victoria. Such a shock. I just can't quite believe it, you know?"

He was a handsome man in his fifties, well tanned, with beautiful silver hair that was thick and lush looking, gleaming. His office was small, much like other editors' offices that she had seen, with stacks of manuscripts, baskets of unanswered correspondence, boxes of manila envelopes, few of them opened. A wall calender displayed an icky May—illustrated by a big-eyed child sniffing a buttercup.

"Had you known her very long?" Constance asked.

"Years and years. We offered her a job here over a year ago, my suggestion. She was a superb editor. Just super."

"She was the magazine editor of Paul Volte's book, I understand. Were you the book editor?"

He nodded, beaming. "A delightful book, purely delightful, wasn't it? She did a wonderful job helping him develop the material, guiding it all along the way. That's what she was so good at. What a tragic loss."

"Did you work together?"

"No, not really. She came here in the middle of May, along about then, and I was gone for nearly ten days in late May. Of course, Paul's book was through production many months before that, while she was still at the magazine. But people acknowledged her role in the tremendous success of the project. A few proposals followed her here from the magazine, things of that sort. People had been stirred by the articles, her work. We expected very good things from her. Such a tragic loss!"

"Were the things that came after her the result of Paul's articles? How could you tell?"

"Well," he said, his broad smile returning, "at least one of them made it abundantly clear. It was addressed to the magazine, to the attention of the editor of Paul Volte's articles. Right there on the envelope."

She smiled ruefully. "That would seem to be clear enough. If it was addressed to the magazine, why did it come here?"

"You know, everyone believes editors pounce on the mail carrier, can't wait to get their hot hands on the treasures they know will be delivered. It isn't like that. Probably when that manuscript turned up it got handed around like a hot potato for a while before Sammy got the bright idea of forwarding it to Victoria. It must have been delivered to the magazine while she was on vacation, before she started working here, or she would have returned it herself then."

"Sammy?"

"Sam Stover. He's at *New World*. He might know something about that manuscript, if you think it's important. I can't imagine why it would be, though. One of thirty thousand that pour in year after year."

She didn't point out that she had not led him to this digression about the manuscript; she had followed, and it now occurred to her to wonder why it had stuck in his mind if it was one of such a great number. "What was unusual about the manuscript?" she asked, taking it for granted something had been, inviting him to take that for granted also.

"Not the manuscript. At least, as far as I know. I never saw it. See, we put it on her desk here as sort of a joke, that and a pile of other stuff, all to be taken care of instantly. A joke. Make her feel as if she was already one of the gang here. But for some reason she singled out that one to respond to. I never saw the proposal, and maybe it was great, but it surprised me that she read it and wrote the guy a note or something. A hell of an editor," he said, and for the first time Constance had the feeling that he meant it.

He said he didn't know why she had gone to the party. He had never even heard of Marion Olsen. He had suspected that Victoria was getting together again with Paul, and he had hoped that was the case, but she had not mentioned any of that to him. In fact, they had said hello in the corridors that last week or so, and that was the only contact they had with each other.

Matter of factly, she asked him where he had been the weekend of the party, and after a pause that held a mixture of disbelief and outrage, he answered. Sailing with two authors and their wives, over to Connecticut. She thanked him nicely and he was excessively polite when he stood up to see her out.

At the door she paused to ask, "Did Victoria have a secretary here, or an assistant? I'd like to ask that person a question or two."

That person turned out to be Beverly Swandon, a plump

young woman with dimples in both cheeks and very curly hair of an improbable chestnut color.

"I remember that manuscript, you better believe. Some joke, loading up her desk like that! As if it wouldn't happen in the normal course of events, you know? But that manuscript that came from Sam Stover, from some nerd out in the boonies. I remember because this guy sends in the manuscript and a week after that he moves, and begins to make phone calls to get his right address on the return envelope. I mean, come on, you don't know you're going to move a week in advance? Yeah. You never heard that the post office will forward mail? Right. But Victoria Leeds took it like a lady and she even wrote him a little note when she sent it back."

"He called here? When? What name did he give?"

"Not here. He called Sam Stover. Anyway, Stover called Ms. Leeds and told her the right address. I never heard a name."

"And she rejected the manuscript?"

Beverly Swandon shook her head. "She put a note on it, something like if he fixed it up, wanted to talk about it in the future, to let her see it again. Anyway, the note was on her memo, you know? 'From-the-desk-of' kind of thing. She didn't put his name on it, just wrote out the couple of lines and clipped it to the manuscript. That's why I never saw a name, I guess. I had to make out a label with the new address. I remember that part. A Washington, D.C., box number. I stuck it over his old address."

"You must have seen his name on the envelope?"

Beverly shook her head; she had reached the limits of her memory, the name eluded her.

It was getting close to five, Constance realized, and she asked Beverly about the rest of the time Victoria had worked here. There was very little beyond the fact that Beverly had liked her a lot, a whole lot, she repeated. She didn't know anything about the party, why Victoria had gone, who Marion Olsen was, or even when Victoria decided to go. She had simply said she wouldn't be in on Friday, and then they found out that she had gone off and got herself killed.

No one should have to be in New York at five in the afternoon, Constance thought a few minutes later, standing outside the

building that housed Magnum Publishers. She was on East
Tenth; Phil Stern lived on West Fourteenth. As far as she could
see there were people, walking, Rollerblading, on bikes, in
trucks, in buses, in taxis, even in private cars that were virtually
gridlocked. People running for the next bus, for the subway entrance, pushing, and creating a strange constant noise that was
partly roar, partly high-pitched voices, brakes squealing, horns
blaring, voices shouting, cursing, singing, even a cornet from
somewhere seemed to belong to the overall sound. She started
to walk. An image presented itself to her mind. She had seen a
cloud of smelts moving up a river once, heading they did not
know where, for a reason they could not explain, but determined. Yes, determined. She walked briskly.

One of Phil Stern's little jokes was that he and Charlie had gone
to school together, and then he had gone into insurance and
Charlie had gone to blazes. Charlie assumed a patient expression; Constance smiled politely; his wife, Alicia, ignored him, but
on the whole the evening was pleasant. Everyone went to bed
early.

Charlie had found out even less than she had, and he had a
long list of names of Victoria's friends and acquaintances. They
both regarded the list with resignation the next morning at
breakfast. They had dawdled in their room until Phil and Alicia
were gone; now they had the lovely old apartment to themselves. Phil had kept this rent-controlled apartment for nearly
thirty years, and it was as fine as ever, even if the windows were
dirty and the woodwork needed a new coat of paint. The rooms
were large and bright with oversized windows, the ceilings were
high, the walls were thick, and it was very quiet.

"Beckman told jokes," Charlie said. Constance groaned in
commiseration. Beckman told the world's filthiest jokes, it was
generally conceded. No one laughed but Beckman.

"There won't be an investigation here?" she had asked in surprise last night, but she understood why not. As far as the city
was concerned, Victoria Leeds was Maryland's problem. New
York would gather up her belongings and ship them off to her
family; case closed. They would hang on to stuff for a time, just
in case Maryland sent someone up to look through things; no
one had objected to Charlie's going through the stuff they had

collected from her office. For all he had gained, he might just as well have stayed in bed, he had added, recounting his day.

"Bergdorf's thinking about retirement. Says they'll raise goats."

"Goats? Does he know anything about goats? Why goats?"

"He likes their eyes. You know, the pupils. He thinks they're really aliens, and they can only see in straight lines, bands, or something like that."

She studied him narrowly. "You're kidding me," she said.

He shook his head. "That's what I said to Bergdorf, but he swore he intends to retire and keep goats. Alien goats!"

She laughed, and after a moment he joined her.

They both went to see Sam Stover, who turned out to be nearly seventy, nearly bald, and dressed in a seersucker suit. Charlie stared at it in awe. He had not seen a seersucker suit for twenty-five years, thirty years. Actually, he couldn't remember if he had ever seen a blue-and-white seersucker suit. It was something you just knew about, learned at your grandfather's knee.

"I'll do anything I can to help you," Sam Stover said. "Victoria was a very special person, very dear to me." He motioned to two chairs that looked as if they belonged in a high school from the turn of the century, heavy, ugly oak, much scarred, and polished from use. He sat behind a desk that was piled high with papers.

Sam Stover was precise in everything he said. He spoke slowly, choosing his words with care, and it appeared that he had never forgotten a thing in his life. He talked at great length about Victoria, how she had been his protégée, his assistant, then his junior colleague, and finally his peer. There had been no enemies, he said firmly; she had not been the type to make enemies. She had been a true professional; any number of careers had been advanced through her efforts with the writers. "It was a good thing for her to move on," he said. "She would have had an illustrious career in book publishing. The magazine, you understand, has been bought out by a Japanese filmmaker, or something of the sort."

He knew exactly what he meant by "of the sort," and it came through as contempt, scorn, derision, beneath civilized consideration. The unspoken words were eloquently expressed in his gesture, the haughty look he assumed.

Charlie finally got around to the last weeks Victoria had been with the magazine, and then the period after she had left. He asked about the manuscript Stover had forwarded to her. "What do you generally do with manuscripts addressed to editors who have left? Is it customary to forward them?"

"Not customary. Not at all. Generally we treat them exactly the same as any other submissions. The publishing world of the magazine is quite different from that of books, naturally. What might be suitable for one would be unsuitable for the other without a great deal of work. But this manuscript, addressed so precisely to the editor of Paul Volte's series, was obviously not meant for anyone else. If there had been even a chance of our taking it, I might have opened it to have a look, but of course, there wasn't."

"Why do you say, 'of course'?"

"Several reasons. One is that we so seldom accept anything that comes in over the transom. That is, freelance, unsolicited, unagented. Life is too short," he added in a brusque tone. "Second, since this person referred to Paul's work, it was to be presumed that the enclosed proposal somehow resembled that, or why draw attention to it, why suggest the same editor should see the new material? We would never have run a second article that in any way resembled such a fine piece as Paul's. Not for many years, anyway, but few on the outside would have known that. And finally, Victoria developed the material with Paul, you understand, and it was possible that the proposal might have been worth her time to develop with this unknown author. That's always a possibility, however remote. It was her option to read it, to send it back unopened, or to pass it on to her first reader, or whatever."

"Lewis Goldstein suggested you might just have wanted to get rid of it, and that was a convenient way, to forward it to Victoria Leeds," Constance murmured.

"Lewis Goldstein is an ass. It would have been easier to put it in the stamped return envelope and send it back to the writer the day it arrived."

"When did the writer call you?" Charlie asked.

"I can't be certain. I think we received the manuscript soon after Victoria left, or she would have handled it herself. Her last day here was the thirtieth of April. I'm certain I had already sent it on to her when this man called me to have me change his address back in May." His voice had gone very dry. Obviously he had never been asked to do anything like that before. "He called and said that he had to have the manuscript back because he had discovered grave errors of fact."

He cleared his throat. "I'm afraid his name meant nothing to me; I had paid no attention to the name on the envelope. I mentioned that the United States Post Office department makes it a rule to forward mail for quite a long time, and he became agitated. I assumed at the time that domestic problems had arisen for him, necessitating the post office box number, and the likelihood was that he would never see the manuscript again if it was delivered to his home address. Therefore, I told him that if it turned up, we would send it to the new address, and that he should write me a letter with that address. He insisted on giving it over the phone, and I jotted it down. It didn't even occur to me to tell him Victoria had moved over to Magnum Publishers. I knew she was out of town, for one thing, but that really was not the reason. I simply didn't think of it. Later, after her return, while we were on the phone I told her about the telephone call and the manuscript. It had already been sent on over to her. I keep a phone log of my outgoing calls; I talked to her on June ninth. I gave her the new address at that time."

It was a miracle that it had ever surfaced again, Charlie thought, regarding the desk. "Had she read it yet?"

"She had. She said it was interesting, might have had something for her, and it was too bad if it had factual errors, but of course that would kill it. She said she would return it. She did not mention the contents, or the subject matter, no more than what I have just said."

"Who sent her the manuscript, Mr. Stover? What was the new address?" Charlie asked. There was no particular reason to pursue this business matter, but there was the remote chance that one of the crew at Tootles's house had lied about having had a contact with Victoria. There was even a chance that it could have had something to do with Paul Volte. Short of plagiarism, Charlie could not think of what that might be, however.

"I thought you might want to know," Sam Stover said and opened a desk drawer. "Naturally I found it for you." He handed a slip of paper to Charlie. The handwriting was elegant and very legible. The name written there was David Musselman.

At two that afternoon they met Sergeant Michael Pressger at the Eighty-ninth Street apartment that Victoria Leeds had leased for the past twelve years. The sergeant was young and very eager. He wanted to rise through the ranks fast, Charlie decided, fending him off as he moved in too close, watching every motion through narrowed eyes, memorizing everything Charlie did, everything he said. No doubt he would re-create it all carefully later. Deliberately Charlie went to a window, studied the view, turned to study the room, even paced it off, and then grunted. The sergeant made a note. Constance glared at Charlie wordlessly; he looked innocent.

The apartment was clean, four rooms, cluttered with too much stuff, but all stowed away as well as the space had permitted. Books, manuscripts, correspondence made up most of the clutter. Two walls had book shelves from ceiling to floor. Her living room appeared to be an extension of her office. The bedroom was almost barren in contrast: a three-quarter-sized bed, chest of drawers, comfortable reading chair and lamp, and a small table laden with books of poetry and plays. In both the living room and the bedroom the tables had marks made by wet glasses, and there was a burn mark on the coffee table in the living room. Constance nodded; just as she had suspected. Victoria had been a wet-glass type. There was an incomplete needlepoint pillow top on the sofa, and a box of colored yarn strands and needles. The kitchen with eating space, and a utility room/second bedroom, finished the apartment. It was all comfortable; Victoria had accumulated things she liked over the years, nice prints on the walls, Monet, Chagall, a Turner; there was a good compact disc player—classical music, jazz; thriving geraniums in bloom lined a windowsill. Two needlepoint pillows on a chair in the second bedroom. . . . Charlie came to a complete stop in the living room before a bas-relief of a face, her face he assumed. He looked at Constance, who nodded.

"Good likeness?" he asked.

"Very. Idealized and romanticized, but she caught her. Toni's

work, I'm sure. She said she had done a study of Victoria's face."
She remembered that Toni had said Paul had bought a second
bas-relief identical to this one; she examined it more closely and
gradually became aware that the sergeant had moved in as Charlie moved away. The officer was breathing on her neck.

"You know anything about computers?" Charlie asked from
across the room, where he was standing at a desk with a computer system.

"A little," the sergeant said.

"I'd like to make a list of the files, not copy them all, just find
out what she was . . . oh, oh."

"What?" the sergeant asked, coming to the desk.

"Not sure. Maybe a gold mine. Look, she used a calendar
program." He was in a menu program, and keyed in the letter
for Calendar. It appeared quickly.

Charlie was able to read through the entries enough to see
that she had recorded: *call from M. Check Marion Olsen. Call
P*. The date of that entry was June 14. June 15 was the date of
her call to Paul Volte to invite herself to Tootles's party.

"I'd like a copy of everything on her calendar from mid-March
on," Charlie said to the sergeant then. He scanned the entries
following the one that had caught his attention. Everything
would need cross-referencing with the addresses in her files, in
her little black book.

"Guess I could make a printout right now," the sergeant said,
studying the layout of the computer and printer.

Charlie moved out of his way and in a minute the printer
blinked awake, cleared its throat, and rattled off several pages.
Charlie noticed without comment that the sergeant made two
copies.

After they left the apartment, Charlie said he wanted to talk to
an old buddy, Curt Mercer, who could very well do most of the
legwork involved in finding and talking to the many people
listed in Victoria's books. Constance nodded. "And I'm off to the
library," she said. "Meet you back at Phil's?"

"Library? What for?"

"They probably have some biographical stuff about Paul
Volte," she said vaguely. "Just curious, I guess."

Actually she wanted to find out when his various successes

had come about, and how many people close to him had died, or left him, and if the two events seemed linked in time. And this was the kind of thing, she well knew, that would be very hard to explain to Charlie. Not that she believed a word of it, either, she hastened to add to herself. Just curious. Very curious.

13

Charlie watched her climb the stairs to the library with a feeling of disquiet. Yesterday when they had gone their separate ways a surge of unease had caught him off guard, but now that had changed; unease had become a real fear. The library steps were crowded with people lounging, reading, eating lunch, watching others, doing nothing, hanging out, and he saw menace everywhere. The fact that they had lived in the city for most of their married life made no difference; the populace had not been armed with assault rifles then, he told himself, and ignored the mocking voice that said *then* was only a few years ago, remember; and, he went on in his silent monologue, murder *then* had been newsworthy, not just a filler on page fifty. As soon as she was out of sight, he started to walk.

He was still preoccupied with the danger of the city, not for him because he had grown up here; it held no more real surprises for him, and he knew it was irrational to be this fearful for Constance. He knew very well that if anyone ever tried to roughhouse Constance, she could easily flatten the guy without mussing a hair or breathing hard. She had studied aikido for many years, at his insistence, he added grimly to himself, and she kept in good shape, and worked out with other aikido partners when she had the chance. Their daughter was almost as good as Constance; he had nearly disgraced them and himself by bawling with pride the first time they had put on a public demonstration. He still remembered the hole he had chewed in his cheek to keep the tears back. But that was different. There was no self-defense against a bullet, or a thrown knife. He wondered if Victoria Leeds would have had a chance with years of self-defense training. A rope over the head, a quick upward yank against the carotids to bring almost instant unconsciousness. He doubted that anyone would have been able to fight back, even Constance with all her skills. He wanted them out of the city as fast as they could manage; he wanted her safe in their own house upstate.

He quickened his pace on his way to hire the help that would allow them to leave. Curt Mercer was a good man, reliable, plodding; he believed investigative work was supposed to be boring, and he accepted without question chores of the sort that Charlie intended to load on him: go see all these people and find out if any of them had known Victoria was going to the party, or why. Or if any of them had a suggestion about why she had been killed, or anything else that might be of help.

He was not happy about the vagueness of the assignment; he had learned that it was best to lay it out precisely: go find out if so-and-so was home Monday from ten to three. Anyone could ask the right questions and find out something like that, while what he was looking for was open, vague, subjective. But he was willing to give it to Curt because he didn't really believe there was anything to learn from her friends. Everyone so far had told the same story: she had not mentioned the party, had not mentioned meeting anyone in particular, had not mentioned anything out of ordinary. He suspected that would continue to be the case. Victoria Leeds had not been a gossip, had not talked much about herself apparently. He was starting to feel that he would have liked her quite a lot; he knew Constance felt that.

When he got back to Phil's apartment, he called Bill Gruenwald, whom he thought of as the tame, friendly sheriff. He gave him the name David Musselman, and the post office number, and they agreed cautiously that maybe they would now learn why Victoria had gone to the party just outside Washington. There was nothing else new, Gruenwald said glumly.

The medical examiner put death at no later than seven-thirty— he had not been able to narrow it more than that. She hadn't eaten anything all day, Gruenwald had said almost apologetically. And the air conditioner had been set to subarctic. Charlie knew enough about autopsies to know that sometimes if you got the year right you were ahead of the game.

He gave the sheriff Phil's number and hung up soon afterward. Then he started to pace.

Constance had been gone for longer than three hours, plenty long to look up Paul Volte. It was nearly five. She would be caught in the gridlock; and it was too far to walk. She wouldn't come by subway, he told himself. She wouldn't do anything that dumb. That's where the guys with the knives and guns were; she knew that. She probably wouldn't get there until after seven, eight. . . . Gruenwald called back.

"Charlie, this Musselman, you know anything about him?"

"Just give it to me," Charlie said in a tight voice. "What?"

"He's dead, Charlie. You know they had two accidents at the condo site? One involved some kids, but the other was a fatal accident. David Musselman fell off a sixth-floor structure and was killed instantly. I thought that name sounded familiar. Right there in the file."

Charlie asked very softly, "When was that, Bill?"

"May tenth." There was a brief silence, and then Gruenwald said, "Someone else has that box number now. Your turn, Charlie. Give."

Charlie told him about the manuscript. "And," he finished, "apparently Musselman called the magazine on about May tenth or eleventh to get the manuscript back. Exactly when did he rent that post office box?"

Gruenwald cursed. "I'll get back to you. When are you coming back down here?"

"Tomorrow," Charlie said. "Nine o'clock shuttle."

They made plans for Gruenwald to meet the plane, and then for the three of them to go see Musselman's widow; she lived in Chevy Chase. Charlie hung up, walked to the window, and stared out at the city, seeing little of it.

It was nearly six when Constance arrived; she was carrying a bag of groceries. Charlie met her at the door, took the bag from her arm and set it aside, and then drew her in close in a hard embrace.

"Hey," she said after a moment. "Wow!" She pulled back smiling, but her smile faded at the look on his face. "Charlie? What is it? What's wrong?"

He shook his head. "Nothing now. I kept seeing you getting mugged, getting thrown under the wheels of a bus, thrown down on the tracks in the subway station. Idle hands, idle minds, Satan's playground, or something like that."

"Oh, Charlie," she whispered. "Oh, Charlie."

"What's in the bag?" he asked then in a hearty voice. "And I learned something from Gruenwald that could blow our case sky-high again, whole new ball game maybe."

"Ingredients," she said, indicating the bag. "I decided to cook some dinner for Phil and Alicia. Least we can do. You know how much hotels cost here in New York these days, if you can get one on short notice?" She picked up the bag and started for the kitchen. "What did the sheriff say?"

There was a counter with stools in the kitchen; he seated himself out of the way and watched her unload the ingredients: a lovely salmon, lingonberries, sour cream, horseradish. . . . Lingonberries, he realized, meant blintzes. His look was reverential when he turned again to her.

"Well?" she asked.

"Well, it seems that Mr. Musselman died on May tenth, for openers. And he worked at the Buell condo complex. He was the fatality we heard about, the reason for tight security now."

She was frowning at him, her hands motionless over the salmon that she had been anointing with lime juice. "May tenth? But isn't that about when he sent the manuscript to the magazine, and when he called? Are those dates all right?"

"I don't know yet. But it makes for an interesting twist. I think we've found the reason for Victoria's party crashing. And she must not have thought he was dead. She returned the manuscript in June, remember, to the post office box."

"Presumably someone collected it," Constance said in a low voice. "Or else it's still there."

He shook his head. "Box is closed out, new tenants."

Phil and Alicia arrived then, and they joined Charlie at the counter, where they had drinks and offered advice to Constance about knives, spices, the location of proper pans and skillets, and she was spared either dodging Charlie's inevitable questions about what she had learned, or else out-and-out lying about it. She knew she was a pretty good dodger, and an incompetent liar.

It had shaken her terribly to see fear on Charlie's face when he caught her up in his arms earlier. He said fear of the dangers of the city, and although that might be what he believed, she did not believe it. They had spent too many years living here for such terror to surface now. But he had been afraid; she had felt his heart thumping, had felt the tremor in his hands when he pulled her to him. At the moment he was laughing at something Phil had just said, the fear pushed out of mind again, so far back that now it would be possible to believe that earlier there had been a simple aberration, a twinge of indigestion, or something equally fleeting and benign. Now it would be impossible to bring it up and talk about it. What fear? he would drawl lazily. Hungry, that's what I was.

It had something to do with Tootles and Ba Ba and that ancient silly Ouija incident, she felt certain. He had buried that, had never breathed a word of it before, but it had soured him for all these years on Tootles and Ba Ba, and had created in him a dread, even a terror that was surfacing now. The fear was inappropriate, out of time, out of place, but that was what made phobias so powerful, their very inappropriateness. Not that this was a phobia, she told herself quickly, well aware that it could turn into one, a phobia that could make an otherwise rational person behave in ways so irrational that treatment could be required. This was an irrational fear that had to be denied, and denial was achieved by transferring the fear away from the self to the other; he feared for her because he could not accept or even examine what had frightened him so badly many years ago.

She thought through this while she prepared the dinner, and chatted with their hosts, and then served and ate the dinner, which everyone agreed was delicious.

As she was drifting off to sleep that night, Constance was jarred wide awake when Charlie grunted and cursed.

"What?" she demanded. "Too many blintzes, too much horseradish in the sauce?"

"What Victoria Leeds said, interpreted by Janet Cuprillo, something about a proposal from a jock. I just got it."

After a second she shivered and groaned. He put his arm around her and drew her close and eventually they fell asleep entwined.

When Bill Gruenwald met them at the terminal in Washington
the next morning, he looked so thoroughly scrubbed, he seemed
to shine. Before the handshaking was completed, he said dourly,
"He rented the box May eleventh."

"Oh," Charlie said with great interest. "Busy day for Mr. Musselman, what with the funeral and all."

"You got it," Gruenwald said. "I'm parked over this way."

Someone calling himself David Musselman had rented a post
office box at the main post office on May eleventh and had kept
it until June twelfth. According to Victoria Leeds's assistant, the
manuscript had been put in the mail to be returned on June
eighth, a Friday. And on June twelfth, someone collected the
mail, and turned in the key, Gruenwald said. No one remembered a thing about him. He had put the key in an envelope and
left it in the box with a typed note saying he no longer needed
it. They hadn't bothered to keep the note, why should anyone?
Gruenwald scowled.

"Once he knew who he was dealing with, he didn't need to
write letters," Charlie said. "And he did call, apparently, on June
fourteenth. Told her to invite herself to the bash, I bet, so they
could meet and talk over the proposal that weekend. And that
would explain Ms. Leeds's presence, and her ducking out for a
date with someone." A date with a ghost, he added silently, and
then instantly denied it. Someone who either claimed to be Musselman, or else claimed to represent him, probably.

Gruenwald drove with unconscious ease, and soon they were
nearing the Chevy Chase developments. "Mrs. Musselman," he
said in a rather flat tone, "has come into a neat little fortune,
couple hundred thousand, plus a settlement from the company.
Three kids, away with grandparents right now. She was having
trouble coping with meals and such." At the next intersection
he turned left, and pulled into a driveway. These houses were
all expensive, with acres of velvet grass, landscaping done by
expensive landscape designers, houses designed by fine architects. Very impressive, and somehow depressing, Charlie was
thinking as they followed the curve in the driveway to the front
entrance of the house. It looked like a set for a stylish Hollywood
movie and real people didn't live in Hollywood sets.

Diane Musselman would have been at home in a movie filmed

here. She was blond and pretty, dressed in a silk pantsuit. Her waist was tiny, her breasts and hips generous, a real hourglass figure, Charlie thought, shaking her hand. She carried a wisp of lacy handkerchief that she touched to her eyes now and then although her eyes were as dry as his. An image of the Barbie doll in Tootles's office swam up in his mind, and he struggled to erase it again.

"I know this is a terrible imposition," the sheriff was saying as she led them into the house, through a spacious foyer with many flowers in oversized vases, and on to a comfortable sitting room. It looked as if no one had entered it since the decorators left.

"I must help in any way possible," she said in a tremulous voice. "Please, if there's anything at all I can do, you must let me. I'll try." She was very brave.

"Yes," Gruenwald said. "Something has turned up that puzzles us. Did your husband ever do any writing? I mean articles for publication, books, things of that sort."

She shook her head, her eyes wide and bewildered.

"Did he have an office here in the house, a study, something like that?"

"Oh, yes. He did a lot of work at home."

She took them to the study, a large room with tan leather-covered chairs, a sofa, two desks, a drawing table . . . many books were on shelves here. One of the desks held an elaborate computer system, printer, a complicated-looking drawing machine. In here, as in the other rooms they had seen so far, everything was very neat.

Charlie and Bill Gruenwald exchanged glances, the gloom they had shared seemed to lift.

"Has anyone touched this equipment since your husband's accident?" Gruenwald asked.

"Someone must have," she said defensively. "Not me. I never set foot in here when he was alive, and I certainly didn't after he was gone. Never. But someone from his office came to get some files or something off the computer and he said everything was gone, erased, blanked out. I forget what he said. Gone. All gone."

Charlie let a sigh escape. He looked at Constance, who was watching Diane Musselman with a thoughtful expression. He knew Constance had not reached across the room to touch him between the shoulder blades, or made any other overt motion to get his attention, but she had got his attention. He lifted his eyebrow so slightly that probably no one but Constance would have recognized it as a signal. She had paused at the doorway; now she came the rest of the way into the room, looking around it with great interest.

"This is such a lovely house," she murmured. "So beautifully decorated and maintained."

Diane Musselman drew herself up straighter and nodded. "Thank you," she said.

"Of course, you couldn't be held responsible for rooms you didn't occupy or use in any way. Like this room, so obviously a man's room, isn't it? But for a reader not to have books on tables, on the arm of the chair, that seems strange. I suppose you had to tidy up before other people came around to collect his files."

Diane nodded. "It was a mess," she admitted.

"How about his bedroom? Did he keep books and papers and things in there, too?"

"Yes, he did. It's still a mess. I just can't seem to bring myself to pick it up. One of these days, of course, I will. The house-keeper is after me to let her do it, but someone has to pick up the important things first. You know?"

"I understand entirely," Constance said. "I think if we're through in here, we might have a look at his other private room, and then we'll leave you in peace. It's been terribly good of you to let us impose like this."

Diane led them through a wide hall with nice pictures of irises and roses on both walls, on to another wing of the house. She walked at Constance's side explaining that it wasn't that they hadn't slept together, but she was so tired so much of the time, what with three children to see to, and the house and all, and he had kept such late hours many nights, and had been such a restless sleeper, thrashing about, keeping her awake. . . . Now and then Constance murmured something soothing.

They reached the second private room that David Musselman had used, and this time when Charlie and Bill Gruenwald exchanged quick looks, they both appeared satisfied with this development. There was no computer in here, but many notebooks, magazines, books on a nightstand by a narrow bed, others on two tables flanking a couch that had a worn blanket draped over the back. The bed was unmade; a stack of books was on one side of it.

"I brought some of this stuff in from the other study," Diane said apologetically. "But then I didn't know what to do with it. We don't usually keep books and stuff on the floor."

"You look so tired," Constance said to her at the doorway. "Show me the way to the kitchen and I'll make you a cup of tea, or coffee. Tell me about the children."

She drew Diane out with her, and the two men went to work.

"How did you know?" Bill Gruenwald asked later in the car heading out toward Tootles's house.

"I guessed," Constance said. Charlie snorted. "Well, there weren't any books in sight in the first room she showed us to, remember? Then his study revealed a reader, a man with many interests. The books were art, poetry, biographies, fiction, books on collectibles, coins, stamps, even carpets, but all put away. I doubt that she ever put a book away in the right place in her life; he must have done it, and that left the question of where were the books he was actively interested in at the time of his death. I thought there must be another room."

Charlie chuckled and slouched down in the seat. Bill Gruenwald turned to look at her directly; he had been watching her in the rearview mirror. He made a saluting gesture and turned his attention back to driving.

"Are you going to tell me what you found?" she asked then.

Bill Gruenwald had asked for a large bag or two, and had brought out two filled with magazines, notebooks, books, maps, drawings. . . . He said he didn't know yet what all was in them; it would take hours to sort it out. They had found a heavily annotated copy of Paul Volte's magazine articles, the series on art and architecture. And they had found the hardcover book, not as heavily annotated, but marked up. Someone had to go through everything, he repeated.

No diary, no outline for the proposal he had sent to the magazine, but in all those notebooks maybe there was something to do with it.

There was a how-to book about submitting a proposal, Charlie said lazily. "Poor guy had it right there in black and white, call up and ask the name of the editor if you have to, but he sent it addressed to The Editor anyway. Chickened out about calling. He had underlined that bit of advice."

They had driven out to the countryside by now, away from the heavy city traffic. "What I have on Musselman," Bill Gruenwald said, relaxing even more at the wheel, "is damn little. We were looking at an accident, remember, no reason to start digging too hard into his past or anything. So, here it is. He was the junior partner of a pretty prestigious firm of architects, made a good living with it, and was good at it, apparently. The condo complex was his, with a lot of help from a flock of juniors who did the plumbing, wiring, floors, the detail work. He was the overall honcho above them. Okay. Buell used that firm a lot for primary design work, but not to see the projects through to completion. Apparently, it can go both ways. So it was a surprise when Musselman came around to check on the roof or some damn thing. We had a lot of hard rain all spring, and he said he was concerned about leaks, and he was around a lot. Ditmar said it was peculiar, but acceptable. Others dittoed that. Strange, but not so strange that anyone gave it more than a passing thought. He died on a Thursday after working hours. The roof was awash that day, and lots of mud had been tracked up. If he was worried about leaks, it made sense for him to go have a look. See what I mean? We were looking at an accident. So he went up there, and he got too close to a slippery edge and fell. Nothing indicated anything but that. No one else was with him, no one knew he was going out to look around that day. A watchman, not Pierce, found his body when he made his rounds right after six. Musselman died between five, when the last workman left, and six-twenty, when he was found."

Charlie did not stir from his slouched position, and in the back seat Constance gazed out the window at the passing scenery, very pretty here, nice grass, good trees, lush-looking farms now and then. No one spoke until Gruenwald said irritably, "All right! We blew it! I can see that now, but at the time? No way. You saw the wife; we got the same story from people he worked with. He didn't have an enemy in the world. No one had a reason to want to harm him. He was in debt, but who isn't? And it

SEVEN KINDS OF DEATH 539

wasn't serious. No drinking or gambling problems. Nothing, period."

"Take it easy," Charlie said. "You blew it, but what the hell?
It looked good at the time and that's all you can do." He pulled
himself up a little bit straighter. "So he dies on Thursday, and
on Friday someone rents the box in his name and calls the magazine to change the return address on the manuscript. You might
be able to find out at his office when someone went out there
to collect the computer files." Diane had looked helpless when
asked for a date. "We've got a busy killer scurrying around ti-
dying up here, straightening up there. Someone who understands his computer enough to clean it out. I sure don't."

"It's a Mac," Constance said from the back seat. "They have
powerful drawing capabilities, very good for all sorts of graphic
work, I guess. I think most people in art or architecture would
understand them, if they use computers at all."

"Well, it's a whole new ball game," Charlie said. "If Musselman found out something funny about the condos and wrote it
up in a proposal for publication, it brings in a whole new bunch
of suspects starting with Max, Johnny, Ditmar, on down to every
foreman, every supplier, God knows who else, backers, bankers.
Jesus! And this person might not have attended the damn party
at all, just met Victoria Leeds at the condo, talked in any of the
rooms, and then after Johnny and group departed, took her up
to the sixth floor and killed her. He could have chosen any time
to leave when Pierce was busy somewhere else."

"I can just see a mad plumber leaving a letter on her bed,
and then taking time out to mess up Marion Olsen's art before
going over to kill Victoria Leeds," Bill Gruenwald said with harsh
bitterness.

In the back seat Constance stared stonily out the side window
at the sparse woods they were passing through.

14

About Musselman's death," Charlie said as they approached the condo area, "did you investigate it yourself?"

"Yeah. I'll show you."

"Stop at the gate," Constance said, "and I'll walk on down to Tootles's house. I want to see her, see how she's doing. You can fill me in later, Charlie."

They had left the Volvo in Tootles's driveway and had to go there eventually to pick it up. Constance had already called the motel they had stayed in before and reserved the same two rooms, and she obviously did not want to peer at a spot on the ground where a man had fallen to his death. Gruenwald stopped, as she had requested, and she left them and started to walk on the shoulder of the road.

"That was a nice piece of work she came up with," the sheriff said, shifting gears, pulling on in through the gate.

"Hm," Charlie said, unhappy that Constance had chosen to go alone, unable to say why it bothered him. It was the middle of the day; Tootles, Babar, the students were the only ones likely to be at the house, not at all like New York. Still, the uneasiness settled over him.

"The rain put them behind this spring," Gruenwald was saying as he drove to the front of the A building—Applegate, Charlie remembered. Max Buell's big, six-year-old Continental was parked there. "A lot of guys weren't working, nothing going on outside, you see, but the painters, plasterers, interior finish people were all busy. Anyway, no one claims to have seen Musselman that afternoon. Could be. He could have driven in, like I just did, parked, and walked in. Elevator up to six, stairs up to the roof." He opened his car door and got out, stood with his hands thrust deep into his pockets outside the building. A sidewalk had been laid, irregular paving stones of a pleasing slate-gray color, bordered on both sides by low-growing plants, nice lawn areas. They walked to the end of the building. "Sidewalk wasn't here then," Gruenwald said. "Junk concrete, bricks, I don't know, just junk littered the ground right here. And this is the place they found him. We've got pictures if you want to see."

Charlie looked from the neatly finished walk up the side of the building; this was on the same side as the deluxe apartments, up there was Six A where Victoria Leeds had died, too. "You'd think someone would have seen him, someone going home or something."

Gruenwald shook his head. "That's what I thought, but they walked me through it. The guys working inside all used the other elevators, the common ones, not the dedicated ones at this end. They stashed their gear in the basement, washed brushes in the basement, stuff like that, and then left by way of the basement doors, the ones closest to where they were. Guys in the other buildings were even less likely to have seen him. Someone driving by at the right moment could have seen him from the road but no one came forward. No one had any reason to be right here until the watchman made his first round, fifteen after six, twenty after, whatever."

"And he didn't let out a peep on the way down?" Charlie asked sourly. "I guess they all wore headsets, listened to music or something?"

Gruenwald flushed and his lips tightened a bit. "Something like that," he said in a cold tone. "Charlie, ease up. It was raining hard. Windows were closed, tarps over any openings, music was on, guys talking and mostly working in inside rooms. No one heard anything."

"It stinks," Charlie said in a colder voice. "Okay, okay. At the time it looked like an accident. But it stinks today. Let's go talk to Max Buell. Not a word yet about Musselman, you agree?"

Gruenwald shrugged, not appeased.

Since they did not have the key to the dedicated elevator, they had to use the common one at the other end, and then walk the length of the sixth-floor hall to the apartment. The door there was standing open. They entered without ringing or knocking.

Max and Johnny were both in the living room of Six A, standing at a table with an open sample book of paint. All the tarps had been cleared away now; the room looked ready for occupancy.

"I heard what you said, and I still say no," Max was saying, as Charlie and Bill Gruenwald walked into the room. "We stick with the original colors throughout unless tenants or buyers say otherwise."

His voice was low, but there was a sharp edge there; it was very clear who was boss. Johnny looked across the room at Charlie and the sheriff, shrugged, and closed the book.

Gruenwald said, "Mr. Buell, could we talk to you for a moment?" He looked at Max, who nodded and sat down at the table.

"Sure," he said. "Johnny, we'll talk about it again later."

"Right," his son said and left, carrying the large book with him. He looked sullen, and his posture was rigid with repressed anger. He did not glance at Charlie or Gruenwald as he walked out stiffly.

Charlie waited until Johnny had closed the foyer/elevator door behind him, and then sat down opposite Max Buell. "Did you tell Spence to arrange the touring show for Tootles? Are you footing that bill?" he asked bluntly. Max leaned back, his face impassive. A good poker player, Charlie thought; he said, "We can find out, you know. All those gallery owners don't owe you a damn thing, do they?"

"What difference does it make?" Max asked finally, giving nothing yet.

"Damned if I know. She doesn't know, does she?"

Finally Max shook his head. "She doesn't know. There's no reason to tell her."

"I agree," Charlie said, in a more kindly voice. "Absolutely, I agree. Why did you do it?"

Max looked from him to Gruenwald, back to Charlie. "She deserves some recognition," he said. "She's overdue recognition, and it wasn't going to happen unless someone made it happen. She's worked all her life for nothing. Not much money, just a little trust fund, no fame, no glory, nothing. She deserves more." He studied Charlie a moment, then asked, "Who told you? Spence?"

"Nope. He would have had his tongue pulled out before he'd talk. You should know that. A combination of things that didn't quite mesh. Spence could have done this anywhere along the line, but he didn't. Not enough money? Maybe. But the fact is that he didn't arrange it until now. All galleries, not state museums, or college museums. Private. Business deals right down the line. And who's the businessman among us, with money to spare for private art shows?" He shook his head. "It didn't take a giant intellect to come up with you."

"She deserves it," Max said again. "She's a brilliant artist who never quite made it. It's not just charity. Some of the pieces might even sell."

Charlie nodded, as if in agreement again. "How is this complex, all this construction, financed?"

Max looked startled at the abrupt change of subject, then he shrugged. "I put up some, up front, then I went for financing, four different banks involved. They pay in installments, so much with foundation digging, so much with outer walls, and so on."

"That's why it was important to have the showing last weekend? Another installment due?"

"Yes. On completion of a major part, one entire building, for example, a big installment is due. It's like a credit line, enough to keep us paying the bills until we start selling and bringing in money. The showing would have included some prospective buyers, as well as the financiers."

"What now? Another tour planned?"

"No. No," he said quickly. "My God, someone died here! Anyway it will be low-key. Nothing showy, not after a tragedy. Nothing to attract media attention," he added dryly. "Our backers are strong about not attracting attention. We'll have them in individually now, two, three at a time at the most. One of their people will just send a representative, an inspector. It will be discreet." He looked at Charlie shrewdly then and added, "I'm not hurting for money, you know. This arrangement is typical, but I could have done the project without it. And I don't lick boots, or various parts of the anatomy to keep the money flowing."

Charlie laughed. "Gotcha," he said after a moment. "Does your son share your feelings?

"Ask him," Max said.

"I want to see Birmingham," Charlie said when they left Max and the A Building. From all over the site the sounds of hammers, saws, music, voices filled the air; next door the Birming-

ham building was relatively quiet, all the major construction
finished. Painters and plasterers, finishers were at work in it.
Charlie led the way down the sloping drive into the basement,
where two men were painting lines on the floor with a machine.
Parking spaces, just like in A. A worker was spraying stenciled
numbers on panels for the dedicated elevators: 1, 2 . . . the number would go on one side of the door that opened in the middle.
The other side already had the letter, B. Exactly like the other
building, except here it was B, and there it was A.

Charlie stood watching for a few seconds, then turned and
nearly bumped into Bill Gruenwald, who was waiting patiently.
"Well?" the sheriff said then.

"Nothing. Just nothing. Let's go."

By the time Constance reached Tootles's house she was in an
icy rage. She bypassed the house when she saw the two young
men and Toni with Tootles and Ba Ba in the side yard. She
walked to the small group. One of the boys was painting a grotesque three-foot-high construction full of oddly shaped holes
that seemed randomly positioned. The birdhouse, she realized.
It had been undercoated and was being painted emerald green.

"We have to talk," she said grimly, taking Tootles by the arm.
She didn't know how long Charlie would be, and she wanted
this over with before he arrived. There was no time now for
niceties.

Tootles looked wary, and pulled against her hand. Constance
tightened her grasp. The others looked alarmed and Ba Ba
reached for Tootles. "Now," Constance said. "Come on. Down
by the creek will do."

She wanted to be away from the others before they started
objecting, and not someplace where Ba Ba was likely to follow
them. She knew Ba Ba would not venture down the path toward
the creek; it was not steep, not difficult, but it was clearly a walk,
and Ba Ba avoided walking; a water chute would have been fine
for her. Constance began to walk briskly, towing Tootles along.

"All right," she said, when they had put several hundred feet
between them and the group at the birdhouse. "I read Paul's
biographies, several of them. You gave it to him, didn't you? After
Gray Axton died, Paul came to console you. He stayed here a
few weeks, and you let him believe that—that gift was transfer-

able, like a bottle opener. Didn't you? He thinks he has your curse, doesn't he?"

"I don't know what you're talking about."

"Don't let's play games," Constance said. "I know what he thinks. I know what you think. Now Toni's trying to talk Paul into giving it to her. And he's just about as unhappy and desperate as you were when you passed it on to him, isn't he? Did you pass it on in some kind of ceremony? Did Ba Ba participate?"

Tootles shook her head, her mouth set, her eyes unfocused as if scanning a very distant horizon.

Constance took her by both shoulders and forced Tootles to look at her. "There was a ceremony, wasn't there?" Tootles brought her gaze back and nodded slightly. "I won't let it happen again, Tootles! Not to Toni. It stops here."

Tootles drew in her breath sharply. Her voice was harsh when she spoke again. "You can't stop something like this. Don't even try. You don't know what you're getting into."

"I can't, but you and Ba Ba can. And you will. My God, you will! I don't intend to stand by and watch another life be deranged by this . . . this superstition."

"I can't do anything to stop it. Even if I wanted to, I don't know how. I can't make Ba Ba do anything. Forget it, Constance."

"You can make Ba Ba do whatever you want; you always could, and you will, or I'll tell Max who messed up your artwork and why," Constance said.

Tootles's face blanched and she suddenly looked very old and haggard. "I don't know what you mean," she whispered.

"You know exactly what I mean. I haven't told anyone yet, but I know. You didn't dare go on tour with that work! And you couldn't just come out and refuse, not after Spence made all the arrangements. What would Max have thought? What would anyone have thought? But you knew perfectly well that most of the work would be scorned." Constance took a quick breath, surprised to find herself so winded. Fury did it to her, she knew. "You messed up this murder investigation; maybe you've made it impossible to find out who killed Victoria Leeds by mixing your personal problems in with her death. Okay, that's done; I won't tell unless you force me to. But, my God, it's going to stop now! Arrange it with Ba Ba. A séance, whatever you want to call it. Invite Paul, and Toni. Don't forget Toni. And me. I want to be there. You make the arrangements yourself and let me know when." She said grimly then, "And at this . . . this séance, Ba Ba is to dismiss the muse, the spirit, whatever she calls it. Do you understand? She is to send it packing. Tell her that!"

Through this Tootles did not move; she was gazing straight ahead with an agonized expression. Color had come back to her face, but she looked ill and almost wild. "How did you guess?"

"Your note to me, the phone call, your desperation. But by the time I got here, the problem, the cause of your desperation, had vanished. You had solved your problem. Destroy the pieces, no show. Simple. The few you left intact are the ones that are good, aren't they? The others—"

"They're junk!" Tootles said harshly. "I did them after Gray died. Junk, that's all they are!" She studied Constance through narrowed eyes. "You really haven't told anyone?"

"No."

Finally Tootles nodded and without another word started back up the path to the house.

Constance breathed deeply a time or two, willing her anger to subside, before she followed. Blackmail, she thought suddenly, her fury instantly renewed; she had been driven to perpetrate blackmail!

Charlie was silent on the short drive from the condos to Tootles's road. Something, he kept thinking. Something he was missing and shouldn't be. He was surprised to see Tootles in the shade of a maple tree, leaning against the trunk, looking for all the world as if she was waiting for him. As soon as she saw that he was in the car, she straightened and waved vigorously.

"Well," he murmured to Bill Gruenwald. "Seems I'm being paged. Why don't you just let me out here? Look, if my guy in New York calls with anything about Victoria Leeds I'll pass it on, and I guess it's time to start going over the books at Musselman's company, as well as Buell's. Musselman was onto something. And it's going to take time, maybe lots and lots of time, to find out what. I sure wish we could keep this whole aspect under wraps for a while."

Gruenwald nodded in complete agreement. "We'll do what we can as quietly as we can. What I'd like right now," he said, coming to a full stop, "is to be a fly on your shoulder. Something's on her mind. See you later, Charlie."

He waved to Tootles, made a tight U-turn, and left. Tootles walked toward Charlie with her hands outstretched.

"I'm going out of my mind," she said, her voice low and husky. "Charlie, please, I have to talk to you. Let's go to the barn, where no one will disturb us. Charlie, this is more than I can bear. I really feel as if I'm going to crack wide open."

He wanted to put his arms around her and pat her shoulder and stroke her back and tell her not to worry. He was startled by the intensity of his desire to help her, to comfort her. He told himself that she was an aging woman without a bit of charm, or grace, or beauty; she was coarse, and a liar, and her feet were dirty. Also she was up to something that he distrusted completely. It didn't matter, he wanted to hold and comfort her. He took her hands.

"Okay, the barn," he said. "And calm down. What's happened? What's got you so upset?"

"A murder! My life's work destroyed. Maybe my life itself destroyed. Oh, Charlie!"

She ducked her head and withdrew a hand to wipe her eyes. Now he put his arm about her shoulders and steered her across the dirt road toward the barn.

The big doors were closed; inside the barn the light was dim. There were the crates that had been roughly opened, the fronts, tops, sides ripped apart to reveal the messes inside. No one had been back here yet to clean up the mess.

She stopped a few steps inside the barn, and suddenly she bowed her head and buried her face in her hands and sobbed. This time he did hold her close while she wept.

"I didn't realize how hard it would hit me, coming back here," she said in a choking voice a few seconds later. "I just wasn't thinking. I'm sorry. I'm all right now."

She groped in her pockets for a tissue and blew her nose, and then walked away from him, to the far end of the building, where there was another narrow door. She opened it and stood in the doorway, taking great long breaths.

With her back to him, she said, "Charlie, will you please take Constance and leave? We made a mistake in hiring you. I'll explain it to Max. I talked a long time with our lawyer today, and he's sure the police don't have enough of a case even to pretend to arrest me."

He had moved closer in order to hear her softly spoken words. "If Max fires us, we'll probably take off," he said. "Why, Tootles? Why do you want that?"

She shook her head, still facing away from him. "You can't understand what my life's been like. You're so orderly, you and Constance, so very much together, so happy with each other. I've never had that, Charlie, not for more than a few months at a time, and then only a few times. Half a dozen months in a whole lifetime! That's what I've had. I have a chance now with Max. Maybe we can make it last. But you have to leave, and Constance has to leave, or it will fall apart again. You're . . . you're a disturbing man, Charlie. I had no idea how disturbing you could still be."

Roughly he took her by the shoulders and pulled her around to face him. "Knock it off, goddamn it! What are you up to?"

She looked straight at him and made no motion to pull free; her hands hung down at her sides. Abruptly he released his grasp of her shoulders and backed away a step, then another.

"I meant what I said, Charlie. I want you out of here as soon as possible. Both of you. She knows how I feel, the attraction I feel, and she . . . she is trying to force me to do something I absolutely must not do, something that will drive Max and me apart, and she understands that very well. Take her away, Charlie. Please. I need this one last chance with Max, one last chance to make some kind of life for myself finally. Charlie, please!"

She did not touch him, did not lean toward him, or make any overt motion, but he felt surrounded by her, within a circle that was Tootles so that no matter which way he looked, which way he turned, how he reached out, he would collide with her.

He shook his head. "Tell me the rest of it," he said, his voice harsh to his own ears. "What does she want you to do?"

"Hold a séance with Ba Ba," she whispered. "And Max won't have it. He really won't tolerate that sort of thing. She has it in her head that Toni is in some kind of danger, and that Ba Ba and I can do something about it by means of a séance. Charlie, I haven't done anything like that since I was a kid. And Ba Ba nearly had a nervous breakdown years ago, fooling around with the occult. It could be dangerous for her. I don't know what's got into Constance's head, why she brought this up. I don't understand, but she says if I don't do it, she'll turn Max against me, and she can. She knows how. She's so clever that way. She knows so much about me."

Charlie had turned to ice. A moment earlier he had been afraid to move, for fear of coming into contact with her; now he could not move even if he had wanted to. Ba Ba and Tootles in their apartment, he was remembering with a sense of dread and fear, summoning something, striking fear into him with their intensity, their belief. And Constance was using her awareness of that incident from his past in some sort of scheme that she had not even bothered to tell him about. She knew he would not go along with anything like that; she knew, and chose to go around him, bypass him, tackle Tootles head-on by herself. Why?

He felt betrayed, and strangely humiliated. Why? he asked himself again. She didn't believe any more than he did that Tootles had had anything to do with Victoria's death, or Musselman's. Why was she harassing Tootles with such an insane demand, believing her to be innocent? Jealousy? He did not accept that, not for a second. There never had been cause for jealousy between them in either direction. If he had not told her about that stupid incident that had terrified him so, she would not have thought of this, he felt certain, and his sense of betrayal and humiliation arose from that knowledge. In some way she was using his past fear.

If this was all a lie of Tootles's, then what for? She must know he would get to the bottom of it. Like most liars, she built her castles on a grain of truth; the truth was that Constance was holding something over Tootles, something big enough to make Tootles appeal to him for help. He believed that was the germ of truth here. If it had anything to do with Toni, or if it threatened Tootles's marriage to Max, or if Max would not tolerate a séance, or Babar was a basket case, none of that seemed to matter. Details. Constance, apparently, intended to force Tootles to hold a séance with her screwball sister Babar; that was the only important thing Tootles had said.

The very idea of it filled him with a deep fear.

Suddenly Tootles put her hand on his arm. "Charlie," she whispered, "I'm sorry. I didn't know this would hurt you so much. I'm so sorry. Just take her home and forget all this. You will, you know. Let the police deal with the murder, get back to your own lives. I won't forget you, Charlie. I won't forget."

Her touch freed him from the block of ice that had encased him completely. He turned to walk back through the barn. "We'd better get to the house."

"You haven't answered me," she said from the open door, a dark silhouette against the bright light.

He nodded. "I know," he said. At the moment he didn't have an answer. He only had questions. When he left the barn she was still standing at the door at the far end.

15

Charlie found Constance with a small group of young people who were not officially students on the back porch of Tootles's house, eating sandwiches, drinking iced tea, talking. Constance patted a wicker sofa, where she had saved him a seat. He shook his head, helped himself to a sandwich, and sat on the top step trying to be unobtrusive. He decided he had succeeded; the boy who had been talking had not paused.

"I said, I agree. You hear me this time? We're all born creative, I give you that much. I've read some of those tests on newborn babies, on preschool children, and so on. I admit up front that something happens to squelch it real early. What I said was that a *good* study would find out first why it doesn't get burned out in everyone if the pressures are all the same in a family, for instance, and, two, why really creative people so often don't do a thing with it."

The other boy shook his head. "That's where you get off the track. You have to make a value judgment about what is or isn't creative. What you really mean is that a lot of people don't do anything with it that the rest of the world is willing to pay money for. A weaver weaving can be creative, a cook cooking, a gardener producing a beautiful garden . . ."

"Bullshit!" the first boy said. "Let me tell you about my

grandmother. She knitted endless booties and scarves and God knows what all, all beautiful, really expert. Creative? Maybe, but she sure would have preferred to be a concert pianist, her ambition at one time, and then marriage, kids, life got in the way. Now and then she played the piano, not very often, and it was terrible to hear her. She would goof up and cry, start over, goof up, and on and on, over and over. I say that's how it is with most of your creative folks, they're hurting to make a real contribution, settling for a pretty cake, or a nice arrangement of roses, or a good paint job on a model car . . . like having your whole body burning with fever and sprinkling a drop of water here or there and making do with it."

He had become very flushed as he talked. Abruptly he lifted his sandwich and took a massive bite.

Toni had not moved during all this. She held a partly eaten sandwich that she seemed to have forgotten. "You have to keep coming back to the capital letters, don't you?" she said softly. "You're talking about creativity with a capital C. Creativity versus creativity; capital A Art versus art."

Charlie found himself thinking déjà vu, the scene he had walked out on thirty years ago, playing itself over again, this time without Tootles, but her input was there, shaping the direction the conversation had taken. Or maybe there really wasn't any other way to talk about what they were talking about.

"It's like the Major Arcana in the Tarot deck," Toni said. "Once they show up, the forces acting on you are outside yourself, uncontrollable. Once you start talking about capital C Creativity or capital A Art you're talking about forces from outside that are uncontrollable, that demand obedience if you want recognition. A pretty garden or a nice scarf can't bring recognition of the sort we're talking about here. A good piece of Art can."

"Even bad Art can," the first boy said. "Most Art is bad, of course. You know the rule; ninety percent of everything is crap, but it gets the recognition and respect it should have as long as you don't cop out."

Constance knew that Charlie would be ready to leave as soon as he finished his sandwich; this was the kind of talk that sent him off in a dead run usually. It had not surprised her to have him choose the step instead of the seat next to her; to have joined her he would have had to walk through the small clump sitting near the table with the food; it might have broken up the conversation. That had been her first reaction to his sitting over there; now she realized, however, that he was looking at her with exactly the same interest and neutrality that he was showing all the others. He was looking at her no more or less than at the others, and she felt he was trying to figure her out exactly as he would try to figure out any stranger who happened across his path.

Charlie was unaware of her scrutiny. He had been thinking about recognition, the importance some people placed on it. Max saying Tootles deserved recognition, attaching more importance to it than to money. Charlie knew theater people who would never dream of going to Hollywood or working for television; they needed the instant feedback of a live audience, the recognition of their talent, their skill, now, instantly. They said television people played to the sponsor, who didn't give a damn what they did as long as they kept an audience and sold product; movie people played to one person, the director. For some people neither of those options was enough, although the money might be very good. Delayed recognition was not enough, either. These young people were giving each other the recognition they all needed, getting it from Tootles, finding it enough for a time, until they were ready to take on the rest of the world. *Which one would succeed out there?* he found himself wondering, looking from one young face to another.

"Your grandmother is a good example of what we were talking about a while ago," one of the boys said. "I mean, for every one who makes it, who doesn't cop out, there are thousands of others with more talent, more skill, more training who don't make it. By itself Creativity is nothing, worthless."

Toni was nodding emphatically. "Luck is what we usually fall back on, but that isn't it, either. Luck is important, but without the other kind of help, no luck or talent or work or determination will put you over the edge."

Her impassioned words were followed by a silence that became prolonged as the young artists all seemed to have turned their attention inward, to contemplate something that had not yet been named.

"What will, then?" Constance asked softly.

Toni turned toward her with a distant look. She opened her

mouth and then snapped her lips together hard, and instead of speaking, she shrugged.

It was over, Constance realized with regret, as the boys got up, dusting off their shorts. She had felt compelled to ask, and for a second she had thought there might be an answer. "We'd best be on our way," she said to Charlie. "You'll give Tootles our number, won't you?" she reminded Toni, who was standing up, stretching. Constance remembered thinking how Toni was the responsible one; Janet had been the bopper. And how they together reminded her of her own daughter, although neither of them had done so singly.

"Oh, sure," Toni said. "No problem. We're off to hang the birdhouse, I guess. When she comes back, I'll tell her."

Toni watched them leave. Constance at the wheel, Charlie slouched down in the passenger seat. As soon as the Volvo was out of sight, she stopped pretending any interest in the silly birdhouse Roger had put together. They all knew he had needed to hammer and pound, and do something with his hands; that had been understood, and they had accepted the monstrosity he had built, but it should now languish in some dark place in the barn.

She wandered back inside the house restlessly. She inspected the dry-erase board, and added Constance's motel number to the other messages, making a heavy black circle around it to attract attention in the hodgepodge of messages already there. She was in the studio a few minutes later when Spence arrived with a dapper little man who looked like the model for the groom on the wedding cake. His cheeks were very pink, his hands delicate and pale. Spence looked like a thug beside him.

"Where's Marion?" Spence asked, at the studio door. The other man was beside him, eyeing everything with great curiosity.

"Taking a walk." Spence had said he would bring out the man from the insurance company, and she knew that Marion had no intention of seeing him. She guessed that Marion had gone all the way to the end of the woods to her little retreat, and that she would stay there until she was certain this man had seen what he needed to see and had gone again. Spence could show him whatever he wanted, she had said before leaving.

In a short while Spence came back alone, and called in to her, "He's gone. If you see Marion tell her the coast is clear."

She grinned. Spence understood Marion better than anyone else on earth, she was certain.

"What's that mean?" Marion's voice floated into the studio then. "Was someone here? Who'd I miss?"

Spence laughed. "I want a drink. You too?"

"Well, maybe, but a small one . . ." Their voices faded to inaudibility.

Toni lay down on the couch in the studio, not to sleep, but only to relax, to rest. The thought of falling asleep out in the open like this made her shudder. She had nailed her window screens in place, and at night she locked her door and wedged a chair under the knob, and still lay awake rigid and fearful hour after hour. But all this would end, she told herself repeatedly, and then what? She tried to think through the next few days, the next months. . . . The house would fill up again, she knew, remembering the mob who had been here when she first arrived. Twelve, fourteen? She didn't even know how many there had been, all talking, all busy. It would be like that again, and this time she wanted to be right here, in the middle of it all, working, critiquing, being critiqued. But first she wanted Paul Volte to come back, because if he didn't return, she would have to go to New York, and she was reluctant to do that, although she would. She had lived in New York for nearly five years, an interlude that she felt now had been snipped out of her life; New York was like a nearly forgotten dream, without value, without interest except for Paul Volte, and if he did not come back, she would go to him. This had to be soon, she knew, without being able to say why or how it could be done, or even if Paul would change his mind and cooperate. All that seemed minor detail-arranging. It would happen, here or in New York.

She had not intended to sleep, but she came awake with a rush of fear that subsided as she recognized Max's voice: "What are you talking about? I don't understand a thing you're saying."

"She will destroy us," Marion said hoarsely. "I can feel it coming. From what she said it seems inevitable. If not me, then you, or even Johnny. It's like a big black cloud hanging there. I want you to fire them both and tell them to leave, no more questions, no more insinuations. Let the sheriff do his job. He's being paid by the government, let him earn it. Or the state police. I thought they had taken charge of the investigation. They have the resources, the manpower to get to the bottom of this without private detectives. Fire them, Max. For my sake. For yours. I wanted to do it, but I can't. You're the one who hired them, they won't pay any attention to me."

There was prolonged silence. Toni realized they were in the small office down the hall from the studio; that door was open, the studio door was open. Even if they had glanced in here, she had been hidden by the back of the couch. Now she did not dare move.

"Honey," Max said finally, "I don't know what in hell's happened between you and Constance, but if you want them out, that's okay with me. Let me talk to Knowlton first, though. It doesn't have to be this minute."

Knowlton was their lawyer, Toni knew, the one who said they needed outside help. He had been very happy with the choice of Constance and Charlie, she understood. She strained to hear what Marion was saying.

"No, of course not this minute. Just very soon. And, Max, promise me something. Promise me you won't talk to her, you won't let her ask you any more questions, or have anything to do with her."

"Damn it, Marion, you've got to tell me what she said! Has she threatened you? Does she think you're involved, after all?"

"No! No, nothing like that. She knows I'm not. It's . . . not me, not you. It's us, the family, everything we've put together, all in danger of crumbling to dust—"

"Jesus Christ!" Spence's gravelly voice interrupted her. "You're talking like a soap-opera queen. It's not good enough, Marion. Even if Max bows out, I'm involved, too, you know. I won't fire them. Goddamn it! You're the only suspect the police have, remember?"

"This is all your fault!" Marion yelled harshly. "You and that stupid show! Why don't you butt out of my life and leave me alone? I don't need you and I haven't needed you for years. Butt out and leave me alone!" Her heavy footsteps pounded down the uncarpeted hallway.

"Shit," Spence muttered. Toni could scarcely hear when he continued, "Sorry about all this, Max. You were handling her just fine. I should have kept my mouth shut."

"Forget it. Do you know what Constance said to start this?"

"Nope. Something Marion doesn't want told, something Constance has ferreted out that she wants buried again. God knows what. Marion usually couldn't care less who says what about her."

"Well, come on. Let's see where she's got to."

Toni lay without motion for a long time after the voices were gone. Constance, she thought, she would be the one to find out things. She remembered how freely they all had talked to her before Victoria's death. She had, and Paul, Spence, all of them, even Max and Johnny. She was so easy to talk to, so understanding. She bit her lip and finally sat up, got up. What had Constance found out?

Constance drove well, careful but not anxious about it; most of the time she stayed right at the speed limit, only now and then exceeding it a little. Her silence was not because she had to concentrate on the road or the car or traffic; it was because she had not yet decided how to tell Charlie what she had done or why. His silence was just as deep; he was searching for a way to tell her he knew she was trying to coerce Tootles to do something he considered if not obscene, then very close to it, and there simply was no good way to say that.

There were silences and silences between them, and most of the time the silences were as companionable as the conversations, but this was a different kind of quiet that had come between them. Too uncomfortable for him to endure. He cleared his throat and said, "Max had Spence put the touring show together."

"Ah," she said, not surprised.

"He paid for all the galleries. Hired them, rented them, whatever they do."

She nodded.

"Tootles doesn't know a thing about that," he finished. "I told Max I didn't see any reason for her to find out."

Constance glanced at him, then faced the road again. "You

remember 'The Gift of the Magi'? You must have read it in school."

He blinked and shook his head. "Give me a hint."

"Oh, it's a lovely little story about a man and wife very much in love but too poor to buy each other Christmas presents."

"Gotcha," he said then. "The long gorgeous hair, the special comb or brush or something."

She nodded. "That's it. Max and Tootles are reenacting it, aren't they?"

"You wouldn't want to give me a little more than that, would you?" His voice was very dry.

She laughed softly. "Tootles messed up that artwork herself, Charlie. She had no intention of taking it on the road because she knew if any critics went to see it, they would pan most of it. She knows very well that she hasn't done work worth showing for many years. But Max doesn't know that, and she can't bear for him to find out she's not the genius he sees. She needs his respect, his adulation even, and this show could have blown it away, or so she thinks. That's what she was so desperate to talk about, it explains the note on the invitation, the phone call, the problem she couldn't see a solution to. Then she did, I'm afraid."

He whistled, thought it over, and finally nodded. "I think you've got it. She could have been working on it ever since they started boxing up the stuff. They boxed it up by day and she messed it up at night. That explains the nutty screws. She loosened them enough to draw attention to them, not because she ran out of time. I bet Palance was supposed to find the mess on Monday when he got back from his camping trip. Wow, thumbscrews wouldn't make her own up to it, would they?"

"Are you kidding?"

He looked at her profile, then back to the road. That was what she had on Tootles, and it was strong enough to make Tootles react. The gift of the Magi, he thought, nodding at the appropriateness. Max couldn't tell Tootles he had arranged the tour, and she couldn't tell him that her work didn't deserve a tour. Those poor stupid jerks, he added almost savagely.

"You know we can't keep that under the table," he said after another few seconds of thought. "It makes a difference, after all, in how we plot a murder. A whole block of time doesn't need factoring in any more."

"I know," Constance admitted. "But I don't know anything for certain. I didn't actually ask Tootles, and she didn't actually say she had done it."

"How careful were you not to put it into words?" he asked, looking at her profile again. He saw a very small suggestion of a smile twitch her lips and vanish almost instantly.

"I don't think I know what you mean," she said, and turned off the road to the access street for their motel. She looked at him with a bright gaze of absolute innocence.

Her eyes widened then and she grimaced. "Damn," she said. "Just damn. You know what we did? We left our suitcase in the sheriff's car. My new clothes. Your toothbrush. Everything we took to New York, or bought there."

"I imagine he'll be around," Charlie said. "Let's order a pot of coffee up in our room and talk our way through this whole mess. You game for that?"

For the next hour or so, they talked, paced their room, drank coffee, made notes, talked some more.

Finally Charlie tossed down the pencil he had been chewing, and went to the window. The coffeepot was empty; his stomach was rebelling, probably not from the coffee as much as from that sandwich earlier instead of a decent lunch, he thought morosely. It was four in the afternoon.

"It's a bigger mess than ever," he said, watching a yellow station wagon maneuver in the parking lot; the driver had made too wide a turn and was backing up ineptly now. Charlie bet with himself that after another try or two the driver would give up on that spot and find a different one.

"Well, maybe not a bigger mess," Constance said, as frustrated as he was, "but certainly a different mess. It seems to me that Tootles must be completely out of the running as a suspect."

"And Max is in," Charlie said, facing her again. "If Musselman found something on him, or the condo, he sure is in."

Constance was digging around her in her purse; she brought out a notebook and flipped through it, then stopped. He watched silently. "Some questions I asked myself a day or so ago," she said. "Like this one: How long would it have taken to mess up the artwork? Now it doesn't matter if that gets answered or not; it doesn't make any difference since she had all the time in the world. And the mystery of where Tootles went, that's another question I can redline. I suppose directly to the barn, where she loosened the screws and finished up whatever she felt still needed doing. Hm."

Charlie waited but when it seemed she was not going to comment beyond that uninformative *hmm*, he cleared his throat. "Well?"

She glanced at him, then back to her notebook. "Why didn't Paul stay with Victoria? That's so sad, and such a waste!"

"Well?" he asked. "You have an answer, don't you?"

"Not one you'll like," she said. "You know when I was at the library, it was to look up Paul. I told you that, didn't I?"

"So?"

"Let me just read the cold hard dates of various things in his life," she said, and started to flip through the notebook again. "Here it is. In 1972, the year Tootles's lover died in Vietnam and *Seven Kinds of Death* was a success, Paul had his first success, about ten months after hers. His first articles were very well received, and his wife left him. In 1975, he won a Chicago literary prize for his first book, and got the job he still has. Not the Pulitzer, but prestigious. Two months later, his father had a fatal stroke. In 1980 his second book was a hit, bigger than the first, and his fiancée died. In 1984 he met Victoria and started the new book that's won so many awards now."

Charlie was staring at her in fascination and disbelief. "You don't buy that there's a connection, I hope," he said when she became silent.

"It doesn't matter one way or the other. It's what he believes. What Tootles believes."

"Right," he said, not quite snapping. "I have a question. How are you going to link all that stuff with Victoria's murder?"

"That's a good one," she said and wrote it down. She looked at him with an almost vacant gaze. "Here's another one. Who put that letter in Paul's room for Victoria?"

"Inside job, all right," Charlie said morosely. "Everyone, all the help, deny knowing anything about it." He frowned. "We don't even know if the note the police found was the same one she received that day."

Constance nodded. "The big question is where did Victoria Leeds go that afternoon? With whom?"

Charlie turned back to the window broodingly. The inept driver was gone, the station wagon safely parked in a different slot.

"You haven't said anything about how Musselman died," Constance said after a few seconds.

"There's nothing to say. Just another death, another dollar, another day. He left his Washington office, and drove out to the condo that afternoon without mentioning to anyone where he was going or why. No one gave it a thought. Next, the watchman found his body at the base of Applegate. It was raining hard. Period."

She was studying his back; something was very wrong, but she could get nothing more than that. Something was wrong. He was too stiff, too distant. Sometimes a case did that to him, but not when there were still so many things that could be learned. This case was still poised at an intersection; it could take off in half a dozen different directions, not a cause for despair just yet.

Usually she could rely on her intuition to guide her in a situation that could become sticky; this time she couldn't because she had not yet told him what she was planning, and there was no way she could tell him that, not yet. He had gone so stiff at her recitation of Paul Volte's career, and his tragedies; that was merely a warm-up, she was afraid, of his reaction when she finally came to tell him everything. First she had to sort it through by herself, find the exactly right way to bring it up, the exactly right nuance of voice, mannerism, attitude. Meanwhile, he was distant, cool, aware that something was missing, something was wrong, and unable any more than she was to do anything about it yet.

Charlie was thinking that if he had met her with a question as soon as possible this afternoon, if he had just said outright, *what the hell are you up to?* then she would have said *what do you mean?* and he would have said he'd had a talk with Tootles, and maybe he could have mentioned her appeal for him to silence Constance, take her away. Then she would have told him what she was planning, and everything would be out, aboveboard, but now, hours later, it was becoming more impossible by the second to discuss any of that. He couldn't explain Tootles to himself, much less to anyone else, even Constance. He could think of no way to bring up that dizzy episode with Tootles in the barn, to try to explain what he had said, what she had said, because now it would sound as if they had met to discuss Constance. Somehow the whole thing had a repellent feel to it that had not been there before. Good old Tootles, he thought sourly.

He swung around then to say, "Let's give the sheriff a call, see if he's free to be wined and dined, and if he'll let us have a go at everything he's gathered to date, starting with Musselman. I keep feeling that we're missing something, and not just our suitcases. Maybe he didn't miss whatever it is even if he isn't aware of it yet."

16

The sheriff's office was forty-seven miles away, too far, he said, for them to drive and then have to drive back. He met them halfway in the little resort village of Potomac Acres. It was a pleasant drive through gentle woods alternating with lush farmland. They met the sheriff at a restaurant. He had brought a packet that included copies of the various reports he had gathered so far. No point in sitting in his office, which was not all that comfortable, he said almost abashedly; they could read the stuff back in their motel. He would have delivered the same packet to them the next day, he said, if they had asked. No one mentioned the fact that the state investigators had practically told him to go fishing, stay out of the way, get lost, let the big boys handle all this.

At their table, waiting for service, they talked about the

weather, which had become hotter and muggier, a storm in the
making, he said. Not until after they had placed their orders,
and finally were eating, did he mention that he had started the
paper hunt for any possible irregularity about the condo financing or building codes, everything he could put together.

"We're, being quiet about it," he said over a dinner of shish
kebab. "What with the shaky S and L's, and people scared about
their own banks the way they are, we don't want any more uneasiness than necessary." The fact that he was doing this without
authorization, and without the knowledge of the state investigators, was not mentioned. "The old man's clean as a whistle
from all accounts," he said. "John Buell is an unknown factor,
he's not even a full partner, just an employee. We're running a
routine credit check on him, but we don't expect much to turn
up. Back to the old man, never any company or personal debts
that didn't get paid on time, no financial troubles that anyone
knows about, no trouble with employees, never a complaint
about shoddy construction, nothing. I doubt we'll find anything
worth toting home."

Charlie sipped his retsina and rolled the pine-pitch flavor
around in his mouth; there seemed to be no liquid, just the
biting taste of fumes. Constance had said no very firmly at the
wine choice, and had settled for a red wine that probably was
okay, he thought, but not really authentic. On the other hand,
her moussaka looked better than his lamb grill. He drank more
wine. He was half-listening to Bill Gruenwald tell Constance
about his ex, who had split when their child was two and was
first diagnosed as autistic. The child was in the hospital part of
the time, at home with him part time. She was beautiful, he said.

Charlie listened, let his mind drift back to the murders, returned to listen again. No doubt, the sheriff was right about the
Buell company. Everywhere they turned, they seemed to run
into a wall: wrong times, no one person available for the right
period, or if anyone was available, there was no motive conceivable.

"For instance," he muttered, "no one in the house could have
killed Victoria, and yet it had to be someone from inside." And,
he continued under his breath, aware that it didn't matter what
he said since no one was paying attention anyway, no one from
that bunch, except Max and Johnny, could have helped Mussel-

man off the roof. But neither of them could have killed Victoria, although anyone could have left the note on Paul's pillow. Not just anyone, he corrected. Anyone from the household, or the hired help. "And you know damn well," he muttered, this time breaking the skin of silence that seemed to separate him from Constance and Bill Gruenwald, "whoever left the note had to have access both to the house and the stationery, and to the typewriter in the condo." Constance and Bill Gruenwald stopped talking and looked at him. "Why roof?" he wondered out loud. "Why not the sixth-floor balcony?" He considered that: the sixth-floor unit again, but why not? Or the fifth?

"Did you check any of the apartments when Musselman took his dive?" he asked Gruenwald.

The sheriff shook his head. "No reason to," he said. "Musselman was on the roof; he left a raincoat up there. Must have been carrying it and put it down, or dropped it."

Charlie asked softly, "Where did he put it down, Bill? Why? Wasn't it raining pretty hard?"

Gruenwald looked unhappy again, the way he did every time Charlie asked about that investigation. He patted his neat mustache, as if afraid it had bristled. "It was raining off and on all day. I don't know why he wasn't wearing it. We found it on part of the housing for the elevator shaft. Look," he pulled a notebook from his pocket and sketched quickly. "This is the layout of the roof. Elevator housing at each end, stairs in the same housing. This end had the door open, not the deluxe apartment side, but this one by the common elevators. We figured he went up the regular elevator maybe to six and took the stairs to the roof. Maybe the rain had let up again. He put his coat down and went to the far side. And maybe he leaned over too far, or his foot slipped; like I said, there was a lot of water up there, and some mud in places. Charlie, that's all we have on it. It seemed like enough at the time." He took a long drink from his stein of beer and set it down heavily. "You tell me why you want the sixth-floor apartment."

"Because you can't tell much about a leaky roof while it's raining if the roof is standing in water. You check the ceilings below, and wait for the water to run off, and then you bring in a licensed roofer. But if he was there to see someone, and if he was pushed, it doesn't make much sense for him and someone else to hold a conference in the rain even if it was intermittent. Better have it indoors on the side where he was found, and that's the sixth-, or fifth-, maybe even the fourth-floor apartment, but then it starts to get chancier to get the right kind of decision about a tumble from the police, the medical examiner. You know, the pros.'' This was not quite a mocking tone, but too close. He regretted it instantly and lifted his wine again.

Gruenwald shook his head. ''That narrows it down to Max Buell, John Buell, the superintendent Ditmar, or maybe one of the foremen. And none of them could have killed Victoria Leeds. Those apartments were all kept locked except when the workmen were in them, and they weren't that afternoon, and the Buells, father and son, had left. That would mean two separate murder cases, one as cold as an icehouse.''

''Locked? Why?''

Gruenwald sighed and looked to Constance as if seeking help. She offered none. ''Okay,'' he said. ''Locked because there were expensive fixtures in place already. And because the Buells had already started to use Six A as an office, with the table and typewriter up there, blueprints, stuff like that. Things they didn't want anyone messing with.''

''Musselman might have had the key,'' Charlie pointed out, and Sheriff Gruenwald looked chagrined. Charlie shrugged.

''You said the Buells had left. Together?''

''No. Max went to Marion's about four-thirty or so. Johnny left right after that, to drive back to the city, where he has an apartment. He seldom stays at Marion's. You know, the girlfriend.''

Suddenly Constance remembered the evening that Paul and Victoria had arrived at Tootles's house, virtually ignoring each other. Victoria had been carrying an overnight bag, her purse over her shoulder, and a red-jacketed book with a paper sticking out. She had put down the suitcase in the foyer and had put the book on a long low table with a clutter of things on it. When Constance followed them up the stairs a little later, Victoria had had the suitcase, and her purse, but not the book.

''Do you have an inventory of Victoria's things from Tootles's house?'' she asked, causing both men to looked surprised at the abrupt turn. ''Maybe you can remember,'' she said slowly. ''A book with a red dust jacket. She was carrying it when she got there, and when she went upstairs she wasn't. I just wondered if it turned up again."

"I'm almost sure not," Gruenwald said, after thinking for a second or two, checking off items on a mental list apparently. "What about the book?"

"I don't know," she said. "I didn't see the title. There was a paper sticking out of it, notebook paper, with writing on it. I wonder if she made notes on the plane, or in the car, and stuck them in the book she was carrying. That's all."

"Would you recognize it again?" Charlie asked.

She nodded.

"Well," he said. "Well. Bill, you game for a visit to Tootles's house tonight?"

The sheriff looked resigned. He glanced at his watch. "I have a few things to do, and then with the drive over, it'll be near ten. That's getting pretty late." His unhappiness was increasing moment by moment.

"We can go look for it," Constance said. "We can let you know in the morning if we find anything. I have to talk to Tootles tonight, so we'll be going over anyway."

The sheriff was shaking his head regretfully. It was one thing to let them see statements, he said, and quite another for them to gather evidence themselves. He would meet them at the house. He looked at Charlie and added, "And wait, okay? Don't start anything without me."

His tone was pleasant, but it was not a simple request; it most definitely was an order. Charlie grinned and shrugged.

Toni was in the office that had once been a dinette, holding the phone with one hand, tracing a pattern in the wood grain of the windowsill with the other, while she listened to the telephone ring in Paul's apartment. Dusk had fallen, bringing with it a stillness in the air that was not peaceful tonight, but more like the low pressure that preceded a storm. All afternoon the humidity had been building, the oppression of the air had increased, and now this breath-holding hush that was not natural had descended. Toni was counting rings. At ten she would hang up, or maybe twelve. But at nine Paul Volte answered.

"It's Toni Townsend," she said in a low voice; she had planned to sound frightened, anxious, and found there was no need to pretend. She was frightened and anxious. "Paul, can you come back, tomorrow if possible?"

"What's happened?" He sounded even more anxious.

She shook her head. "I'm sorry. I didn't mean to scare you. Nothing really, and yet . . . I don't know what's happening. Marion wants to fire Constance and her husband, the detectives. She had a fight with Constance, I think. But I don't really know. Anyway, that will just leave the sheriff and the state police here, and they think she did it, and I guess they'll arrest her, or something."

"Is Max going along with her?"

"I guess so. He can't tell her no and make it stick. If this is what she wants, he'll do it. Spence doesn't want to, but they'll make him, I know. There's no reason for him to hold out. But the two of you could. I know if you were here to back up Spence, he'd keep them working on this. I . . . I'm really, afraid for her, Paul. You know, she's so smart about so many things, but she's acting crazy about this. She's being so dumb. I'm sure she doesn't realize that she's in danger. And if Constance has really found out things, this is the worst possible time to fire her. Paul, we need to have all this over, done with. Can you come?"

They talked only another minute or two; he hung up first, and before she could replace her handset, she heard the telltale click of another phone on her line. She drew in a sharp breath and closed her eyes hard; what had she said, what had he said? Her hand that had been holding the phone was wet; her mouth was dry. Finally she turned toward the door to see Spence standing there, leaning against the doorframe.

"What the hell do you think you're up to?" he demanded.

"Trying to save Marion," she said fiercely. "If no one else cares, I do."

Spence was studying her openly the way he might study an art object whose authenticity he questioned. He straightened and started to leave, then paused a moment. "Toni, sweetie, if I were you, I'd be awfully careful about not letting on that my ears were bigger than anyone realized. Know what I mean?"

She watched him walk away. His back was very broad and strong-looking; he kept in good shape, like someone who worked out often and regularly. She shivered and at the same moment a gust of wind blew hard against the screened window, entered the room, stirred dust, stirred her hair, made the hairs on her arms stand up; she hugged herself hard. Just the one gust blew now, and when it was gone, everything seemed even quieter than before. Her shivering increased, as if with a deep chill. Who had been listening? Not Spence. There were phones all over the house; anyone could have lifted one in time to overhear her call.

She left the office and went into the bathroom and washed her face with cold water. When she returned to the hall, she could hear the low mumble of voices from the studio—Roger, Bob, Jason, maybe one or two more from Claud's classes. She should have gone to check out everyone instantly, she thought then. By now whoever had listened would be far from any telephone, probably. Resolutely she started to walk toward the main part of the house, the living room, and Marion. She had to tell her before someone else did, or before Marion brought it up, if she had been the one on the other phone.

Marion and Ba Ba were both reading; Spence was wandering around the room studying one piece of work after another. He stopped and put his hands in his pockets when Toni walked in. She could hear Max and Johnny talking over some business problem in the adjoining room, the television room, they called it, although no one ever seemed to turn on the set. Max and Johnny had been discussing some problem all evening. Toni drew in a deep breath and then said cheerfully, "Paul is coming back tomorrow for a day or two. I was just talking to him."

Spence grinned at her. She lifted her chin with defiance and sat down close to Marion. *Seven Kinds of Death* was still in the center of the room, as if it had become a permanent part of the furnishings. Any day now an ashtray might appear balanced on it somewhere, or a glass with melting ice cubes.

"Did he say why?" Marion asked. "What does he want now?"

Toni shrugged and did not dare look at Spence. "He's worried," she said. Then swiftly she said, "I told him you were letting Charlie and Constance go and that alarms him, I think."

"For God's sake!" Marion exclaimed, jumping to her feet. "Why is it that everyone is taking it as a sacred duty to butt into my business? What do you mean, talking about me with Paul? Who do you think you are? Isn't that a touch presumptuous, you little ninny?"

Toni leaped up and cried, "I did it for you, Marion! You don't seem to realize that they could arrest you! You're the first one they picked, and nothing's happened to make them change their minds. And, yes, it's presumptuous! I know that. I'll leave in the morning if you tell me to."

Ridiculous, she wanted to scream. She was crying like a baby, tears streaming, nose running, her voice choked and thick. Suddenly Marion put her arms around Toni, stroked her hair, saying, "Shh. Shh. There, there." And she was crying harder than ever.

"Constance won't hurt you," she said in her choking voice. "She likes you too much to hurt you. And she's smart. Let her find out who did it and end all of this. What would we all do if anything happened to you?" It came out in bits and pieces, interrupted by gasps for air, interrupted by shuddering inhalations and exhalations, interrupted by having to blow her nose, and then by hiccups. And all the while Marion held her and stroked her hair, her back.

"I'm sorry, baby," Marion said finally when Toni came to a stop. "I'm so sorry. I didn't realize how upset you were. You've been so good, so calm and collected, holding it all back. Let it out, baby. That's all right. Just let go."

Toni wept harder. She was not at all sure when the act had stopped, when she lost it, but now she could not seem to control herself at all. She leaned into Marion and let herself be held and babied, and she sobbed.

At the door Charlie tightened his grasp on Constance's hand, as they stood silently watching. Across the room in the doorway to the television room Max and Johnny were watching, as was Spence Dwyers at the far wall, and Babar sitting on the edge of a chair, her mouth opened slightly. Toni wept; Marion murmured to her, and no one else moved.

How long this had been going on Charlie didn't know, and how long it might have continued he couldn't guess, but it was interrupted at that moment by the sound of boisterous voices behind him.

"You chowderhead! Give it back!"

A boy came running from the studio wing; he was carrying a sketchpad. Behind him a second boy was tearing after him, yelling. They came to a stop when they saw Charlie and Constance.

The one in front grinned and said hi, the other one grabbed for the sketchpad, and they both turned and walked back the way they had come. As soon as they reached the turn in the hall, the chase resumed; pounding footsteps thundered on the uncarpeted floor.

Toni had pulled away from Marion at the noise; when she saw Charlie and Constance in the doorway, she turned scarlet, ducked her head, and raced past them, ran up the stairs. In her shorts and tank top, blushing furiously, she looked like a child fleeing punishment.

"Well," Charlie said then as he and Constance entered the room. "We were passing by, the door was open, and here we are. Hello, all. How's tricks, Tootles?"

She glared at him and didn't even glance at Constance. "Too bad you wasted your time. I'm going to bed."

"What a shame," Charlie said. "You'll miss the sheriff. We'll give him your regards."

She stopped all motion. "The sheriff is coming? Why? Now what?"

Charlie shrugged. "I guess he'll tell you when he gets here." He pretended not to notice that Constance was roaming the room glancing at stacks of books, books on shelves, on tables, some on the floor.

"Will you tell your wife that this isn't a public library?" Tootles snapped, and sat down again.

"Well, I don't have to wait up for the sheriff," Ba Ba said and heaved herself up from the chair; it was not easy for her.

Constance had gone nearly all the way around the room. She smiled at Max and Johnny and walked past them. "Ba Ba," she said, "are you going to be around all weekend?"

Ba Ba glanced swiftly at Tootles, then at Max. "I don't know. Why?"

"I might have a party, and I'd really like for you to come."

"A party! My God, are you insane? A party?"

"Well, a very special party, and for very few people. You're all invited, of course, and Paul will be as soon as I can reach him."

"Is that why he's coming?" Ba Ba asked.

Constance was examining a few books that were holding a pottery bowl. She straightened and said, "So he's already planning to come? How nice. When?"

"Toni said tomorrow. But if you asked him . . . did you ask him yet?"

Constance shook her head. "I will when he gets here."

"Tell her, Max," Tootles said harshly then. She was sitting stiffly, her fingers drumming the arm of her chair, one foot tapping furiously. "Just tell her what we decided."

"Well now," Max said in a placating way, "I don't think we decided yet, did we? Spence thinks we should hold off—"

"Goddamn it! *I* decided! Constance, get your ass out of my house. You're fired. And take lover-boy with you! Now!"

Constance scanned the room, paying no attention to Tootles. Then she saw a book with a red dust jacket in the chair Ba Ba had just left. Unhurriedly she moved toward the chair. Charlie was still near the doorway, watching her with a faint grin. He saw the book now, she knew; neither of them mentioned it.

She picked up the book and sat in the chair regarding Tootles. She glanced at the spine of the book, a fantasy romance, and then put it down on the table by the chair. She glanced at Charlie with an expression that told him it was the wrong book; neither of them would have been able to say how she communicated this, but the message was sent and received.

"You know, Tootles," she said calmly then, "I doubt they'll arrest you, after all. Several things have turned up that seem to rule against it. So if you want us to leave, naturally, that's your choice. But my party is really my business. Tomorrow night sounds good. In our motel. It will be a little cramped, but not too bad. I'll have to set a time after I see Paul, find a time that will be possible for everyone. Ba Ba, is nine too early, too late?"

"But I haven't even accepted," Ba Ba said indignantly. "And if Marion thinks it's a bad idea, so do I."

"But Tootles plans to be there," Constance said easily. "Don't you?" She turned her pale eyes on Tootles, who stared back at her with anger and resentment. The silence held for a second, another; neither woman shifted her position. Finally Tootles looked away.

"Not there. Here. After dinner. Nine-thirty," she said harshly.

Constance nodded, and then turned her gaze to Charlie to see that his face had become wooden, his eyes flat black, not reflecting any light at all, like two little dull stones. She had seen that expression many times when he confronted a suspect, or a particularly distasteful crime; until now she had never seen it directed at her.

They all looked past Charlie then as gravel was crunched in the driveway in front of the house. Moments later the sheriff and two deputies appeared at the door. One of the things he had done after leaving them, apparently, was to get a proper search warrant.

He was super efficient that night, almost to the point of being rude. "Ms. Leeds was carrying a book with a red jacket when she arrived here," he said, producing the warrant. "She put the book on the table in the foyer. Did any of you see it after that? Did you move it?"

"What book?" Tootles asked. "I don't know what in hell you're talking about now."

"Who might have cleared off that table?" he asked.

"Jesus!" Tootles cried. "I don't know! Ask Alice Weber!"

He nodded. "I will."

Ba Ba lowered herself into a chair, and then turned to look at Constance with horror. "You thought I had it, didn't you? My book there. You thought that was it!"

"Good God," Johnny muttered. "Dad, this is the last straw. I'm going home. We can finish up in the morning."

He went back into the television room, and one of the deputies followed him and began his search there. Johnny put papers together, stuffed them into his briefcase, and started out.

"If you don't mind," the sheriff said. He reached for the briefcase, and after a slight hesitation Johnny handed it over. Gruenwald looked inside, gave it back, and motioned to the second deputy, who walked out with Johnny.

No one else in the room moved or spoke as the sheriff's men continued to search. Gruenwald stayed in the living room until one of the deputies called him to the foyer. He moved the few steps to the foyer, then turned and said, "Ms. Leidl, would you mind?"

Constance got up to join him, acutely aware of the eyes that were watching her every motion. The book the deputy had was orange-red, too thin, too tall. She shook her head.

The fourth time she was called, she hesitated, then slowly nodded. "I think so," she said. The book was a collection of Byron's poems.

Gruenwald opened the book, and began to riffle through the pages. A piece of paper fell out. It was notebook paper folded in half. They watched it fall; he picked it up gingerly with a pair of tweezers as if it might explode, and very carefully he opened it, using the tweezers and his pen, not getting fingerprints on it. On the paper was what appeared to be a map of Tootles's property, and the condominiums across the road from her retreat. Constance felt Charlie near her and glanced at him, but he was gazing fixedly at the paper.

Gruenwald slid the book and paper into an evidence envelope, and said, "It was in the studio mixed in with a bunch of magazines." He nodded to the deputy. "Nice going." Then he went to the doorway to the living room. "Thank you, Mrs. Buell, Mr. Buell. We'll be leaving now. Sorry to have bothered you again." He nodded to Charlie and Constance and left.

"Well," Tootles said. "Son of a bitch, what the hell is going on? Can anyone tell me that?"

Max took her hand and held it, and asked Constance, "You saw her with the book?"

"Yes. I remembered earlier this evening. She had it with her when she came."

"So what the fuck difference does it make?" Tootles cried. "Jesus Christ, I feel like I'm in a Beckett play. Doesn't it matter to you that nothing makes sense anymore?" She yanked her hand away from Max and jumped up. "I'm going to bed. This is a madhouse, and you're all loonies. All of you!" She stamped from the room. Ba Ba struggled to her feet and lumbered after her.

Max looked apologetically at Constance and Charlie, and they started for the door. "Our cue," Charlie said. "Good night, Max. She'll calm down pretty soon. Just take it easy."

It wasn't that she needed help in walking out of the house, across the porch, along the walk to the driveway and their car, Constance thought a few seconds later; she was perfectly capable of walking alone. Just as she was perfectly capable of opening the passenger seat door and sliding into the Volvo. And, she thought grimly, she was also perfectly capable of maintaining a silence just as long as he was. She gazed straight ahead and did not say a word.

17

In their room, still distracted, still silent, Charlie put Sheriff Gruenwald's manila envelope down on the coffee table and regarded it morosely. He picked up the phone to order a large pot of coffee.

Constance watched him adjust pillows, rearrange the light at the end of the sofa, and kick off his shoes before he reached for the envelope. She sat across the table from him. "I don't think you should come to Tootles's house tomorrow night," she said.

He looked up from the papers he had started to sort through. "Why not?"

"You'll hate it. Besides, it really has nothing to do with the murders. With death yes, but not with murder."

Charlie put down the papers and leaned forward, with both hands pressed hard on the tabletop. "Do you know what happened over there tonight?" he asked. His voice was low, but there was a biting intensity in the words, in the way he looked at her. When he became this intense, he sounded like a foreigner who had not quite mastered English, had not yet acquired an ease of pronunciation: he clipped the words, exaggerated the vowel sounds, sounded like a stranger.

"What do you mean?"

"That silly girl has placed you in danger," he said, even more controlled than a moment ago. Anyone from outside would think he was being as casual as the morning weather report, but she knew, and was startled by the subdued vehemence that seemed even more dangerous for being checked so thoroughly.

"And you topped it by telling Tootles she probably won't be arrested," he added. "My God, between the two of you, you're inviting the killer to have just one more go at it."

She started to respond sharply, but choked her words back and instead considered what he was saying. Toni had said she, Constance, had found out things; and she, Constance, had certainly told Tootles she probably wouldn't be charged. She bit her lip in exasperation.

Charlie got up to answer the door when a knock sounded. He paid the waiter as Constance made room for the coffee on the table. When they were alone again, she poured for them both.

"You really think it's someone over there now?"

"I don't know. But I think anything that's said over there might as well be broadcast. What are you planning for your party?" Some of the tightness had eased, but he was still too tense.

She looked at the coffee cup she held and said in a low, hesitant voice, "I think Tootles and Ba Ba and Paul fooled around with séances, or crystal balls, or the Ouija, something like that years ago, and Tootles gave Paul her muse. The dates are right, their attitudes about it, everything. His book is filled with it. Anyway, I think . . . no . . . I *know* that Toni is going to try to get Paul to pass the muse over to her. And it's a jealous muse, maybe even a crazy one. Toni's . . . she's too young and too innocent to have that burden shoved off on her." She watched his expression harden as she spoke, and she heard a sharp edge in her voice as she responded more to his expression than to anything he might say. "I said you would hate it. And I also said I don't think you should be there. Remember?"

"And I don't intend to let you be with that crew without me," he said flatly.

"If you go, will you promise you'll leave it to me? Not interfere in any way? Just observe?"

He looked at her with his hard flat eyes and slowly shook his head. "No promises. I don't think you know what you might be letting yourself in for. Why are you doing this? Do you even know why?"

"I was there when Victoria got killed. It seems that I should have been able to do something, but I didn't. Apparently Victoria was shut out because Paul believes or says he believes that toll has to be paid. I saw Tootles accept the curse and adjust her life to accommodate it. It has to stop. I didn't do anything to help Victoria, but this time I know what I can do. I don't think Toni deserves what she'll be getting."

"You sound as if you believe in it."

She shook her head. "I told you before, it doesn't matter what I believe. It's what they believe. I said it has nothing to do with the murders, but it has a lot to do with death. It has to stop. Even if none of that's true, Toni deserves a chance at a real life, one that includes art and love, maybe a family, whatever she chooses. She deserves that much out of life. What if she were Jessica, Charlie?"

Not fair, he wanted to yell. Not fair. And she knew it. Either of them would do whatever was required for their daughter's sake, but she hadn't seen Tootles and her little sister in action, and he had. God help him, he had. "Okay," he said finally. He stood up and reached across the table, took her cup and saucer from her hands and set them down, and then drew her close enough to kiss. "Whatever it is, we're in it together, remember? I won't promise to keep still, but God, I'll try. I most definitely will try."

"That's all a guy can do," she said softly, and this time she kissed him.

She was relieved that the light had come back to his eyes. Where did he go when they turned hard and flat, nonreflective like that? So far away she was afraid that one day no words would bring him back, no hand would reach him, no warmth would restore him to life. A deep shudder passed through her; she had been thinking of him as dead when his eyes became stonelike. And that was almost right, she knew; the warm, human, loving man vanished and left an iceman in his place. She also knew that she was afraid of the iceman, who used to appear more and more often and stay longer each time. The battles in his sleep had been between the two, the iceman and Charlie; nightmares, the tossing and turning, the insomnia he had preferred to dreaming, all battles for possession—Charlie or the iceman. She knew that victory had never been assured, never from the first foray to the day he turned in his city ID, to the present. The iceman waited, would always be waiting. And if that was believing in possession, she thought, then she was a firm believer, after all.

Charlie poured himself more coffee and took out a notebook, looked over a list he had made. "Let's try the first-things-first on them all," he said. He had a theory that Constance could tell from a brief meeting exactly what was bugging anyone; nothing she said could shake this idea. He called it her first impressions, first-things-first theory. She sighed dramatically, but did not protest; sometimes useful things came out of it.

"Okay," he said. "Tootles."

"Scared to death Max will find out she'd rather teach than do art, and she believes she can't do art anymore."

Charlie nodded. Part of the game was that he should not express surprise or disbelief until later. "Max," he said.

"Easy. He thinks she's a genius and is really afraid she'll find out that he arranged the tour and then she'll think it was because he doubts her worth, and thought he had to buy recognition for her. He's terrified that he'll lose her."

Charlie made a noncommittal noise, then said, "Spence."

"He never stopped loving her," Constance said, surprising herself. "He would do anything to keep her well, happy, his friend, whatever, to keep the welcome mat out for him. He wants her to be happy with Max."

"Anything?" he asked softly.

She nodded. "Anything."

"Paul?"

"Consumed by guilt. And self-doubt. He doesn't know if he is really talented or not, whether he deserves any success, if he was responsible for Victoria's death." She considered this, then added, "He really needs professional help. I don't know how deep his depressions are, but . . ." An absent expression settled on her face. She raised her hand slightly, and Charlie leaned back waiting.

After a time she looked at him with a puzzled expression. "You know Victoria really didn't talk nonsense; that comes from the way Janet interprets what she heard. Right?" She did not wait for his nod. "Checking out a smoke. Something about where there's smoke, there's fire, and that became going out for a cigarette. Proposal from a muscleman, Musselman, jock. And then there's the curious 'ironic pose' paraphrase. Remember? Where is the note about what she said?"

She found it in her notebook. "Yes. I wrote her words: 'Paul's ironic pose was wearing him down, and making him tired.' Remember the book she had with her? Byron's poetry. Charlie, try: Byronic pose, and wearing thin, and tiresome."

He thought about it, then muttered, "Paul's Byronic pose is wearing thin and getting tiresome. Maybe. But so what?"

"She saw through him," Constance said slowly. "His tragic figure was amusing to her because she didn't believe in it. That's one of the things that baffled me. Her attitude toward him. Amusement." Another thought occurred to her and she sighed deeply, almost theatrically. "Eventually, someone is going to have to talk to Janet, try to get the real words she heard."

They considered this in gloomy silence for another few seconds. "It doesn't change anything, does it?" she murmured finally, and nodded toward his notebook.

He glanced at the open page. "Johnny?"

She hesitated only a moment. "Afraid of his father. He wants to be his father desperately, I think. Tired of being junior. Ambitious and a bit timid, a bit weak. Away from Max probably he's altogether different, though."

He ran his finger down his list, and she said, "There's still Toni." He looked at her, waiting. He had not included Toni because he had seen no reason to do so; she had been accounted for from four-thirty on the day Victoria was killed. He had not included Babar because murder was just too damn physical for her. She would more likely talk someone to death.

"Toni would do anything almost to get what she thinks Paul has, the muse, the wild talent. She thinks she's nothing without it," Constance said. She shuddered. "What a terrible desire, to want something you believe will kill people you love. What a terrible price she's willing to pay. Or else, she doesn't really believe it would bring her suffering," she added thoughtfully. She turned her gaze to Charlie and asked, "When do we start to realize the bill will come due, really and truly it will? She doesn't believe it yet. I don't think she believes she'll ever be in love."

This had gone off in altogether the wrong direction, he thought grumpily. He did not want to talk about this "gift" or "curse." He did not want to talk about suffering artists or about art and its price tag. He snapped his notebook shut. "Good stuff, all of it," he said then, forcing a grin. "Now, to work. You want to do Gruenwald's reports in any systematic way, or just dive in for now?"

They just dived in.

By twelve Constance's vision was starting to blur, and for no good purpose, she thought glumly as she got up to walk around the room, to stretch. Everything she was reading she had heard already; absolutely nothing was new, nothing had not been brought up, discussed, dismissed. She stood at the window and watched the western sky flare with distant lightning that was closer now than it had been half an hour ago. She began to hope their silly cats were indoors. Sometimes the cat door jammed. But the Mitchum boys would be watching out for them, she told herself, and still hoped the cats were inside. Poor Candy was terrified of storms, and Ashcan would be a wreck. Anything out of the ordinary threw him into a panic; their absence for so many days would make him feel he had been deserted forever, and now a storm to verify that the gods were indeed after him. And Brutus, she thought with resignation, would become a monster if he was locked out during a storm. He would make life hell for the other two cats if the storm wasn't already doing it.

She didn't even know if there was a storm in New York, she told herself then, and turned away from the window to see Charlie staring off into nothing with a fixed, distant expression. Lightning flashed again, closer, this time followed very quickly by a rumble of thunder. Moving in, she thought. Charlie apparently had not noticed.

She took her seat again, continuing to watch him, saying nothing. She hoped he wouldn't decide to go for a walk. Sometimes he did when he was in this phase, thinking something through from every possible angle, and then over again, and again, finding and answering the questions, the problems, the sticky points.

A new streak of lightning was so bright that it glared in the room and this time the thunder was simultaneous. Charlie blinked and glanced at the window. "Tell me again about finding Victoria's body," he said. "Start with entering the building."

She began, but now the thunder and lightning, and gusty wind driving rain hard against the windows made talk impossible. She reached for his hand and drew him up. "Watch," she said, pulling him closer to the windows, but not too close. Her mother had always said, *Don't draw attention to yourself during a thunderstorm.*

"It's going to storm," he said.

She laughed and put her arm around his waist; he put his hand on her back, let it slide down to rest on her buttock, and they stood and watched the storm build. It was a tornado-spawning storm, she thought, as the wind blew harder in violent bursts, then died down and blew even harder moments later.

"We could go down to the bar," Charlie said, and she knew he was thinking tornado weather, too. At that moment the lights flickered, flickered again, and went out. "We definitely will go down to the bar," Charlie said then. He had no intention of being on the seventh floor with a blackout, no elevators, and just one nut with a match trying to find the stairs. On the other hand, he knew precisely where the stairs were. He always checked out the stairs, the fire-extinguishing system, and usually he was not happy with what he found, but at least he knew how to get out.

He held her hand and they left the room and entered the absolute darkness of the hall, where already voices were asking where the stairs were, what happened to the lights, did anyone have a match . . .

Charlie had his little penlight, and down the hallway two flash-lights started dueling. He saw that one was being held by a kid, nine, ten years old, and that it was a Teenage Mutant Ninja Turtle flashlight; he grinned and tugged Constance by the hand. Let the kid save the universe, he thought, opening the door to the stairs.

The lounge was dimly lighted by candles, and was much nicer this way than it had been before. The problem would be the air conditioning, Charlie knew, but it was not a problem just yet. He saw Constance to a booth and then went to get them both an Irish coffee. The coffee, he said, because it could be a long night and in a little while the coffee would be cold without elec-tricity to keep it heated, and the Irish because what the hell, it could be a long night.

"You were telling me about finding Victoria's body," he said when he sat down across from her. She told him about it again.

The storm seemed very far away now. No lightning flash pen-etrated the lounge, and the thunder was muted, the wind van-quished by masonry and steel. In a while someone opened a door out front, and another one in the back, and a breeze flowed through.

"Think back to the elevator ride up," Charlie said, gazing past her with a faraway look. "When Max found the roses, did Tootles admit she had sent them?"

After a moment Constance shook her head. Tootles had looked embarrassed, she remembered.

"Right. And she told you that Johnny ordered them in her name. Everywhere we've turned, we keep running smack dab into Tootles and her lies, don't we? Why would she lie about that?"

Constance felt her throat tighten painfully. "What are you thinking?"

"We both came here believing she wouldn't murder anyone. I think she's counting on that more than she'd admit. But she would, you know, given the right incentive, the right circumstances. Look at her, an aging, nearly penniless woman, a failed artist who is running a school that could be put out of business any day, and along comes a rich man who is crazy about her. She hooks him and she'd do anything to keep him, even destroy her own life's work. Then, suppose one day Max comes home in a state of shock. Musselman's found out something, they argued, Musselman got shoved off the balcony, and Max will go to prison. Protecting Max would be incentive enough, I believe." He paused, as if considering his own words.

"You're making the state's case," Constance said in a low voice.

He nodded, still looking beyond her. "Everywhere, the roadblocks we run into are hers," he said. "She threw everyone off the track by messing up her own work. She ordered the flowers, and then denied it because she has to maintain the attitude that she doesn't give a damn about the condos, or anything to do with them. A lie. Of course, she cares desperately. Max is her financial freedom and first Musselman and then Victoria Leeds threatened to strip it from her. And," he added soberly, "she could have slipped an extra key to the condos to Victoria Leeds, told her to go up there and wait for her so they could talk. When Johnny's group arrived, it would have been a simple thing for Victoria to keep out of sight." He drew in a breath and shook his head sadly. "And it was Tootles, remember, who invited Paul, believing he was still Victoria's lover. Invite one, get both."

"But she claims that Johnny insisted on asking Paul."

"The problem," he said thoughtfully, "is that she says a lot of things, and you have to root around them like a pig after truffles trying to decide which is true, which is a blatant lie."

"You're scaring me, Charlie. You really are."

He pulled his gaze back from that distant horizon and focused on her. "About that party you intend to throw, the séance, let's discuss it."

"I won't let you talk me out of it," she said hotly.

Charlie started to say something, but the lights came back on; they both blinked after the dimness. A group of people entered the lounge, laughing, talking. "Let's go up," he said, reaching for her hand across the table. "There's a lot to discuss. You know, we should use candles more often, travel with them, use them every evening."

His face had turned soft, his eyes seemed to glow. Absurdly she felt a touch of warmth on her cheeks. Then her indignation at his betrayal of Tootles flooded in and she would have withdrawn her hand, but his grasp tightened and they stood and walked from the lounge hand in hand.

When Constance got up the next morning, she found Charlie in their sitting room with a tray that contained a large pot of coffee, sweet rolls, a doughnut, juice, and half a grapefruit. The grapefruit was for her, she knew. He was sprawled on the sofa, the telephone at his ear, another doughnut in his hand, grinning like a kid completing his baseball card collection. She blew him a kiss and went back for her shower, and to dress.

"Well," she asked, rejoining him a few minutes later, toweling her hair.

"Well indeed. This is the way. Push a button and it's breakfast. Why don't we ever have doughnuts at our house? Push another button and the sheriff says, yes sir, I'll get right on it. Push another button and a beautiful blonde strolls through."

She picked up a pillow and threw it at him. He ducked, laughing. She left to comb her hair.

"What did you tell the sheriff?" she asked, when she came back this time and poured herself coffee.

"Not a thing yet. We're to meet him at five, compare notes, here in the lounge. Funny thing is the sheriff can investigate Musselman's death all he wants, but not the Leeds murder.

That's state territory. Tough. Anyway, that leaves us a whole day to get our act together. Just so we get back by five. What'd I'd like to do is meet Debra Saltzman and her friends."

She tasted the grapefruit. It was so acidic, so green she felt her whole body cringe; Charlie laughed. "I told you they're bad for you. Have a doughnut."

When they went down to the lobby they found two messages in their box, one for each of them. Charlie read his first: *I can tell you something about the crates that were opened. I'll be in my office at the school from eleven to twelve. Meet me then.* It was signed Claud Palance.

Constance read hers aloud: *You have to come to the retreat at eleven-thirty. I have to talk to you. Don't bring Ch. Come alone. T.*

Charlie nodded gravely, thanked the desk clerk, took Constance's arm and they walked out into the day that had been remarkably freshened by the storm. "Divide and conquer," he murmured as they walked to the car. "Get me out of the way and work on you. God only knows what ammunition she planned to use."

"Both of them?" she asked. "You really think so?"

"Don't you?"

After a moment she nodded. Tootles's work; she really was getting desperate.

"Now, let's see," he said behind the wheel a moment later. "Out that way, turn left, five, six miles to the shopping mall. Right?"

She knew he did not need any confirmation. They drove directly to the mall and went into a discount store, where he bought some paint thinner, turpentine, a sponge, a large bunch of hideous plastic flowers, and a bottle of cologne. He surveyed his purchases thoughtfully, then nodded, and they paid for them and left. It was ten-thirty.

The day was starting to warm up and would become very warm before dark, he felt certain, but now it was nice. Sparkling clean after the rain; a few trees had blown down here and there, but there was no drastic damage. A good cleansing storm.

"It's about an hour in to Washington," she said, thinking about it. "We've never been to the Space Museum, you know.

We could do that." They had an appointment to see Debra Saltzman and Sunny Door at three-thirty.

"Righto," he said and turned the key.

The day had been designed to make him feel humble and small,
he decided late in the afternoon. First the Space Museum had
achieved this nicely, putting him out there where he was of less
importance than a single raindrop in the ocean. Lunch had been
in a restaurant where the headwaiter was pseudo-French, the
worst kind, and regarded Charlie as a tourist from Nebraska or
worse. And then Debra Saltzman's apartment, penthouse apartment, he corrected himself. It seemed that her father was *the*
Saltzman, heir to one of the great fortunes—his daddy had invented one of the dry soup mixes and had gone on to dry salad
dressing mixes, dry juice mixes . . . It was enough to make Charlie's head ache. Debra was dressed in a silk pantsuit with a halter
under the jacket; Sunny was in a running outfit with a green
stripe down the leg. Both looked exceedingly rich.

"What I'd like," he said to them, "is just a straight account of
exactly what you saw and heard when Johnny Buell took you to
the condo that night. Okay?"

"You think the killer and Victoria Leeds were already there,
don't you? The papers said that's one of the theories," Sunny
said, leaning forward in her chair, her eyes gleaming. Two spots
of red flared on her cheeks, then faded, leaving a beautiful, controlled apricot tan.

Charlie thought of it that way, a controlled tan, done to a turn,
ripe for the picking . . . gravely he nodded. "That's exactly what
I think. And I think there's a good chance that something you
saw, or didn't see, something you heard, or didn't hear, might
provide just what we need to wrap it up."

"See?" Sunny said to Debra with a toss of her head. Her hair
flowed like brushed silk with every movement she made.

"The point is we didn't see or hear anything," Debra said
coolly.

"Maybe," Charlie said. "Maybe you know more than you realize. Let's start with approaching the gate."

Watching, Constance thought how very good he was with
these young women. He was not deferential in a way they were
used to. He had dismissed the apartment, which was breathtak-

ing, with a stunning view of the city, just as he had dismissed
the slight inflection with which Sunny had said her last name
Door. Names, fortunes, none of that interested him, it was clear,
but what did interest him was the quality of their perceptions,
what they had seen, what they had heard, what they had thought
of it all. Constance doubted if anyone ever had treated them with
intellectual interest in their young lives.

And what it came out to, she also thought, was a repeat of
what they had learned already. No one saw or heard anything.
He took them to the gate, through it, down into the basement,
up the elevator, and so on until they were back in the Continental and on the way to the city once more. Nothing new. No
one else was there. Debra had left her purse in the elevator when
they went into the apartment, she had started to go back for it,
then didn't because they would leave in just a second anyway.
Left it where? he asked. On the shelf under the mirror, she said.
She put it down to comb her hair, and forgot it. He nodded. On
to the smell of paint in the apartment, the tarps, the curved
hallway. . . . What had they talked about with the watchman?
Both women filled in the brief conversation; it had lasted only
a minute or two and then Johnny had come back.

Both young women had treated his interrogation as an ad-
venture when it began, but they were bored with it quickly,
bored with having to back up to fill in details that seemed so
minute they couldn't make any difference. Like where everyone
stood in the apartment, in the elevator, on the ground waiting
for Johnny to come back. Debra said he wanted to know their
lines of sight, didn't he? And why didn't he just say so if that
was it? He nodded. That's it, he admitted, and they worked with
a little sketch, then another. Where were they when Johnny
opened the trunk and tossed in his briefcase? Sunny had looked
inside; the trunk was big and empty. Debra had watched a con-
trail point to the city. Where were they when Johnny went back
inside? Standing by the car, talking. No one passed them there.
Did they actually see Pierce follow them to the gate when they
drove out?

"He was walking after us," Debra said. "I saw him, and we
didn't see anyone else," she said finally in irritation. "Believe
me, I wouldn't lie about it. What for? We didn't see anyone!"

Finally he thanked them, and he and Constance rode the elevator down twenty-two floors and emerged to the street, where it was hot and muggy and crowded with tourists. You could tell the tourists because of the cameras, and the women didn't wear hose, and they were sunburned to a degree that looked painful.

"Well," Constance said judiciously, "you told them what they didn't see or hear could be important."

He laughed. "Let's get on the road. This is a sauna."

They were nearly an hour late for their meeting with Bill Gruenwald. He was drinking a beer when they arrived; he looked tired and discouraged.

Charlie was tired, too; he had not counted on the tourists, on the heavy traffic, on the heat that had increased mile by mile as they neared the city. It was not fair, he thought vehemently, for Constance to look the way she did after such a day. She was in beige pants and a beige top with a white belt, white sandals; she looked as if she had stepped out of a cool advertisement only minutes ago. He was dirty, sweaty, crumpled, and the tension he had put aside all day had returned vengefully, much worse, he was certain, than it would have been if he had admitted it throughout the day instead of shunting it off like that.

He liked Bill Gruenwald and didn't want to play games with him, but on the other hand Gruenwald had been ordered off the case, and Charlie needed him. Game time, he told himself unhappily.

18

Sorry we're late," Charlie said as they neared the booth.

Gruenwald stood up and glanced at his watch. "Forget it. Technically, I'm off work. I know a little place you might like, few miles down the road. Good food there. Buy you a beer."

"He really doesn't want to be seen with us, does he?" Constance murmured in the car a few minutes later, as Charlie followed the sheriff along a narrow winding country road that was a series of sharp curves.

"Nope. I reckon he's vulnerable politically. Case goes haywire, he gets it in the neck. Way it goes."

The sheriff's turn signal began to flash; Charlie slowed down. They left the blacktop road for a newer one of glaring white concrete, and just ahead there was a sprawling log structure with a sign: Harley's Haven.

"We are there," he said, pulling into the parking lot behind Bill Gruenwald. A few other cars were in the lot, which was quite spacious, and looked well used. Watch out for weekends after nine, Charlie thought. When he glanced at Constance it was to see a look of concentrated absence on her face. That was how he thought of it; she was not home, but off somewhere thinking. She could concentrate herself away during lectures, during Christmas-rush shopping, during movies, during his long discursive discussions with Phil Stern, his lifelong friend, anything.

Once or twice that expression had come during one of their infrequent arguments; he had stormed out of the house wanting to kick a cat or dog, or take a swing at a lion, something. When he returned, she could pick up the argument exactly where they had left off, and he never would learn what had taken her away briefly.

He touched her arm, bringing her back as cool and poised as ever. But he knew that if she had not yet finished whatever it was, it would be up to him to carry on the conversation with Bill Gruenwald, who would never realize she was paying no attention at all.

Inside Harley's Haven there was a nice dance floor, and two dining rooms, one separate from the music area; it was dim and quiet at this hour. They sat in there. A red-haired man came out from the back to greet them. "How's things, Bill? What'll it be?"

"Paddy," Bill Gruenwald said, then nodded to Charlie and Constance and mentioned their first names. "Dos Equis for me."

"Good ribs coming along," Paddy said. "Belinda's cooking, you know, her own sauce?"

Gruenwald groaned. "I'll hang around for them." When they all had ordered their drinks, he said to Constance, "Spare ribs barbecued by Belinda is one of the reasons some folks around here aren't hurrying very fast to get to heaven. When she goes, they'll trail along after her."

Charlie and Constance decided they would hang around and

wait for the ribs also. Bill Gruenwald began to talk about some of Charlie's cases he had followed: he asked intelligent questions. Charlie gave him reasoned, intelligent answers, and Constance went back to her "other space," where she could think undisturbed.

They were well into the ribs before she came back fully. The ribs were as good as promised. They came with a sweet/sour cole slaw, biscuits, green beans cooked with ham most of the afternoon, boiled new potatoes, collards with vinegar and green onions and a bowl of fresh black-eyed peas.

It was time to slow down, Charlie knew, or he would have to stop long before he wanted to. Trouble was, he wanted to eat for a week; the motel restaurant, decent as it was, left an empty spot after every meal there. Mediocre food did that, left an emptiness, and you just ate more and more trying to find the one thing that would touch and fill that hole, and never did.

"Charlie," Bill Gruenwald said, "Belmont is getting antsy. I think he'll hold off until early next week and then go calling with a warrant."

"Good heavens!" Constance said indignantly. "With what? He can't have any more than he did yesterday, or the day before that."

Bill Gruenwald nodded. "That's one of the problems. He isn't getting anything else, and he's got Marion Olsen; a motive, the ruined art pieces; time, she's the only one who had the time."

"Have you given him anything about Musselman yet?" Charlie asked.

"Tried. Only way that makes much difference is if the reason is political; someone paid off someone for the variance, or else graft; you know, order it at a buck, write down two, pocket one, pay one. Either way, it gets political and nasty. Belmont doesn't like politics mixed in with his murders, one of the problems. And he wants that to stay the way it was closed, accidental death. Even if we came up with something besides accidental death, he seems to think it's a different case altogether. And it could be, you know. *This* case concerns a bunch of nutty artists, that's how he sees it."

"Well, it really does," Charlie said. "A nuttier bunch you aren't likely to find. Look, come to the party tonight. You want to see nuts in action, be there."

Gruenwald hesitated. "A party?"

"Party. Séance. Whatever. I don't intend to take part, old buddy. I intend to sit it out in the dining room, or back porch, or somewhere." When the sheriff still hesitated, Charlie dipped his fingers in his water glass and then wiped them carefully. You couldn't get barbecue sauce off without water, he thought, and this was not the sort of place that brought hot lemon-scented towels or water bowls. He paid close attention to the task of cleaning his hands as he said, "If I were you, Bill, I'd be there tonight. I mean, if I didn't have anything better to do, no new movie in town that needs my immediate attention, no hoodlums on big mean bikes roaring around, no shootings in the saloons, why then I'd consider this a sort of special deluxe entertainment opportunity and I sure would be there."

"What time?" Bill Gruenwald asked resignedly.

"We probably shouldn't arrive together. And we plan to get there about nine-thirty. Maybe you could have a reason to drop in, you know, a few more questions to ask Max or Spence or someone. You ever find out what time Spence left his shop that Friday?"

"Yeah. Five. Made great time, got to the house at ten to six."

"Uh-huh. Anyway, party time, nine-thirty or so. Am I remembering right? Was there blueberry pie on that menu?"

All through dinner Toni watched Paul Volte; whenever he glanced in her direction, she quickly looked away, but then found herself watching him again. He ate very little and drank wine and looked sad. It made her want to cry for him to look so sad all the time. A few times when Ba Ba addressed him quite directly, he had looked so blank it was as if he had gone deaf.

Johnny was tired, he had announced at the start of the meal; he said nothing more after that.

Spence was going on about two artists who had got in trouble with NEA over what some called obscene art, and they defended as antiwar statements. Spence was hanging their show next week, he said unhappily, and he expected pickets, demonstrations, God knew what all. Fire bombs, he added gloomily.

Only Max seemed normal; he listened to Spence with interest, and he watched Marion with such affection that it was touching to see.

And Marion was angry about something. She scowled and cursed and banged her glass down too hard, and let her silverware clatter too often, but she didn't really say anything.

All in all it was a very strange and awkward dinner; as soon as it was over, Marion said, "Paul, Ba Ba, I need to talk to you. Let's go to the office."

Toni helped Mrs. Weber clear the table and scrape dishes in the kitchen. A few minutes later when she returned to get the tablecloth, she saw the sheriff at the table with Johnny and Max, looking at a crude map.

"Hi," the sheriff said. "Are we in the way here?"

She shook her head. The tablecloth had been folded and pushed across the table to the end. Slowly she picked it up, gathered the napkins, and started to leave.

"Like I said," the sheriff was saying, "we figure they must have already been inside the complex by seven. You had to unlock the gate to drive through, but did you look at the other door, the single door?"

Johnny shook his head. "I never gave it a thought. It was closed, or I would have noticed, but I didn't examine it."

"Of course not. No reason to. Pierce says it was locked at six, but I wonder if he really tried it, or just gave it a glance."

Max said sharply, "If he said it was locked, it was. He's a good watchman."

Toni went on into the kitchen. She felt as if something that had just started to loosen in her throat had tightened all the way again. Why didn't they finish? Be done with it? She wanted to scream at the sheriff with his bland voice, his bland face, his silly little mustache. . . . Without warning, she was seeing his face then, not the way it had looked just now in the dining room, but strangely different, with a deep hurt, a deep secret: a private self she had not seen before.

She dropped the tablecloth on the kitchen worktable and wandered out of the room, down the hall toward the studio, thinking of nothing at all, but examining the face that had presented itself to her, turning it this way and that in her mind, following a line that started at the corner of the eye, down the side of his face where it was smoothed out by his rather high cheekbone . . .

As she passed the closed office door, she could hear raised

voices, including Spence's, although Marion had not even invited him to the little talk. Toni continued past the door, on to the studio, to her workspace at a long table against the wall.

Not soapstone, too soft, too smooth. Gneiss, or even sandstone. A reddish sandstone, with yellow in it. She reached across the table to a lump of modeling clay, but when she drew it closer, the image vanished. Now she could see only the bland sheriff with his bland mustache, his bland eyes. She stared ahead at the wall; there was a crack in the paint, small bits had chipped off exposing the undercoat that was whiter than the finish paint. She pinched off a bit of clay and pressed it against the crack. She filled in the crack from as high as she could reach to where it disappeared behind the table. Tears flowed down her cheeks as she plugged the crack with the soft gray clay.

Then she heard a door slam and Marion's harsh voice yelling, "Goddamn it! There's no choice! We do it her way! You hear me? And you behave or I'll get you by the balls and I won't let go! And Ba Ba, you screw up with this and I'll slap you silly from here to Christmas! You got that straight?" Her voice receded, still at full volume apparently, but she was hurrying away, her bare feet making no noise.

Toni ran to the bathroom that was between the office and studio; she closed the door, locked it, and then pressed her forehead against it hard. After several very deep breaths, she turned and washed her face, and felt she was as ready as she was going to get that night. It was time for Constance and Charlie to show up, party time.

19

Charlie entered the dining room, his hands deep in his pockets, scowling fiercely, to hear Sheriff Gruenwald say to Johnny, "All we really know is that Victoria Leeds must have got into the condominium before you took your group in. There just wasn't time enough afterward." He looked at Charlie. "Hi, what's up? Oh, I forgot, they're having a party or something?"

"Or something," Charlie snapped. "I was invited to go somewhere else." He cocked his head, listening. "They can't seem to make up their minds where they want the party to happen."

Across a narrow hall from the dining room, with both doors standing wide open, was the television room. The voices became clearly audible:

"This will do just fine," Constance said. "Plenty of chairs, that card table is about right, don't you think?"

"It's okay," Ba Ba said in a lower voice that sounded sullen.

"Good, let's just arrange things in here." Constance was being inhumanly cheerful and brisk.

Charlie sat down at the dining-room table and glanced at the sketch Bill Gruenwald had made of the condo complex, Tootles's little retreat, the path through the woods. He did not linger over the sketch, but was listening intently to the voices from the dining room.

"How we used to do it," Constance said, "was to have the two Ouija enablers sit at the table, and the others sit around them holding hands. You have to promise not to say anything, or make a sudden movement. You know, respect for the method, the people using the Ouija, the others in the room, and so on. Agreed? Max, I'm not sure you'll like this. Wouldn't you rather join Charlie, wherever he is?"

Max's voice rumbled, nearly inaudible, but he was protesting, that much was clear.

"All right," Constance said, "but you'll have to abide by the rules, just like everyone else." There was a pause; he must have nodded or somehow agreed silently. She went on, "Whoever is at the end should be prepared to take notes if there is a message. Spence, would you do that? At this end, maybe. Do you have a notebook or something, a pen? Just put it where you can get at it without having to leave the group."

Charlie got up and crossed the hall, to stop in the doorway, where he could look into the television room. There was a grand piano, a large television, many cushions on the floor, several overstuffed chairs and a sofa, and additional cane chairs with woven seats. Constance was standing at a card table, where Tootles and Ba Ba already were seated with the Ouija board and planchette between them. Tootles looked murderously angry. The others had drawn a line of chairs close to the table. Now Constance sat down next to Toni and took her hand, Max took Constance's hand, and after a second Spence sat down and took Max's other hand. Paul was ashen; he moved like a robot with jerky motions when he crossed to sit by Toni.

Charlie was aware that Bill Gruenwald and Johnny Buell had joined him at the doorway. He took Johnny's arm and pulled him away, his finger to his lips. Back in the dining room he said in a low voice, "They'll close the doors if they catch us snooping. Listen." Babar's voice carried to them clearly.

"Is anyone there? Hello. Is anyone there?" A lengthy silence followed. "Sometimes you have to ask through the Ouija," Babar said, and another silence followed.

"You guys were talking about how anyone got into the complex?" Charlie asked Bill Gruenwald in a very low voice. The sheriff nodded; Charlie lifted his eyebrows in surprise. "That's the easy part," he said, still speaking softly. He listened again, then said, "They, the killer and Leeds, must have seen Buell and his group enter, and simply went through when the gate was open. A step off the access road, behind the trees, and it was done. He left the building open when he took the group upstairs. How long does it take to get inside, duck out of sight?" He cocked his head, and put his finger to his lips again. He took the few steps to the door to the music room and stood there silently. Johnny and the sheriff came after him.

"It's not working," Tootles said flatly. "I can't help it if it doesn't work. There's no way to make anything happen."

Constance was thinking back to her girlhood, a time when she was thirteen or fourteen, one of a group of high school girls who had stayed up all night playing with Tarot cards, the Ouija, palmistry. There had been a lot of giggling, and not a little apprehension and even fear that was always denied as quickly as it became recognized. They had been in the Olsens' basement rec room. Ba Ba had not been allowed to join them; she had been too young at eleven or possibly twelve.

Constance had not played with the Ouija since that night so many years ago. One of the girls had become hysterical, she recalled; how easy it had been then to become hysterical, to have other girls patting, touching, kissing, even envying the one who had succumbed. How they had longed to faint. One good faint would have been worth two cases of hysteria.

Toni's hand in hers had been trembling earlier, but now was still, and had even warmed up. She removed her hand from Toni's, gave Max's hand a little squeeze, and then withdrew from his grasp. His hand had been warm and firm from the start.

"Let me try," she said to Ba Ba, who still looked furious.

"I'd rather not," Ba Ba said. "When it's a bad night, it's best to leave it alone."

"Oh, we don't know that it's really a bad night, do we? Maybe Tootles is just too upset. And she has every right to be upset. It's been one thing after another, hasn't it?"

Glaring, Tootles stood up and went to the chair Constance had just left. She took Max's hand, and then Toni's. "Let her have a go at it," she said in a tight voice. Constance smiled at her, then at Ba Ba.

Toni had been afraid, then she had known nothing was going to happen. The way Marion had been sitting, the stiffness of her shoulders, the set look on her face, her whole attitude had said clearly that there was nothing to be afraid of because nothing was going to happen. Now the fear leaped back, redoubled, quadrupled, overwhelming. Constance would make something happen, she knew. She could not control the trembling in her hands. Marion tightened her grasp on one side, while on the other side Paul's hand was shaking every bit as much as Toni's.

"Is anyone there?" Ba Ba demanded, the same words as before, but with a difference; now it was a challenge.

Constance laughed. "Let's ask with the planchette."

After they moved the planchette around the board to ask, an interval passed that seemed too long to endure; no one moved; the planchette did not move. Babar looked sleek and fierce, Constance relaxed and bright-eyed with interest. Then the little planchette began to slide. Constance glanced at Spence, who was staring at the Ouija with a look of disbelief. When she nodded at him, he released Max's hand to pick up his pen and notebook. Standing in the doorway, fists clenched, Charlie felt a stirring of memory, a stirring of an atavistic reaction to the strange and unnatural that raised the hairs on his arms, down his back. Abruptly he turned and went back to the dining room.

"Jesus," Gruenwald muttered. "I didn't know people still believed in stuff like that. Isn't your wife a Ph.D. psychologist? Does she believe in that?"

Charlie glared at him. "Why don't you do your job and let her do hers," he said in a low mean voice. "You need some more pointers? How about the rope? Trace it. Who around here has rope, and why? Trailer tie-down? Camping rope? Boating? Why nylon? Because it makes a tidy little package that can go into a purse, or a pocket? Were the ends burned to stop raveling? Trace the ash, lighter fluid, barbecue starter, gasoline? What was used? A match? Candle? Gas burner? Cigarette lighter? God, the labs today can tell you the name of the gas company! Have you even thought to look over clothes, see if you come up with fibers, nylon fibers in pockets, for example, or fibers from her clothes on the knees of someone's pants? Why don't you just get on with your job and don't worry about what my wife believes?"

Gruenwald tightened his lips into a thin line. He started to gather up the papers he had spread on the table. Johnny Buell looked at him, then very quickly away, as if embarrassed for him.

"Who is there?" Constance asked in the next room. Charlie went to the door again. Constance had a strained expression; she was pale. She had not counted on this, she was thinking. Ba Ba had gone into a trance that was legitimate; she was in a somnambulistic trance from all appearances, and the planchette was racing around the board.

Charlie's fists tightened. *Something was wrong.* Late into the night they had talked; he had gone over that other time with her, reviving all the terror he had felt that day when Babar had summoned a ghost, a spirit, a something, and it had touched him with fear and loathing. Last night Constance had said, "If this is going to work at all, it has to be as real as it was to you the first time you saw Ba Ba at the board. You have to let it run without interference or nothing will happen. She's probably even better now, more experienced at this, but we're more experienced, too, Charlie." She had said that he no longer was that young kid, groggy with fatigue, stupefied with coming out of a deep sleep into something weird. Last night it had sounded reasonable. Now, watching with his fists balled so hard that his forearms were starting to spasm, all he could think was *some-*

thing was wrong. Constance was too pale; he could see a sheen of sweat on her upper lip, the way the tendons in her neck were too tight, the fierce set of her jaw. The thought came to him with the force of a blow to the solar plexus: *she would be the target.*

The planchette moved faster and faster spelling out words: Y—O—U—C—A—L—L—E—D—B—E—F—O—R—E—I—C— A—M—E—I—A—M—S—T—I—L—L—H—E—R—E

"If you are here, you can hear my voice," Constance said clearly. "You have to leave, go back where you came from. No one here needs or wants you any longer."

I—W—I—L—L—N—O—T—L—E—A—V—E—P—A—U—L

"Tell it to go away, Paul," Constance said. "Just say the words. Tell it."

The planchette began to skitter across the board, back and forth jerkily, not pausing anywhere long enough to see if it was on a letter, skidding to the edge, back; then suddenly it flew off the board and landed in Ba Ba's lap. She did not move; her hands remained suspended before her as if her fingers were still resting on the planchette. Slowly her hands were lowered until her fingertips touched the Ouija board. Her face did not change expression; she looked like a Buddha contemplating nirvana.

"I won't leave," Ba Ba said in a thick unrecognizable voice. "Paul needs me. Paul wants me."

Charlie's stomach spasmed at the sound of that voice.

"Tell it!" Constance demanded, facing Paul, who was shaking violently.

"Get out," he cried then. "Just get the fuck out. Go back to the hell you came from! Leave me alone! Get out!" His voice rose to a near scream. "Get out! Get out!"

"No!" Toni moaned. "I want it. Don't leave!" She tried to wrest her hand free from Tootles's grasp.

"Jesus God," Gruenwald whispered.

His words, so close to Charlie's ear, yanked him back from a wild plummeting fall toward that other room out of the past. For a moment the two scenes appeared superimposed on one another. He shut his eyes hard, and when he opened them again the past was gone.

Max was as rigid as death, as was Tootles. She was holding

Toni's hand in a hard grip. And Toni looked ready to pass out; her pale face had taken on a bluish cast. She twisted her hand away from Paul; he jumped up, clutched the table holding the Ouija board, and screeched at it.

"Get out of my life! Get out!"

The Ouija board seemed to jerk convulsively; it twisted and spun around and slid across the card table and sailed off to the floor. The silence and stillness that replaced the frenzy stretched out until, abruptly, Paul slumped, rocking the table that he still clutched with both hands. He didn't fall, and after a second he straightened again. Constance felt as if she had been released from an enveloping restraint. She flexed her fingers.

"It's gone," Paul whispered hoarsely. "It's gone!"

Charlie let out a breath he had not realized he had been holding. Toni moaned again and ducked her head. After a second Constance picked up the board and returned it to the table. Ba Ba stirred and put the planchette on the board. She looked dazed.

In the doorway Charlie felt his muscles start to relax, leaving him feeling exhausted with a dull ache here and there; he turned and went back to the dining room, followed by Johnny and the sheriff.

"Jesus," Gruenwald said again in a low voice.

"It . . . there's more," Ba Ba whispered.

Constance wanted to deny it, to cry out, *No!* This wasn't part of the plan; Ba Ba's part was finished. But Ba Ba was rigid, staring straight ahead as if entranced again. "Let's make sure it's gone," Constance said, and she heard her voice as strained and as unfamiliar as the voice that had come from Ba Ba only moments earlier. "Ba Ba?" They positioned their hands. There was a brief silence and then she said, "Is anyone there?"

Gruenwald and Johnny went back to the door to watch; this time Charlie did not join them. Every instinct was crying out to stop this, stop it now, stop it completely, and never start it again. He felt hot and cold all at once, and he could almost feel the pallor of his face; sweat between his shoulder blades chilled him, and he knew he would not be able to stand in the doorway and watch again.

"Spence," Constance said in her unfamiliar voice.

It took a long time, the letters all ran together as they had

SEVEN KINDS OF DEATH   597

done before; the planchette sped up and it was hard to make certain the letters were all noted. Constance said each one when the window paused over it. When the message stopped, Spence read what he had written:

Tell Diane manuscript is in drawer with Buffalo nickels.

"Are you still there?" Constance asked the board. There was a long silence. "It's over." She removed her hands from the planchette. Ba Ba stirred and straightened her fingers; she looked very relaxed and sleepy.

"What the devil does that mean?" Spence asked, studying the message. "Something to do with her work?"

"Whose work?" Tootles asked.

"Victoria Leeds's apparently. Who else works with manuscripts?" Then he added, "Well, Paul does. You know a Diane?"

Paul shook his head. His face looked waxen.

"She's trying to help find her killer," Ba Ba said in a sepulchral tone. "We have to find out who Diane is and pass the message on to her."

"Anyone here know a Diane?" Spence asked.

"Who has a collection of Buffalo nickels?" Paul said. His voice was so harsh it was nearly unrecognizable. "Come on, enough's enough. Forget it. Marion, I'd rather like a drink. You mind?"

"No, by God, we all deserve something. Come on."

"Well," Gruenwald said in the dining room, "your wife puts on a good party, Meiklejohn. I'll be on my way. See you around."

Charlie nodded. He wiped the sweat from his forehead; he felt gray and very, very old.

Johnny looked as shaken as Charlie felt. He muttered something about a drink, and wandered out of the dining room, headed for the living room, where voices sounded faint, very distant.

"Diane Musselman," Gruenwald said in a low voice. "Goddamn it! What the hell are you up to?" He sounded mean and dangerous. "I'll phone Belmont to stake out her place. Damn you, Charlie! Jesus Christ!" He hurried away.

"Drink," Charlie thought clearly then. Drink. He wanted a drink very badly.

"I knew you'd be good," Ba Ba was saying to Constance when he entered the living room. Max was pouring drinks. Toni was on the sofa and no one else was in sight. "I could tell," Ba Ba was going on. "You shouldn't fight it, Constance. It's a God-sent gift that can do good things."

Drink, Charlie thought again. He took Constance's hand; it was icy. "Are you okay?"

She nodded. Charlie's gaze happened upon Toni, huddled on the sofa, watching Constance with bitter hatred.

Charlie stiffened, listening, then dropped Constance's hand. "Wait here," he said curtly, and raced to the foyer, out to the porch, in time to see the white Corvette throw gravel as it left the driveway too fast and sped off down the dirt road. He already had his keys in his hand as he ran to the Volvo and snatched the door open, jumped in and tore off after the Corvette before anyone else got off the porch.

The little sports car was faster than the Volvo, and it was being driven by a maniac. Charlie kept it in sight, but did not catch up; he made every turn, every curve, and kept it in sight. At first he had thought they were heading toward Chevy Chase, but very soon he realized he was lost. Although he had a good sense of direction, and would be able to find himself if he had just a glimpse of a map, or if he had driven these roads in daylight, he was driving twisting country roads in the dark, and the roads were narrow, some blacktop, some concrete, some dirt, with mileposts instead of names. Names would not have helped, he had to admit to himself as he made another right turn. He kept most of his attention on the car he was following, but there was enough left over to keep in sight the headlights behind him, pacing him. Bill Gruenwald, he thought, hoped.

All right, he reasoned, Gruenwald had called Belmont or some of his own deputies by now; they would have someone keeping an eye on the Musselman house. Maybe. His lips tightened. They *would* have someone keeping an eye on the house; they'd better.

Up ahead was a lighted area, a gas station, tavern, even, by God, a stoplight, he realized, closing the distance between his car and the Corvette.

Constance watched Charlie speed off after the Corvette, followed closely by the sheriff's Ford. She watched until all the lights were gone, and then turned to reenter the house.

"What the devil is going on?" Max stood at the door, also watching.

"I don't know," she said. "It seems everyone decided to go out for a ride."

"Johnny too?" Max sounded disgusted. "Now what?"

"Not me, too," Johnny said, coming from the shadows of shrubs in the yard. "I gave my keys to Paul. He was pretty upset and his rented car was packed in between the Volvo and your car, Dad. It just seemed easier to let him take mine until he cools off." He laughed. "He'll be surprised when he realizes that Charlie and the sheriff both are on his tail."

"Good Christ," Max muttered and went back inside.

Constance and Johnny followed him.

All right, she thought, all right. All she had to do was keep everyone in sight until Charlie and Bill Gruenwald returned. She knew that, but everyone else wanted to wander. Max vanished and returned; Tootles and Spence had been gone, and came back together from the office; Ba Ba wanted to talk to Constance and she kept trying to dodge her. Toni just shivered on the sofa and watched Constance with dull hatred. And Johnny was in and out of the kitchen, also dodging Ba Ba, looking more and more often at his watch as the minutes crawled by.

"Shit," he muttered once. "I thought he'd want to take a spin to the village or something. I didn't think he planned on staying out all night."

"Constance, you really should just try the crystal ball, just once," Ba Ba said. "I just know you'd be sensational with it."

"Who is Diane?" Spence asked, and Ba Ba shrugged.

Constance asked him if he would drive her back to the motel in a little while.

"Whistle when you're ready," he said agreeably.

She went to the office and found a piece of paper, and an envelope and scrawled a note to Charlie, sealed it, and put it in her pocket, just in case. She was not certain she would trust it to anyone here, she realized. Tootles would certainly read it, and Ba Ba and Toni were doubtful. Meanwhile she would keep it in her pocket.

Forty minutes dragged by; no one had relaxed, or sat still more than a few minutes at a time while they waited. Even Ba

Ba had become silent and looked fatigued, when suddenly Johnny stood up and said, "Dad, this is too much. Mind if I borrow your car and go home? If and when Paul comes back, feel free to use the Corvette."

Silently Max fished out his keys to the Continental and handed them over. He looked terribly tired. Johnny mock-saluted and left the room. Constance turned to Spence and said, "Me too. Would you mind?"

He looked at her curiously, then shrugged. She said to Max, "If Charlie comes back here tonight, will you give him a note for me, please?" She handed the envelope to him. "Thanks. Good night, everyone."

As soon as the Corvette reached the brightly lighted area of the tavern and gas station, Charlie braked, jerked the Volvo to the side of the road. A moment later the dark Ford pulled up behind him. Gruenwald emerged.

"What?" he asked.

"It's Volte," Charlie said in a hard, tightly controlled voice.

"Paul Volte?"

"Yeah. How fast can we get back to the house? You know a better way than the way we just came?"

When Spence got his car headed up the driveway, Max appeared at the passenger side door. "I'm going, too," he said. "Unlock the door."

Spence glanced at Constance. After a second she nodded and he unlocked the door with his control panel. Max got in the back seat.

"I suppose you want me to follow the Continental," Spence said, driving out to the road, making his turn. The taillights were at the intersection; they vanished.

"Yes," Constance said. "I don't think it will be far." She did not look at Max in the back seat; he did not speak again.

The Continental turned in at the condo complex. "You'll have to pass him," Constance said. The other car was stopped at the gate, Johnny was opening it. "Max, do you mind?" she said and ducked down in the seat. In the back seat Max leaned over out of sight. They passed the Continental just as it was pulling inside the complex. "Now stop," Constance said. "Let's back up, right to the gate, and go on foot." She looked at Max. "Why don't you wait for us?"

"No!" He was out of the car before Spence had set the hand brake.

When they got to the driveway to Applegate, the Continental was going down the ramp to the basement. Constance hurried, with Spence at her side, Max trailing a step or two behind. Pierce, the watchman, was standing at the driveway down to the basement. He had looked puzzled a moment earlier, now he looked totally bewildered. Constance held her finger to her lips, and he looked past her to Max, who nodded. Pierce shook his head and moved back a few steps, leaned against the building silently, and watched.

They took the stairs. At the basement level, Constance kept going down until they exited at the sub-basement. There was a dim light, and eerie shadows cast by the rows of storage compartments. It was silent. She glanced at the footwear of the two men; running shoes on Spence, soft-soled sandals for Max, and her own sandals would not make noise, she knew. They left the stairwell and looked down the first row of storage compartments. Empty. Silently they moved to the next row, and this time, Constance dug her fingers into Max's arm and drew him back. Toward the far end Johnny was opening one of the doors.

She had her witnesses, she was thinking, but what could they see from here? Only that he was taking something out. But if they got closer and he ran, then what? She pulled Spence back a bit farther and whispered, "I'm going down the other aisle and get closer."

She could handle him, she was certain. He was big and muscular, but she had the skill, years of training, and she had the edge of surprise.

She had reached the halfway point of the rows when she heard the metal storage door slam, and then his footsteps, heading for the stairs at the other end. She started to run.

"Hold it right there, Mr. Buell. If you don't mind."

The sheriff? Now she fairly flew to the end of the aisle and came to a stop. Charlie was standing there, leaning against a storage compartment, and at his side was Sheriff Gruenwald, holding a gun. Charlie looked past him to Constance; a very wide grin split his face.

"What the fuck are you doing down here?" Johnny demanded. "This is my building! Get the hell out of here!"

"Let's not get too excited," Sheriff Gruenwald said. "What is that you removed from the storage compartment?"

"None of your fucking business. What, you got a warrant or something? You going to shoot me in the back when I leave? This is my property, you pissant sheriff! How do you think you can explain coming here and threatening me? Man, when I get hold of my lawyer—"

"You'll do what, Johnny?" Max's voice was heavy, wooden. "Whose building? What do you have there, Johnny?"

Johnny spun around at the sound of his father's voice. His voice rose to a near falsetto when he cried, "You did this? You called him! Why? I didn't do anything you wouldn't have done in my place! I didn't!"

Max was walking down the aisle toward him. "Give it to me, Johnny. What is that? A bundle of clothes? Give it to me."

Johnny moved a few steps toward him, and then he swept out his arm and knocked Max to one side, against one of the metal storage compartments, and he ran. At the end of the aisle, Spence stepped forward and hit him once on the jaw. Johnny dropped and was motionless.

And somehow during this, without awareness of her own actions, or Charlie's, Constance had moved to his side, and he had put his arm around her and was holding her very close.

20

At ten minutes before ten the next morning Charlie and Constance pulled into the condominium grounds. The superintendent Ditmar met them at the curb in front of Building B— Birmingham. Or maybe Baloney, Charlie thought, taking the envelope Ditmar held out to him. It contained the computer card keys to the elevators and various rooms.

"I turned off the electronic door-closer system, just like you said I should," Ditmar said. He hesitated, as if he wanted to ask them if it was true. He shook his head, then turned and walked back toward his little trailer/office.

Charlie opened his trunk and took out the shopping bag with his purchases from the previous day. "This won't take long," he said to Constance. "If they get here before I finish, keep them out here. Okay?"

She nodded and watched him enter the B building with his bag of tricks. Bill Gruenwald and state police investigator, Lieutenant Belmont, arrived together a few minutes later. She greeted them and relayed the message: Charlie would be along in a minute or two.

Howard Belmont was fierce-looking this morning. His forehead was furrowed with deep lines, and his lips were nearly invisible. Bill Gruenwald looked as though he had slept very little, but he was calm and peaceful, almost as if he had taken a week's supply of tranquilizers. She suspected that he had not needed any.

"He began to talk," he said. "Not enough yet, and his lawyer put in an appearance and stifled him, but he started. Once they start, they usually keep on." He ignored the state officer. "And there was a pretty wrinkled note to Victoria Leeds in the pocket of the pants. They had a date for five o'clock. His stuff is in the lab now."

Charlie walked from the building then and nodded pleasantly to Bill Gruenwald and the lieutenant, who eyed him as if he suspected rabies. "Good morning," Charlie said cheerfully. "Let's get the show on the road, gentlemen. What I'll do is give you what I have, and then split."

No one protested. "Okay," he said. "Let's pretend. We are the little group that Johnny Buell brought over here the night he killed Victoria. Right? Honey? You want to drive?" Constance got behind the wheel; the others got inside the car. She made a U-turn and drove slowly down the ramp to the parking basement of the B building.

"Pretend two things," Charlie said. "First, that this is Building A, and next is that we had to use the electronic thingie to open the gate to the basement."

Constance drove to the other end of the basement, headed up the ramp to the street again; she stopped and pulled on the hand brake.

"And here we are," Charlie said. He got out and opened the door for the sheriff and the lieutenant. "We'll take the elevator up to six. I have the key for it."

He opened the door; they got in and the door closed again. Very soon the opposite door opened, and he led them out into the larger foyer. "Keep in mind that all these buildings are exactly the same," he said, leading the way, past the curved hall that would accommodate bookshelves, to the doorway to the living room. "Wait here," he said, "and don't touch anything. Wet paint, you know." The odor of paint was very strong; tarps were heaped on the floor in a table-shape. "I improvised the furniture. The tables have been put away somewhere," he said, walking quickly past the tarps, into the dining room, where he picked up the shopping bag, and then rejoined them. He held it up and said, "Briefcase. And now out."

They retraced their steps silently, back to the elevator, down to the basement, back inside the car. Constance drove up to the street and stopped again.

"Whoops," Charlie said. "Let's check the other apartments. You can come too," he added. He still had the shopping bag. Bill Gruenwald was looking bored; the lieutenant's face was red and his eyes nearly closed. He looked as if he had high blood pressure, and it was rising second by second. When Charlie entered the building on the first-floor level, they all followed him. This time they entered the elevator with the big brass number five.

At the fifth floor Charlie moved swiftly; he went through to the living room, where tarps were arranged in such a way they resembled a table. The paint smell was strong. Bill Gruenwald and Lieutenant Belmont exchanged glances. If this wasn't the room they had just left, it was identical to it, down to the tarps on the floor. Charlie very quickly rolled the tarps to make a bundle, and not quite running, but moving fast, he left the apartment by way of the door to the hall. He jerked his head in an invitation for the others to follow as he hurried to the end of the hall and opened the staircase door, and started up. No one spoke.

At the sixth floor Charlie used his borrowed key to open the apartment and led them to the living room, where more tarps had been draped over sawhorses, another tablelike shape, and where one tarp had been rolled into a cylinder that could have been a body on the floor.

Gruenwald came to a dead stop. Charlie hurried past the tarps, carrying his bundle, and dumped it in the dining room on the floor. As soon as he unrolled the tarps, the odor of paint rose and spread. He picked up the sponge he had soaked in turpentine and put it in a plastic bag that he closed with a tie, and then shoved into his shopping bag. Still moving silently, he motioned again for them to follow him. They got into the dedicated sixth-floor elevator, where a bunch of fake flowers was on the shelf under the mirror. The odor of the cologne he had sprayed on them was stifling; this time Charlie punched B for basement. When they got down and left the elevator, he went along the row of doors lifting off the panels with floor numbers stenciled on them. They were being held only by finishing nails that fitted very loosely into the holes drilled for screws. Only the number six was relatively tight. It took five seconds to remove that one. He leaned the panels against the wall, and went up the stairs to the first floor and from there out to the street, where he stopped at the Volvo, opened the trunk and tossed the shopping bag inside.

Gruenwald had a dazed look on his face. "Voilà!" Charlie said. "Sleight of hand. The case of the disappearing body. Now you see it, now you don't."

"That son of a bitch," Belmont muttered. "That lousy son of a bitch!"

"I should have tumbled sooner," Charlie said. "Everything pointed to him."

Gruenwald snorted. "Come on. Let's have a look at those numbers."

They went back down to the basement and this time examined the numbered panels. "Nothing's very fancy down here," Charlie said. "That threw me, I guess. The brass numbers up on the ground floor are pretty hard to ignore and they're on to stay. But these are stenciled on the panels. Same stencils used for parking spots, and for the storage compartments in the subbasement."

Gruenwald and Belmont studied one of the panels carefully. They went to the elevator doors and examined one of them just as thoroughly. One side of each door had the panel with the big B already stenciled on it; there was nothing to indicate what floor the elevator served. Until the numbered panels were attached, each door was a blank ride.

"All those identical doors," Charlie said, "no way you can guess which is Six B, which one's Five B, and so on. And this building's identical to the A building. This section looks exactly the same as this section of A building; the painting has progressed to the same place it was over there. The only door that was marked was the door to the stairs. A big six on any of the doors, the other numbers loosely in place, that would have been enough to carry the illusion. One thing missing in their testimony was the arrangement of roses."

Gruenwald thought, then nodded. "No one in that group mentioned flowers," he said.

"I know," Charlie said. "I asked them specifically about the elevator, what they saw, heard, the works. No roses. No flowers. The girls put their purses down on the shelf and primped a little in the mirror. Debra even left her purse on the shelf when they went into the apartment. They couldn't have done that if the flowers had been there.

"And there's nothing upstairs to indicate they were on five instead of six," Charlie said. "The apartments are so much alike no one would have noticed that the elevator was a few feet off to the side. Out the windows they'd see treetops, what they expected. Inside both apartments, there were conference tables. So, the mention of wet paint and the turpentine on rags and the tarps on everything was to make sure they would stay put, as well as make sure they truly believed that they had been in Six A and there had not been a body on the floor. The paint smell was another giveaway, but I didn't notice. Everyone said there was a smell of paint, but what people smelled was thinner, turpentine, and all the interiors are latex, water-based. No turpentine anywhere. The painters washed their brushes in the sub-basement, and I missed that. Anyway, there shouldn't have been any odor immediately identified with paint. No one should have smelled turpentine, and they did; they should have smelled roses, and they didn't.

"So they went up to Five A, where he had set the stage complete with briefcase, and down they came again, ready to swear they had been in Six A. He returned to move the tarps out of Five A, fix the numbers on the elevator doors, and the stage was set to give him a lovely alibi. Planned to the last detail. Then Tootles crossed him up by ordering the flowers, a little surprise for Max. And she crossed us up by lying about them, saying Johnny had ordered them. I called the florist," he added. "She picked them out in person." That was the trouble with Tootles, he thought then; you had to check and double-check every statement she made, and life was too damn short.

They walked out to the street level and stood near the Volvo.

"What about last night?" Belmont demanded. "What the hell were you doing last night?"

"One of the things I hammered at the girls about," Charlie said, "was where everyone was standing, sitting, looking at all times. They saw him open the trunk of the Continental and toss his briefcase inside. There were no clothes in the trunk, no work clothes at all. I never mentioned clothes, or flowers, of course, but there it was, like a puzzle piece that's defined by the hole. Just something else missing from their testimony. That night, if he had to borrow the Continental to pick up his pals at the train station, his work clothes should have been in it, or else in the apartment. He went back to the house to switch cars, remember? Still in his work clothes then. Victoria Leeds came to meet him, thinking she had a date with Musselman probably, and he killed her. He changed into party clothes, but what happened to the work clothes? We figured that if we charged him up with the séance, got him in an emotional state, and then if I baited you," he said to the sheriff, "about following up on lab work and physical evidence, he might do something foolish. I hoped he would take the hint and decide to get rid of the clothes if he hadn't already done that. I thought they might be somewhere around here, but there are a lot of places to hide stuff around a construction site." He shrugged. "Probably he never had a chance to collect them without risking being seen, you sure can't hide much in that little Corvette, so he needed the Continental again. He came down to get the evidence, maybe the only physical evidence there is. Makes me think he believes there's something incriminating there. But it was stupid of him. He should have waited."

They almost always did something stupid, he thought, almost as if they wanted to leave a trail, get caught.

"If we hadn't turned around and come back, he'd have got away with the clothes," Gruenwald said. "Shit, *that* was a dumb thing to do, warn him like that."

Charlie suppressed a grin and nodded meekly. With Constance at one end of the aisle, and Spence at the other, Johnny had had absolutely no chance of getting away. Zilch chance, he added to himself.

"If the manuscript turns up and if it has pretty damning things to say about the job here, or about Johnny, we can nail that to his hide, but if it doesn't . . ." Belmont was gazing thoughtfully into the distance, no doubt hearing a defense attorney mock his case.

"What Johnny could be most afraid of," Constance said, with no warning that she had been noodling with that topic, "is his father. This job is rather like probation for Johnny, isn't it?" She was not inviting comment. Her clear pale eyes were focused on the Volvo, or the trees beyond it, or the horizon, or nowhere.

"Put yourself in his place and you can follow his thought processes pretty accurately," she said after a moment. "If this job goes well, Johnny takes over the company, Max more or less retires, and Johnny's future is rather rosy. He has a girlfriend who is used to a life-style that is elevated, to say the least. He must be desperate to become a full partner, start his plan to expand. If he made a suspicious deal with anyone who could monkeywrench the whole thing, it's understandable that he might panic. He has to keep Max from learning anything that would keep him from becoming a partner, taking charge." She brought her gaze back to the small group, back to Belmont. "So, I think you'll be all right for motive. Musselman died because he knew something that Johnny couldn't afford to have published; Victoria because she knew what it was."

Charlie always thought she went at things backwards. If you get the who and the how, he liked to say, the why pops up at you like a Halloween spook. But she needed the why or she was inclined to distrust the who and how.

"There must be a reason why Max has kept Johnny as an employee, not a partner," she said, just as if he had been arguing with her. "And Johnny knows that Max would dissolve the company rather than turn it over to his son if there's anything crooked in the background; Max is maybe the second most honest man I know."

Charlie grinned and she looked surprised and added crisply, "My father is the first."

Gruenwald glanced at his watch and said, "What about the art that got ruined?" Charlie shrugged. "Maybe he'll explain that," Gruenwald said. "Trying to create a motive for Marion Olsen? Maybe. Well, I have guys over at the Musselman house, making a search. If there's a manuscript, they'll find it. I'm going over there now. You coming, Howie?"

"You kidding?" The lieutenant looked like a kid who had brought a baseball only to learn that the game of the day was basketball.

"And we have to wrap up things at Tootles's house," Charlie said. "Let's get at it, and take off."

Toni met them at the front door. Constance felt very sorry for this young woman who had shadows in her eyes that had not been there a week ago. Toni looked at her coldly, then spoke to Charlie. "They're expecting you," she said. "In the television room. It's the only room in the house that the reporters can't see into."

She had started to walk away when Charlie said, "Hold on a sec, will you? How's Max?"

She shrugged. "Resigned. He doesn't seem surprised, just hurt and resigned." She hesitated a moment, then said, "Now they're saying Johnny got in trouble a few years ago, in college, something about stealing tests. Ba Ba told me, but it seems that everyone else knew all about it."

Toni had finished growing up, Constance thought, watching her when she led them into the house, her shoulders straight, her head high; and Toni would not forgive her.

Charlie took Constance by the arm and they all went to the television room, where Ba Ba was pouring coffee. She looked different, too, aloof and distant, so calm she looked doped. Tootles and Max entered the room, and Spence and Paul followed them. It was a subdued group.

"I'll keep this short," Charlie said as soon as they were all seated. Max was pale and remote, much more distant than Babar, and Tootles had been crying hard. Her eyes were swollen and bloodshot. She held Max's hand in a death grip.

"I'll give you everything I gave the police," Charlie said. "Some of this they would prefer to keep under wraps for the time being, but they didn't hire me, you people did. They are always afraid that if their suspect knows what they have against him, he will manage to counter it. That's beside the point right now." No one moved; he could have been addressing a workshop, a class who knew a test would follow. He told them the mechanics of how Johnny had killed Victoria and arranged his own alibi at the same time. "The clothes probably will settle it," he finished. "Or they could find traces of turpentine in his briefcase, or a section of rope. They might go after him for Musselman's death, but maybe not. They will look for the manuscript, naturally, and if it turns up, they may reopen that case and tie the two together. If it doesn't . . ." He shrugged. "We'll wait and see."

There were a few questions, not many. No one looked directly at Max, who stared ahead stonily. Suddenly Max said, "I was too hard on him. His mother was always too soft, and I tried to make up for her, and went too far."

Gently Constance said, "We always think that, don't we? It's my fault. Whatever my child has done, I'm really to blame. It must be in the genes. I imagine killing Musselman was an accident, don't you? But after that . . . he chose, Max. You couldn't go back to day one and reorder his life, make him be someone else. And the man he became chose his actions." She paused, then said, "And, Max, on Monday or Tuesday, they were planning to arrest Tootles for the murder of Victoria Leeds. When you are blaming yourself, casting back for what you said, what he said, what you did, what he did, back through the years, you may find a place where you recognize a turning point, an ultimatum of some sort that you'll feel you should not have pressed. If that happens, just keep it in mind that he knew Tootles was the one they would arrest."

For a time he studied her face without any readable expression on his own, then he nodded, and put his arm around Tootles's shoulders. He nodded again.

"Well," Charlie said, "Gruenwald will be back around, there will be more questions, statements to make and sign, all the routine will be observed. But it's really over." He reached for Constance's hand, but she shook her head.

"One more thing," she said. "The séance was a fake through and through. You should all know that. I arranged it, and I manipulated it from beginning to end." Ba Ba gasped, and Toni jumped to her feet, shaking her head. "Tell them, Tootles," Constance said. "Tell them."

Tootles moistened her lips, but remained mute.

"Ba Ba moved the planchette in the beginning," Constance said grimly. "To give it credence. To make it believable. And I moved it later."

Tootles was staring at her, pale down to her lips. Constance continued to regard her until finally she nodded. "She arranged it," Tootles said.

"Why?" Toni cried. She turned toward Paul Volte. "What you said . . . part of a charade?"

Before Paul could speak, Ba Ba wailed. "I never! It moves by itself! I didn't do it! And you didn't know anything about a coin collection. How could you have known something like that?"

"We saw David Musselman's study," Constance said. "We saw his books on collectibles. Including coins. I don't know if he has such a collection, but he has collections of other things. And he would not have got rid of the manuscript. Architects are trained to be conservative. To conserve, save. He would have saved a copy of the manuscript."

"Good God!" Spence said. "You set a trap for him. Diane is Musselman's widow?"

Constance nodded. "It was a trap. The first part had to look real so he'd accept the rest. Ba Ba is so good with the Ouija; it looks so real when she does it. There isn't any jealous muse, no curse, no gift of the gods. Is there, Paul?"

He had been standing by a chair, holding the back of it with a white-knuckled grasp. Wordlessly he turned and walked out of the room, his shoulders hunched; he looked ancient moving away from them.

"No muse," Constance repeated softly. "Victoria Leeds knew that. Her death had nothing whatever to do with him. She left him months ago because she had come to understand the barrier was his doing, his choice. We think what she said to Janet was that his Byronic pose was tiresome.''

She stopped when it became apparent that Toni was no longer listening. Staring at the empty doorway, she was as immobile as a piece of art, her face blank; she seemed oblivious to the lengthening silence in the room. Finally she took a step forward.

Abruptly Tootles pulled Max's hand away from her shoulder and stood up. "Just where are you going?" she demanded harshly.

Toni did not even glance at her. "I'm leaving," she said in a dull voice.

"Right!" Tootles yelled. "Leave! You know where you'll end up? In Hollywood making cute little figures that can chase other cute little figures off cliffs and get a chuckle out of cute little kids high on Saturday morning cartoons."

Color flared in Toni's cheeks; before she could say anything, Tootles drew in a long breath and went on almost savagely. "*I* never told you it would be easy. *I* never promised you a magic wand, or a mysterious muse to sit on your shoulder, or a goddam talisman to make life easier. *I* told you it would take a lot of fucking hard work."

Her gaze swept the room, art on every flat surface, art hanging from the ceiling, crowding the windowsills, in every corner. Her gaze hardly even paused at her own work, *Seven Kinds of Death*, but continued to take in all of it.

"You do it yourself," she said in a lower, even harsher voice, "or it doesn't get done. Your hands, your eyes, your sweat. . . . If your fingers bleed you put on Band-Aids; your feet hurt, take off your shoes; your head aches, take an aspirin, but *you* do it. No fucking magic. And you look at it and you say, it wouldn't be here without *me!* Maybe it's good and you say, I did that. Maybe it's a piece of shit, and you say, I did that. Another little hole in the universe is plugged up, and you did it. You look at the world and your hands tell us what you see there, and you say, I'm here! I did that."

Charlie took Constance by the hand. Quietly they walked out of the room. Tootles's voice followed them to the porch, the driveway.

They had got into the Volvo when Spence appeared, ambling

toward them in his slouchy way. He put his hand on the door by Constance. "If that was a show last night, you guys sure missed your calling. Some act!"

They both waited. This wasn't what he had followed them to say.

"You didn't clear up the problem of the ruined sculptures," he said.

Very distinctly they heard Tootles scream, "Ba Ba, shut the fuck up!"

Charlie grinned and leaned forward to look past Constance at Spence. "The sheriff thinks Johnny might have done it to supply a motive for Tootles."

Spence's ugly face brightened. "Yeah," he said softly, then again, "Yeah! Johnny must have done it." He reached in to shake Charlie's hand, and then leaned forward to kiss Constance. "You guys are pretty terrific," he said, and shambled away, back toward the house.

Charlie started the car. "Son of a bitch," he murmured. "He knows, doesn't he?"

"I think Spence knows a lot," she agreed.

He started to drive, and smiled when her hand found its way to his thigh. He didn't know which he wanted to do most, go home, or drive to the nearest motel.

"Home," she said lazily. His grin widened and he covered her hand with his.

A few months later a special-delivery parcel came addressed to both of them. It was a large and heavy box, marked fragile. Charlie carried it to the kitchen table to open it. It was a bas-relief of Constance, done in a creamy ivory marble. He stared at it for a long time, uncertain if he liked it or not. After a quick drawing in of her breath Constance touched it, moved her fingers over the cheeks, along the chin.

When he looked up from the piece to her, there were tears in her eyes, and he suspected that the work was very good. It was not idealized, not romanticized. The face was strong and rather implacable, and although the bones were very fine, there was an androgynous quality overall. The eyes were cast downward a little. The eyes were knowing, not just looking, but also seeing. It was almost frightening, that feeling of awareness, as if the stone eyes could see through the many layers of defenses that shielded most people from view.

He put his arm around Constance's shoulders, and he was glad that when he looked at her, that piece of stone was not what he saw. He did not voice this because he was almost certain she already knew.